BUG BOYS

Outside and Beyond

Also by Laura Knetzger

Bug Boys
Sea Urchin (Retrofit Comics)

BUG BOYS

Outside and Beyond

By Laura Knetzger
Colors by Lyle Lynde

RH
GRAPHIC

Bug Boys: Outside and Beyond was drawn with pen and ink on Bristol board and Photoshop.

Cover art, text, and interior illustrations copyright © 2016, 2017, 2018, 2021 by Laura Knetzger

All rights reserved. Published in the United States by RH Graphic, an imprint of Random House Children's Books, a division of Penguin Random House LLC, New York. Originally published in the United States in black and white and in different form by Czap Books, Providence, Rhode Island, in 2015.

RH Graphic with the book design is a trademark of Penguin Random House LLC.

Visit us on the Web and sign up for our newsletter!
RHKidsGraphic.com • @RHKidsGraphic
LauraKnetzger.com

Educators and librarians, for a variety of teaching tools, visit us at RHTeachersLibrarians.com

Library of Congress Cataloging-in-Publication Data is available upon request.
ISBN 978-1-9848-9678-0 (trade) — ISBN 978-0-593-12535-9 (library binding) — ISBN 978-1-9848-9679-7 (ebook)

Designed by Patrick Crotty
Colored by Lyle Lynde

MANUFACTURED IN CHINA
10 9 8 7 6 5 4 3 2 1
First RH Graphic Edition

A comic on every bookshelf.

To Bob and Deb

Special thanks to:
Kevin Czap
Mark Friedman
Kris Mukai
Stuart Solomon
Christopher Wessel

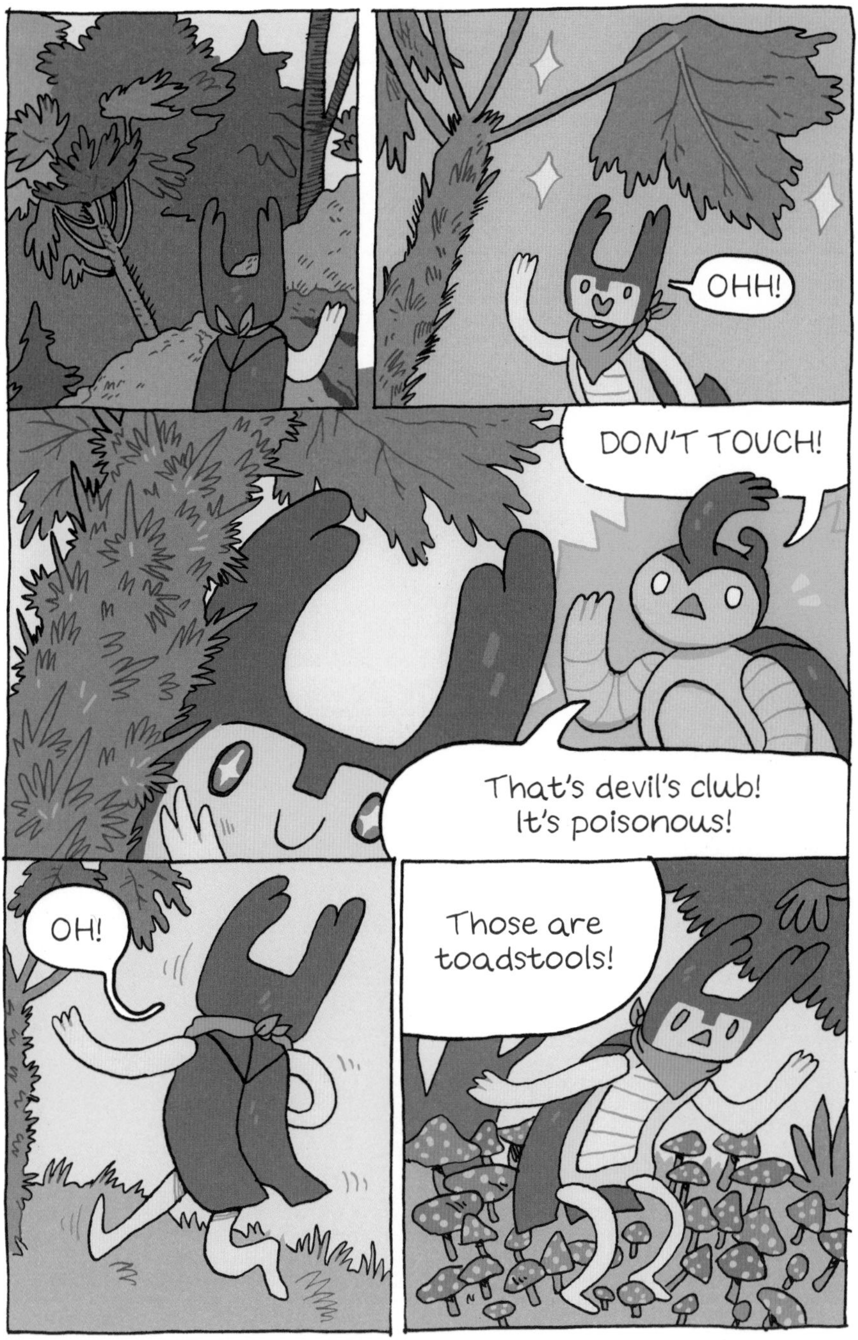
OHH!
DON'T TOUCH!
That's devil's club!
It's poisonous!
OH!
Those are
toadstools!

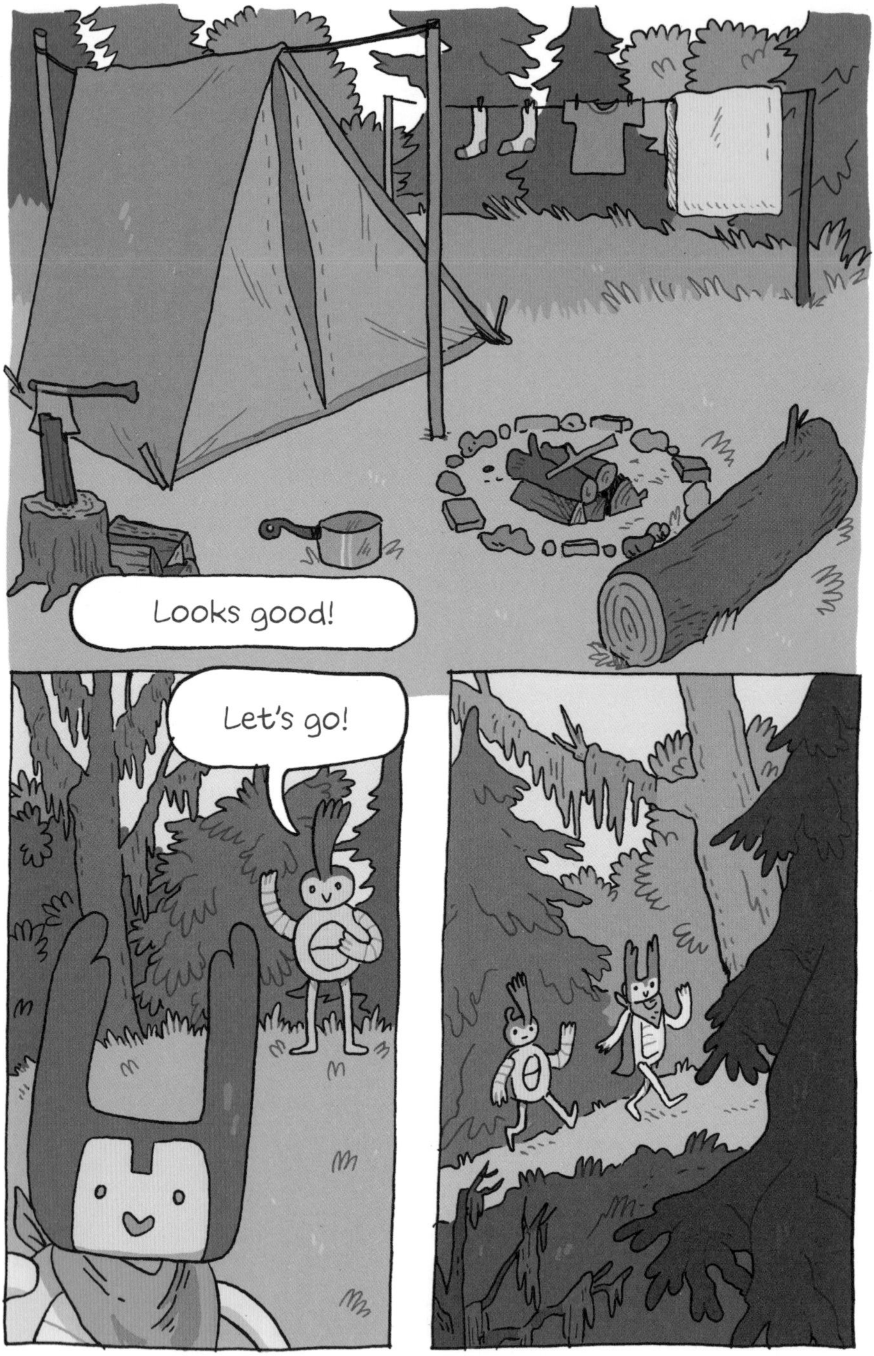
Looks good!
Let's go!

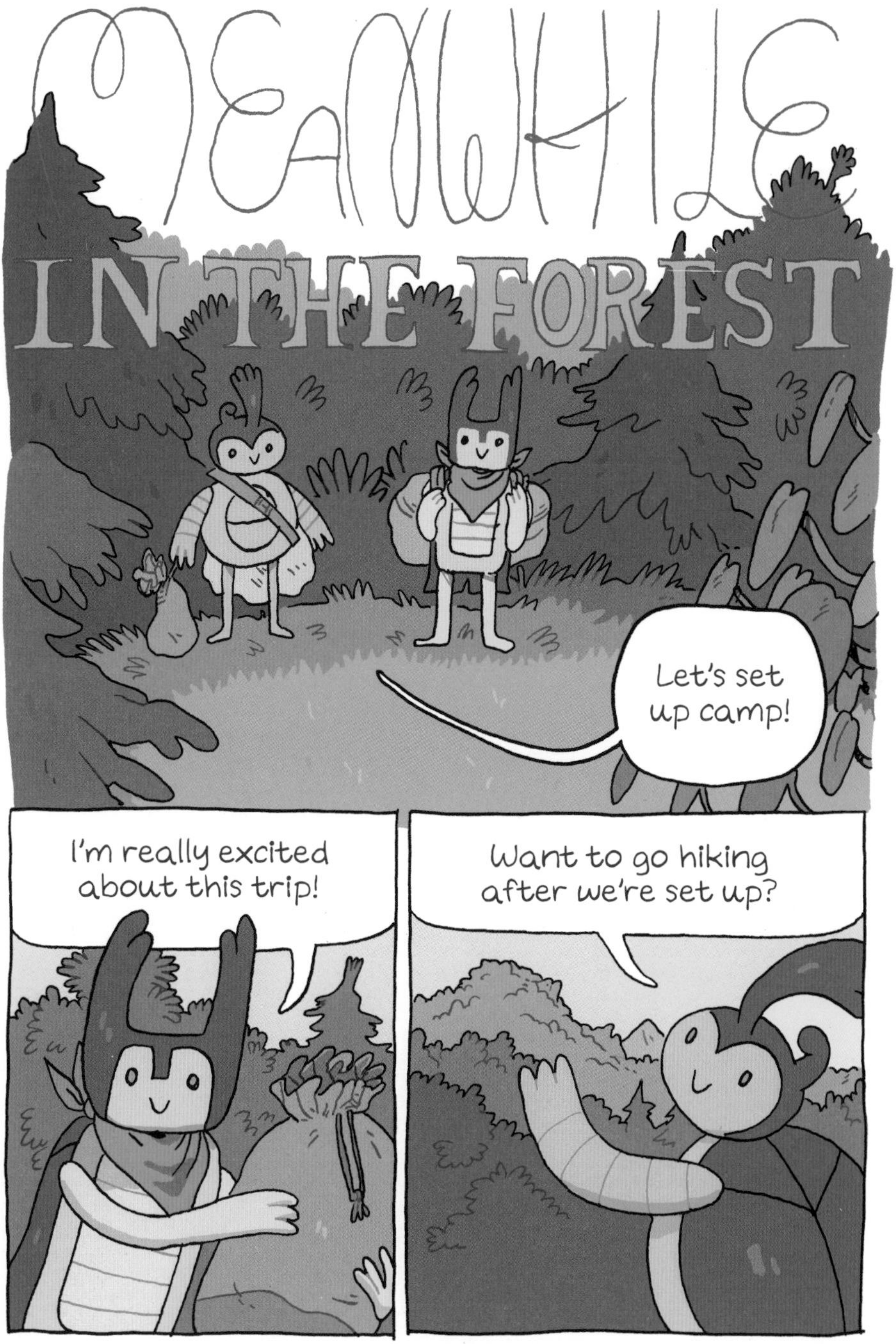
MEANWHILE
IN THE FOREST
Let's set up camp!
I'm really excited about this trip!
Want to go hiking after we're set up?

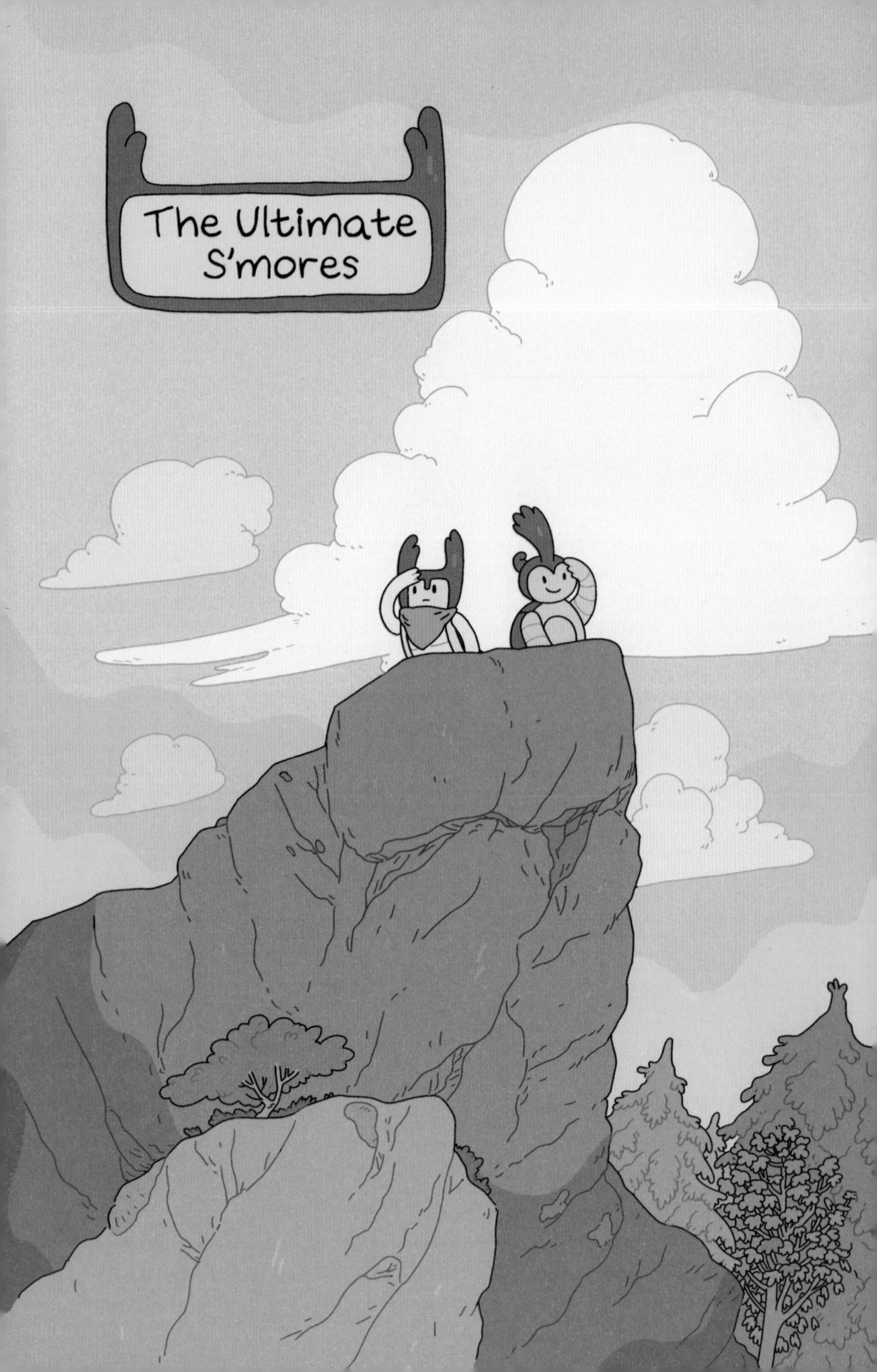
The Ultimate S'mores

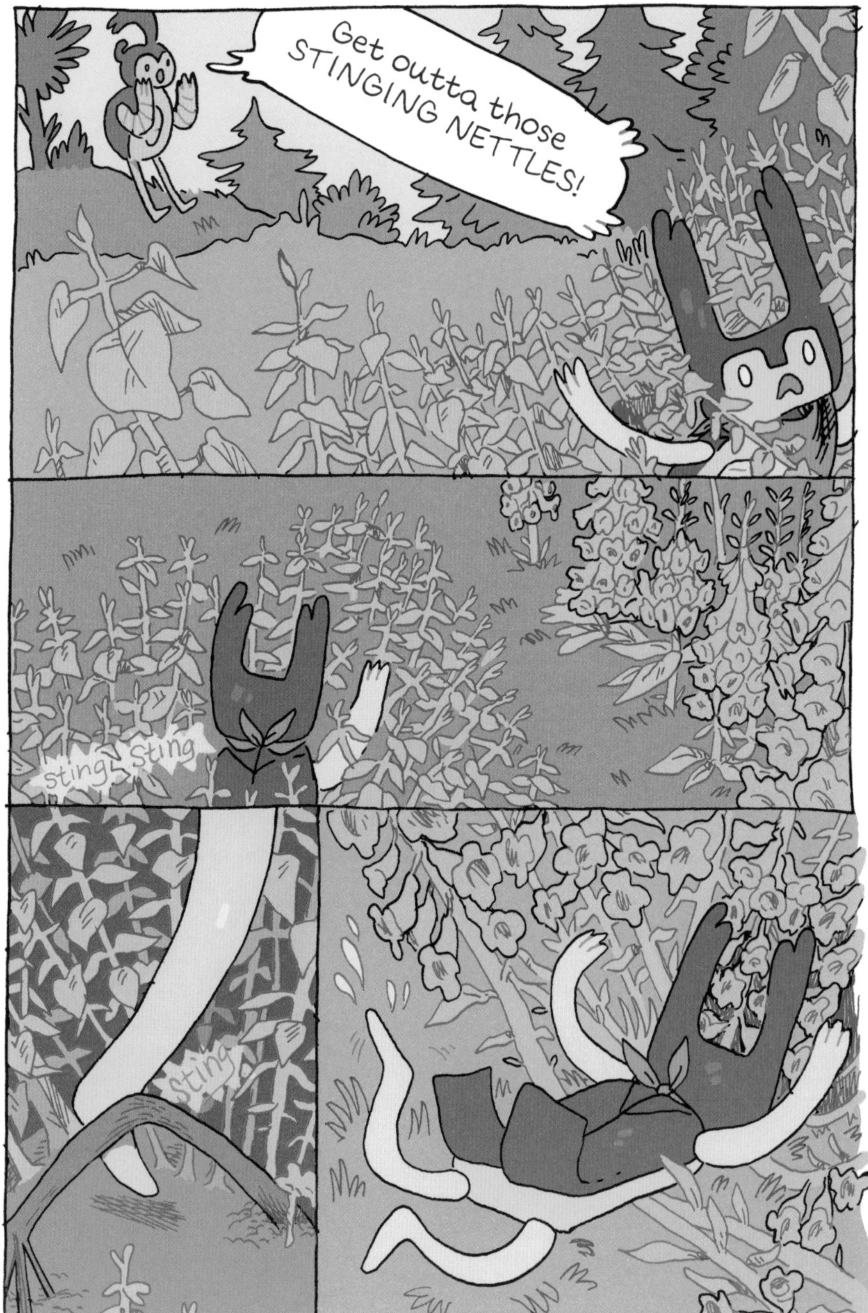
Get outta those
STINGING NETTLES!
sting
sting
sting

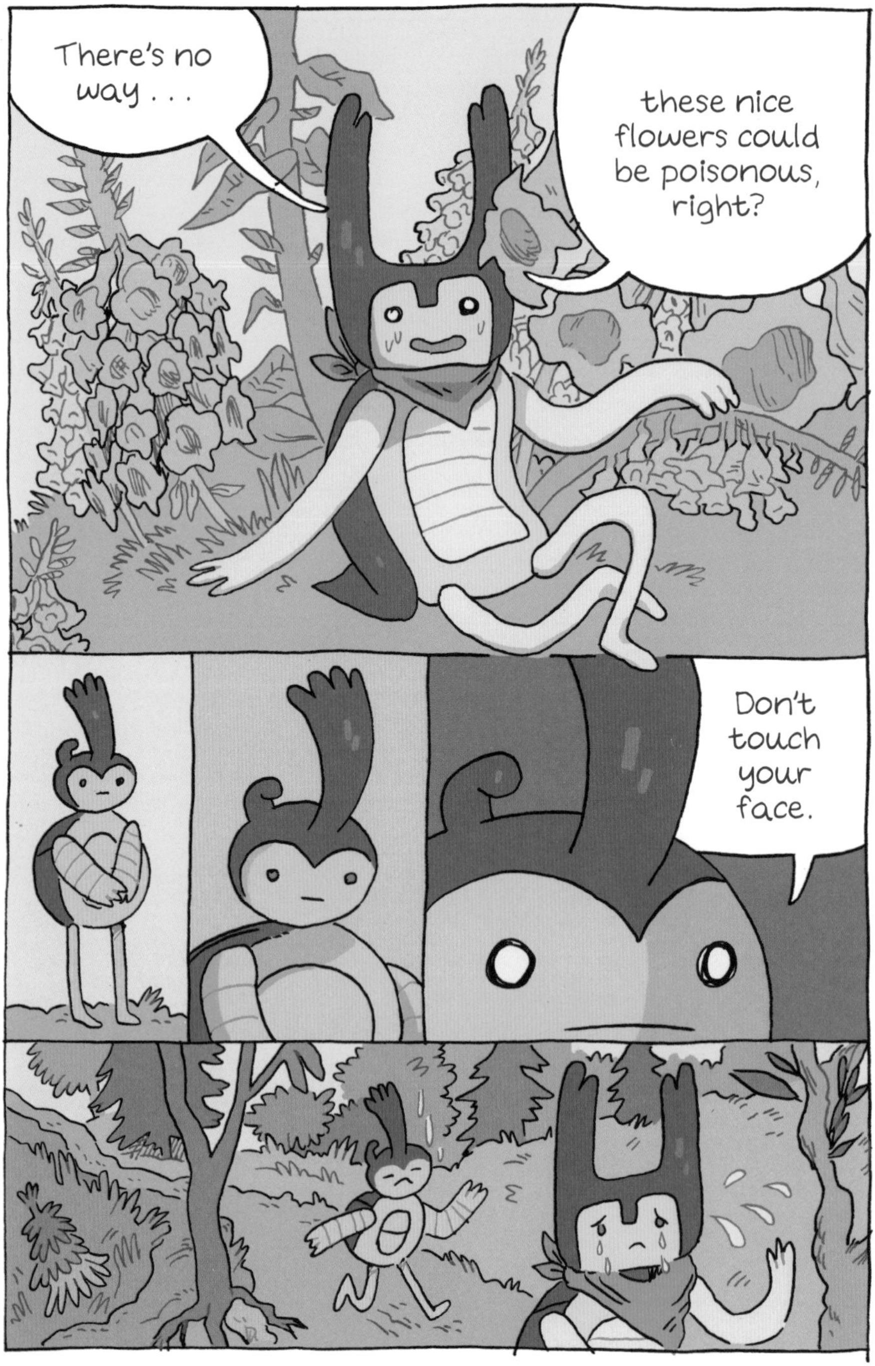
There's no way . . .
these nice flowers could be poisonous, right?
Don't touch your face.

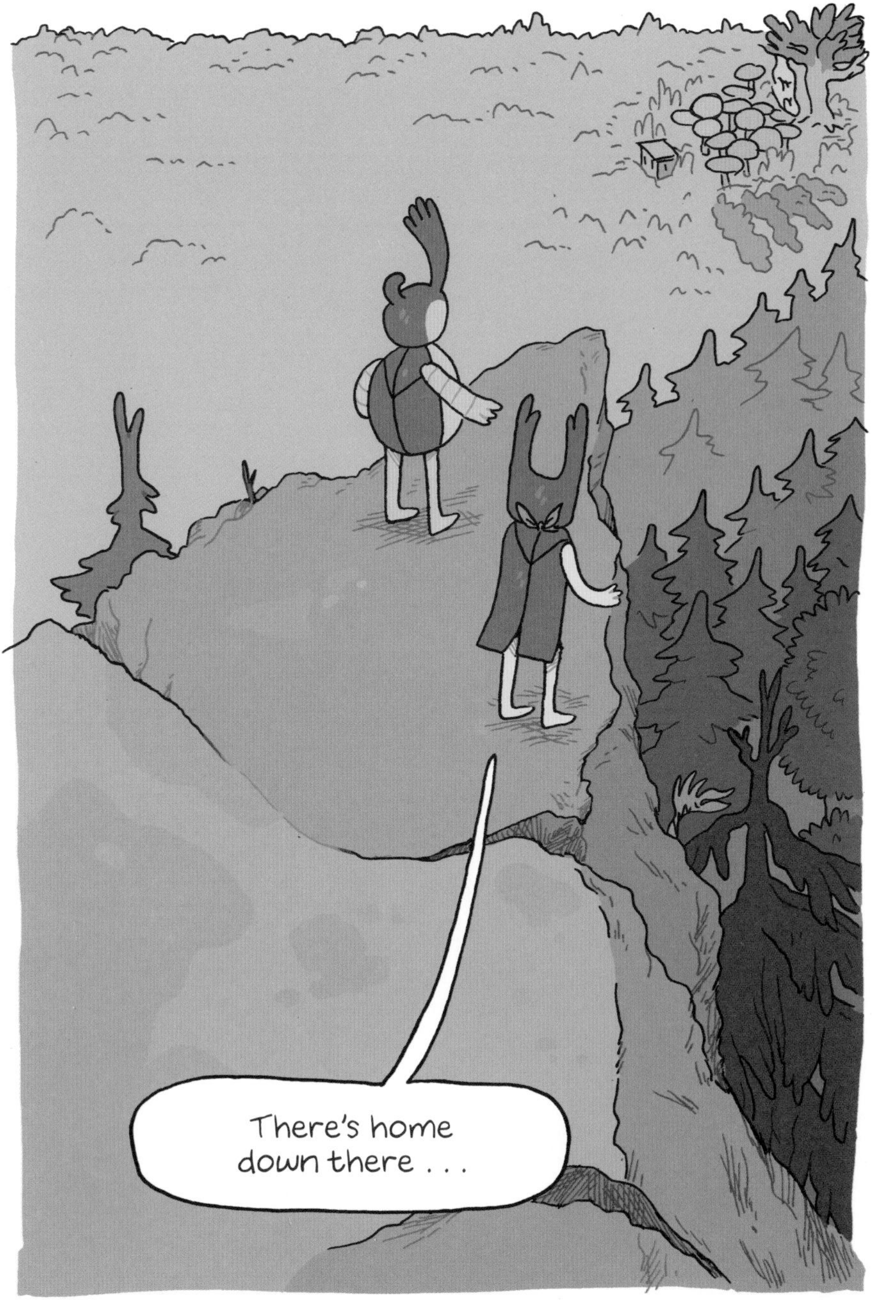
There's home down there . . .

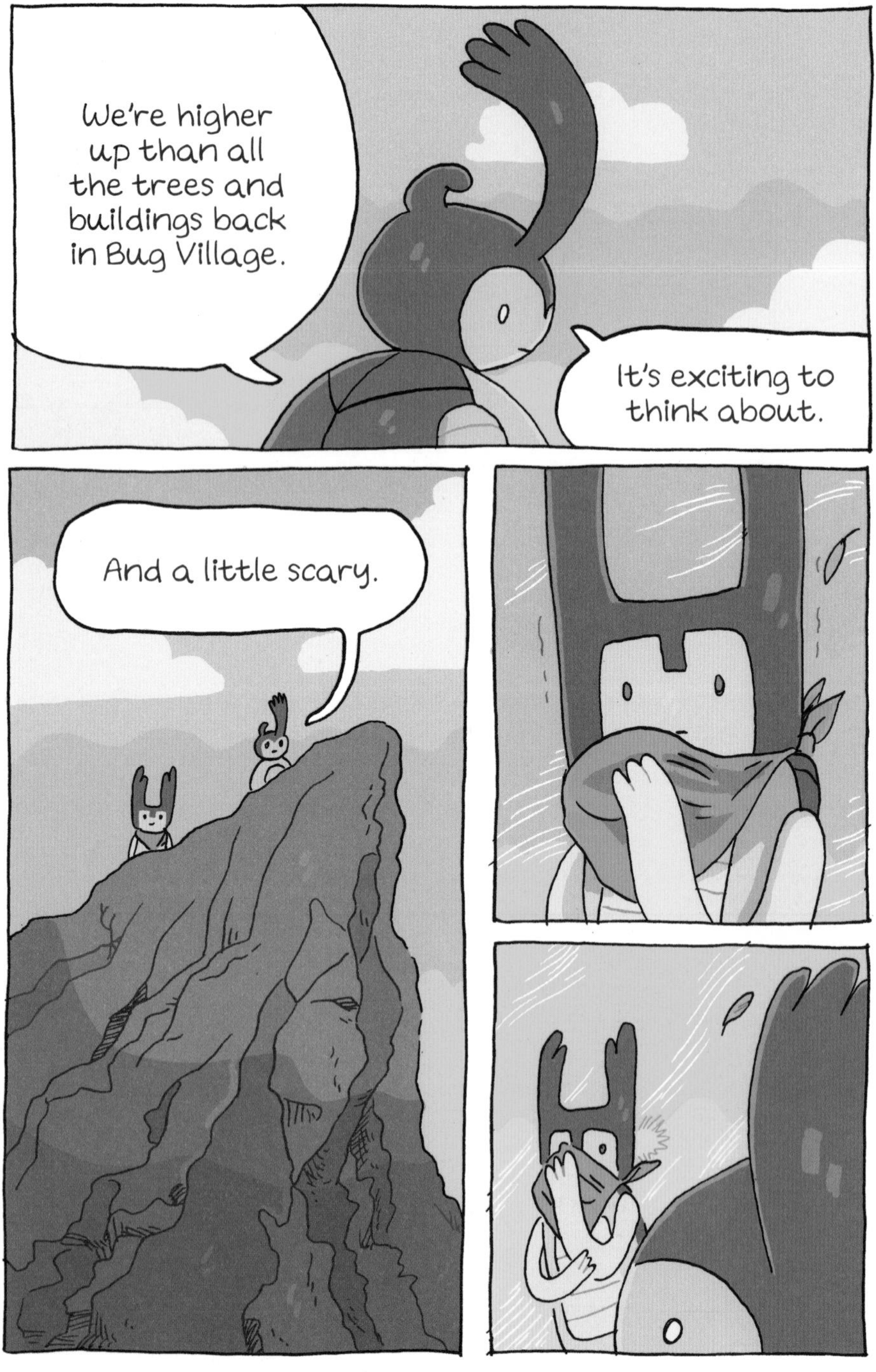
We're higher up than all the trees and buildings back in Bug Village.
It's exciting to think about.
And a little scary.

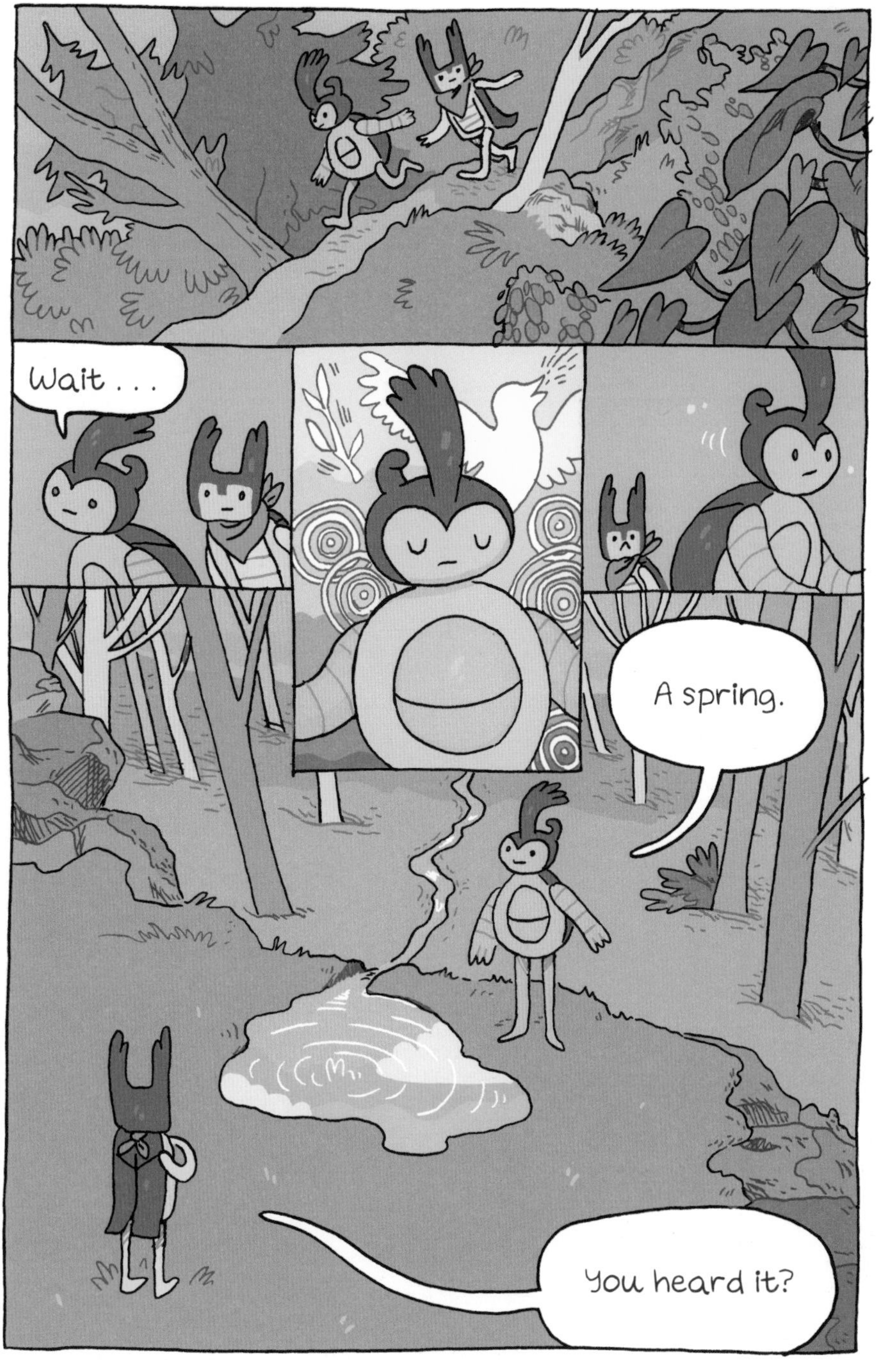
Wait . . .
A spring.
You heard it?

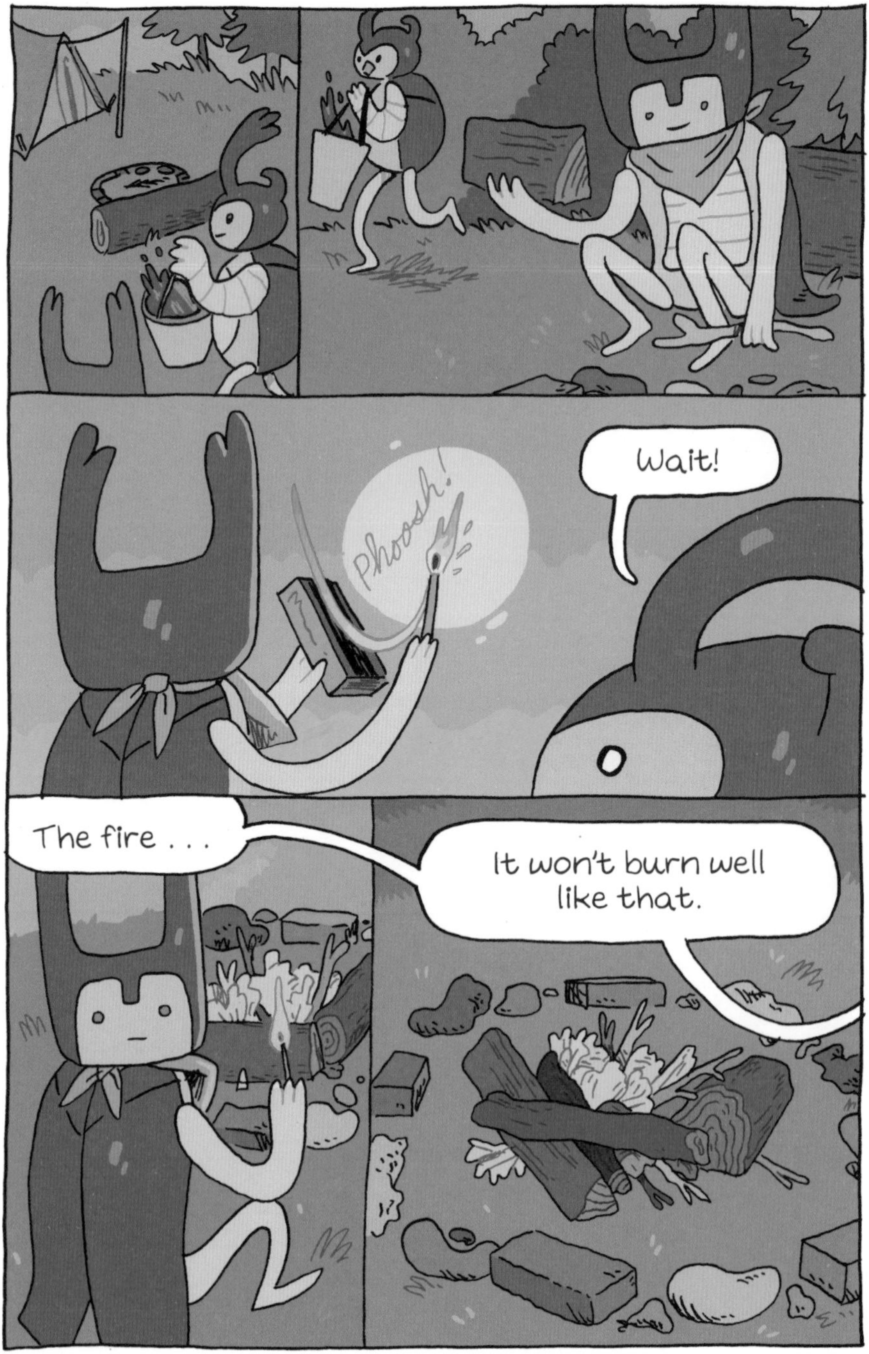
Phoosh!
Wait!
The fire . . .
It won't burn well
like that.

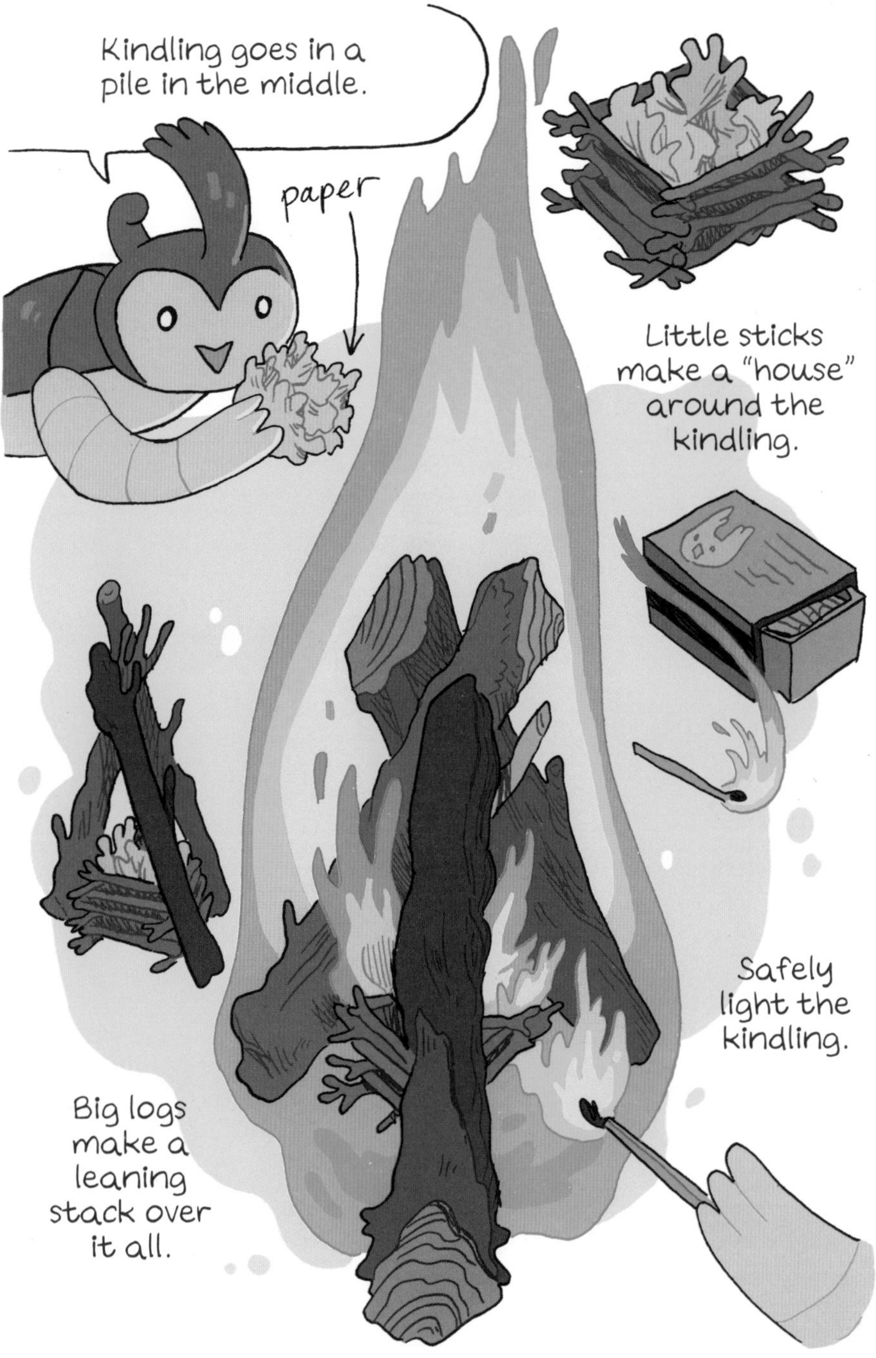

Kindling goes in a pile in the middle.
paper
Little sticks make a "house" around the kindling.
Safely light the kindling.
Big logs make a leaning stack over it all.

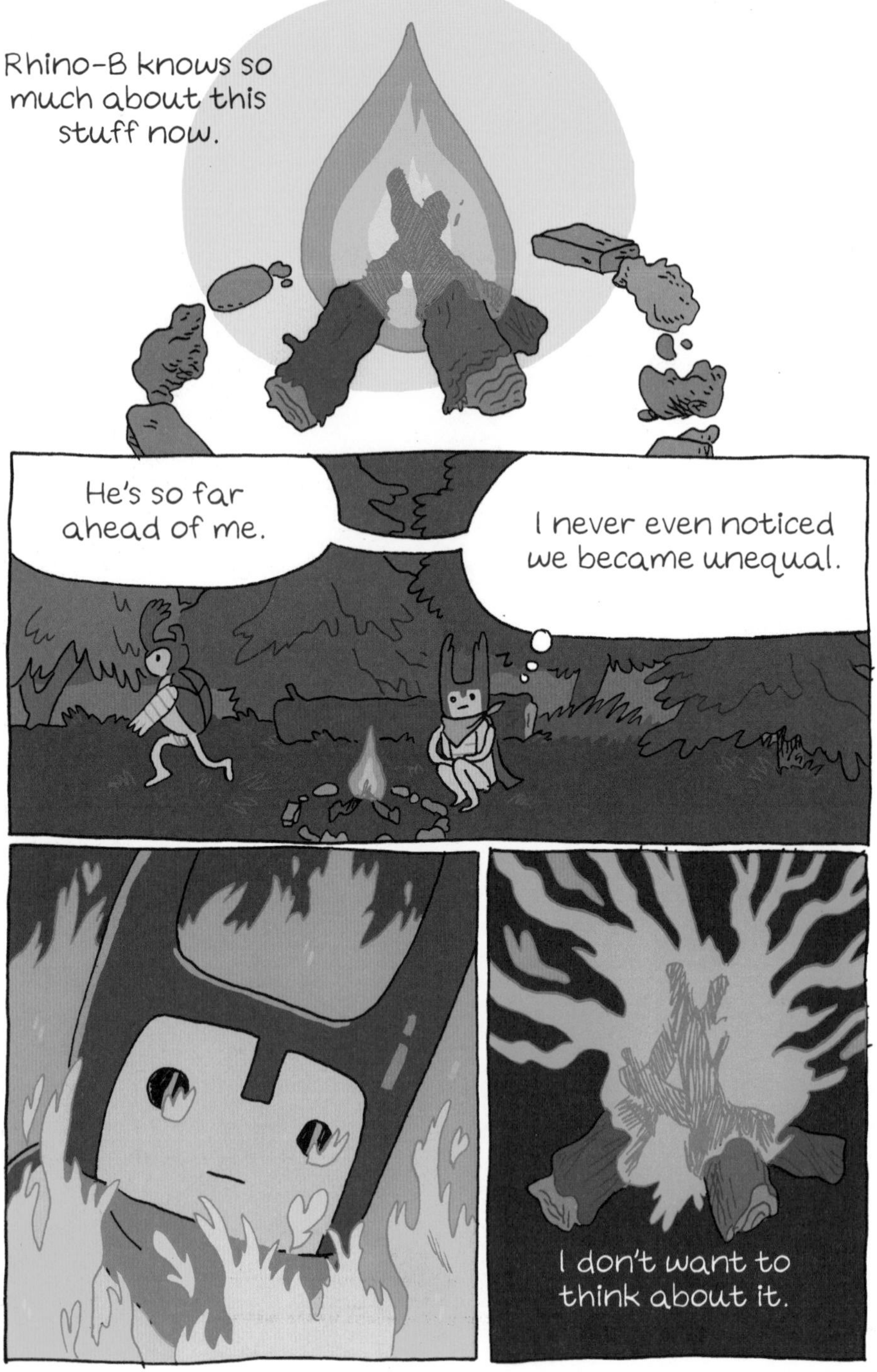

Rhino-B knows so much about this stuff now.
He's so far ahead of me.
I never even noticed we became unequal.
I don't want to think about it.

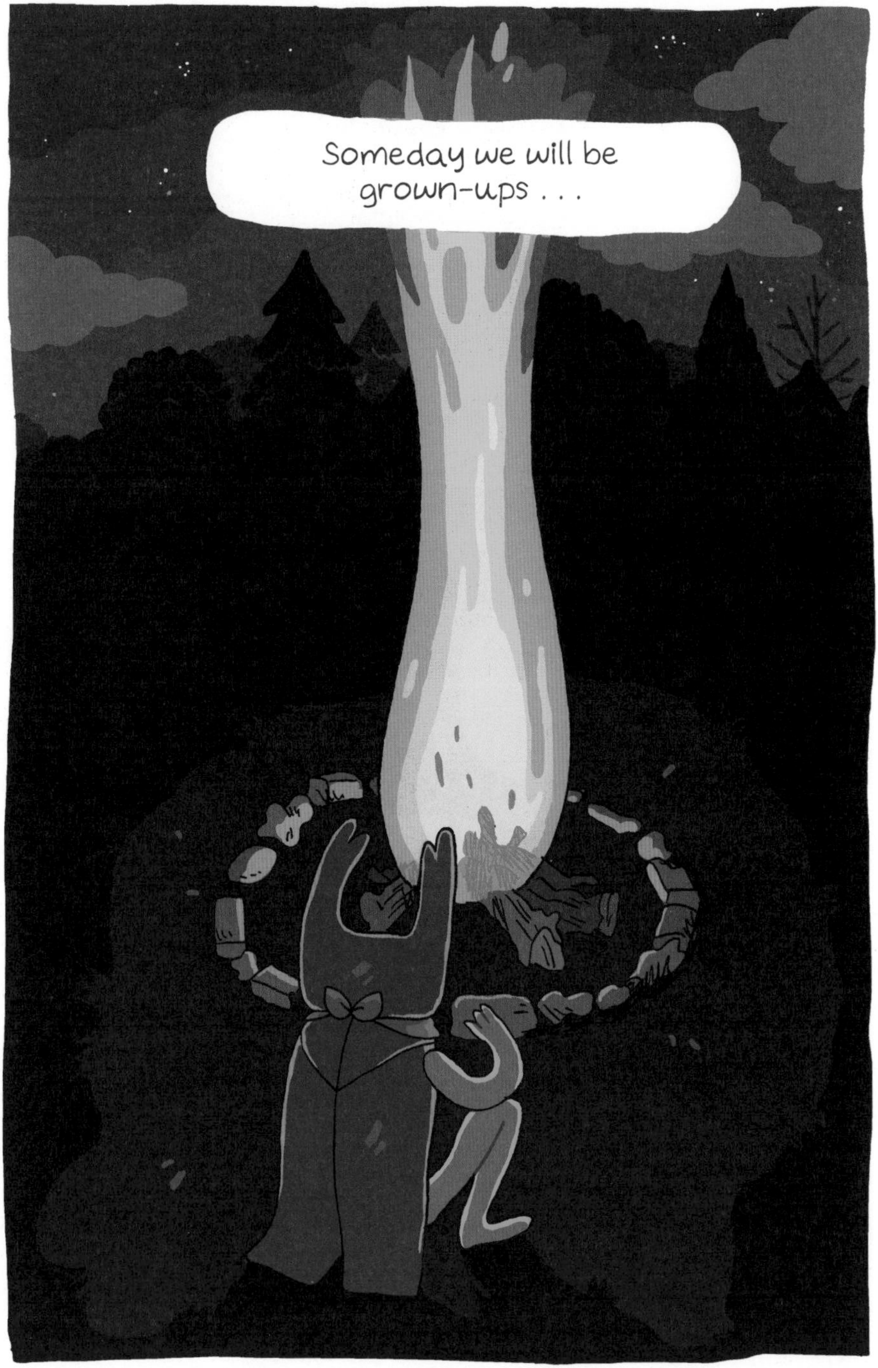
Someday we will be grown-ups . . .

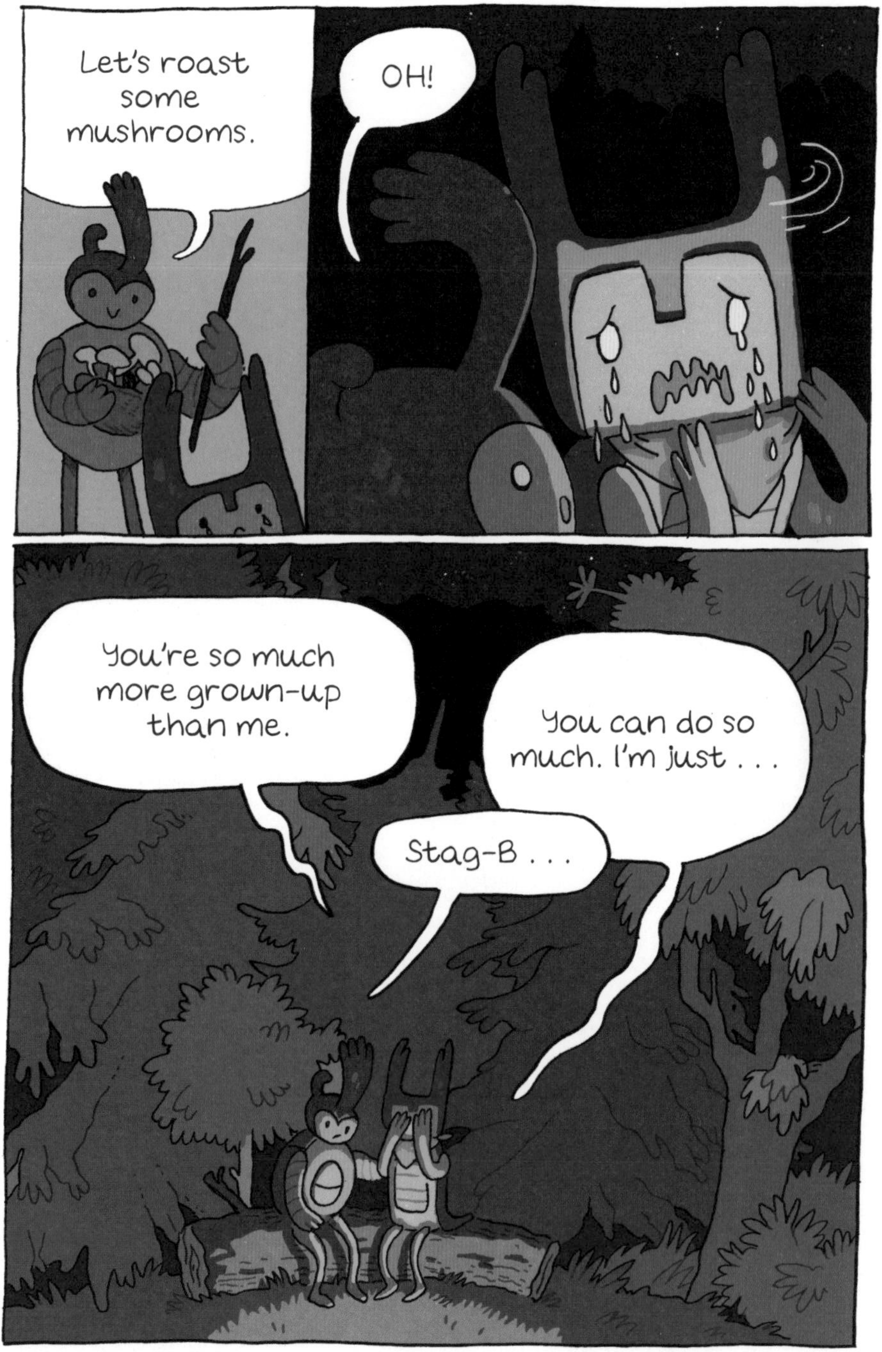
Let's roast some mushrooms.
OH!
You're so much more grown-up than me.
You can do so much. I'm just . . .
Stag-B . . .

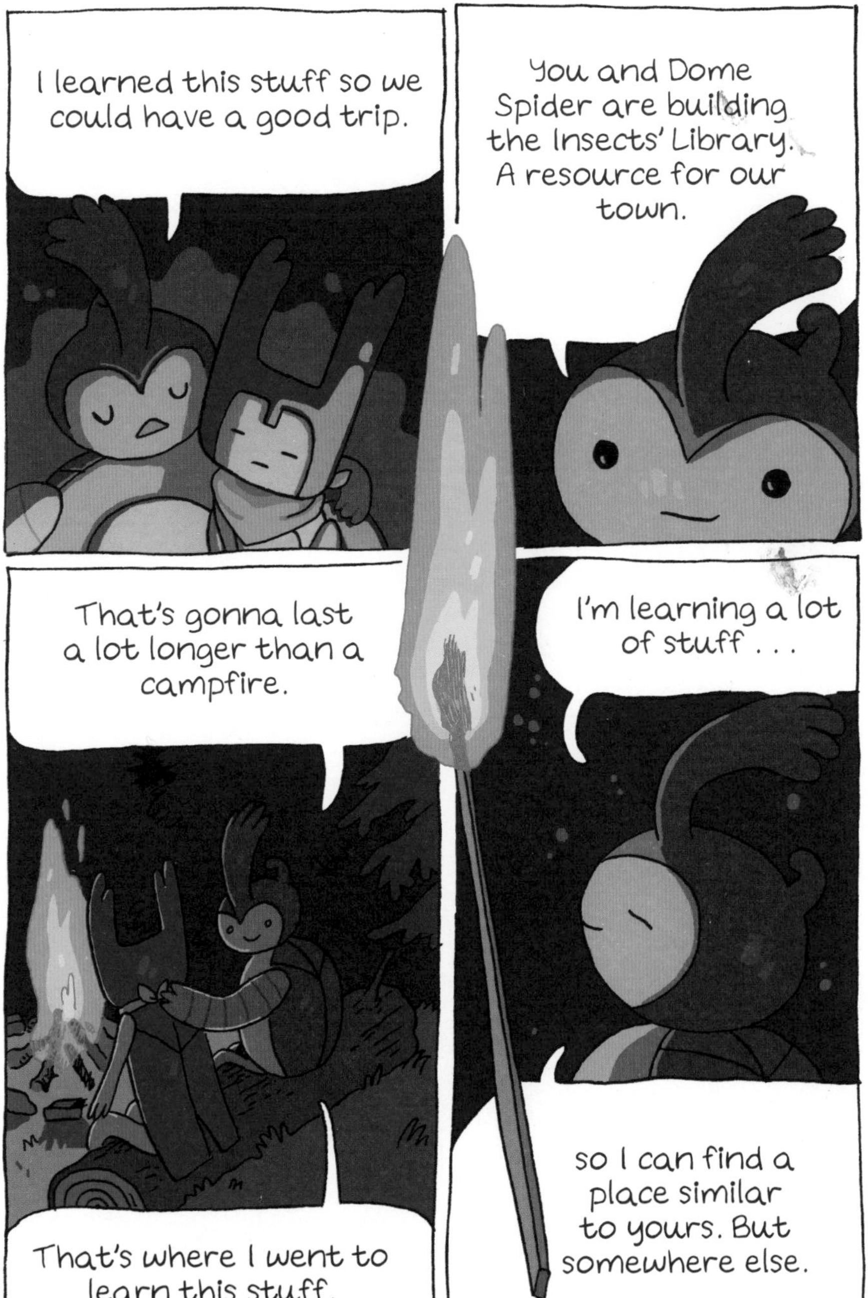
I learned this stuff so we could have a good trip.
You and Dome Spider are building the Insects' Library. A resource for our town.
That's gonna last a lot longer than a campfire.
That's where I went to learn this stuff.
I'm learning a lot of stuff . . .
so I can find a place similar to yours. But somewhere else.

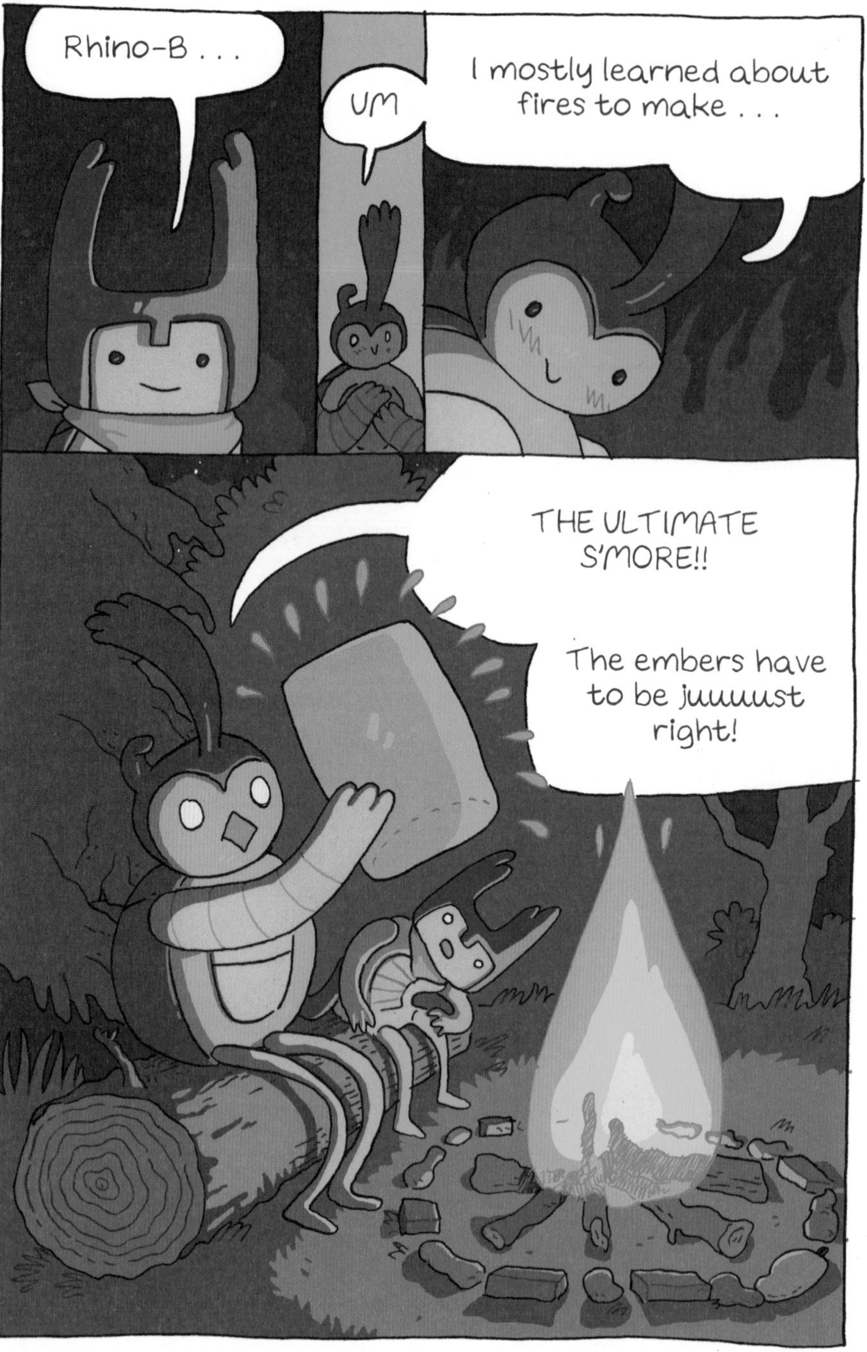
Rhino-B . . .
UM
I mostly learned about fires to make . . .
THE ULTIMATE S'MORE!!
The embers have to be juuuust right!

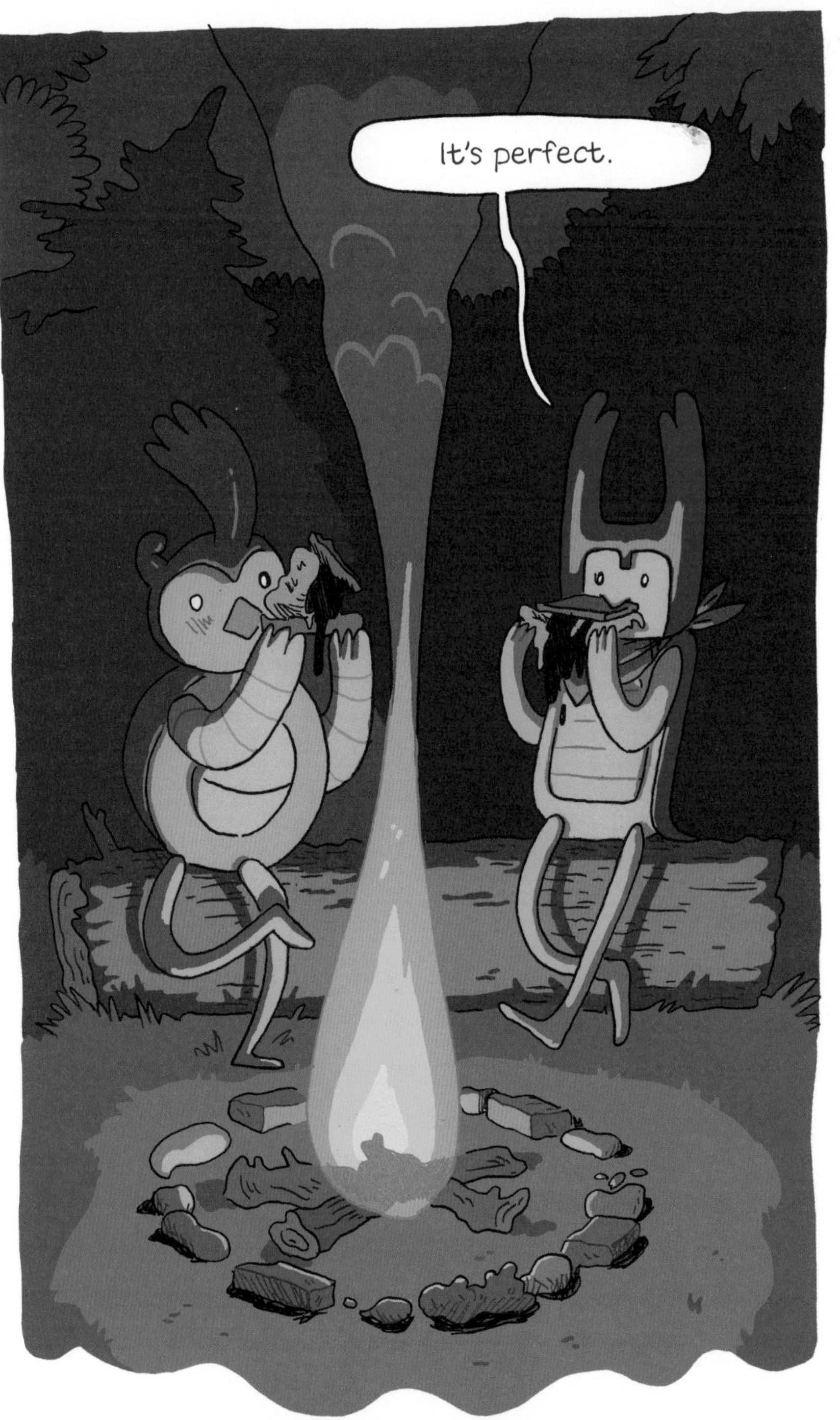
It's perfect.

DRAGONFLY QUEST
Morning! Letter!
Oh!
I'm Dragonfly. I'm twelve Bug years old.
Bye!
My favorite subject is geography.

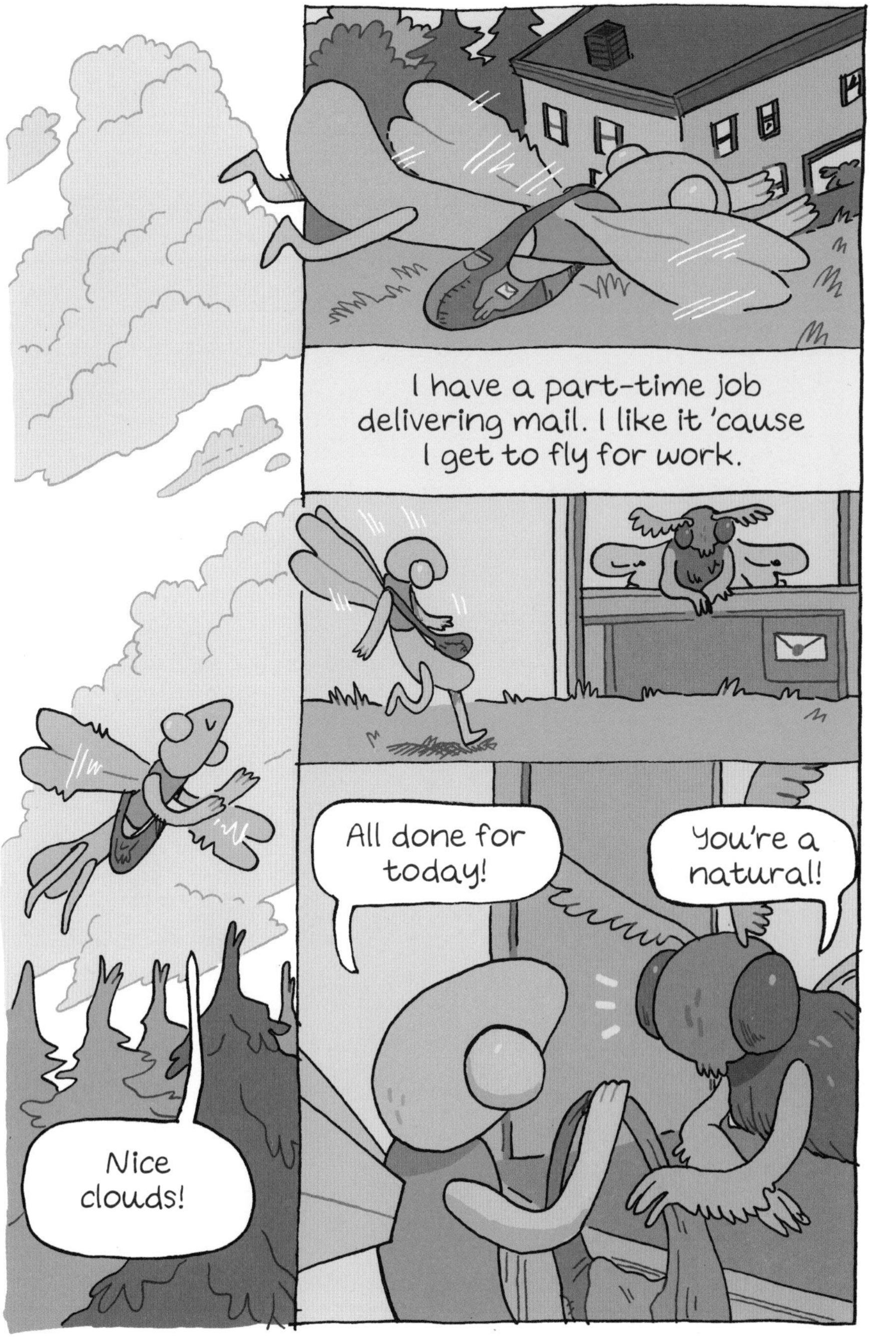
I have a part-time job delivering mail. I like it 'cause I get to fly for work.
All done for today!
You're a natural!
Nice clouds!

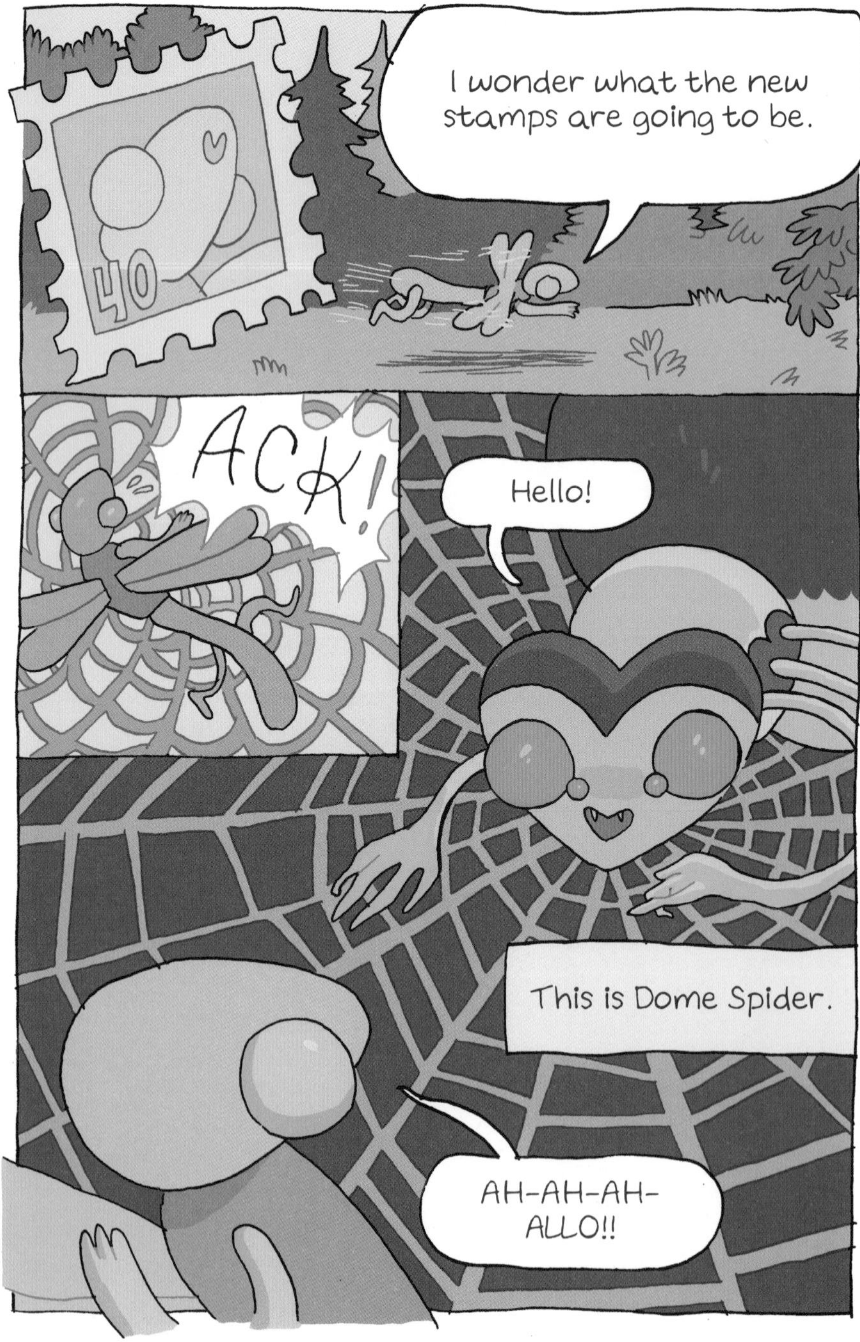
I wonder what the new stamps are going to be.
40
ACK!
Hello!
This is Dome Spider.
AH-AH-AH-ALLO!!

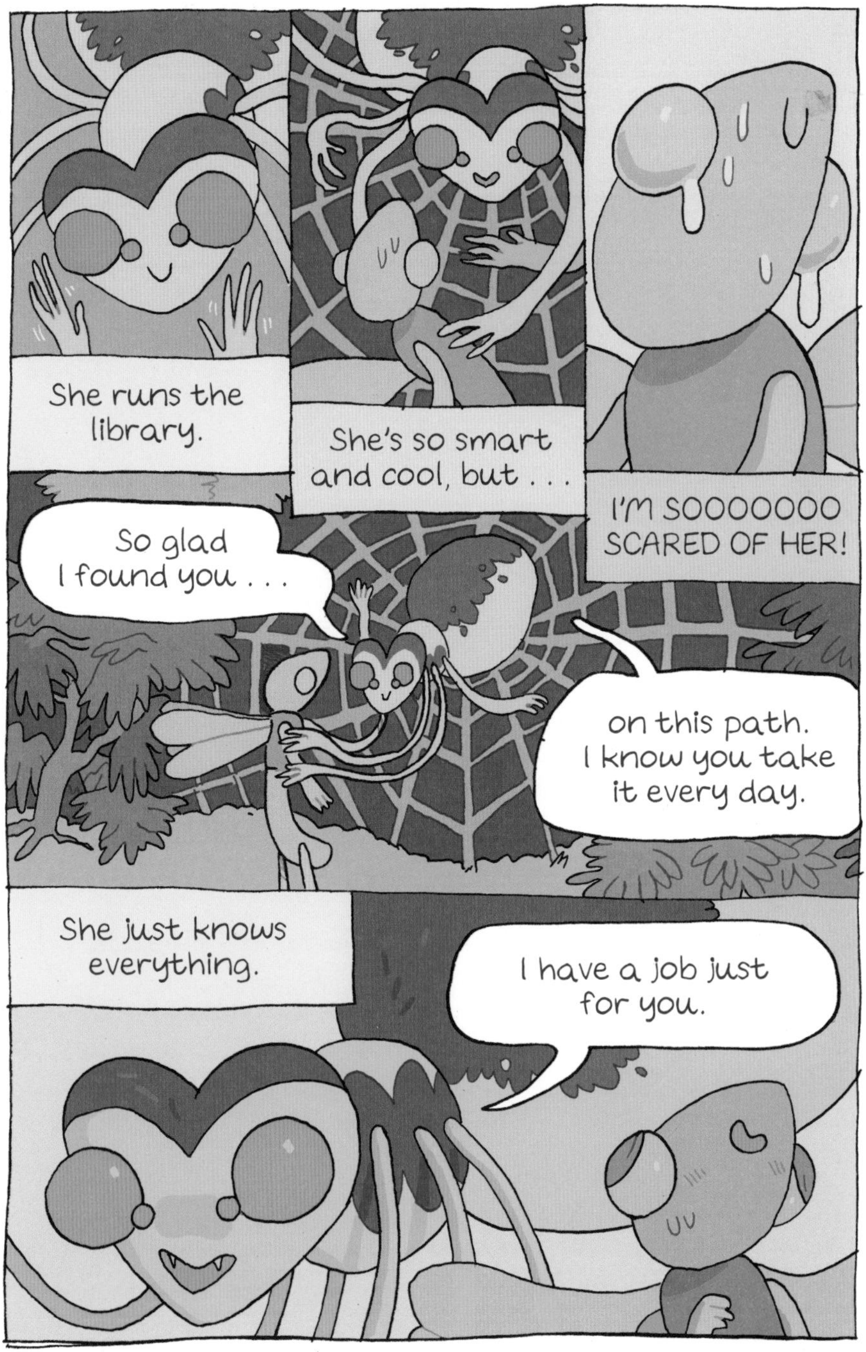
She runs the library.
She's so smart and cool, but . . .
I'M SOOOOOOO SCARED OF HER!
So glad I found you . . .
on this path. I know you take it every day.
She just knows everything.
I have a job just for you.

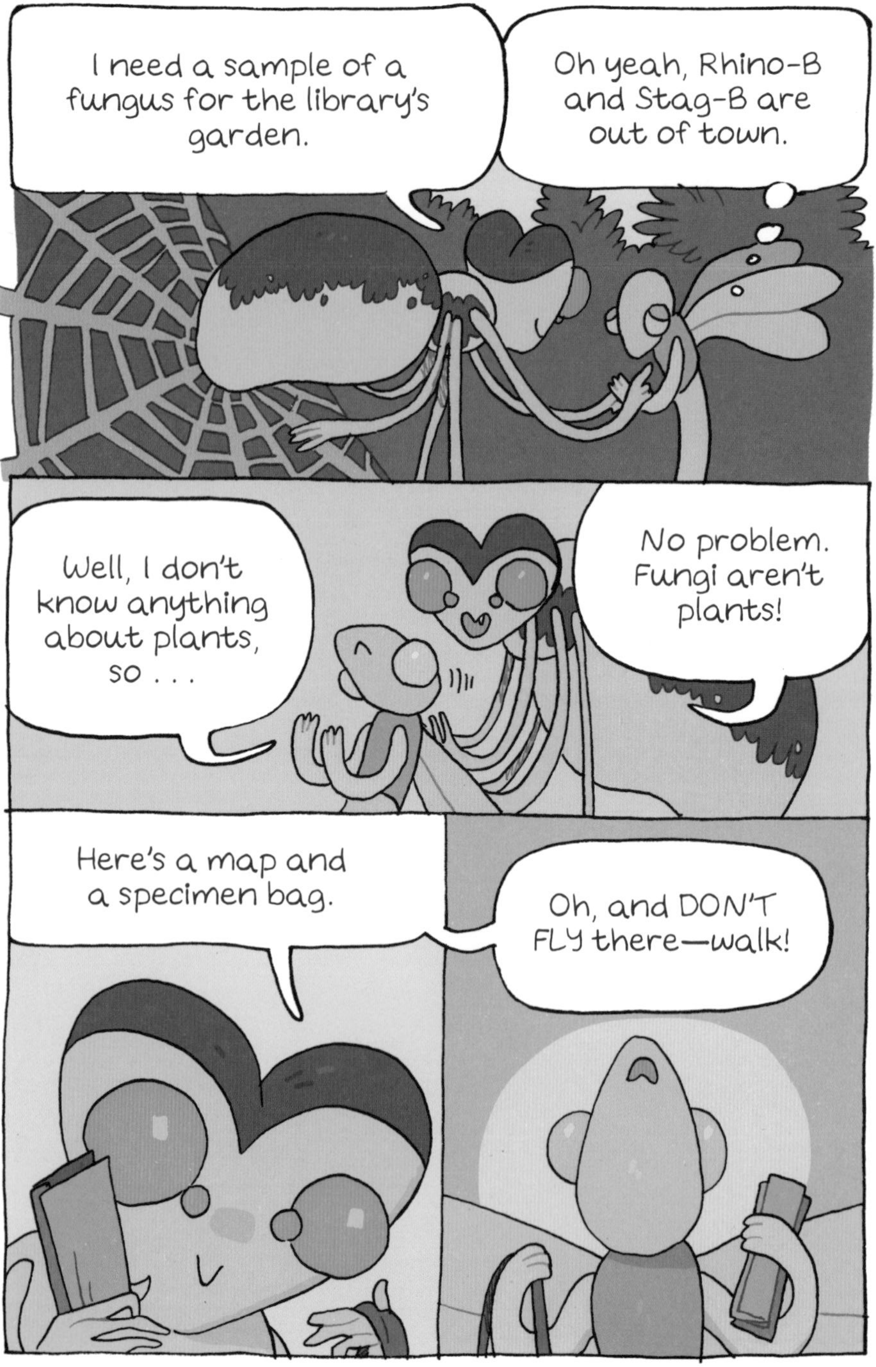
I need a sample of a fungus for the library's garden.
Oh yeah, Rhino-B and Stag-B are out of town.
Well, I don't know anything about plants, so . . .
No problem. Fungi aren't plants!
Here's a map and a specimen bag.
Oh, and DON'T FLY there—walk!

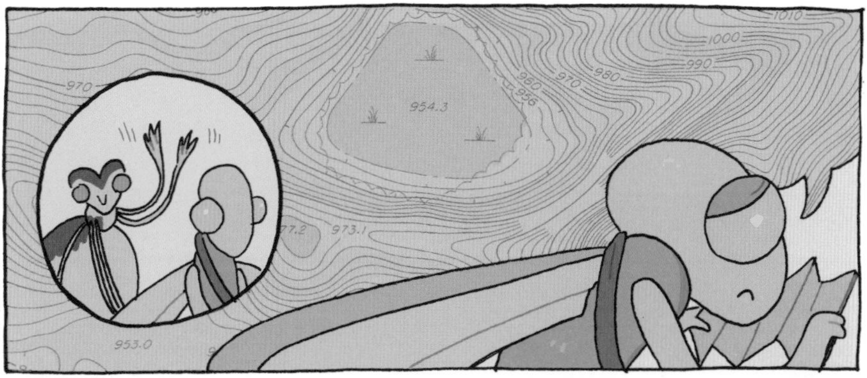
970
954.3
1010
1000
990
980
970
960
956
977.2
973.1
953.0

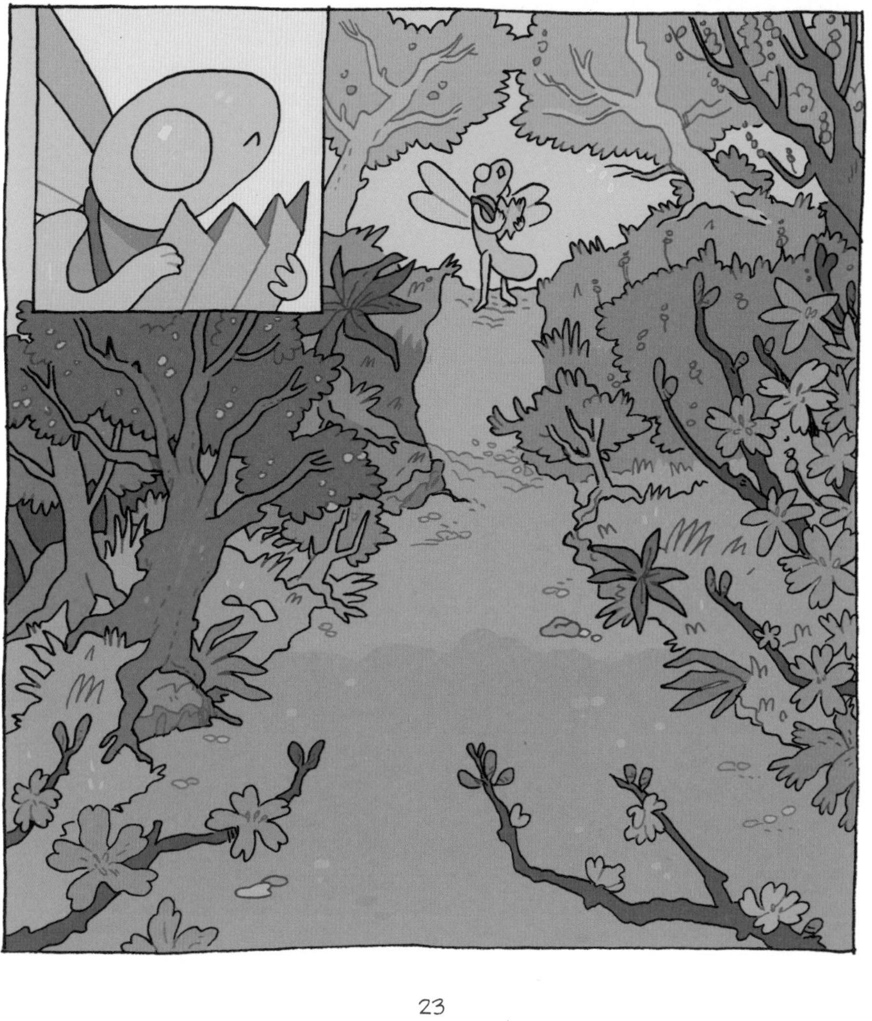

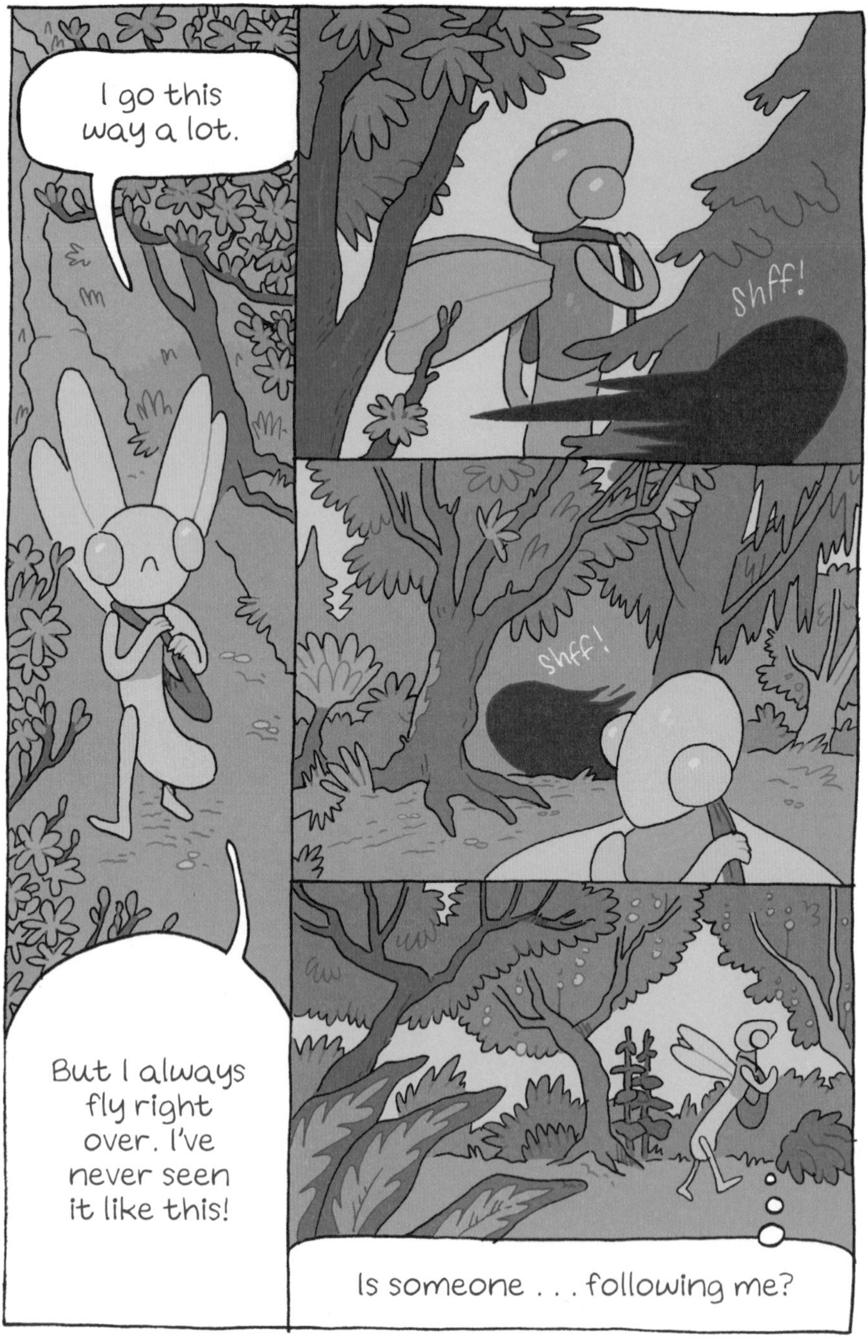
I go this way a lot.
shff!
shff!
But I always fly right over. I've never seen it like this!
Is someone . . . following me?

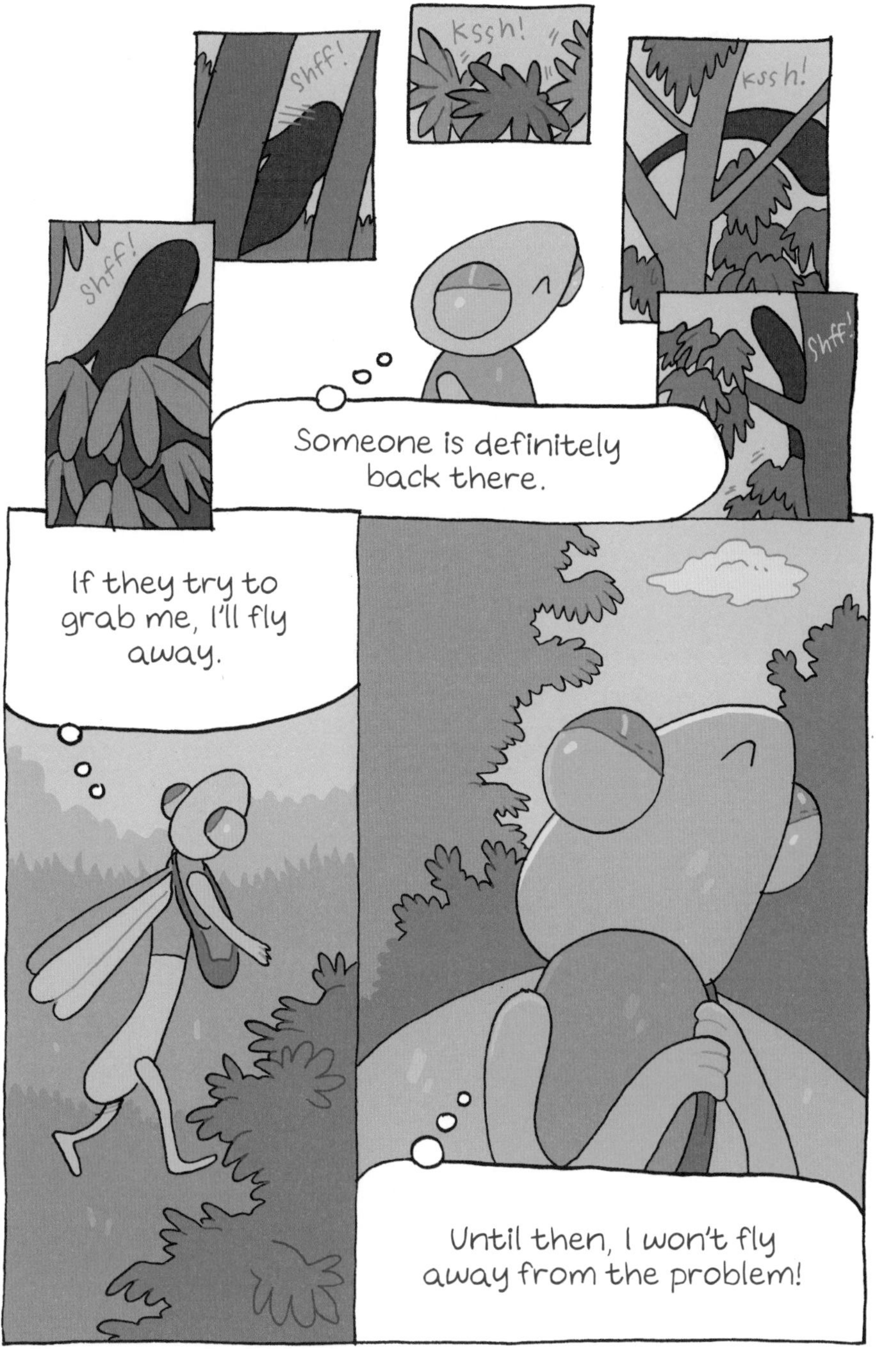
shff!
shff!
kssh!
kssh!
shff!
Someone is definitely back there.
If they try to grab me, I'll fly away.
Until then, I won't fly away from the problem!

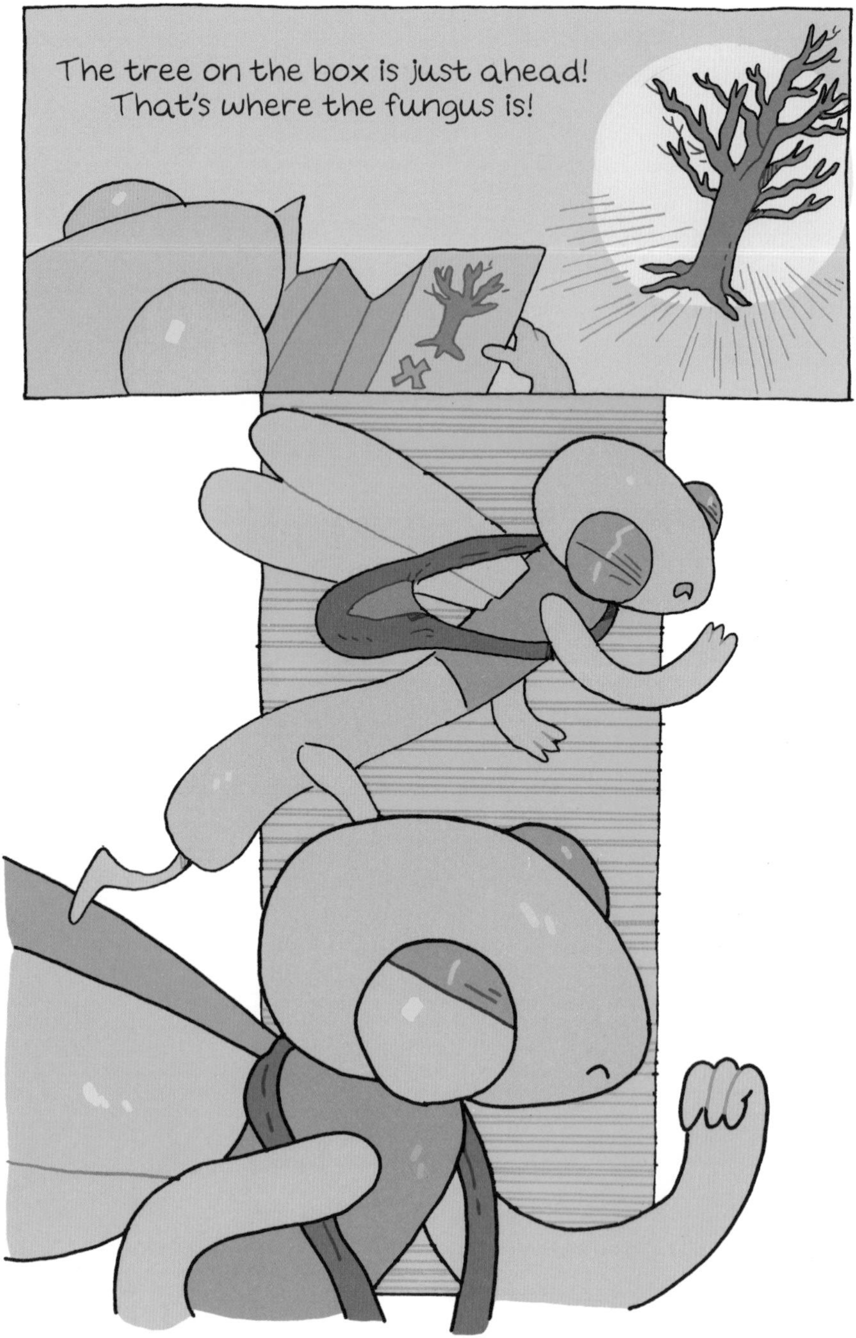
The tree on the box is just ahead!
That's where the fungus is!

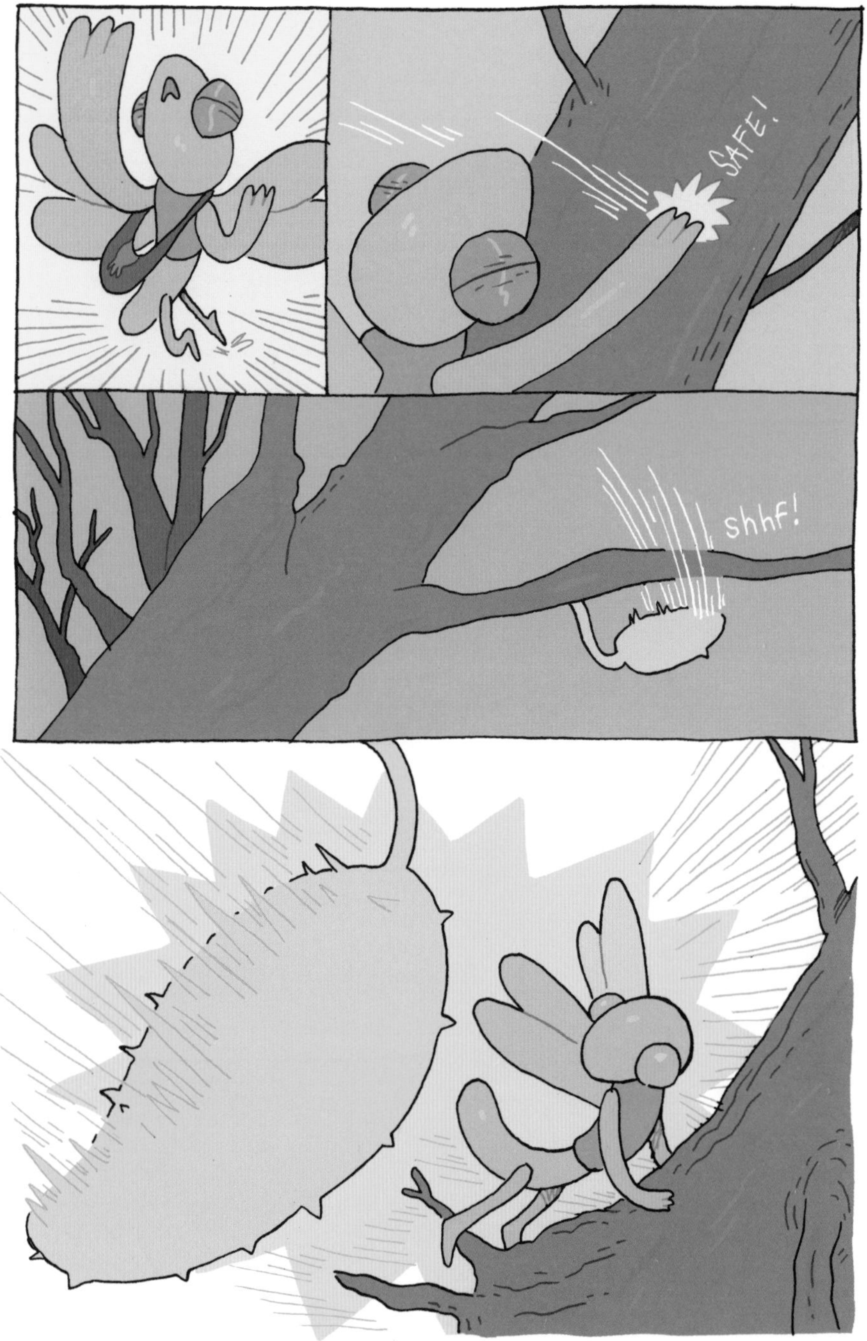
SAFE!
shhf!

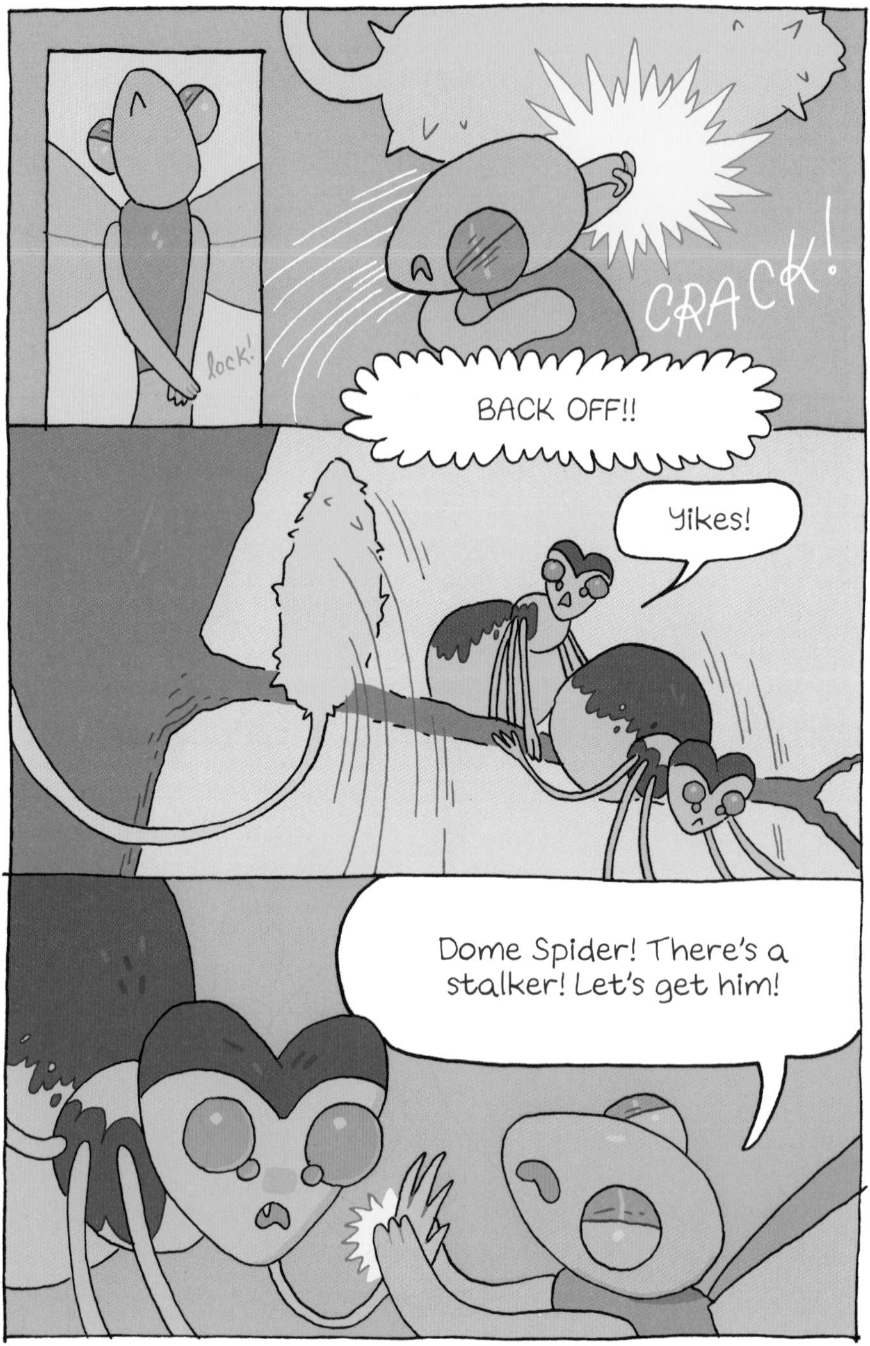
lock!
CRACK!
BACK OFF!!
Yikes!
Dome Spider! There's a stalker! Let's get him!

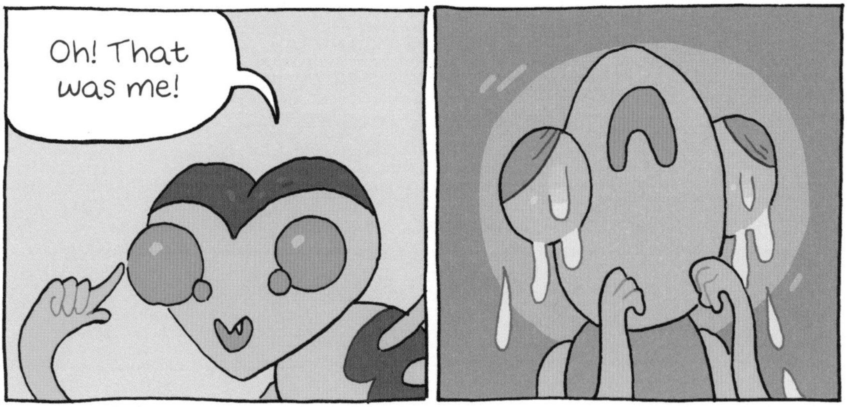
Oh! That was me!

Don't worry! An adult you trust was there!

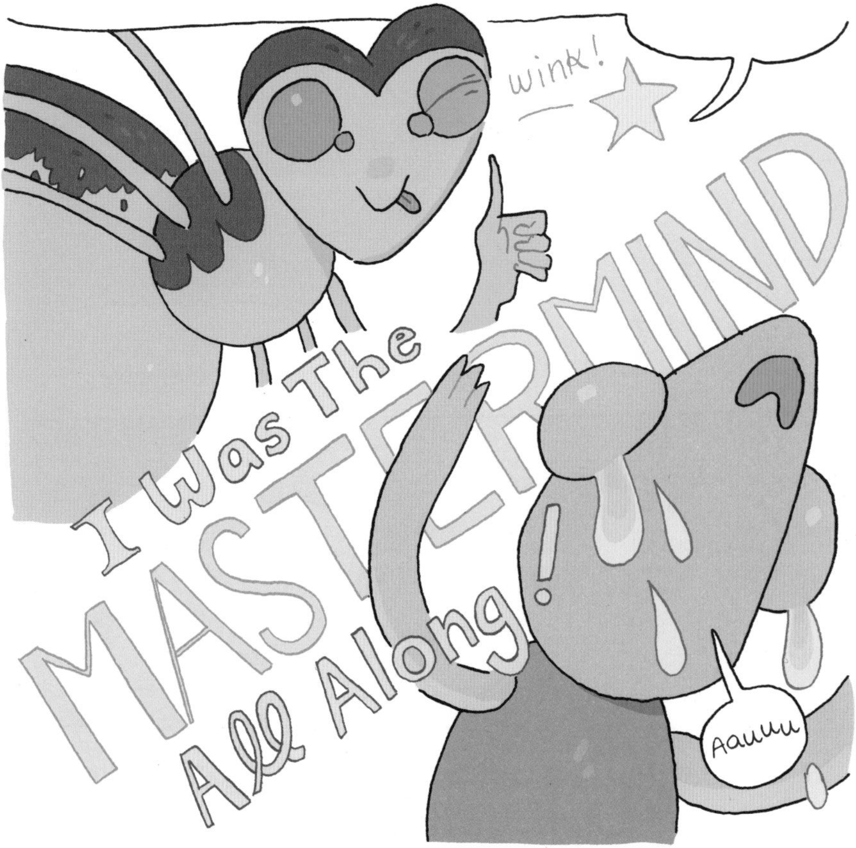
wink!
I Was The MASTERMIND All Along!
Aauuu

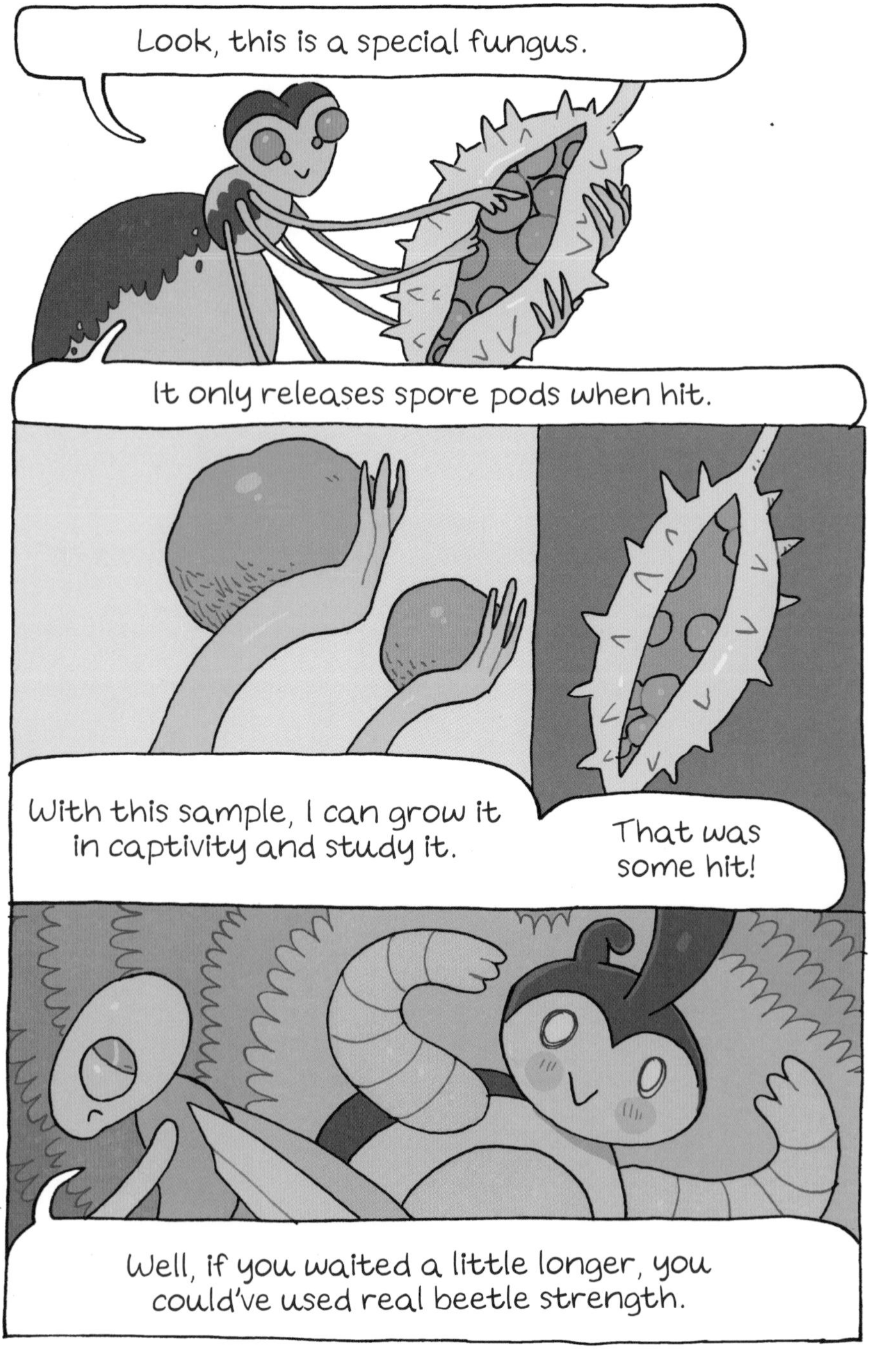
Look, this is a special fungus.
It only releases spore pods when hit.
With this sample, I can grow it in captivity and study it.
That was some hit!
Well, if you waited a little longer, you could've used real beetle strength.

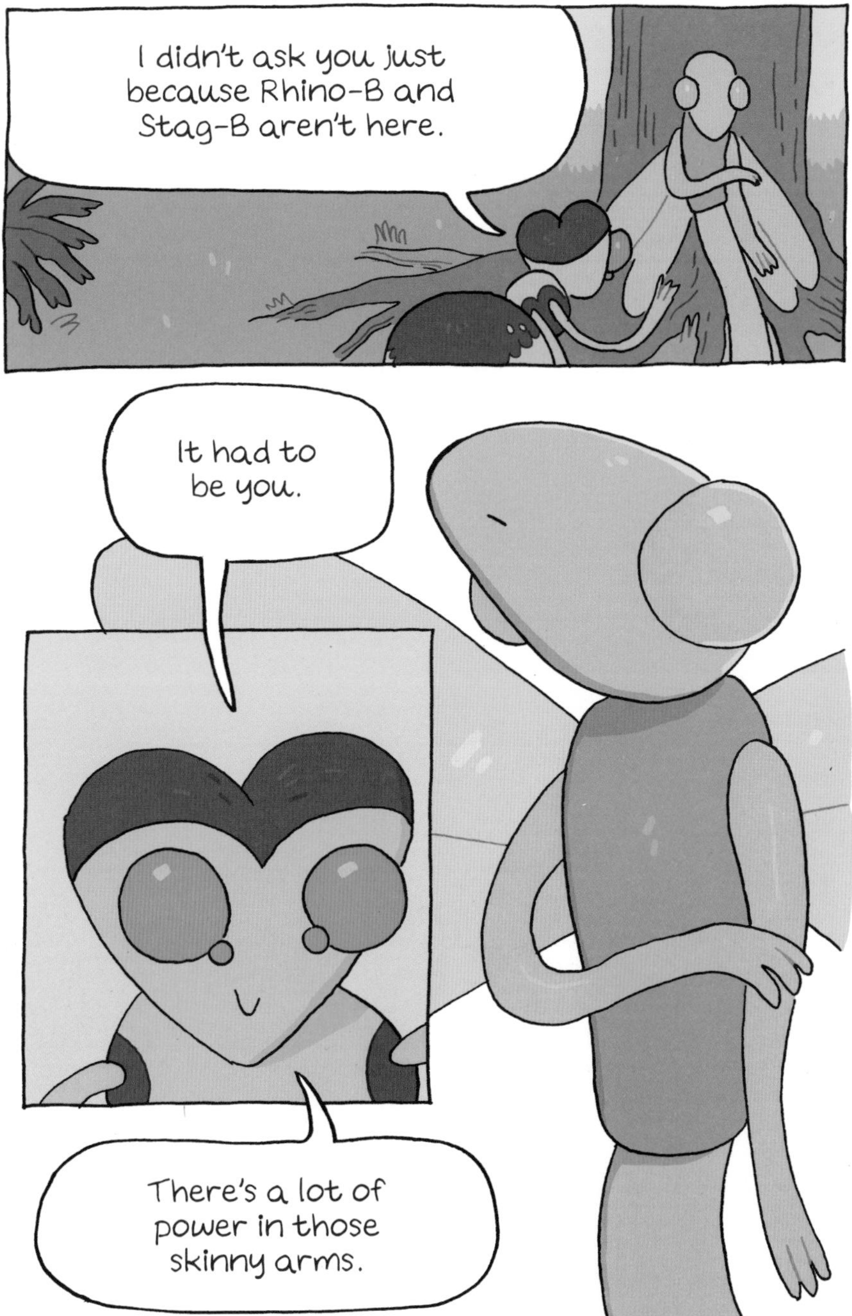
I didn't ask you just because Rhino-B and Stag-B aren't here.
It had to be you.
There's a lot of power in those skinny arms.

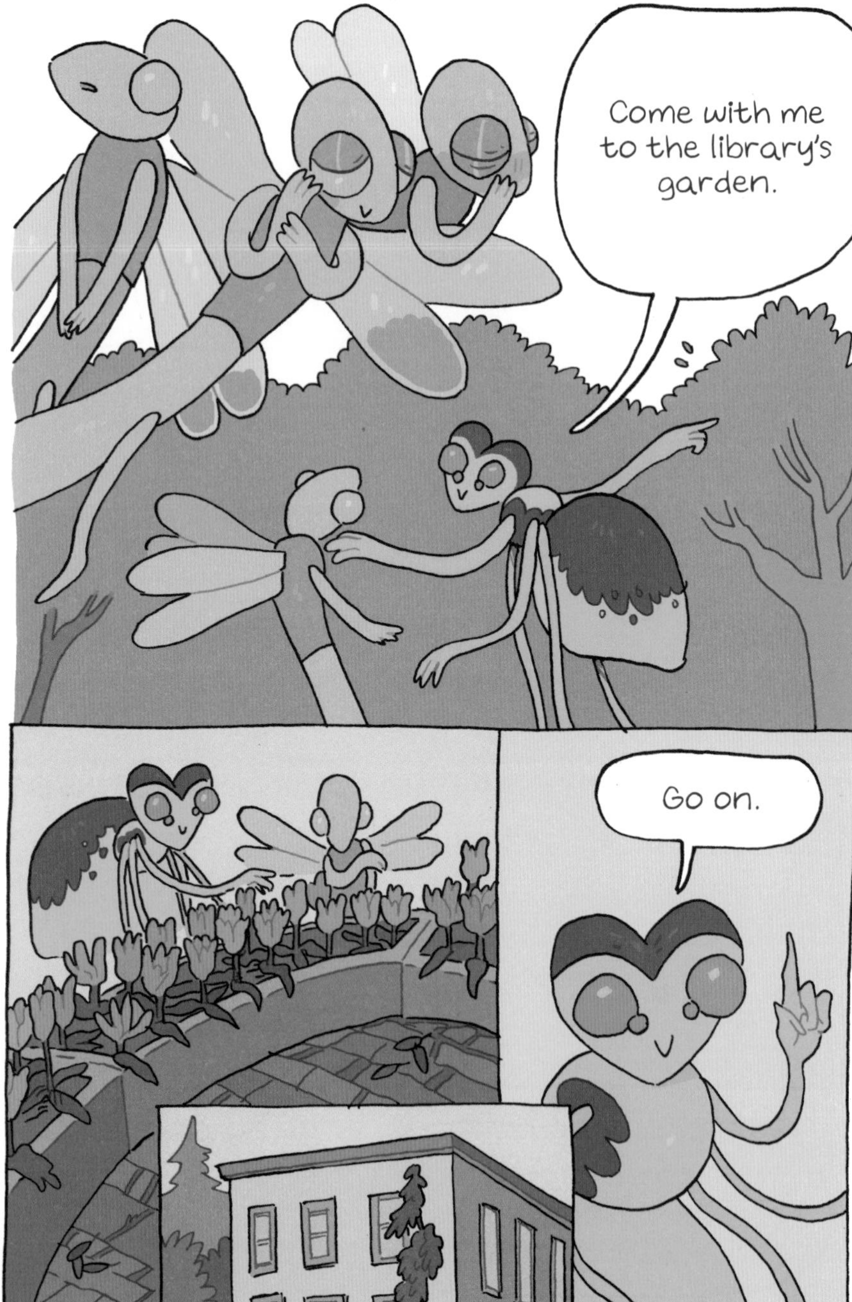
Come with me to the library's garden.
Go on.

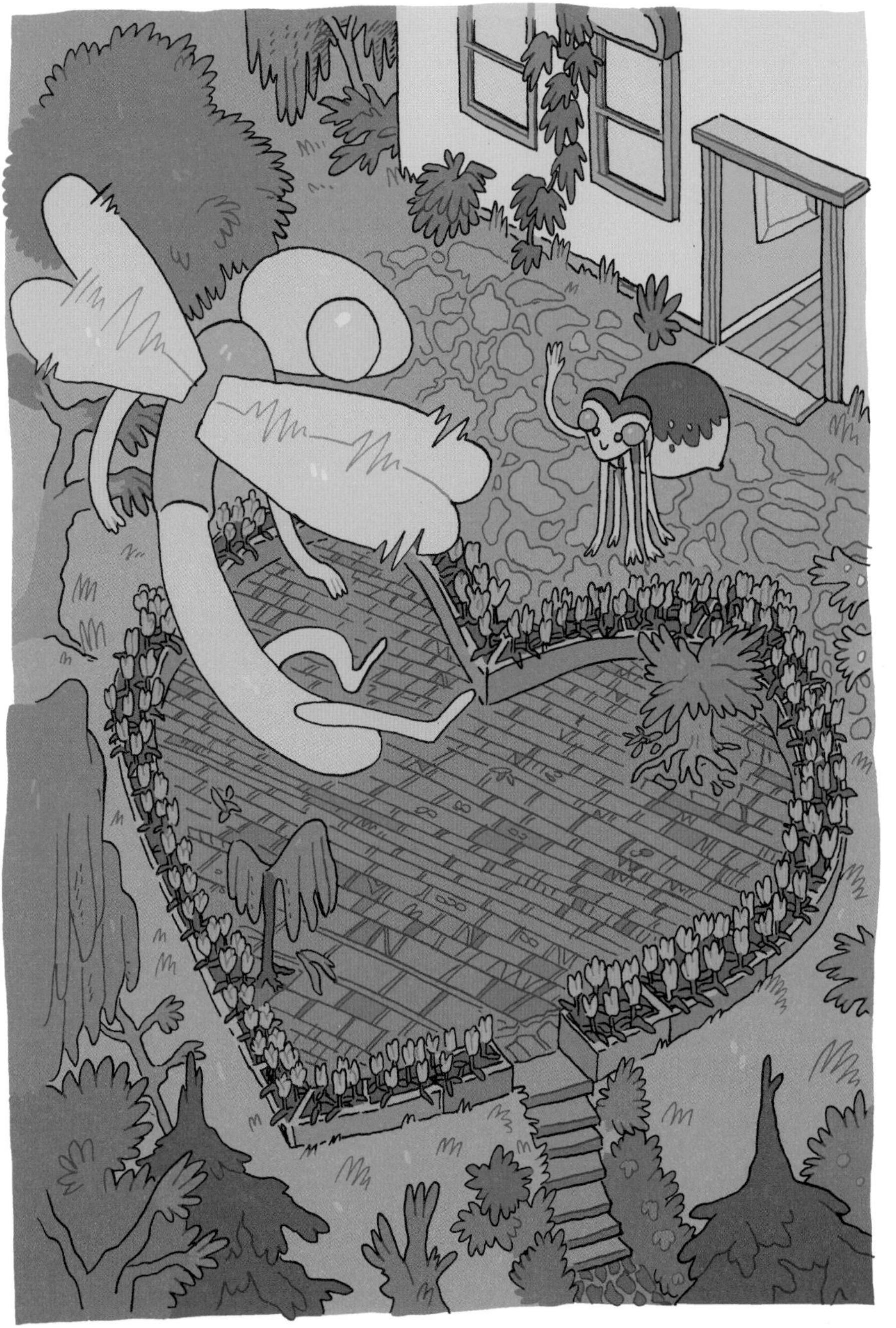

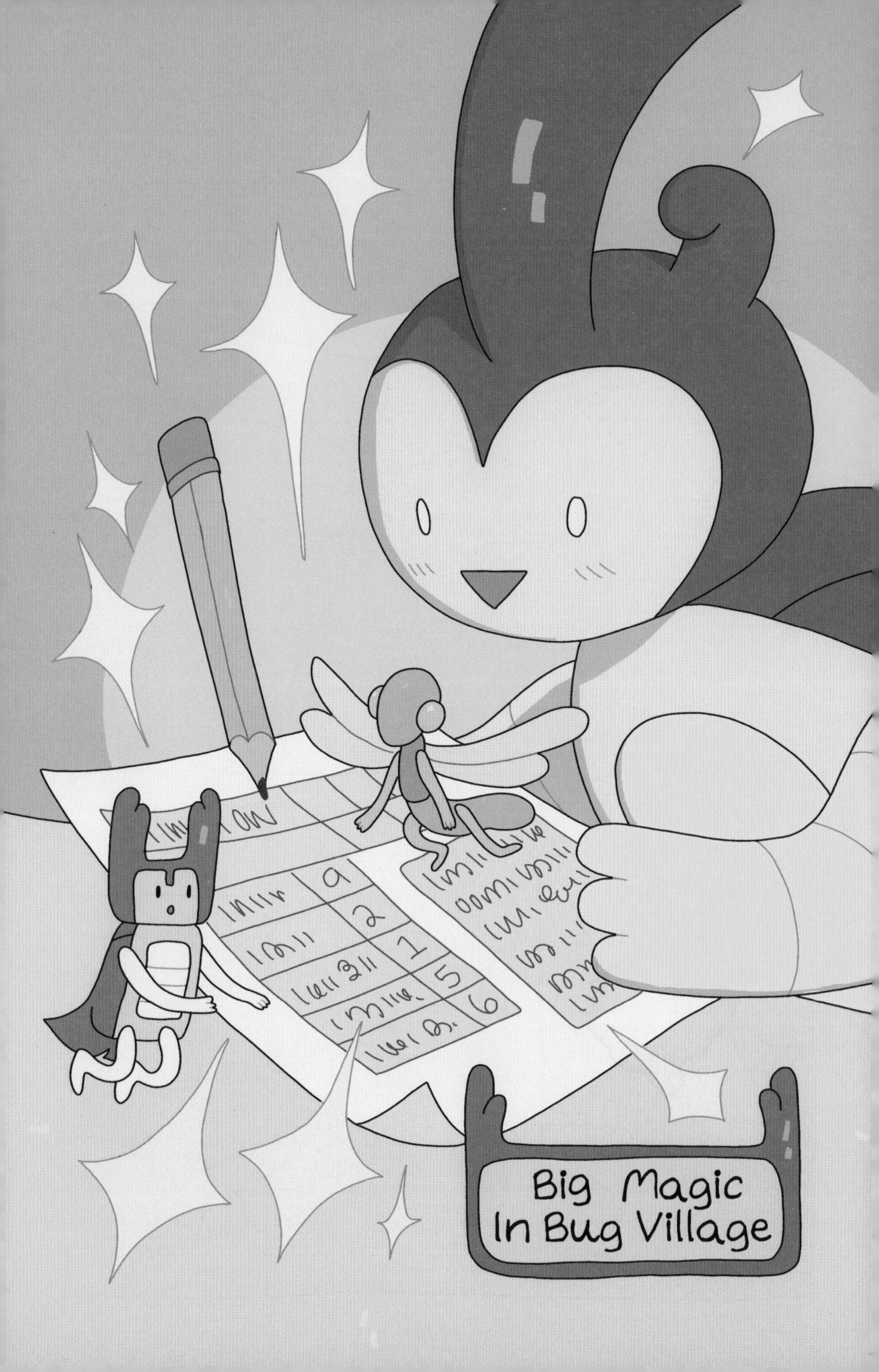
Big Magic
In Bug Village

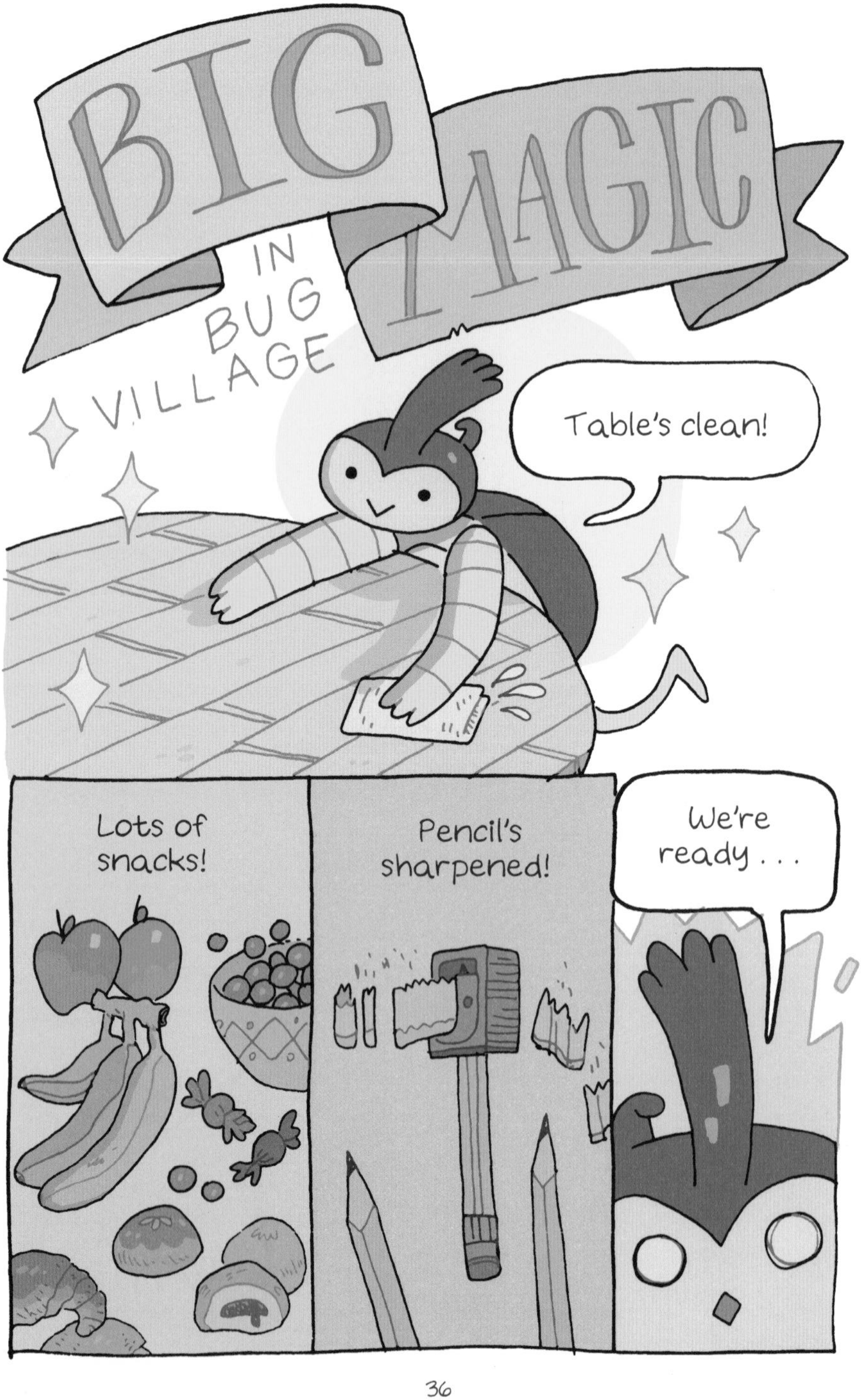
BIG MAGIC
IN BUG VILLAGE
Table's clean!
Lots of snacks!
Pencil's sharpened!
We're ready . . .

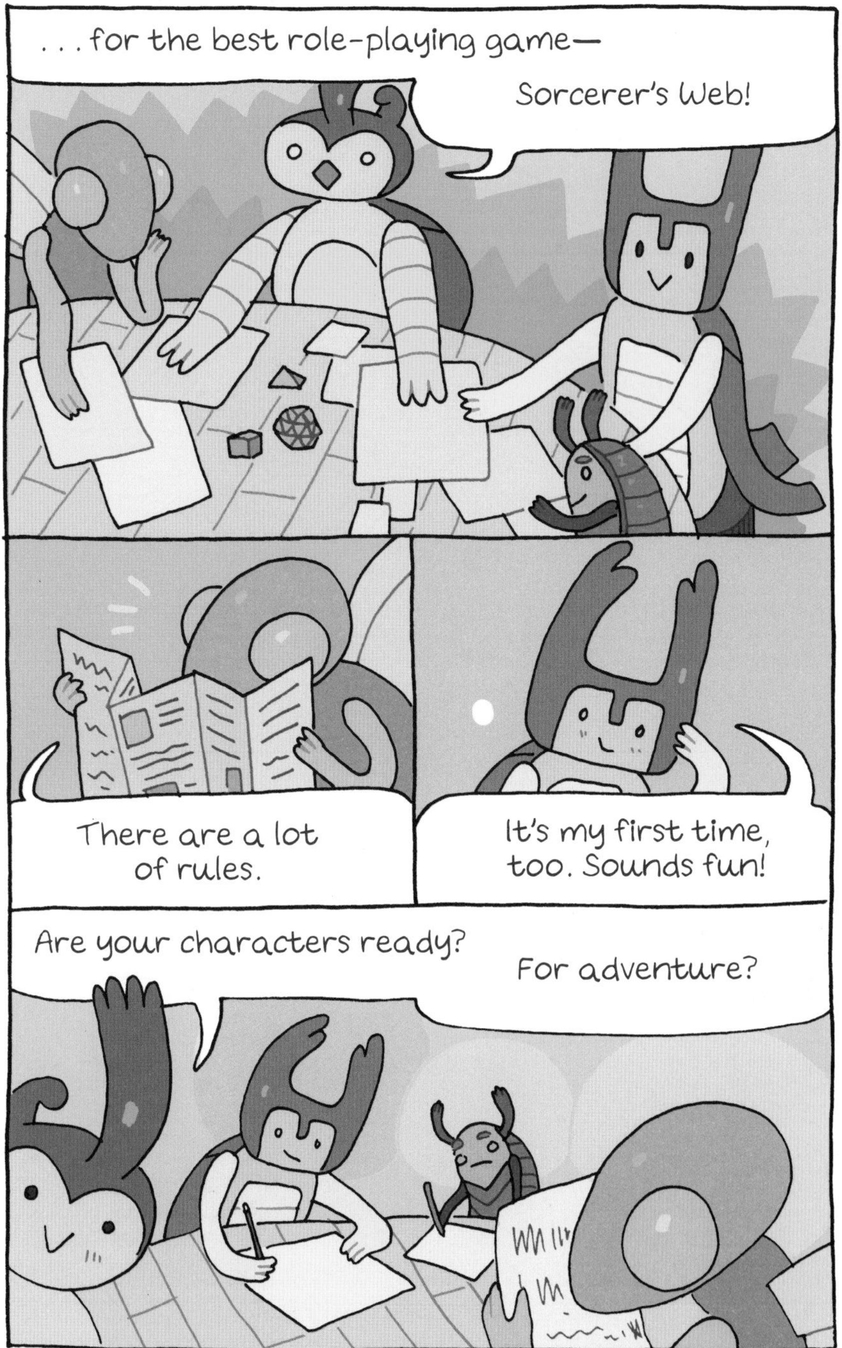
. . . for the best role-playing game—
Sorcerer's Web!
There are a lot of rules.
It's my first time, too. Sounds fun!
Are your characters ready?
For adventure?

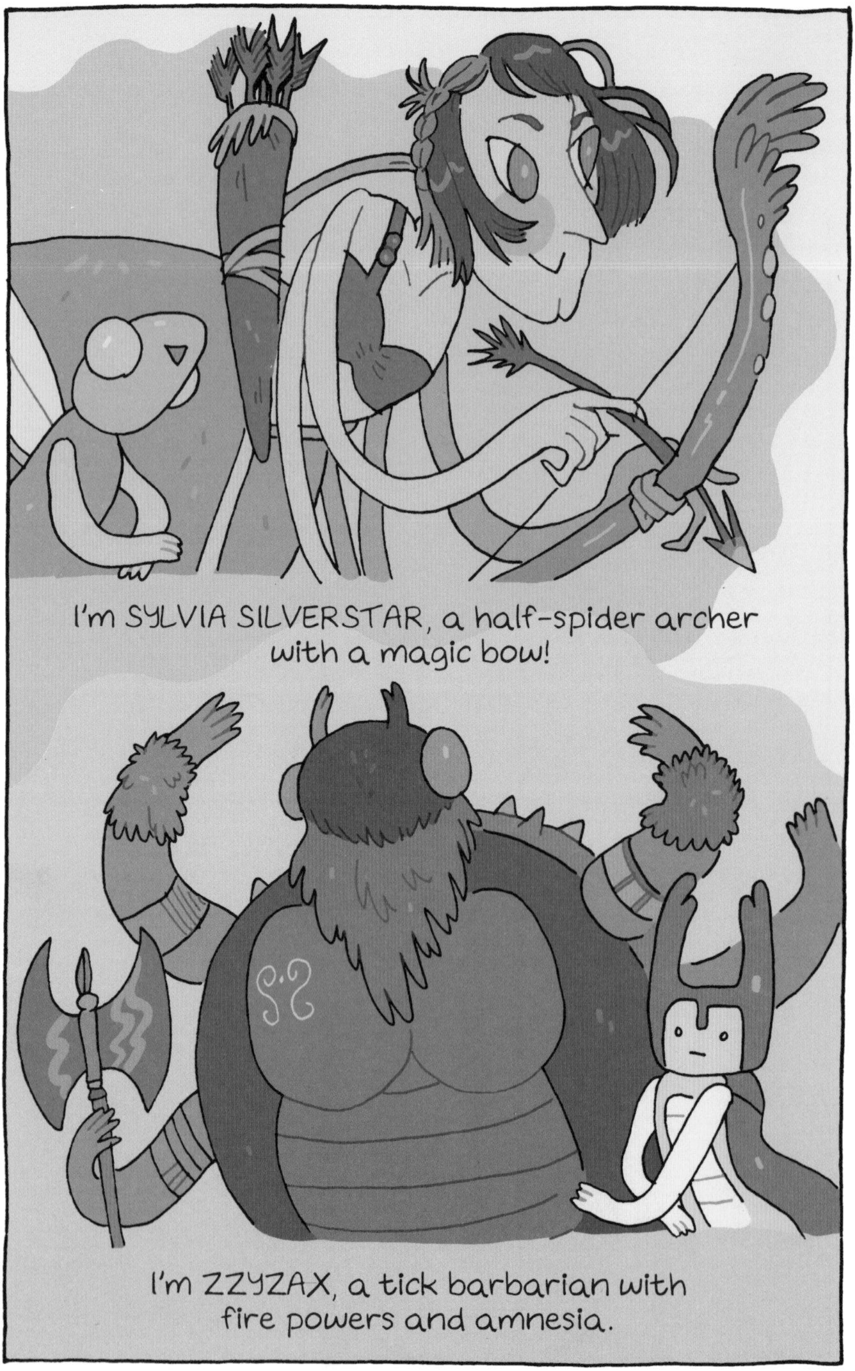
I'm SYLVIA SILVERSTAR, a half-spider archer with a magic bow!
I'm ZZYZAX, a tick barbarian with fire powers and amnesia.

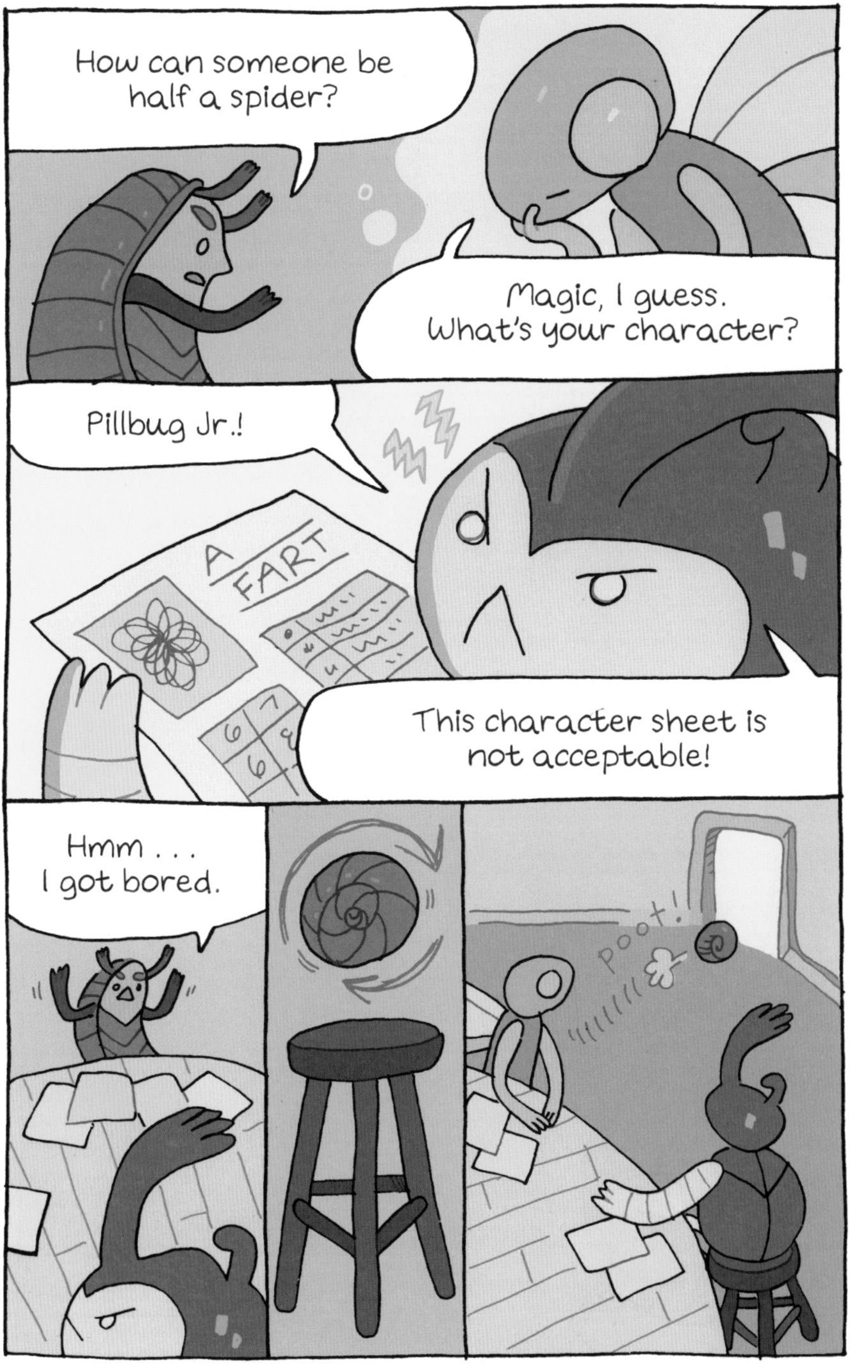
How can someone be half a spider?
Magic, I guess. What's your character?
Pillbug Jr.!
A FART
This character sheet is not acceptable!
Hmm . . . I got bored.
poot!

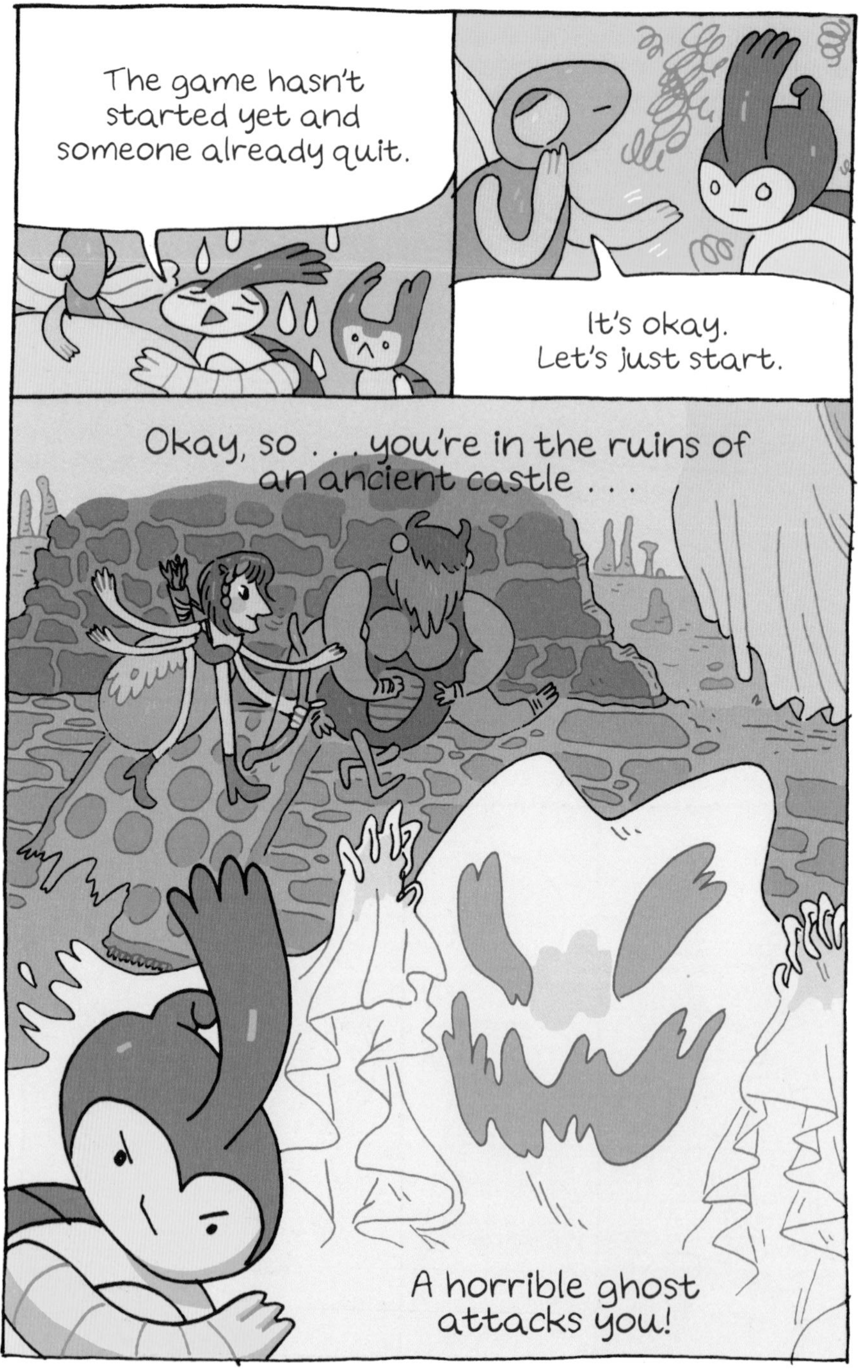
The game hasn't started yet and someone already quit.
It's okay. Let's just start.
Okay, so . . . you're in the ruins of an ancient castle . . .
A horrible ghost attacks you!

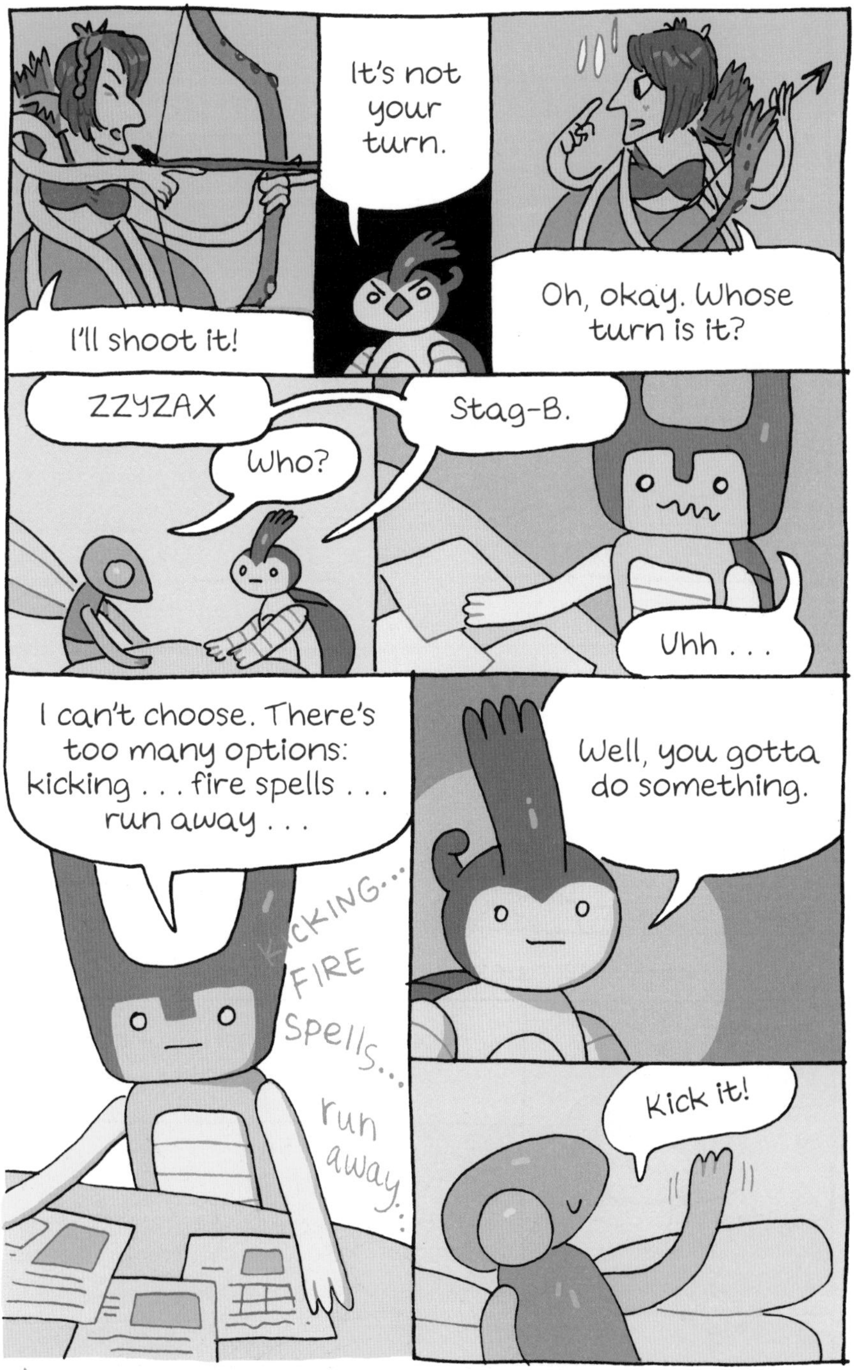
I'll shoot it!
It's not your turn.
Oh, okay. Whose turn is it?
ZZYZAX
Stag-B.
Who?
Uhh . . .
I can't choose. There's too many options: kicking . . . fire spells . . . run away . . .
KICKING...
FIRE
Spells...
run
away...
Well, you gotta do something.
Kick it!

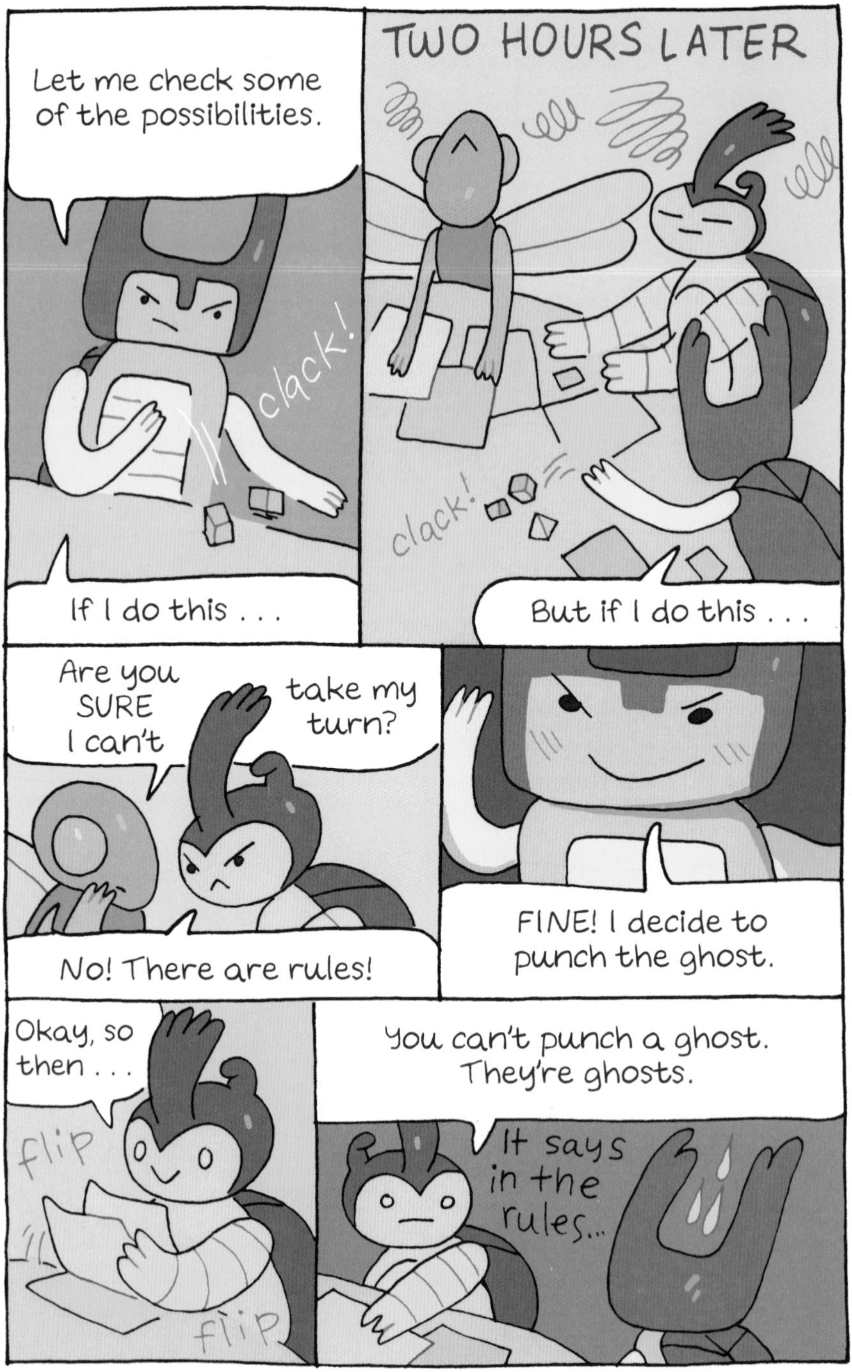
Let me check some of the possibilities.
clack!
If I do this . . .
TWO HOURS LATER
clack!
But if I do this . . .
Are you SURE I can't take my turn?
No! There are rules!
FINE! I decide to punch the ghost.
Okay, so then . . .
flip
flip
You can't punch a ghost. They're ghosts.
It says in the rules...

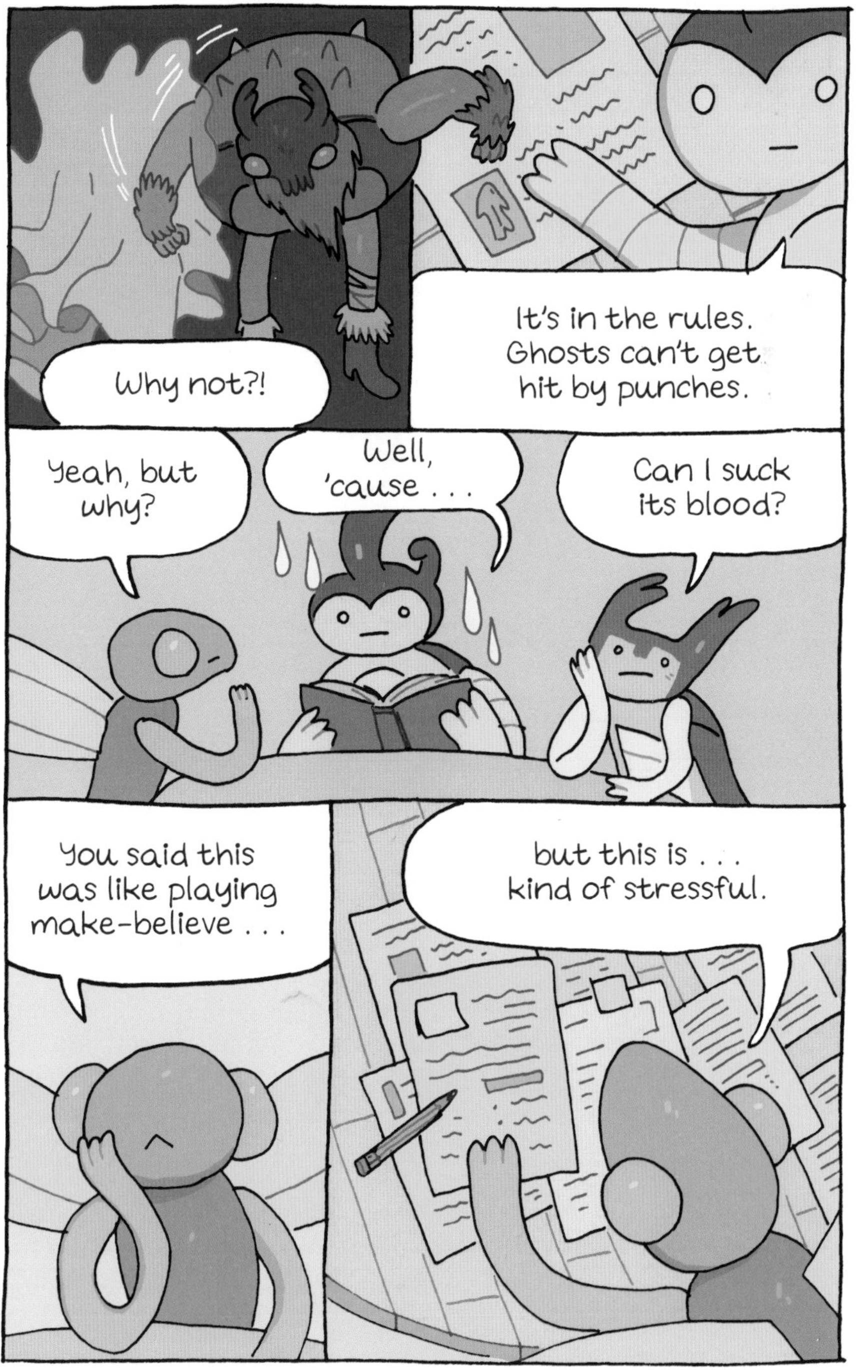
Why not?!
It's in the rules. Ghosts can't get hit by punches.
Yeah, but why?
Well, 'cause . . .
Can I suck its blood?
You said this was like playing make-believe . . .
but this is . . . kind of stressful.

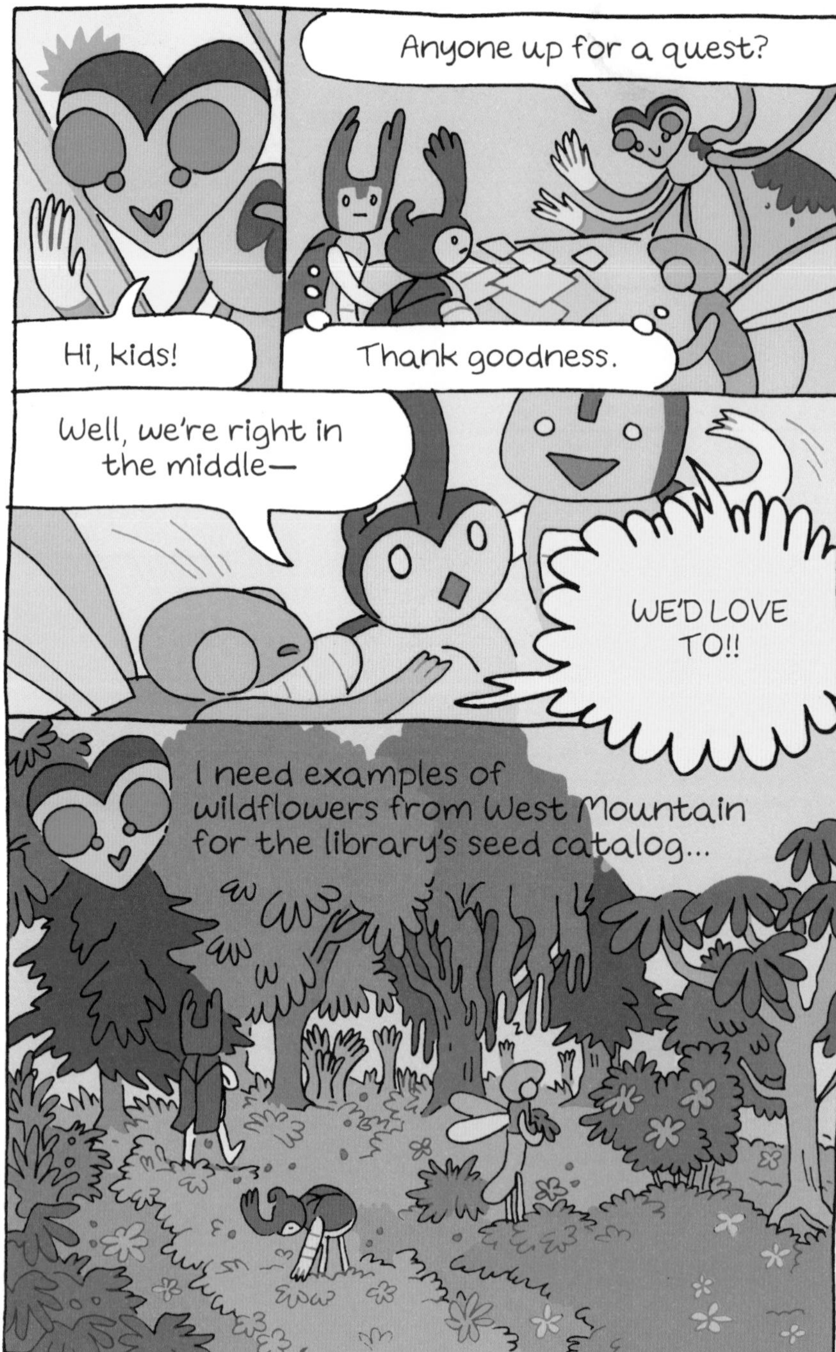
Hi, kids!
Anyone up for a quest?
Thank goodness.
Well, we're right in the middle—
WE'D LOVE TO!!
I need examples of wildflowers from West Mountain for the library's seed catalog...

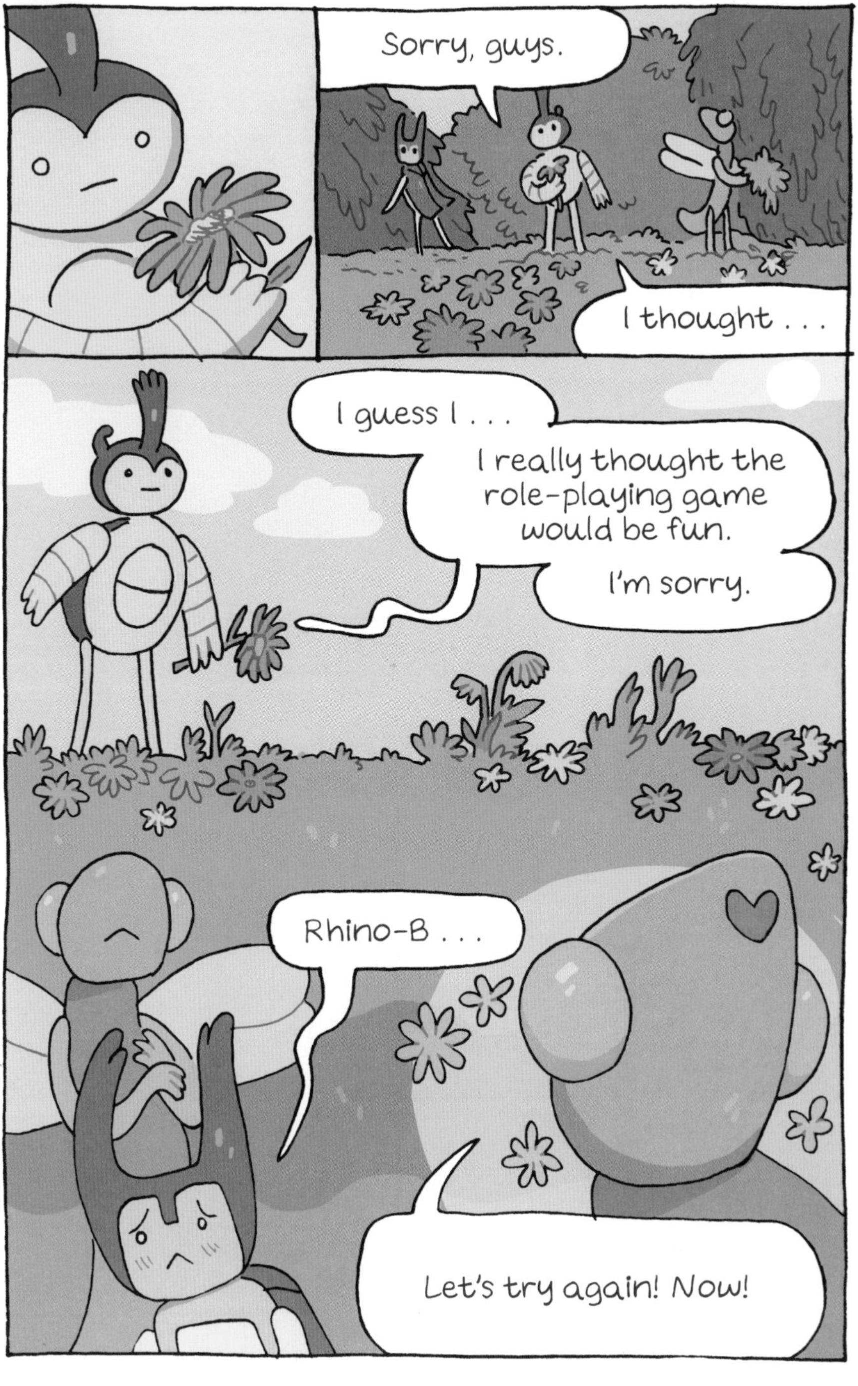
Sorry, guys.
I thought . . .
I guess I . . .
I really thought the role-playing game would be fun.
I'm sorry.
Rhino-B . . .
Let's try again! Now!

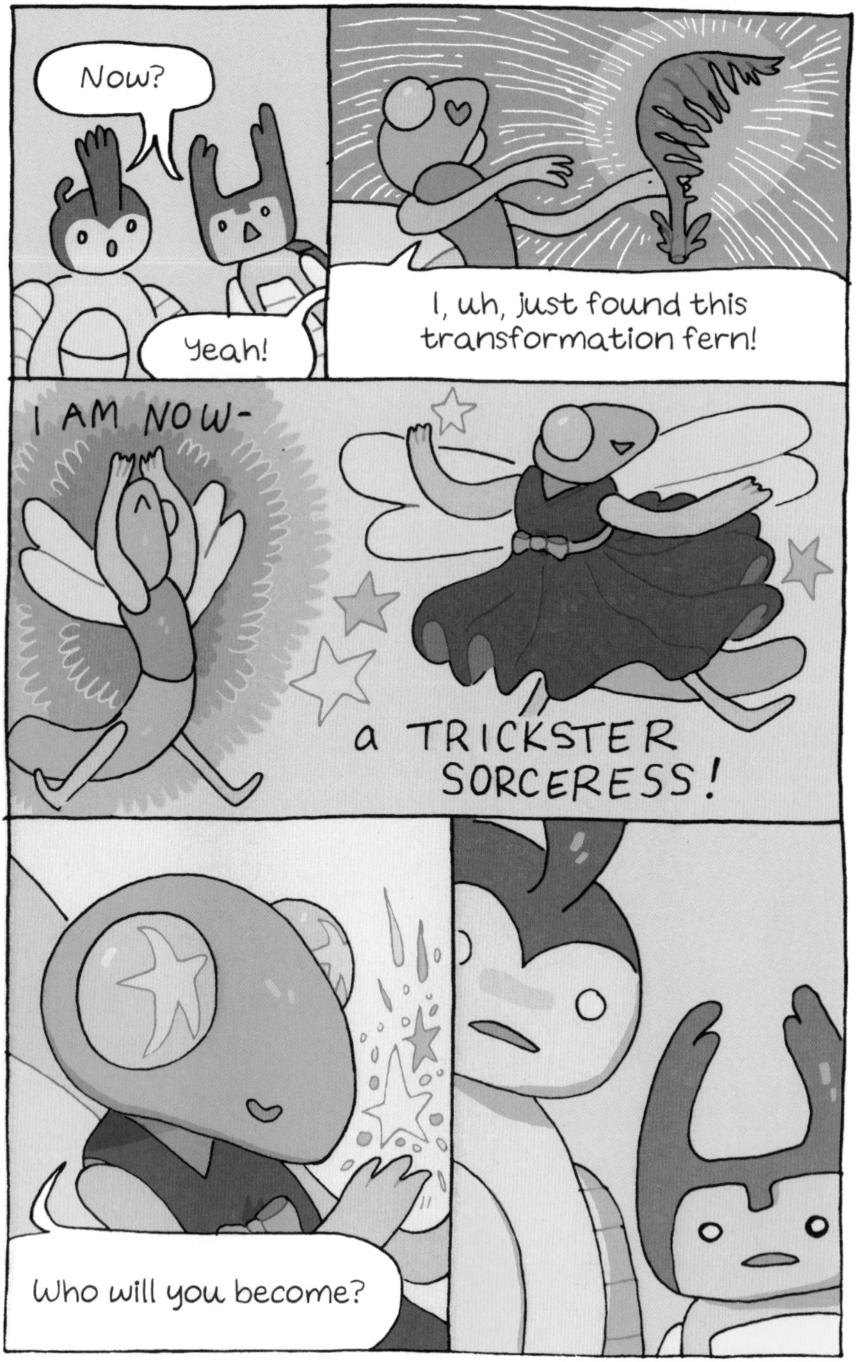
Now?
Yeah!
I, uh, just found this transformation fern!
I AM NOW-
a TRICKSTER SORCERESS!
Who will you become?

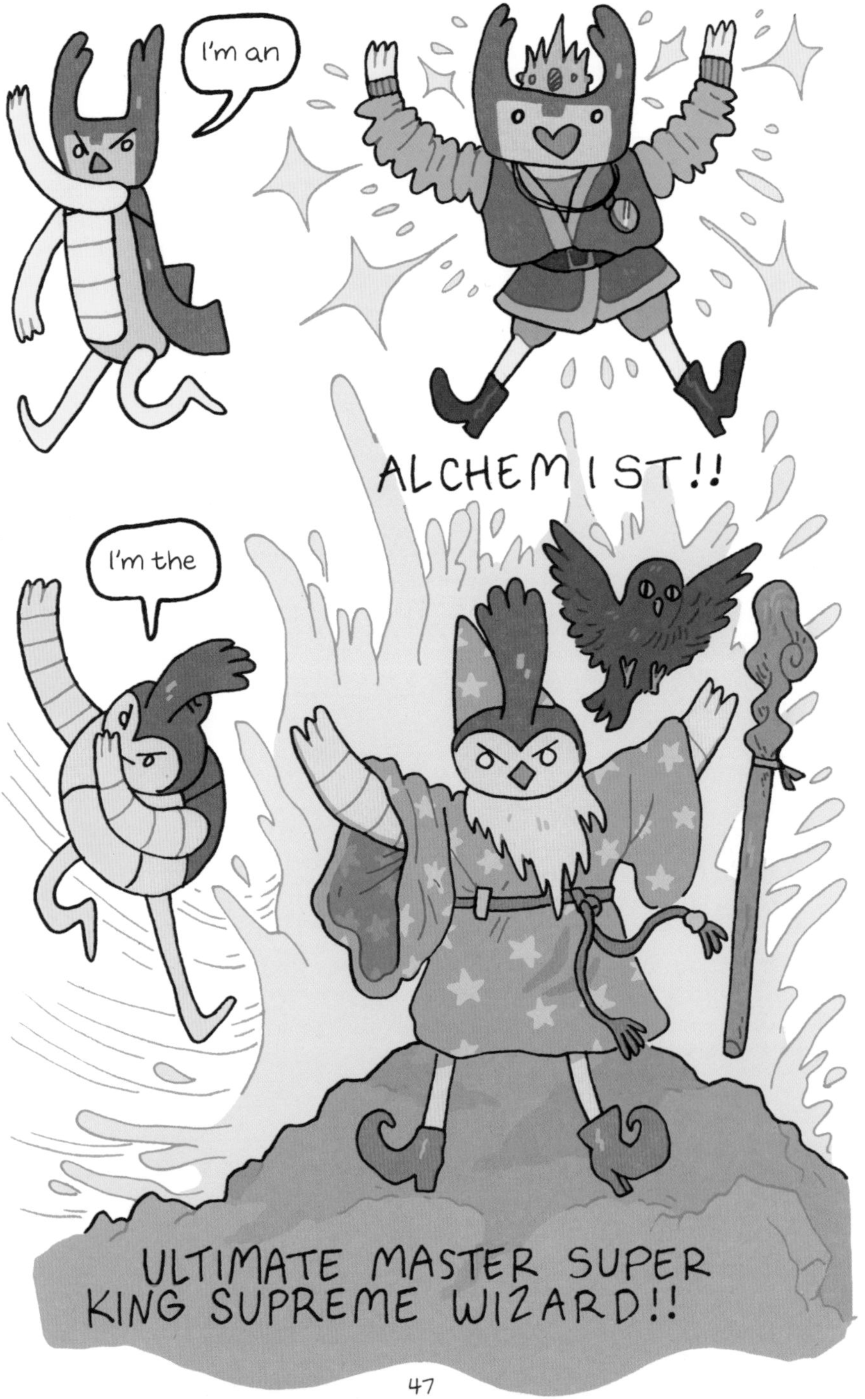
I'm an
ALCHEMIST!!
I'm the
ULTIMATE MASTER SUPER KING SUPREME WIZARD!!

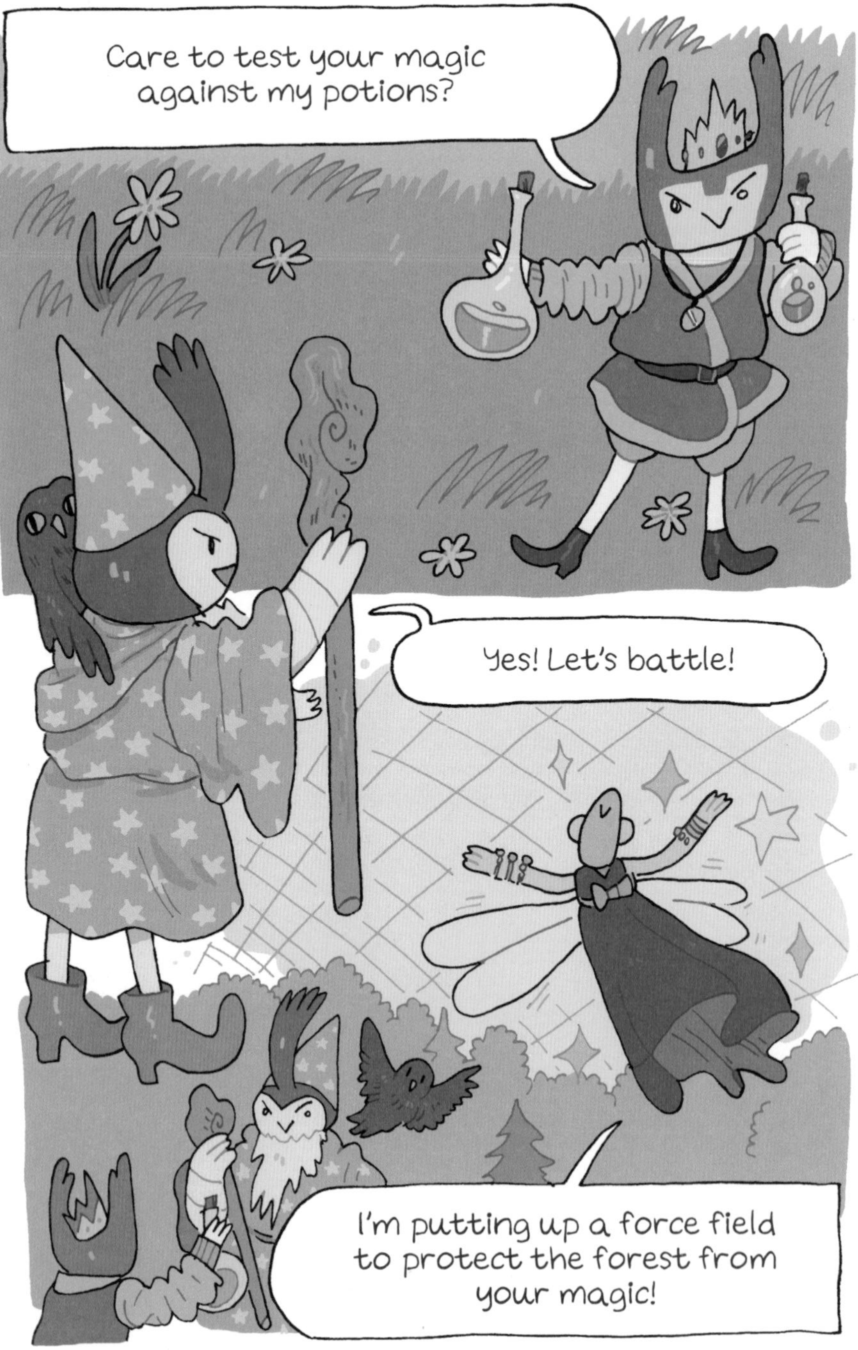
Care to test your magic against my potions?
Yes! Let's battle!
I'm putting up a force field to protect the forest from your magic!

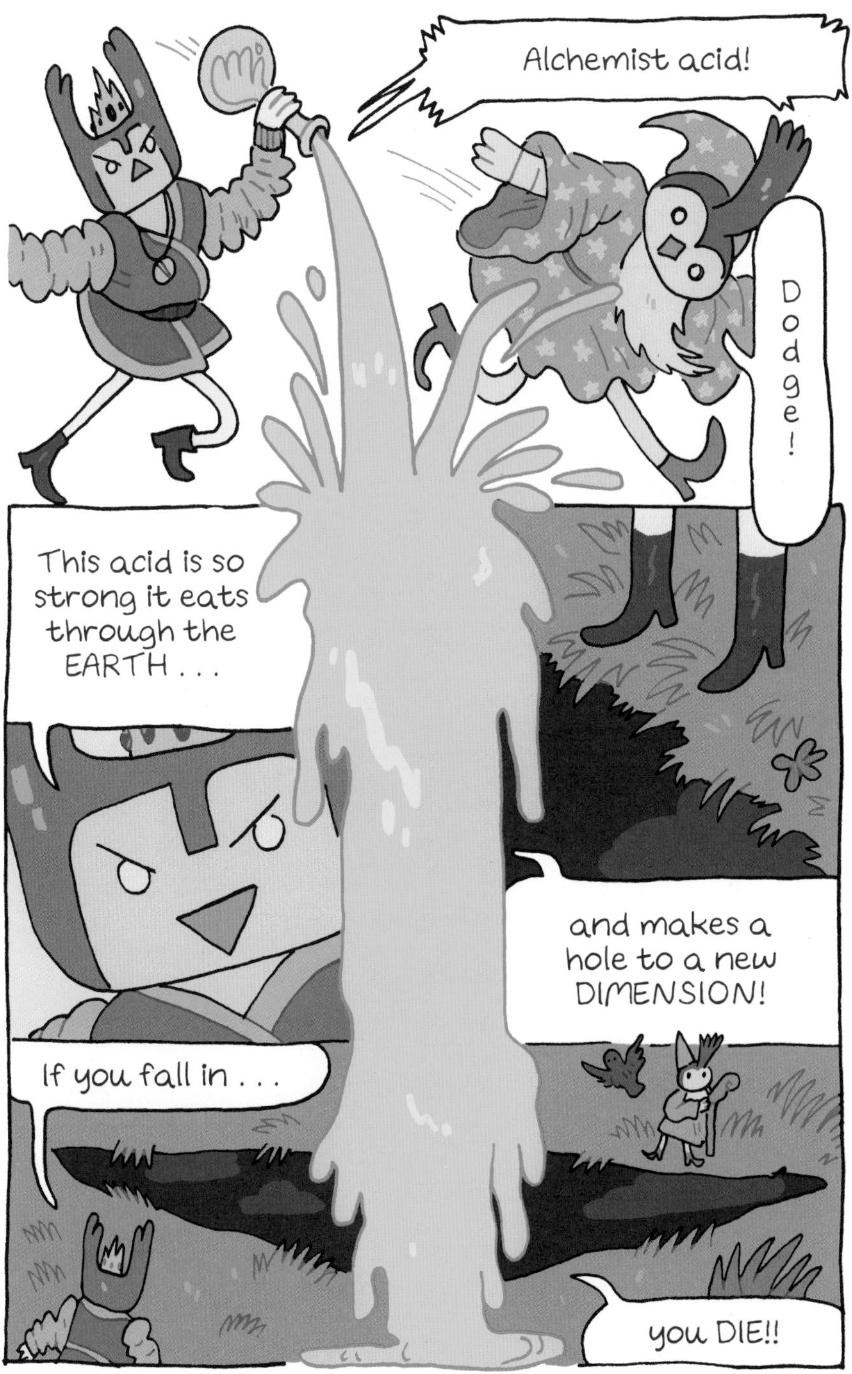
Alchemist acid!
Dodge!
This acid is so strong it eats through the EARTH . . .
and makes a hole to a new DIMENSION!
If you fall in . . .
you DIE!!

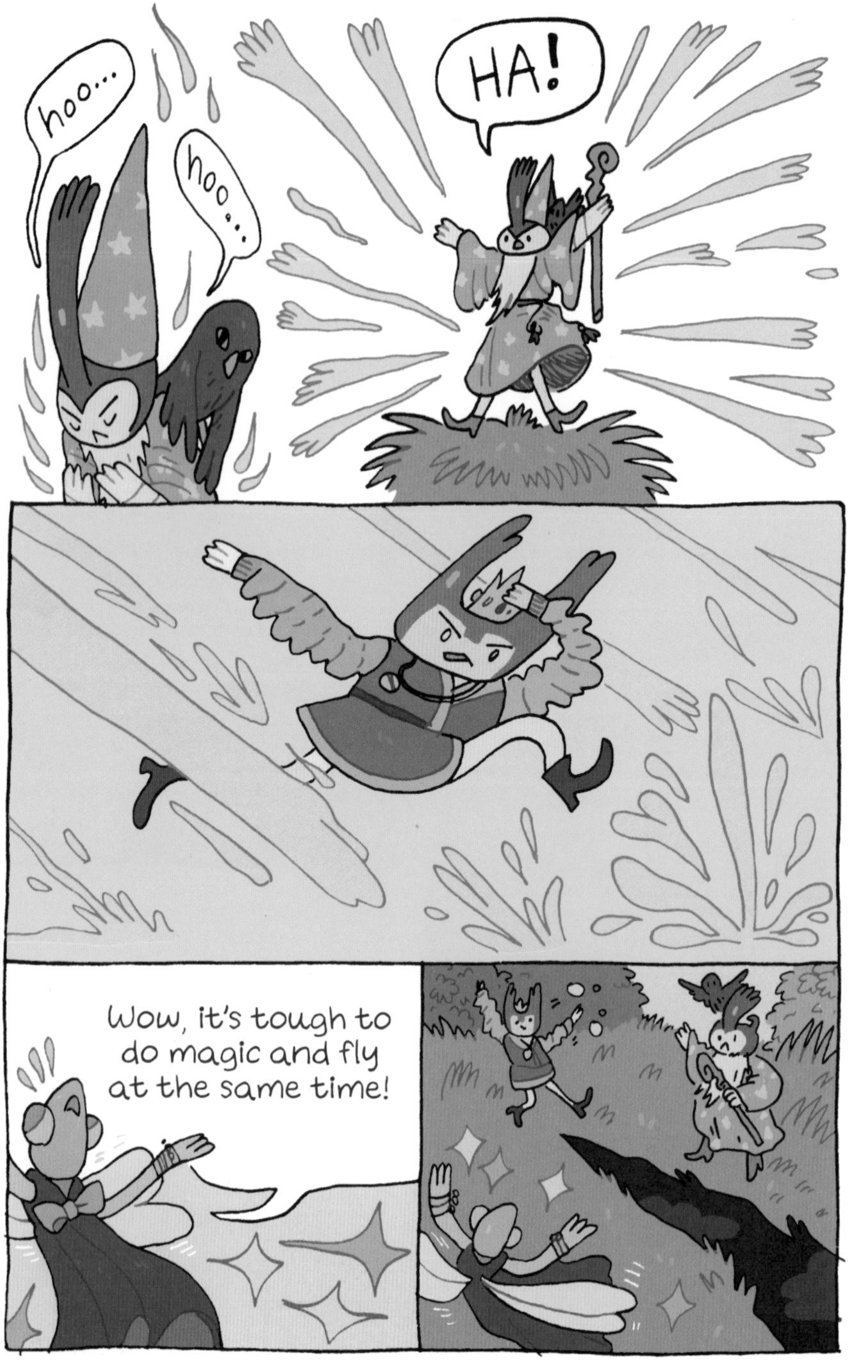
hoo...
hoo...
HA!
Wow, it's tough to do magic and fly at the same time!

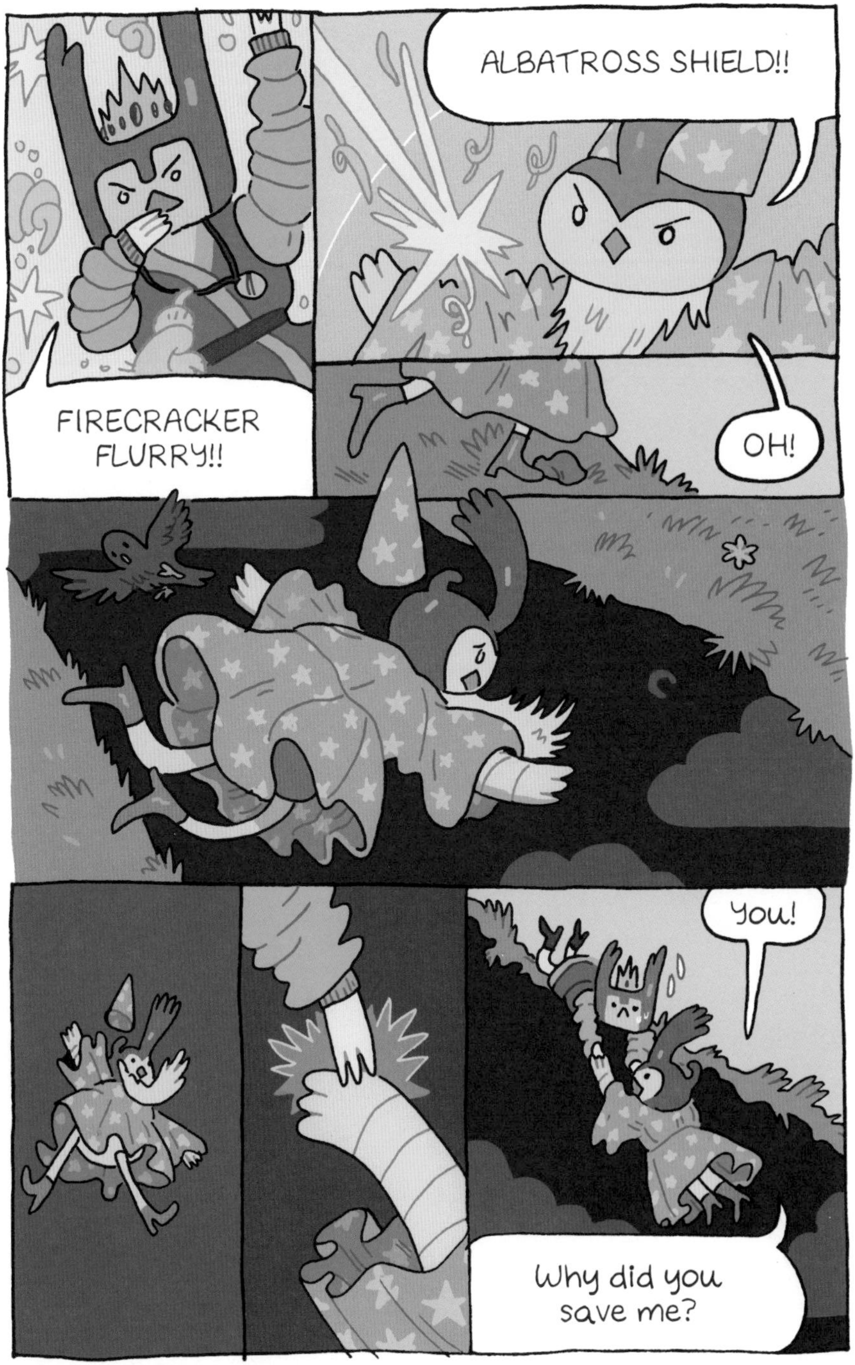
ALBATROSS SHIELD!!
FIRECRACKER FLURRY!!
OH!
You!
Why did you save me?

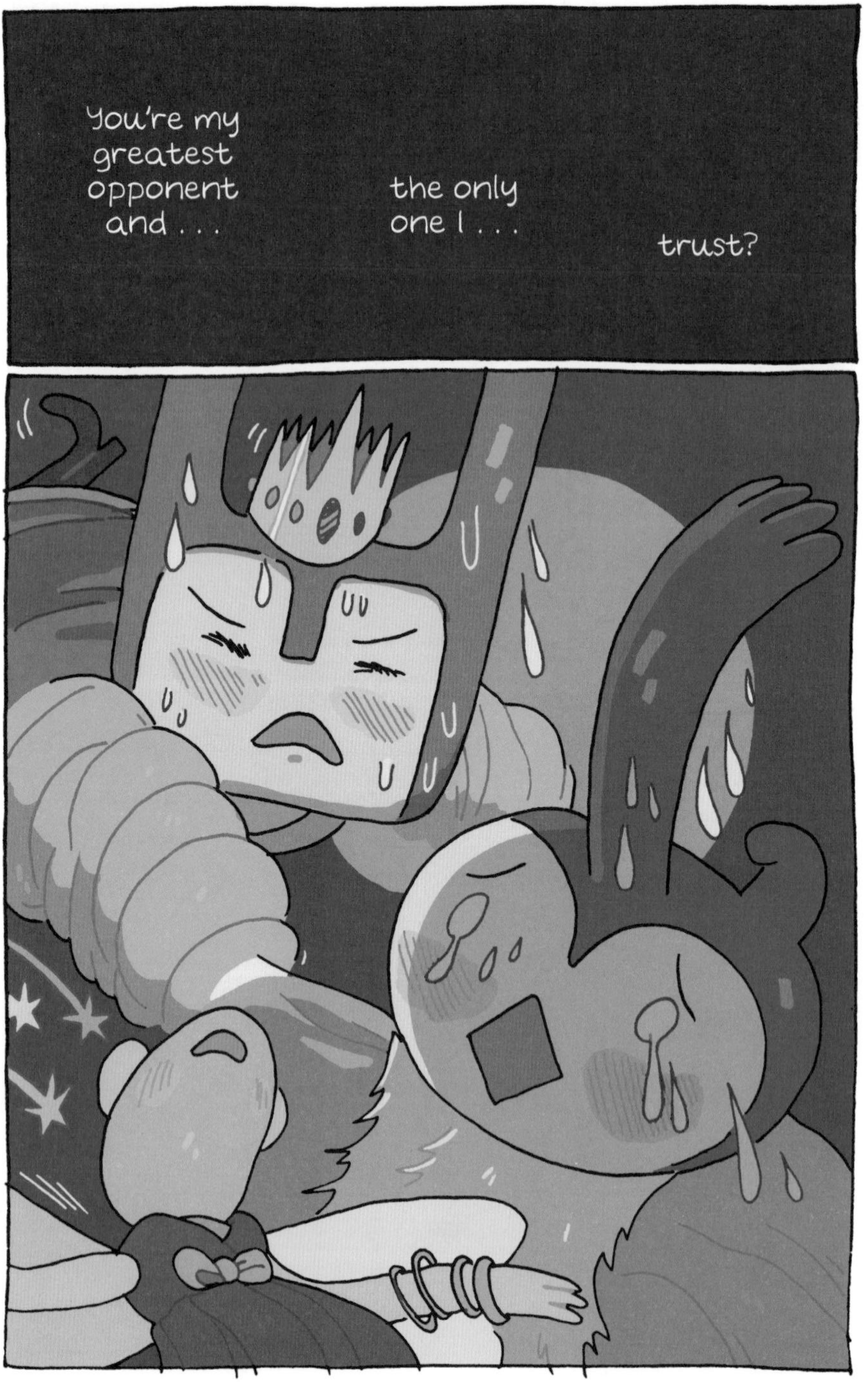
You're my greatest opponent and . . .
the only one I . . .
trust?

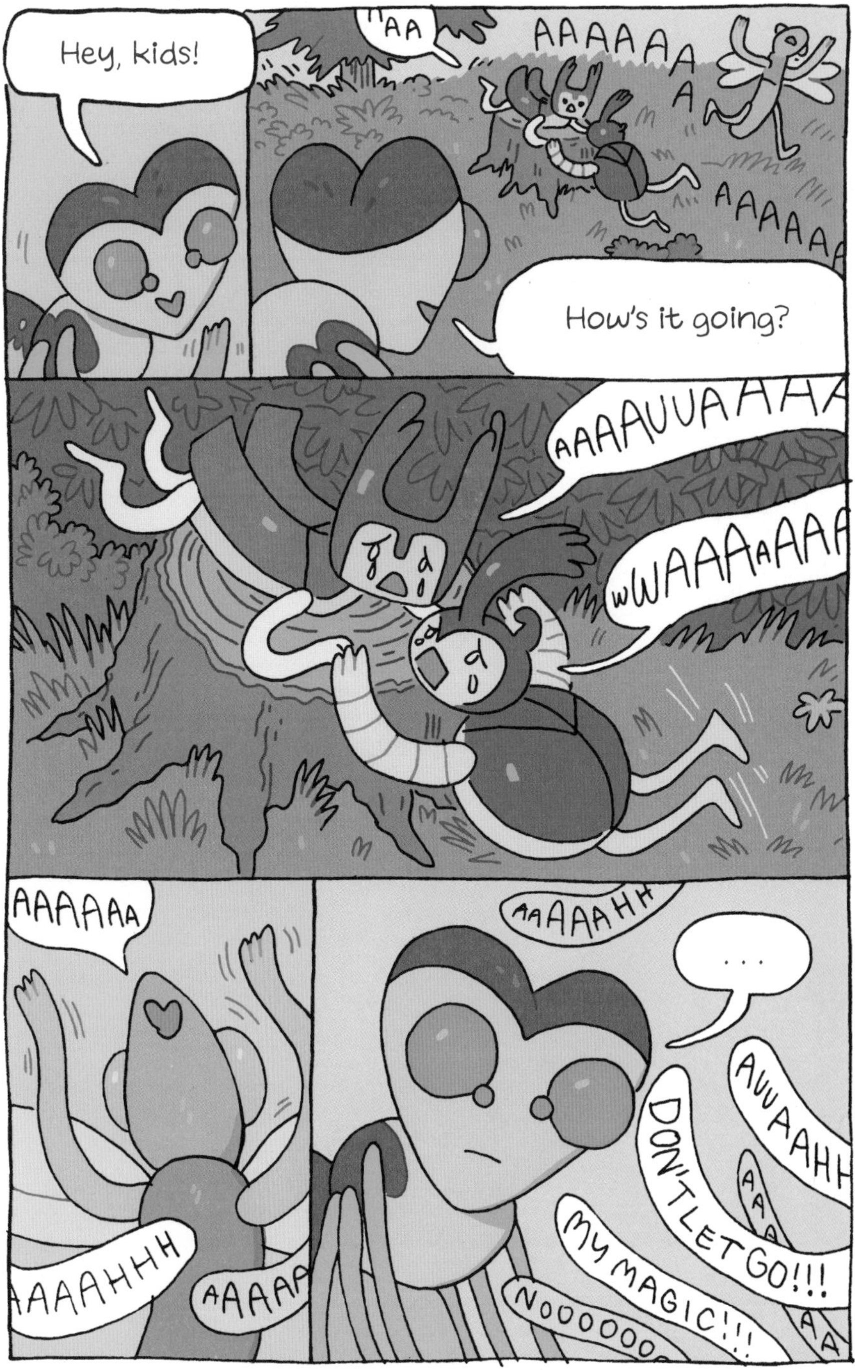

Hey, kids!
AA
AAAAAAA
AAAAAA
How's it going?
AAAAUUAAAA
wWAAAaAAA
AAAAAA
AAAAHH
AAAAHHH
AAAA
...
AUUAAHH
AAA
DON'T LET GO!!!
MY MAGIC!!!
NOOOOOOO
AA

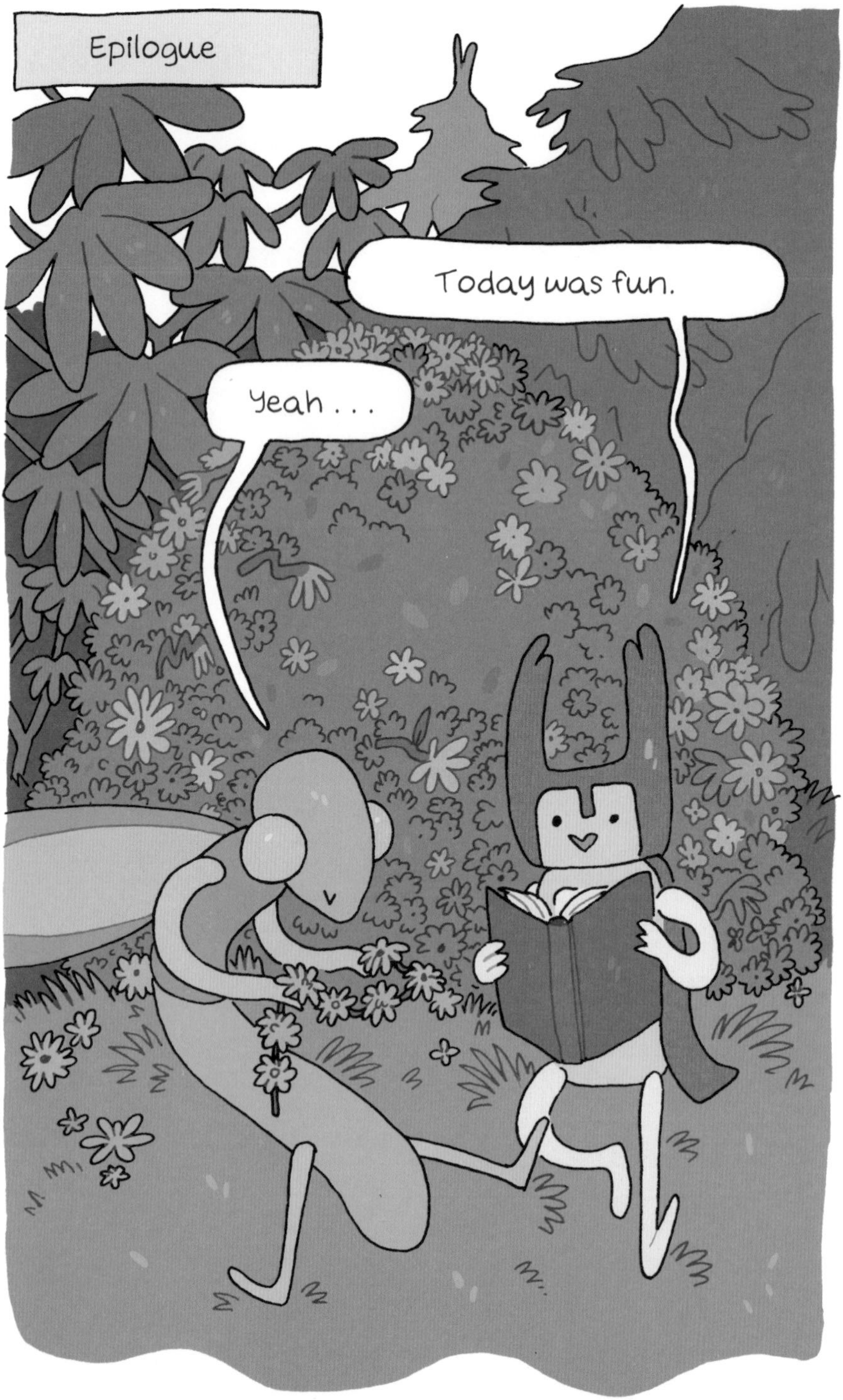
Epilogue
Today was fun.
Yeah . . .

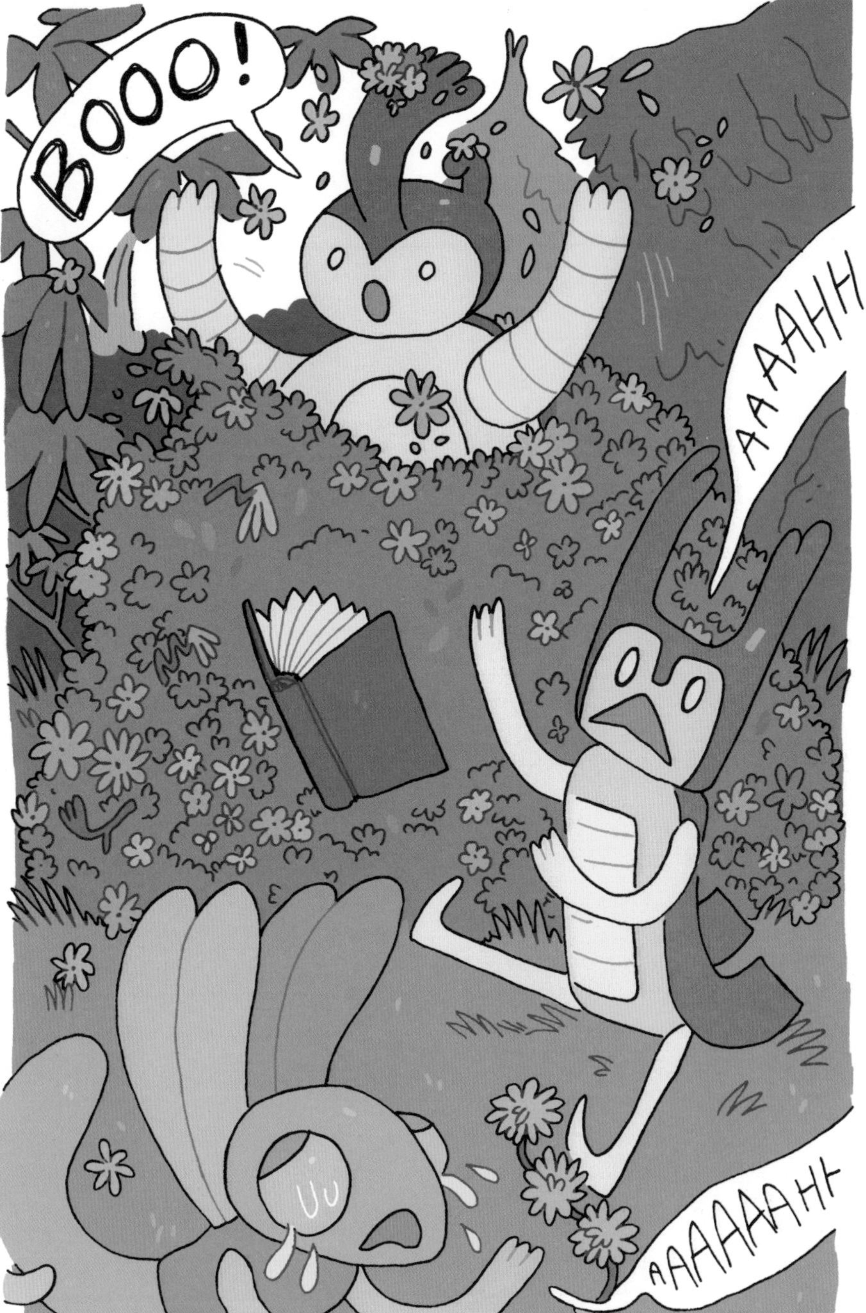
BOOO!
AAAAHH
AAAAAAH

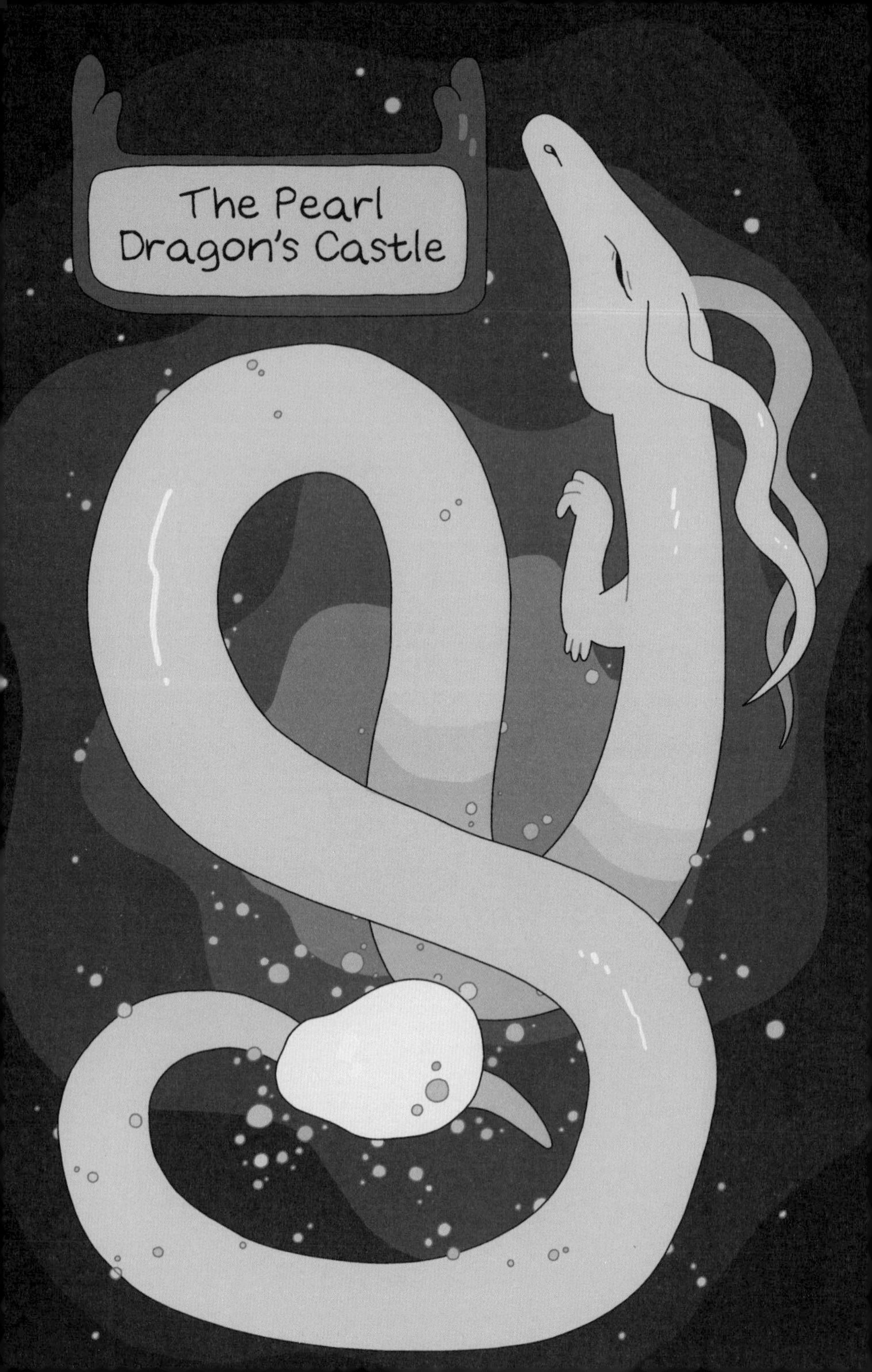
The Pearl
Dragon's Castle

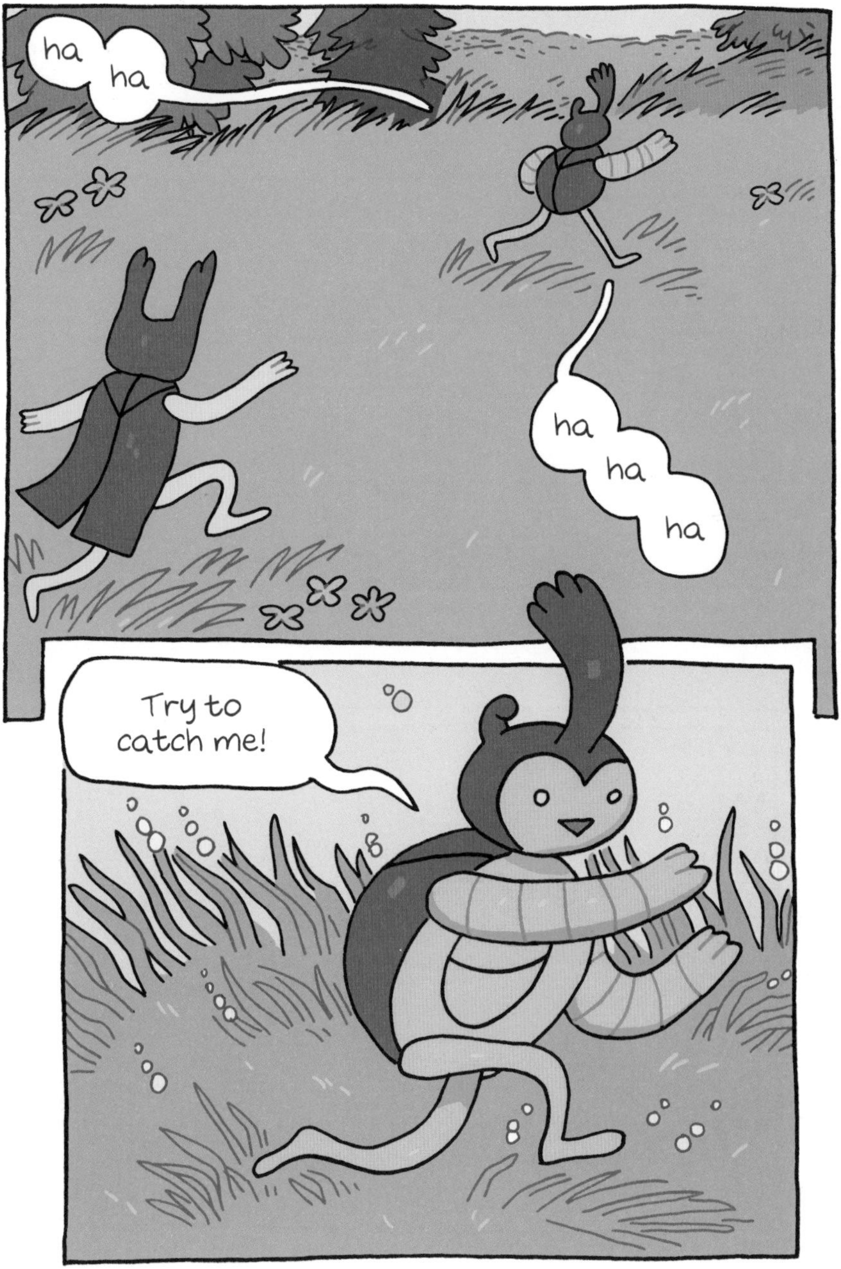
ha
ha
ha
ha
ha
Try to catch me!

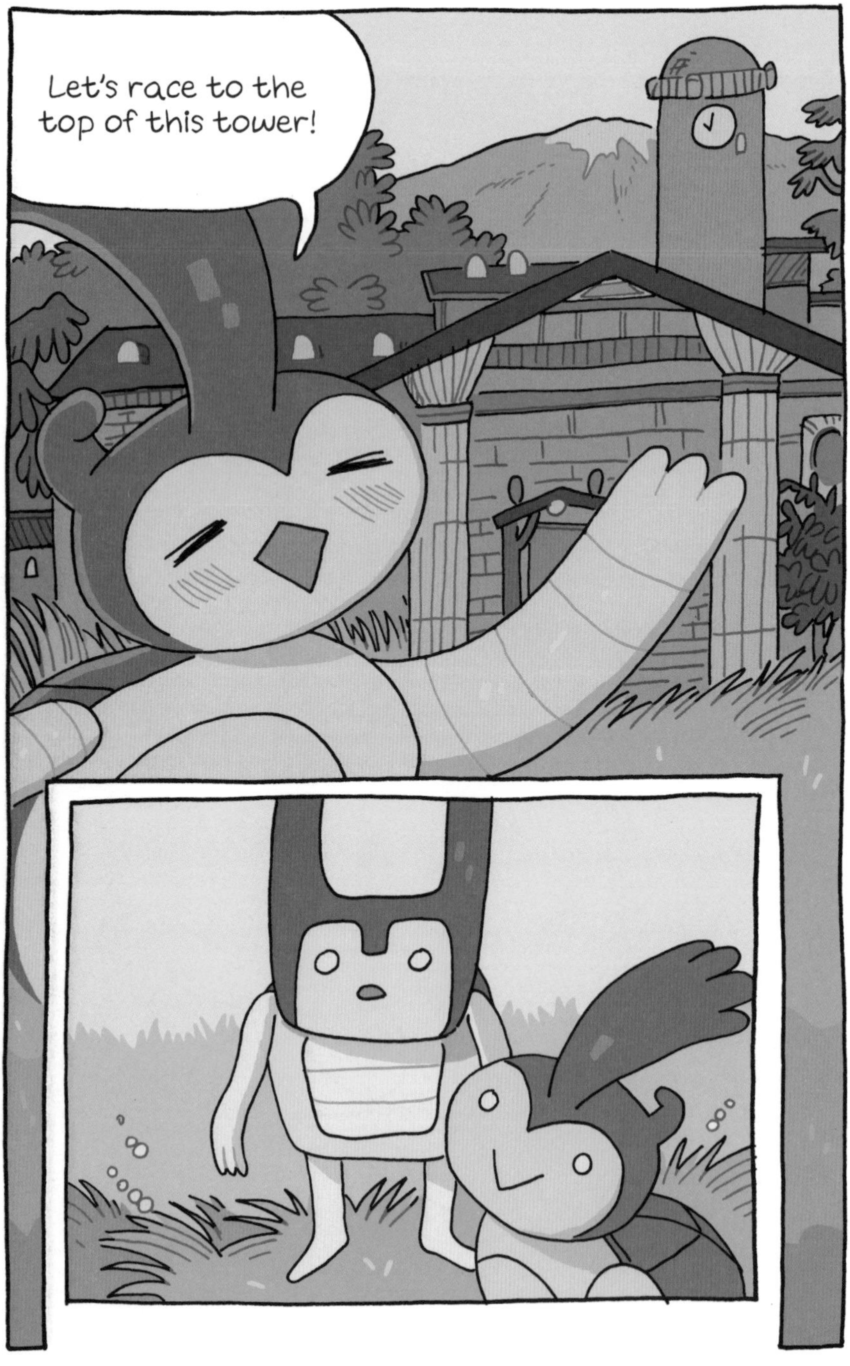
Let's race to the top of this tower!

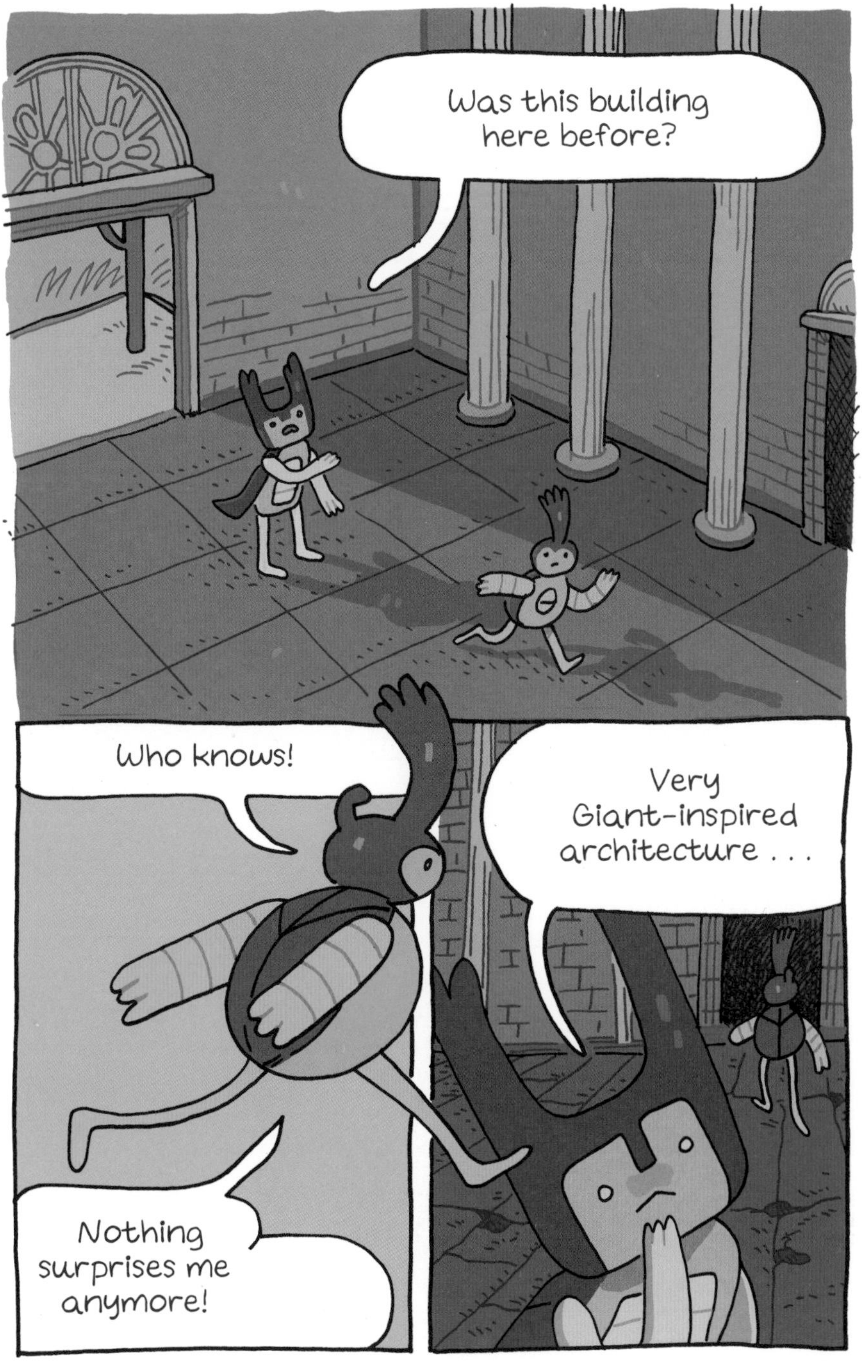
Was this building here before?
Who knows!
Nothing surprises me anymore!
Very Giant-inspired architecture . . .

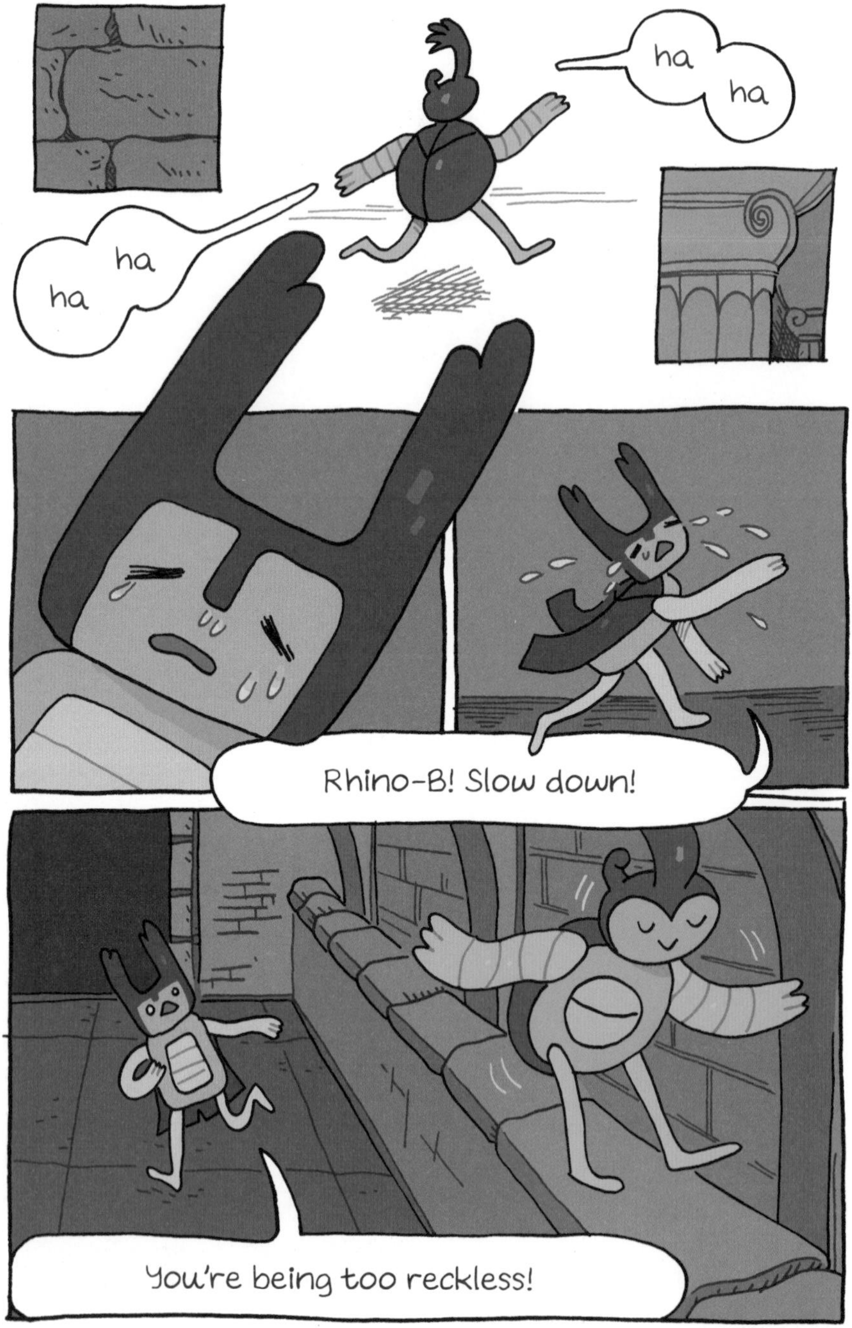
ha
ha
ha
ha
Rhino-B! Slow down!
You're being too reckless!

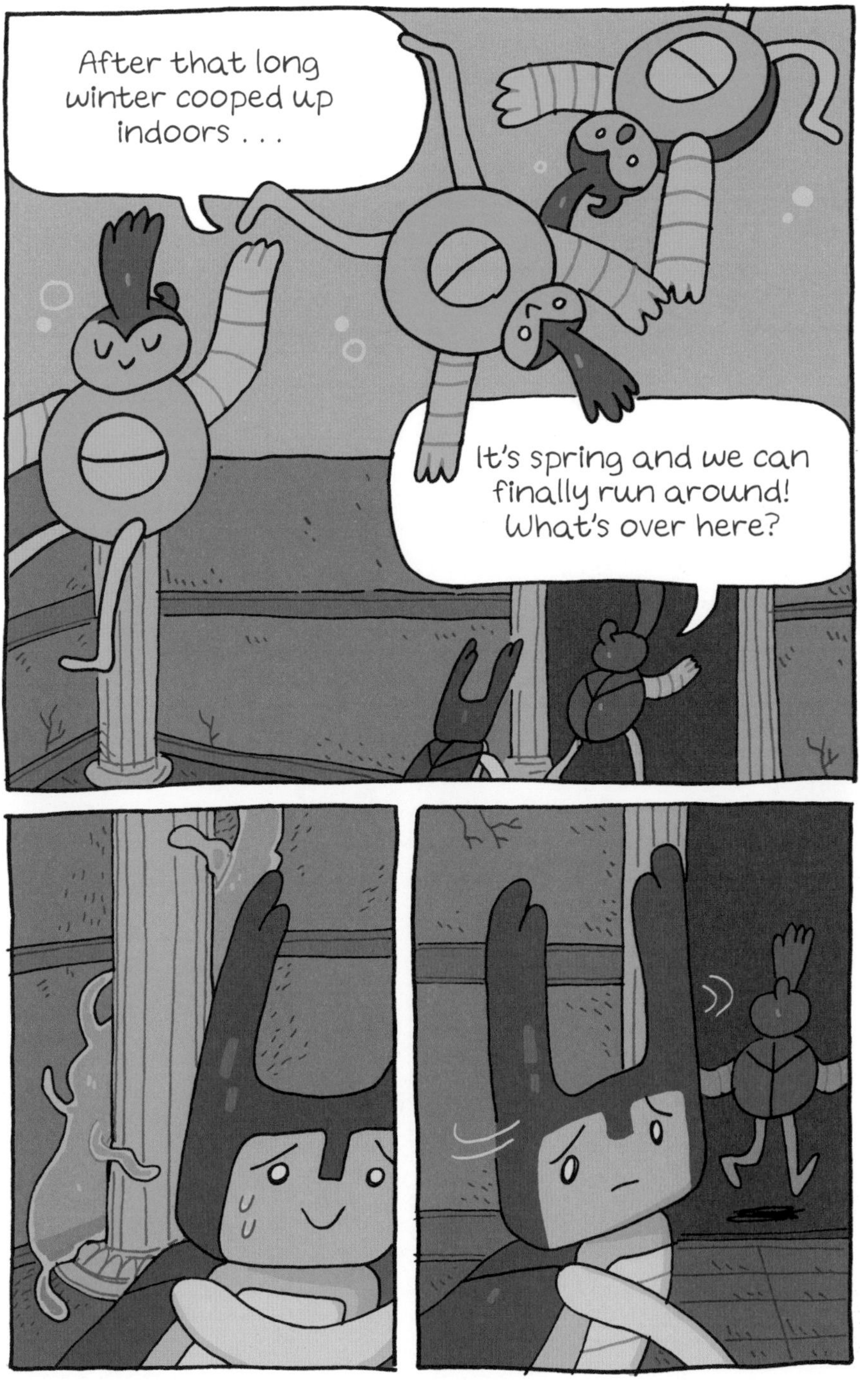
After that long winter cooped up indoors . . .
It's spring and we can finally run around! What's over here?

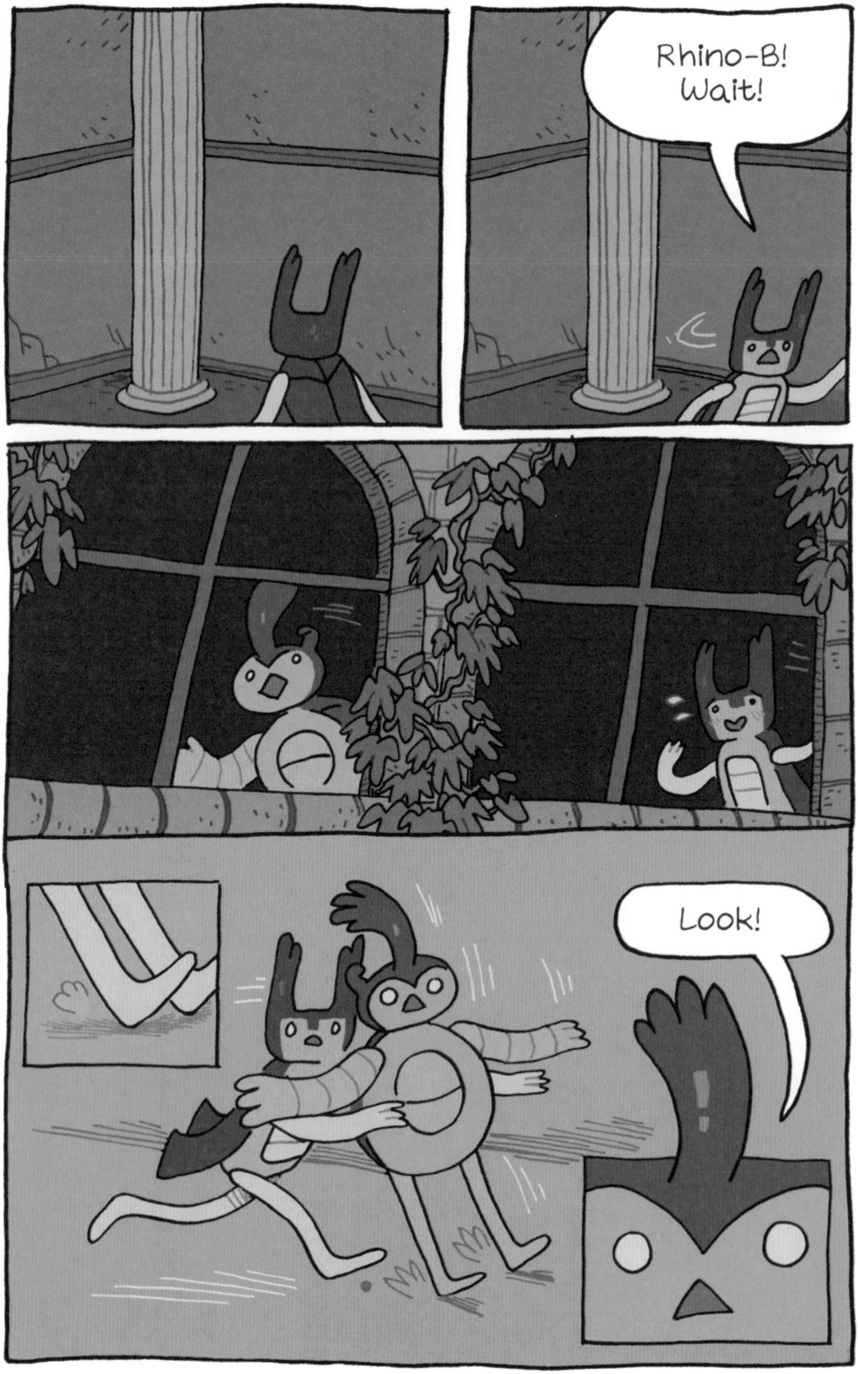
Rhino-B! Wait!
Look!

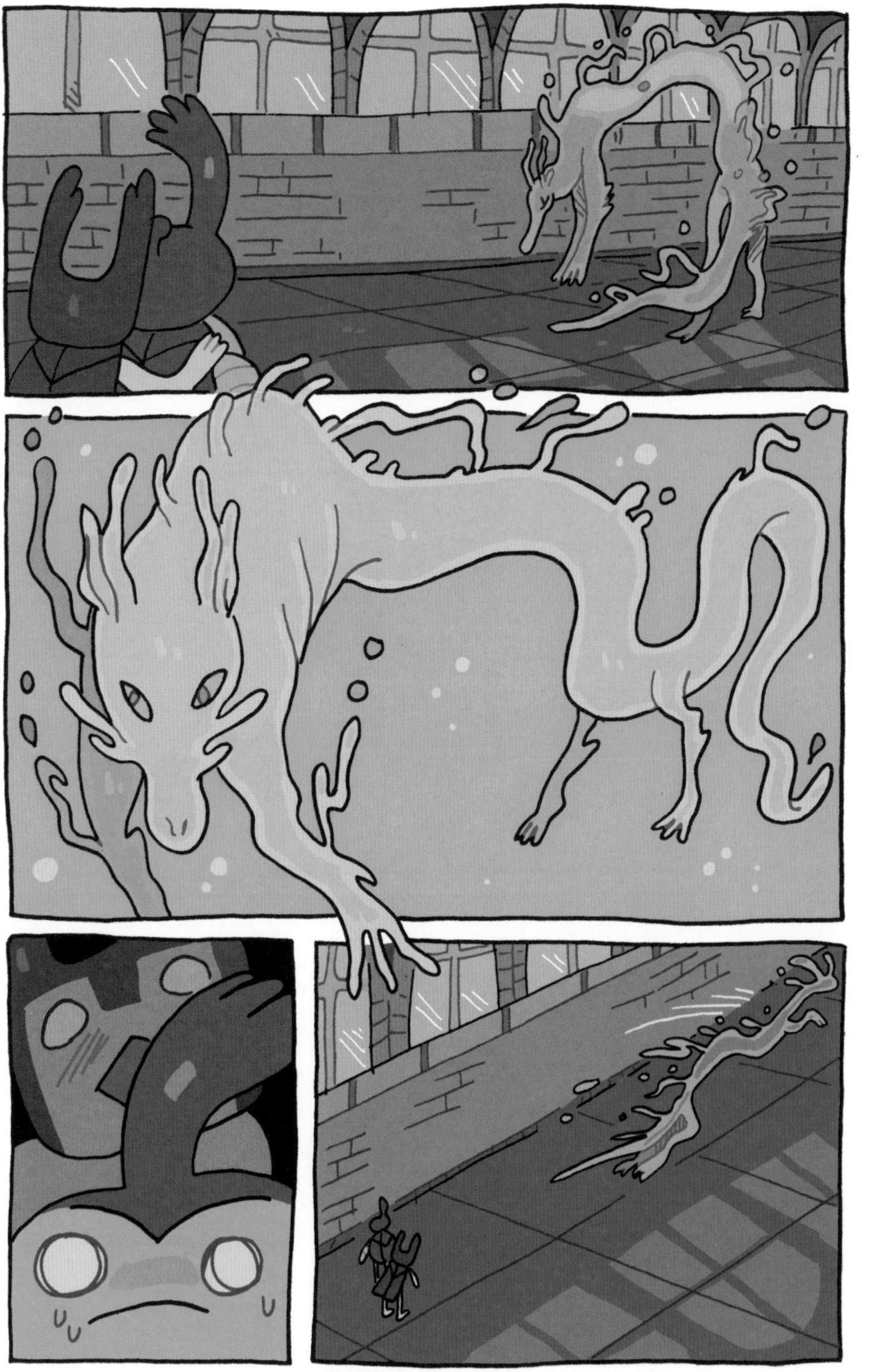

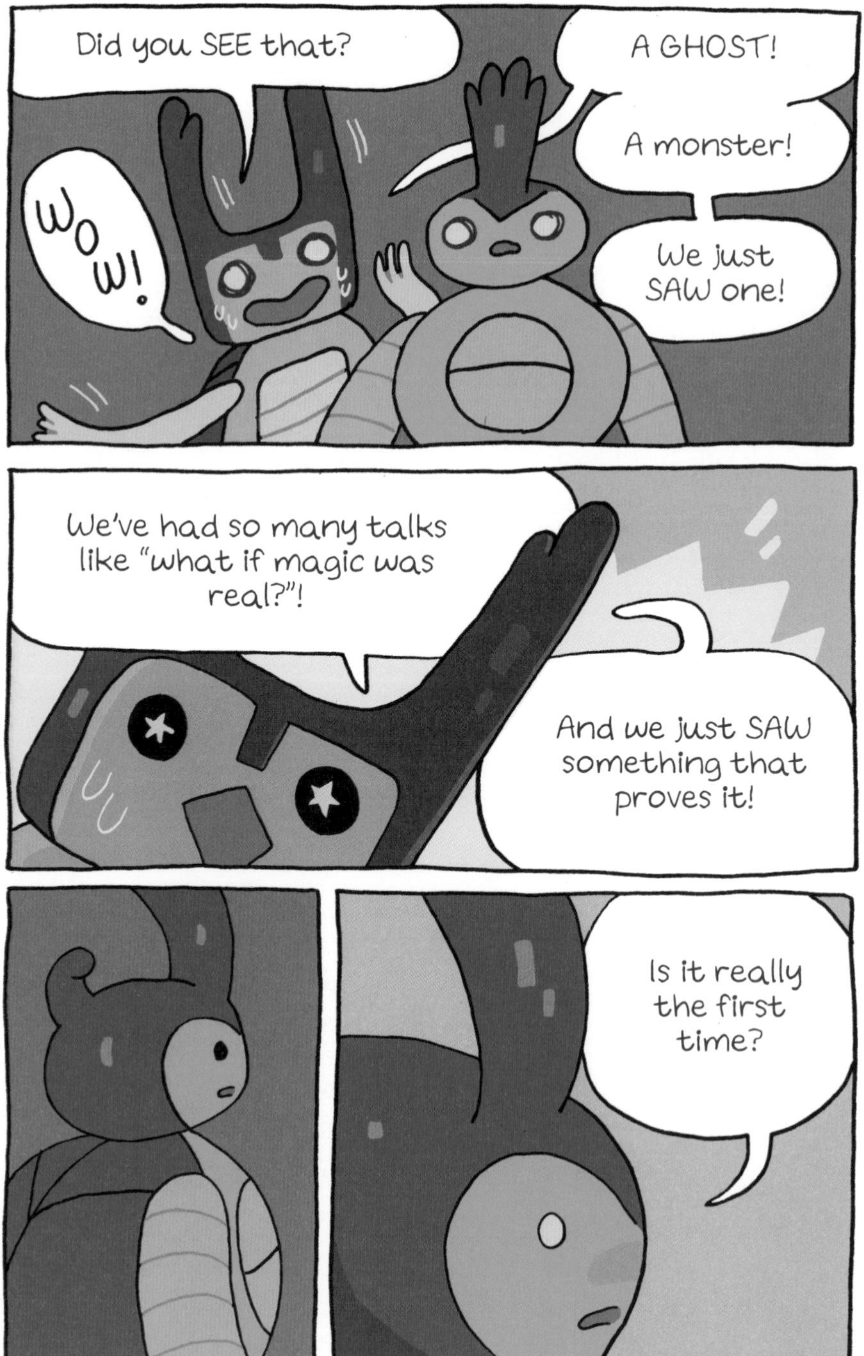
Did you SEE that?
WOW!
A GHOST!
A monster!
We just SAW one!
We've had so many talks like "what if magic was real?"!
And we just SAW something that proves it!
Is it really the first time?

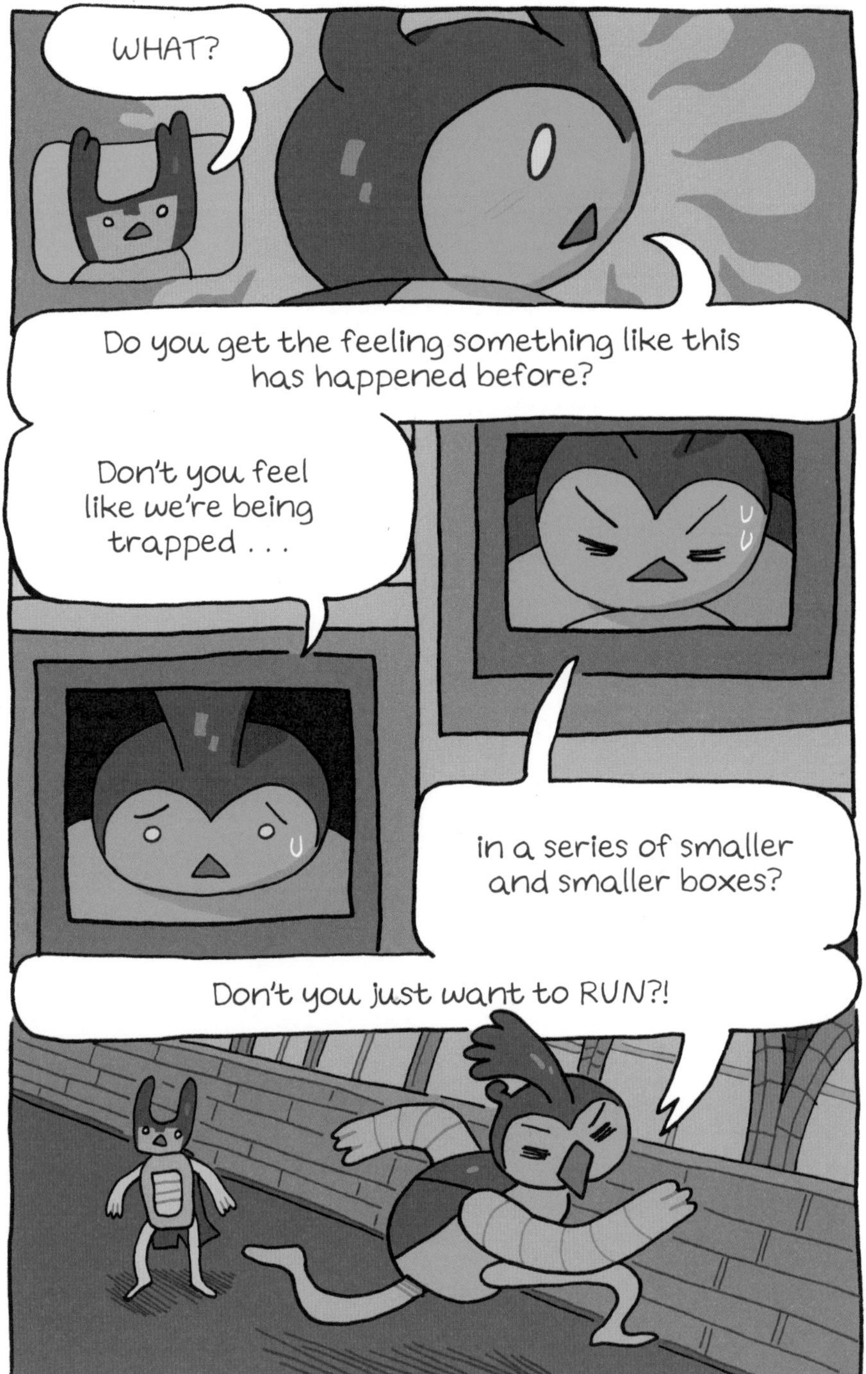
WHAT?
Do you get the feeling something like this has happened before?
Don't you feel like we're being trapped . . .
in a series of smaller and smaller boxes?
Don't you just want to RUN?!

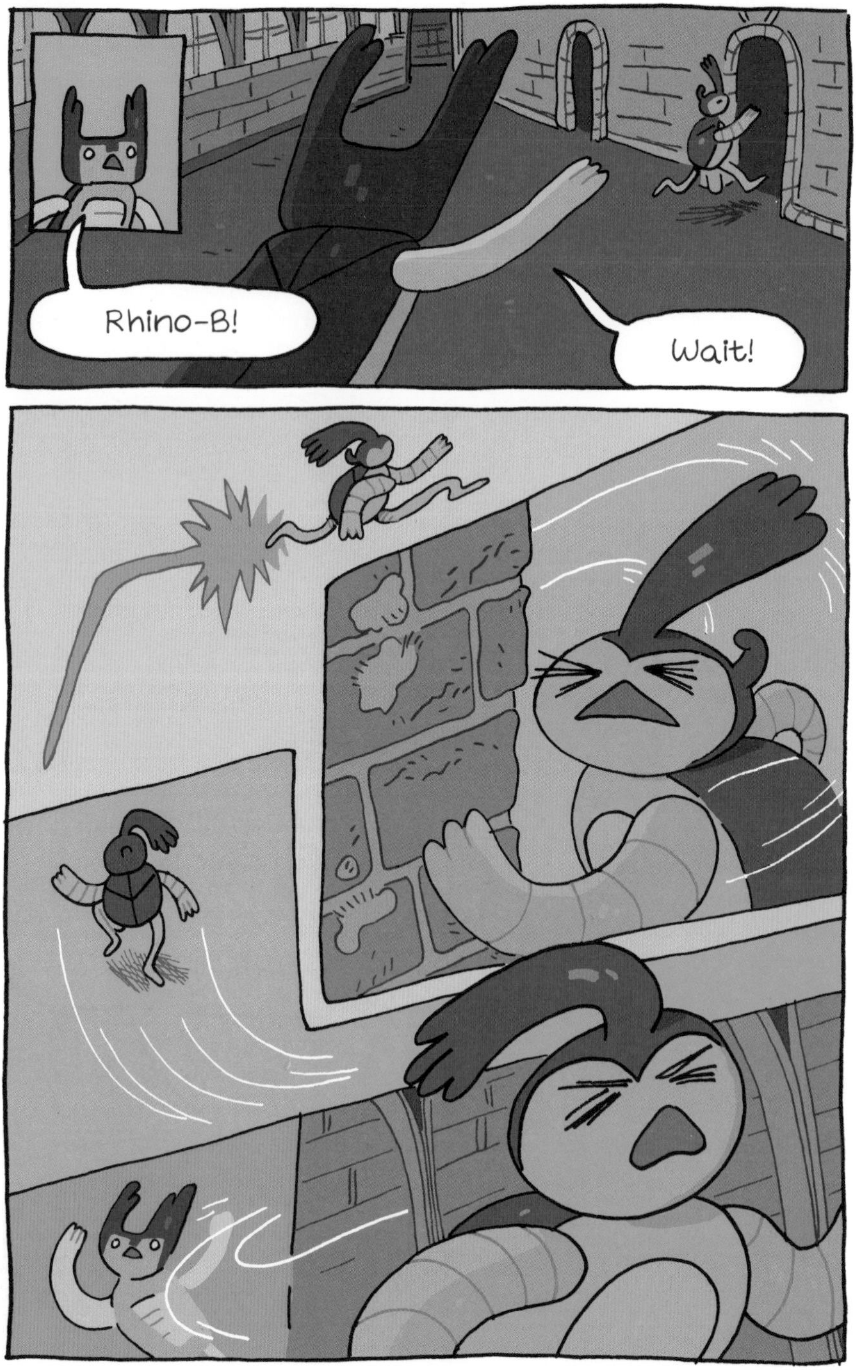
Rhino-B!
Wait!

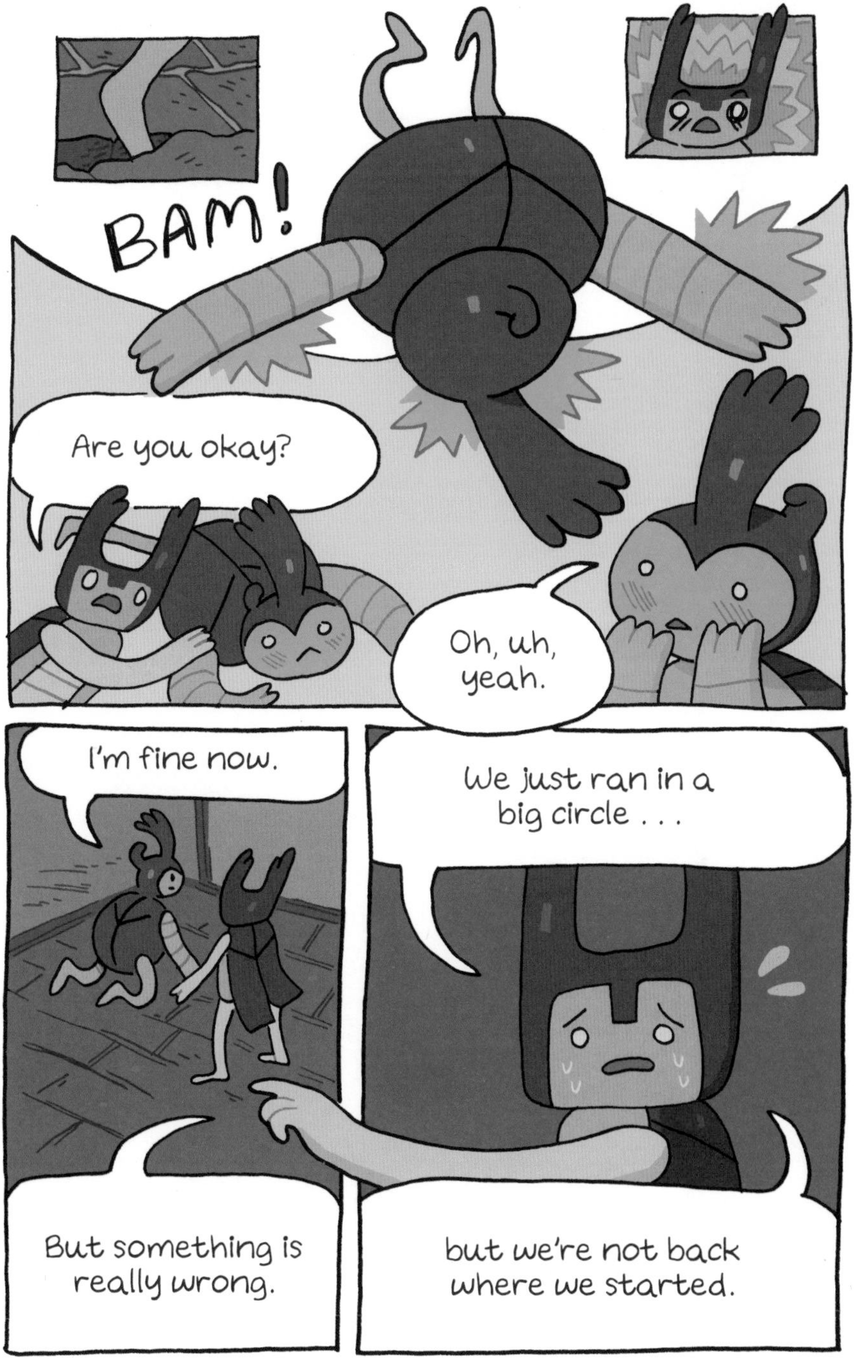
BAM!
Are you okay?
Oh, uh, yeah.
I'm fine now.
But something is really wrong.
We just ran in a big circle . . .
but we're not back where we started.

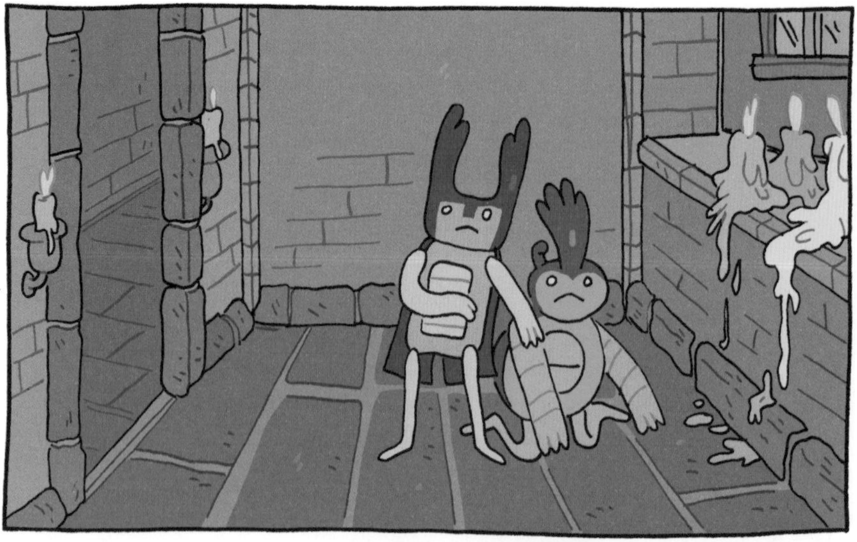

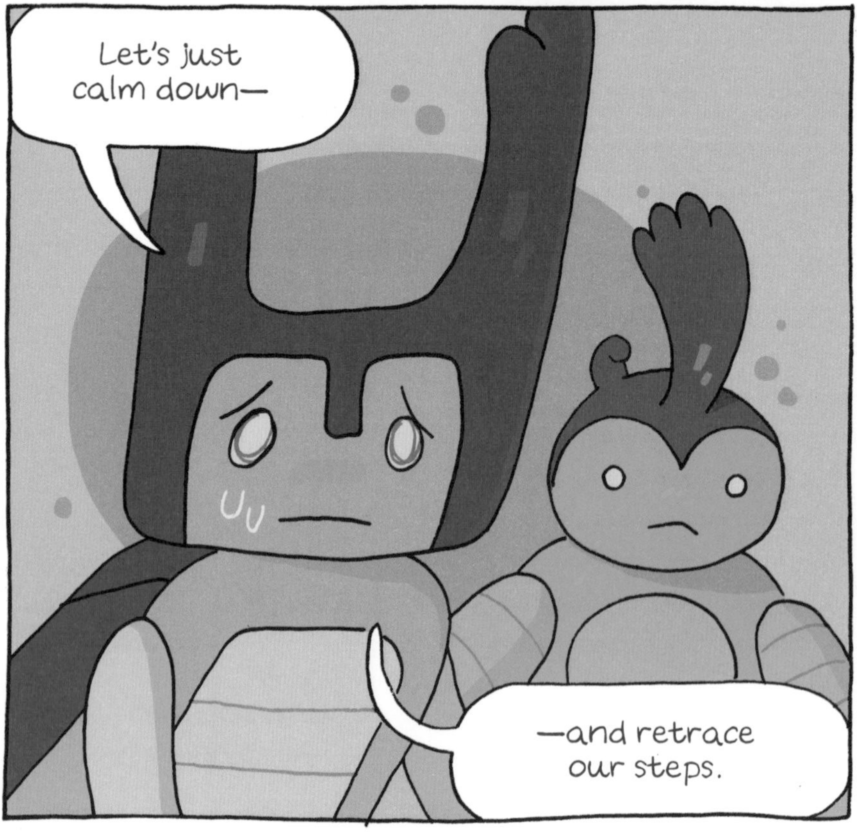
Let's just calm down—
—and retrace our steps.

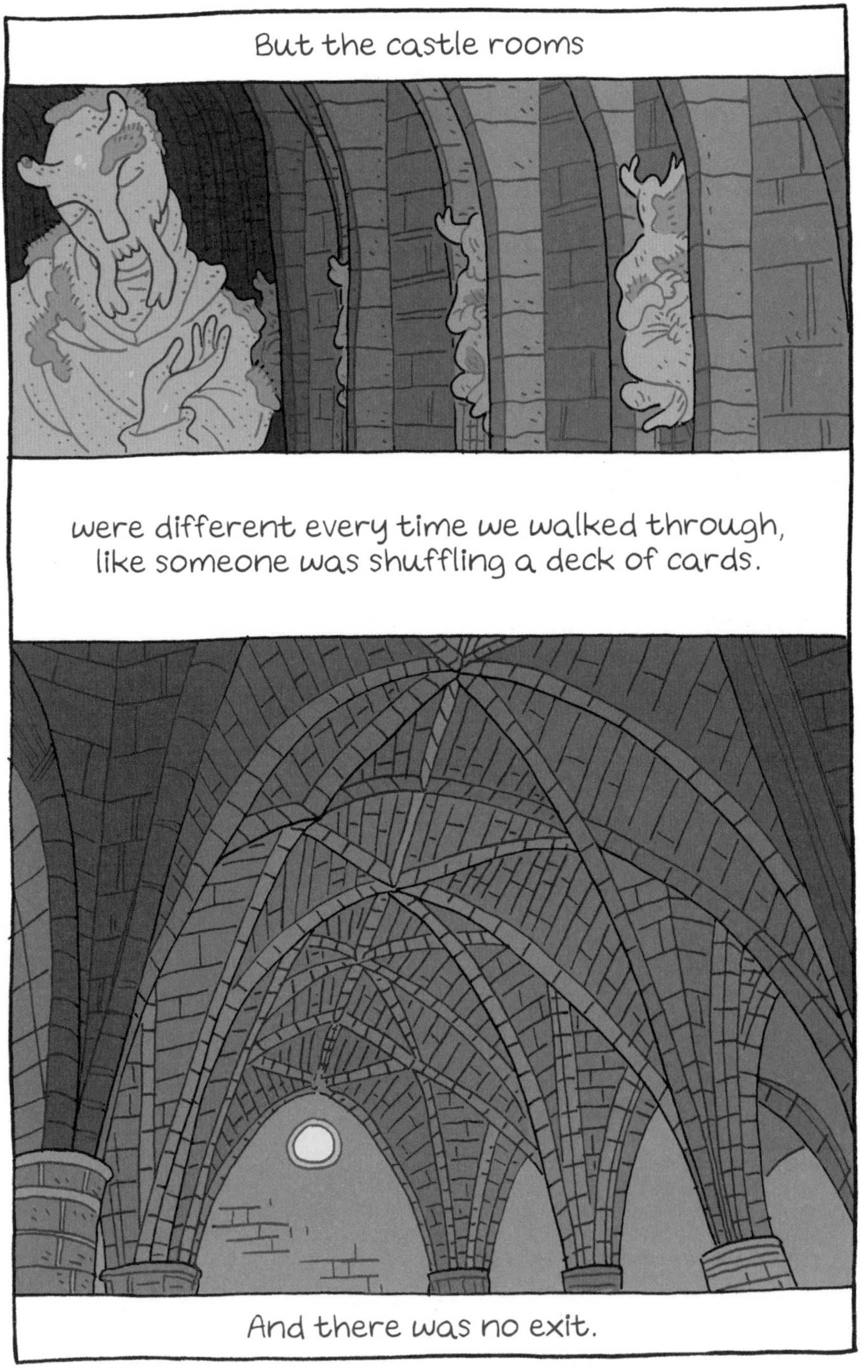
But the castle rooms
were different every time we walked through, like someone was shuffling a deck of cards.
And there was no exit.

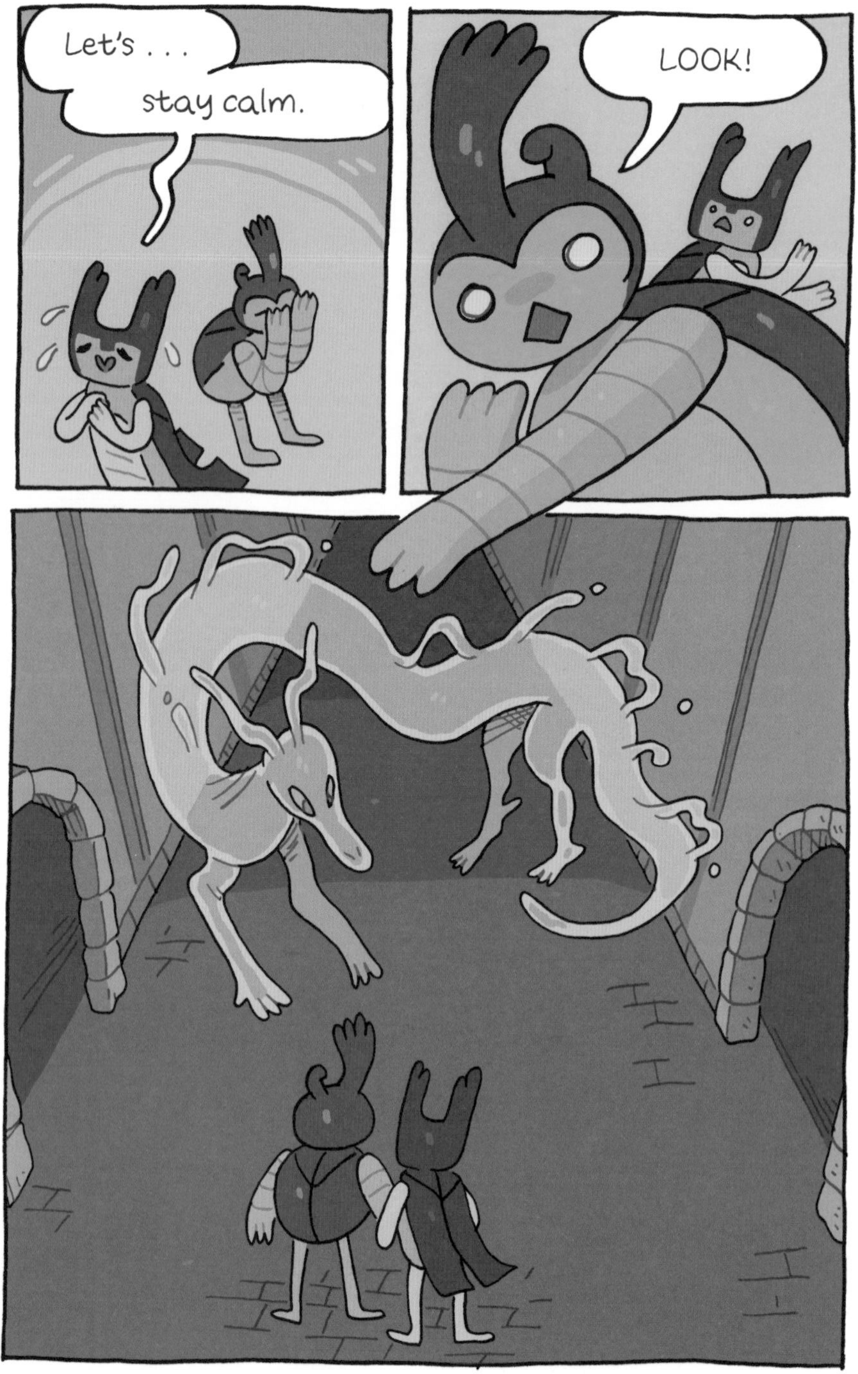
Let's . . .
stay calm.
LOOK!

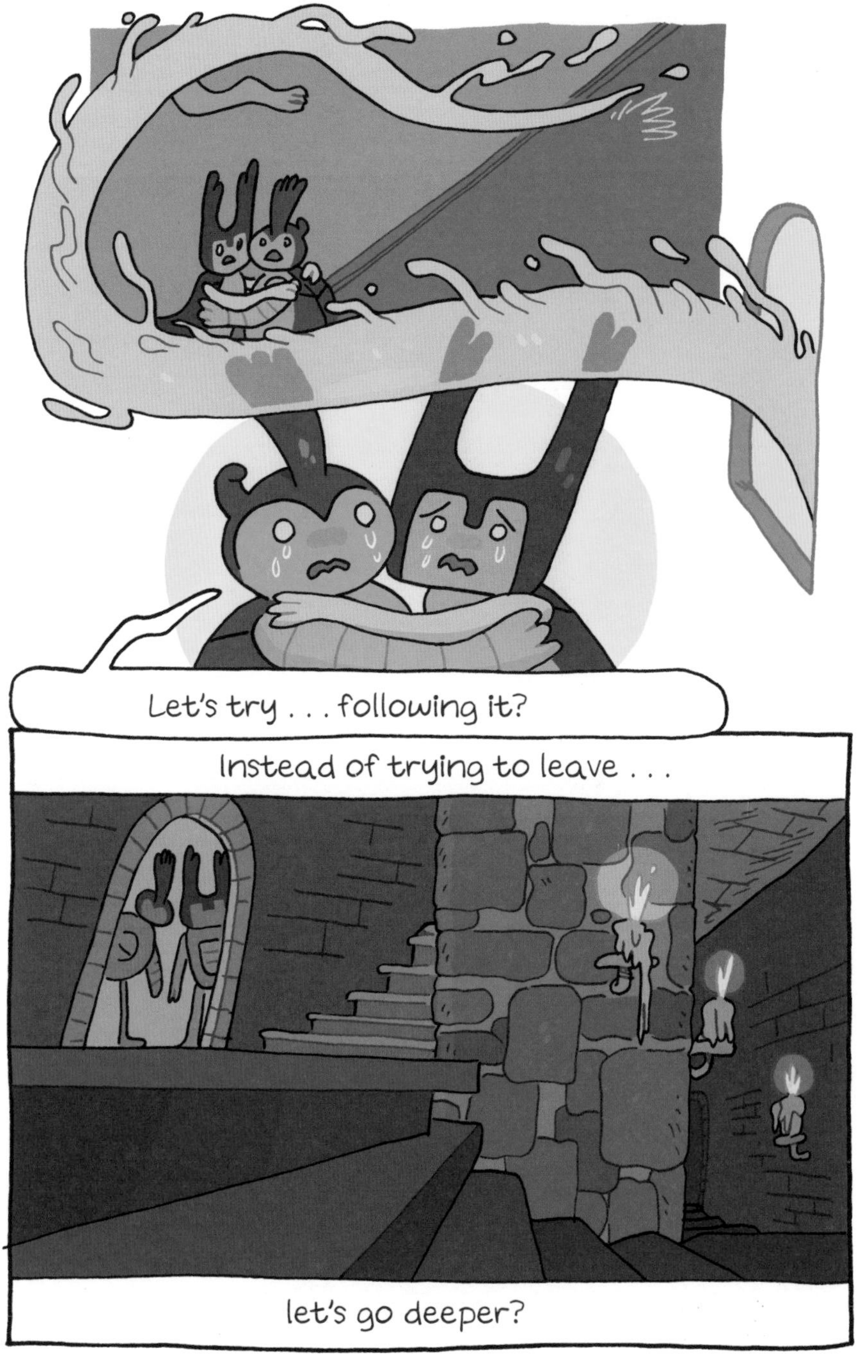
Let's try . . . following it?
Instead of trying to leave . . .
let's go deeper?

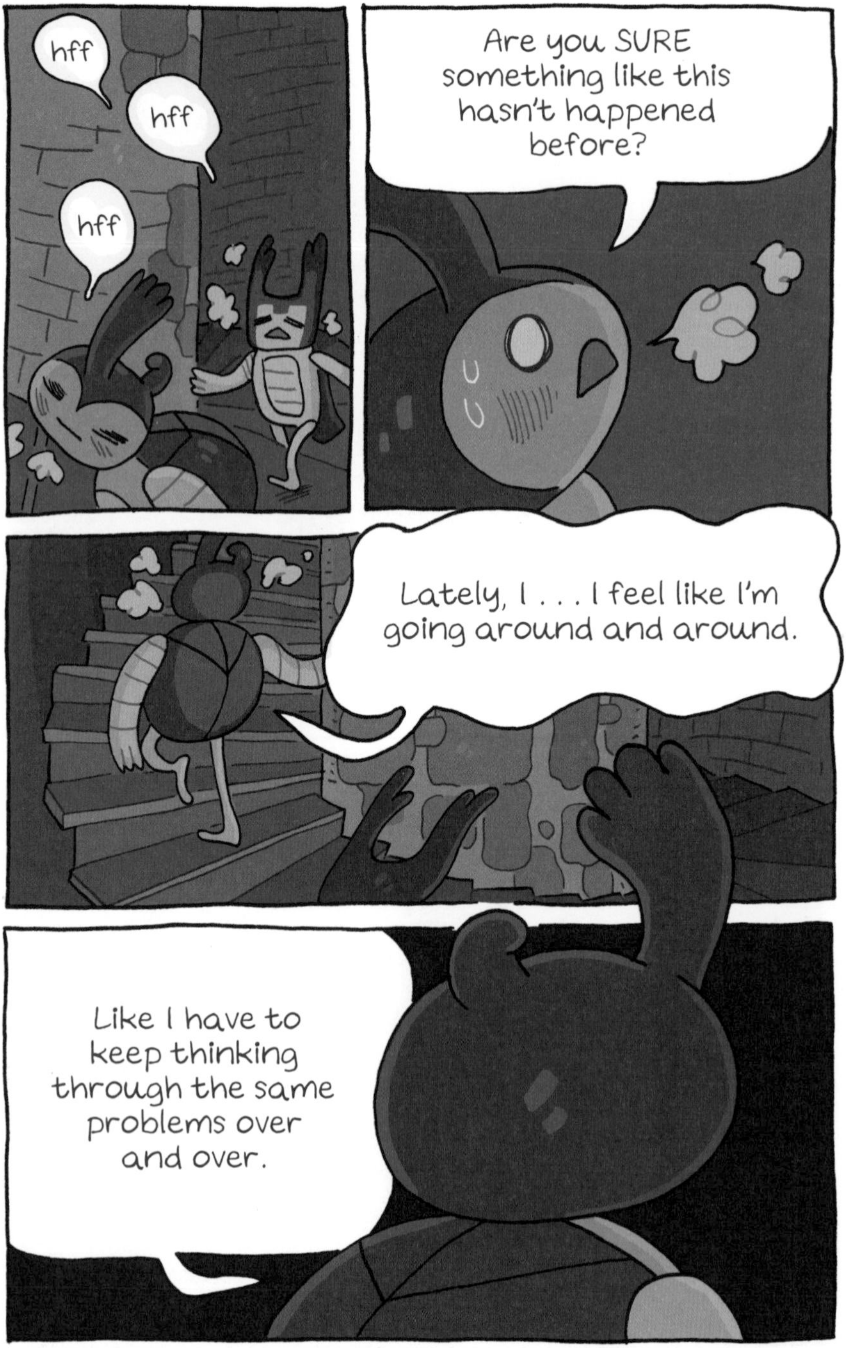
hff
hff
hff
Are you SURE something like this hasn't happened before?
Lately, I . . . I feel like I'm going around and around.
Like I have to keep thinking through the same problems over and over.

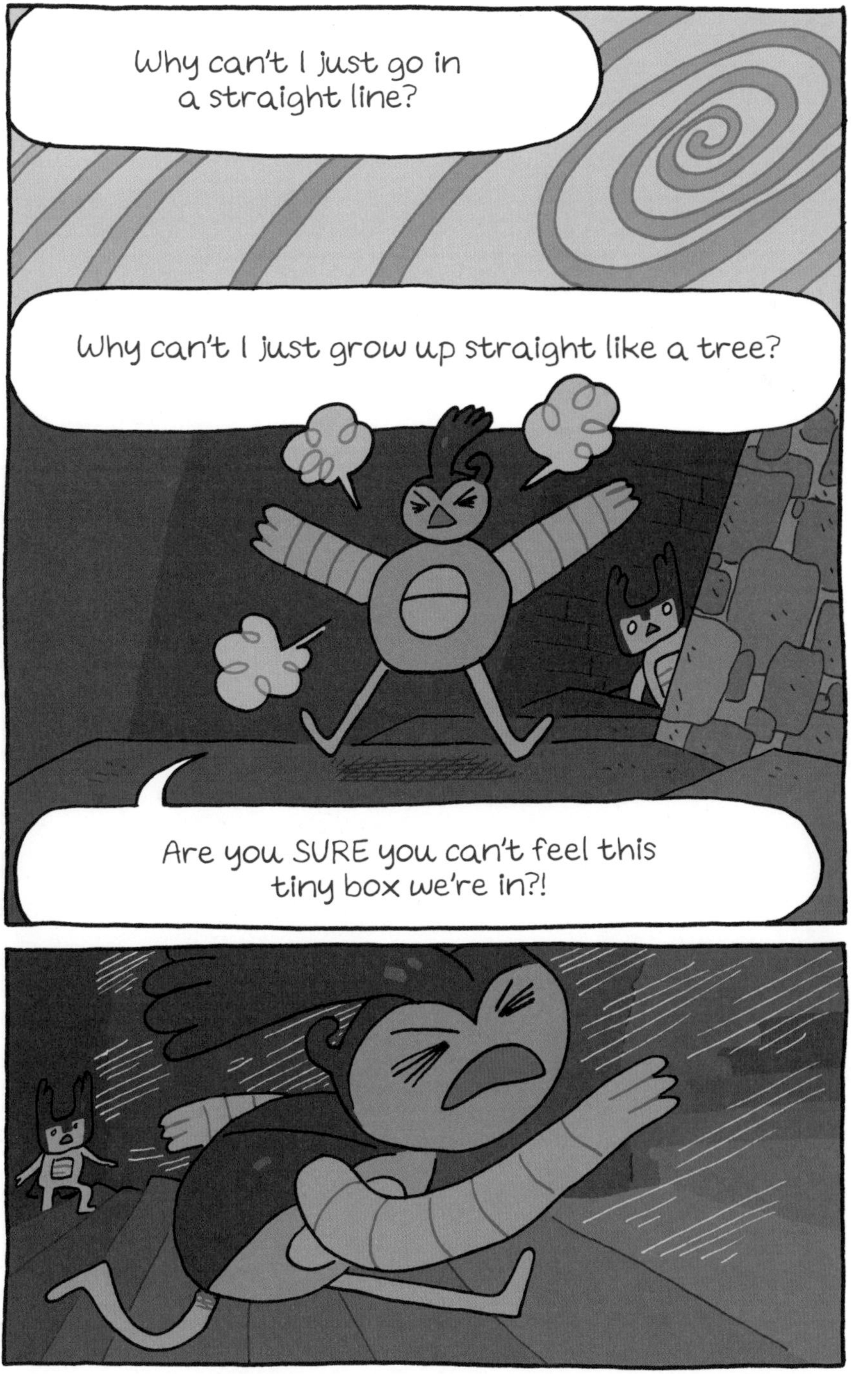
Why can't I just go in a straight line?
Why can't I just grow up straight like a tree?
Are you SURE you can't feel this tiny box we're in?!

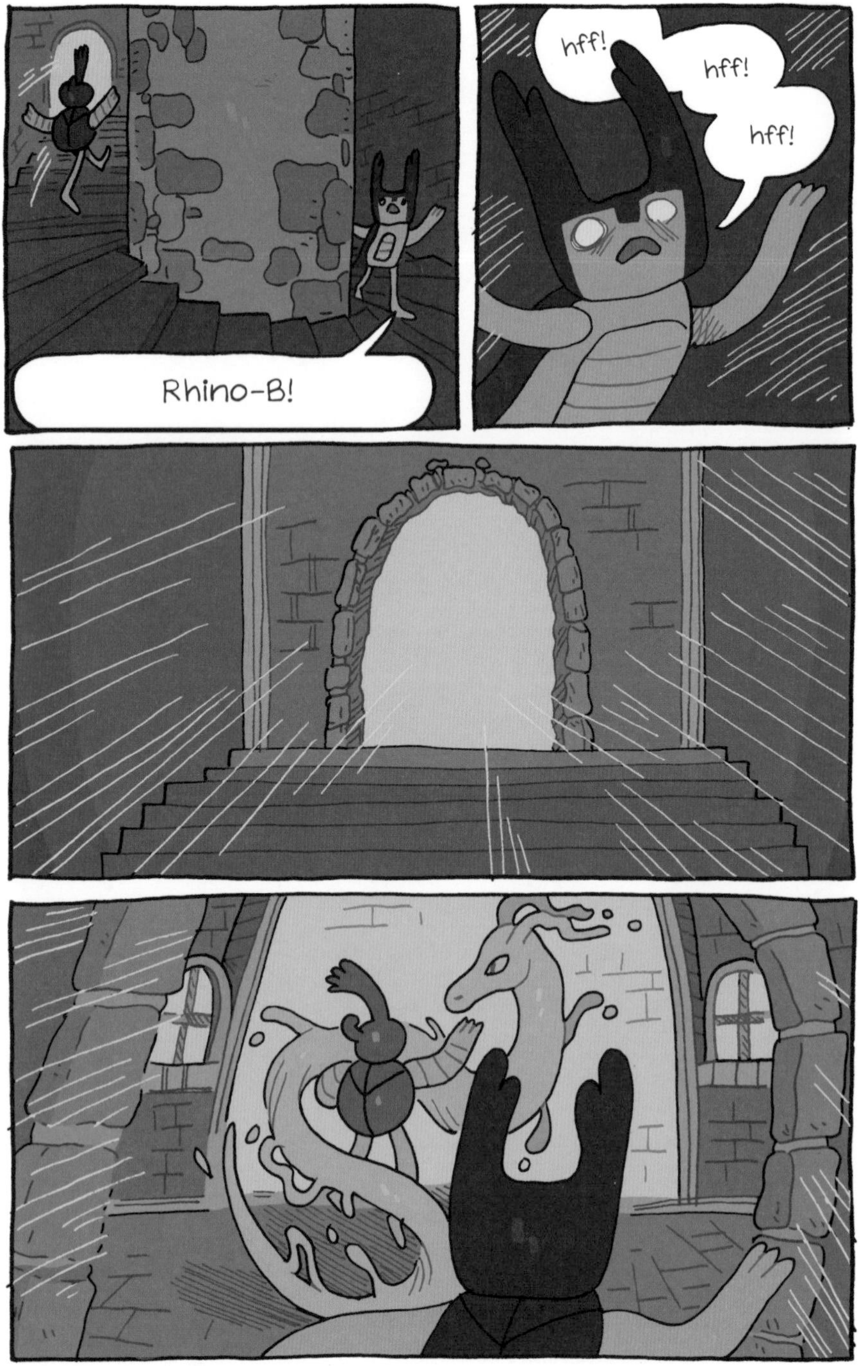
Rhino-B!
hff!
hff!
hff!

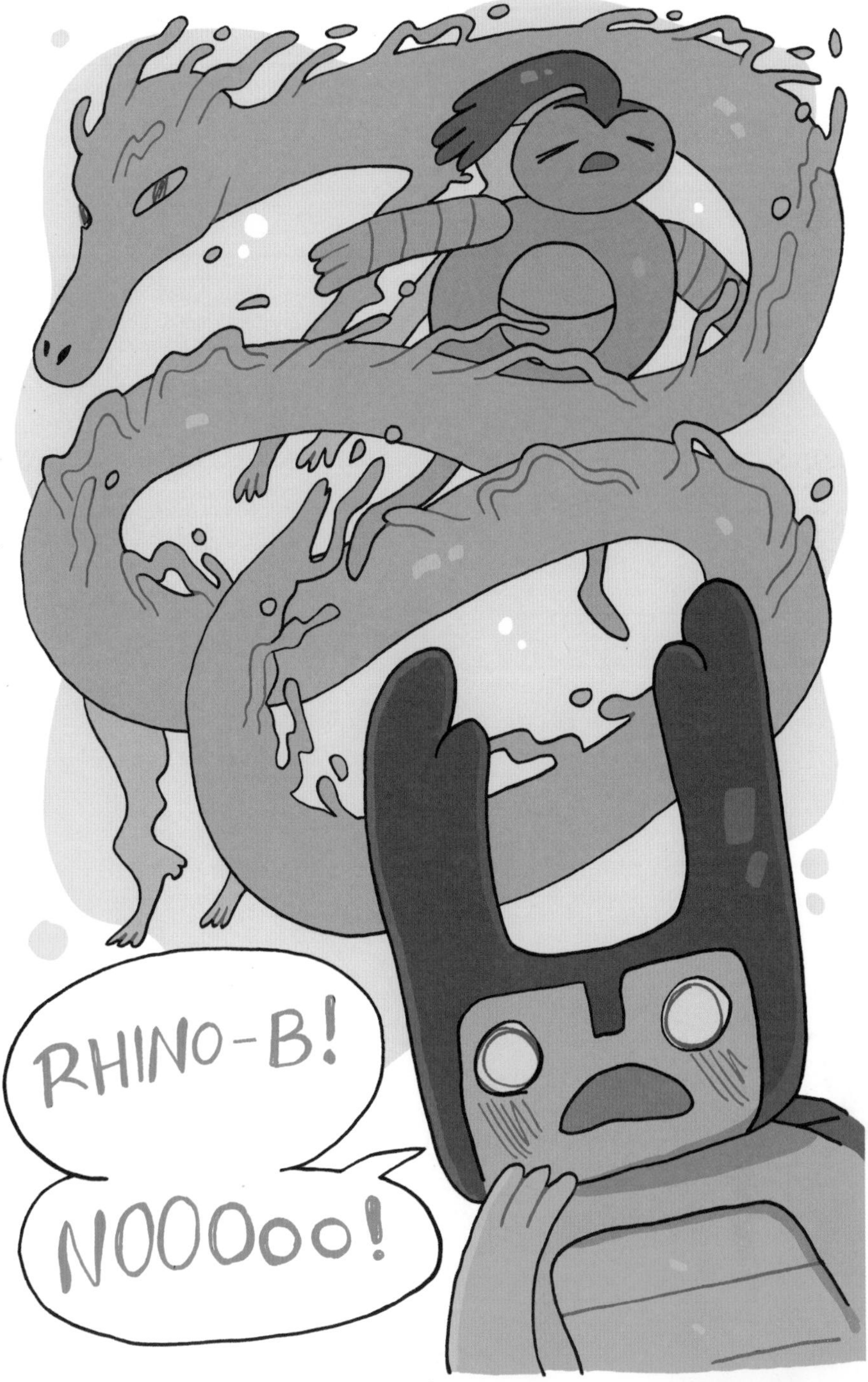
RHINO-B!
NOOOoo!

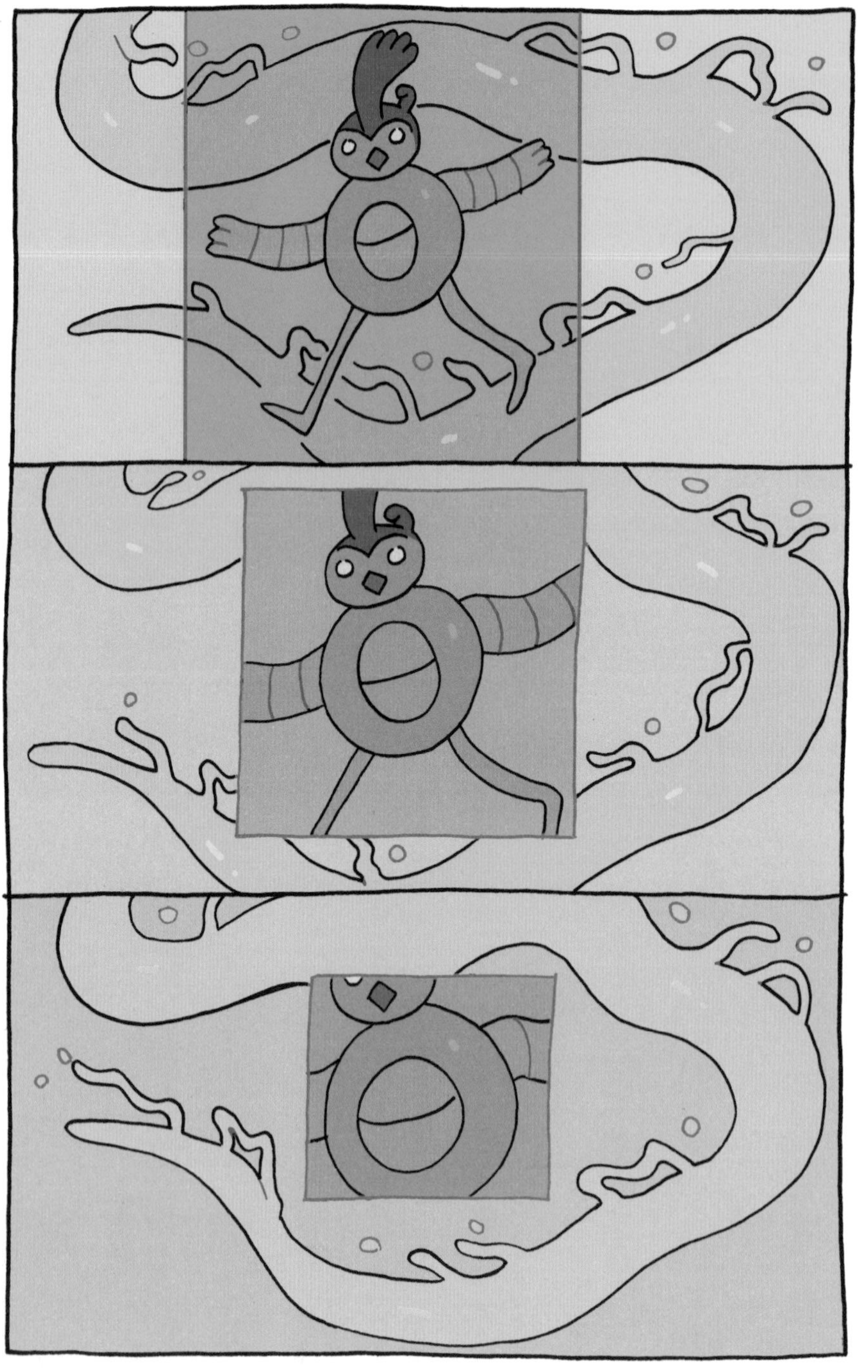

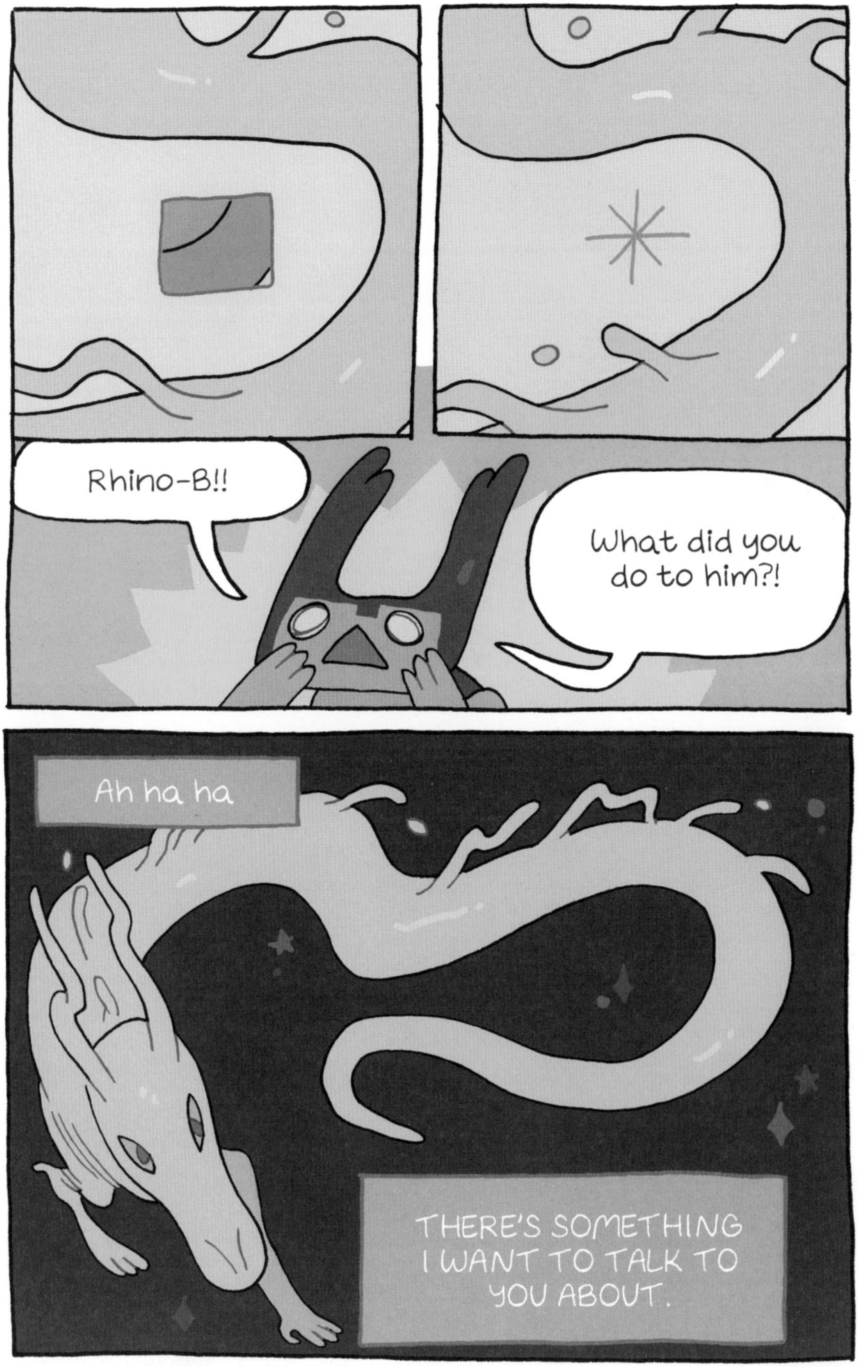
Rhino-B!!
What did you do to him?!
Ah ha ha
THERE'S SOMETHING I WANT TO TALK TO YOU ABOUT.

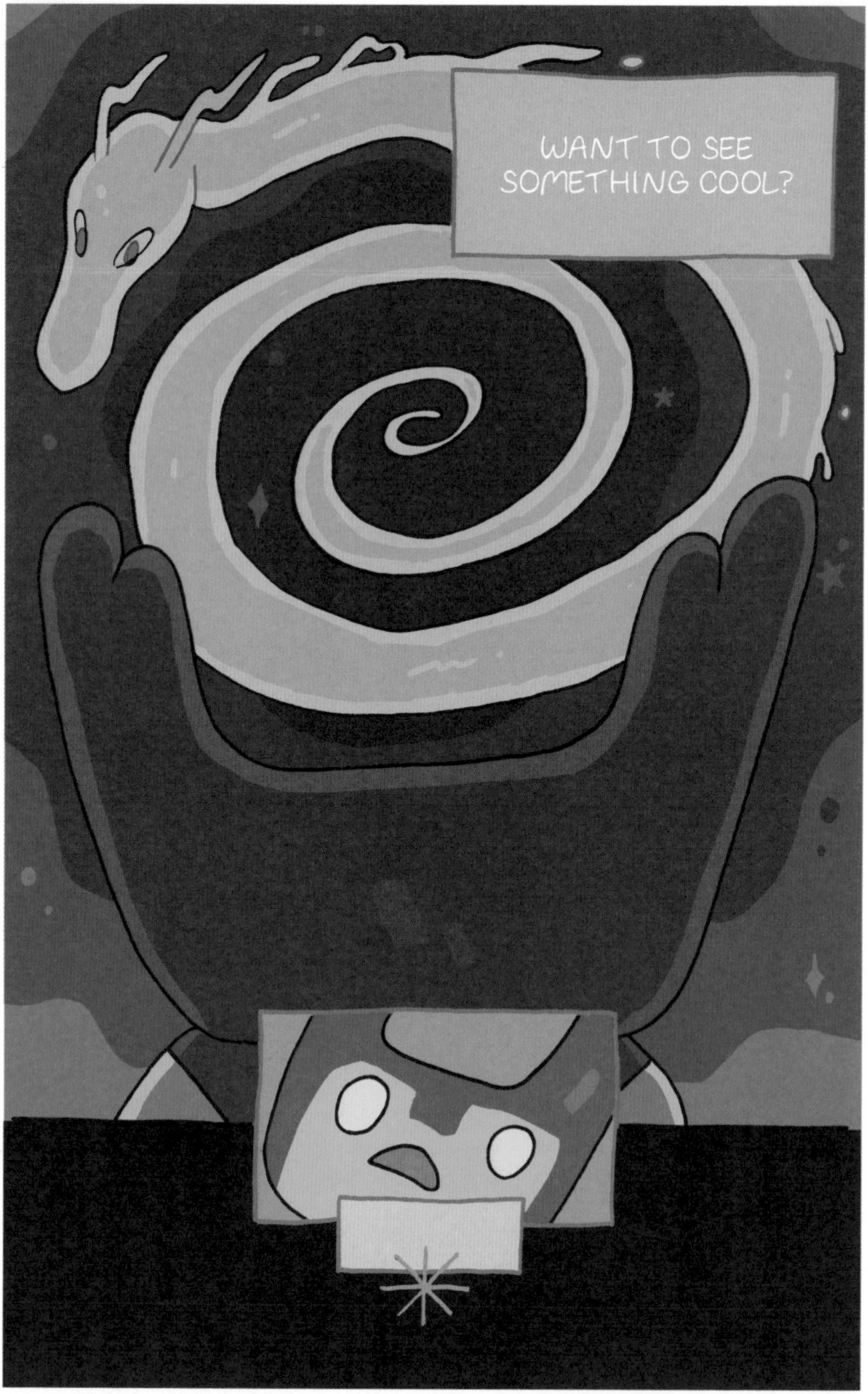
WANT TO SEE SOMETHING COOL?

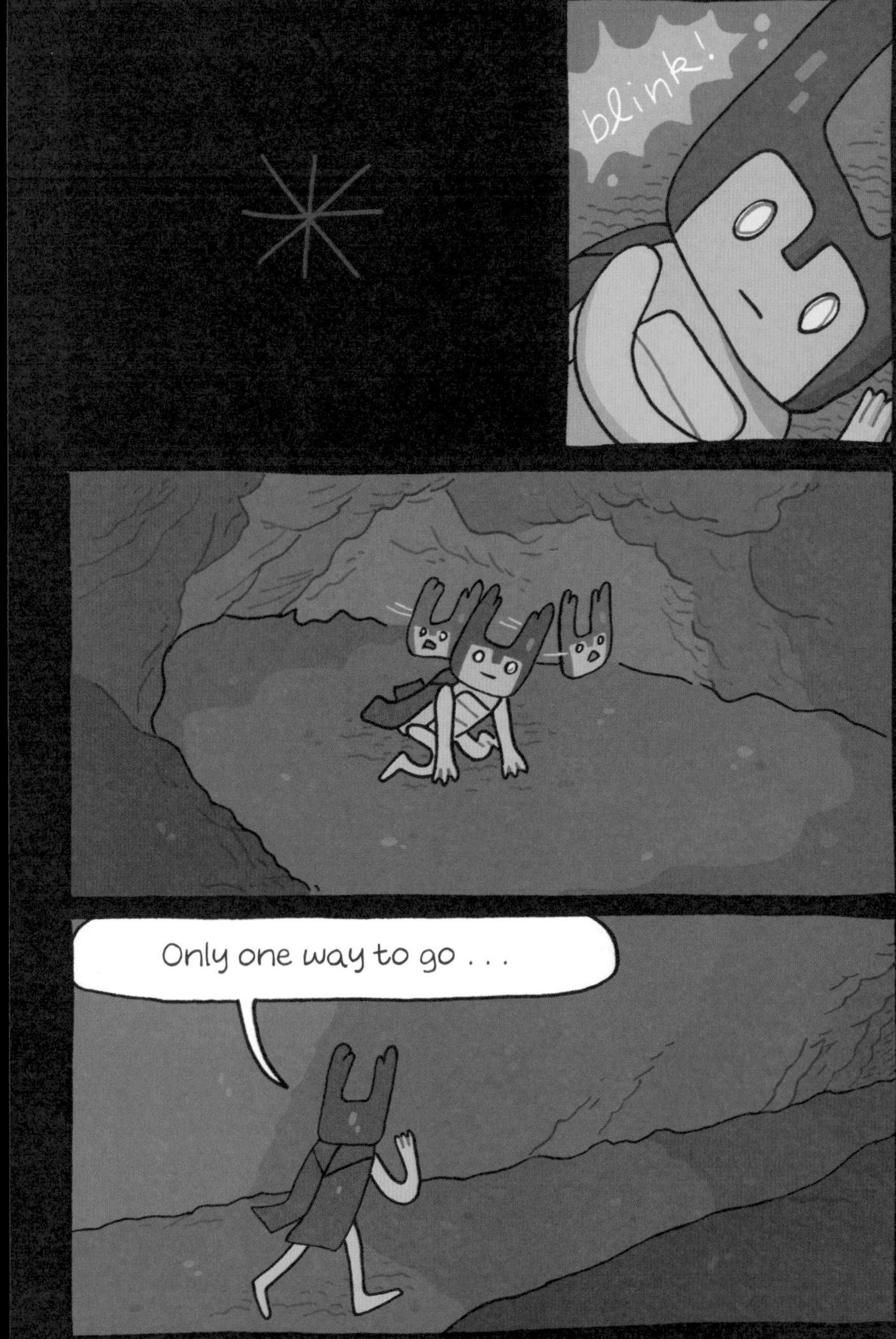
blink!
Only one way to go . . .

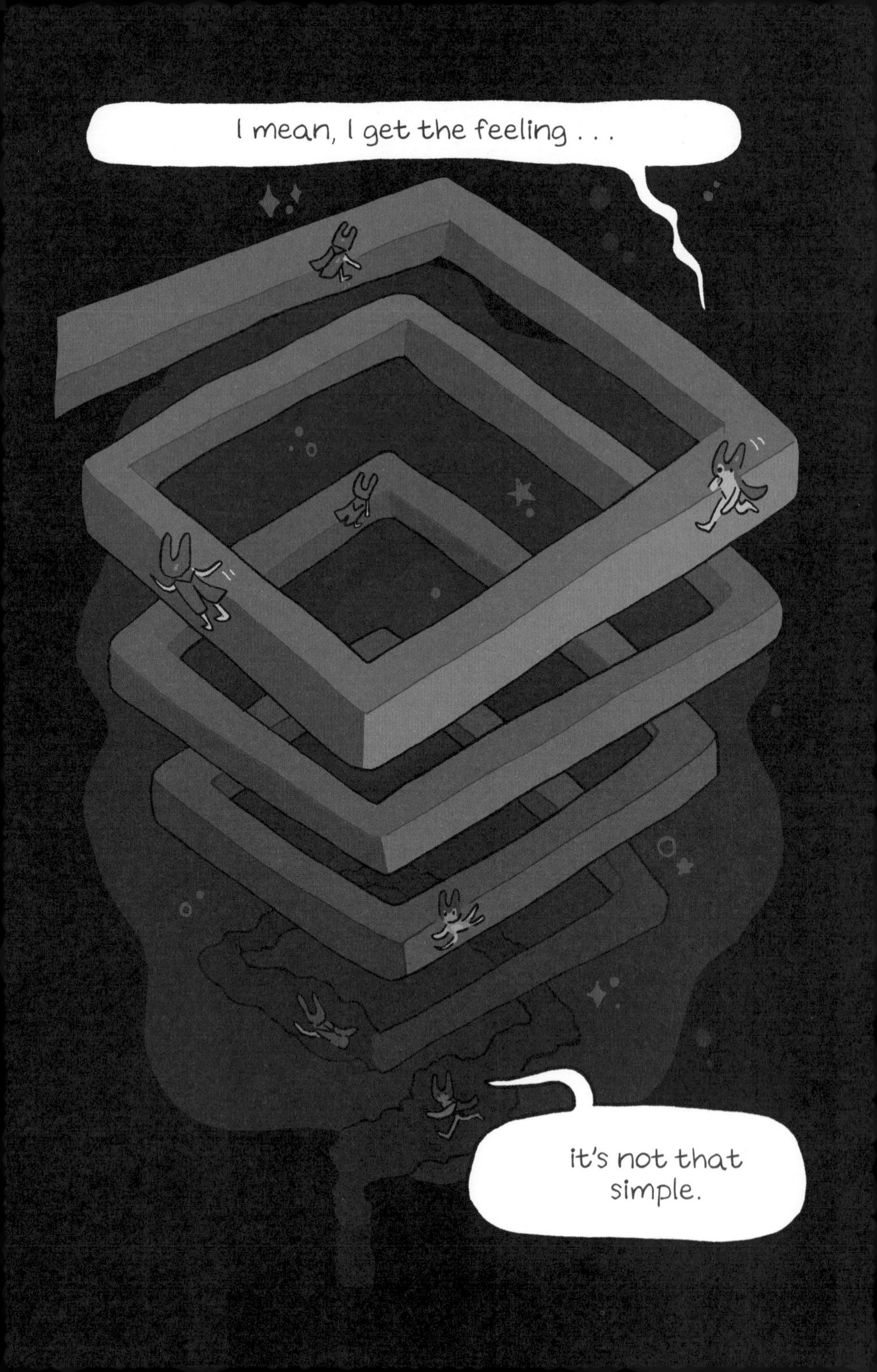
I mean, I get the feeling . . .
it's not that simple.

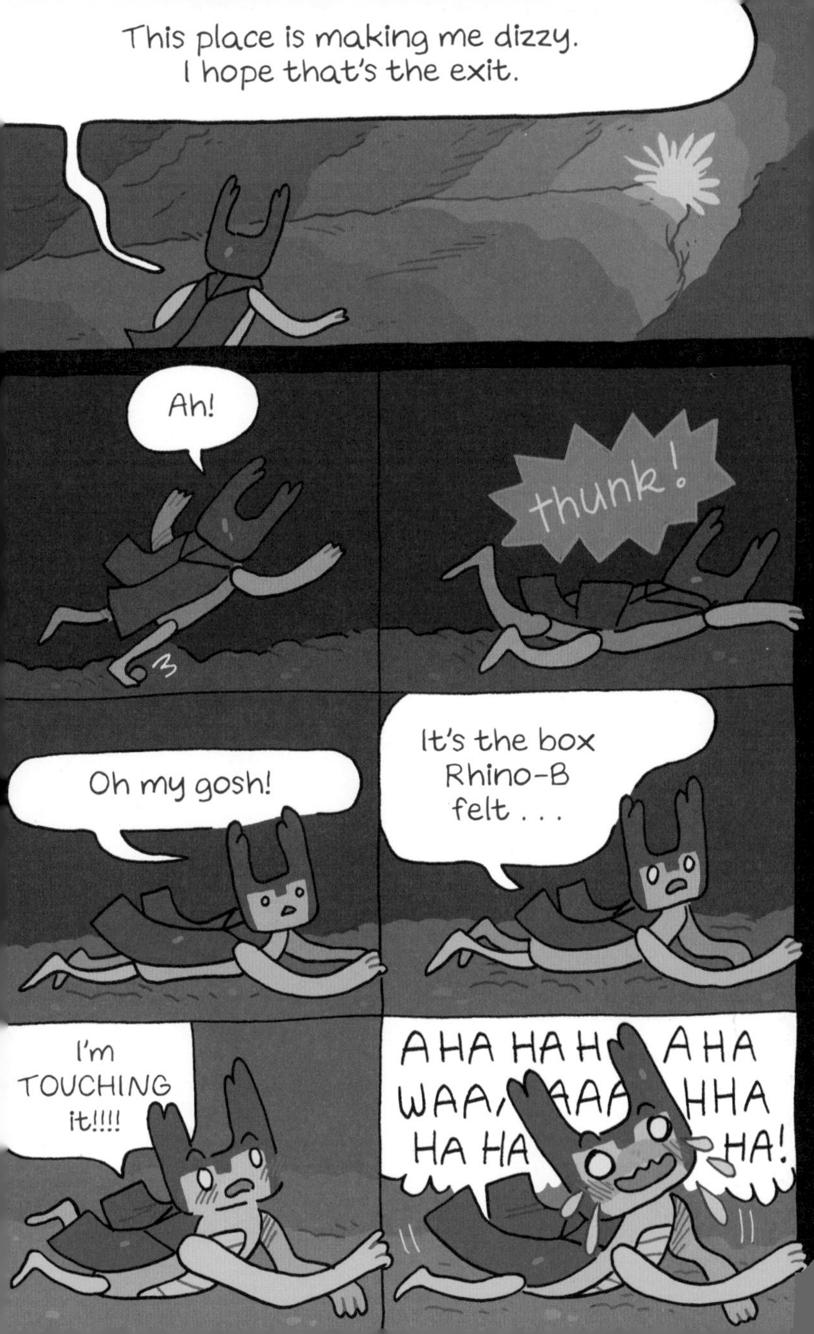
This place is making me dizzy. I hope that's the exit.
Ah!
thunk!
Oh my gosh!
It's the box Rhino-B felt . . .
I'm TOUCHING it!!!!
AHA HA HAH AHA WAA, AAA HHA HA HA HA!

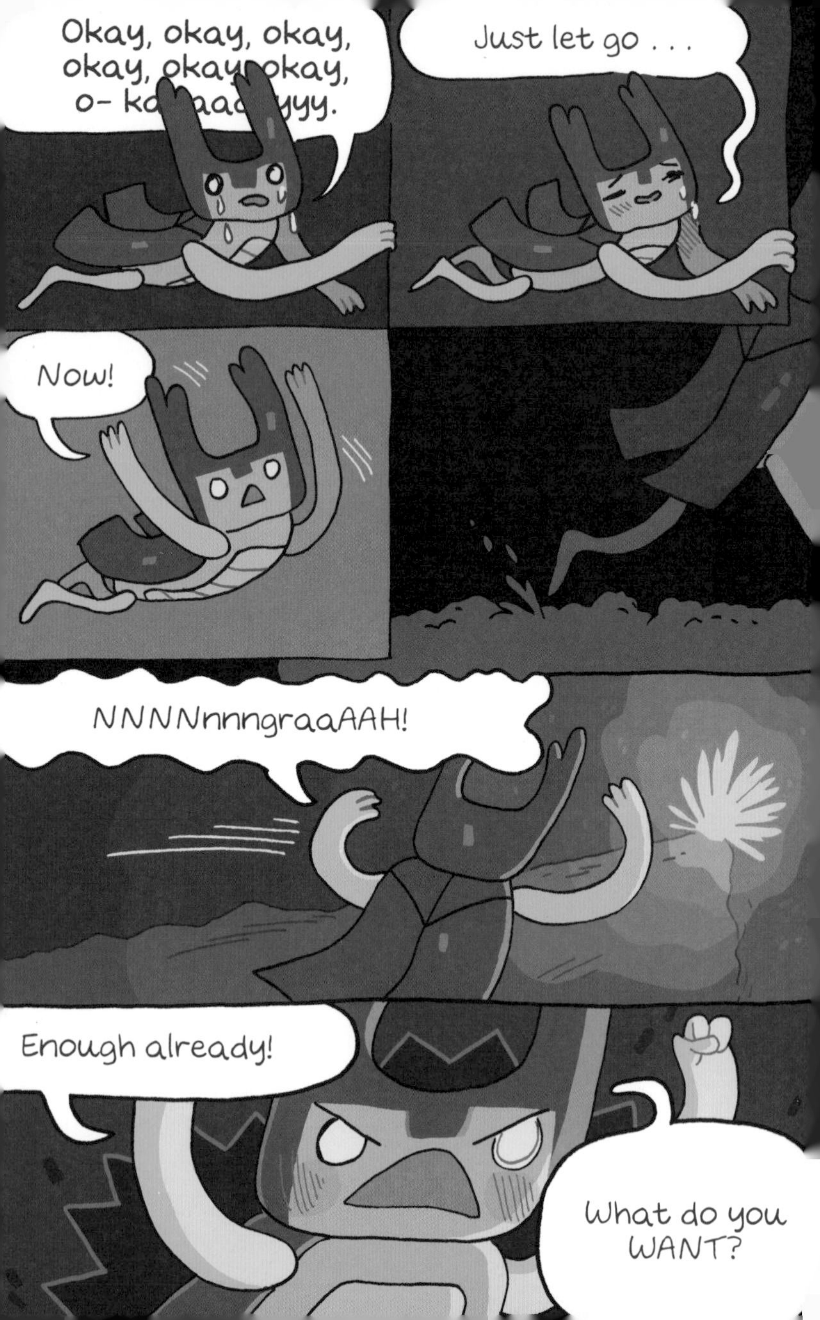
Okay, okay, okay, okay, okay, okay, o- k aa yyy.
Just let go . . .
Now!
NNNNnnngraaAAH!
Enough already!
What do you WANT?

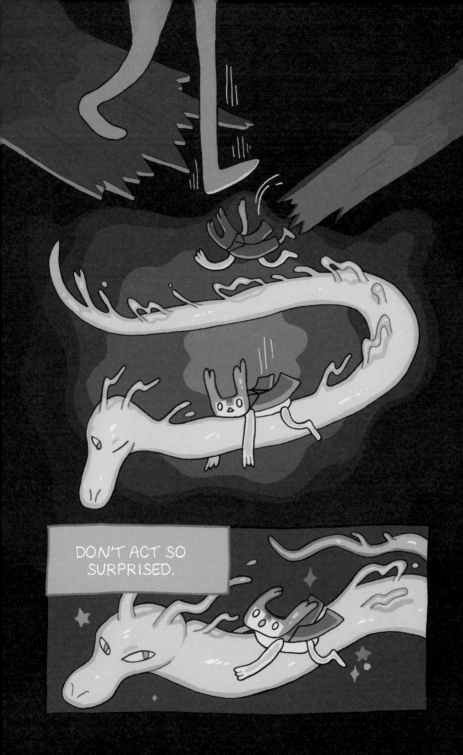

DON'T ACT SO SURPRISED.

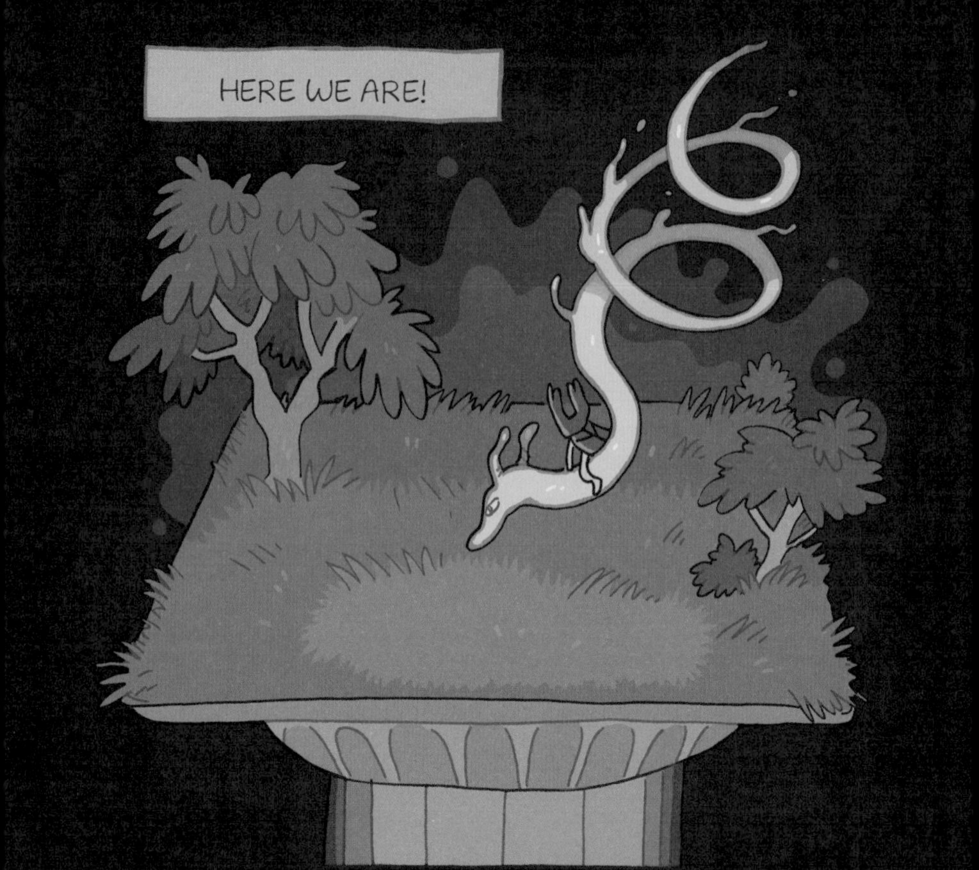
HERE WE ARE!

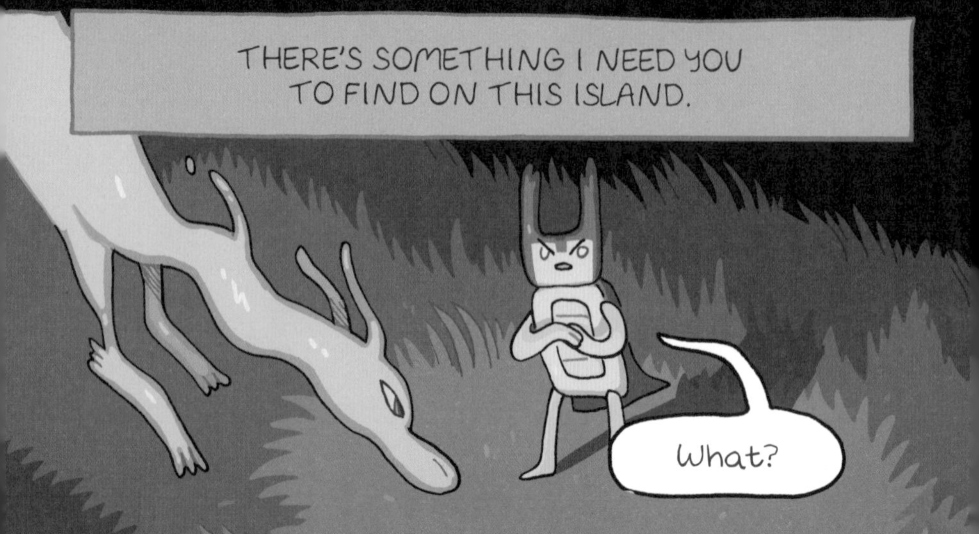
THERE'S SOMETHING I NEED YOU TO FIND ON THIS ISLAND.
What?

THE TRUTH.
YOUR TRUTH.
Where's Rhino-B?
START DIGGING!
NOT THERE!
NOT THERE, EITHER!

So you DO know where it is.

YOU TOO. THINK MORE.

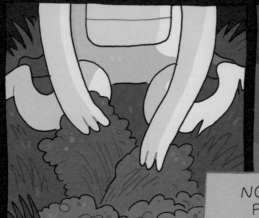

NOT THERE! STOP PLAYING DUMB.

YOU'VE MET SOMETHING LIKE ME BEFORE, RIGHT?

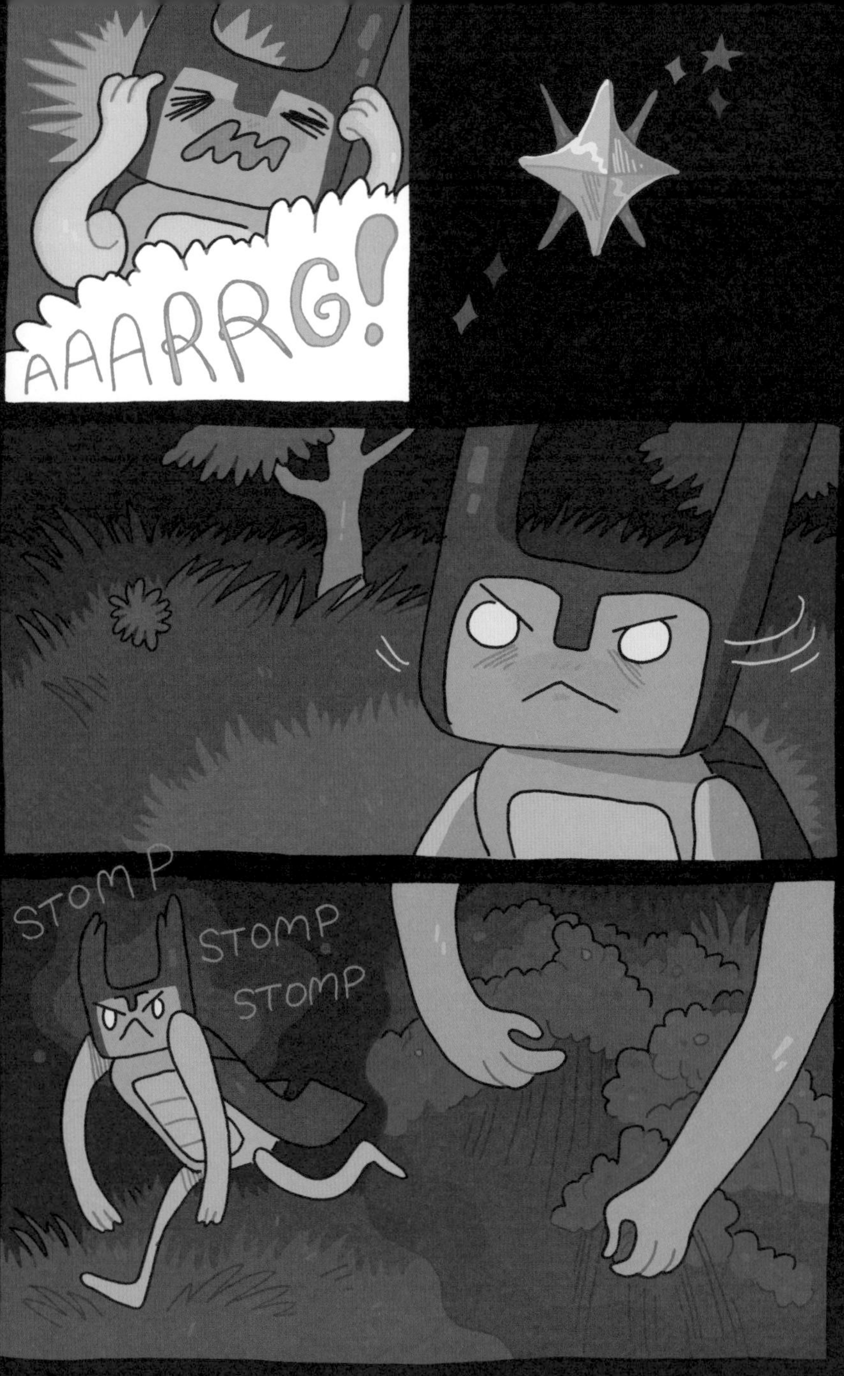
AAARRG!
STOMP
STOMP
STOMP

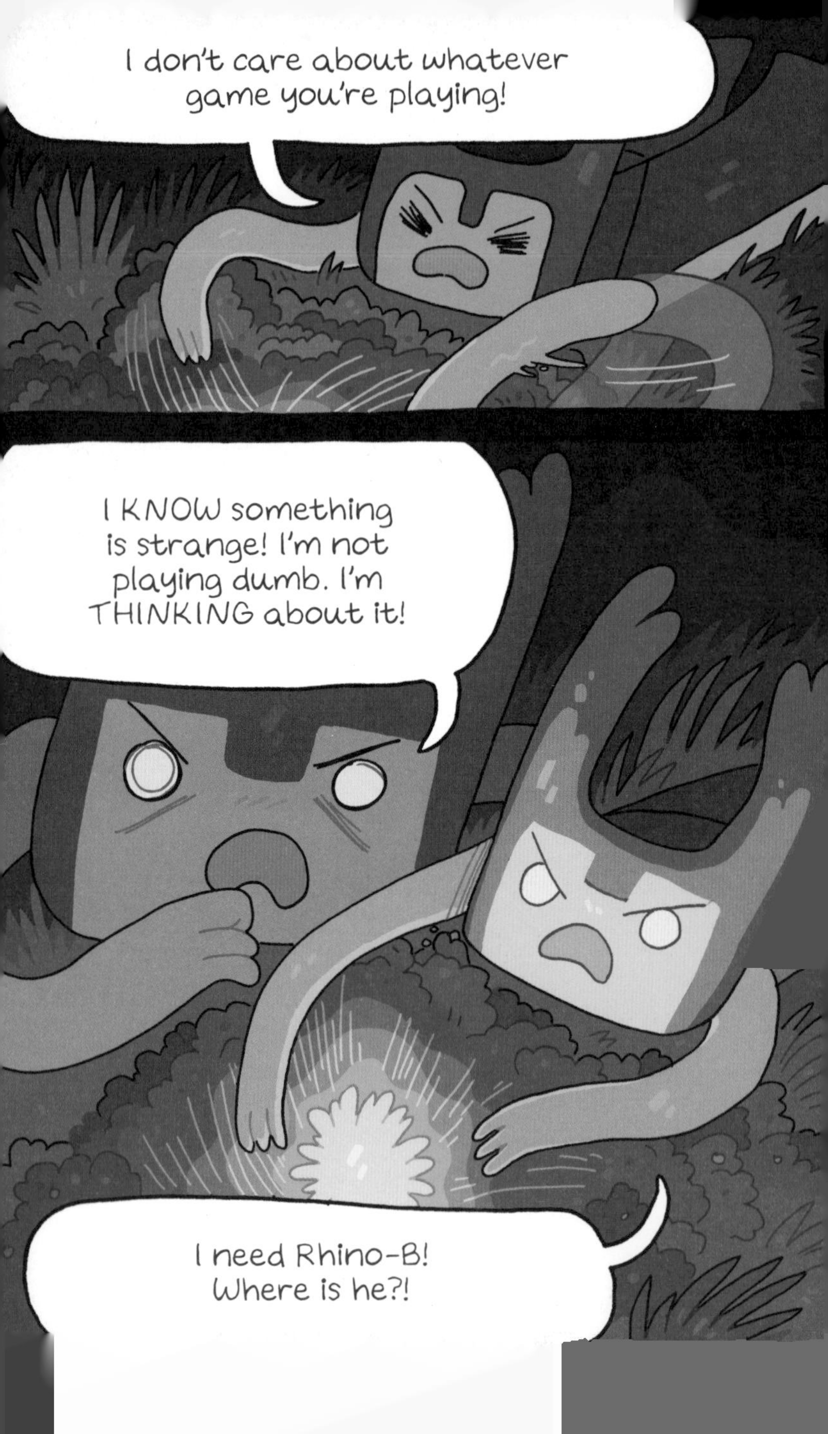
I don't care about whatever game you're playing!
I KNOW something is strange! I'm not playing dumb. I'm THINKING about it!
I need Rhino-B! Where is he?!

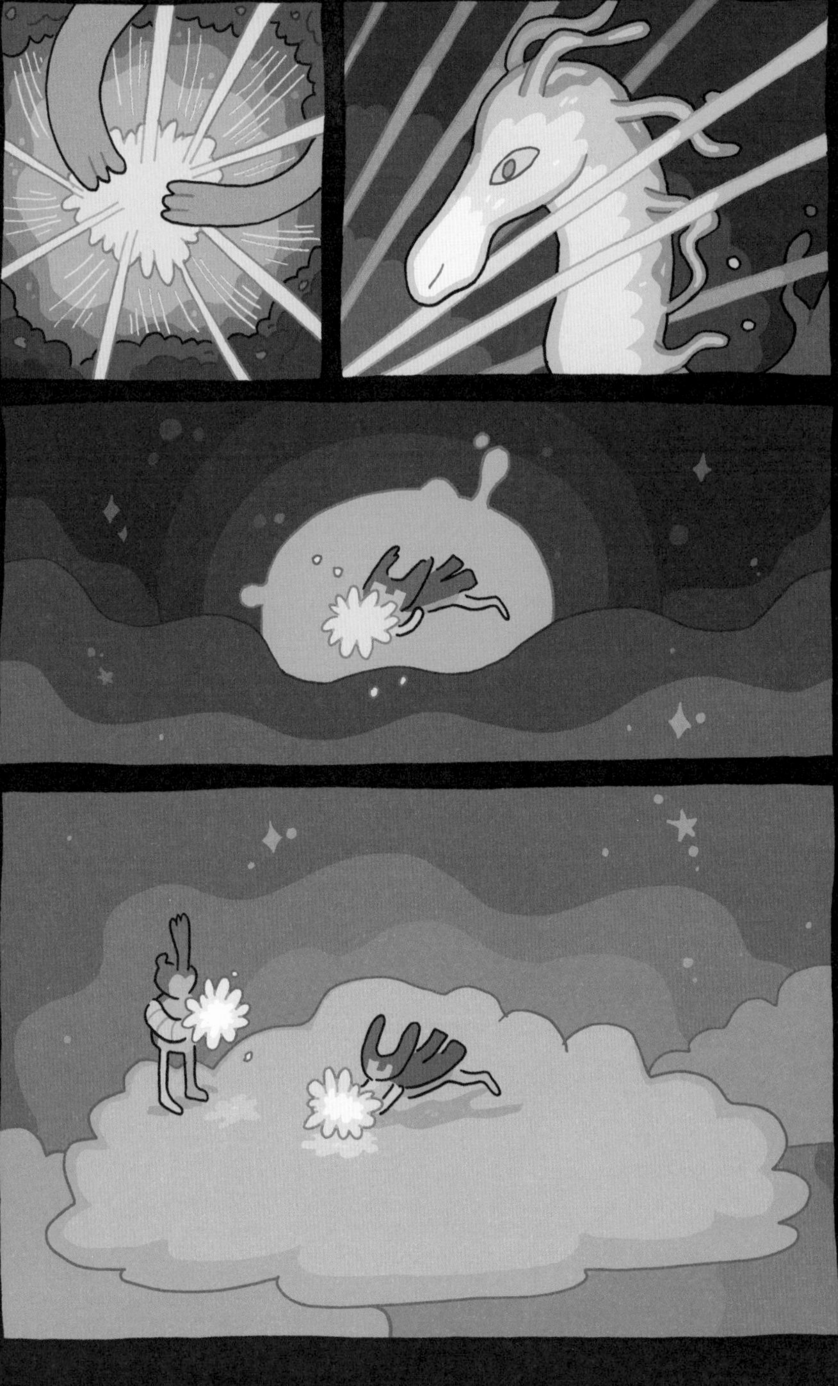

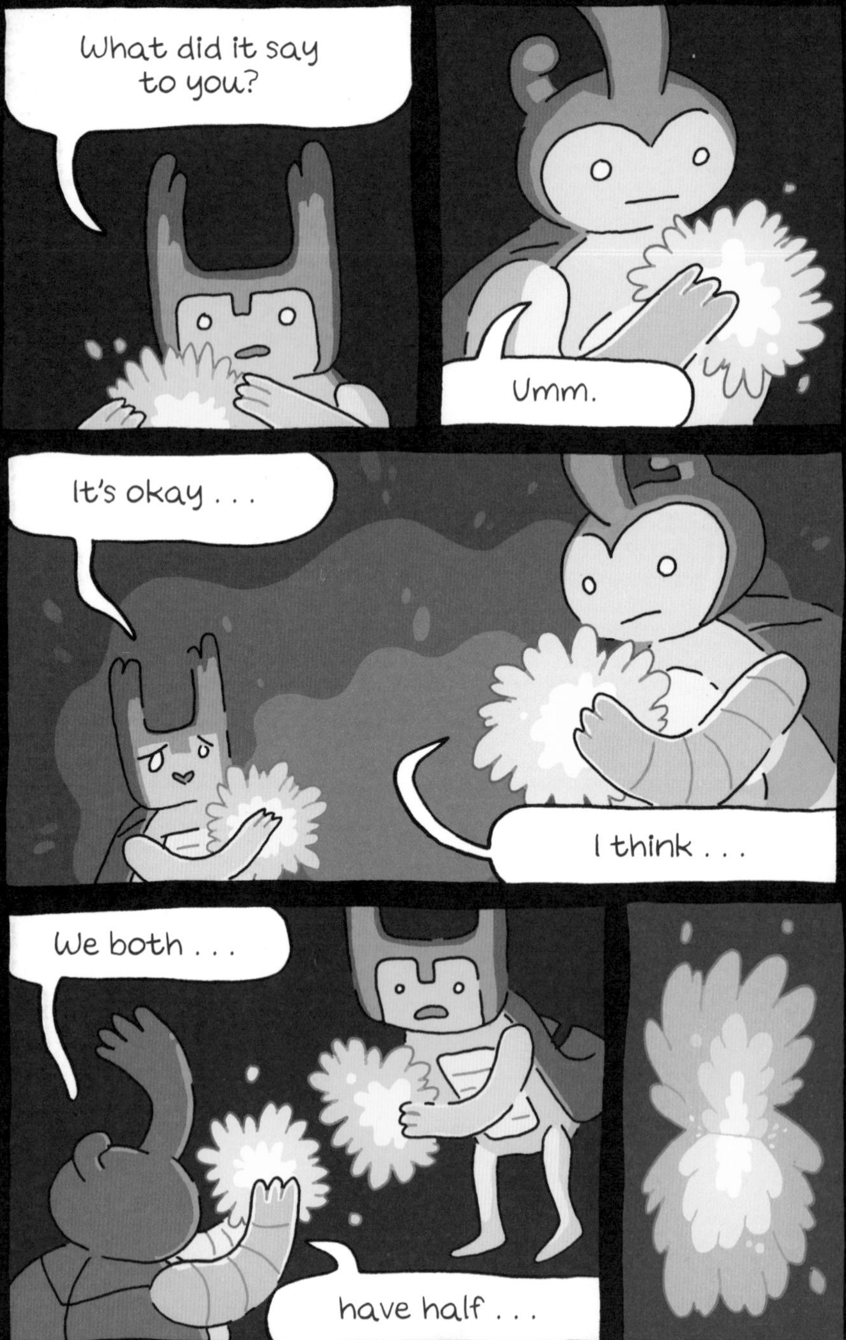
What did it say to you?
Umm.
It's okay . . .
I think . . .
We both . . .
have half . . .

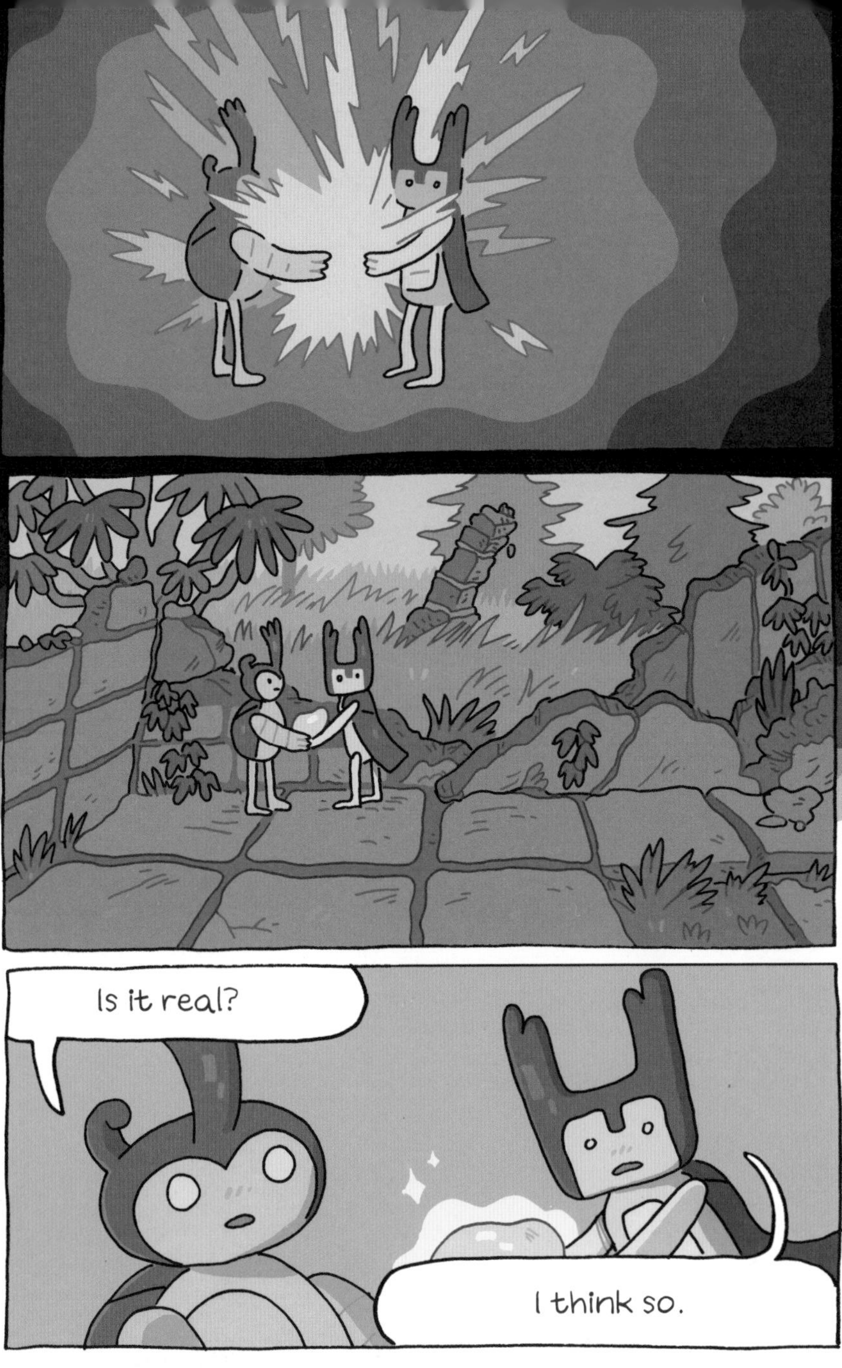
Is it real?
I think so.

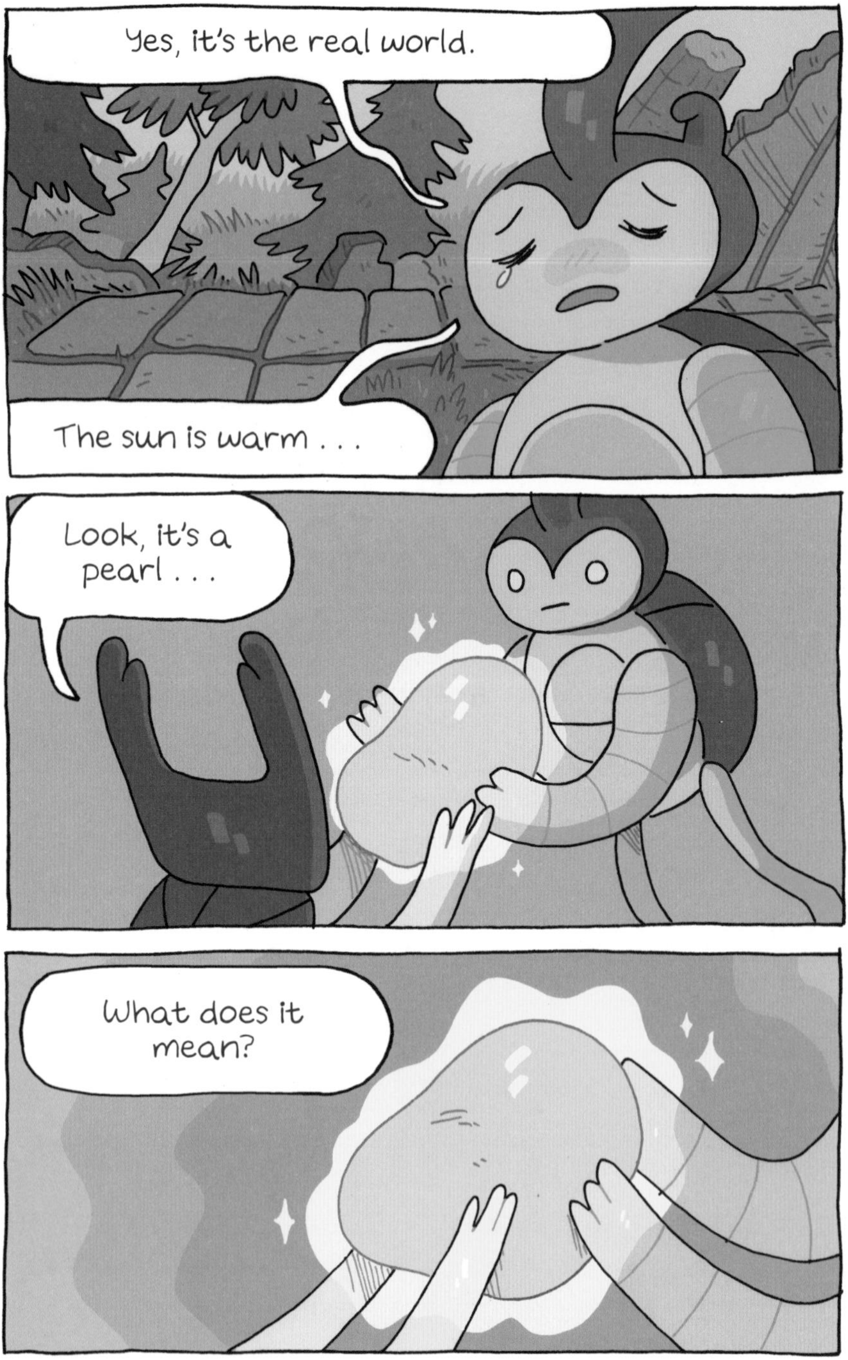
Yes, it's the real world.
The sun is warm . . .
Look, it's a pearl . . .
What does it mean?

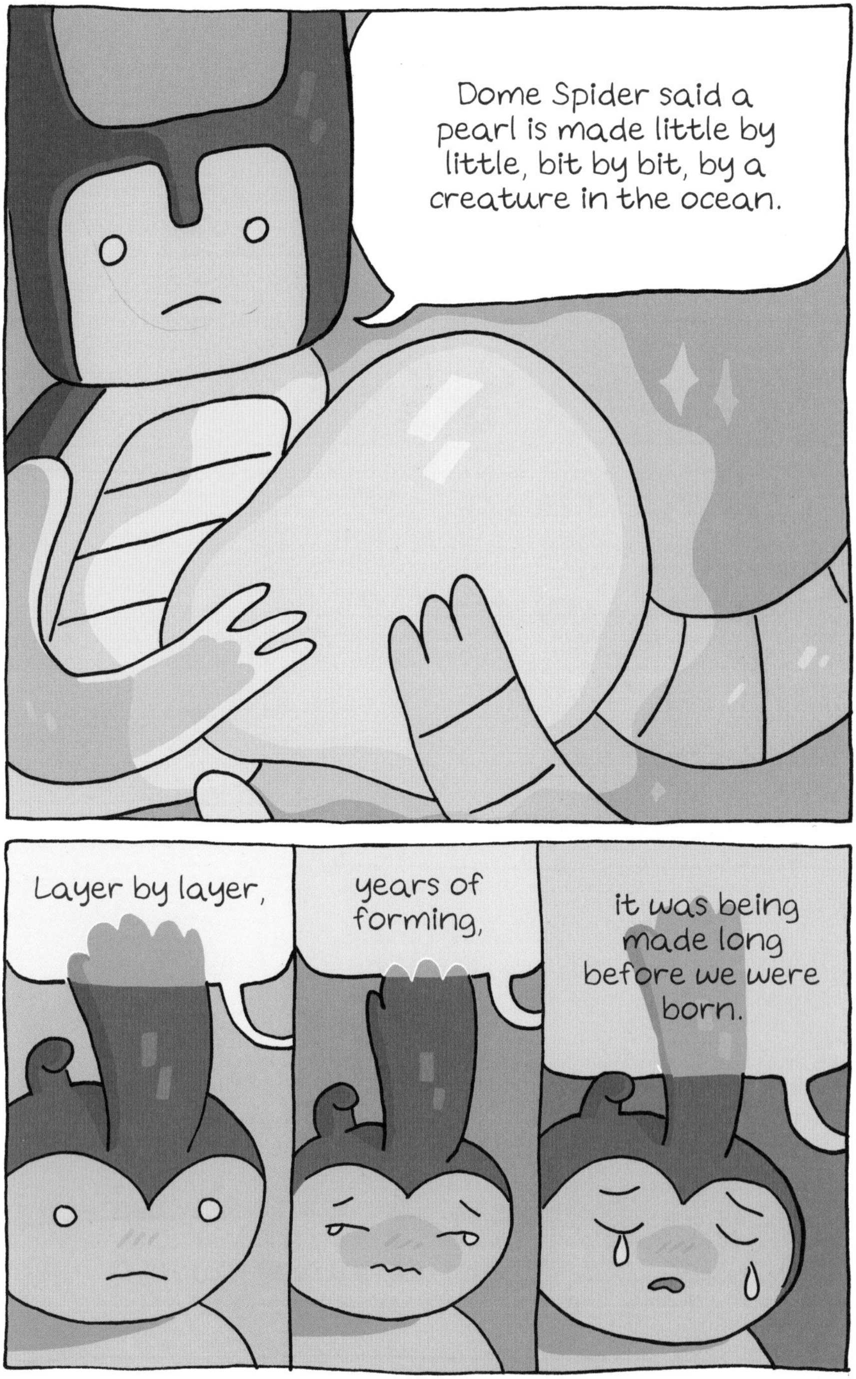
Dome Spider said a pearl is made little by little, bit by bit, by a creature in the ocean.
Layer by layer,
years of forming,
it was being made long before we were born.

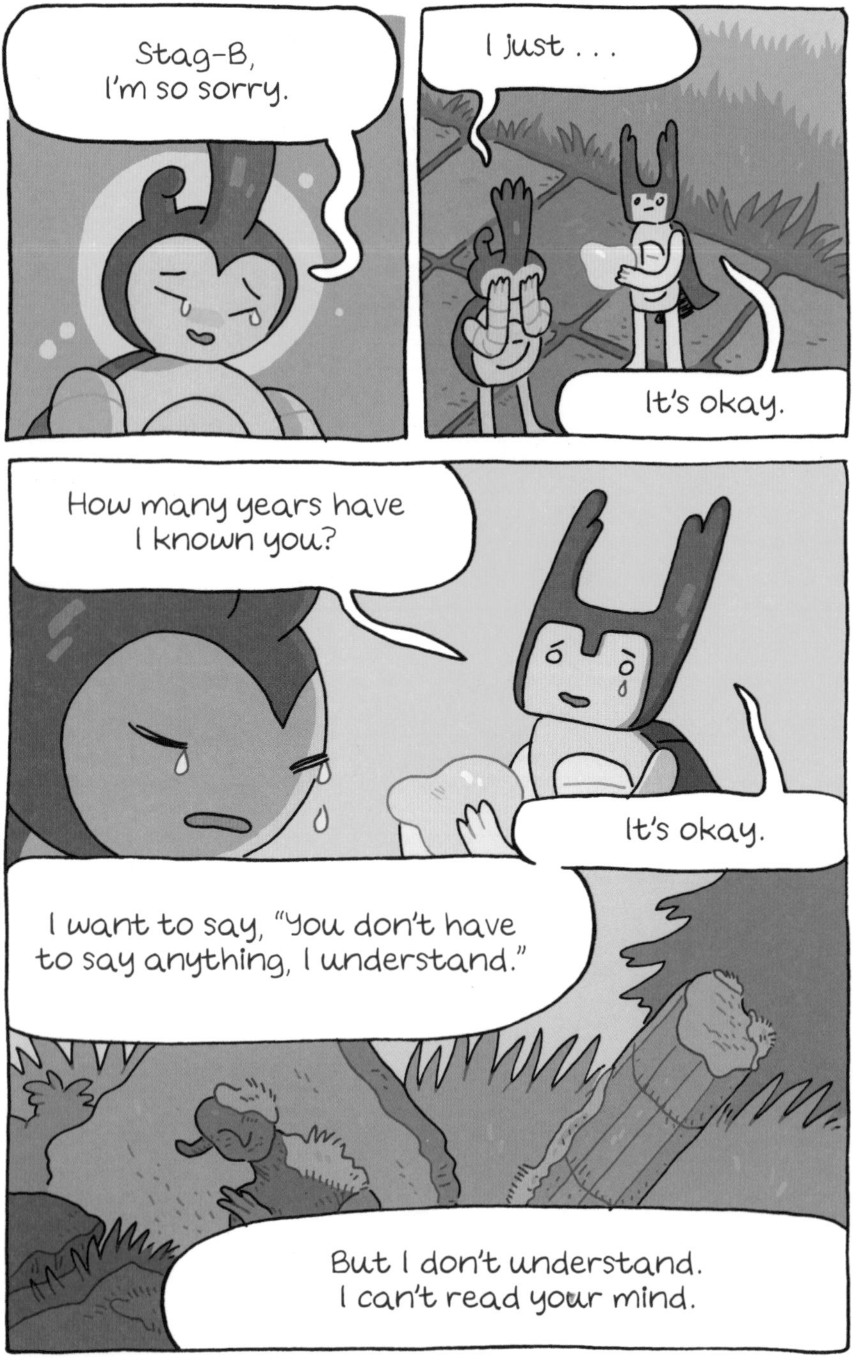
Stag-B,
I'm so sorry.
I just . . .
It's okay.
How many years have
I known you?
It's okay.
I want to say, "You don't have to say anything, I understand."
But I don't understand. I can't read your mind.

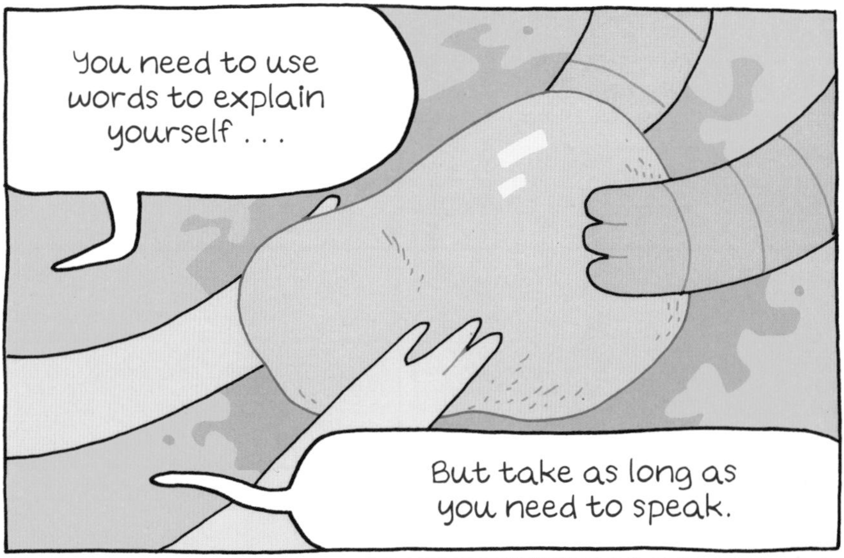
You need to use words to explain yourself . . .
But take as long as you need to speak.
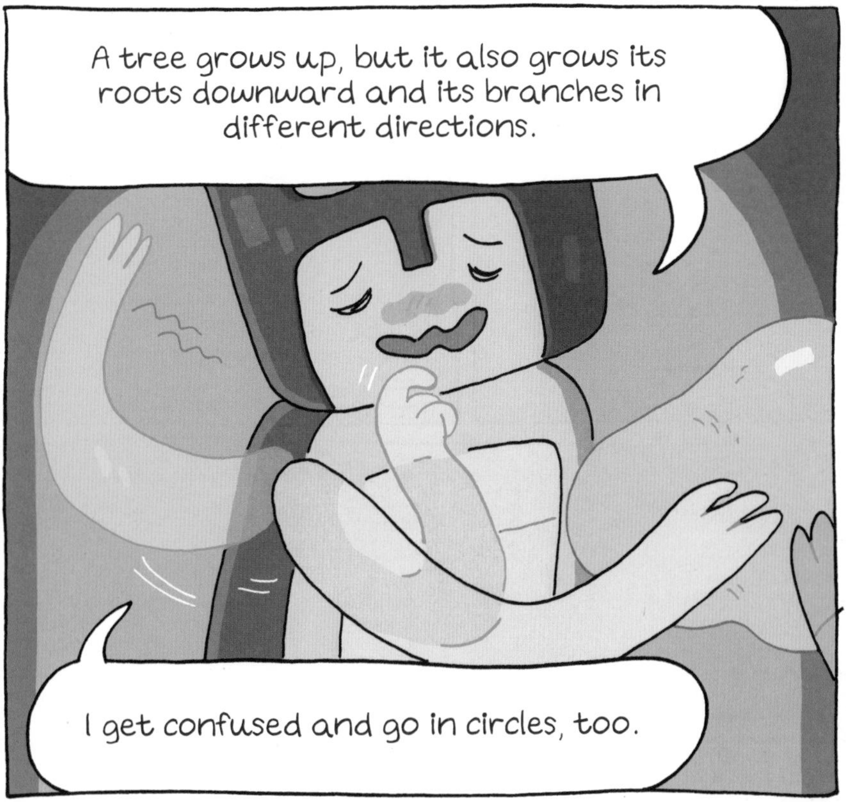
A tree grows up, but it also grows its roots downward and its branches in different directions.
I get confused and go in circles, too.

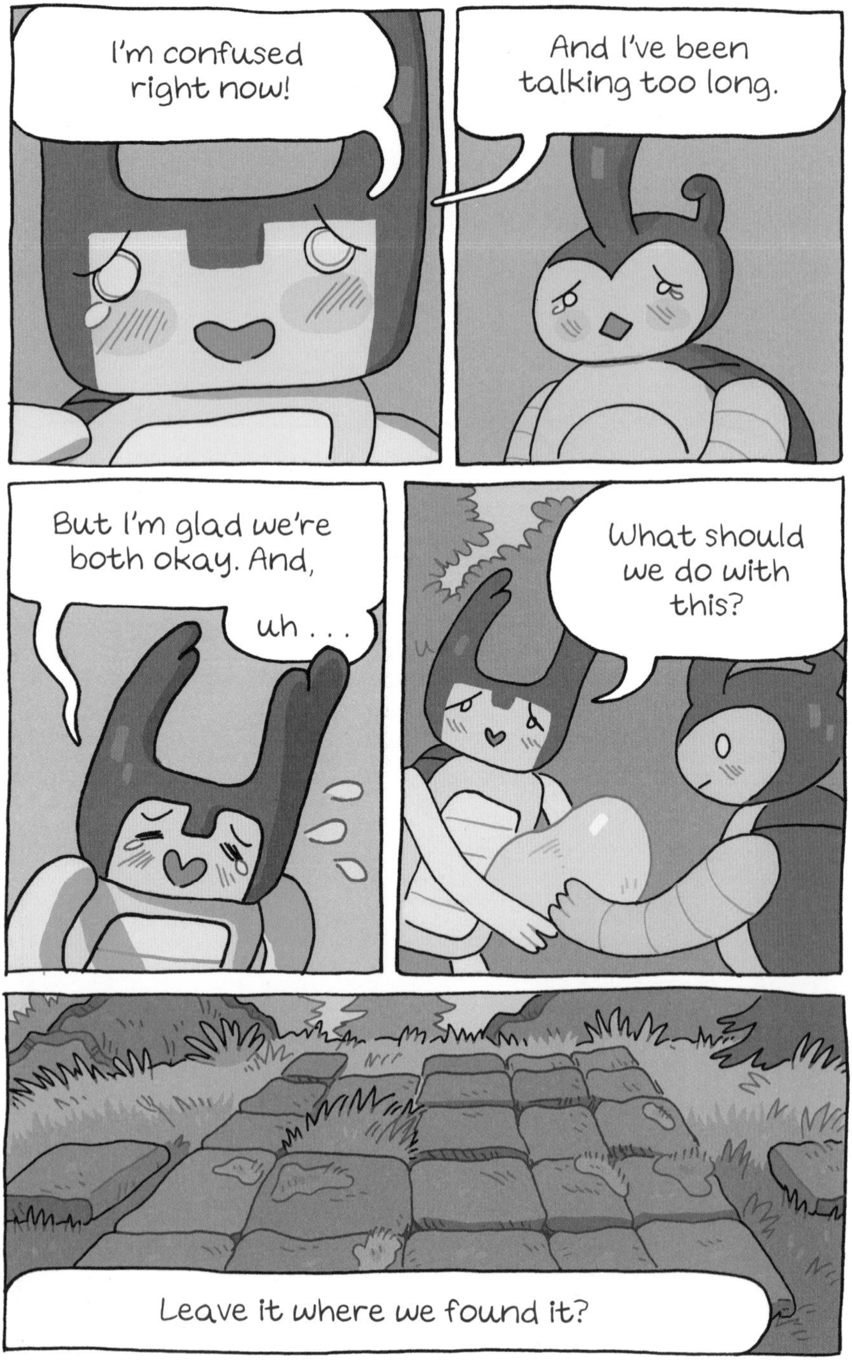
I'm confused right now!
And I've been talking too long.
But I'm glad we're both okay. And,
uh . . .
What should we do with this?
Leave it where we found it?

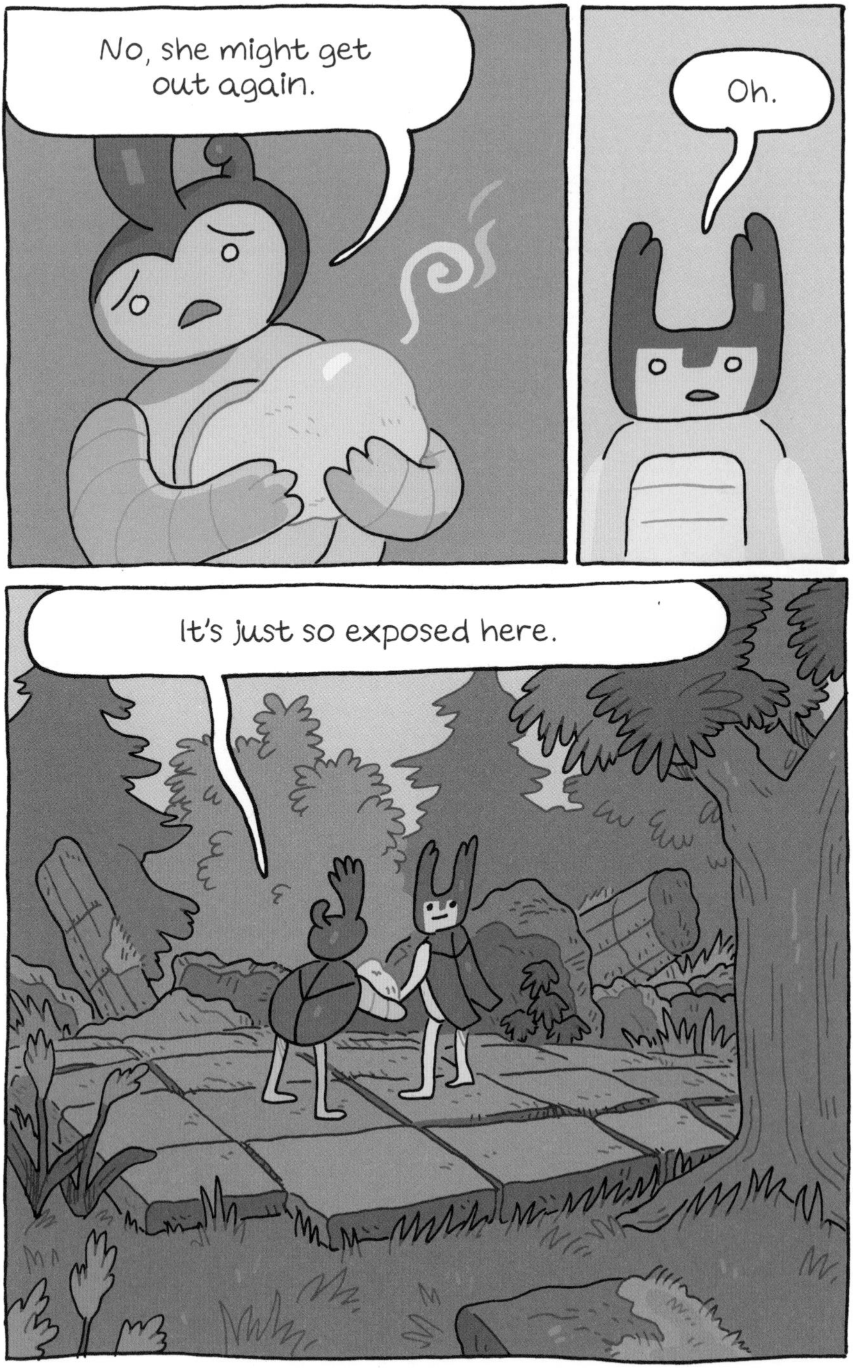
No, she might get out again.
Oh.
It's just so exposed here.

We went back to Bug Village.

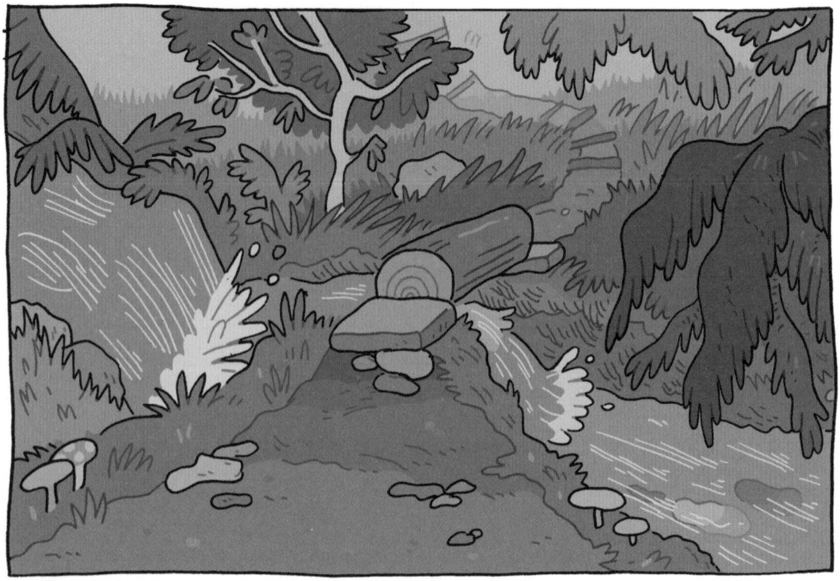

And we left the pearl at the Insects' Library.

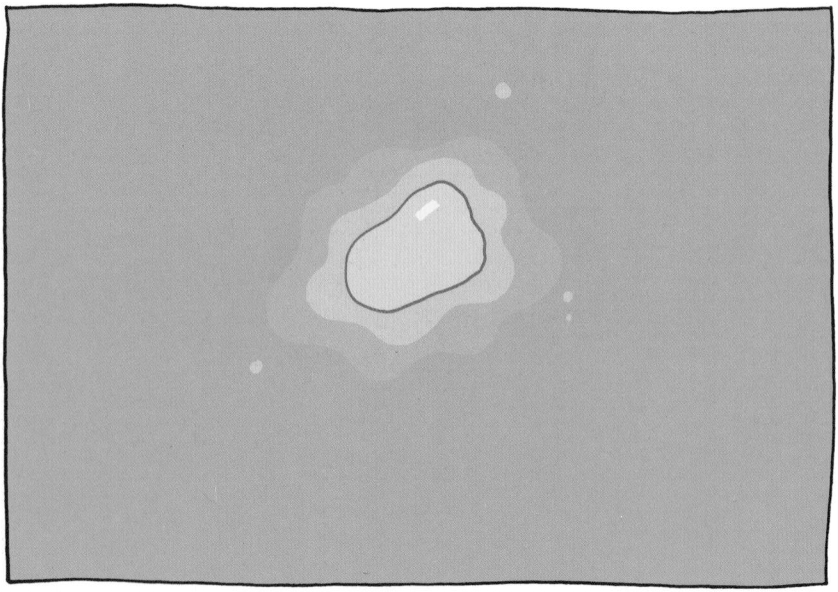

Rhino-B built a place for it on an old shelf in one of the storage rooms.

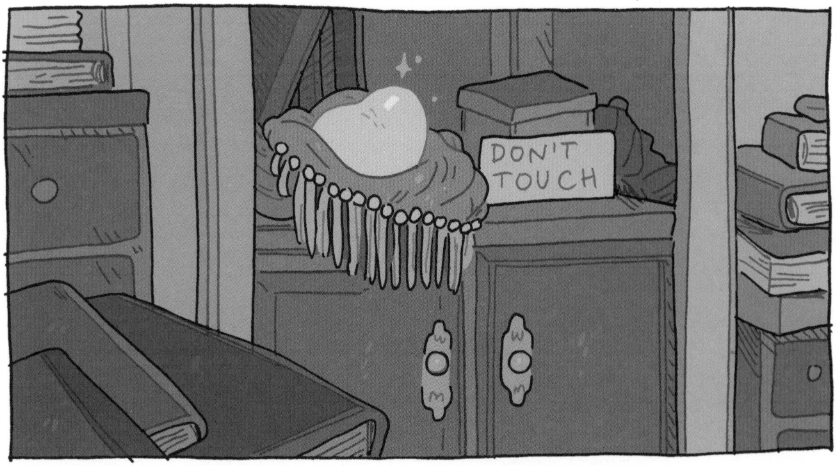
DON'T TOUCH

So she wouldn't get too cold.

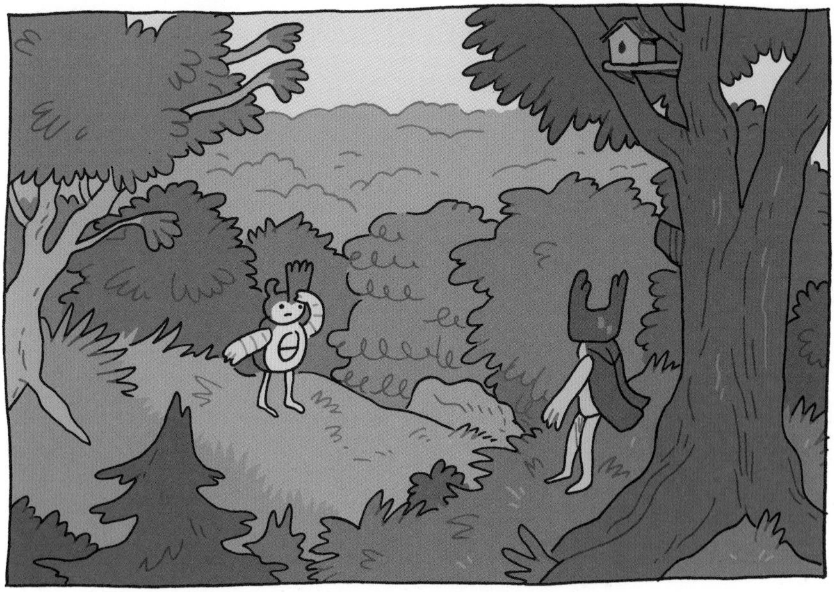

When we went back to that area, we couldn't find the ruins again.

In any case, we went home.

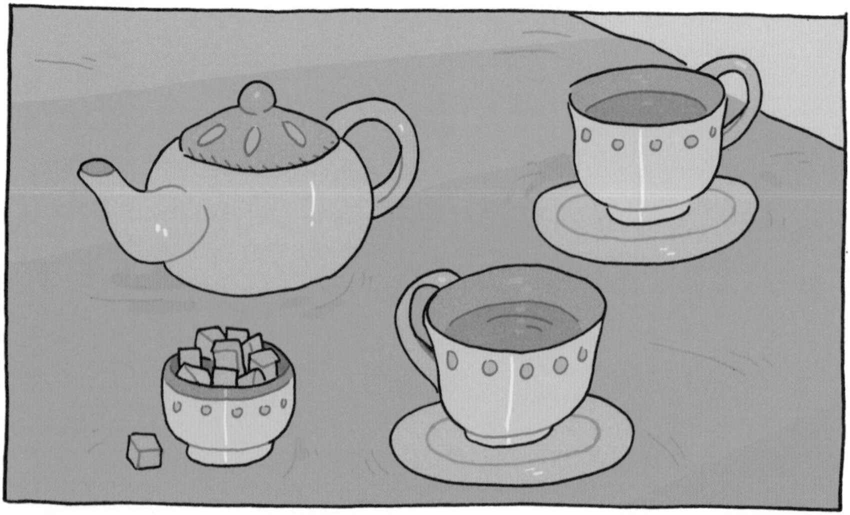

And had a long talk.

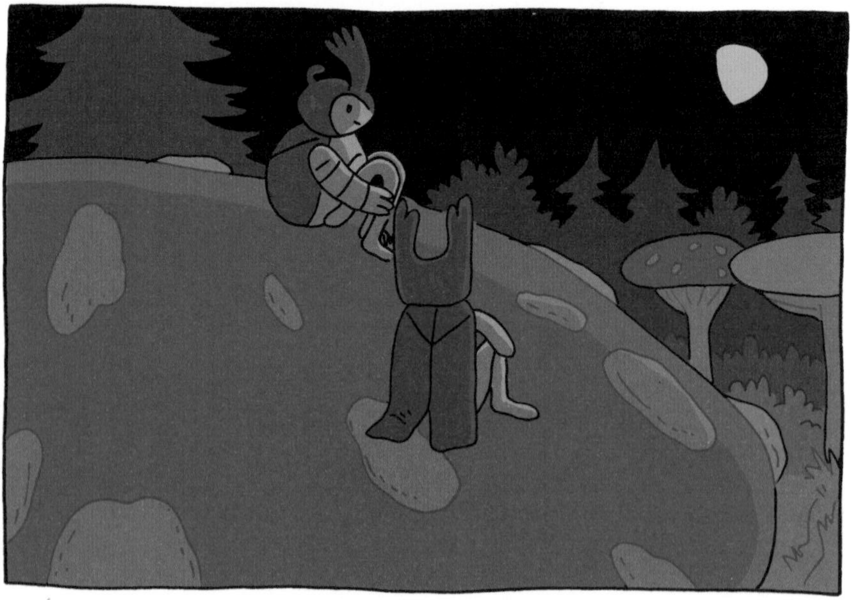

And looked at the moon.
And slept soundly.

(only read past this
page if you want to
know what the ghost
said to Rhino-B.)

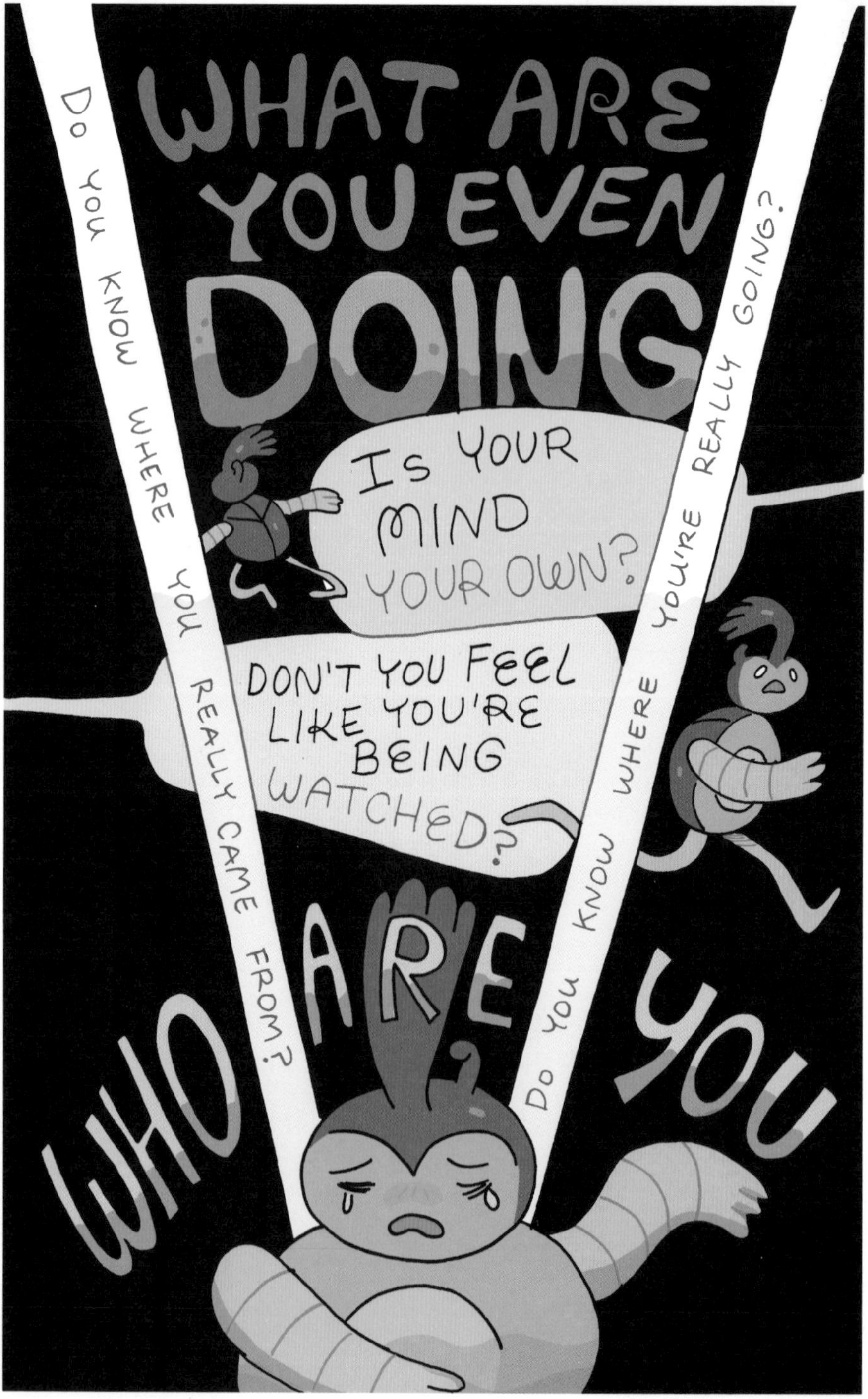
WHAT ARE YOU EVEN DOING
DO YOU KNOW WHERE YOU REALLY CAME FROM?
DO YOU KNOW WHERE YOU'RE REALLY GOING?
IS YOUR MIND YOUR OWN?
DON'T YOU FEEL LIKE YOU'RE BEING WATCHED?
WHO ARE YOU

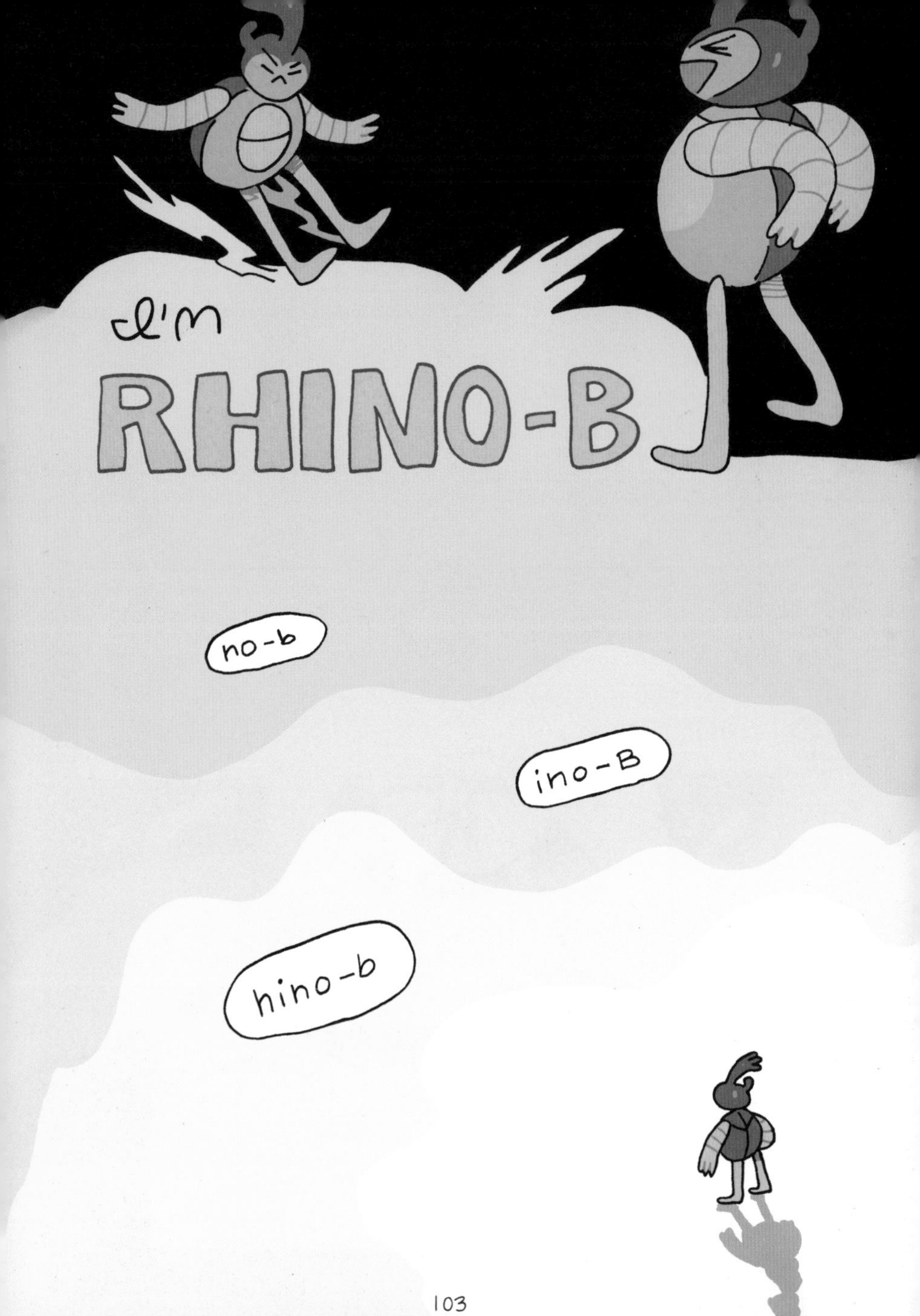
I'm
RHINO-B
no-b
ino-B
hino-b

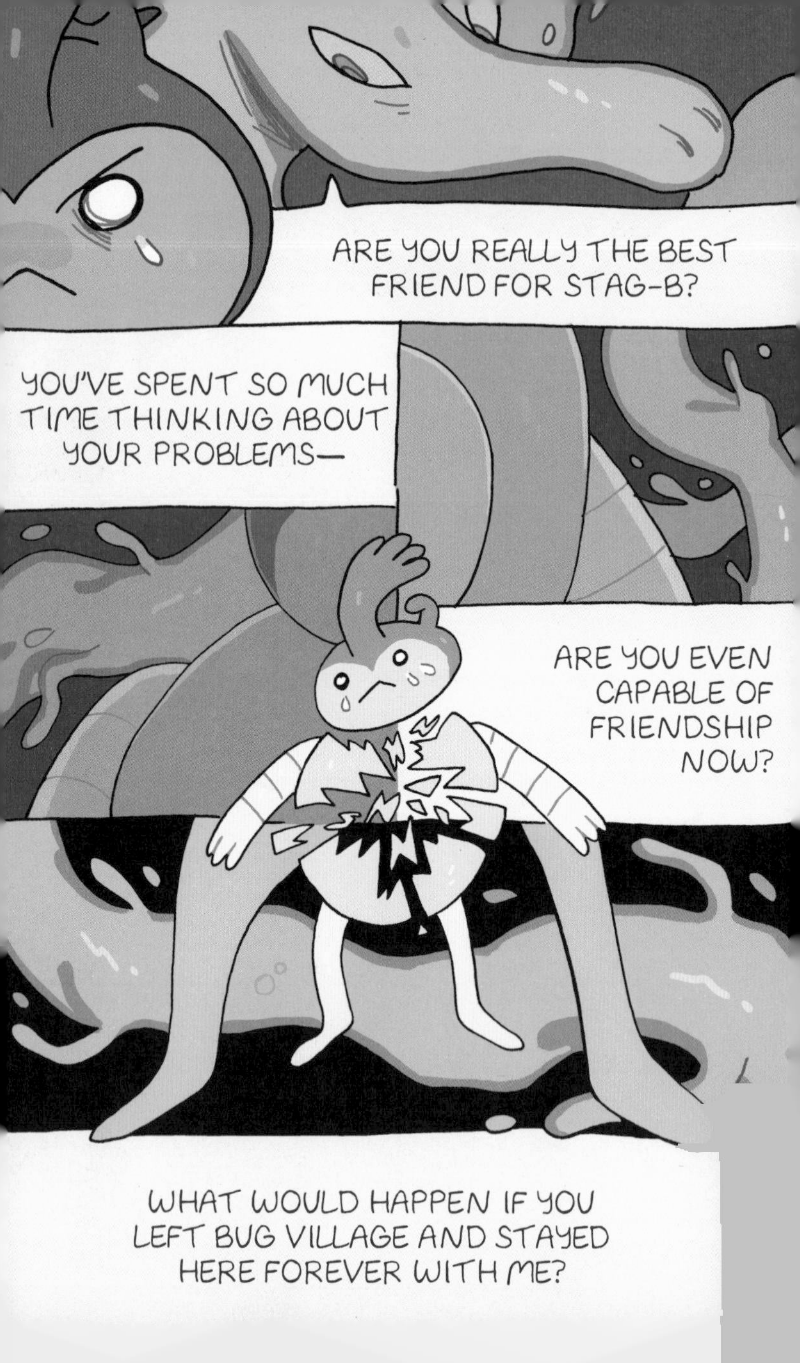
ARE YOU REALLY THE BEST FRIEND FOR STAG-B?
YOU'VE SPENT SO MUCH TIME THINKING ABOUT YOUR PROBLEMS—
ARE YOU EVEN CAPABLE OF FRIENDSHIP NOW?
WHAT WOULD HAPPEN IF YOU LEFT BUG VILLAGE AND STAYED HERE FOREVER WITH ME?

YOUR DOUBTS ARE ALIVE, YOU KNOW.
DON'T YOU SEE WE'RE THE SAME?

We're NOT!

You don't have the answers I need.
I'll find them someday.

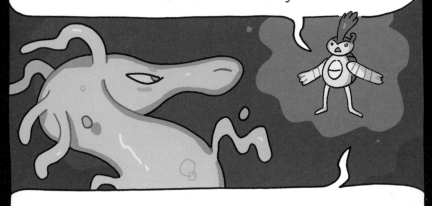

You're lonely. You're buying
time to keep me here.

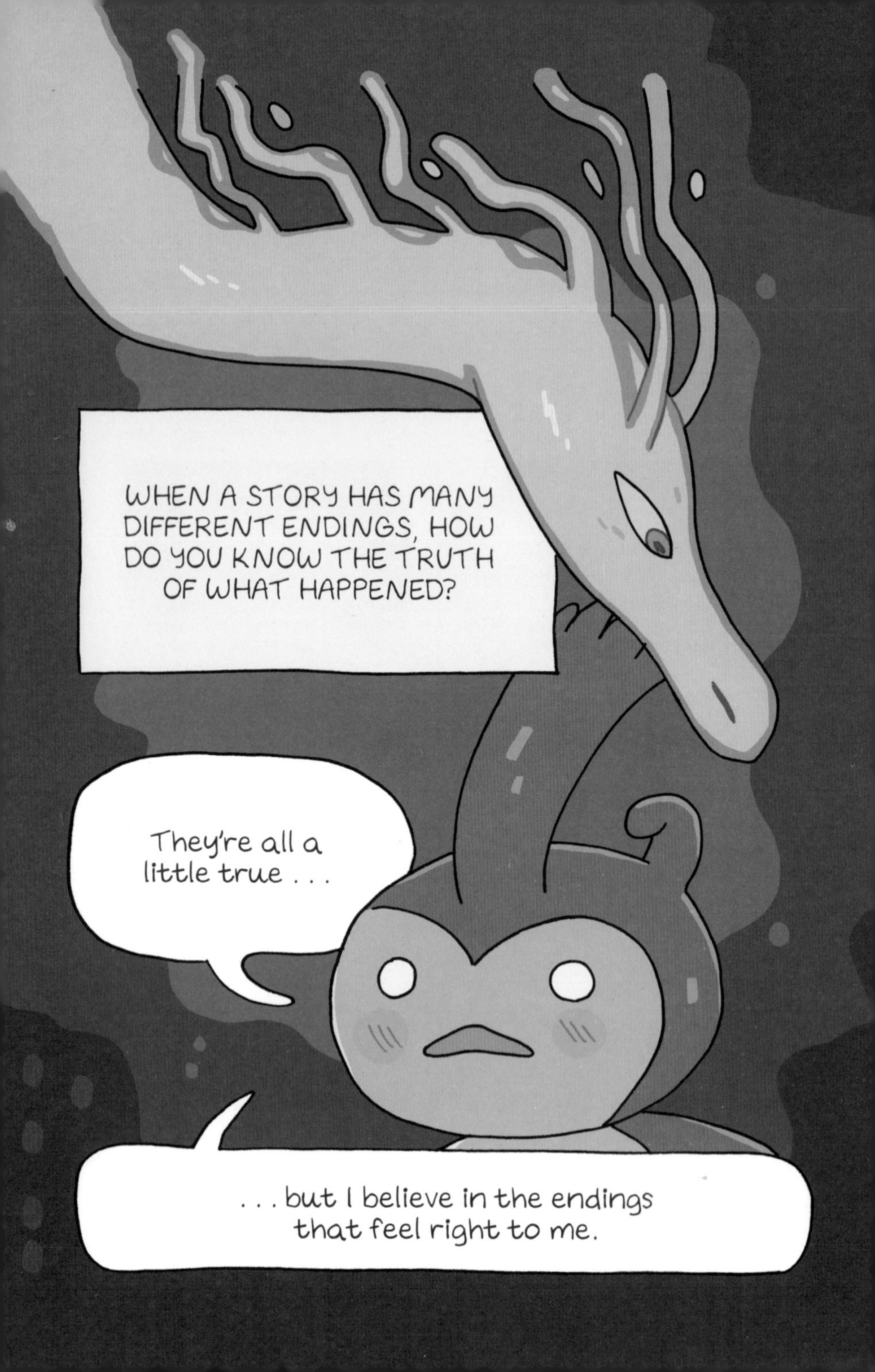
WHEN A STORY HAS MANY DIFFERENT ENDINGS, HOW DO YOU KNOW THE TRUTH OF WHAT HAPPENED?
They're all a little true . . .
. . . but I believe in the endings that feel right to me.

I like the endings where everyone goes home . . . and things don't change too fast.

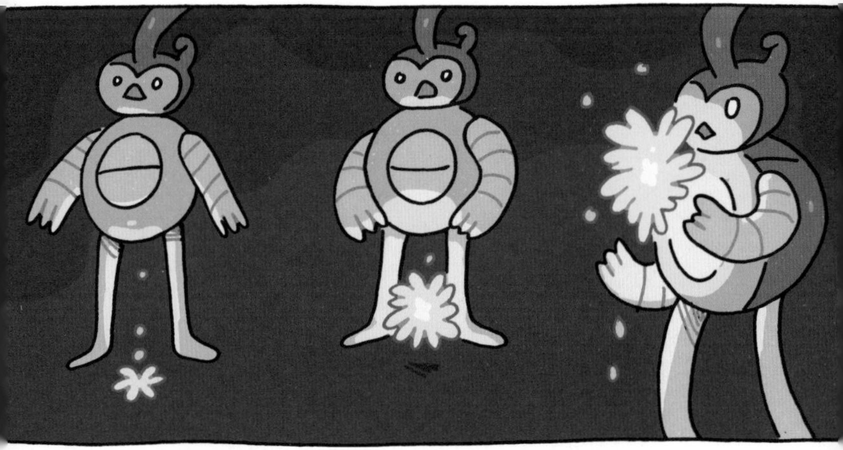

And everybody gets just enough of their happy ending . . .

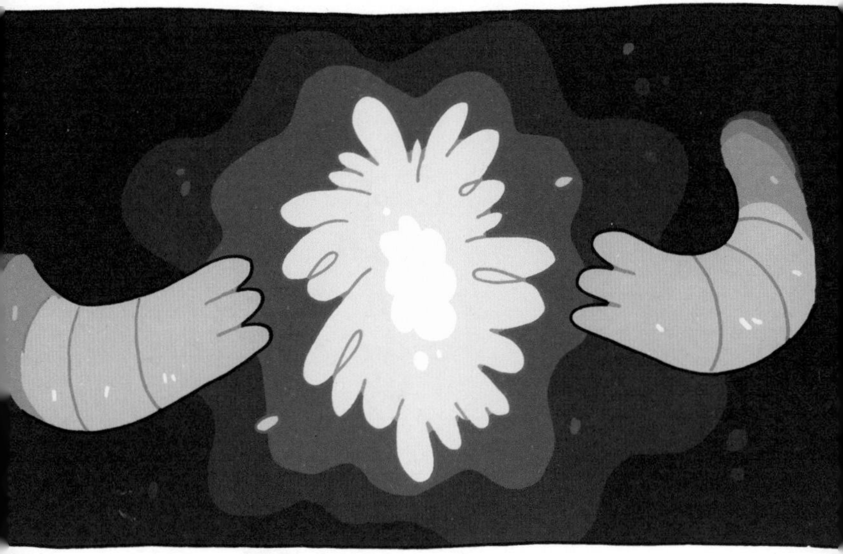

Even if it's just a story, I believe.

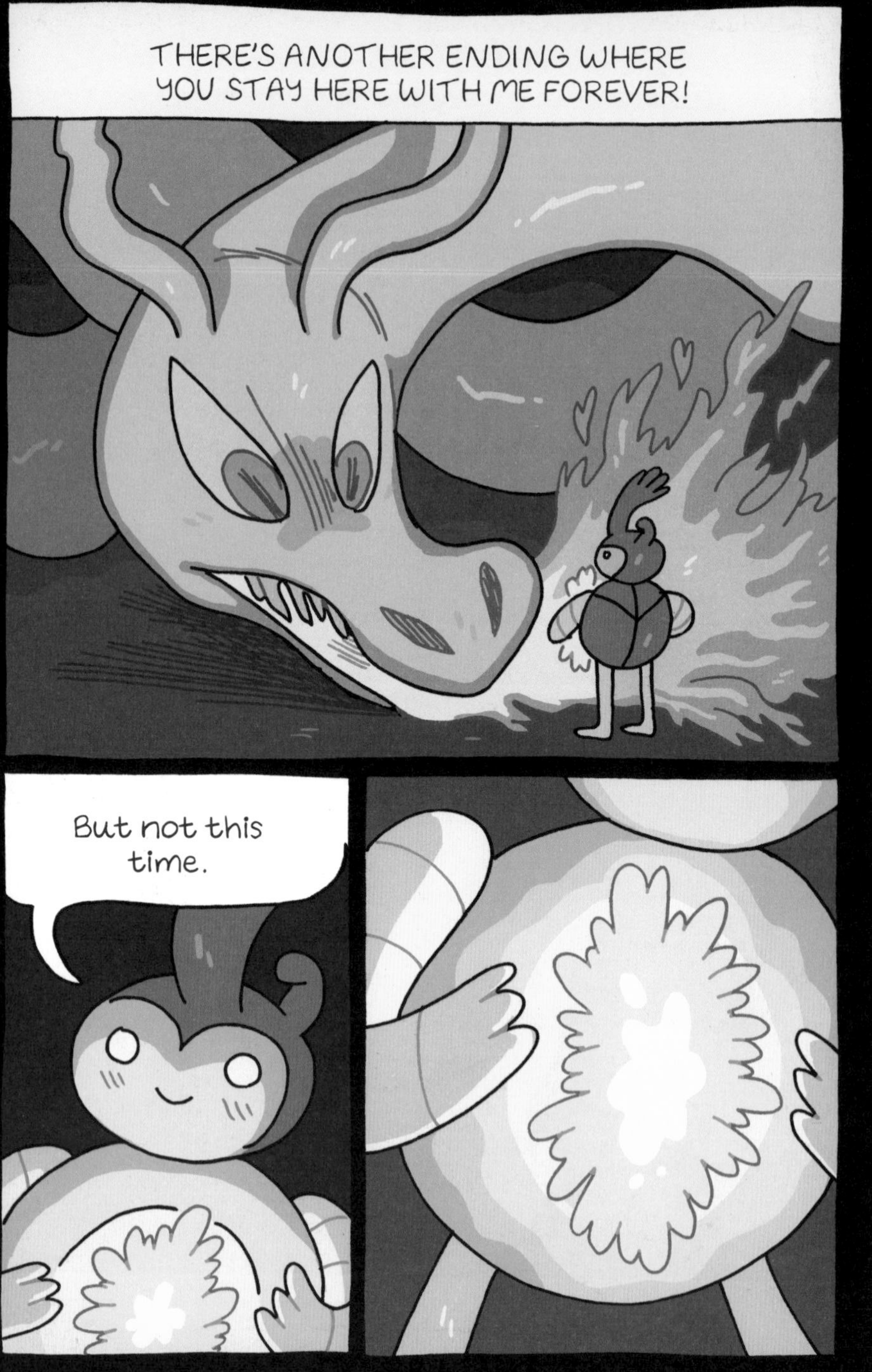
THERE'S ANOTHER ENDING WHERE YOU STAY HERE WITH ME FOREVER!
But not this time.

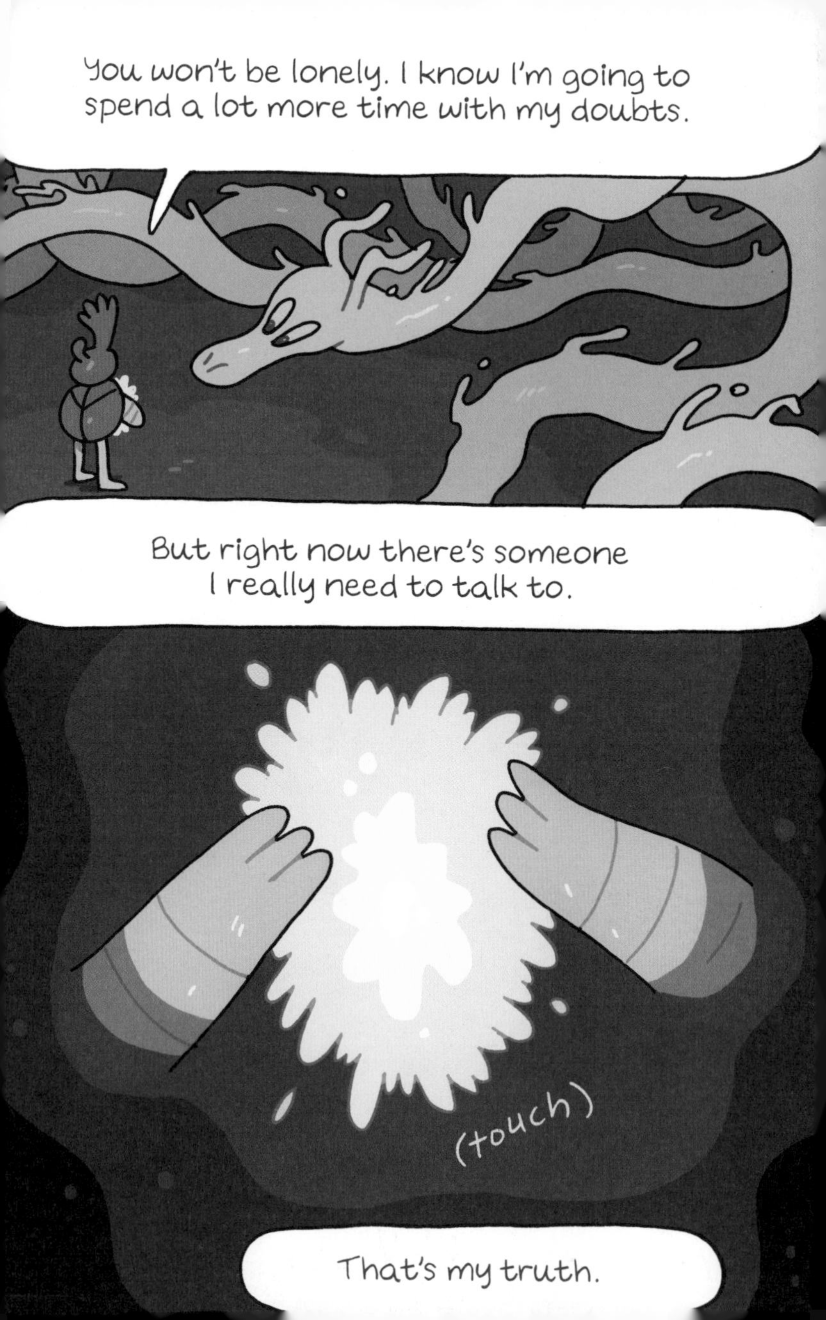
You won't be lonely. I know I'm going to spend a lot more time with my doubts.
But right now there's someone I really need to talk to.
(touch)
That's my truth.

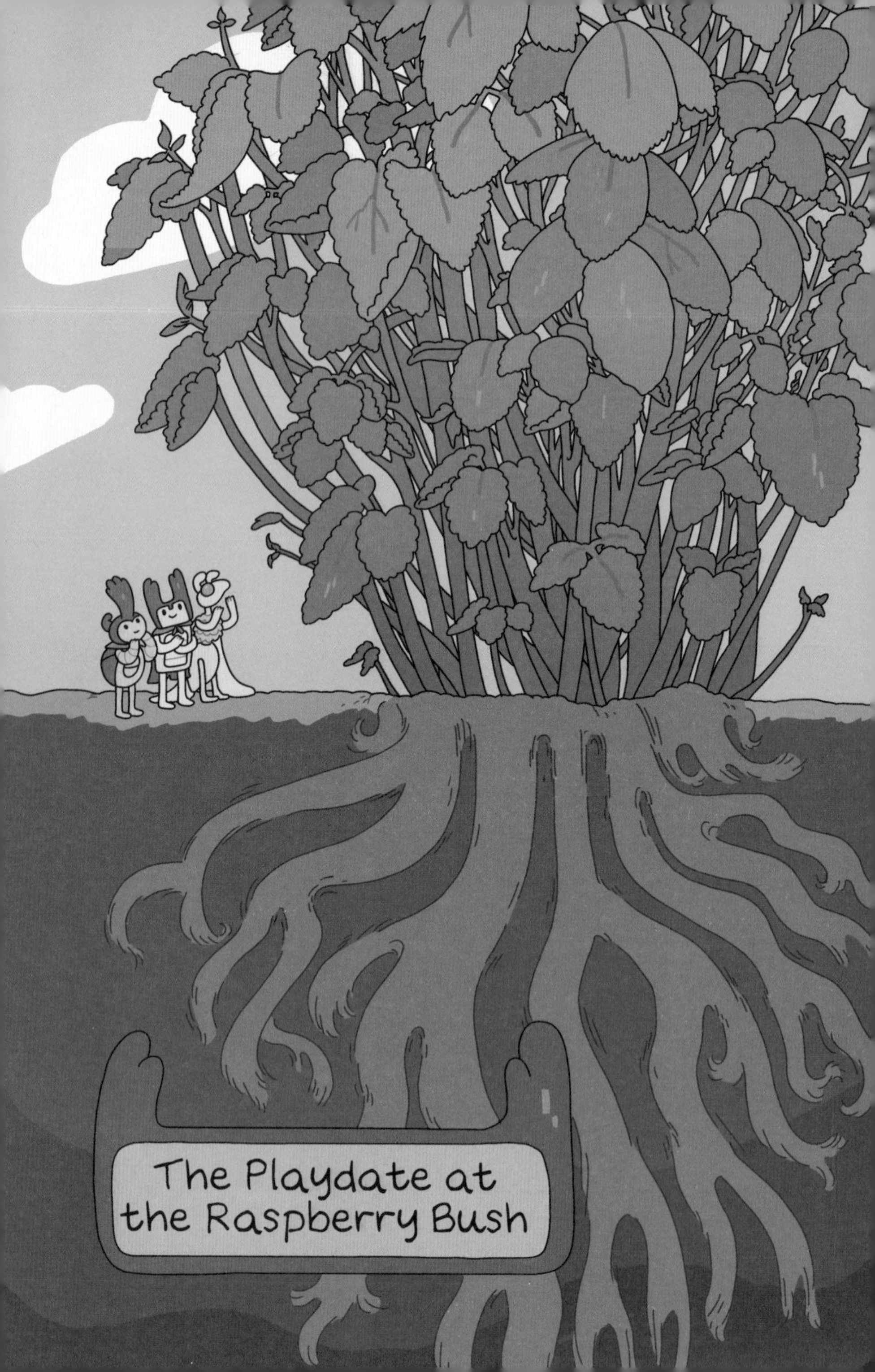
The Playdate at
the Raspberry Bush

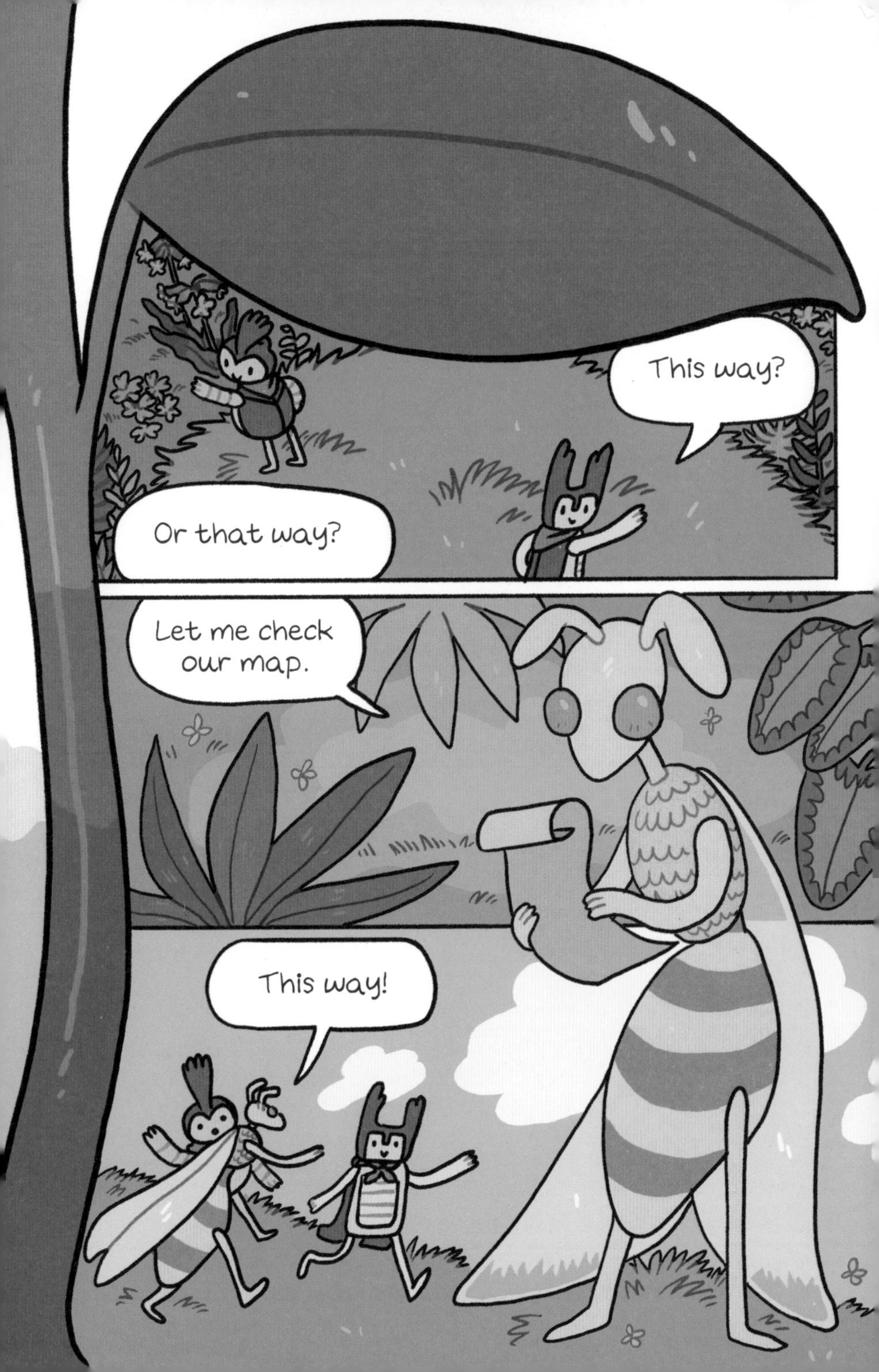
This way?
Or that way?
Let me check our map.
This way!

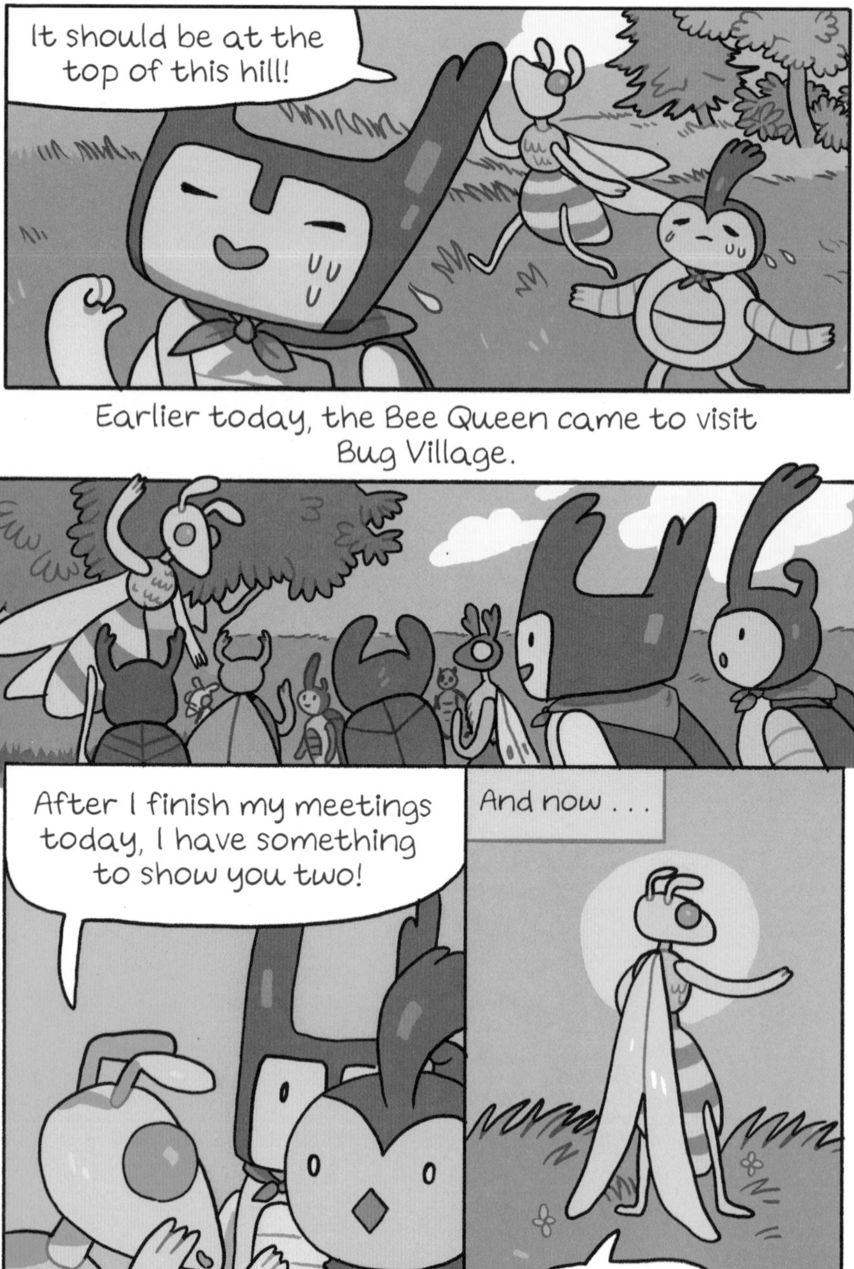
It should be at the top of this hill!
Earlier today, the Bee Queen came to visit Bug Village.
After I finish my meetings today, I have something to show you two!
And now . . .
It's here!

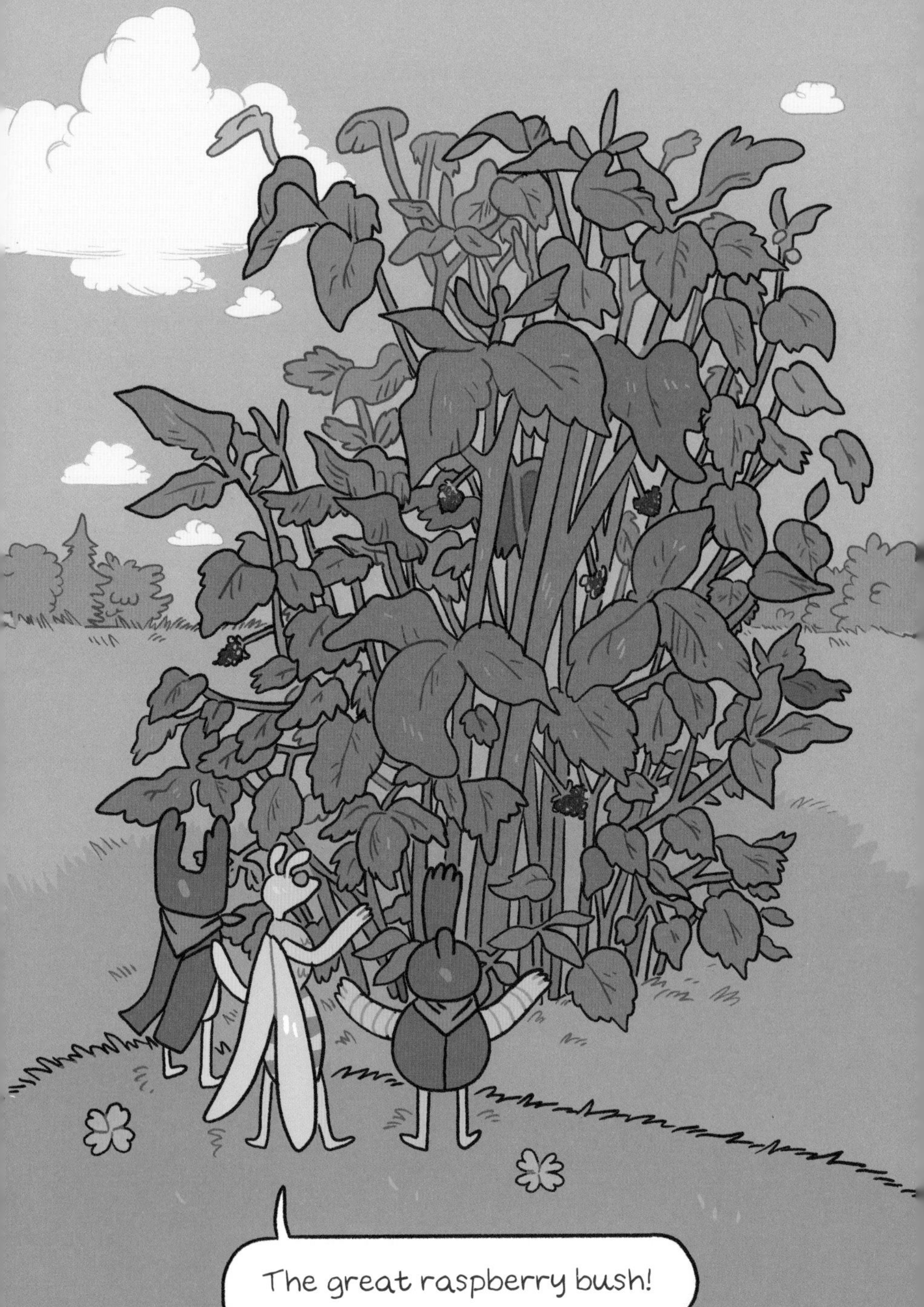
The great raspberry bush!

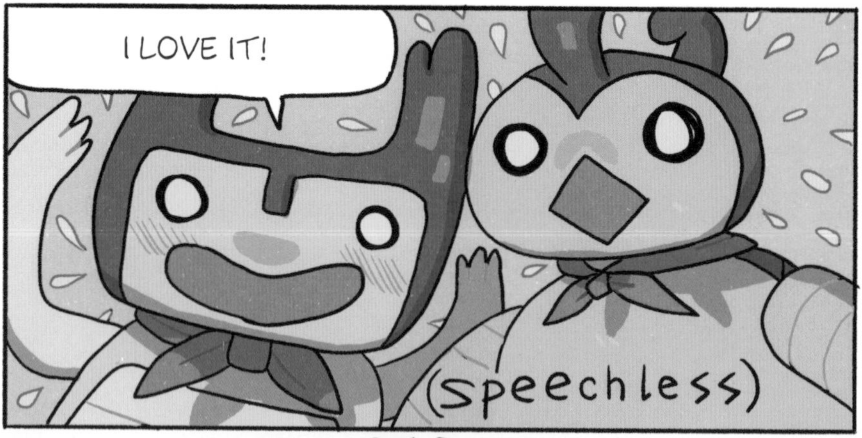
I LOVE IT!
(speechless)

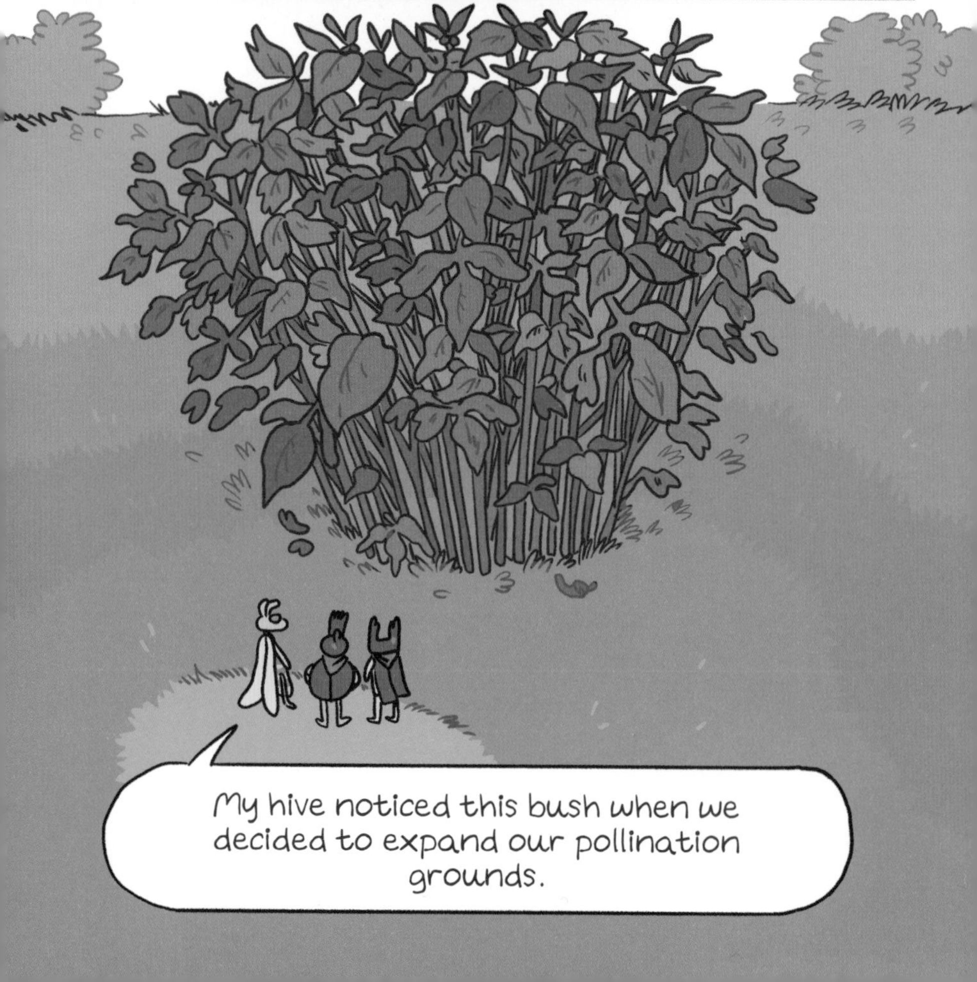
My hive noticed this bush when we decided to expand our pollination grounds.

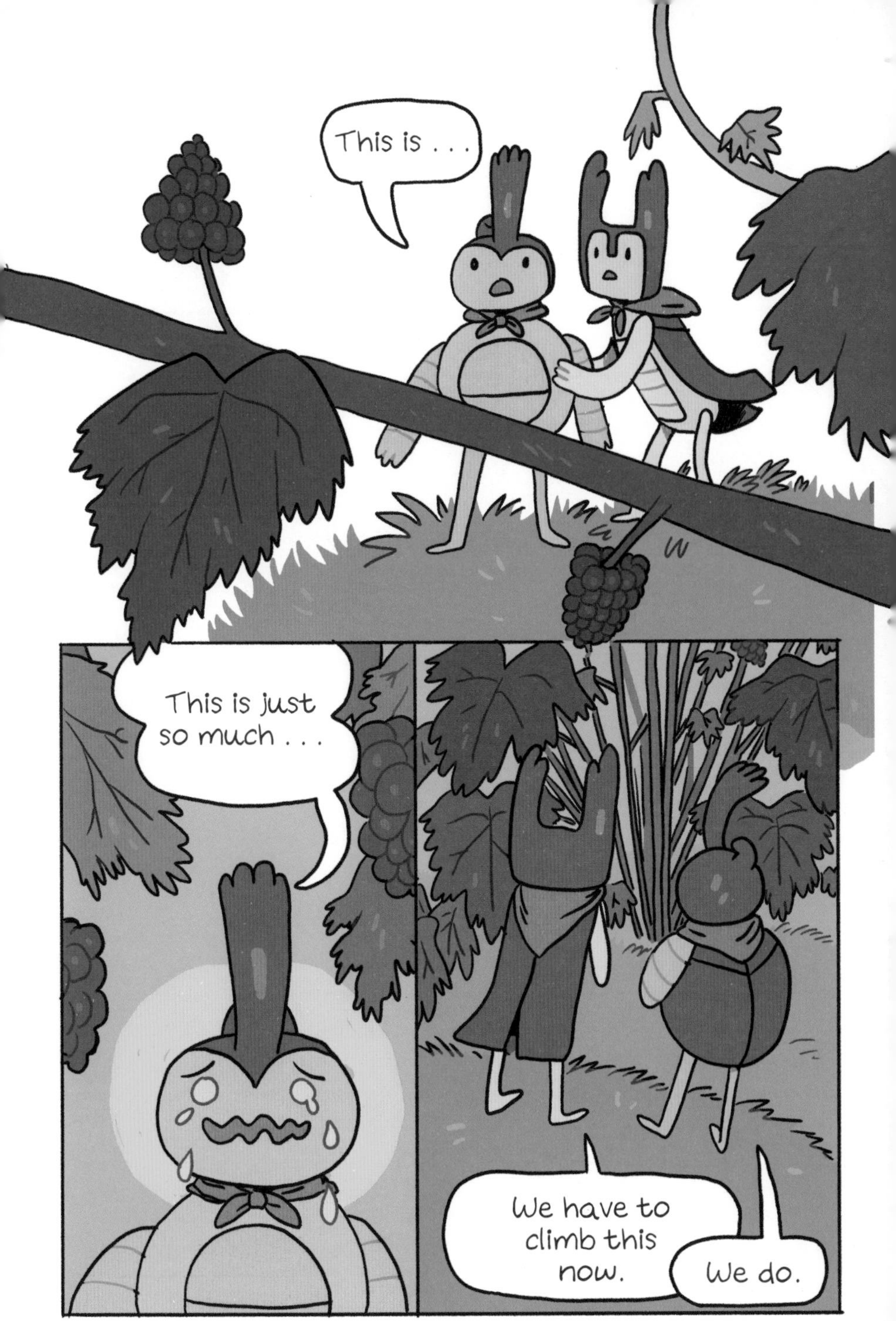
This is . . .
This is just so much . . .
We have to climb this now.
We do.

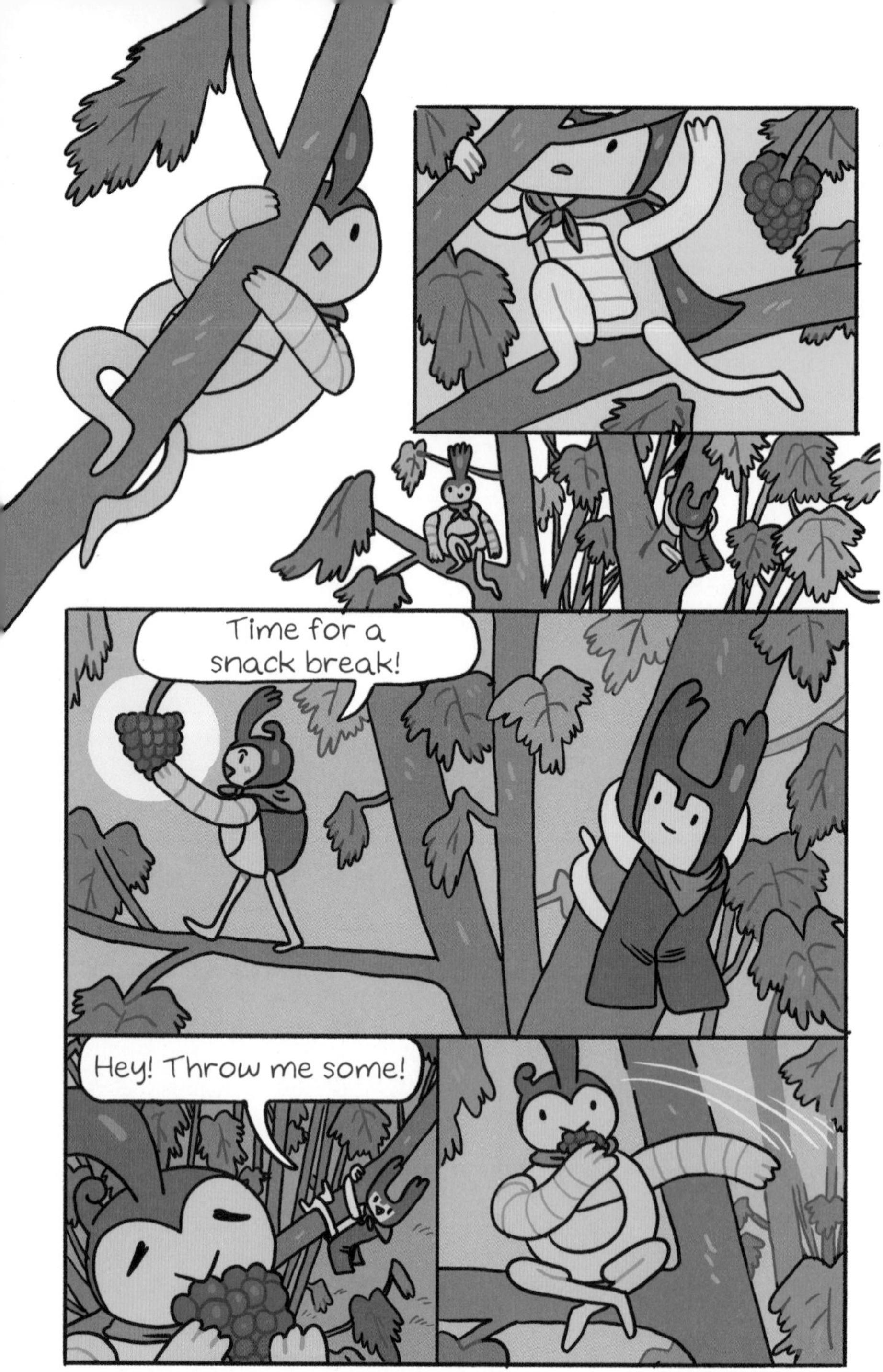
Time for a snack break!
Hey! Throw me some!

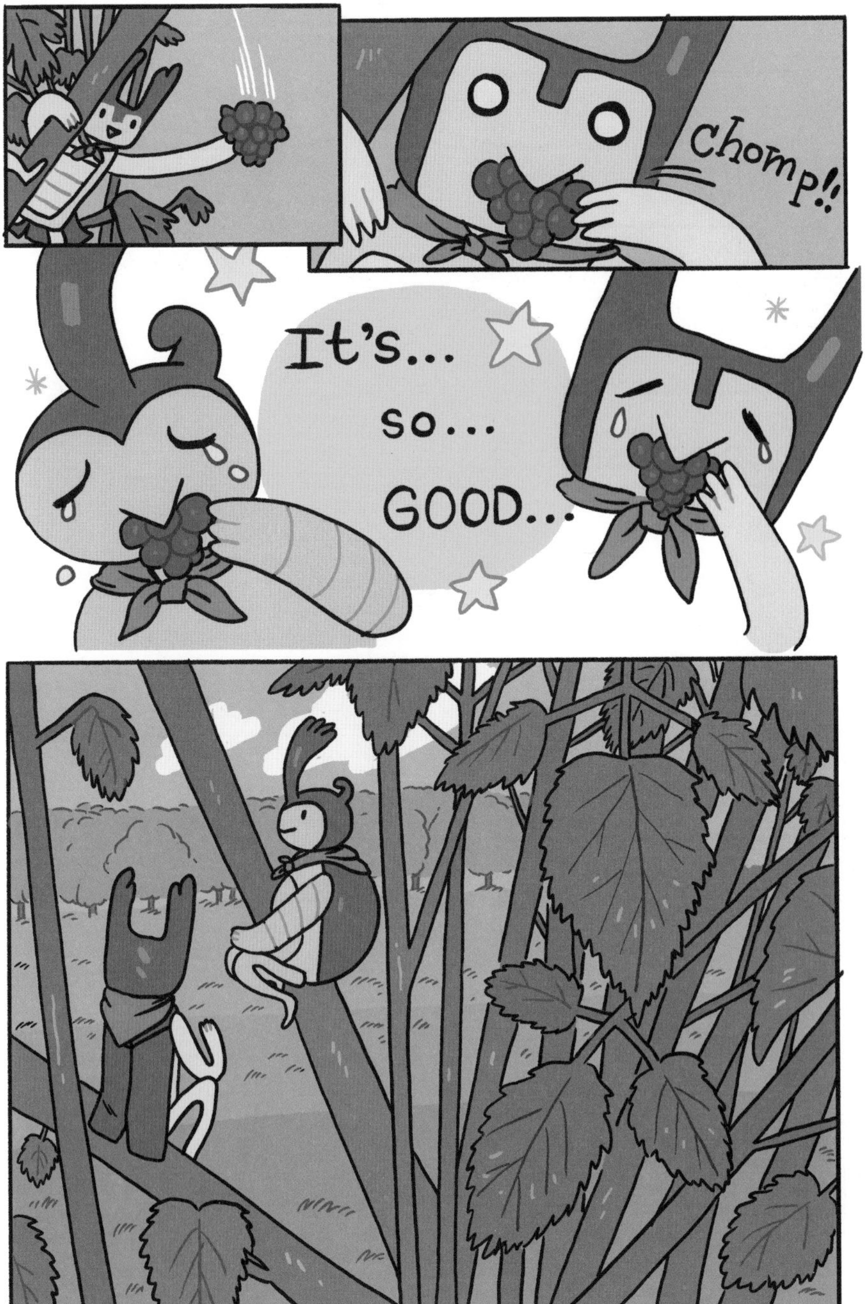
Chomp!!
It's...
so...
GOOD...

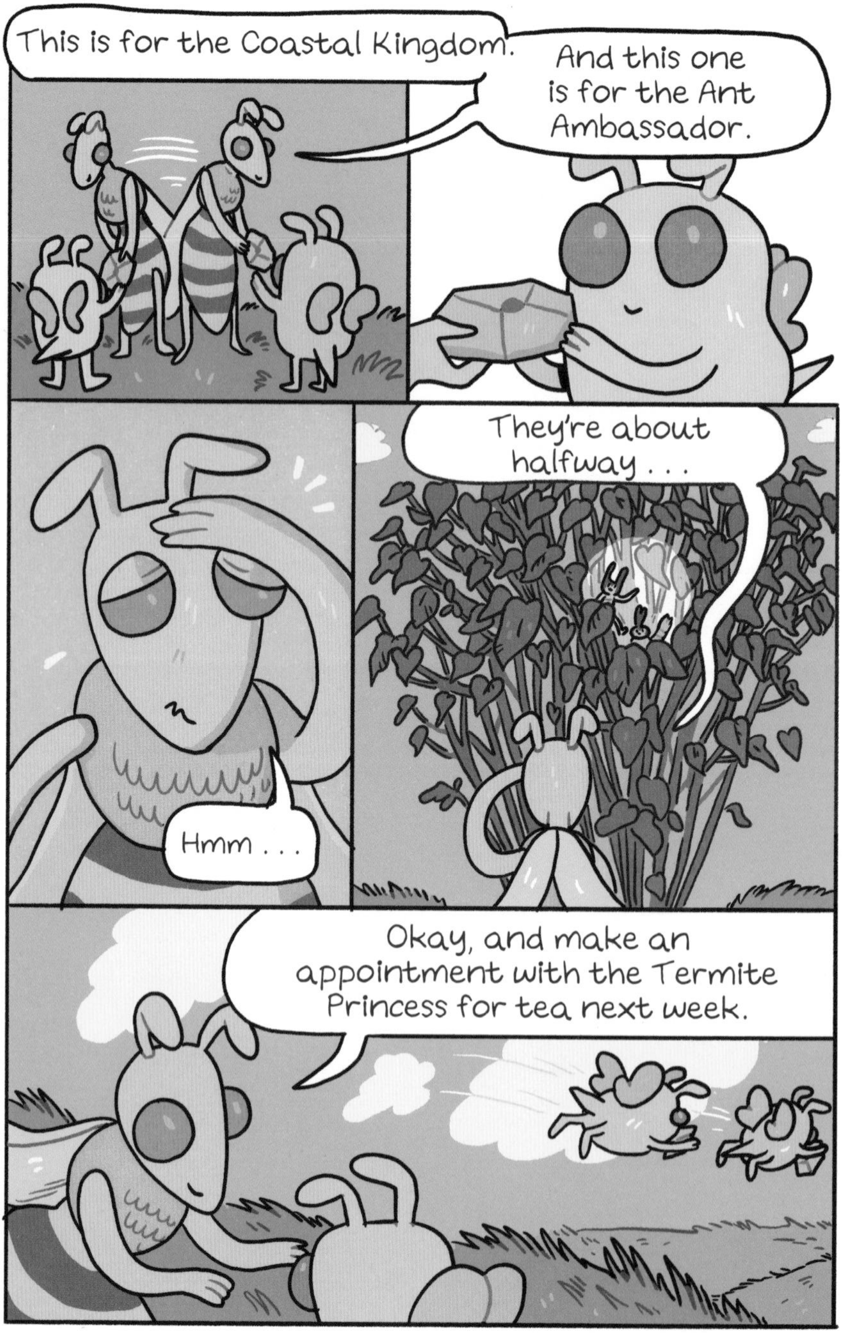
This is for the Coastal Kingdom.
And this one is for the Ant Ambassador.
Hmm . . .
They're about halfway . . .
Okay, and make an appointment with the Termite Princess for tea next week.

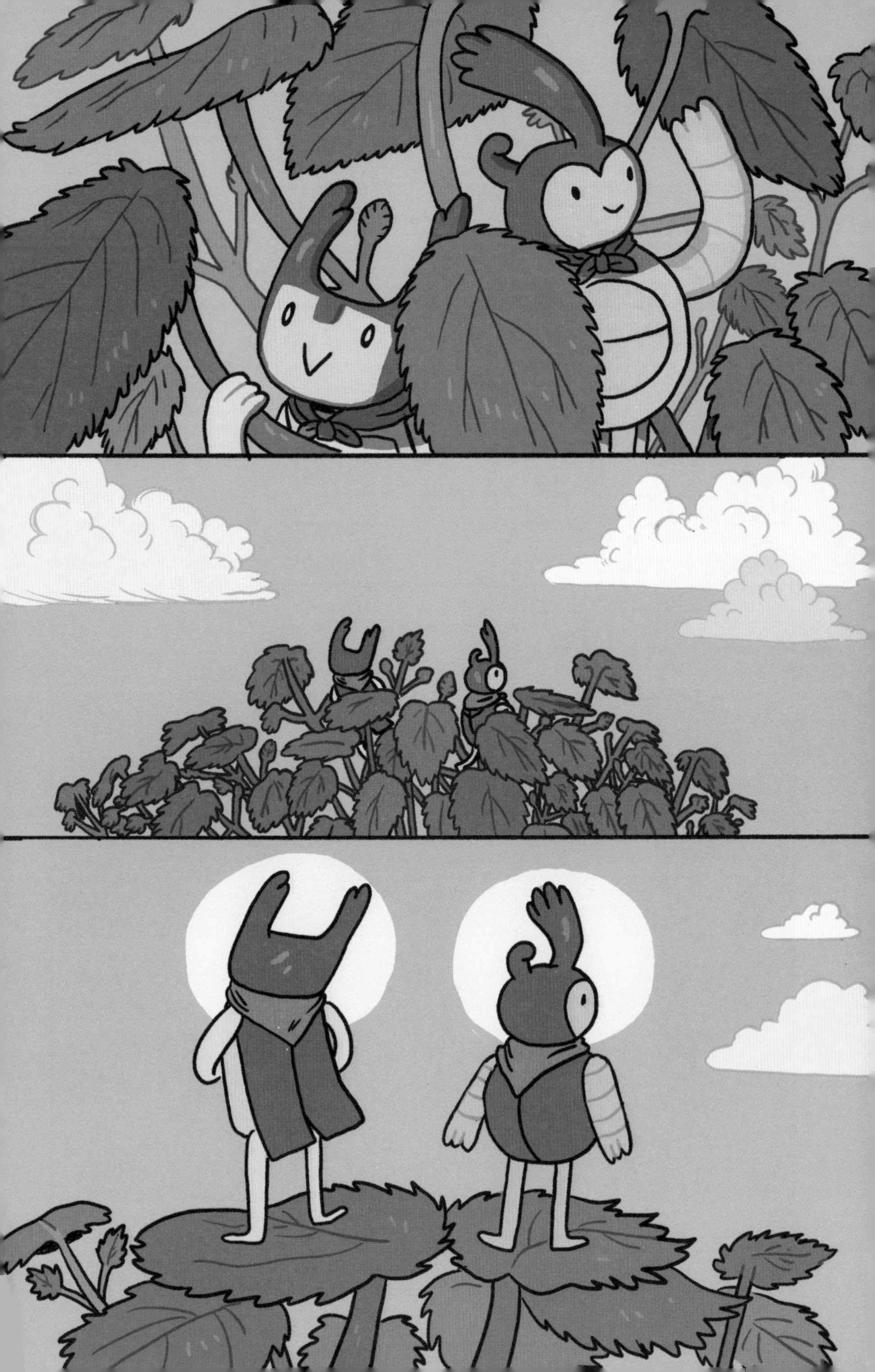

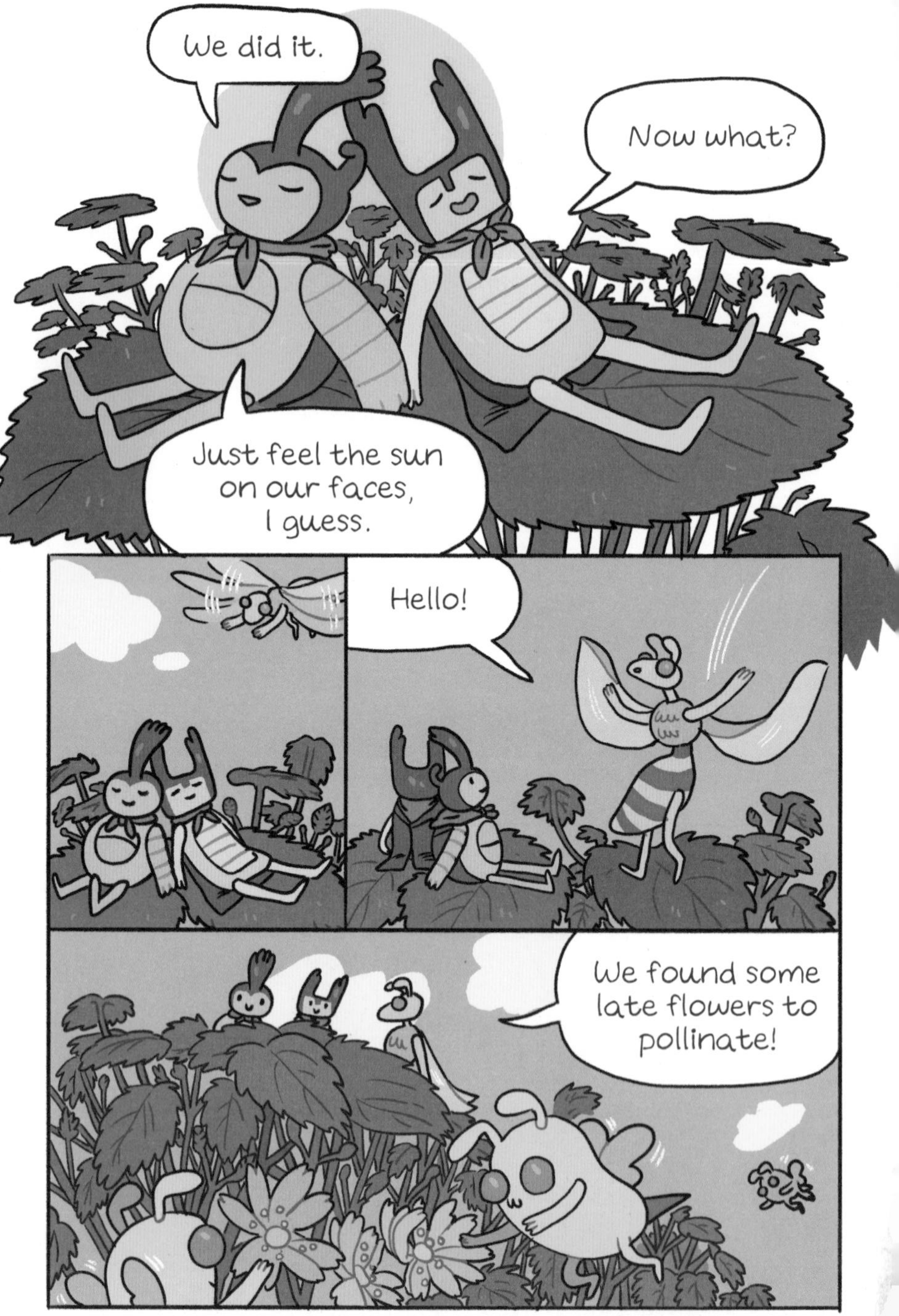
We did it.
Now what?
Just feel the sun on our faces, I guess.
Hello!
We found some late flowers to pollinate!

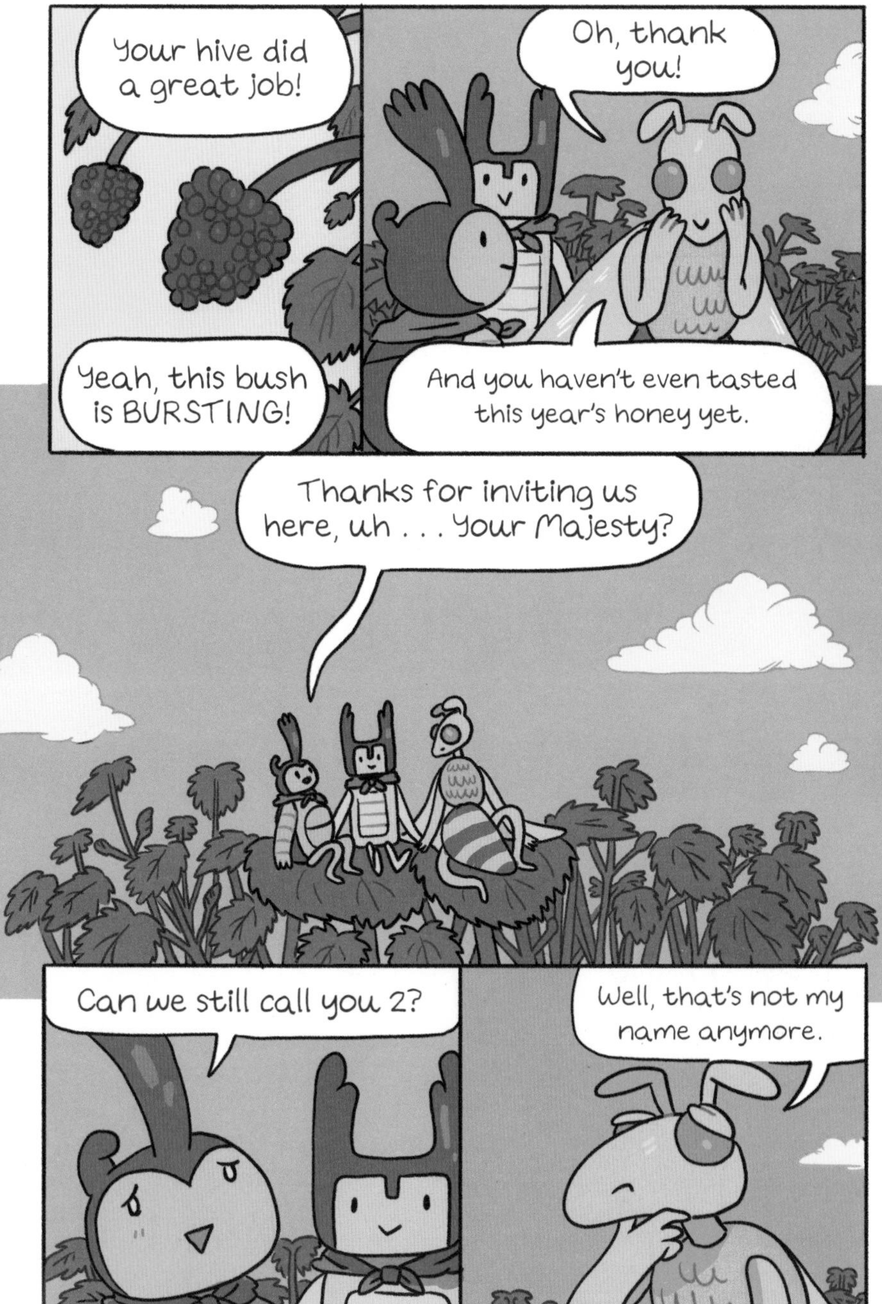
Your hive did a great job!
Yeah, this bush is BURSTING!
Oh, thank you!
And you haven't even tasted this year's honey yet.
Thanks for inviting us here, uh . . . Your Majesty?
Can we still call you 2?
Well, that's not my name anymore.

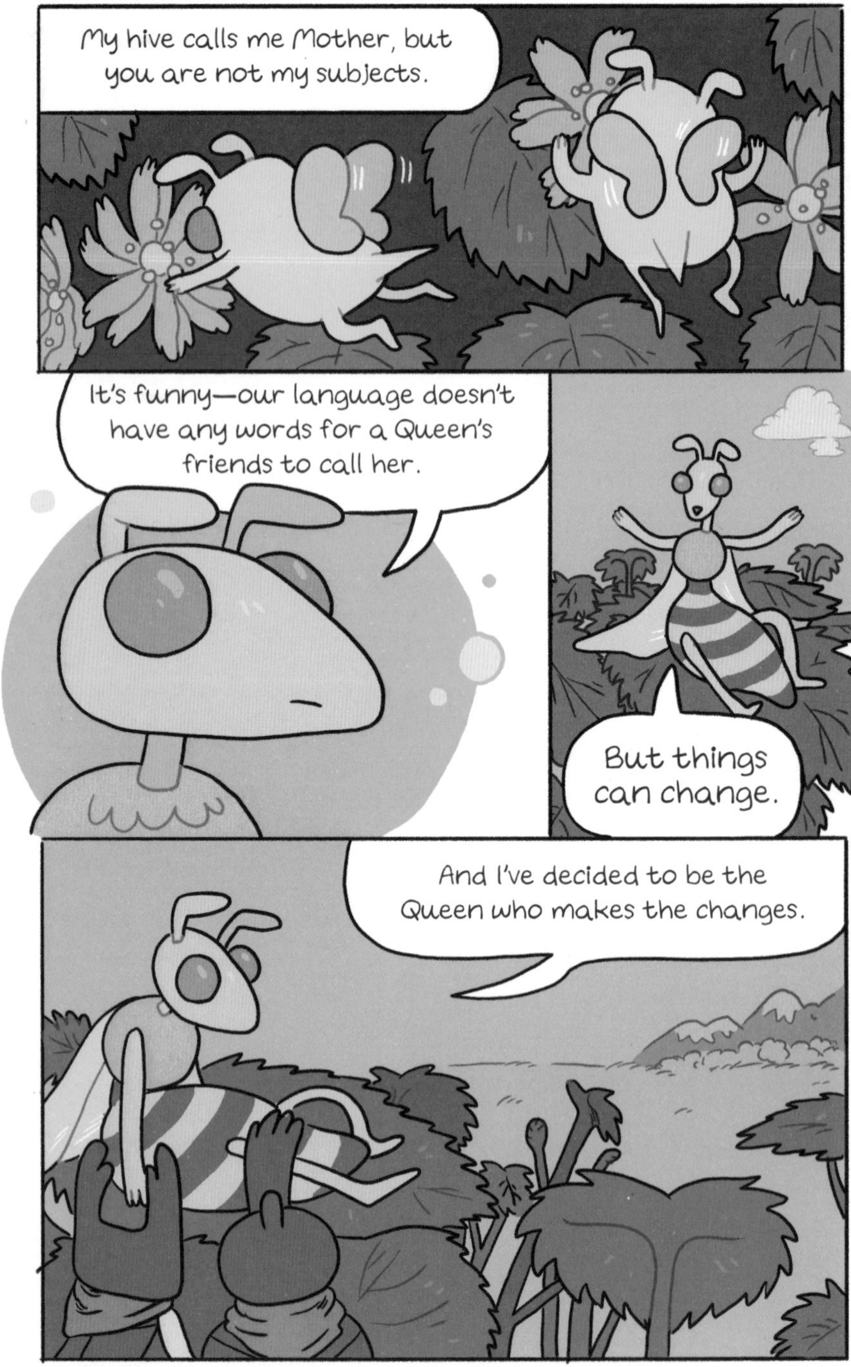
My hive calls me Mother, but you are not my subjects.
It's funny—our language doesn't have any words for a Queen's friends to call her.
But things can change.
And I've decided to be the Queen who makes the changes.

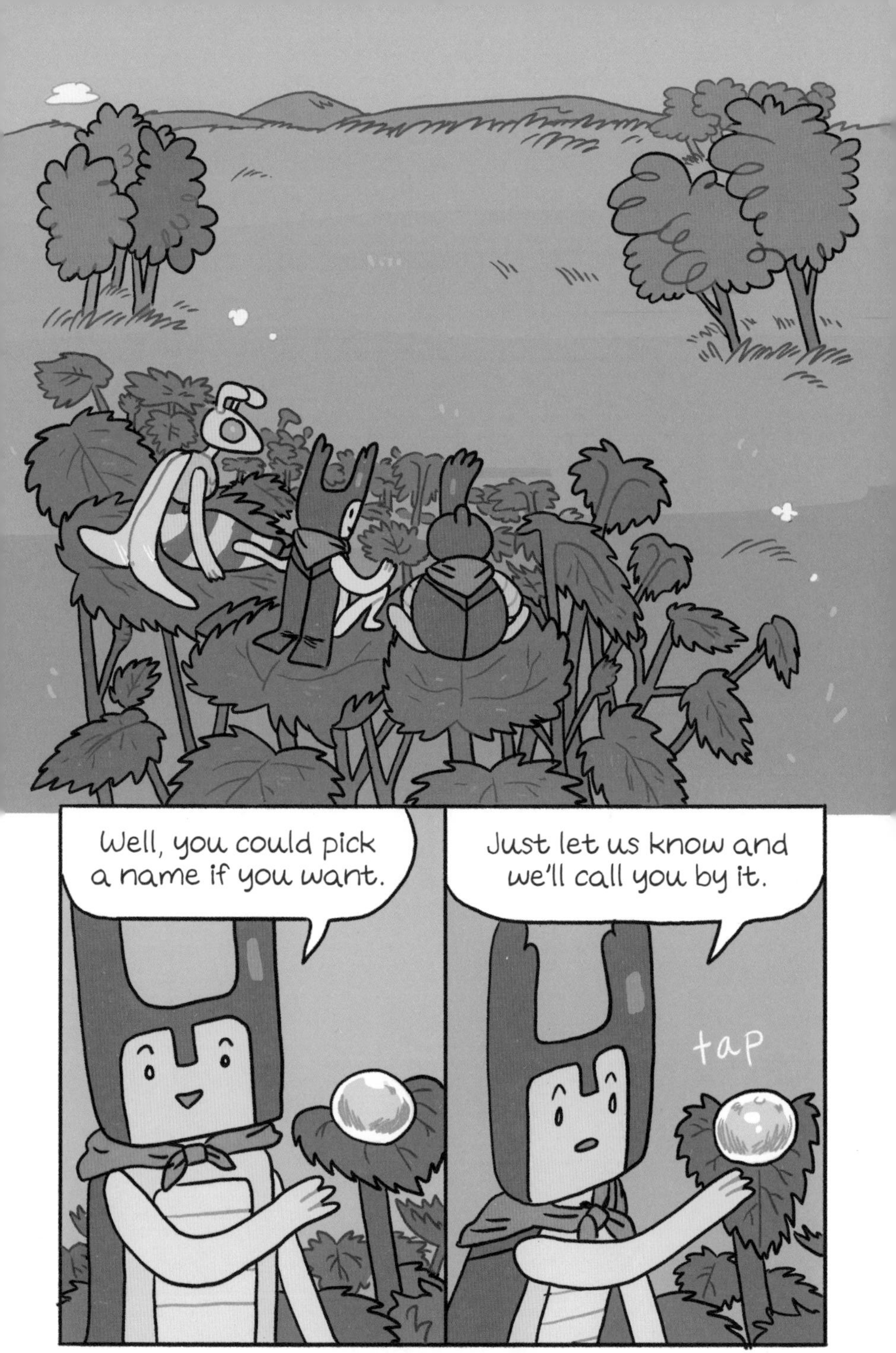
Well, you could pick a name if you want.
Just let us know and we'll call you by it.
tap

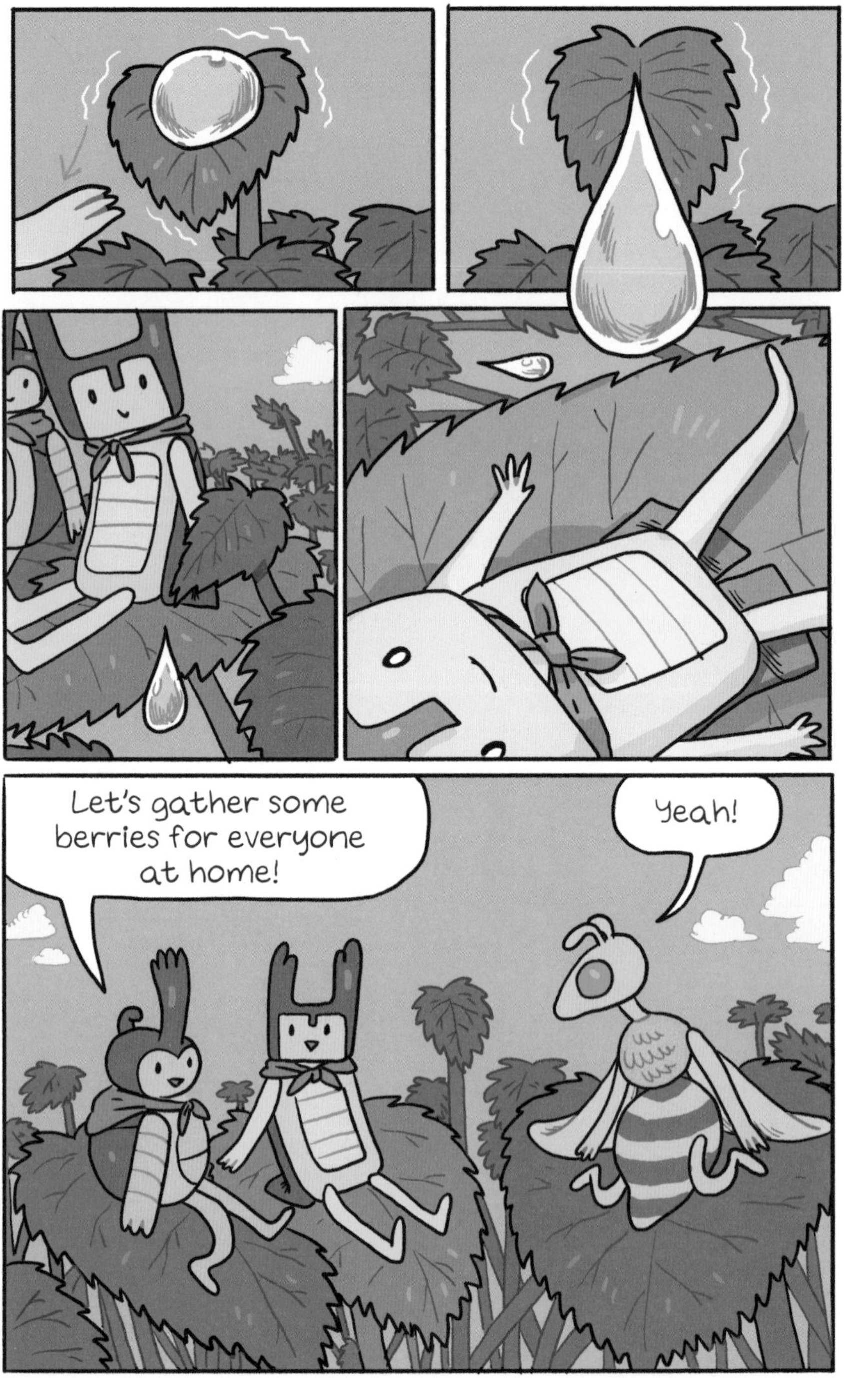
Let's gather some berries for everyone at home!
Yeah!

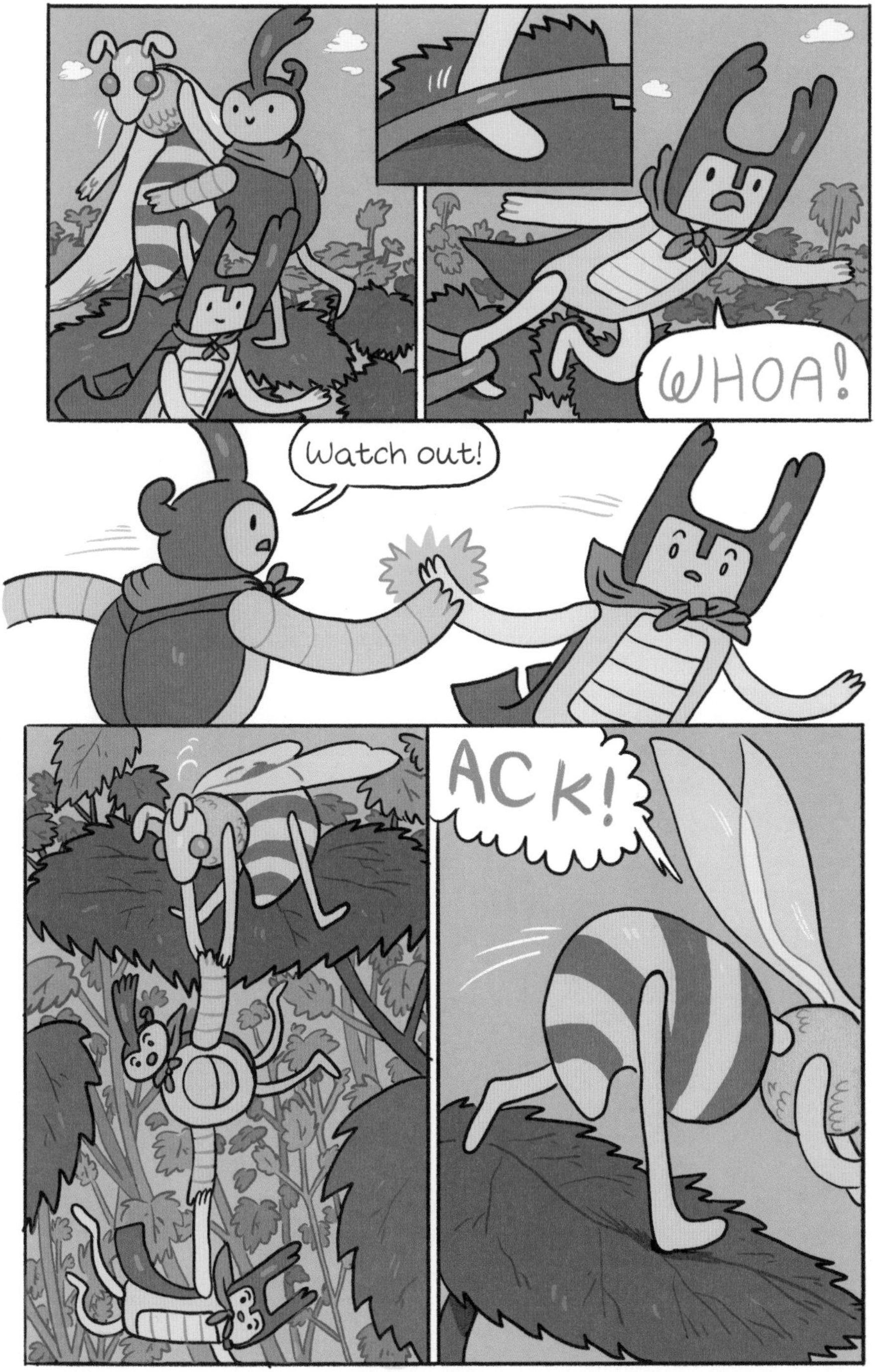
WHOA!
Watch out!
ACK!

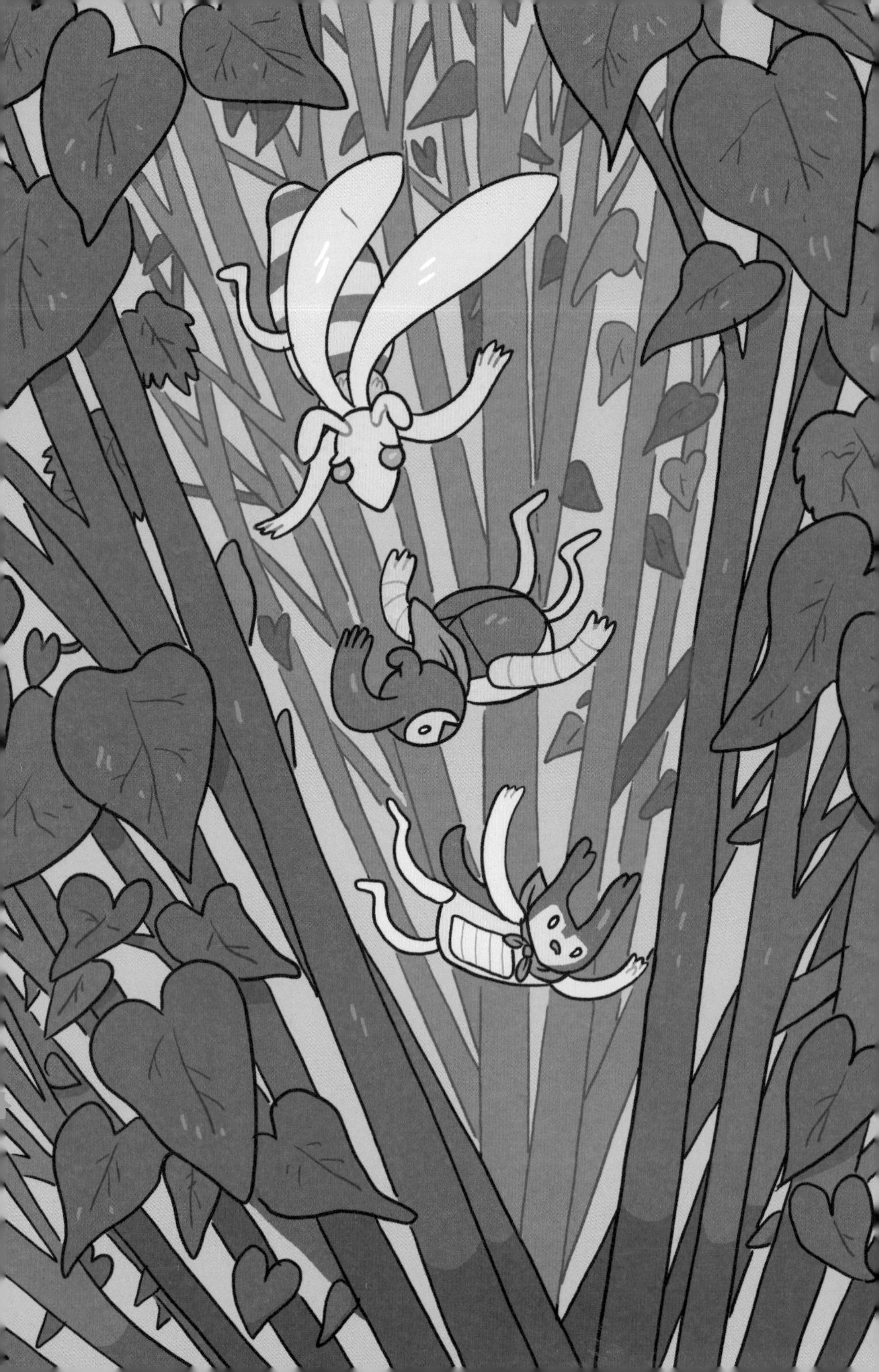

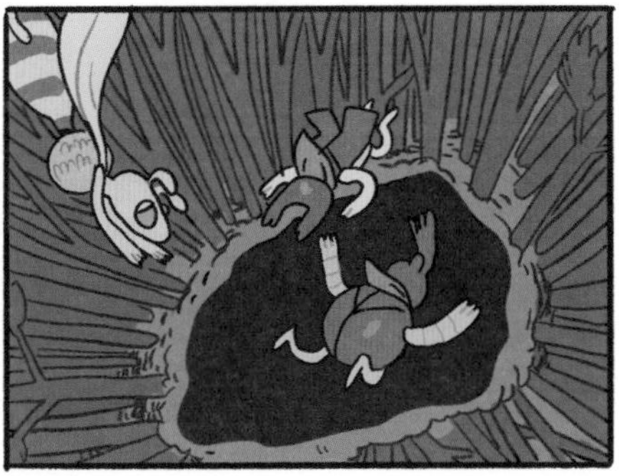

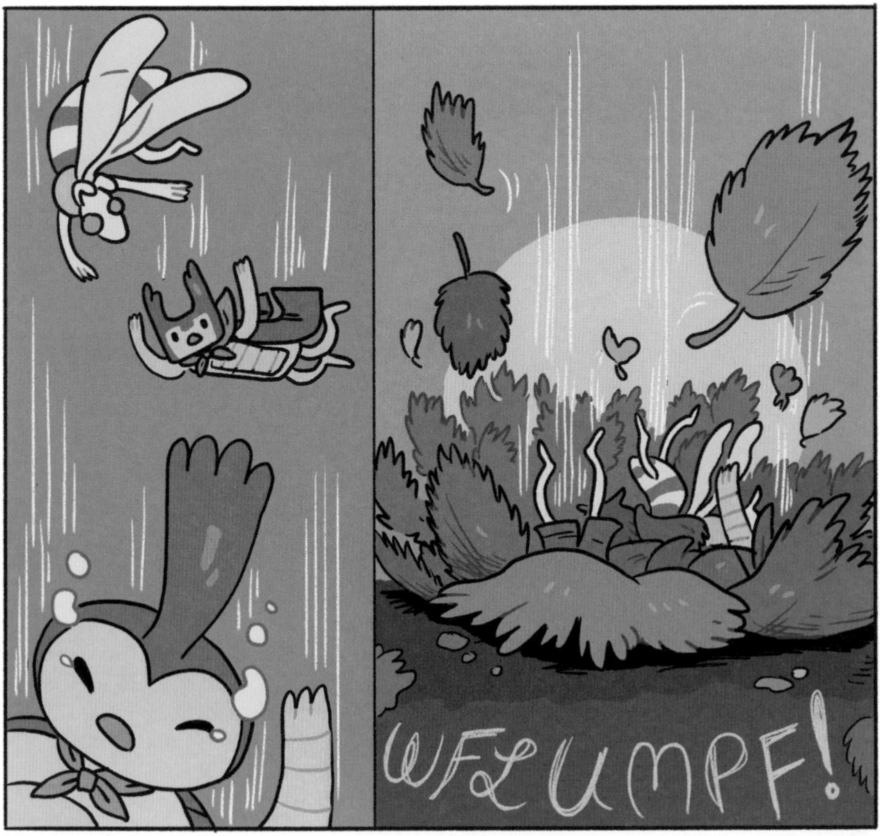
WFLUMPF!

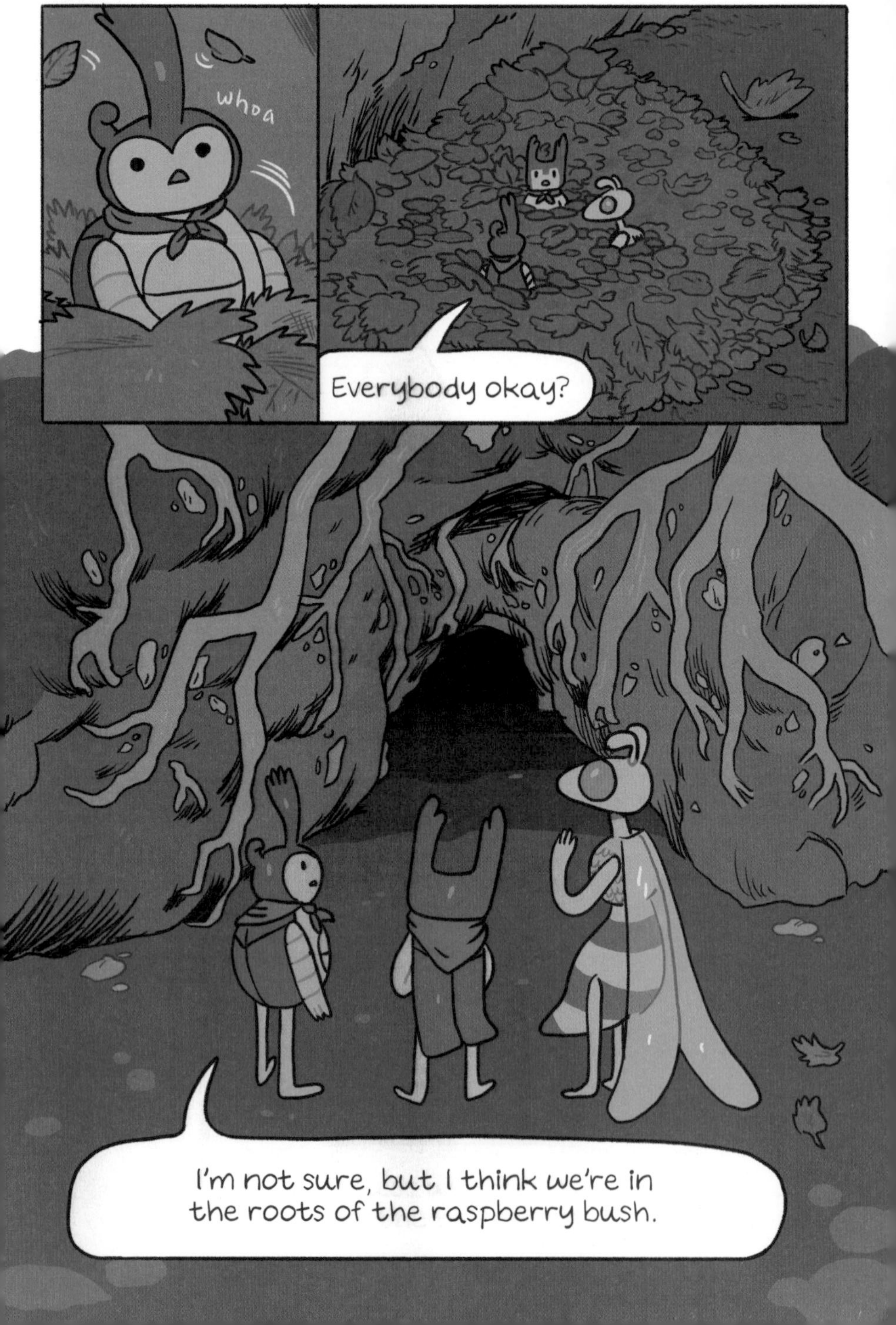
whoa
Everybody okay?
I'm not sure, but I think we're in the roots of the raspberry bush.

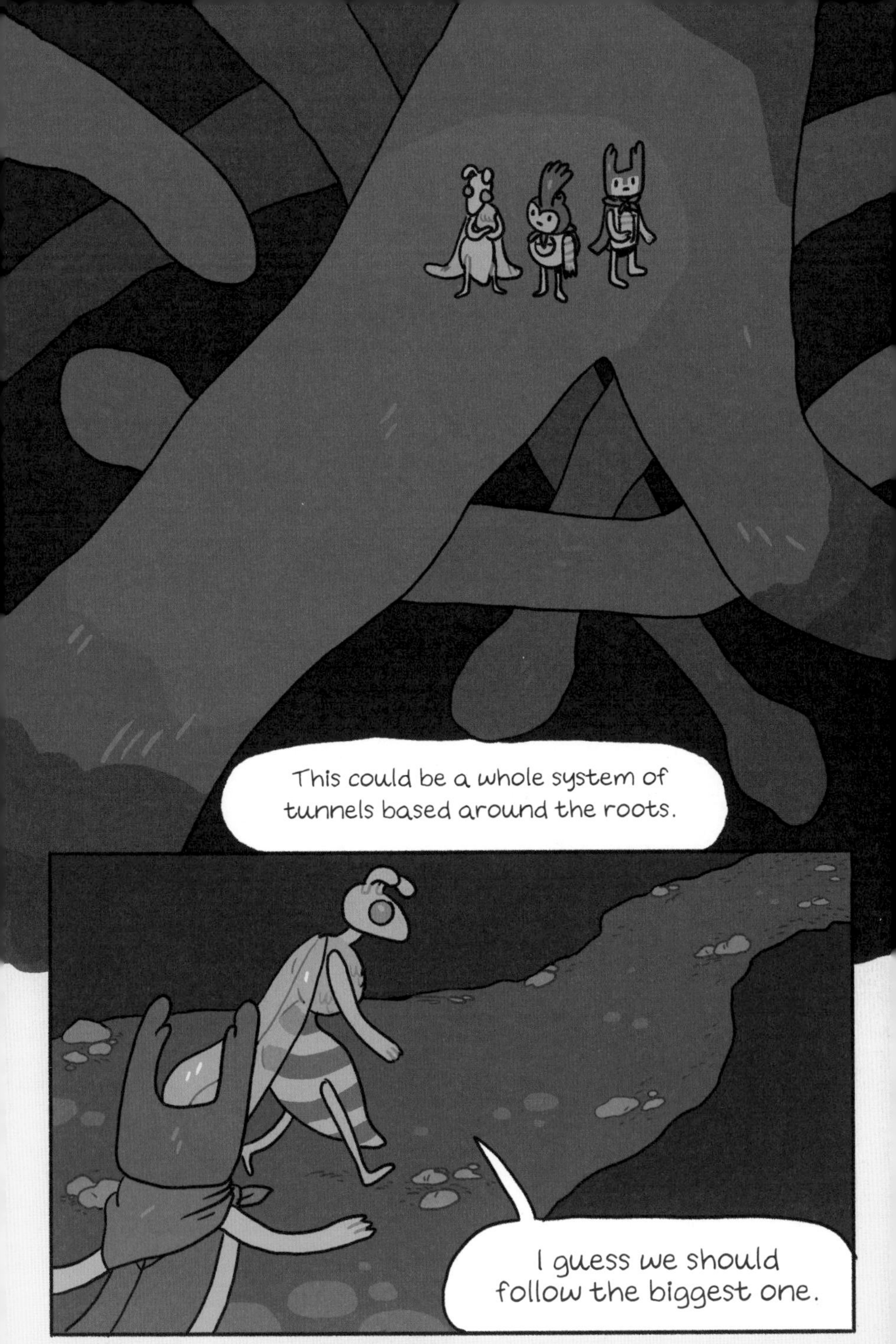
This could be a whole system of tunnels based around the roots.
I guess we should follow the biggest one.

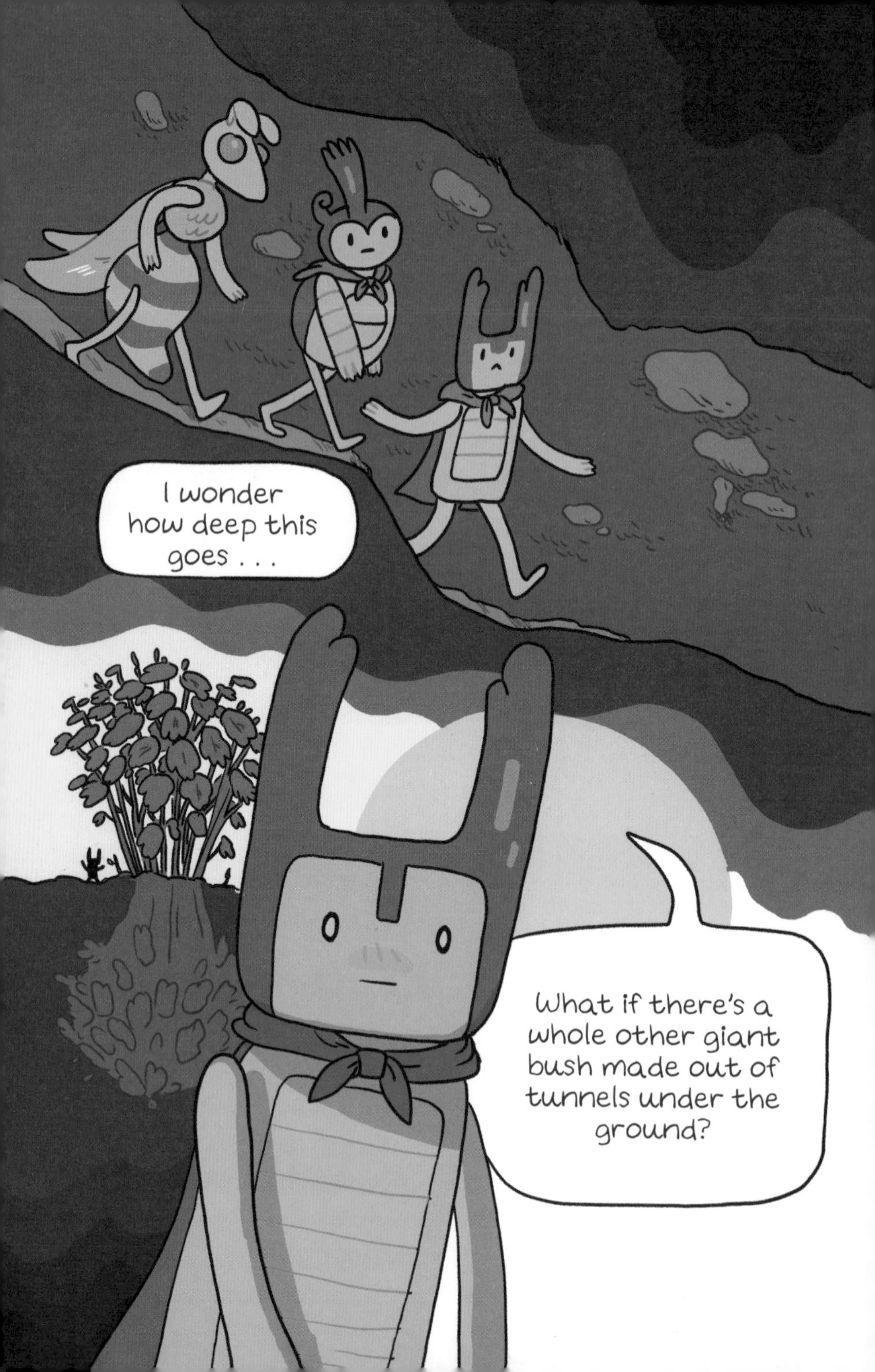
I wonder how deep this goes . . .
What if there's a whole other giant bush made out of tunnels under the ground?

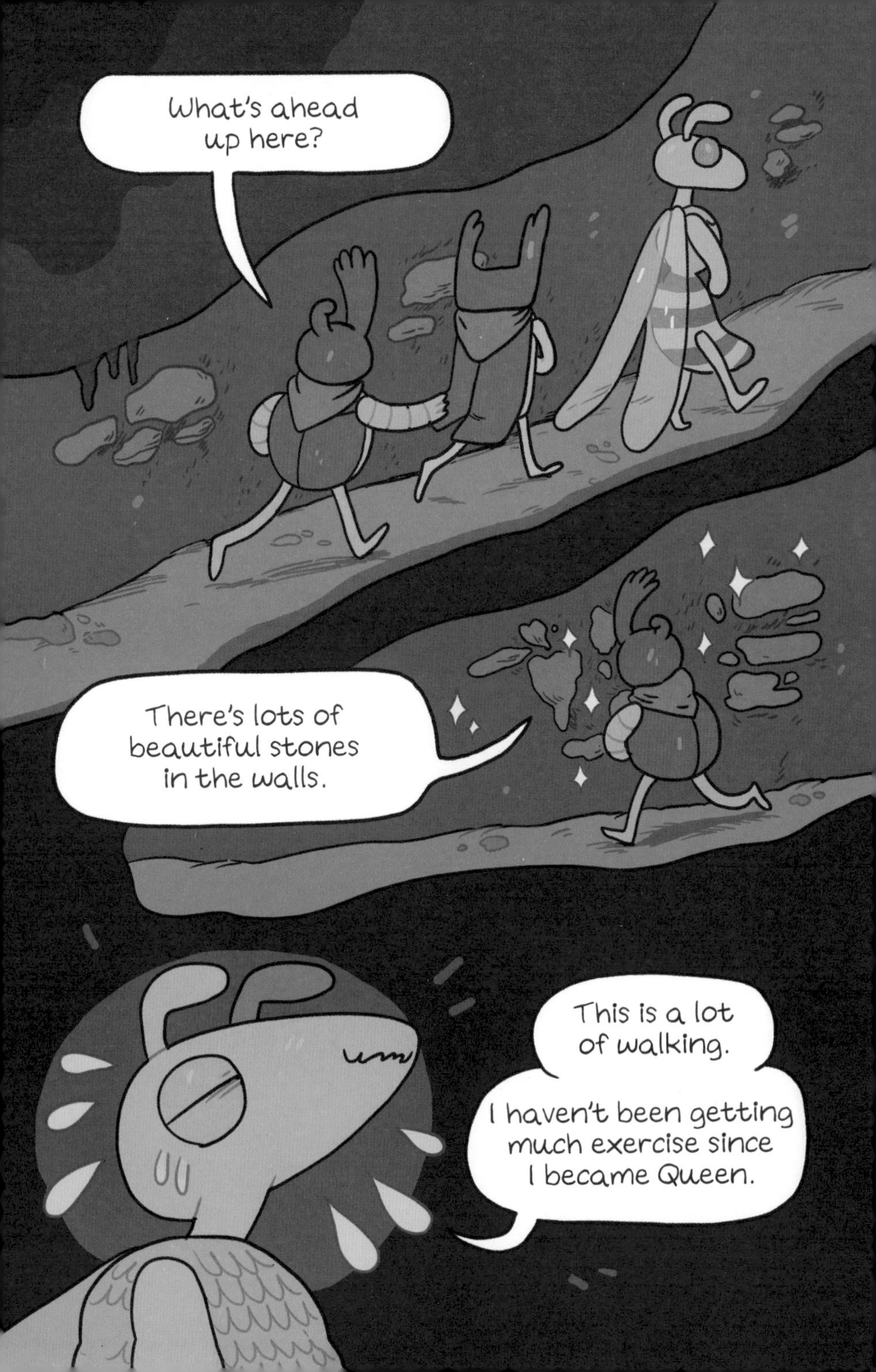
What's ahead up here?
There's lots of beautiful stones in the walls.
This is a lot of walking.
I haven't been getting much exercise since I became Queen.

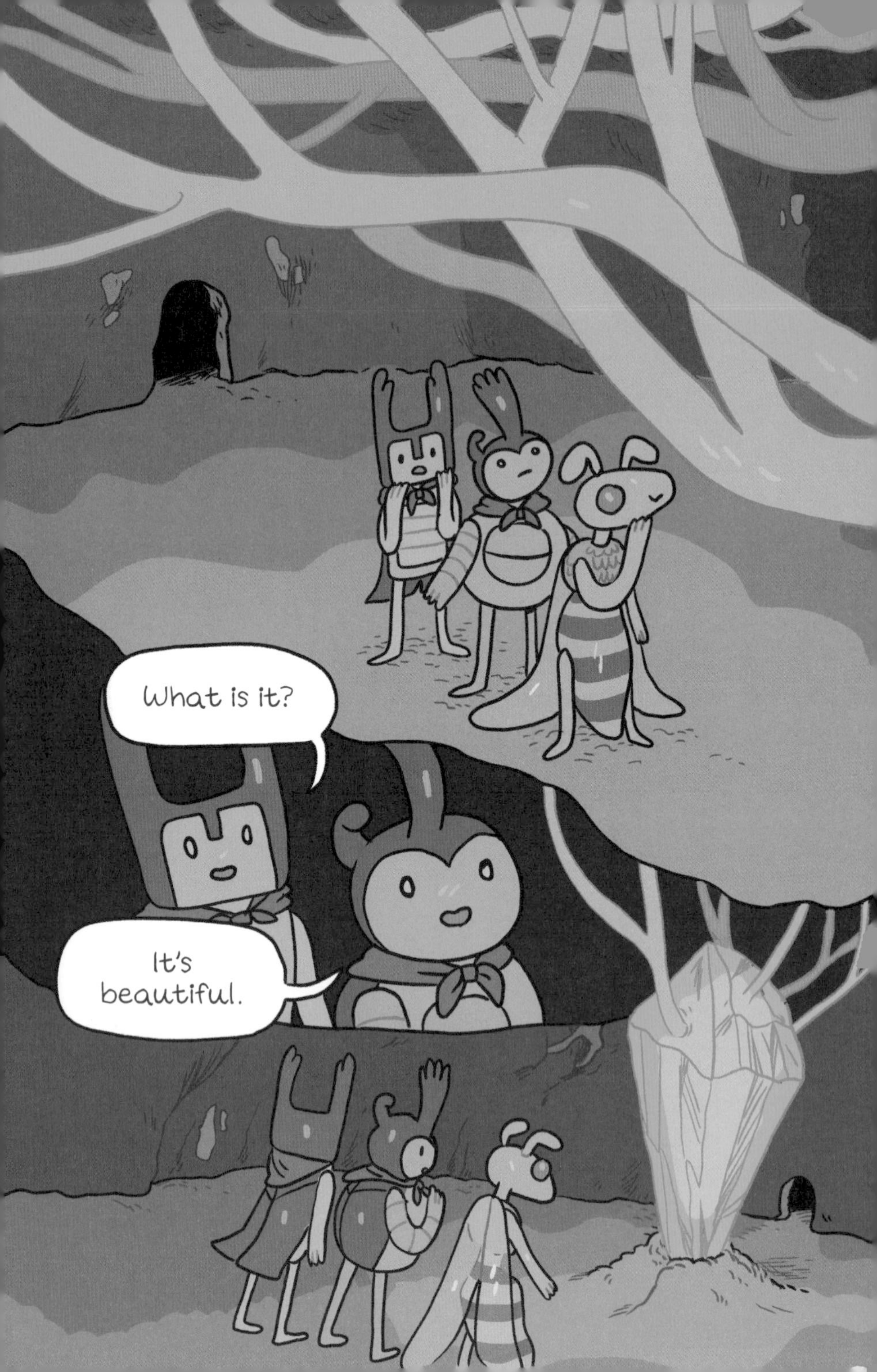
What is it?
It's beautiful.

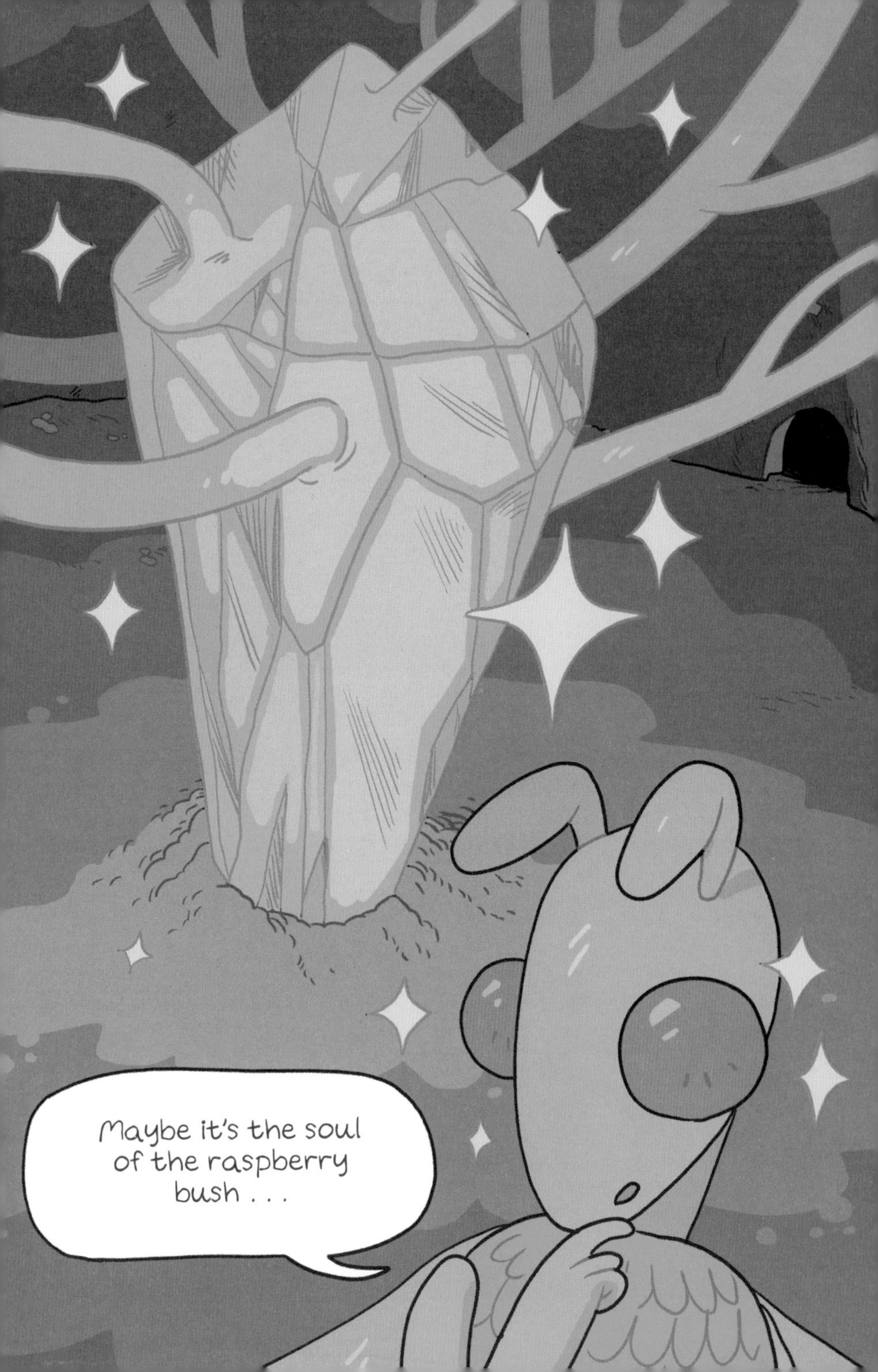
Maybe it's the soul of the raspberry bush . . .

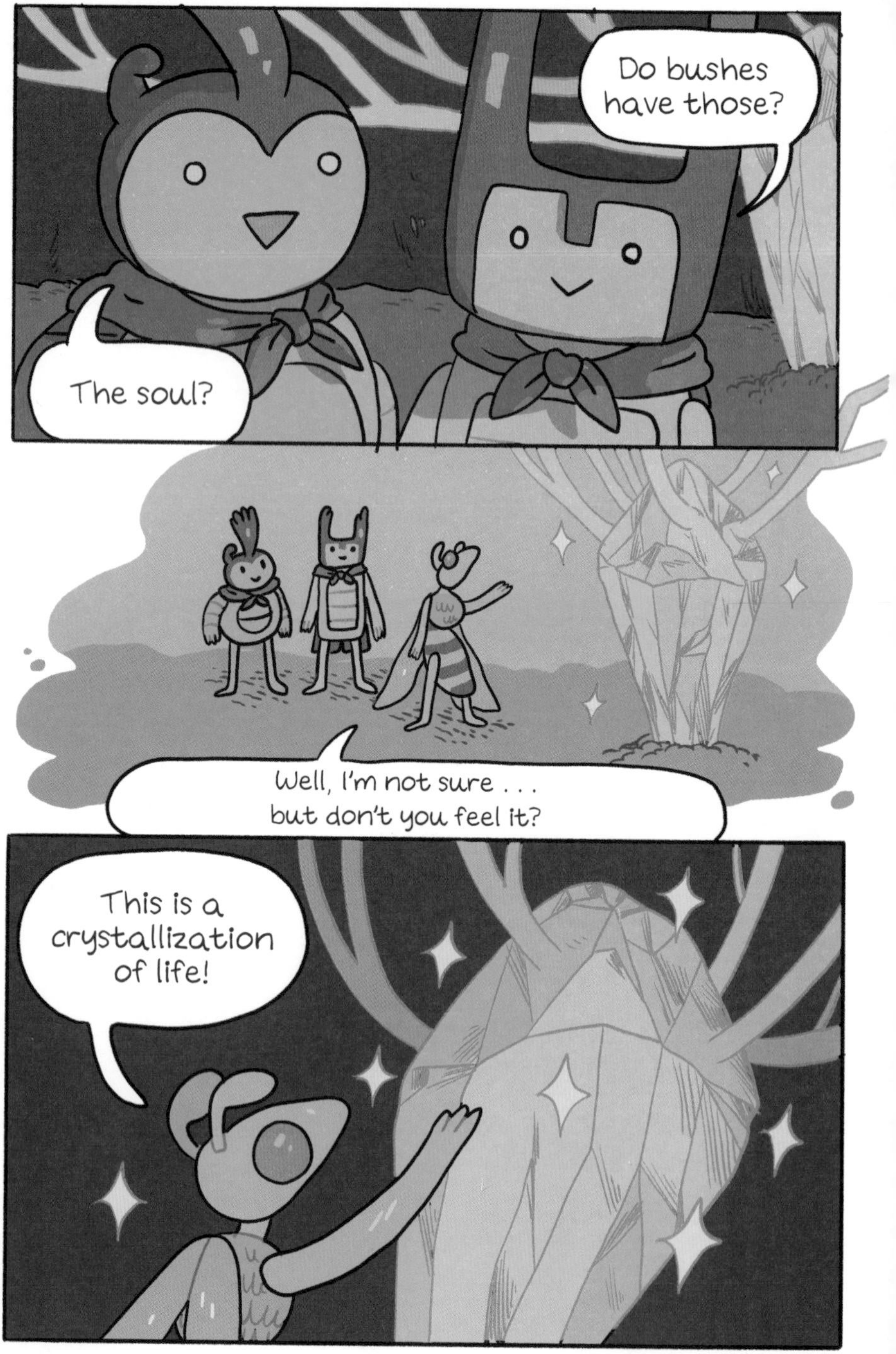
Do bushes have those?
The soul?
Well, I'm not sure . . . but don't you feel it?
This is a crystallization of life!

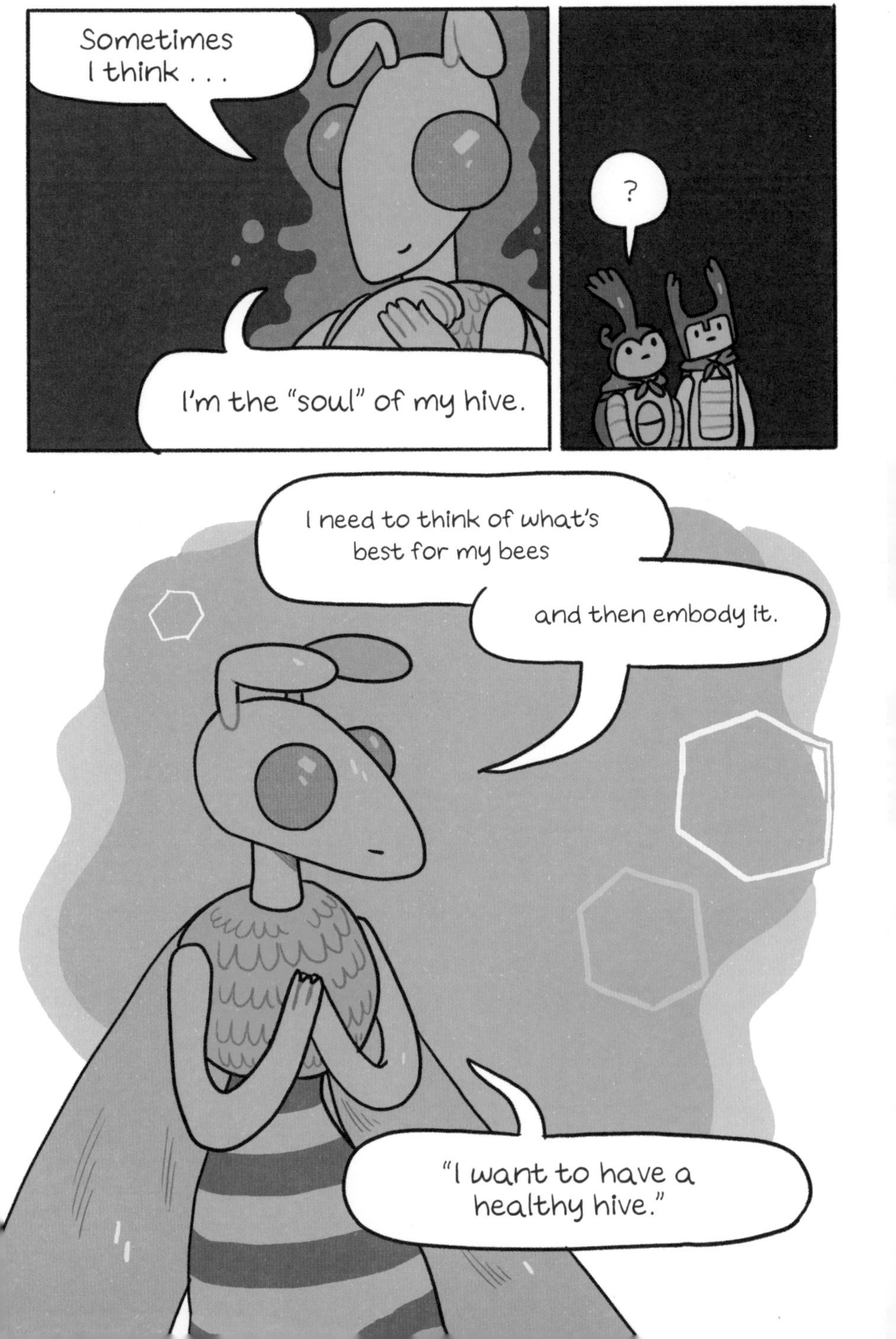

Sometimes I think . . .
I'm the "soul" of my hive.
?
I need to think of what's best for my bees
and then embody it.
"I want to have a healthy hive."

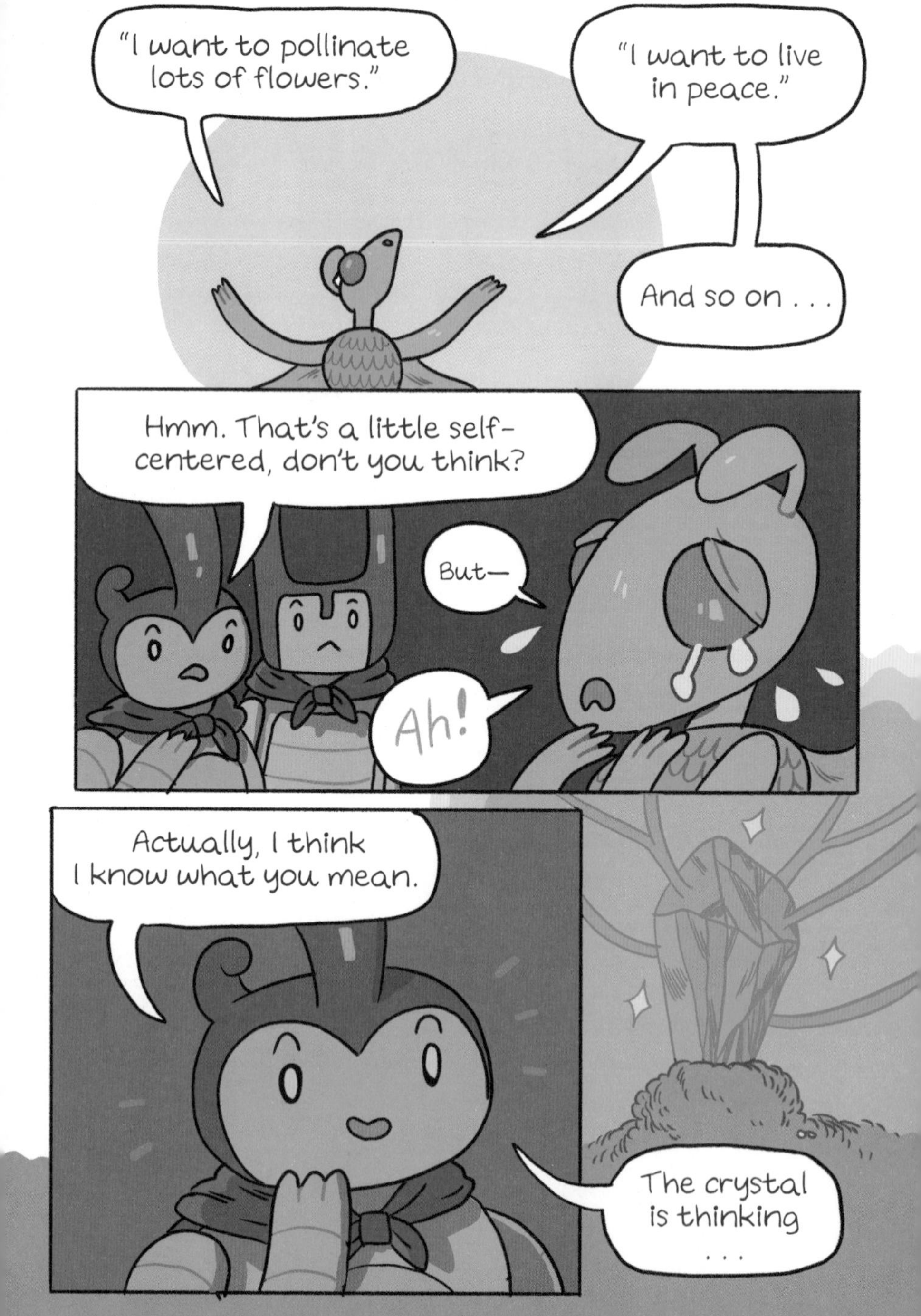
"I want to pollinate lots of flowers."
"I want to live in peace."
And so on . . .
Hmm. That's a little self-centered, don't you think?
But—
Ah!
Actually, I think I know what you mean.
The crystal is thinking . . .

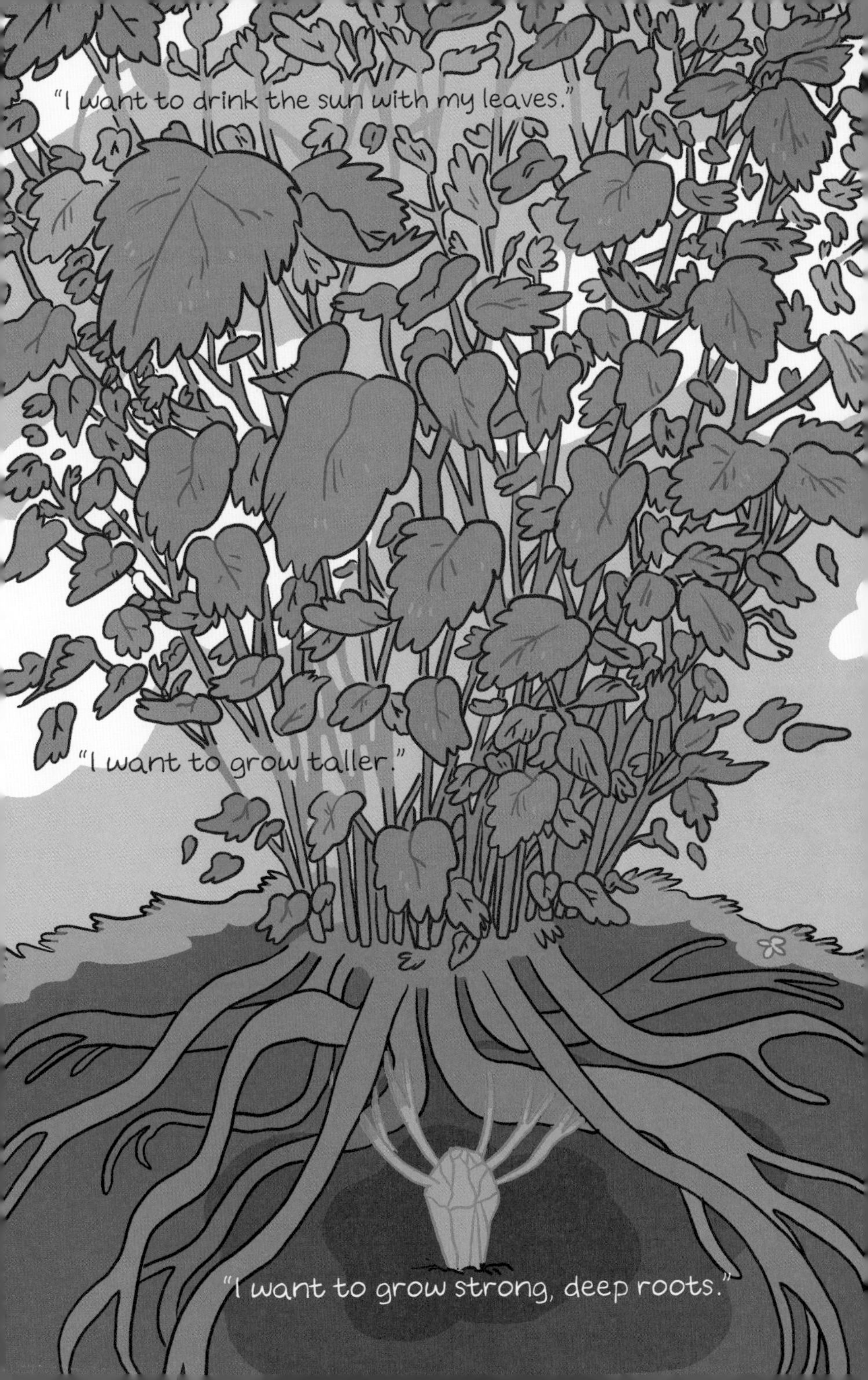
"I want to drink the sun with my leaves."
"I want to grow taller."
"I want to grow strong, deep roots."

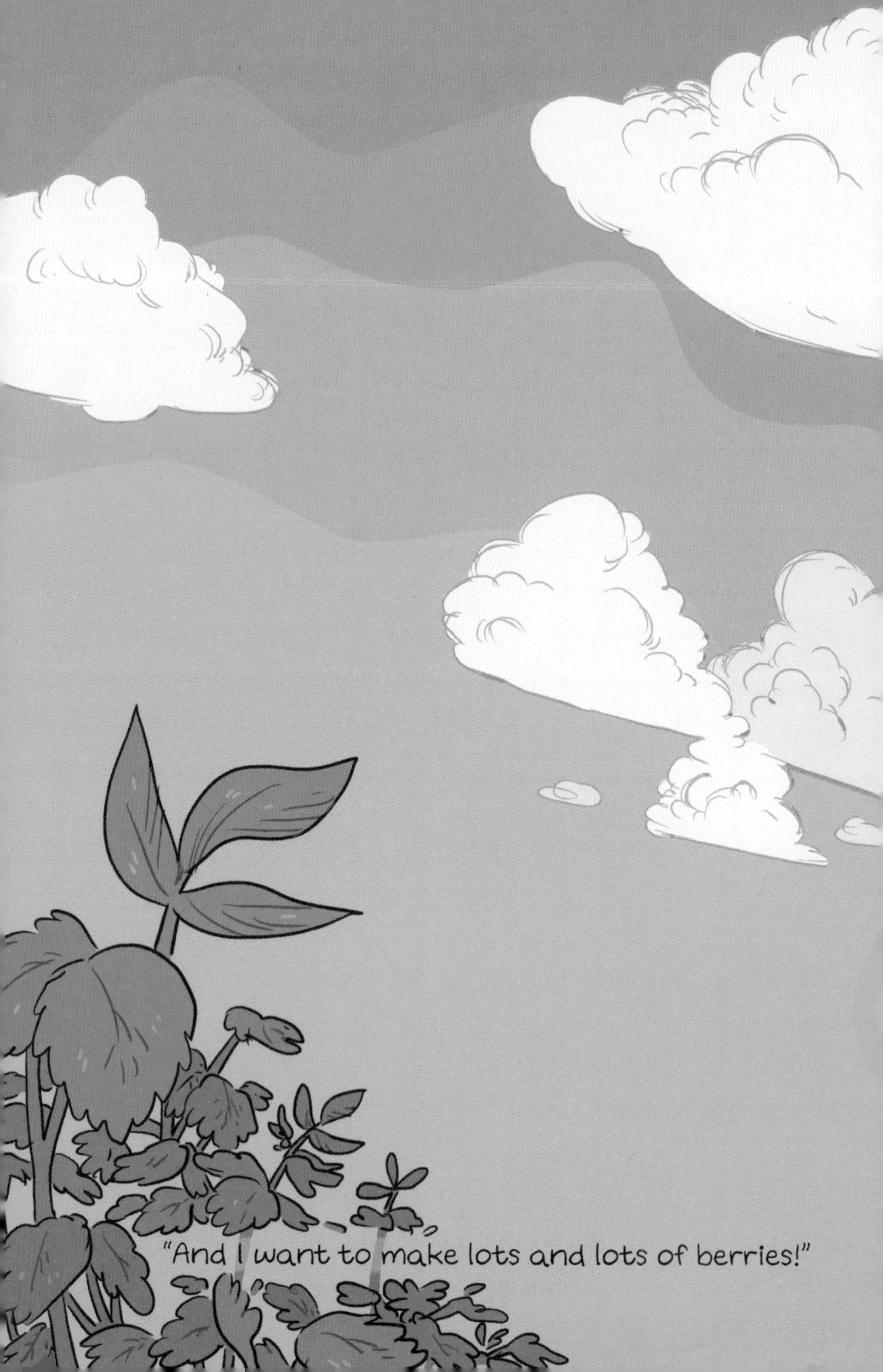

"And I want to make lots and lots of berries!"

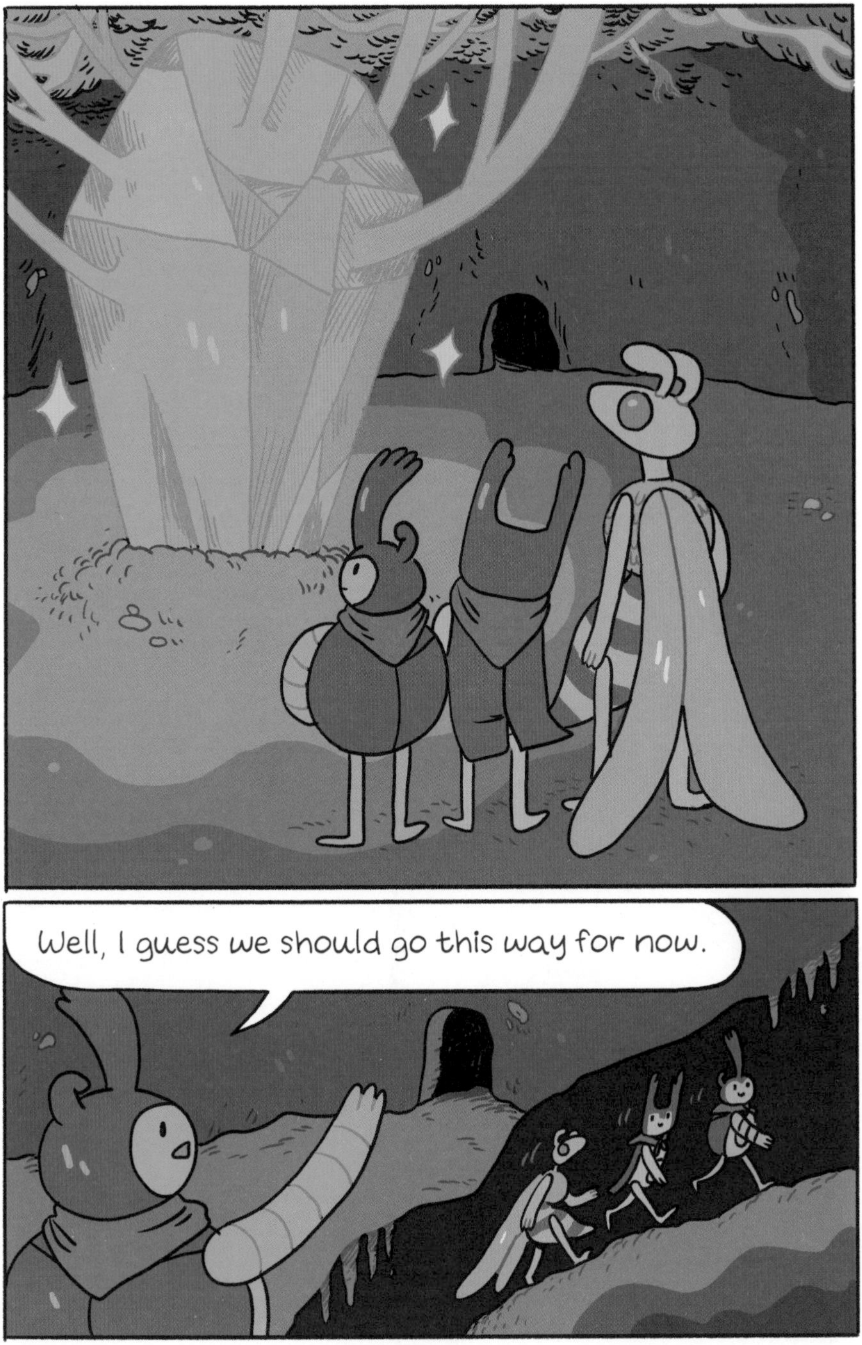
Well, I guess we should go this way for now.

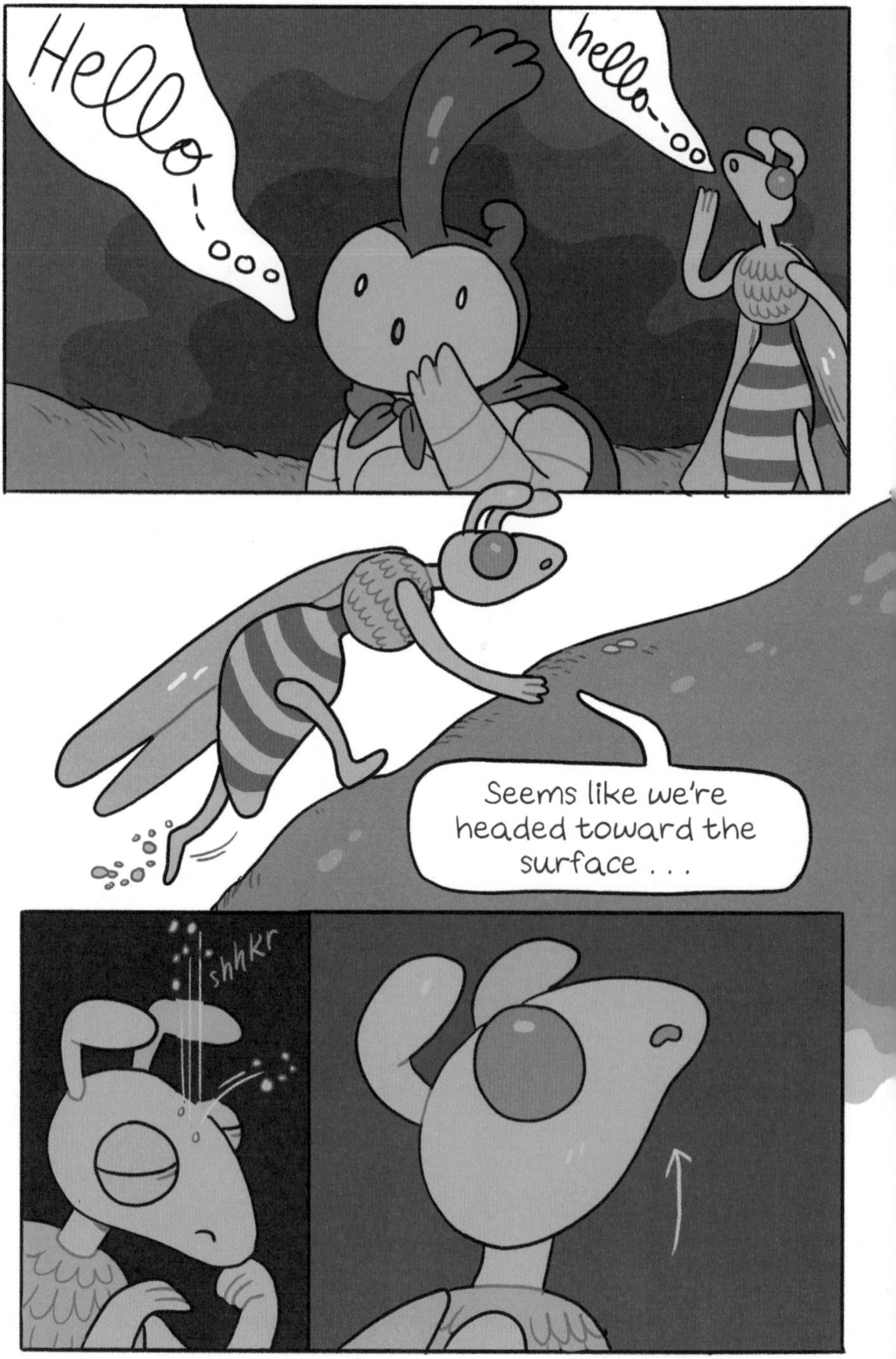
Hello-ooo
hello-ooo
Seems like we're headed toward the surface . . .
shhkr

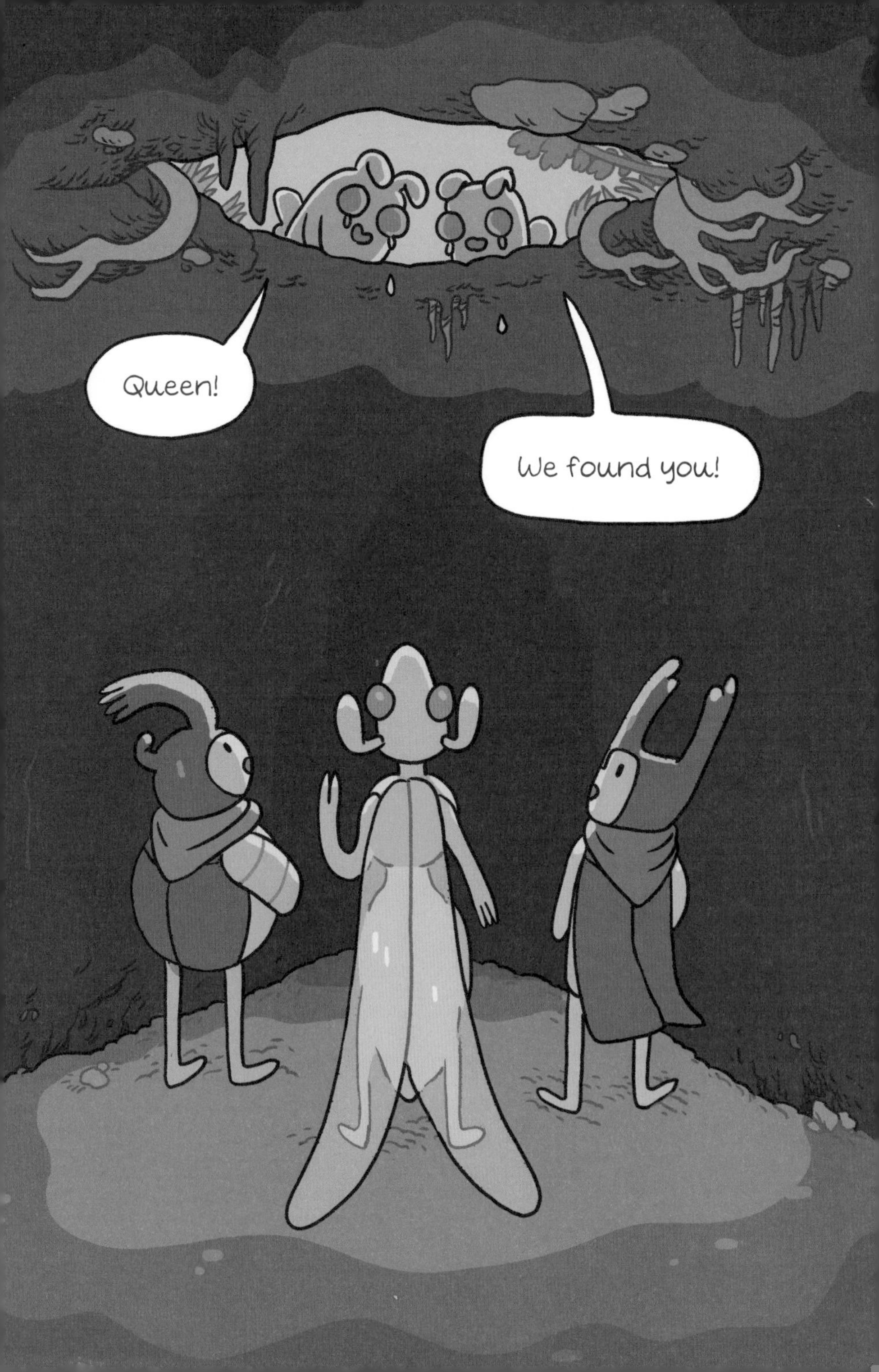
Queen!
We found you!

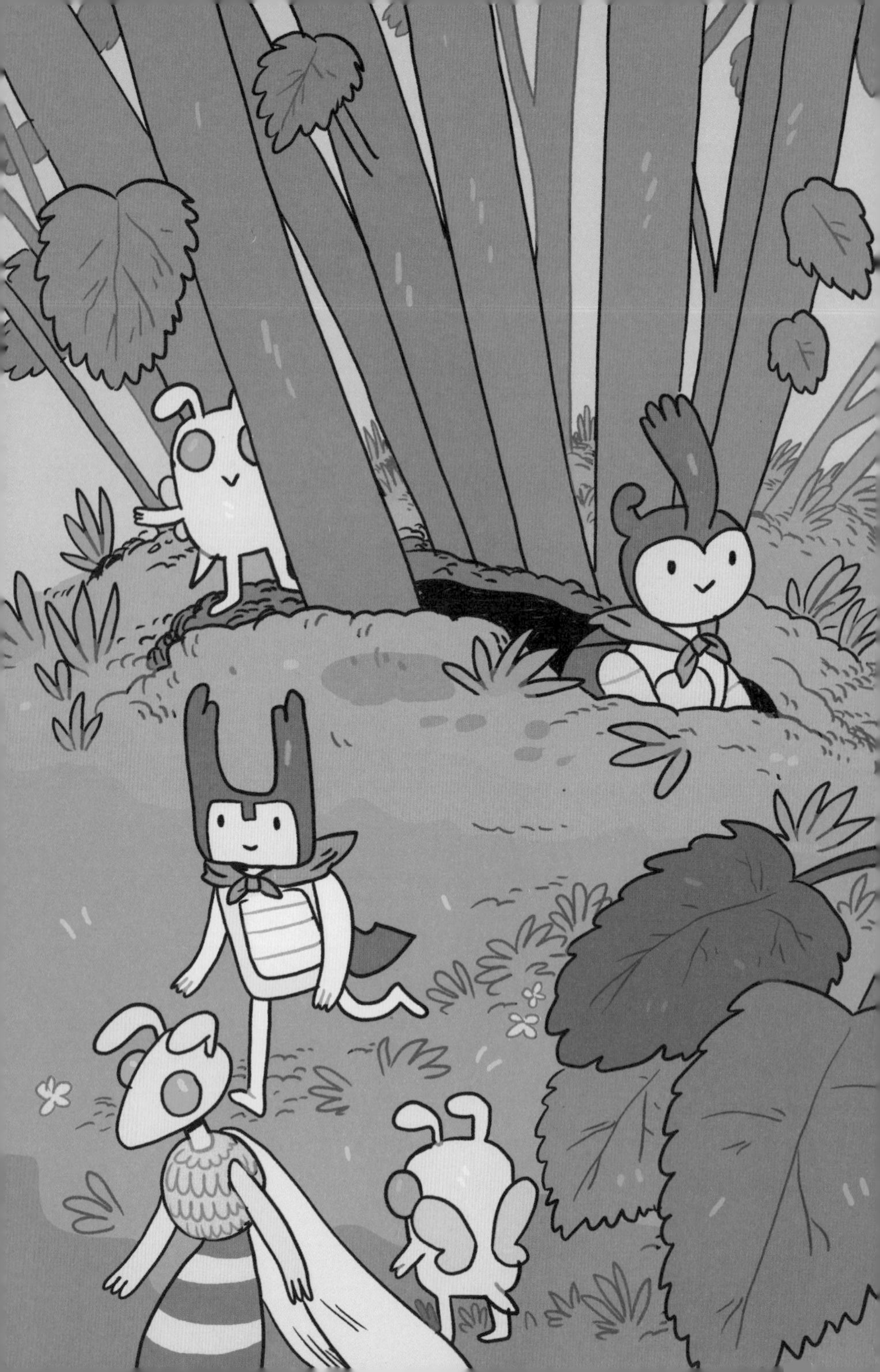

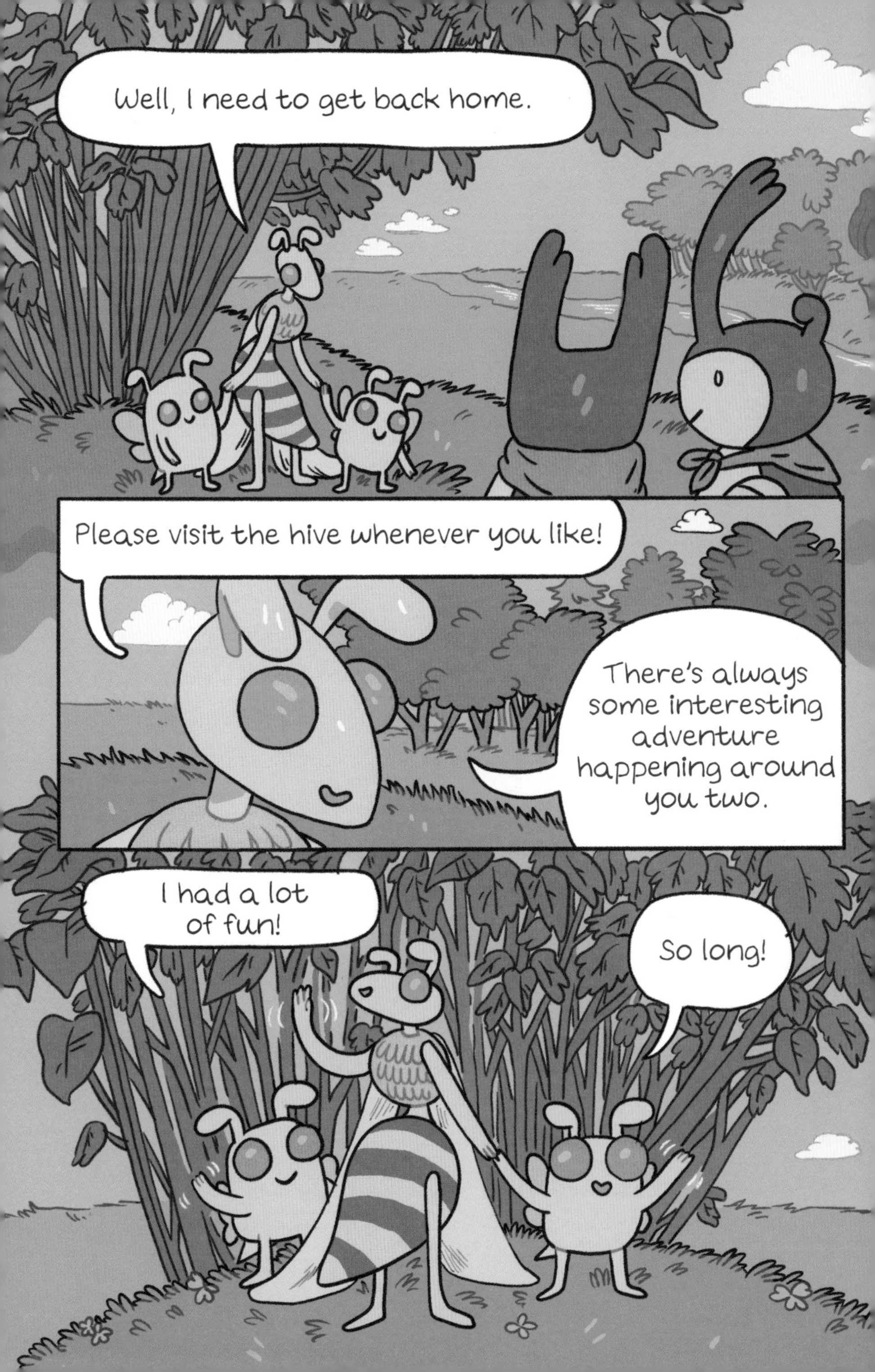
Well, I need to get back home.
Please visit the hive whenever you like!
There's always some interesting adventure happening around you two.
I had a lot of fun!
So long!

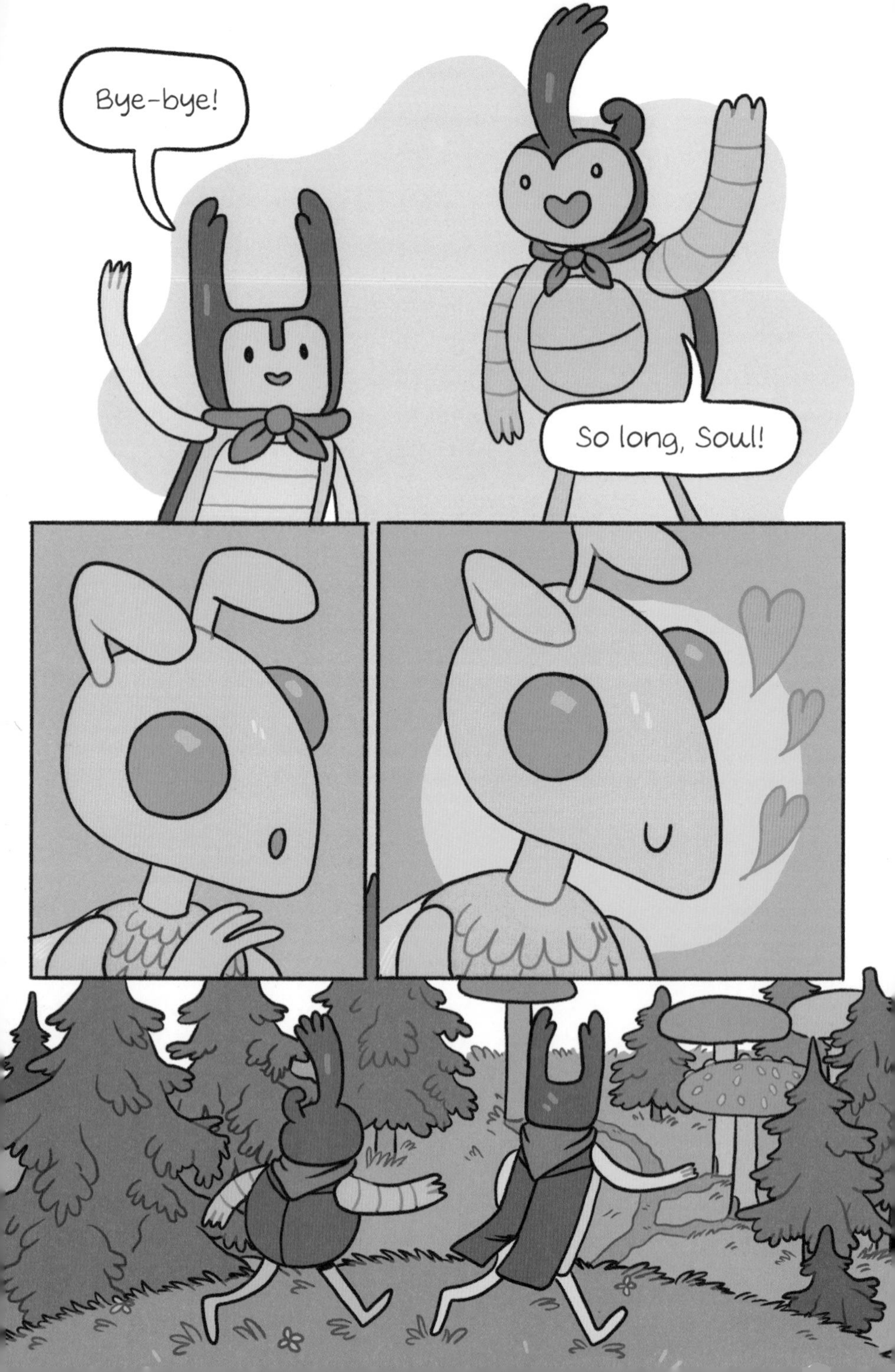
Bye-bye!
So long, Soul!

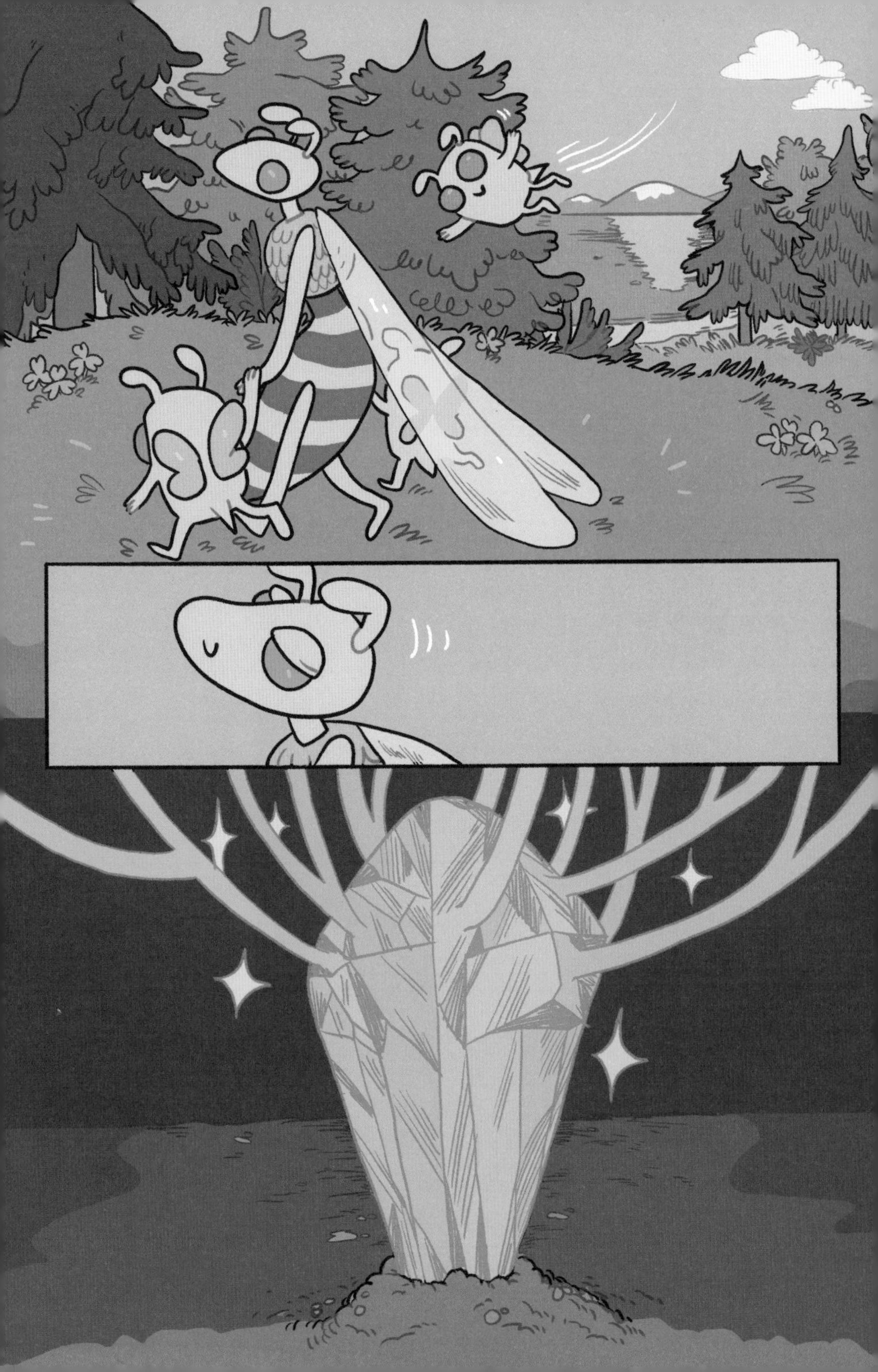

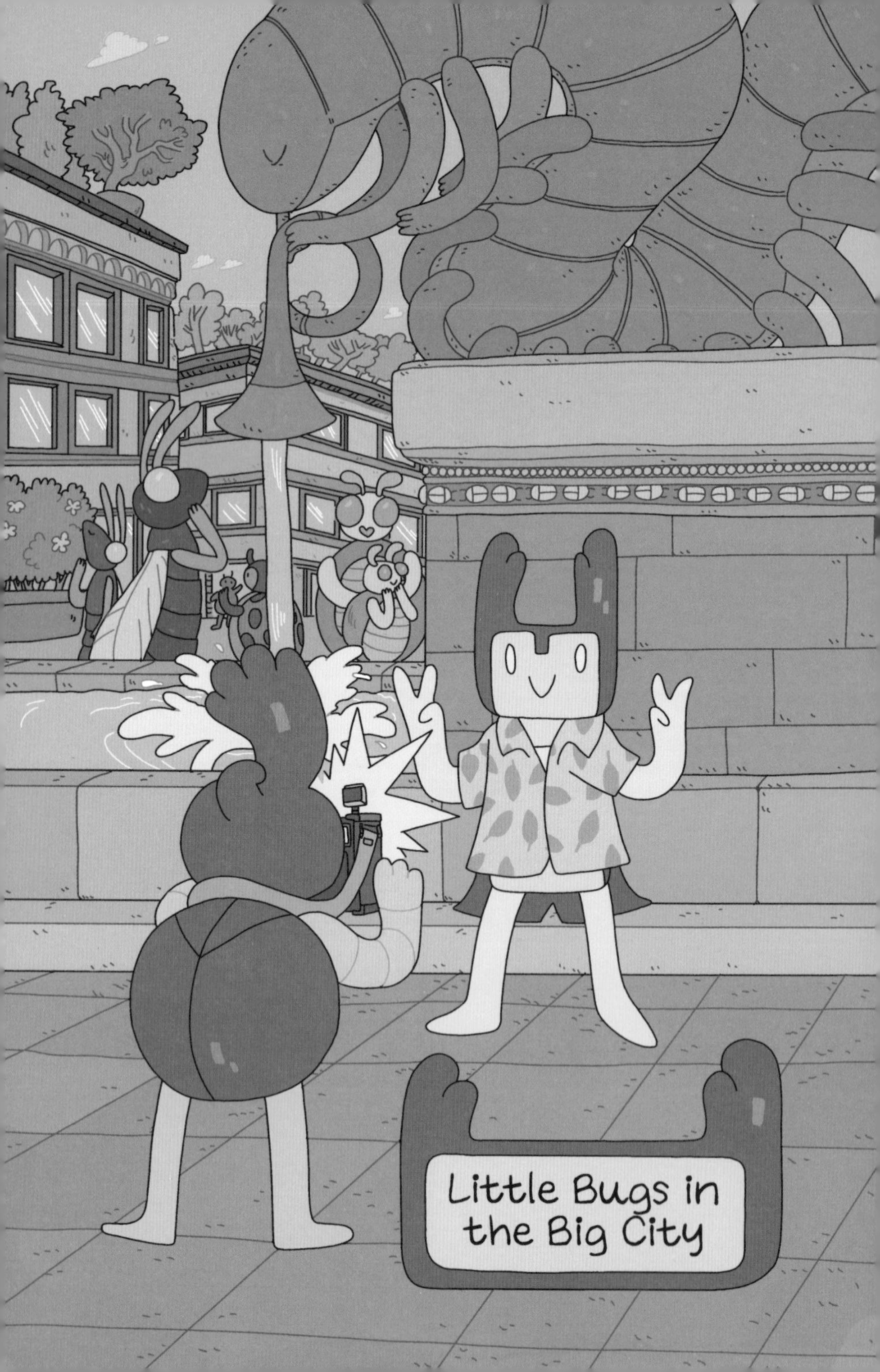
Little Bugs in the Big City

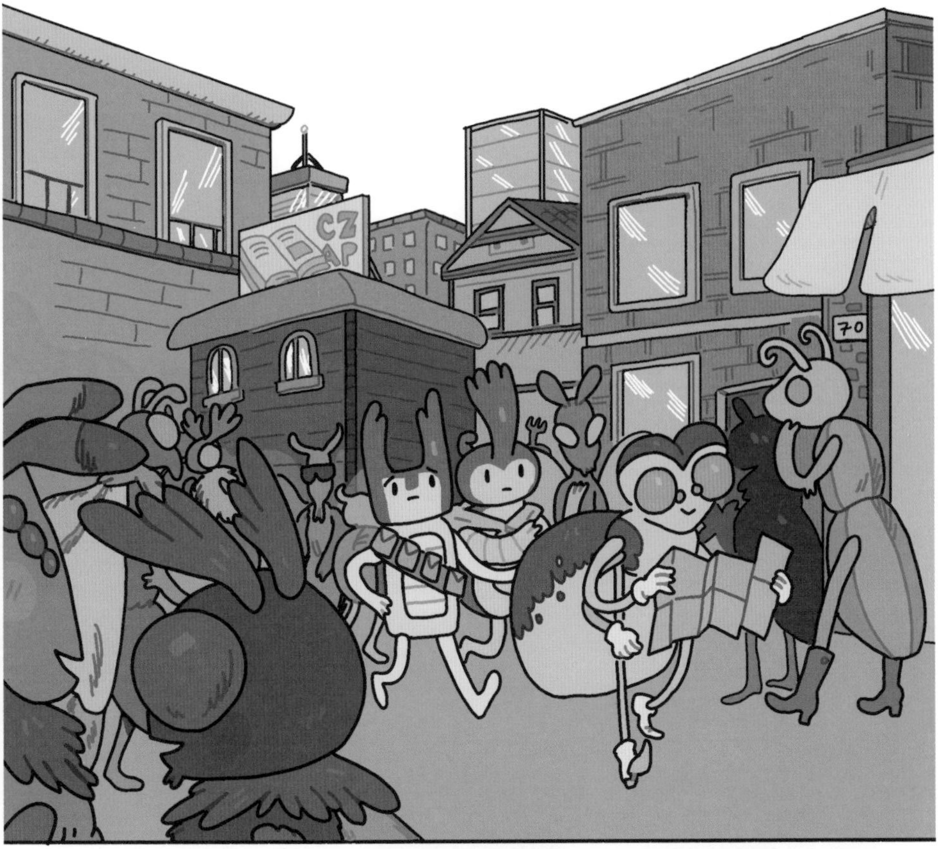
CZ
AP
70

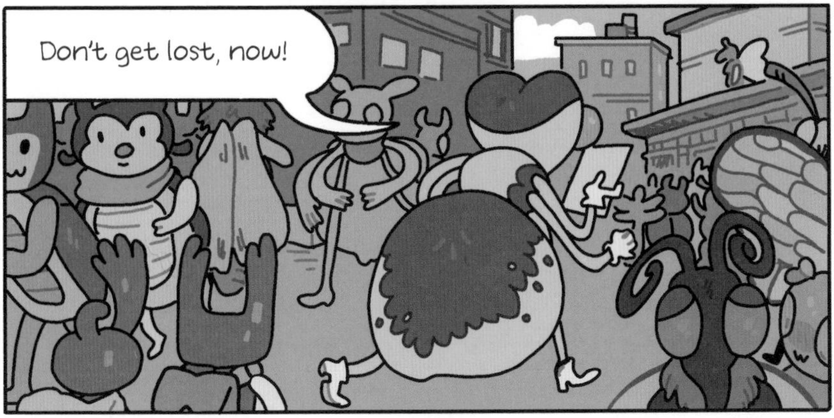
Don't get lost, now!

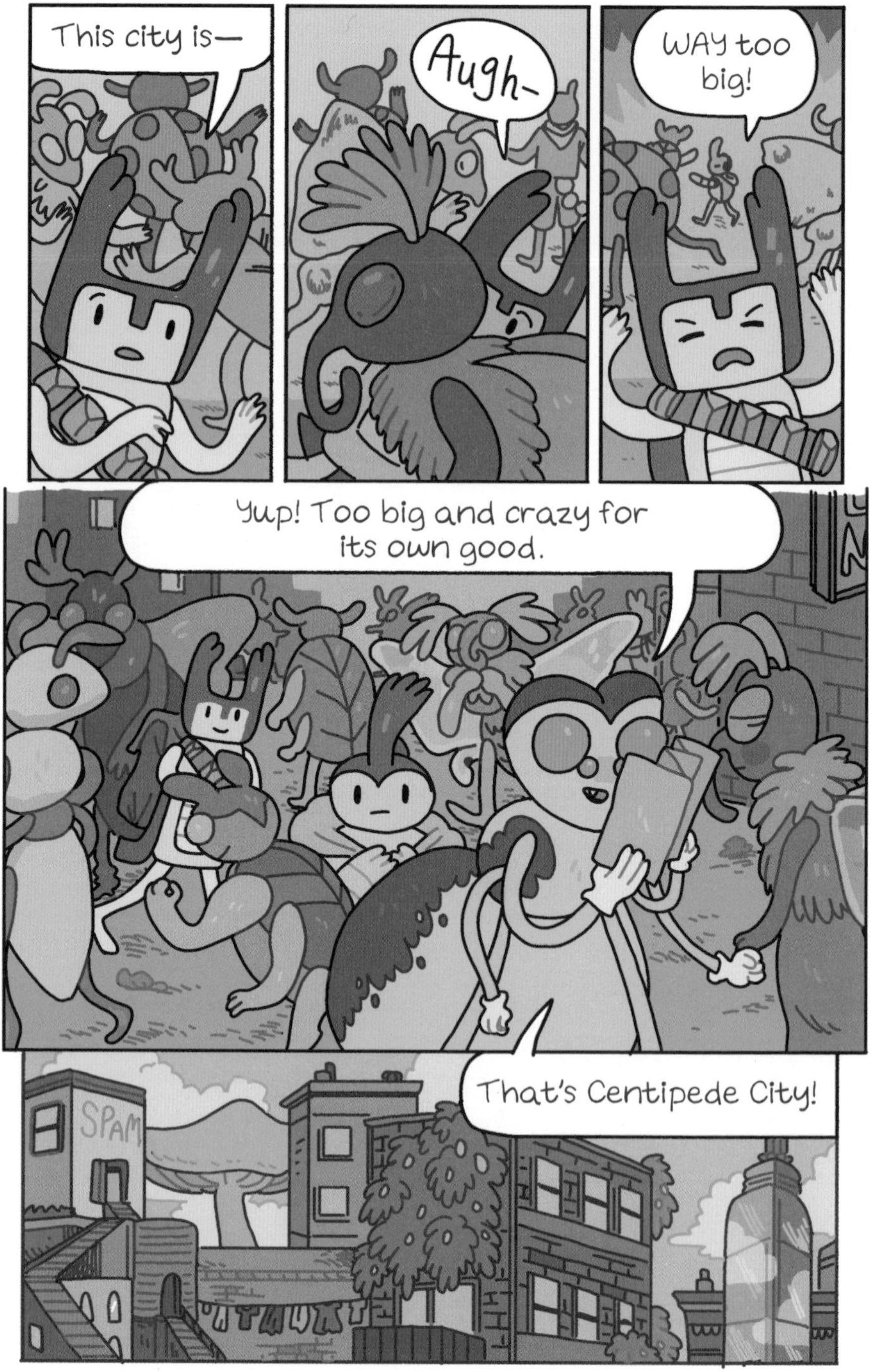
This city is—
Augh-
WAY too big!
Yup! Too big and crazy for its own good.
That's Centipede City!
SPAM

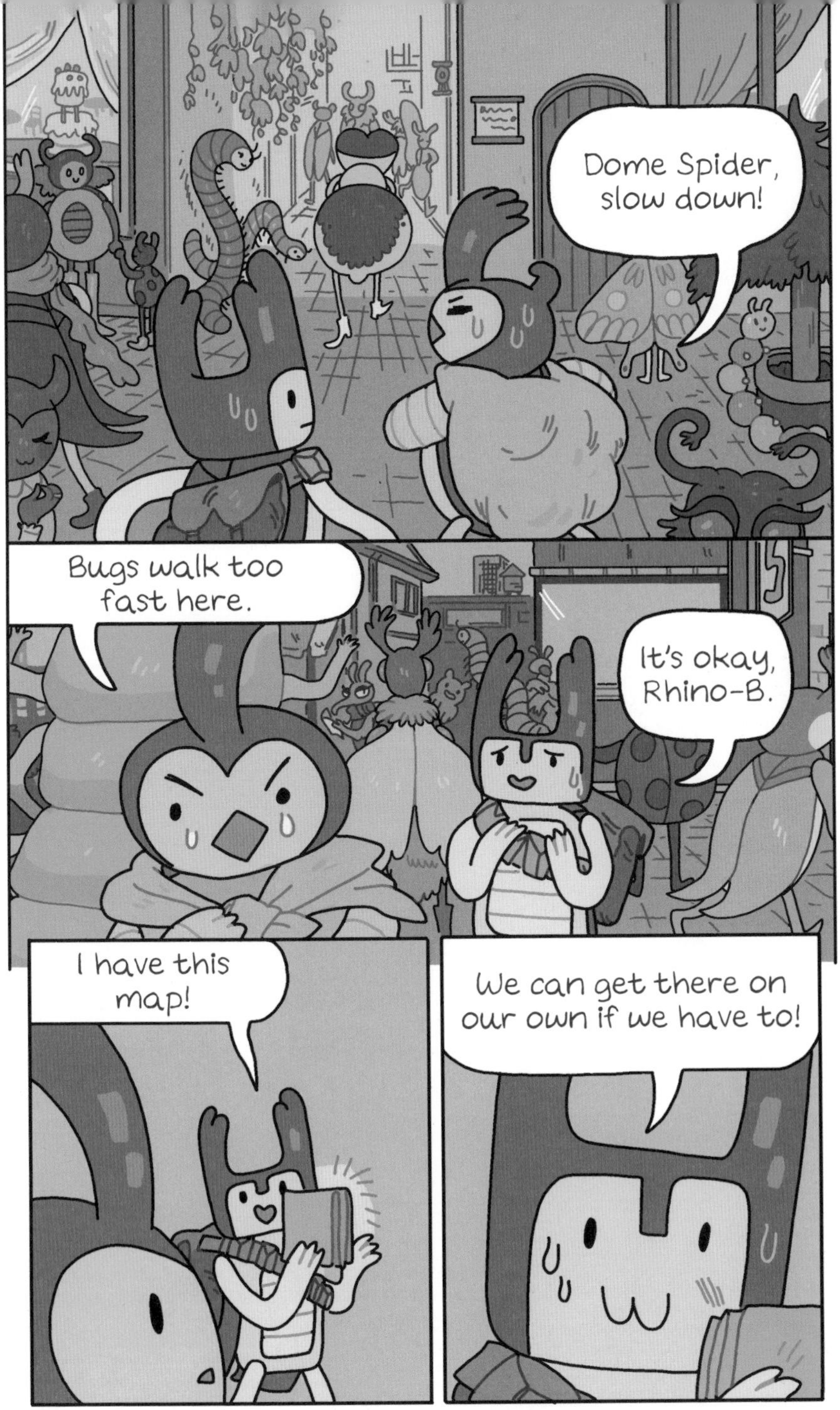
Dome Spider, slow down!
Bugs walk too fast here.
It's okay, Rhino-B.
I have this map!
We can get there on our own if we have to!

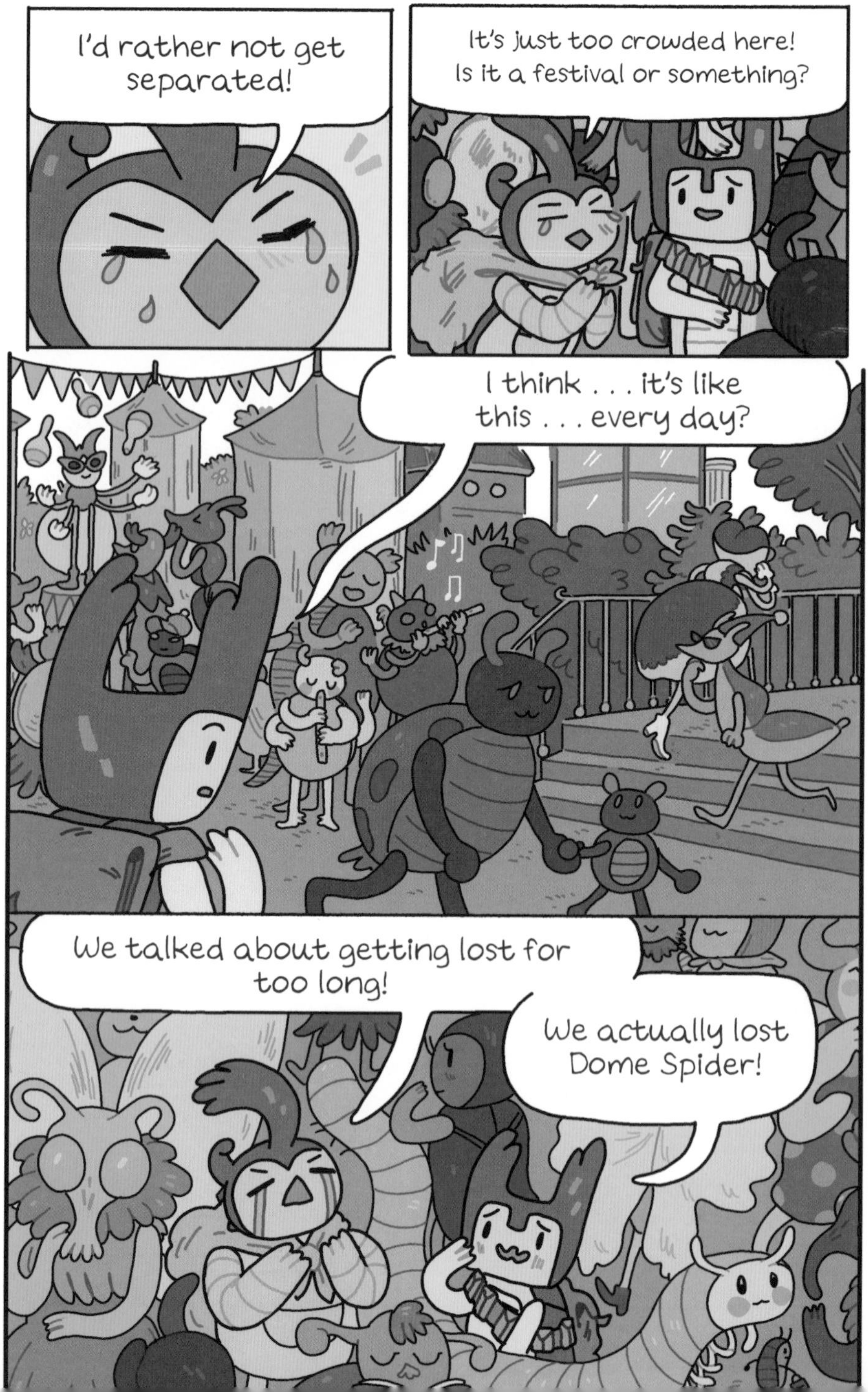
I'd rather not get separated!
It's just too crowded here! Is it a festival or something?
I think . . . it's like this . . . every day?
We talked about getting lost for too long!
We actually lost Dome Spider!

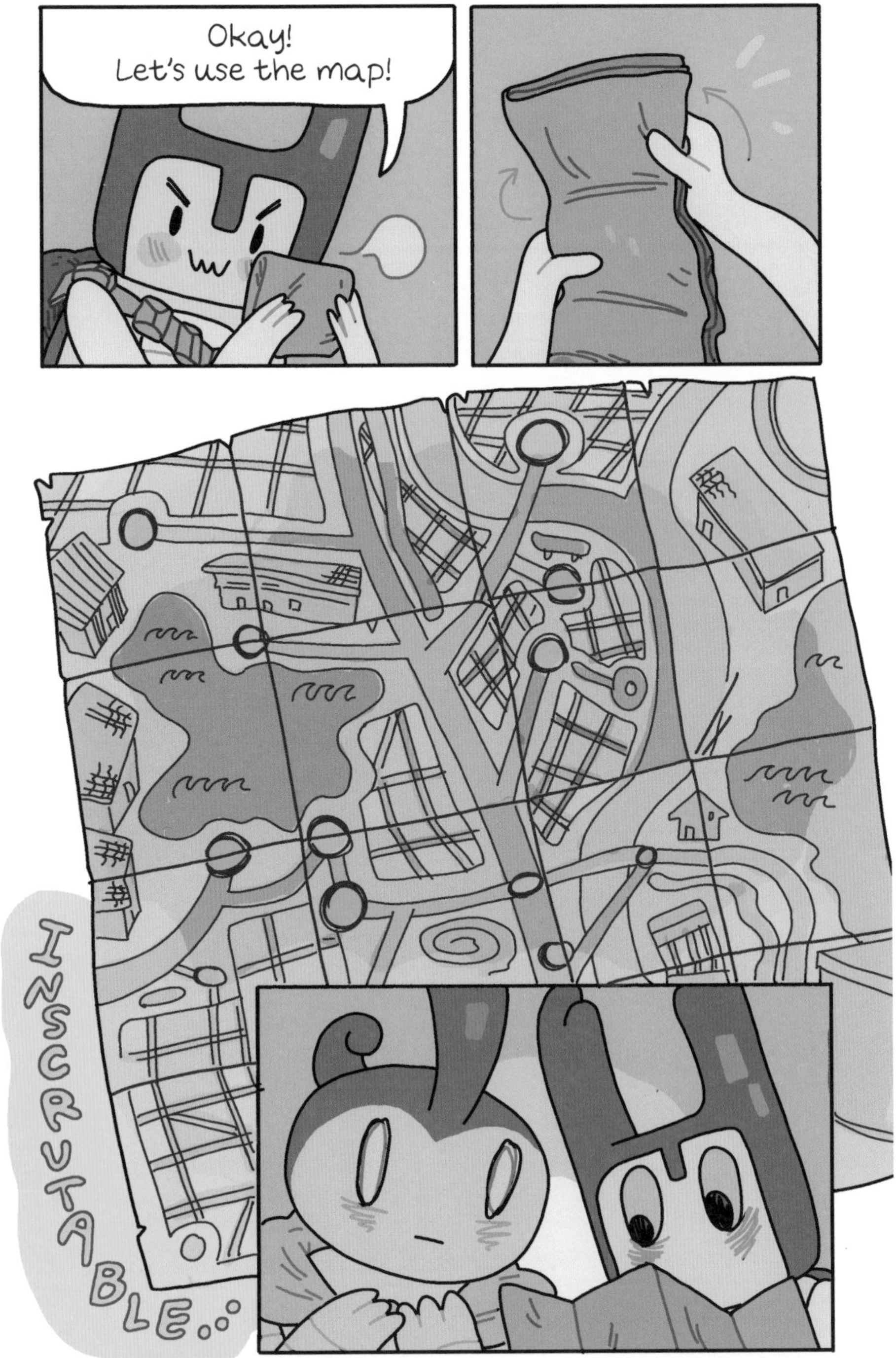
Okay!
Let's use the map!
INSCRUTABLE...

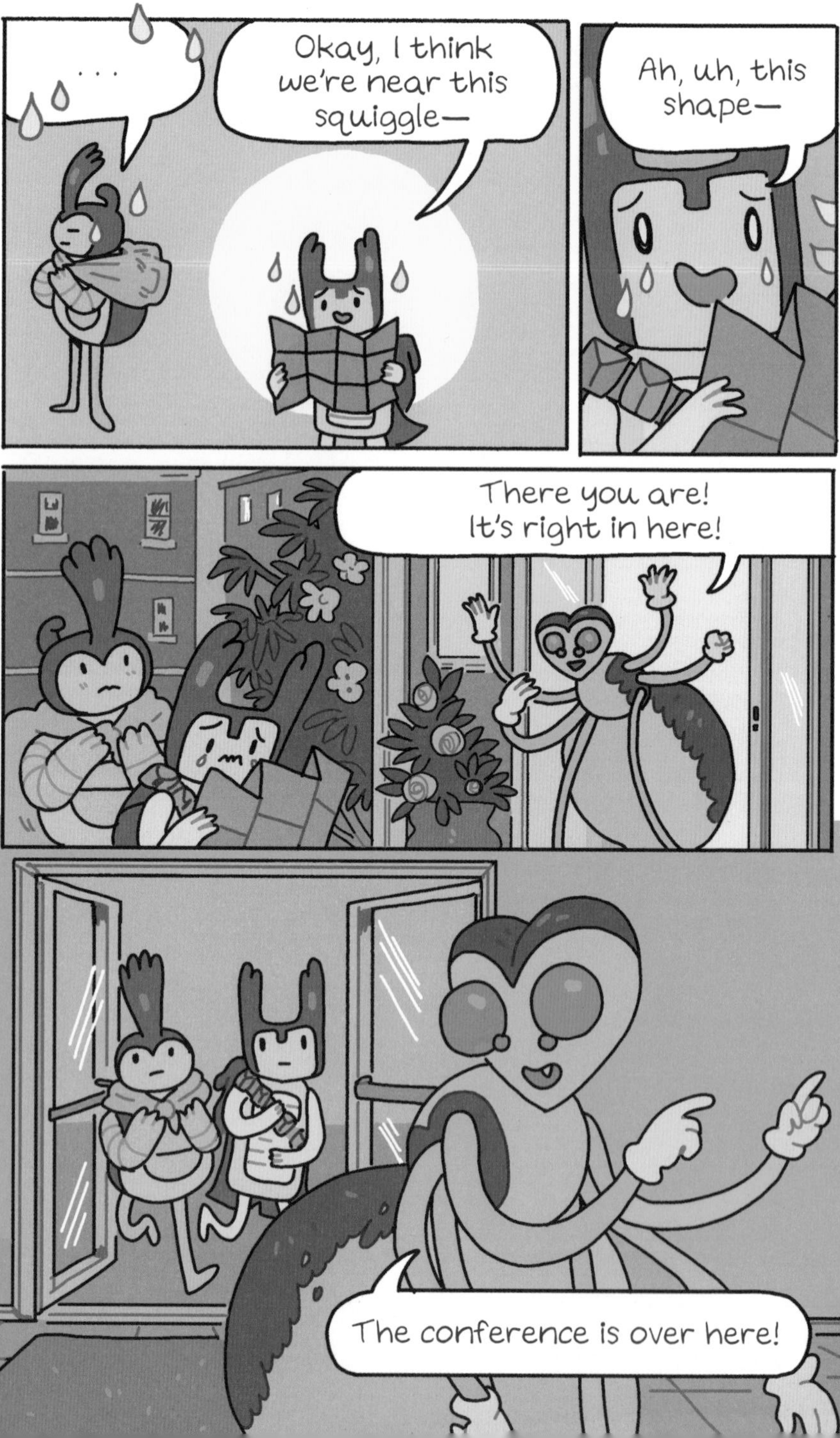

. . .
Okay, I think we're near this squiggle—
Ah, uh, this shape—
There you are! It's right in here!
The conference is over here!

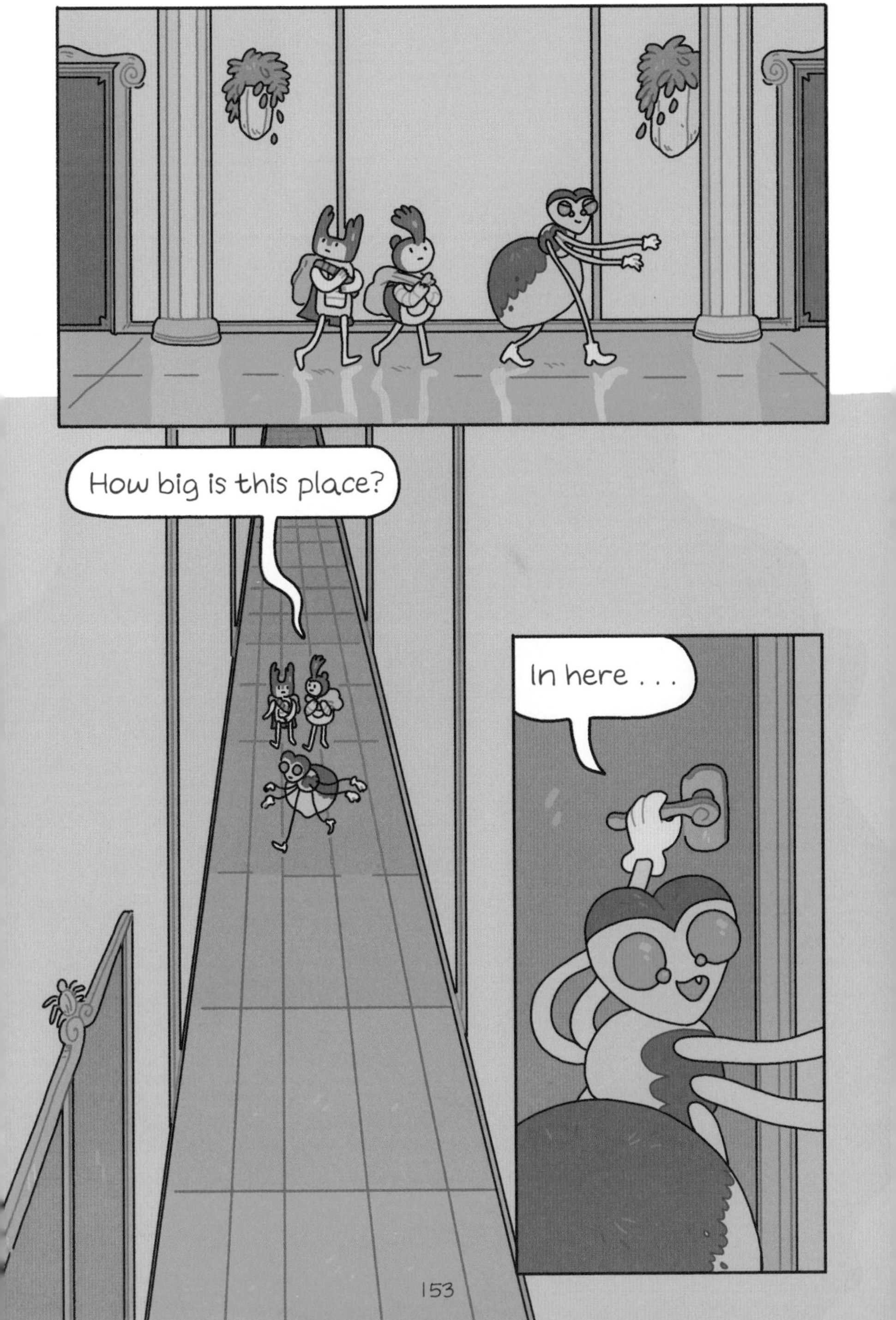
How big is this place?
In here . . .

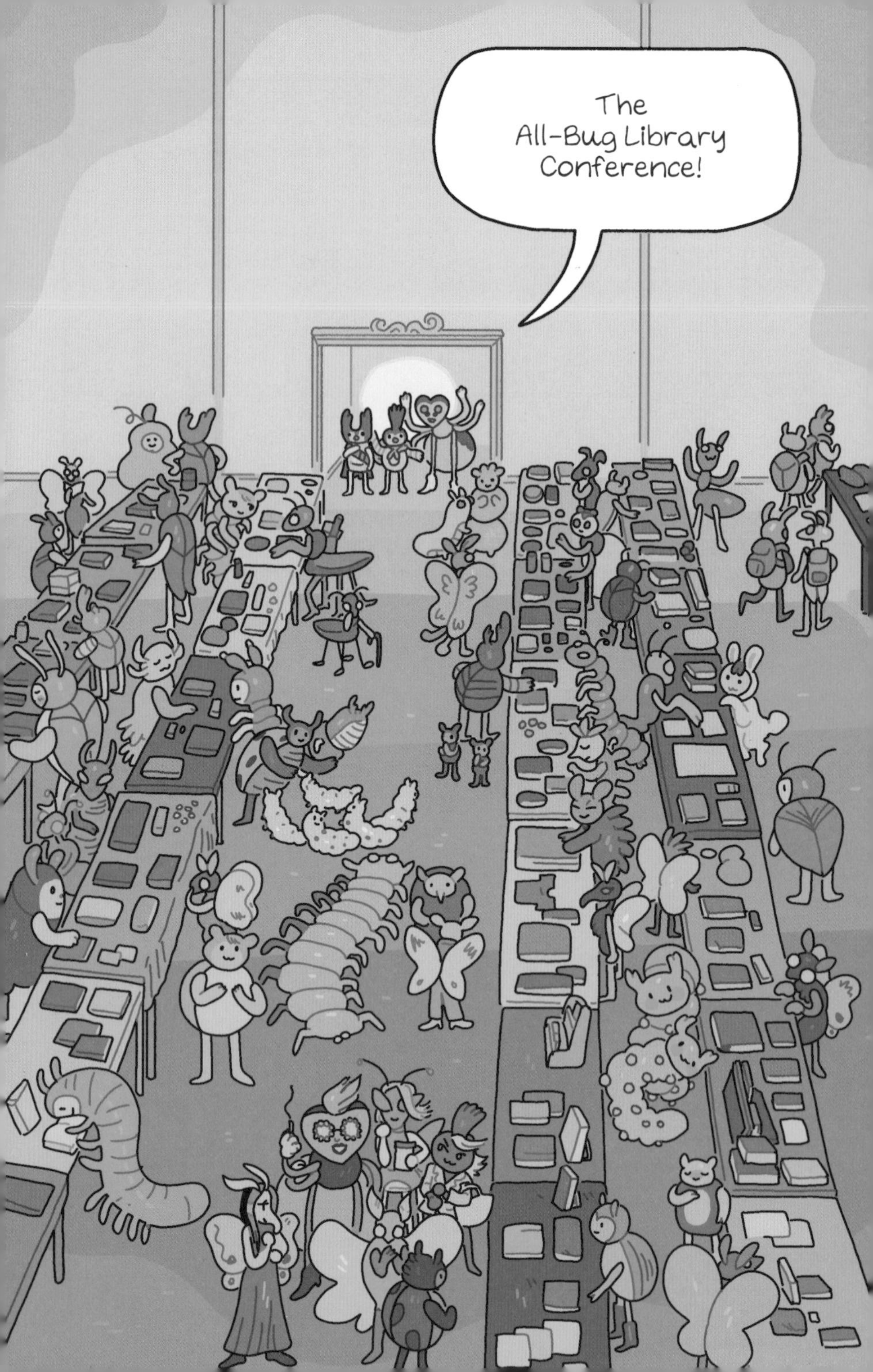
The All-Bug Library Conference!

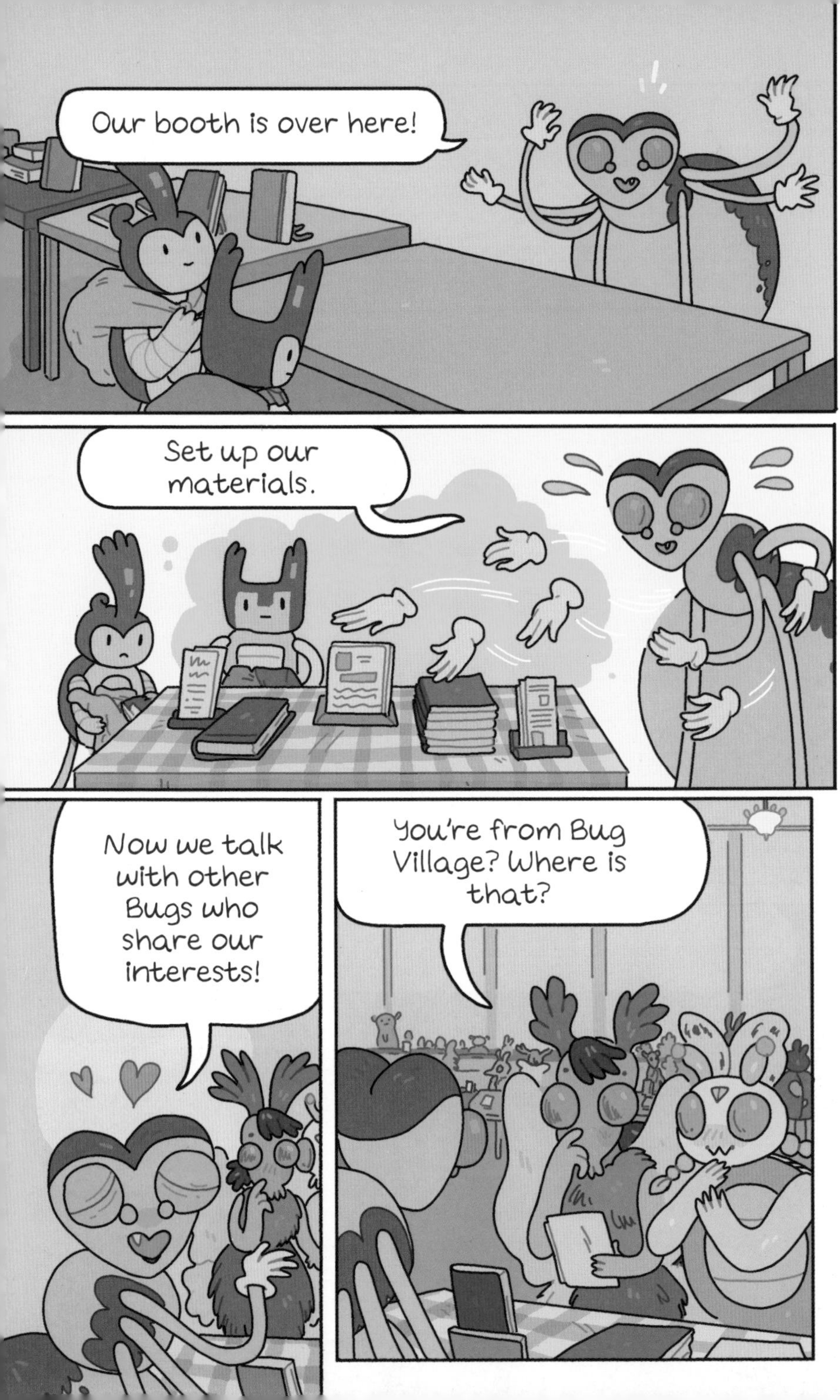
Our booth is over here!
Set up our materials.
Now we talk with other Bugs who share our interests!
You're from Bug Village? Where is that?

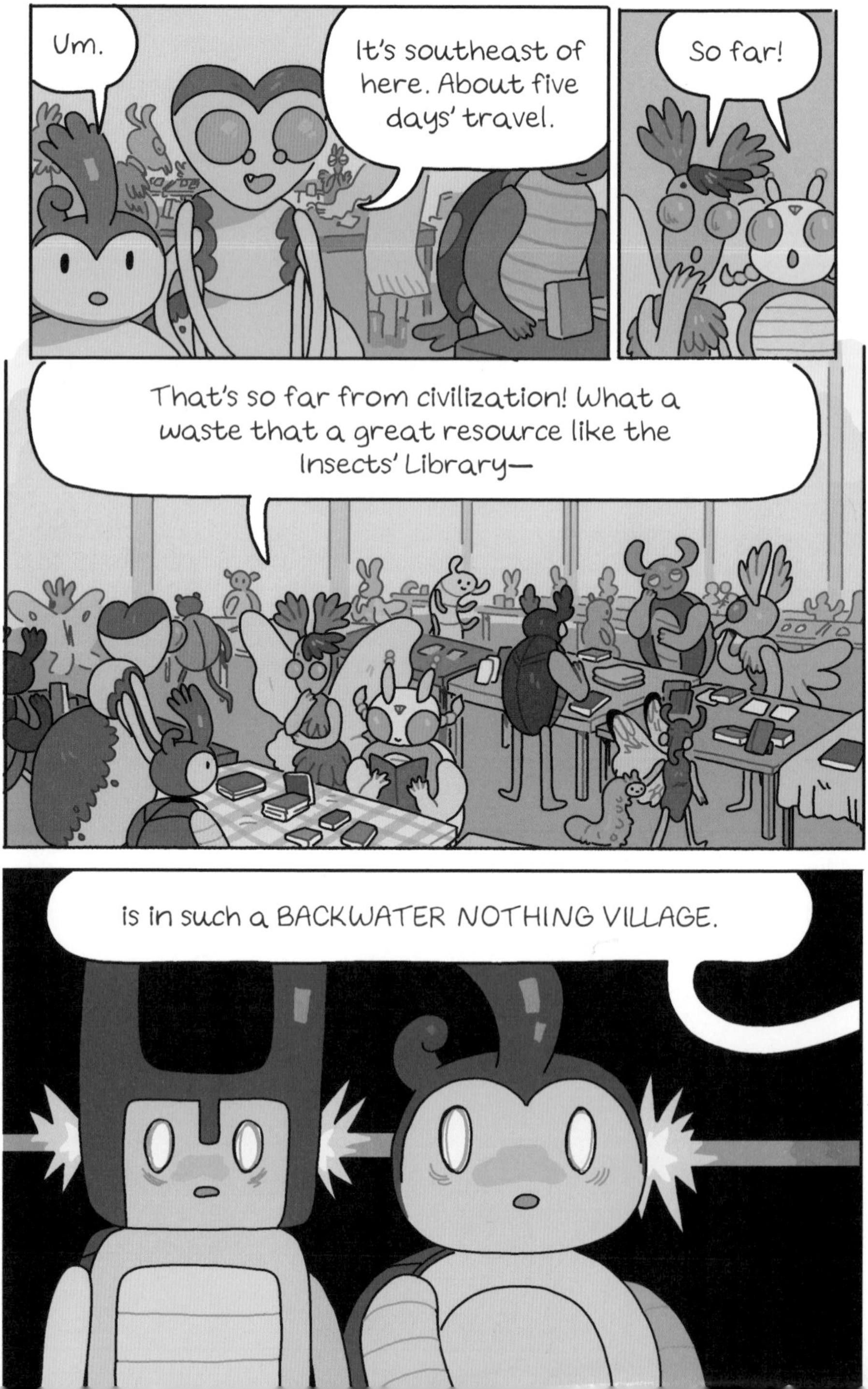
Um.
It's southeast of here. About five days' travel.
So far!
That's so far from civilization! What a waste that a great resource like the Insects' Library—
is in such a BACKWATER NOTHING VILLAGE.

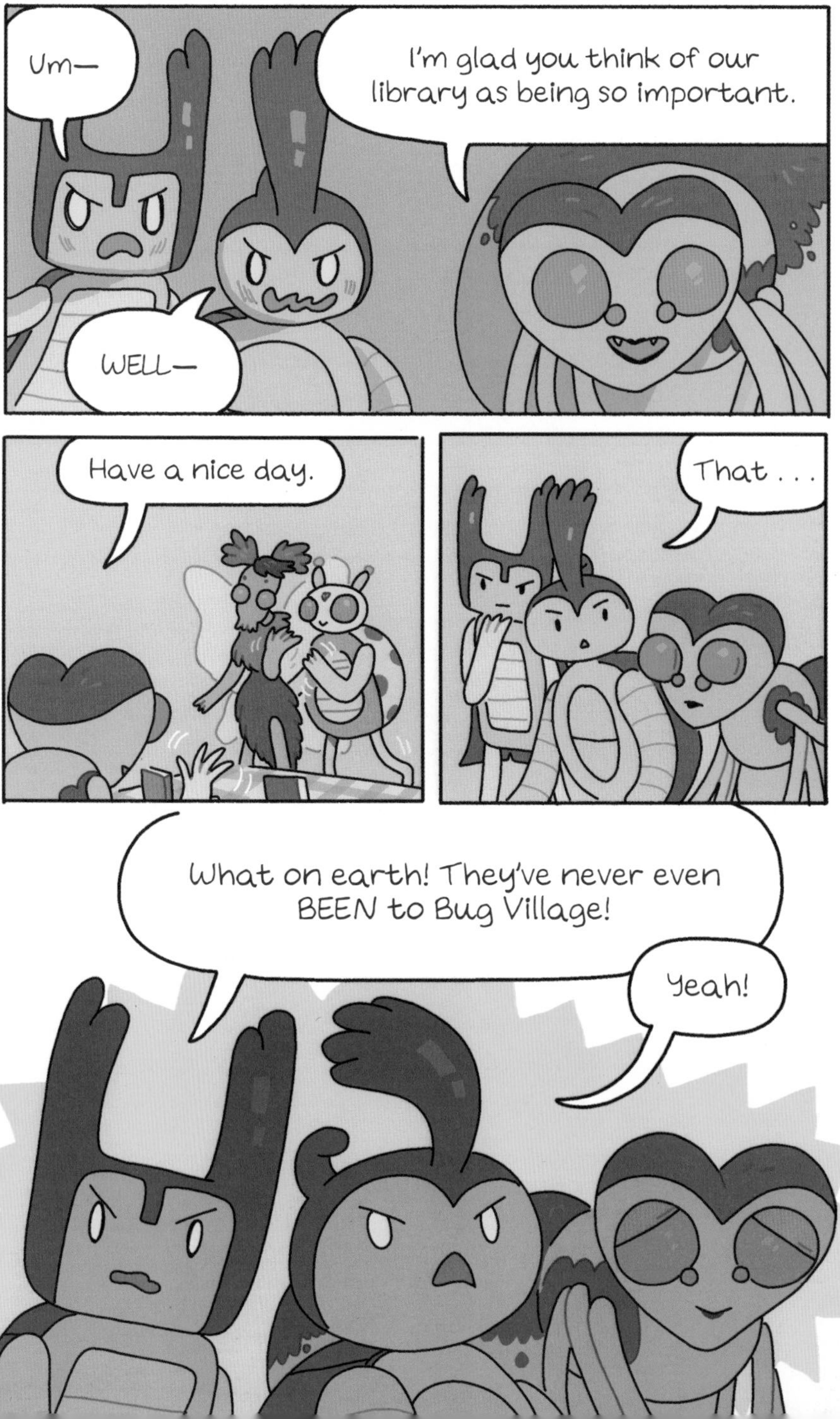
Um—
I'm glad you think of our library as being so important.
WELL—
Have a nice day.
That . . .
What on earth! They've never even BEEN to Bug Village!
Yeah!

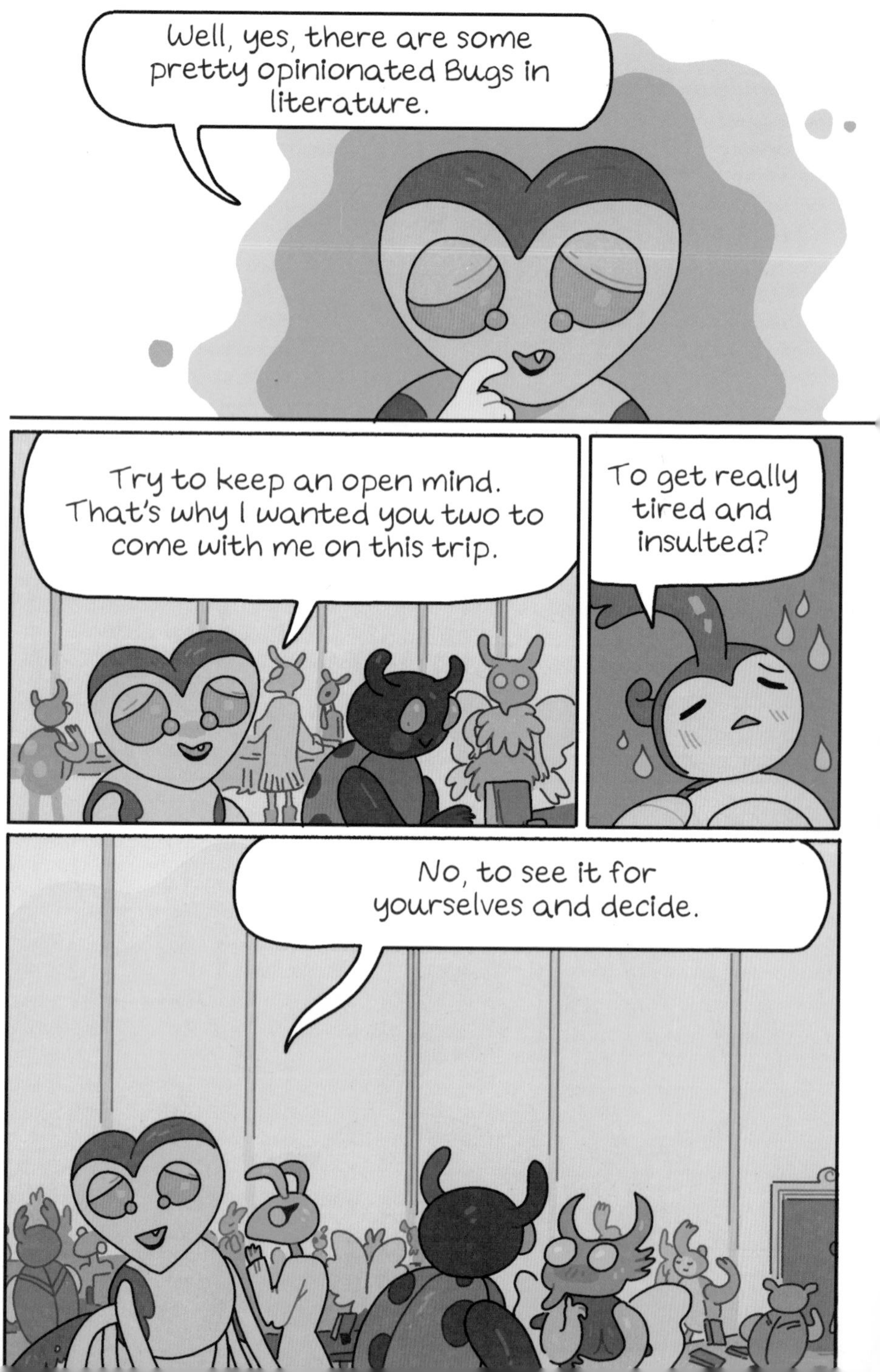
Well, yes, there are some pretty opinionated Bugs in literature.
Try to keep an open mind. That's why I wanted you two to come with me on this trip.
To get really tired and insulted?
No, to see it for yourselves and decide.

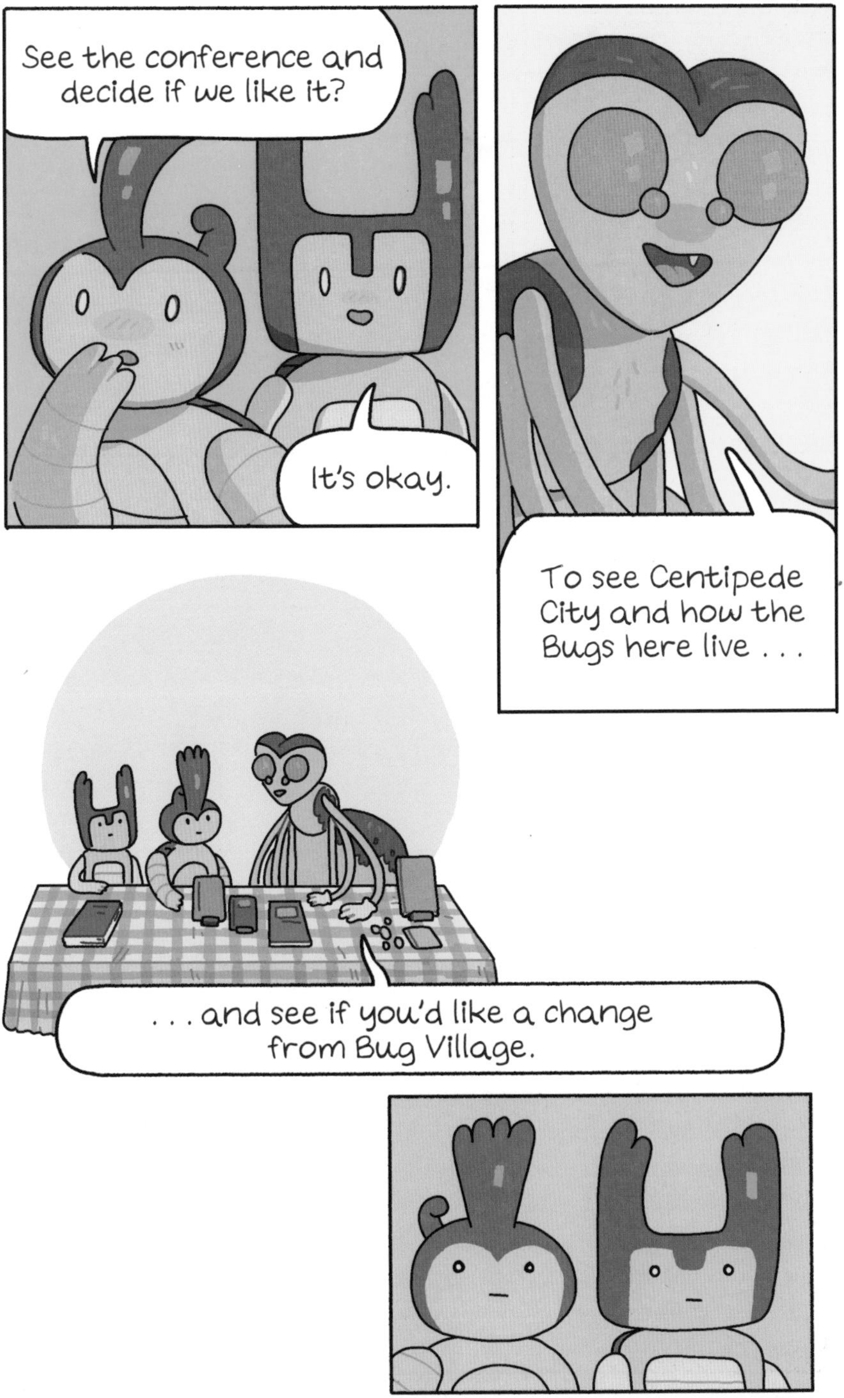
See the conference and decide if we like it?
It's okay.
To see Centipede City and how the Bugs here live . . .
. . . and see if you'd like a change from Bug Village.

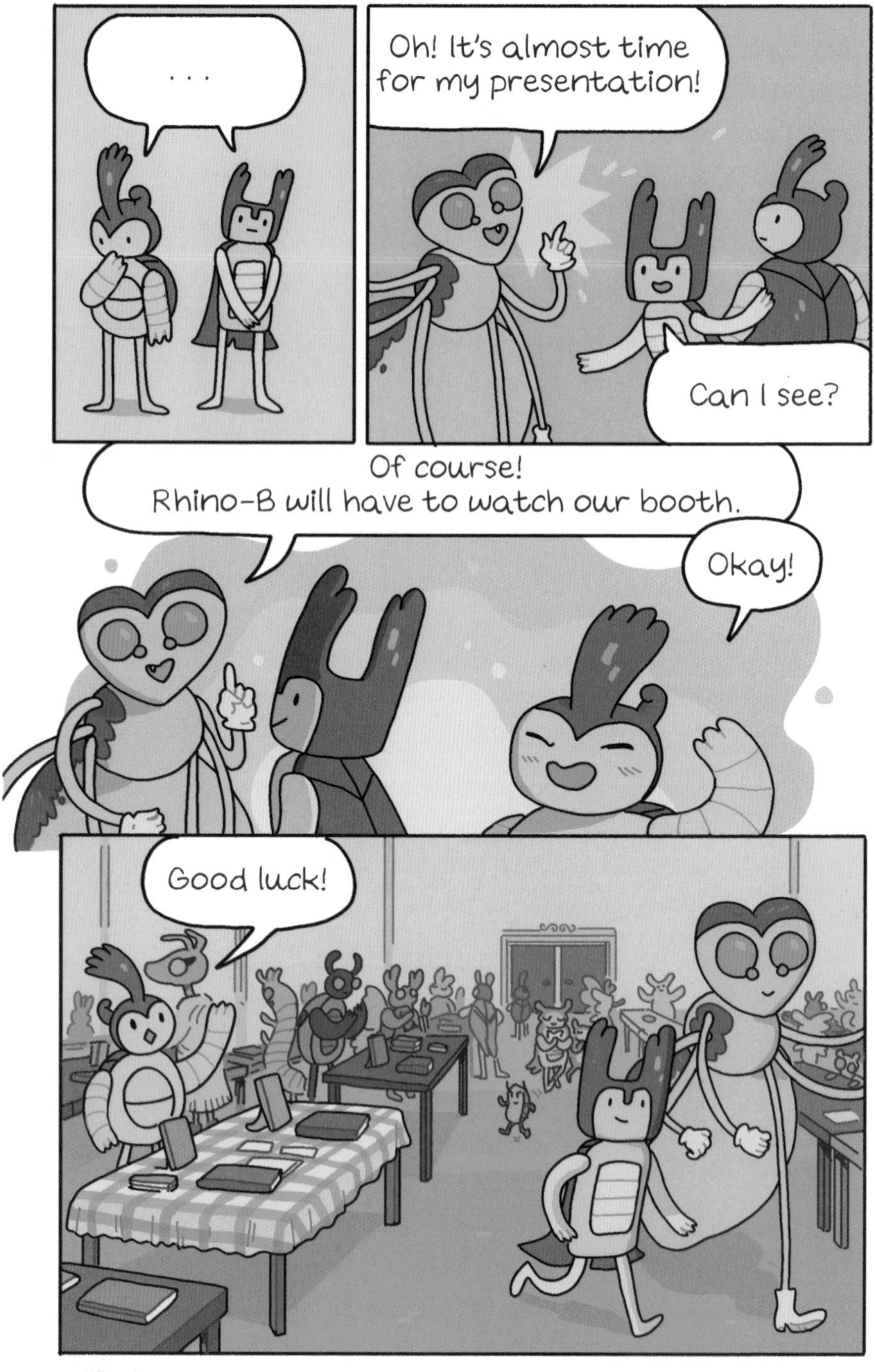
...
Oh! It's almost time for my presentation!
Can I see?
Of course! Rhino-B will have to watch our booth.
Okay!
Good luck!

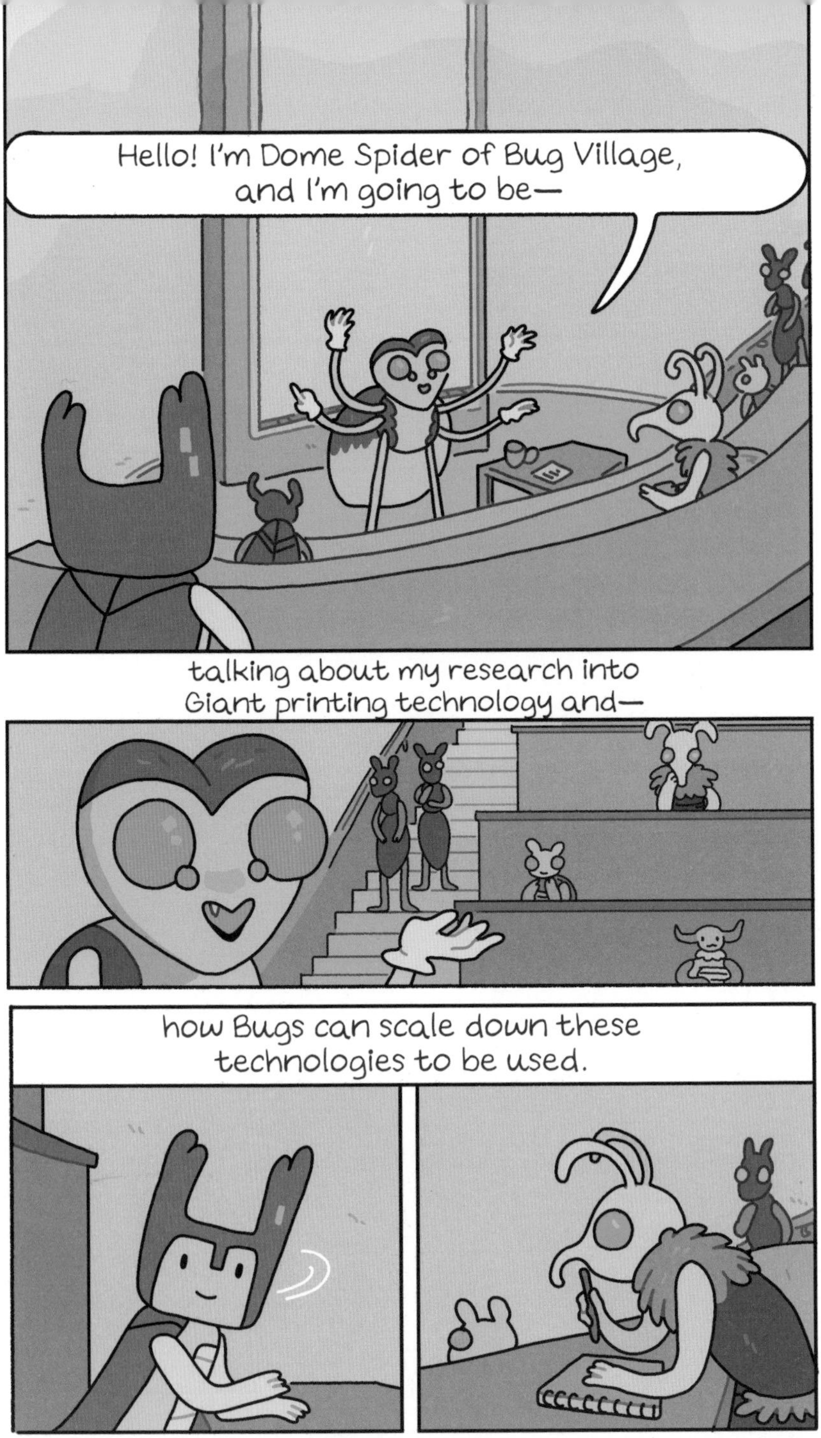
Hello! I'm Dome Spider of Bug Village, and I'm going to be—
talking about my research into Giant printing technology and—
how Bugs can scale down these technologies to be used.

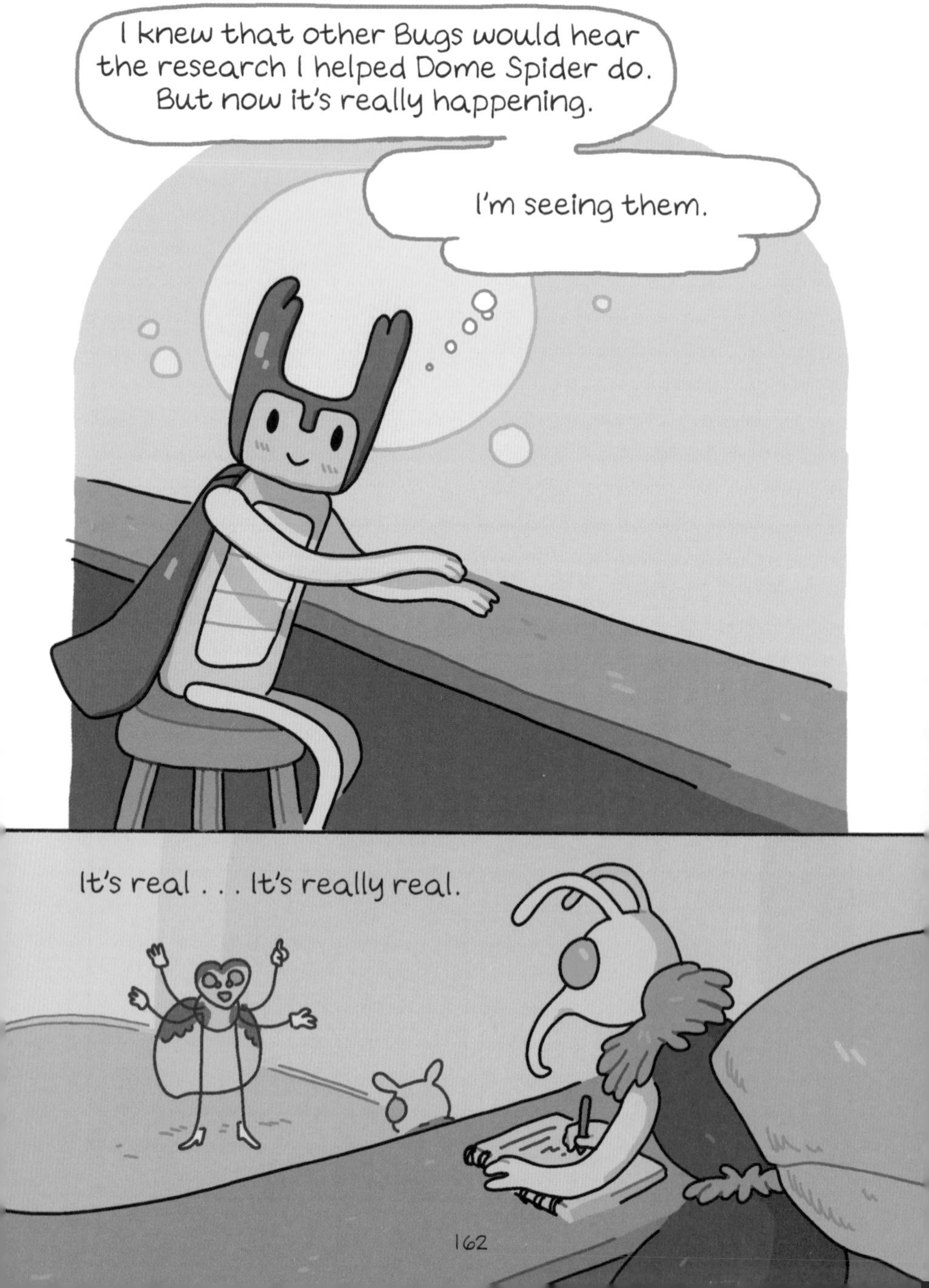
I knew that other Bugs would hear the research I helped Dome Spider do. But now it's really happening.
I'm seeing them.
It's real . . . It's really real.

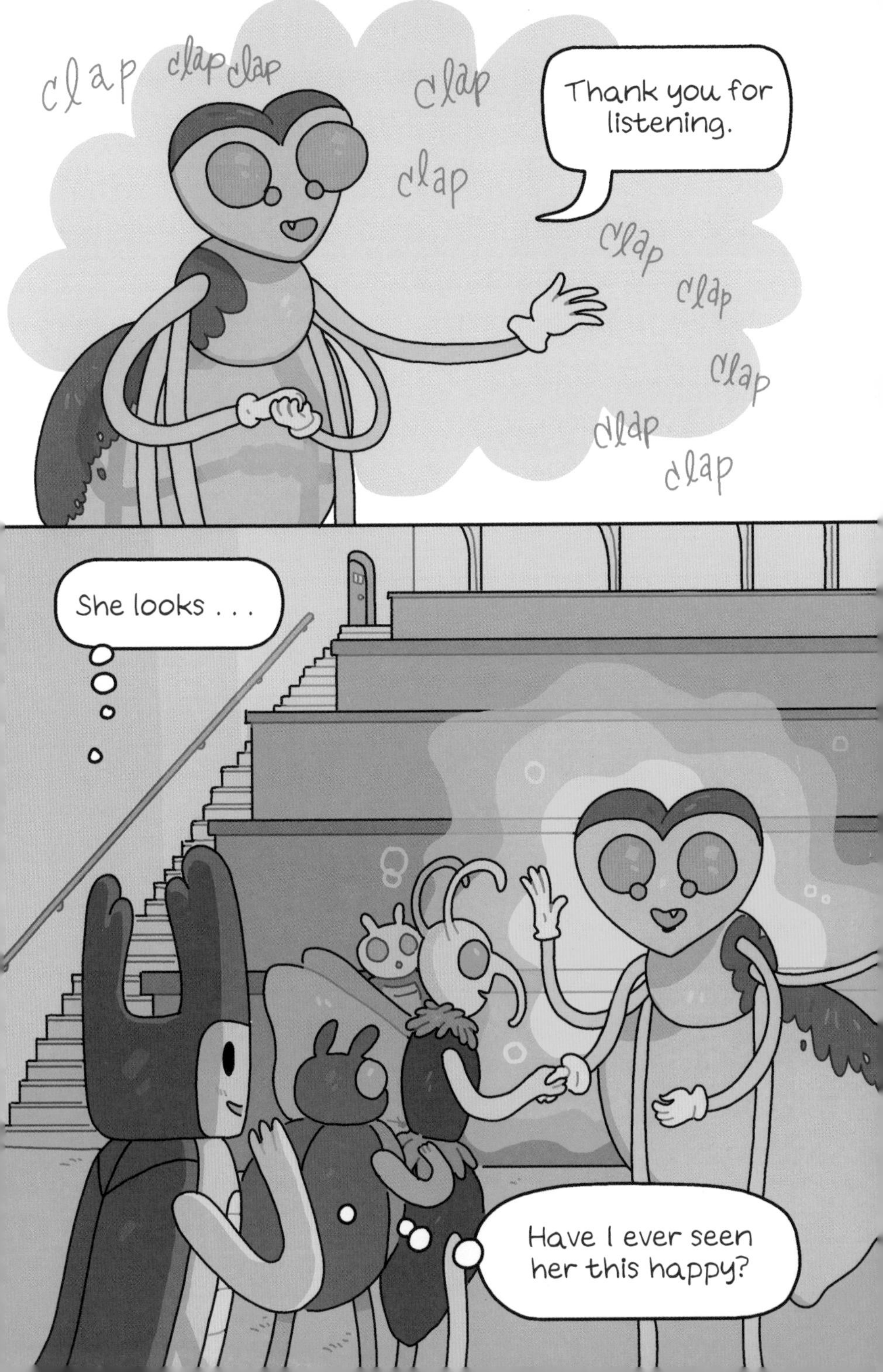
clap clap clap
clap
clap
Thank you for listening.
clap
clap
clap
clap
clap
She looks . . .
Have I ever seen her this happy?

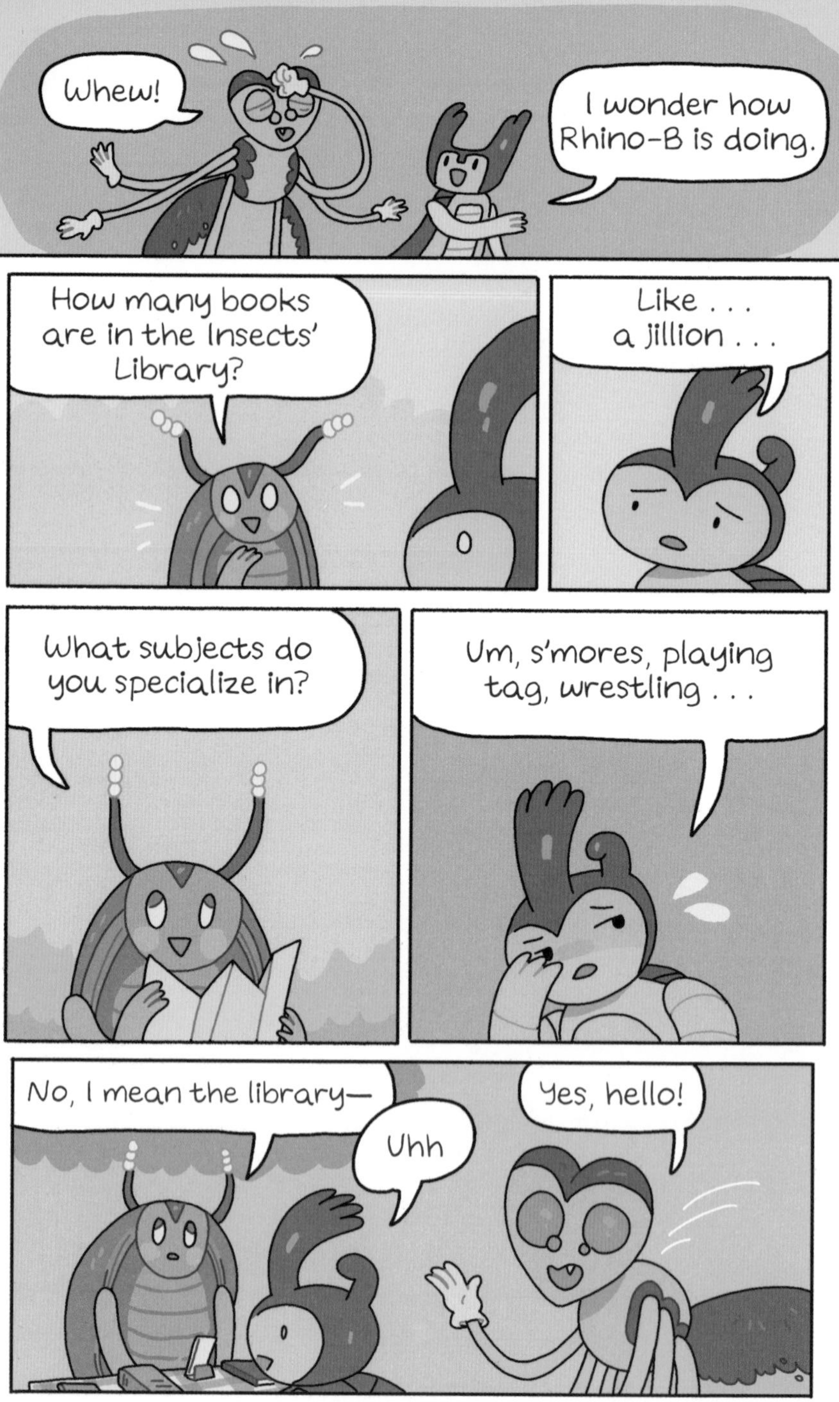
Whew!
I wonder how Rhino-B is doing.
How many books are in the Insects' Library?
Like . . . a jillion . . .
What subjects do you specialize in?
Um, s'mores, playing tag, wrestling . . .
No, I mean the library—
Uhh
Yes, hello!

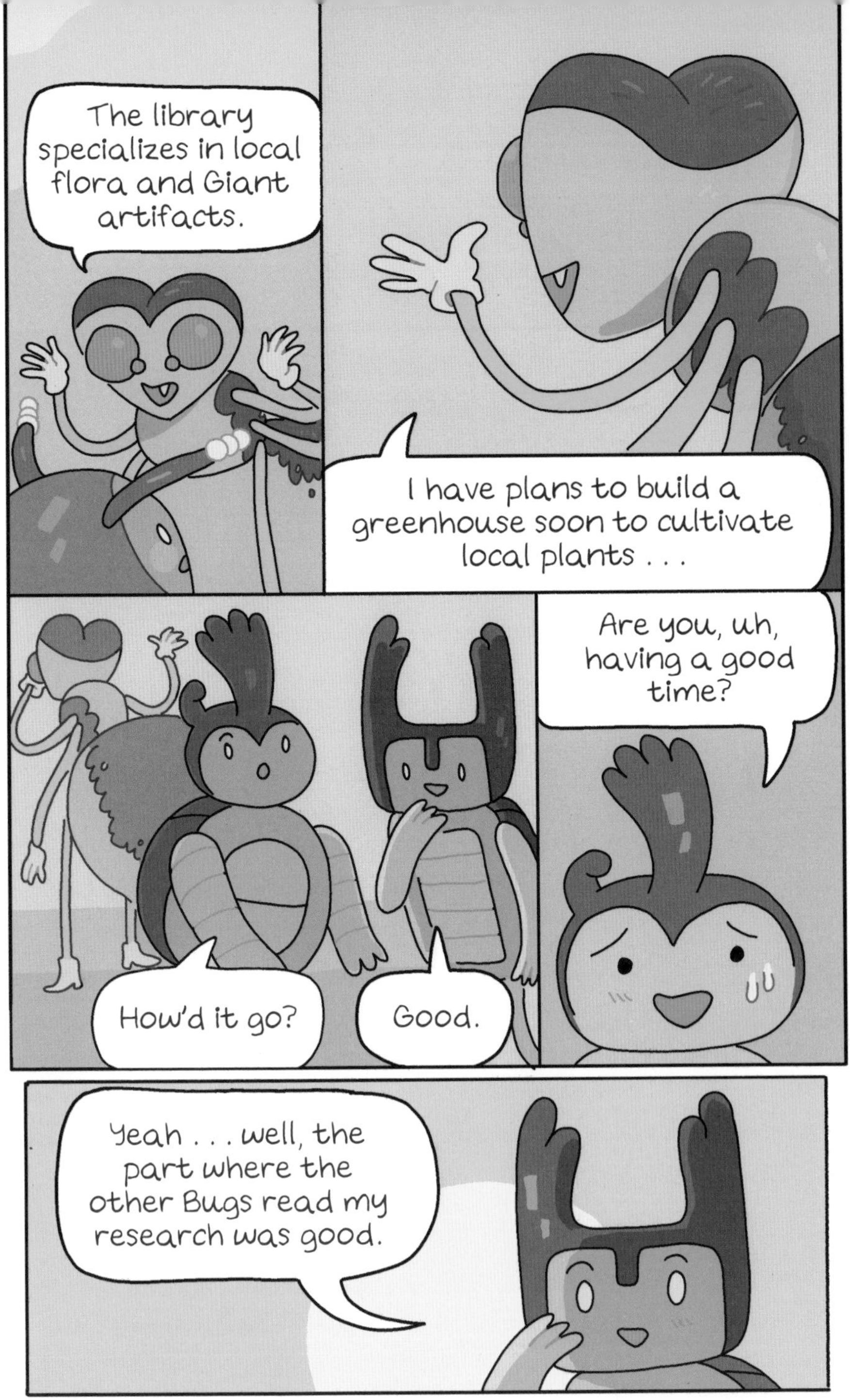

The library specializes in local flora and Giant artifacts.
I have plans to build a greenhouse soon to cultivate local plants . . .
How'd it go?
Good.
Are you, uh, having a good time?
Yeah . . . well, the part where the other Bugs read my research was good.

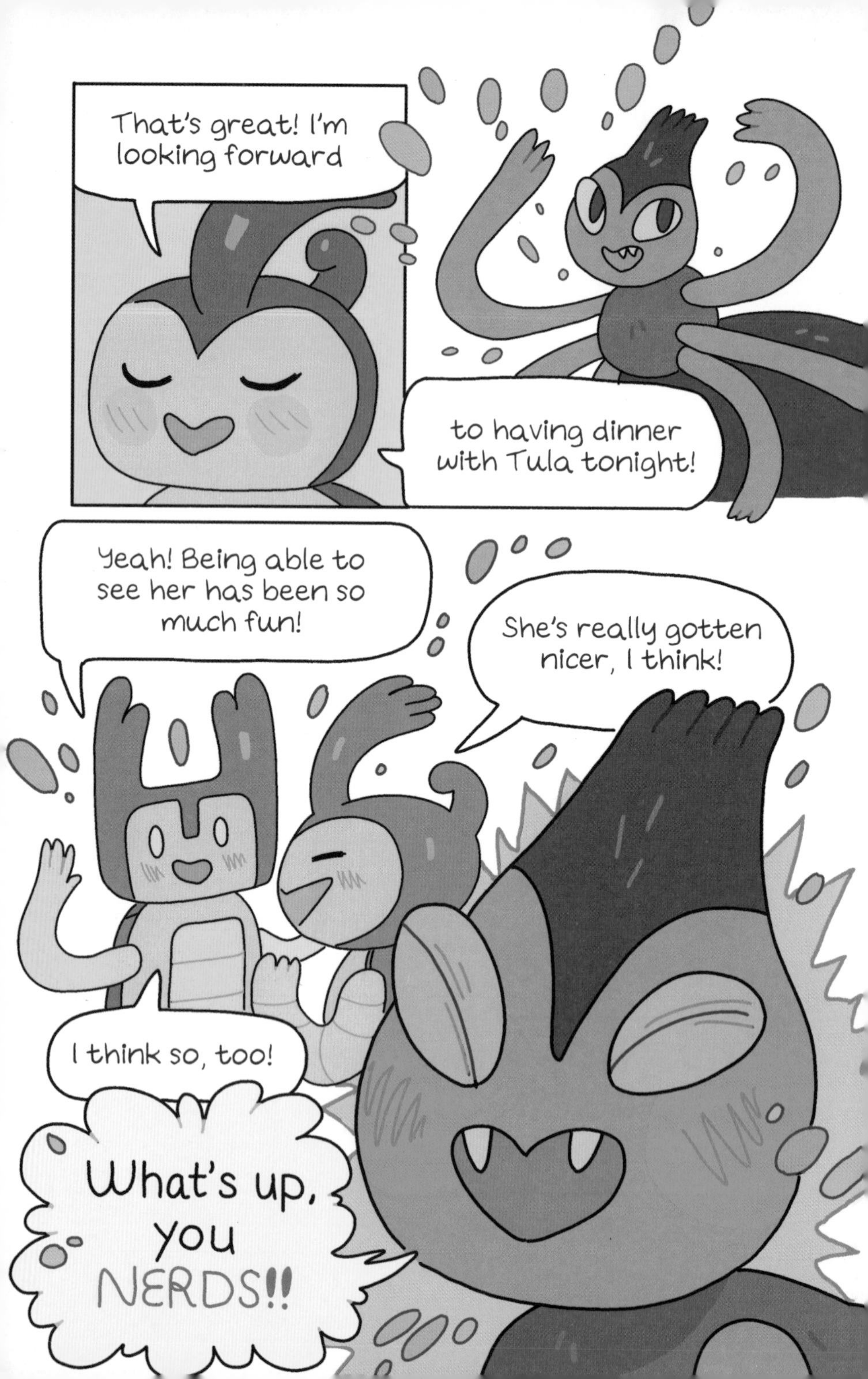
That's great! I'm looking forward
to having dinner with Tula tonight!
Yeah! Being able to see her has been so much fun!
She's really gotten nicer, I think!
I think so, too!
What's up, you NERDS!!

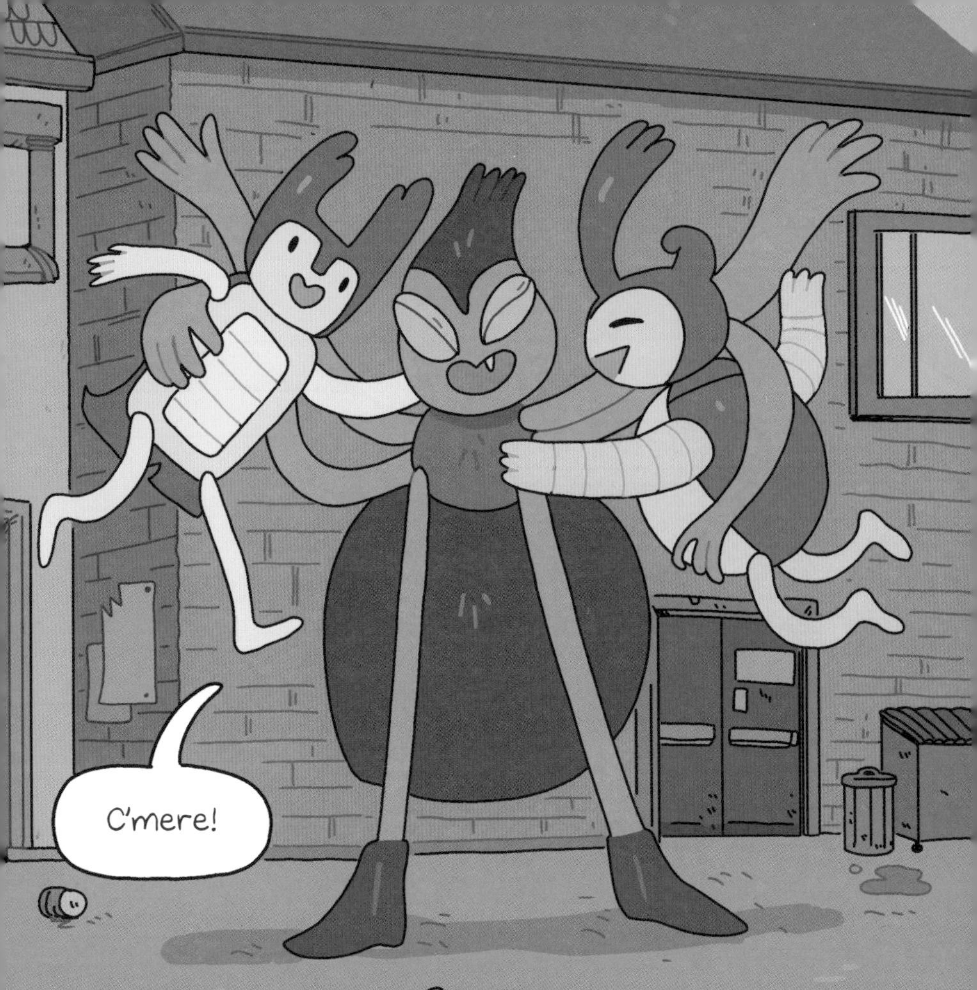
C'mere!
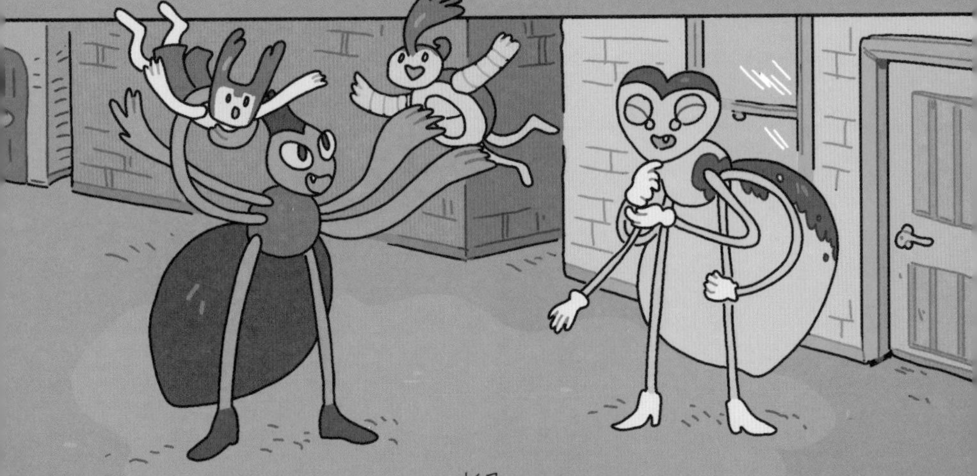

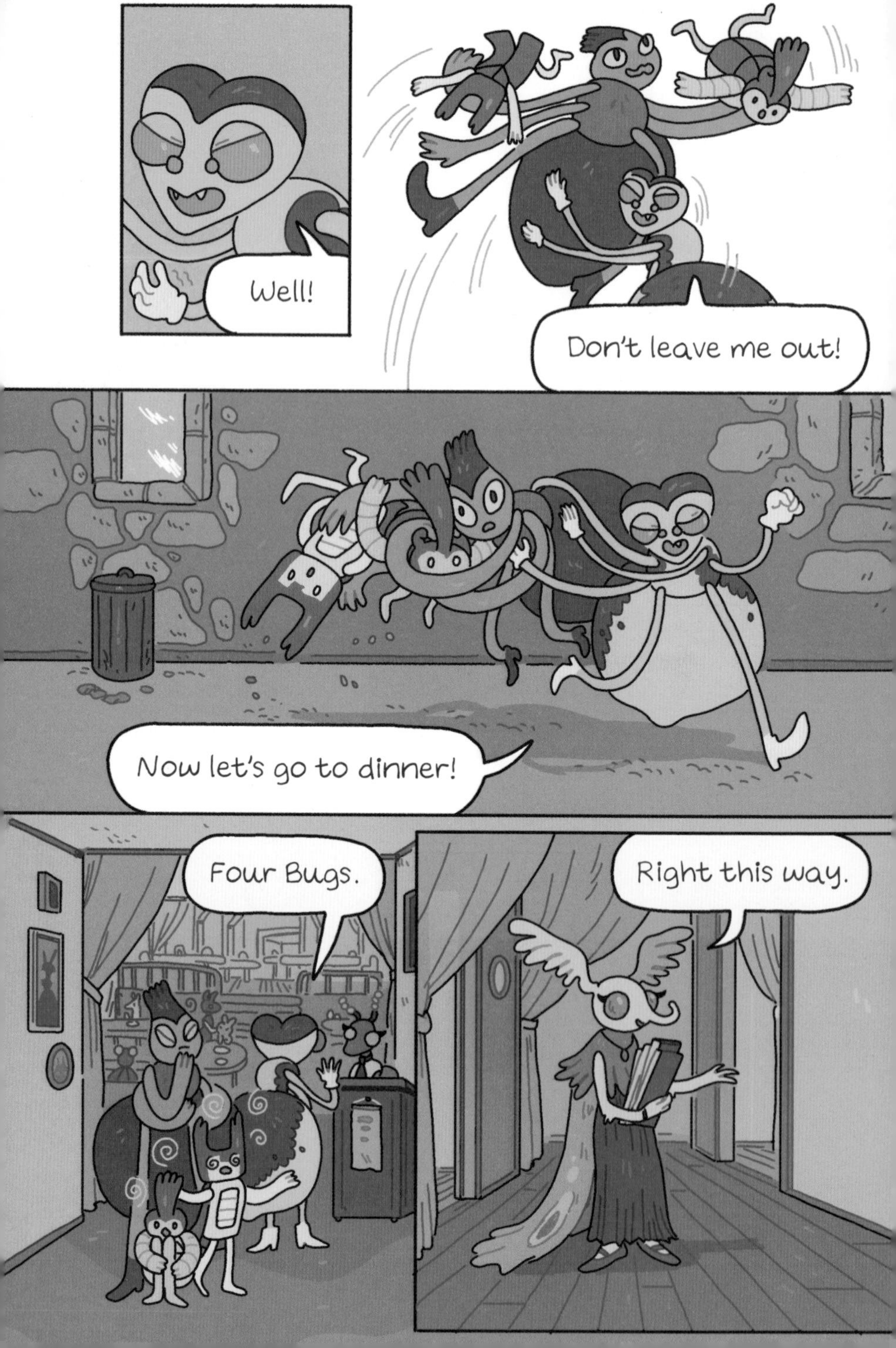
Well!
Don't leave me out!
Now let's go to dinner!
Four Bugs.
Right this way.

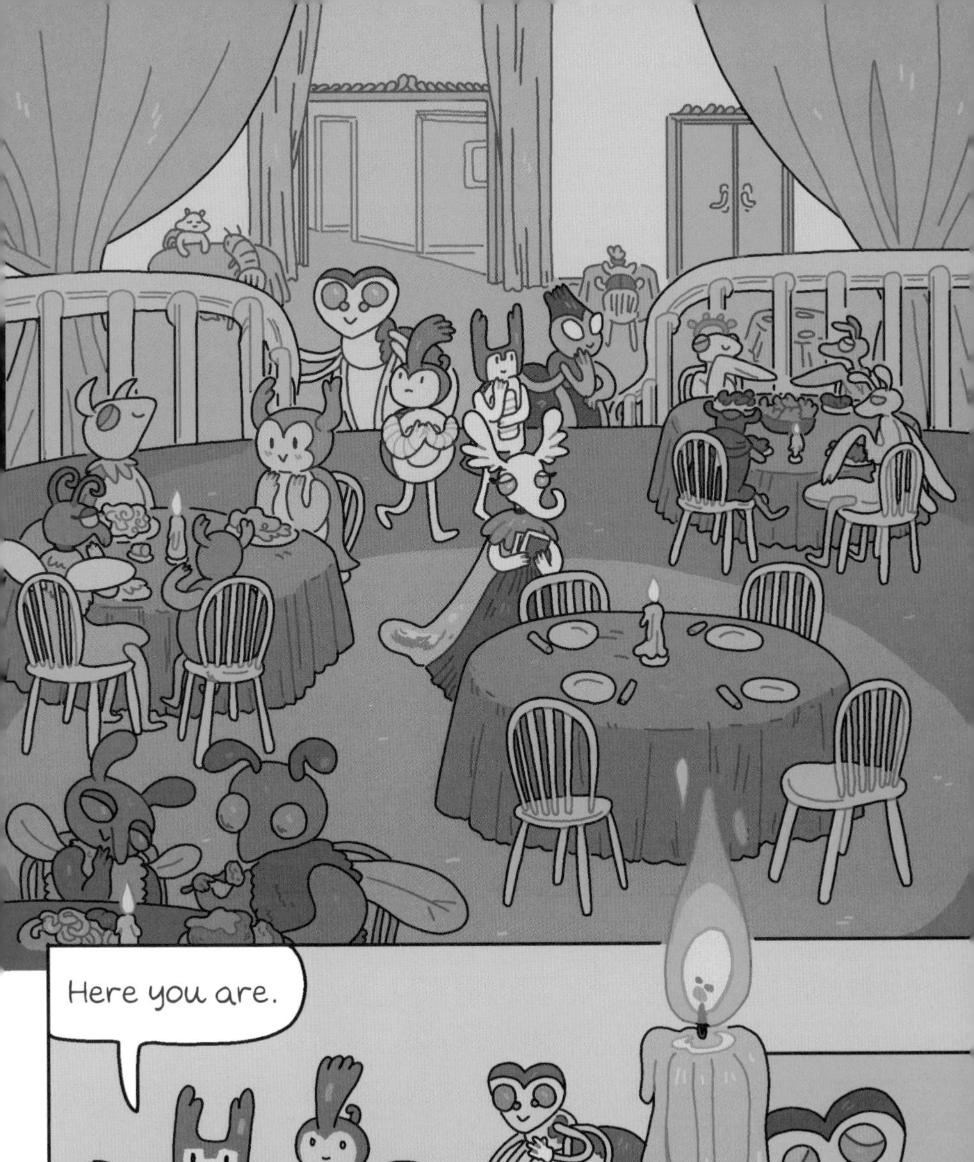

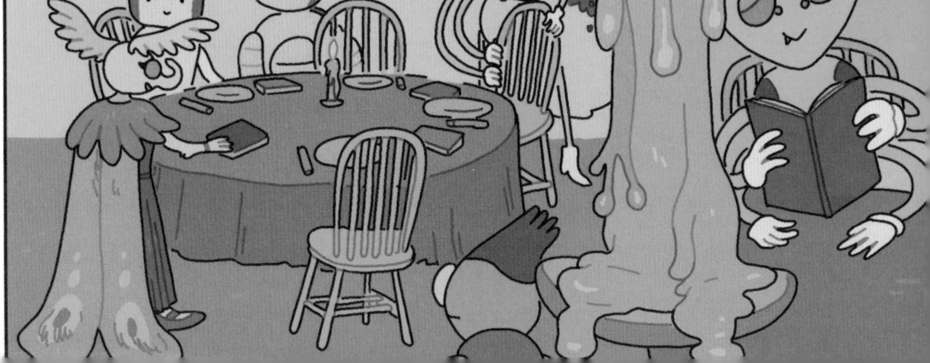
Here you are.

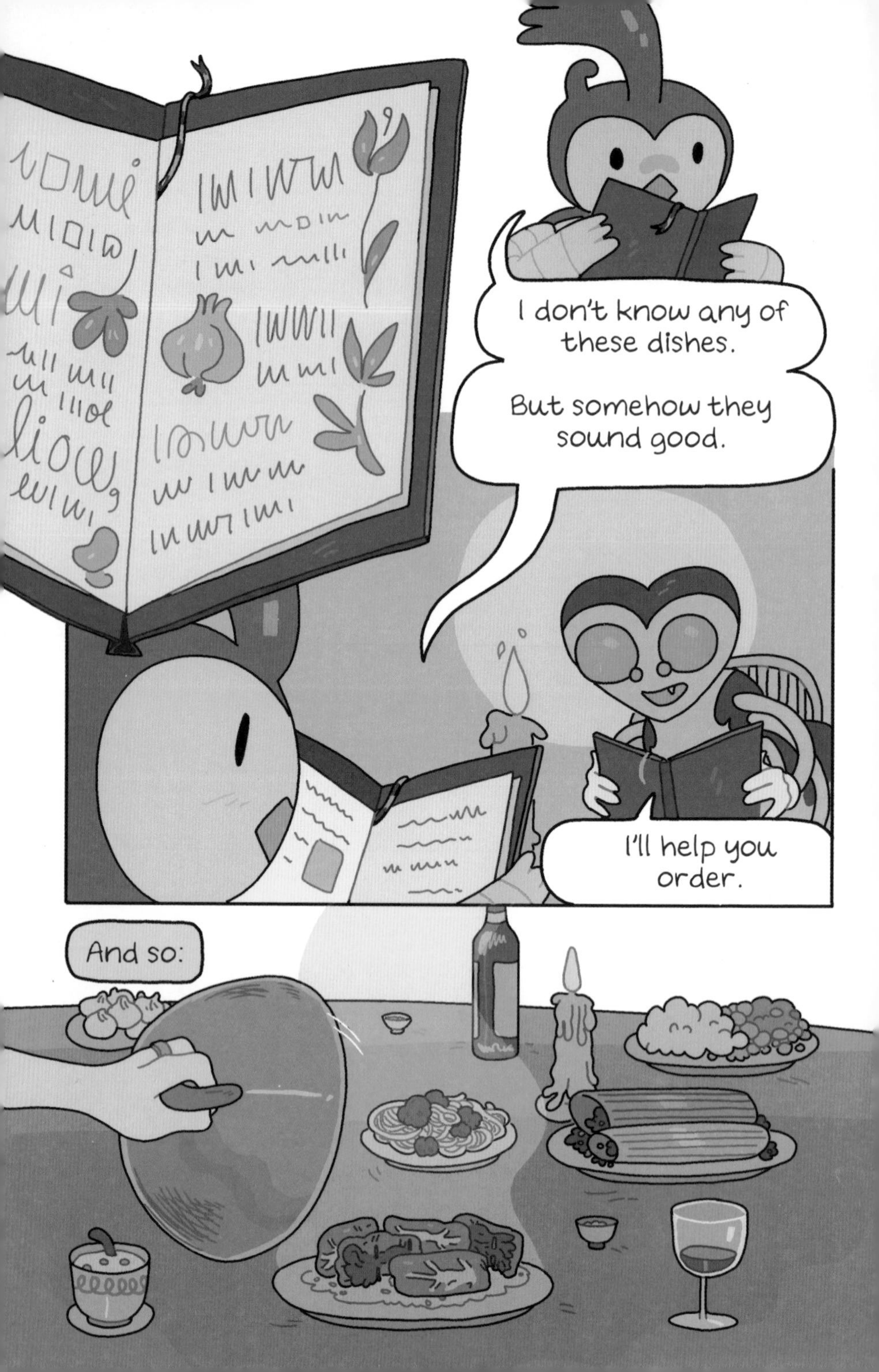
I don't know any of these dishes.
But somehow they sound good.
I'll help you order.
And so:

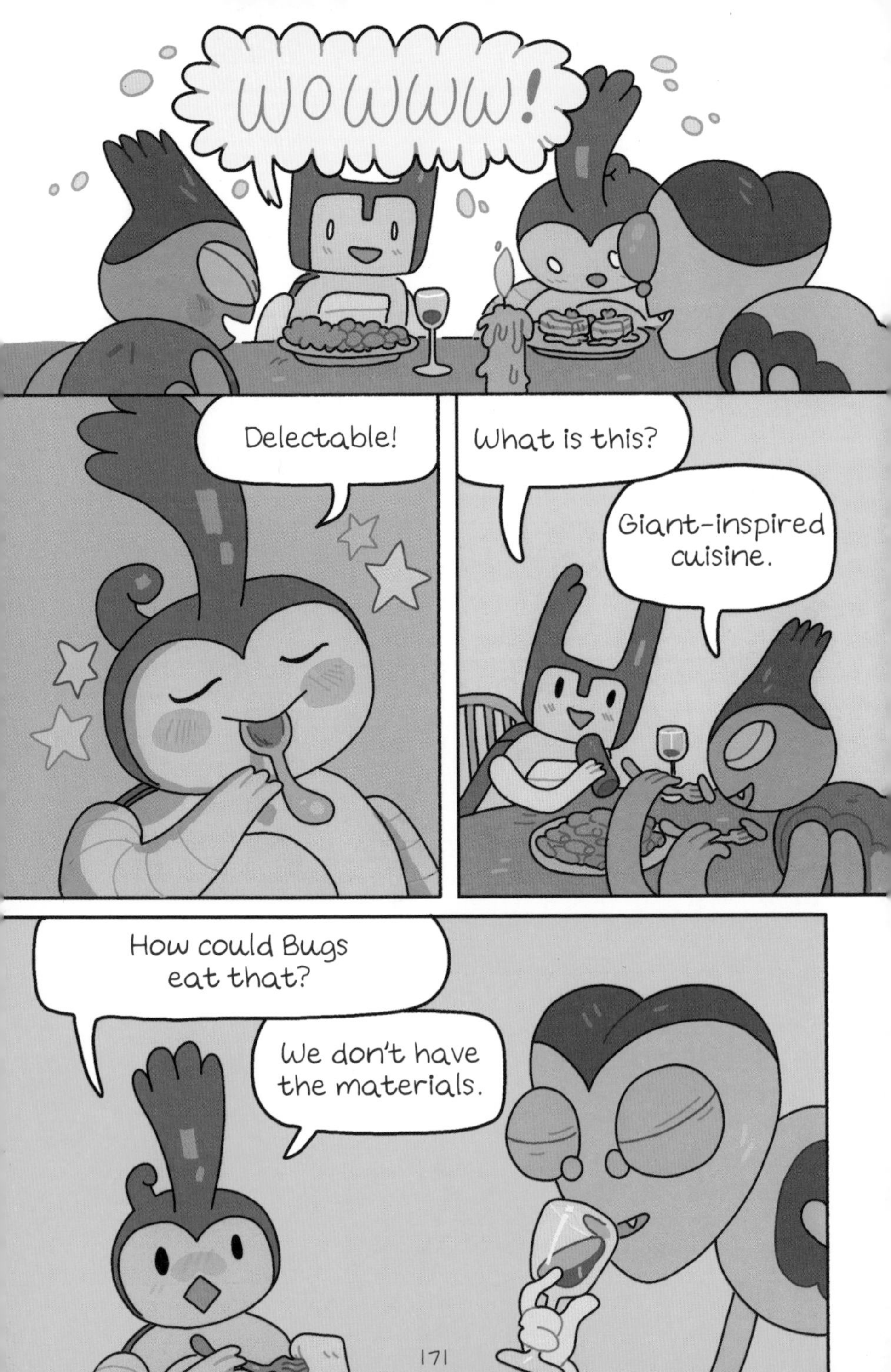
WOWWW!
Delectable!
What is this?
Giant-inspired cuisine.
How could Bugs eat that?
We don't have the materials.

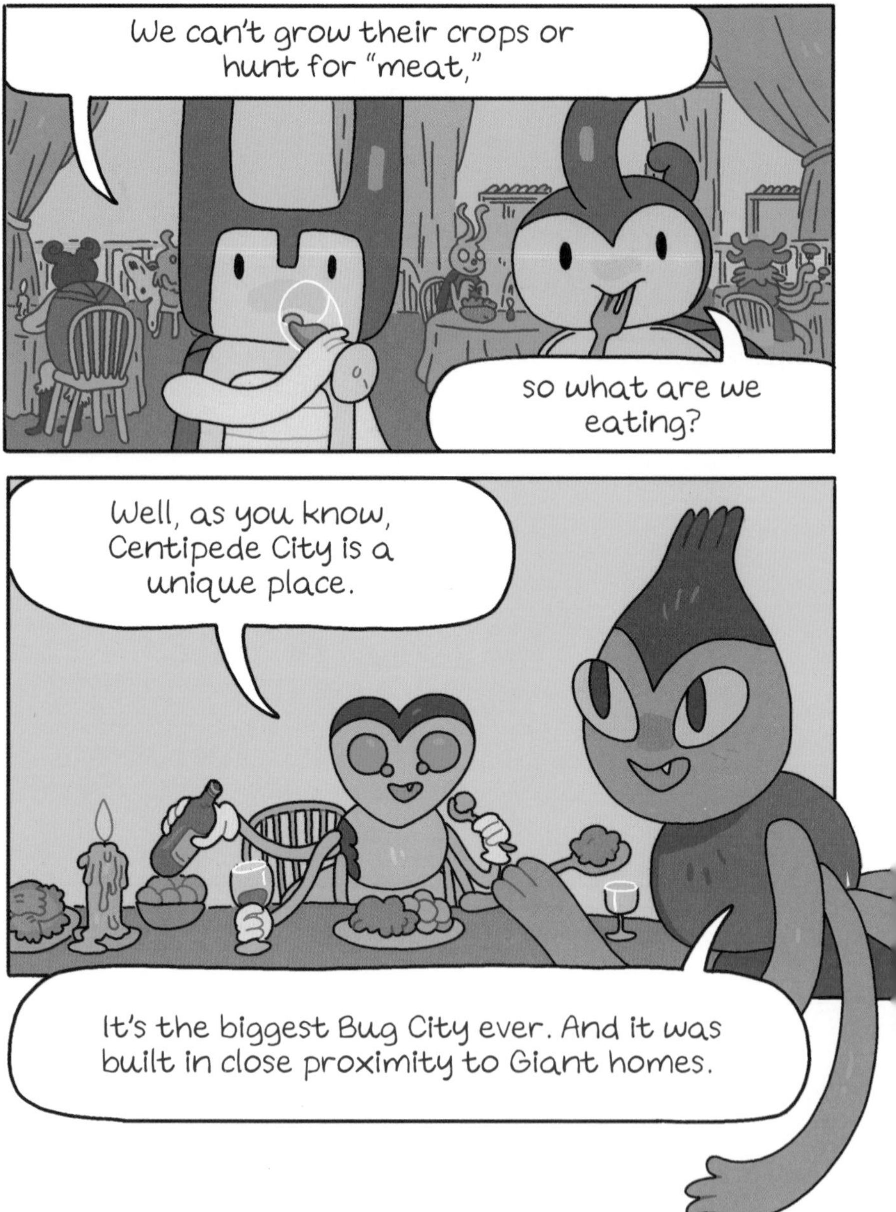
We can't grow their crops or hunt for "meat,"
so what are we eating?
Well, as you know, Centipede City is a unique place.
It's the biggest Bug City ever. And it was built in close proximity to Giant homes.

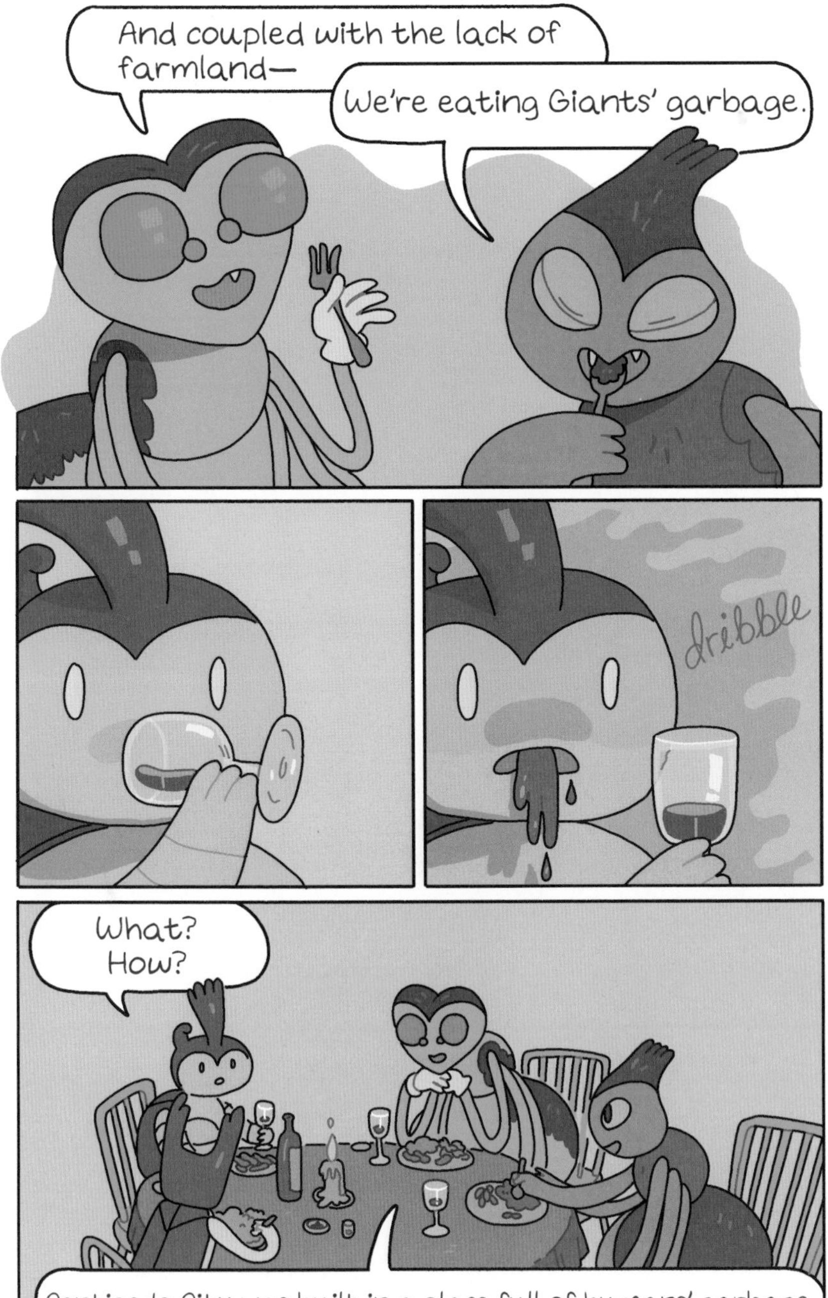
And coupled with the lack of farmland—
We're eating Giants' garbage.
dribble
What? How?
Centipede City was built in a place full of humans' garbage.

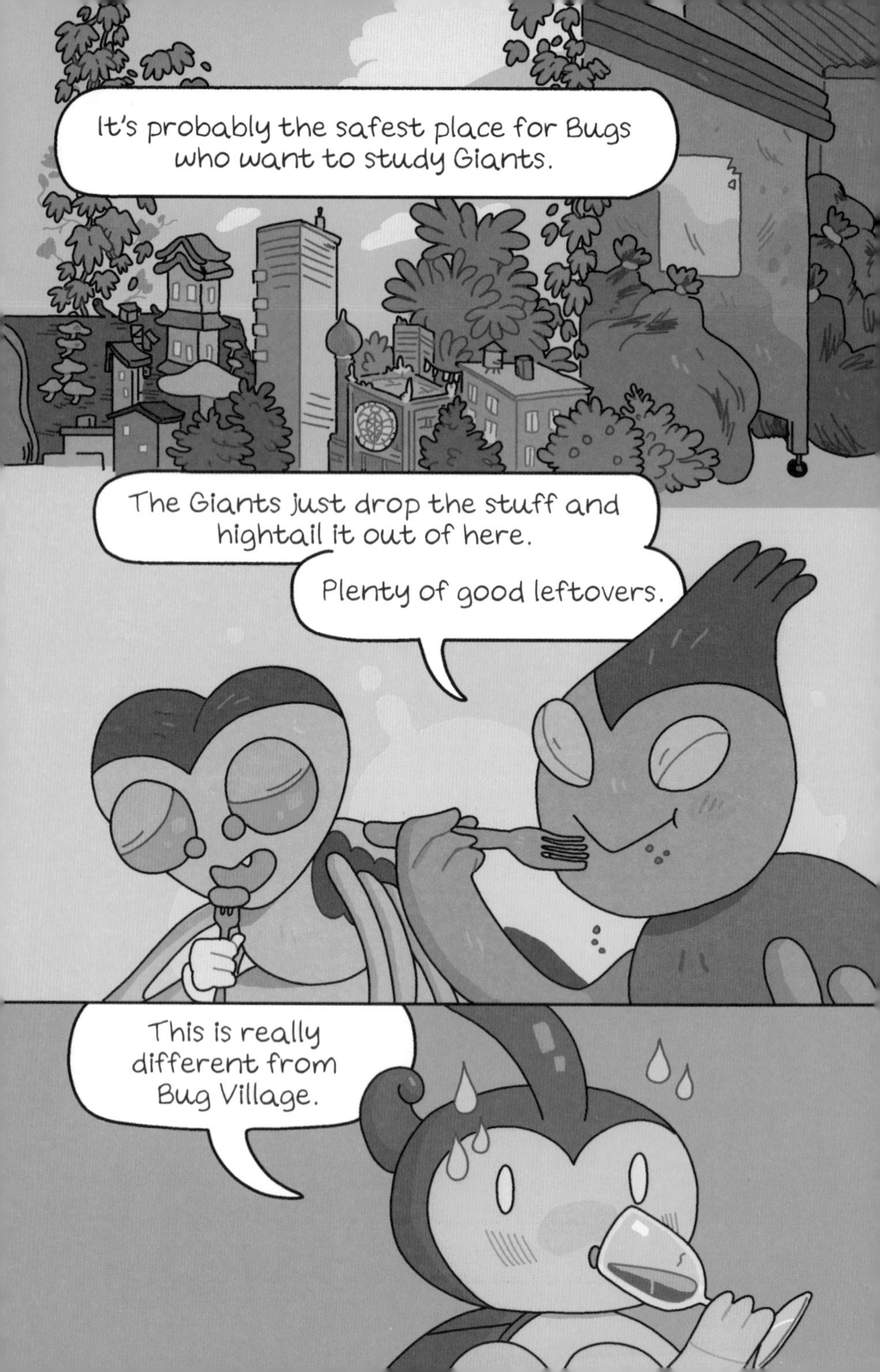
It's probably the safest place for Bugs who want to study Giants.
The Giants just drop the stuff and hightail it out of here.
Plenty of good leftovers.
This is really different from Bug Village.

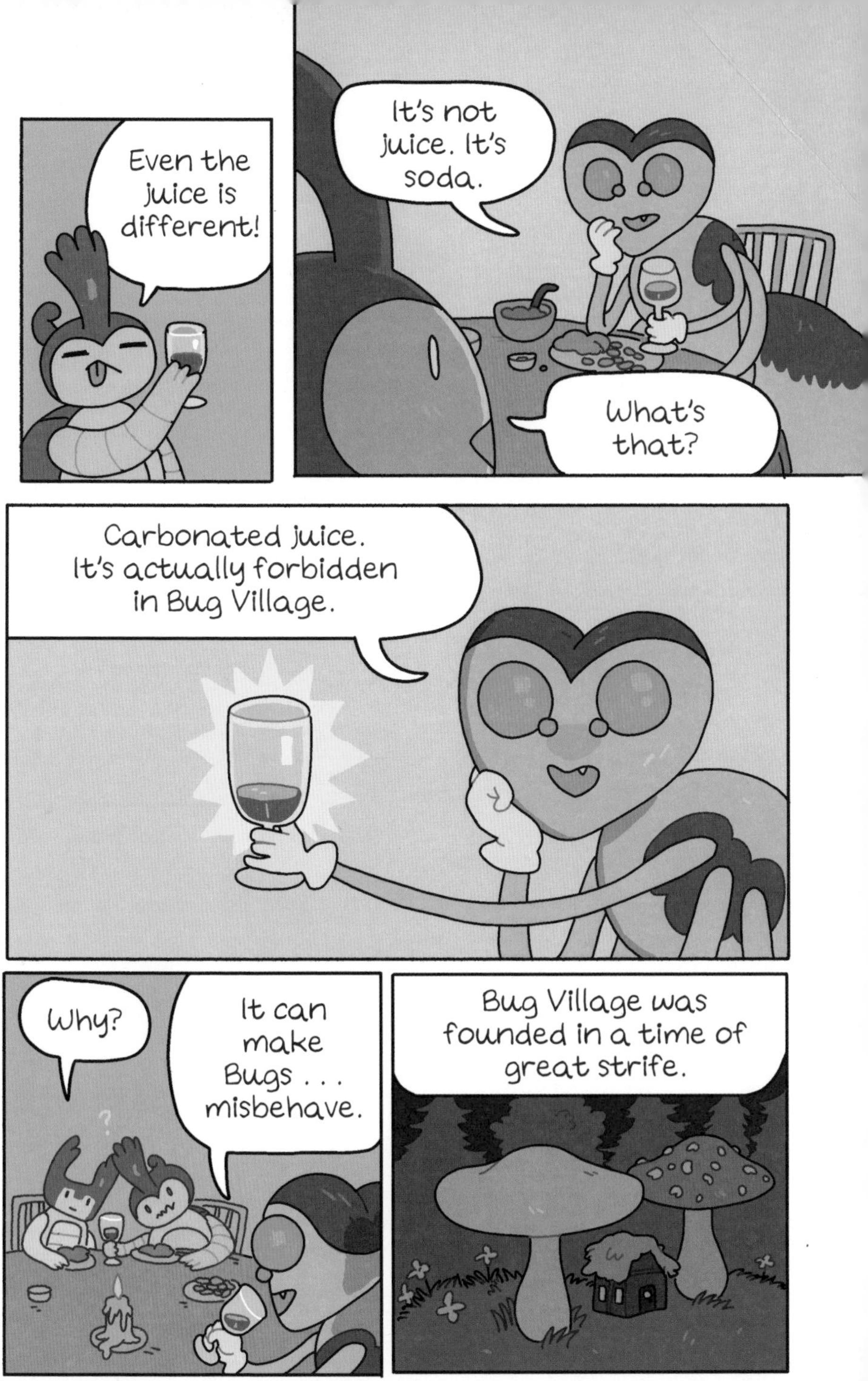
Even the juice is different!
It's not juice. It's soda.
What's that?
Carbonated juice. It's actually forbidden in Bug Village.
Why?
It can make Bugs . . . misbehave.
Bug Village was founded in a time of great strife.

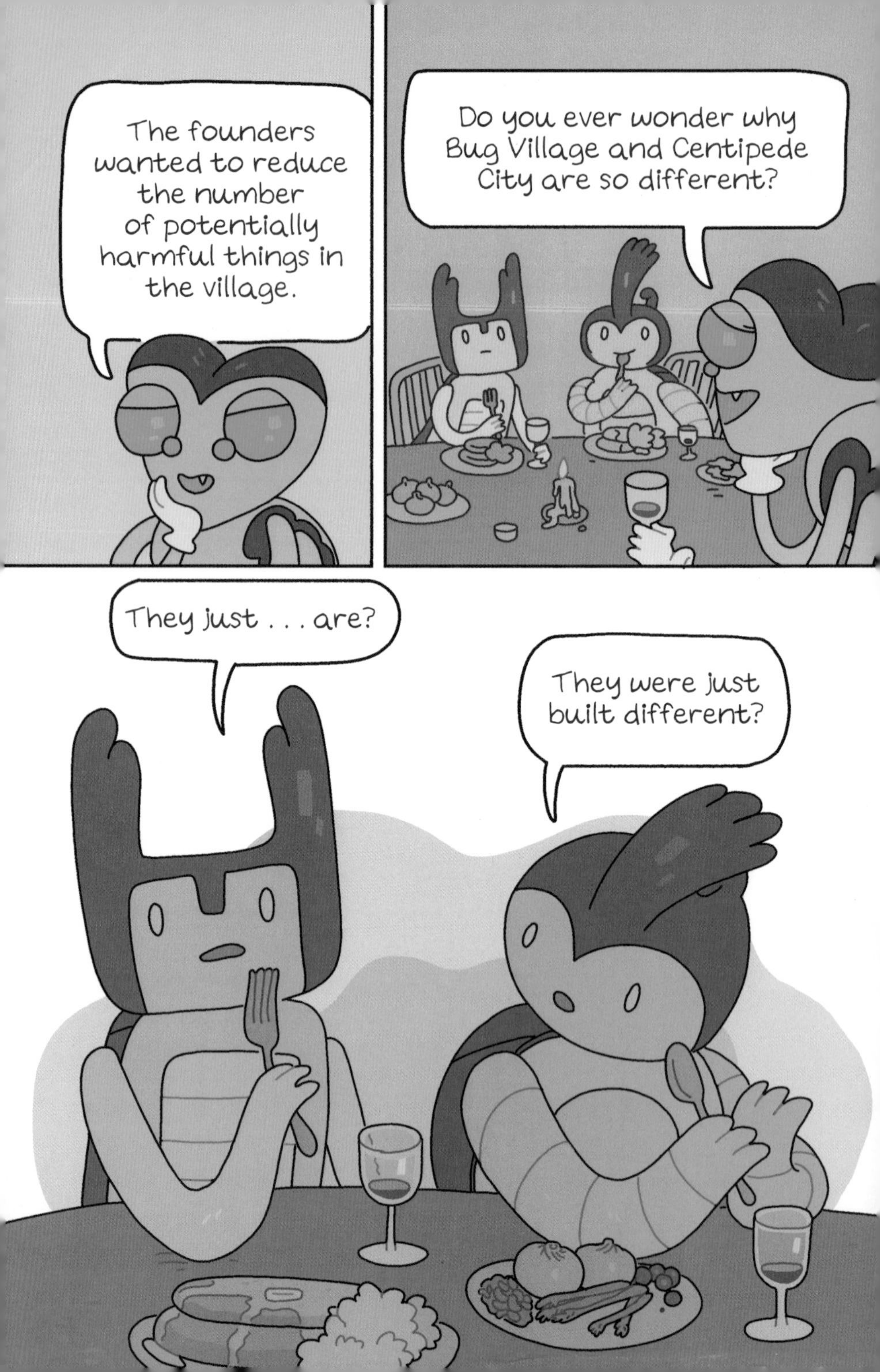
The founders wanted to reduce the number of potentially harmful things in the village.
Do you ever wonder why Bug Village and Centipede City are so different?
They just . . . are?
They were just built different?

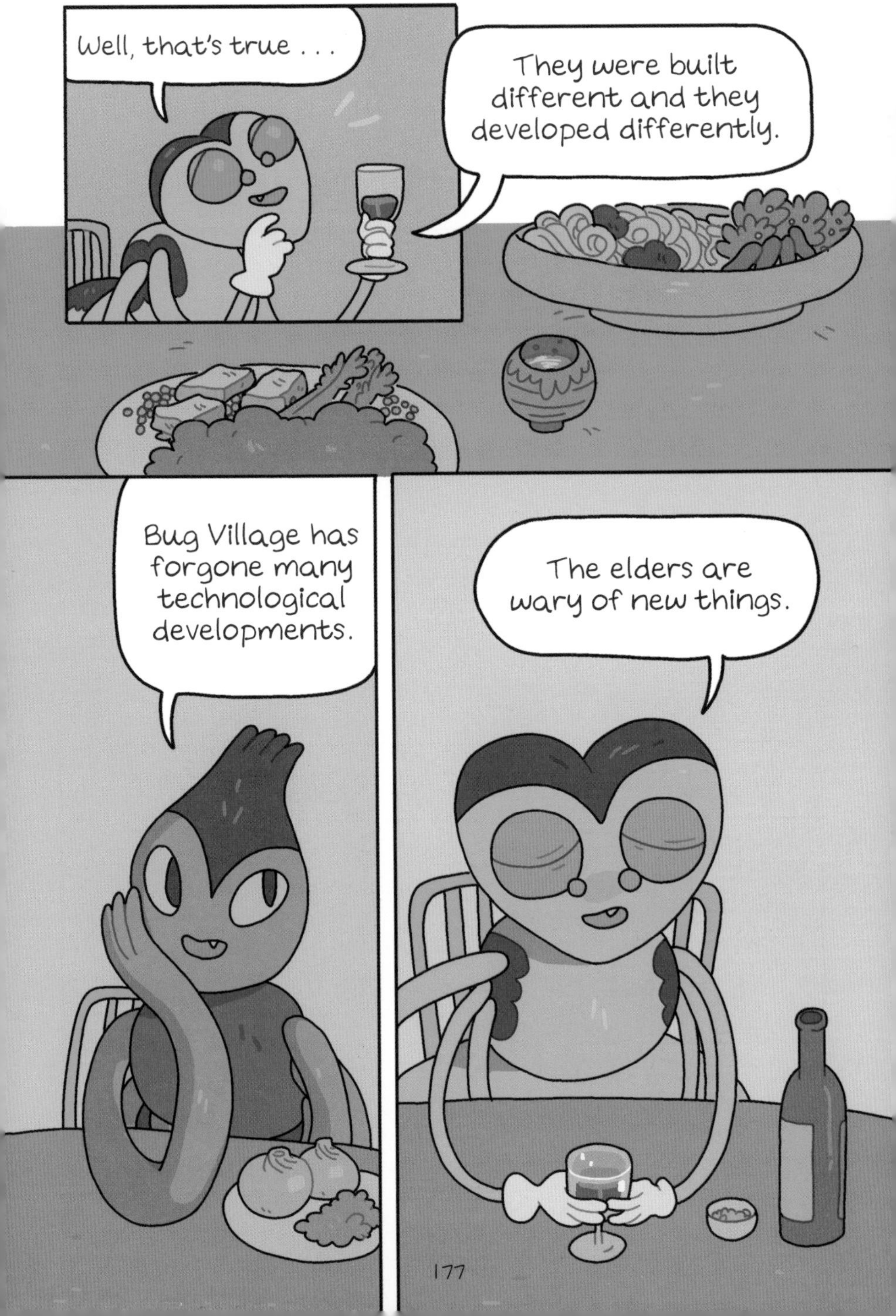
Well, that's true . . .
They were built different and they developed differently.
Bug Village has forgone many technological developments.
The elders are wary of new things.

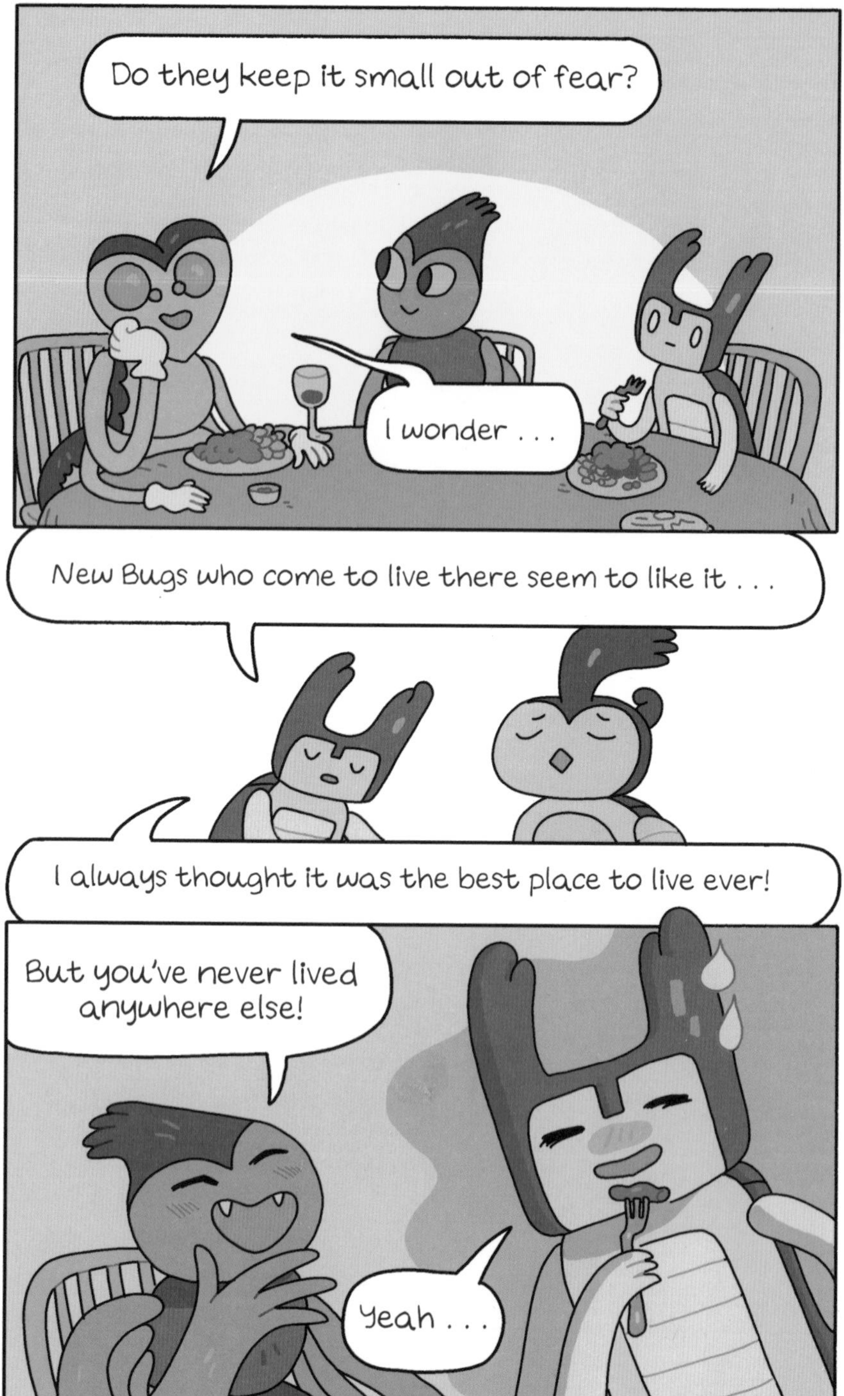
Do they keep it small out of fear?
I wonder . . .
New Bugs who come to live there seem to like it . . .
I always thought it was the best place to live ever!
But you've never lived anywhere else!
Yeah . . .

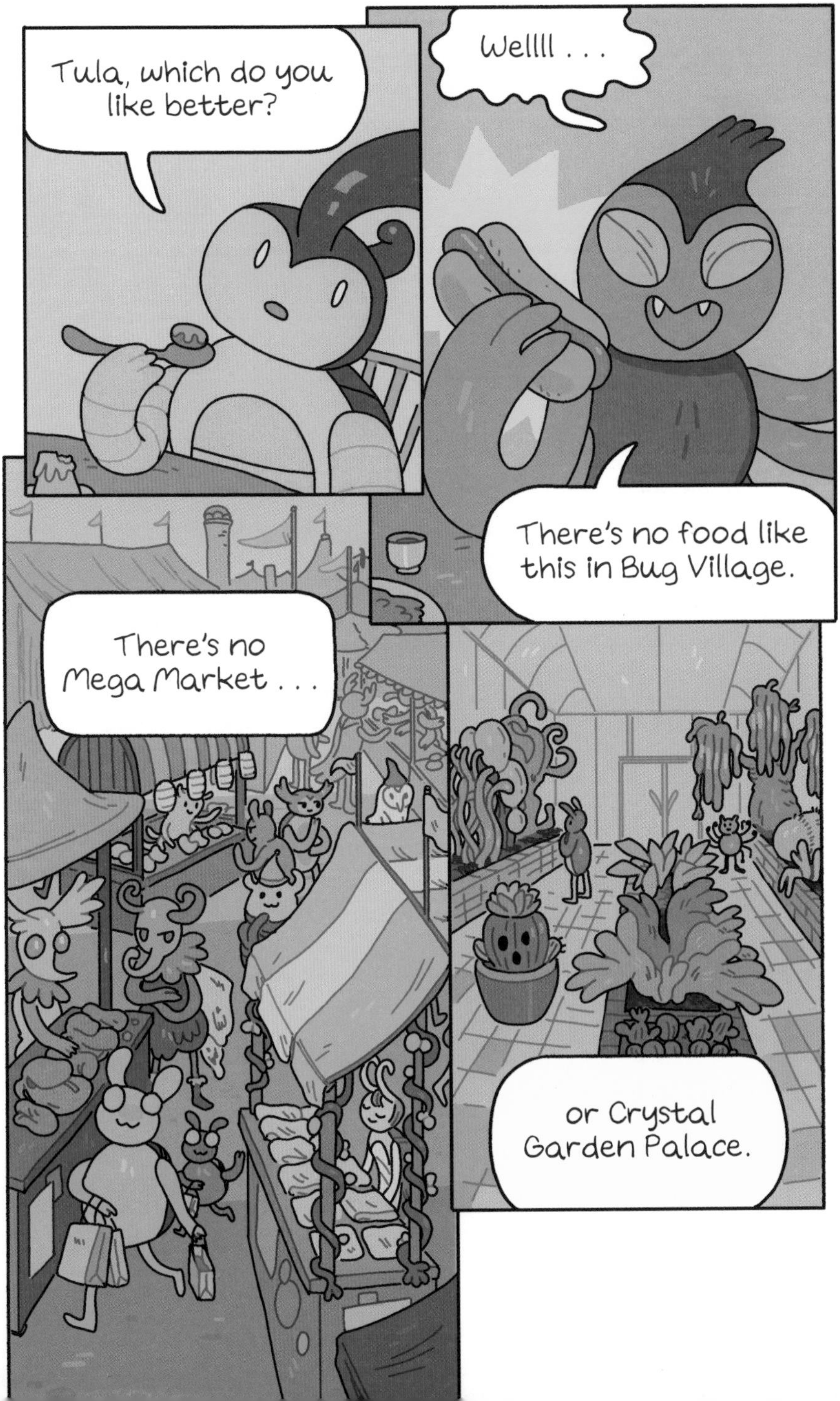
Tula, which do you like better?
Wellll . . .
There's no food like this in Bug Village.
There's no Mega Market . . .
or Crystal Garden Palace.

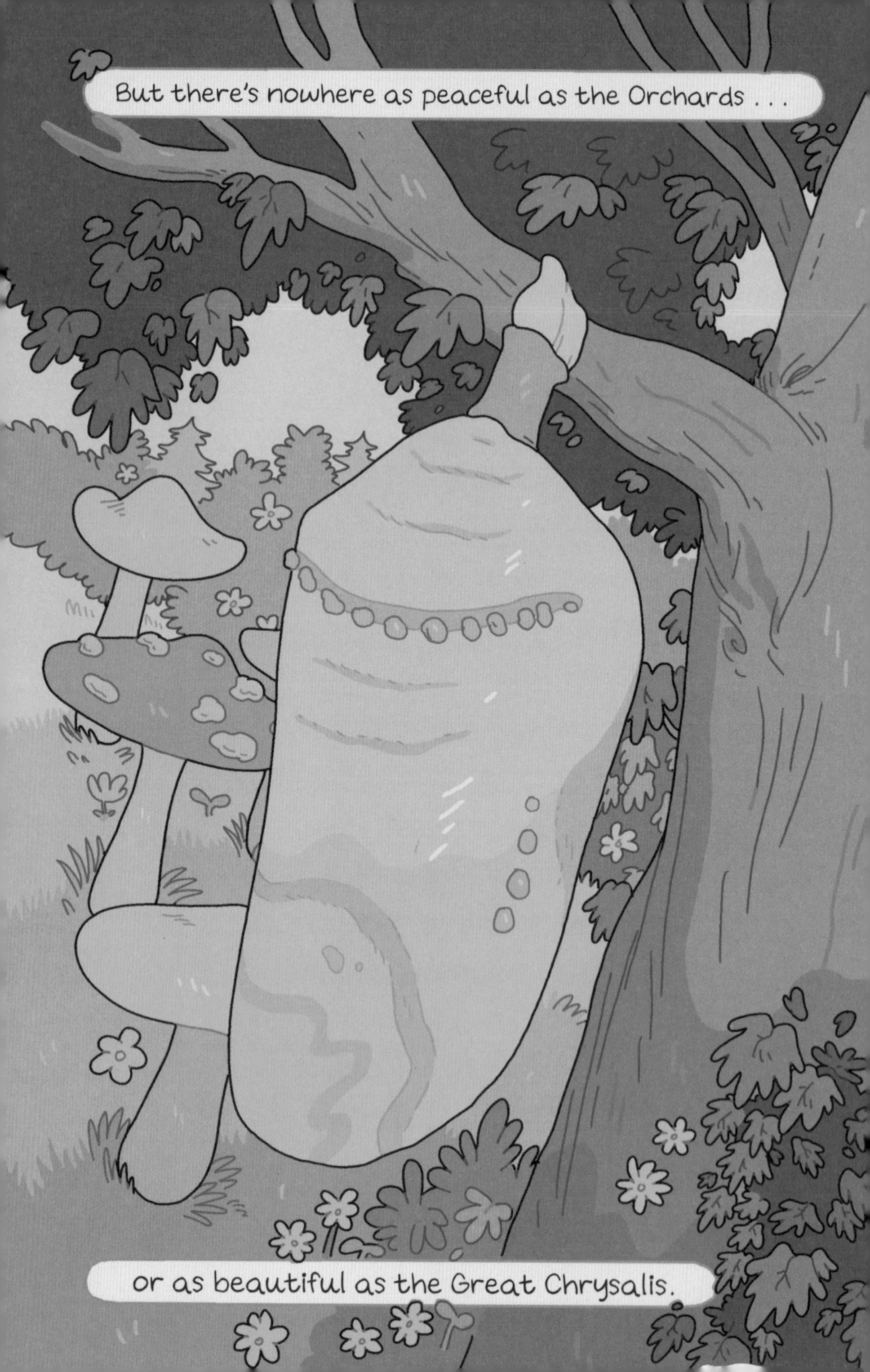
But there's nowhere as peaceful as the Orchards . . .
or as beautiful as the Great Chrysalis.

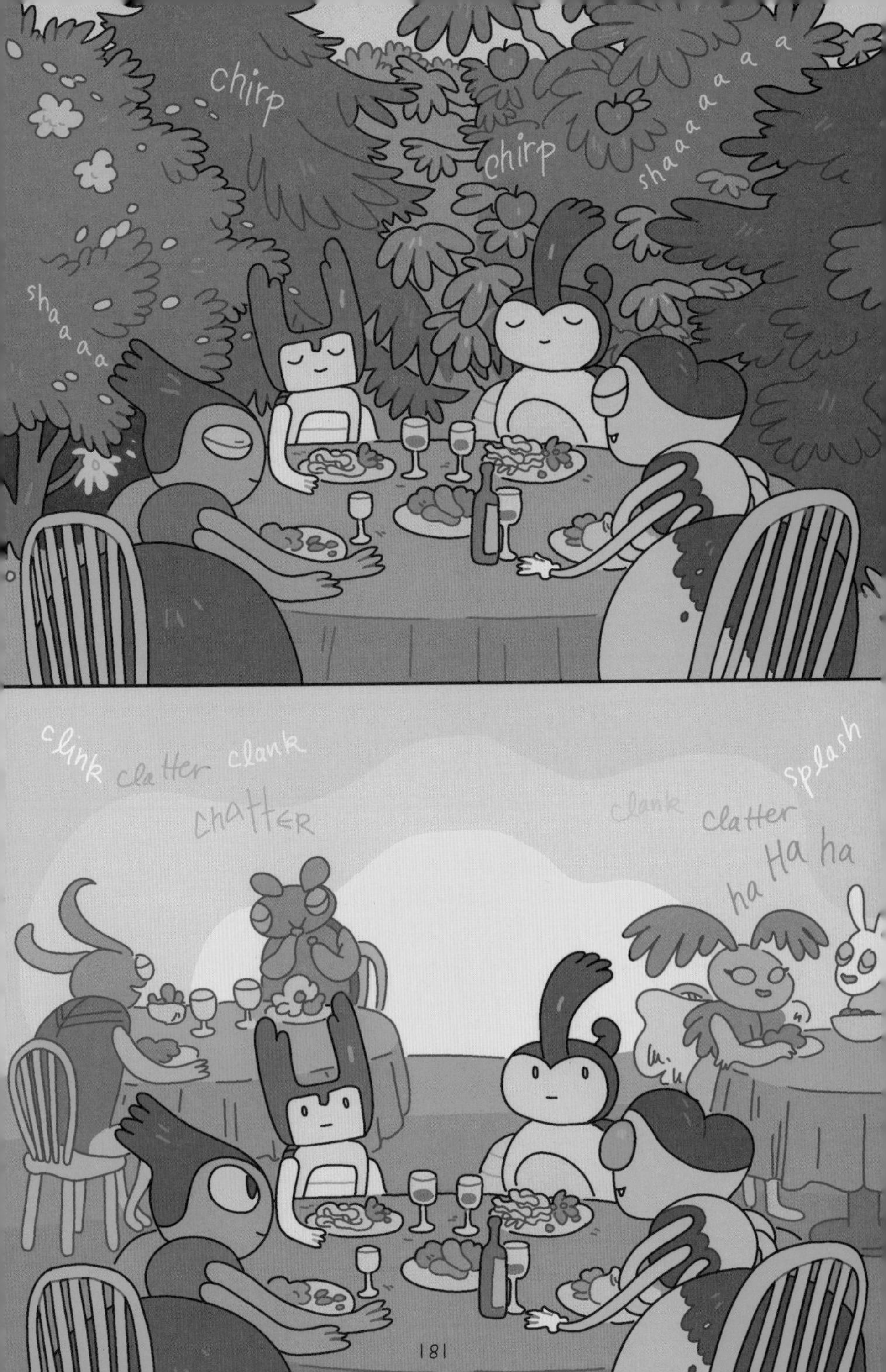
chirp
chirp
shaaaaaaa
shaaaaa
clink clatter clank
chatter
clank clatter
splash
ha Ha ha

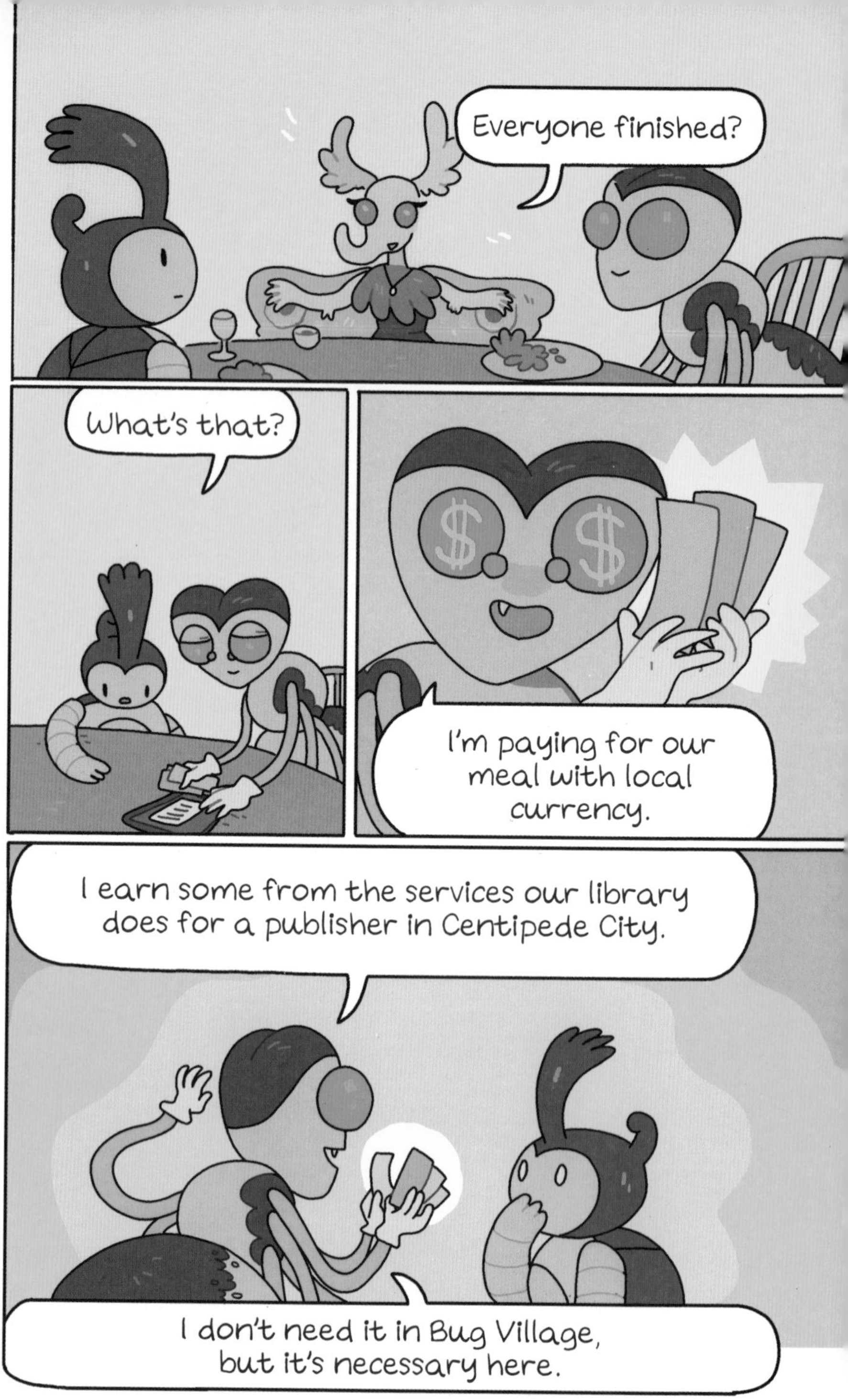
Everyone finished?
What's that?
I'm paying for our meal with local currency.
I earn some from the services our library does for a publisher in Centipede City.
I don't need it in Bug Village, but it's necessary here.

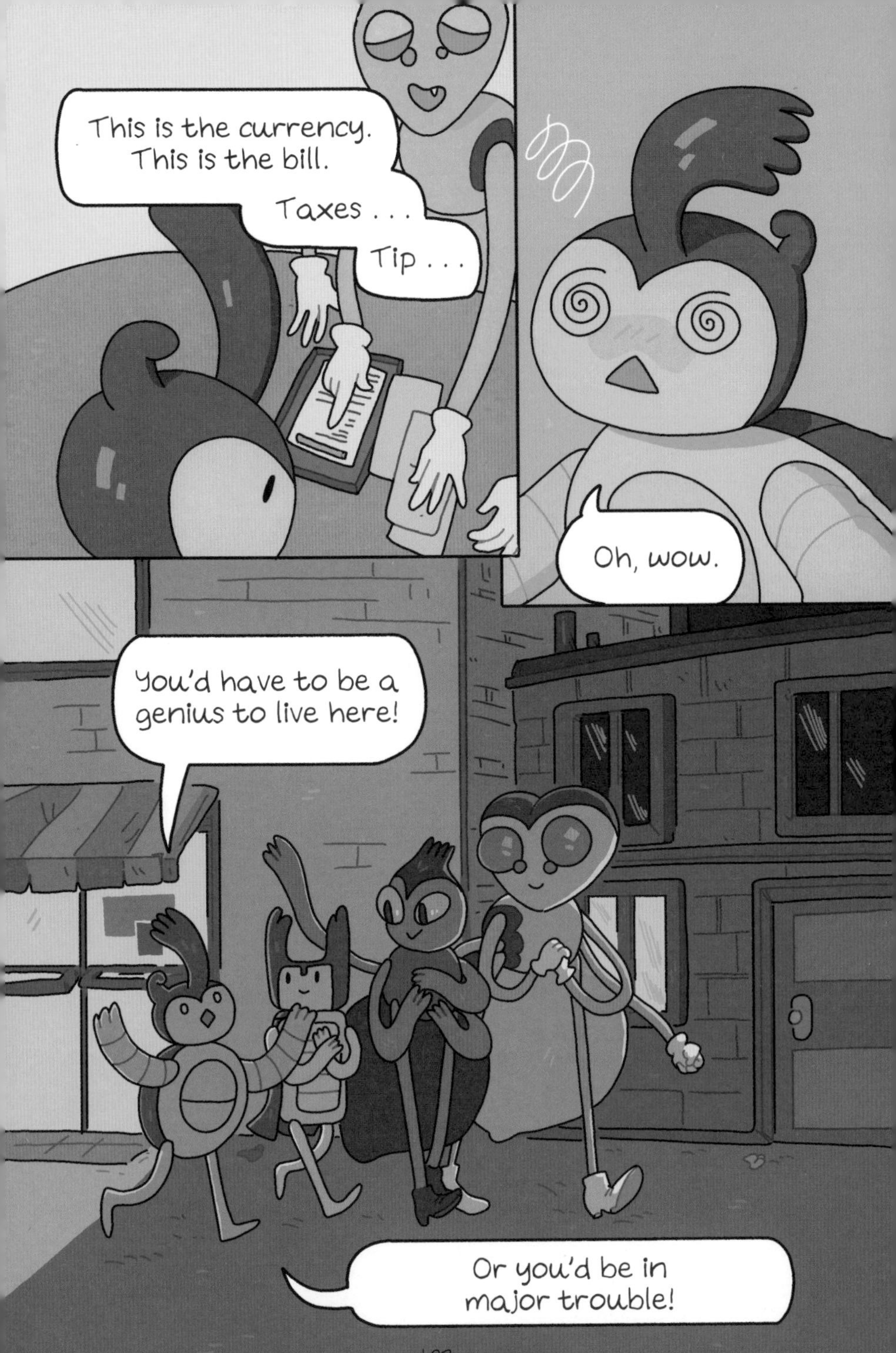
This is the currency. This is the bill.
Taxes . . .
Tip . . .
Oh, wow.
You'd have to be a genius to live here!
Or you'd be in major trouble!

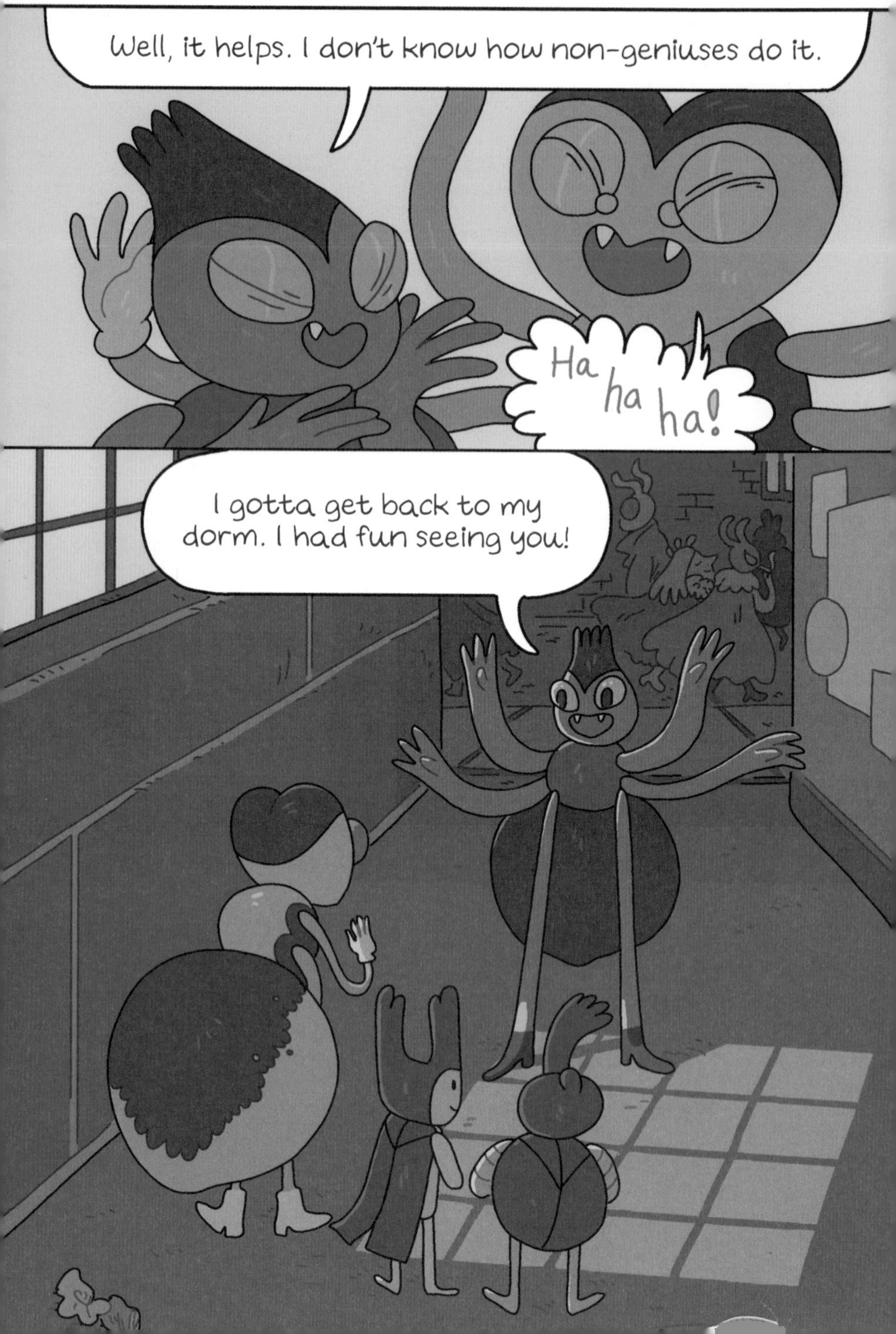
Well, it helps. I don't know how non-geniuses do it.
Ha ha ha!
I gotta get back to my dorm. I had fun seeing you!

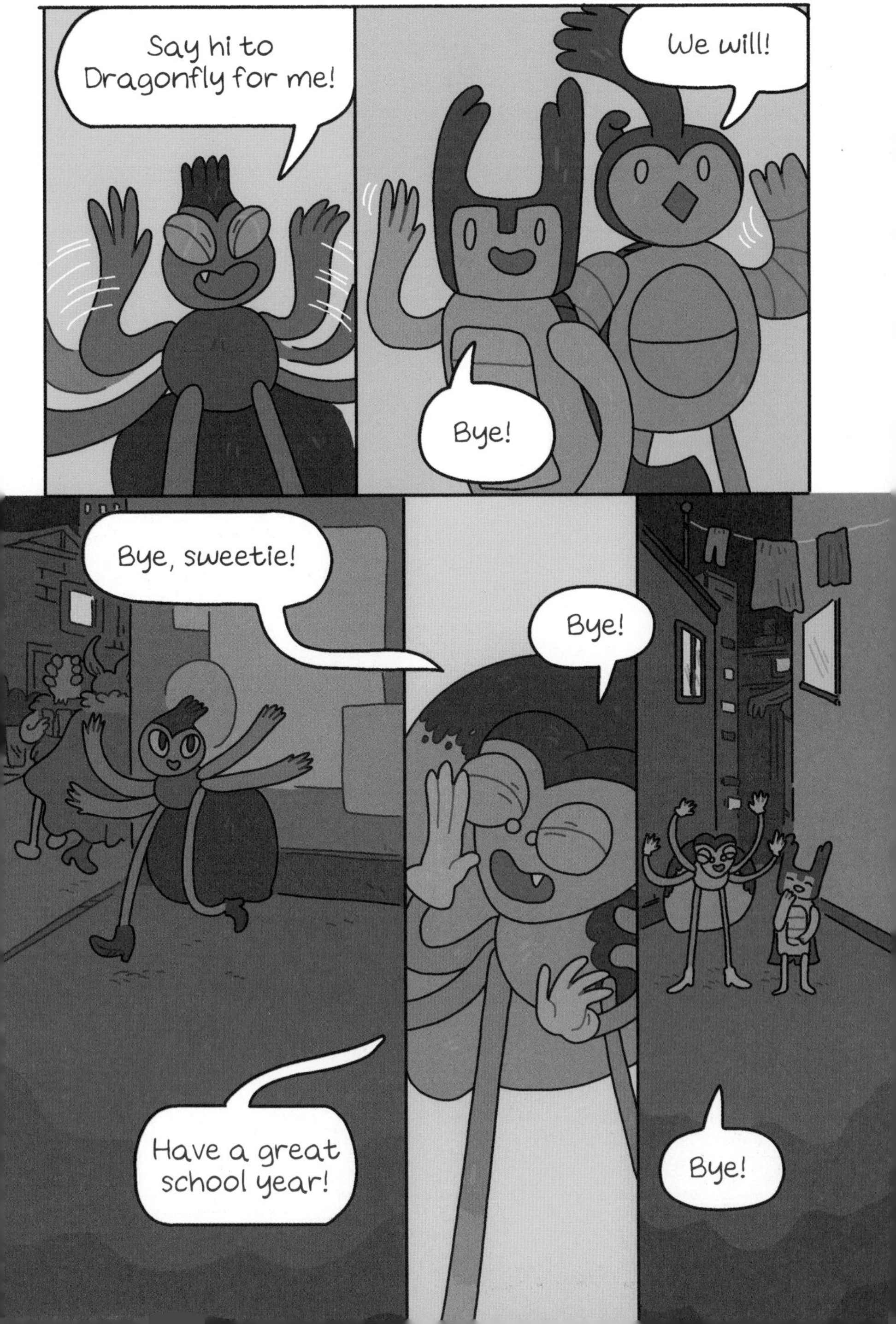
Say hi to Dragonfly for me!
We will!
Bye!
Bye, sweetie!
Have a great school year!
Bye!
Bye!

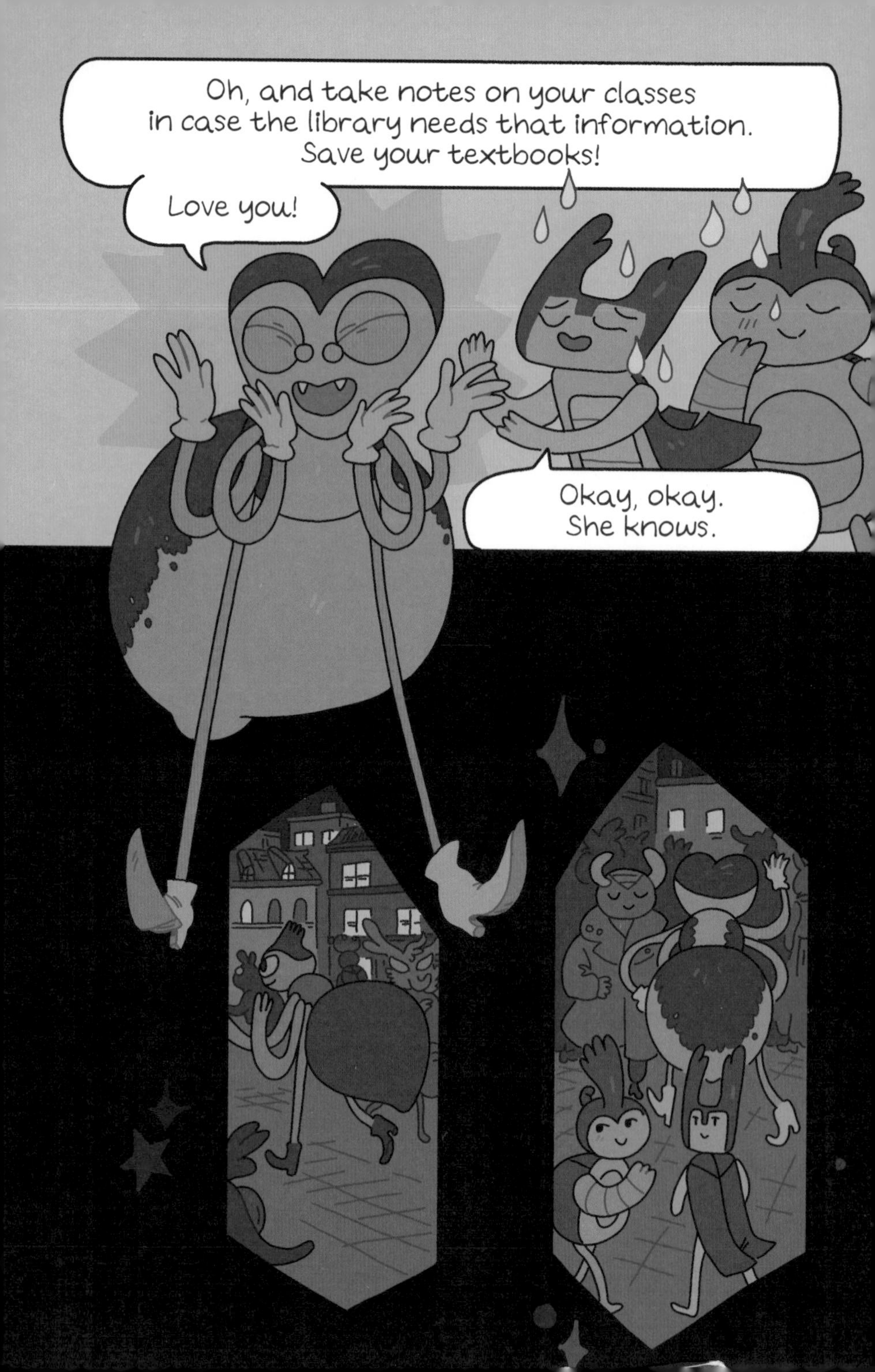
Oh, and take notes on your classes in case the library needs that information. Save your textbooks!
Love you!
Okay, okay. She knows.

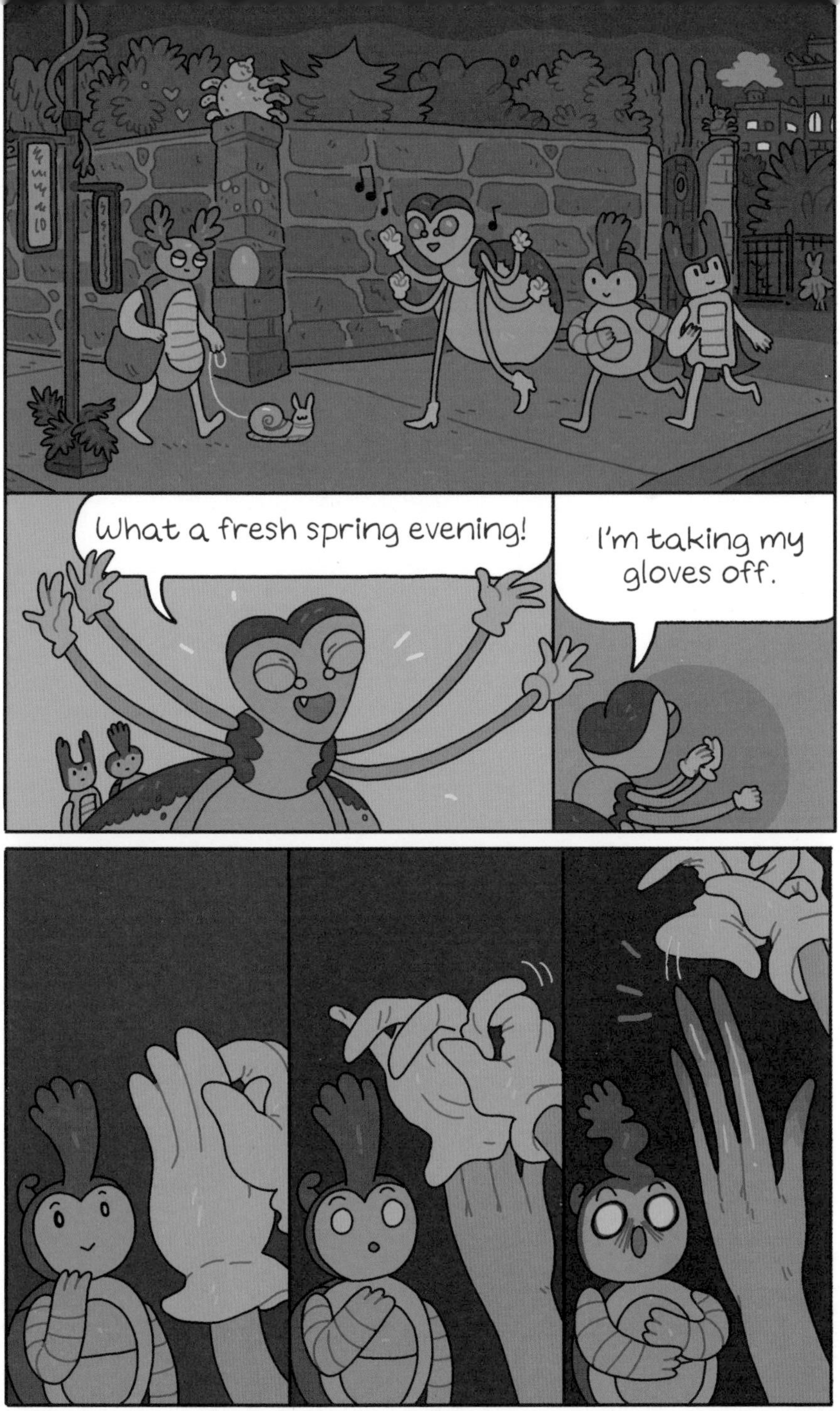
What a fresh spring evening!
I'm taking my gloves off.

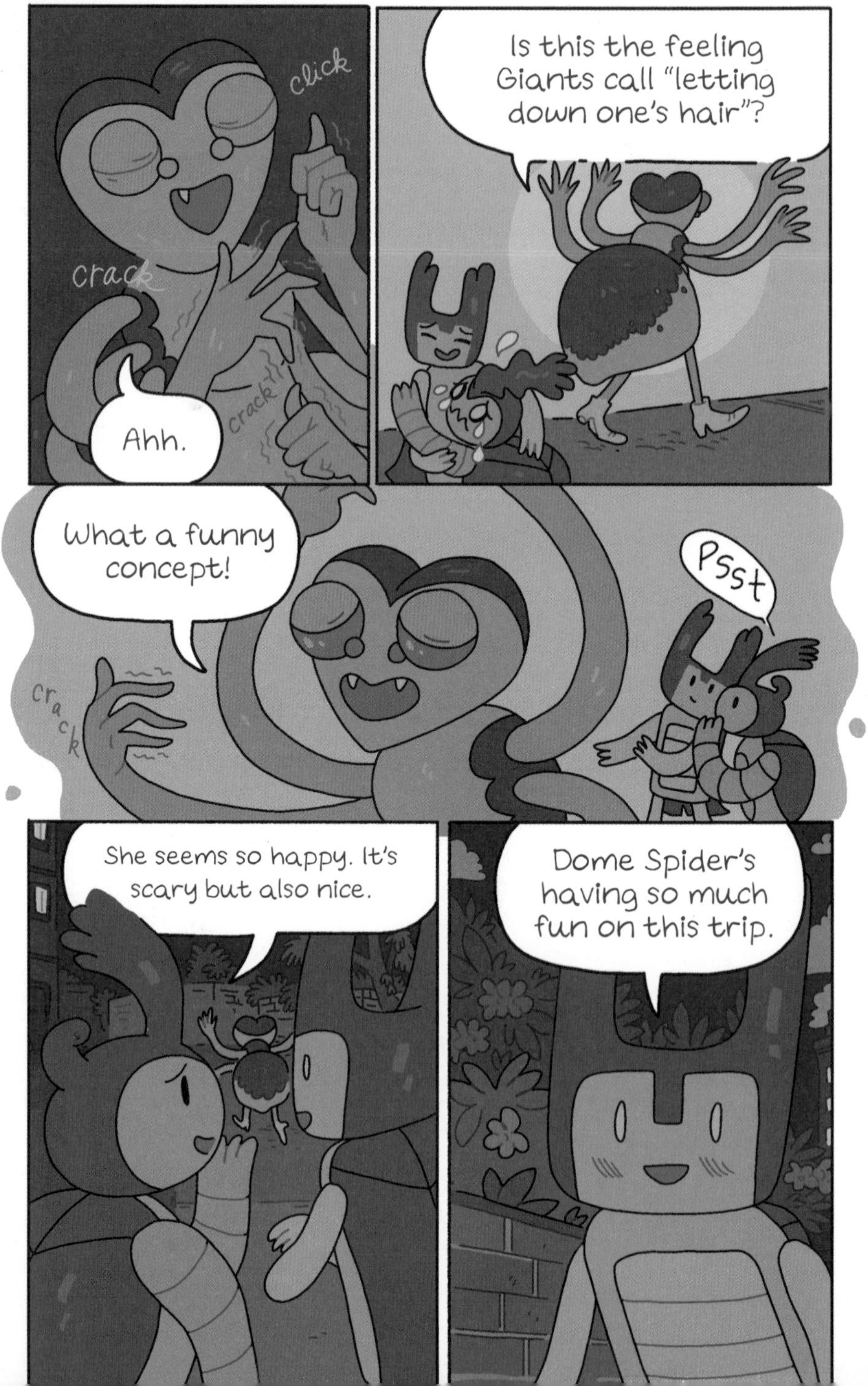

click
crack
crack
Ahh.
Is this the feeling Giants call "letting down one's hair"?
What a funny concept!
crack
Psst
She seems so happy. It's scary but also nice.
Dome Spider's having so much fun on this trip.

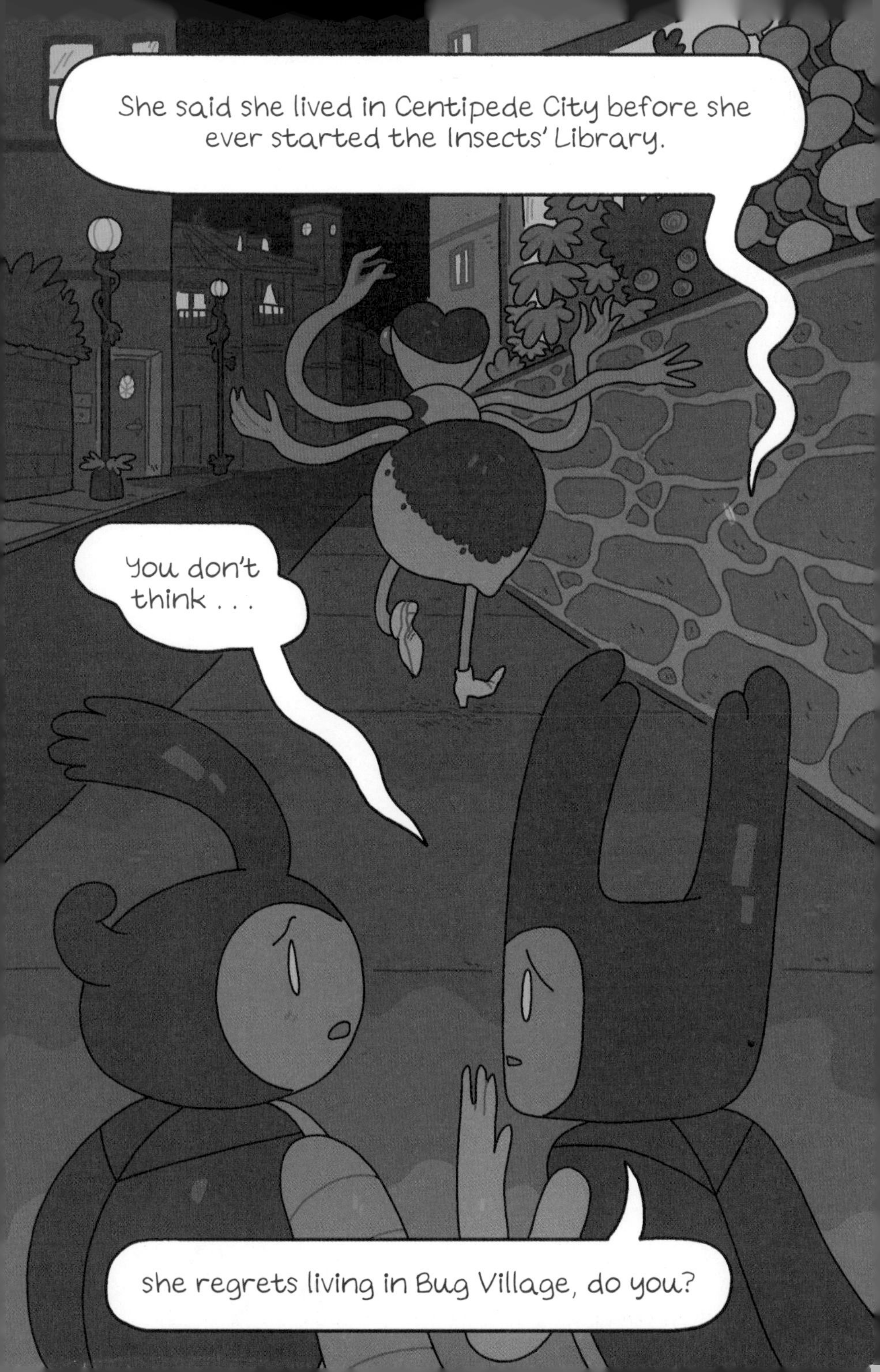
She said she lived in Centipede City before she ever started the Insects' Library.
You don't think . . .
she regrets living in Bug Village, do you?

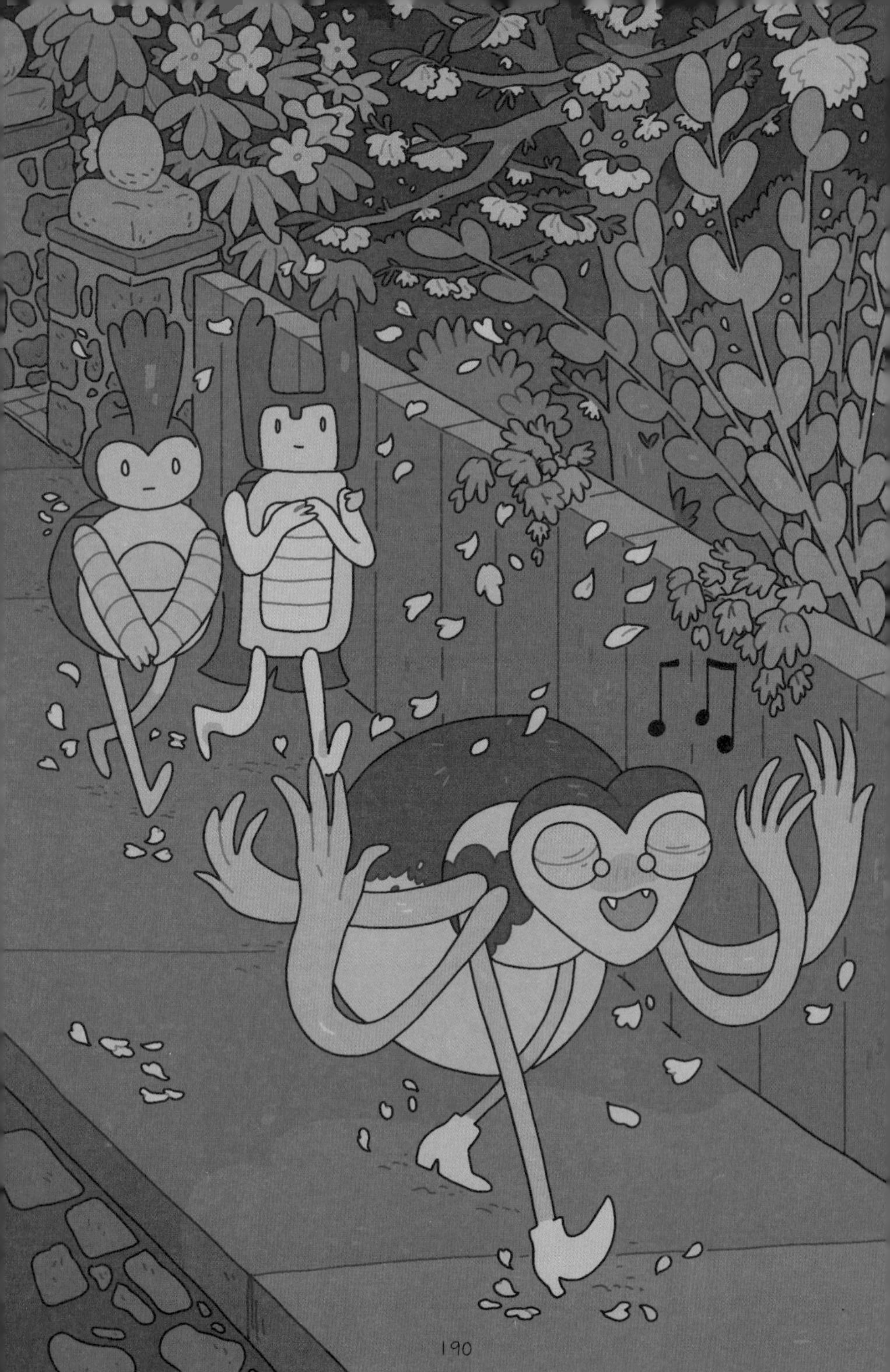

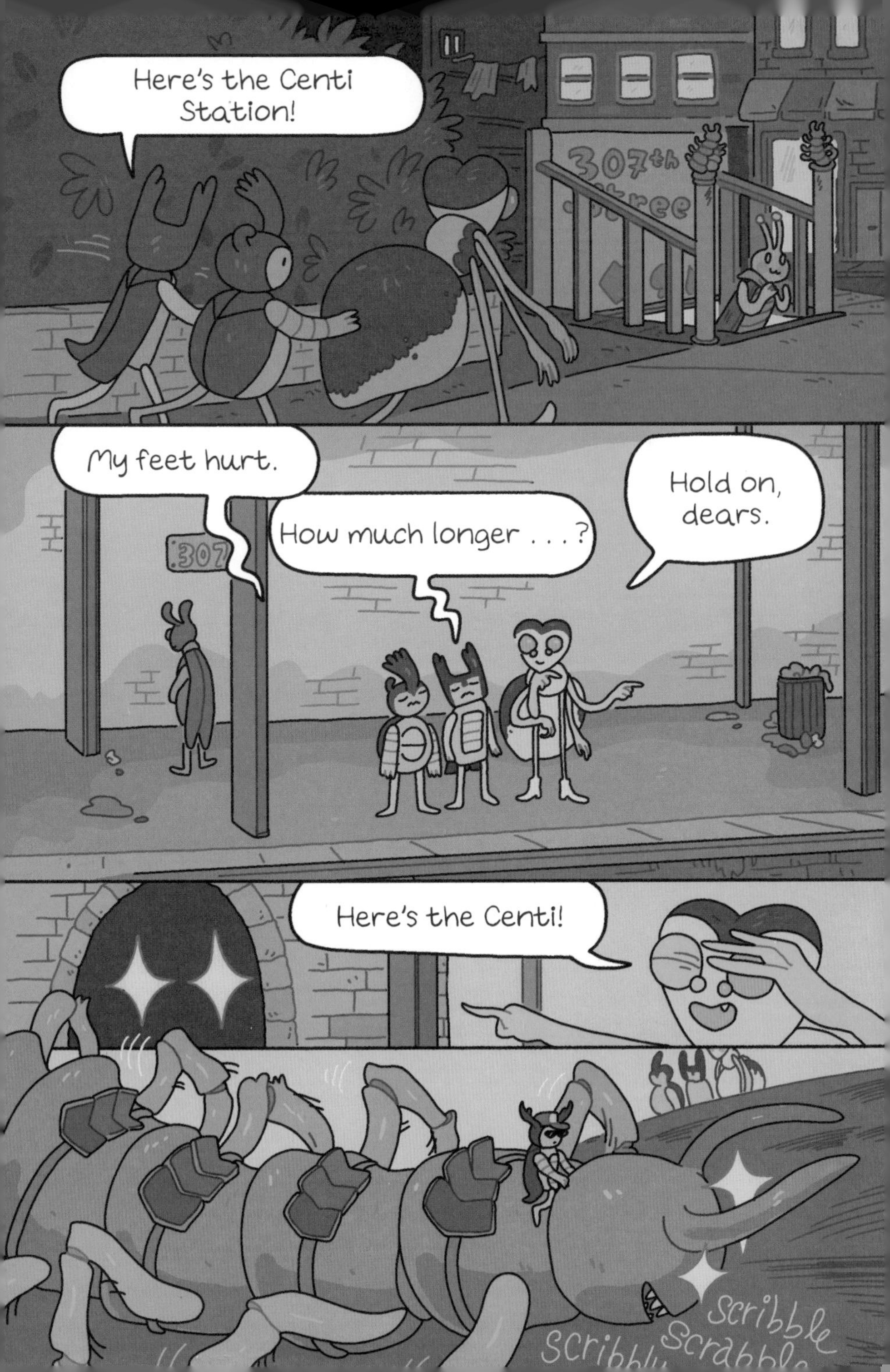
Here's the Centi Station!
307th
My feet hurt.
307
How much longer . . . ?
Hold on, dears.
Here's the Centi!
Scribble

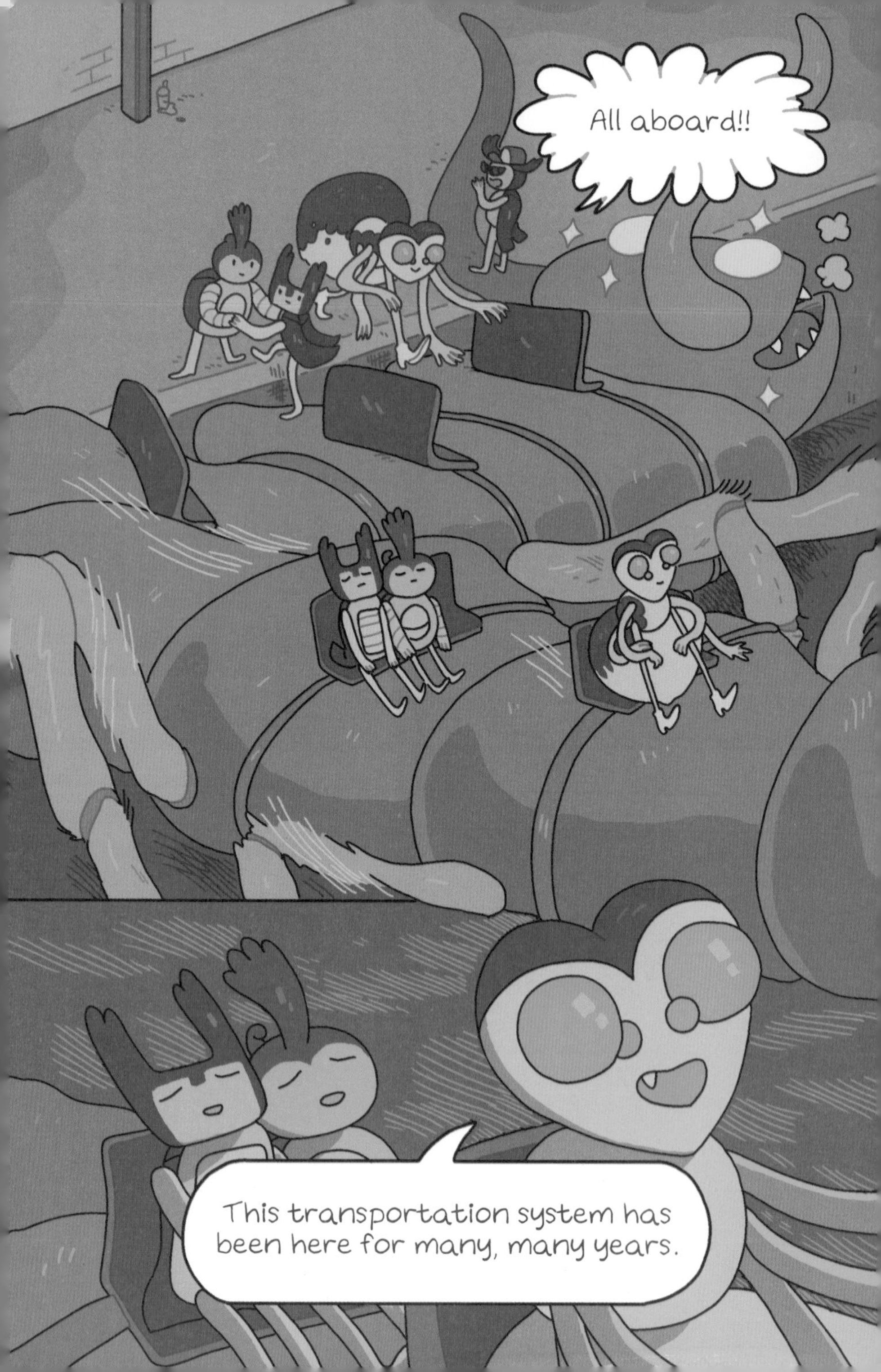
All aboard!!
This transportation system has been here for many, many years.

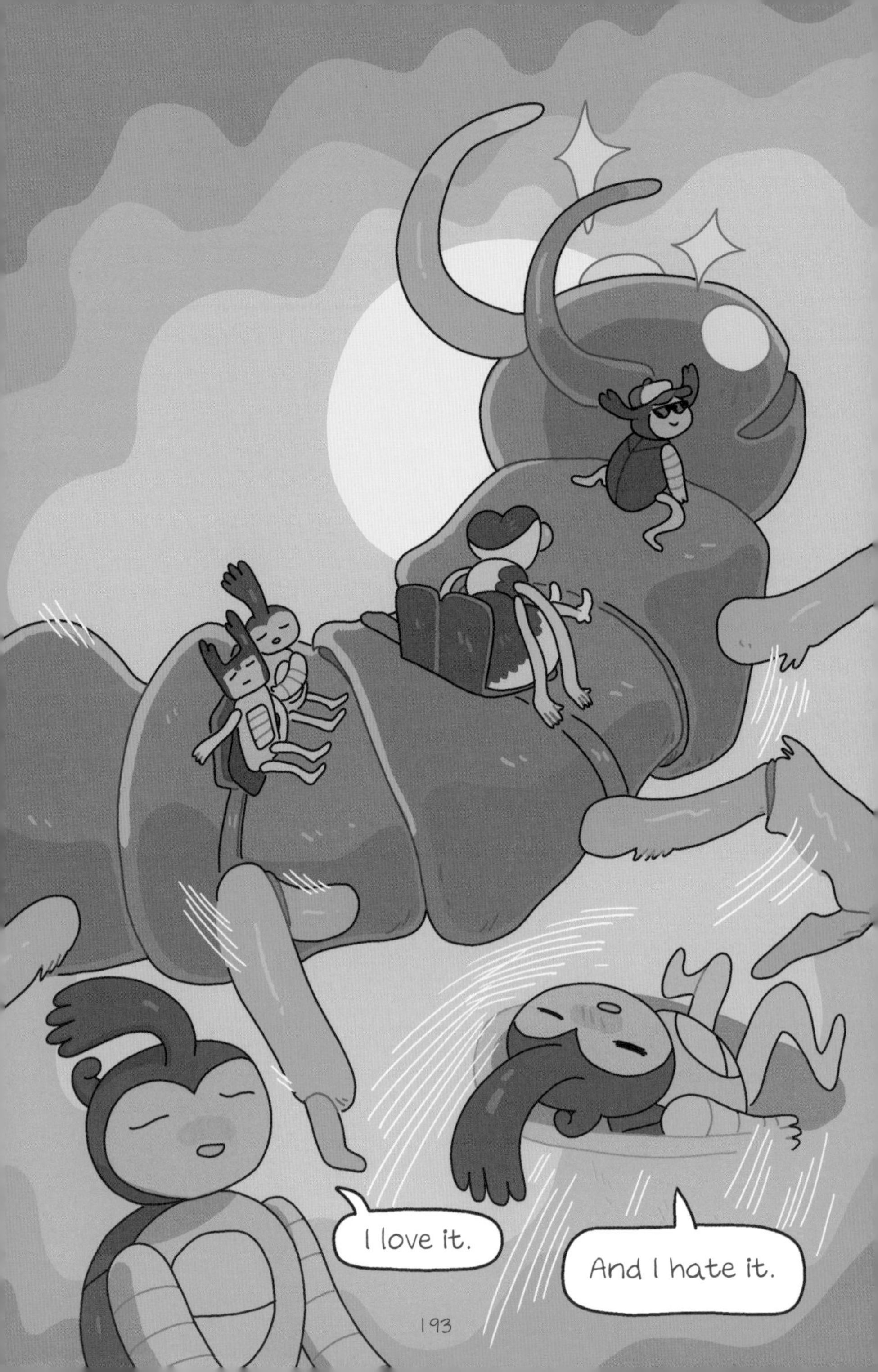
I love it.
And I hate it.

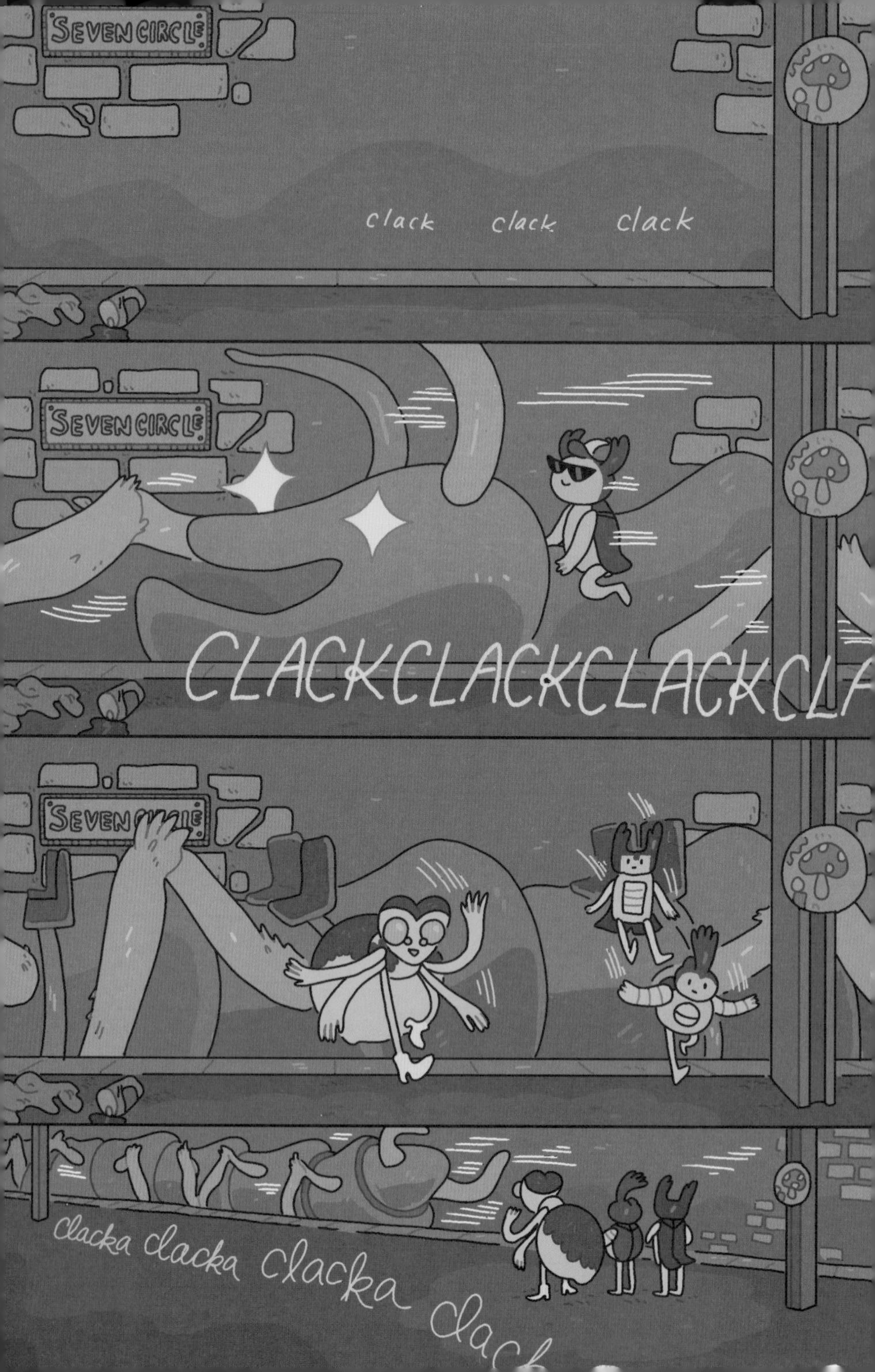
SEVEN CIRCLE
clack clack clack
SEVEN CIRCLE
CLACKCLACKCLACKCLA
clacka clacka clacka

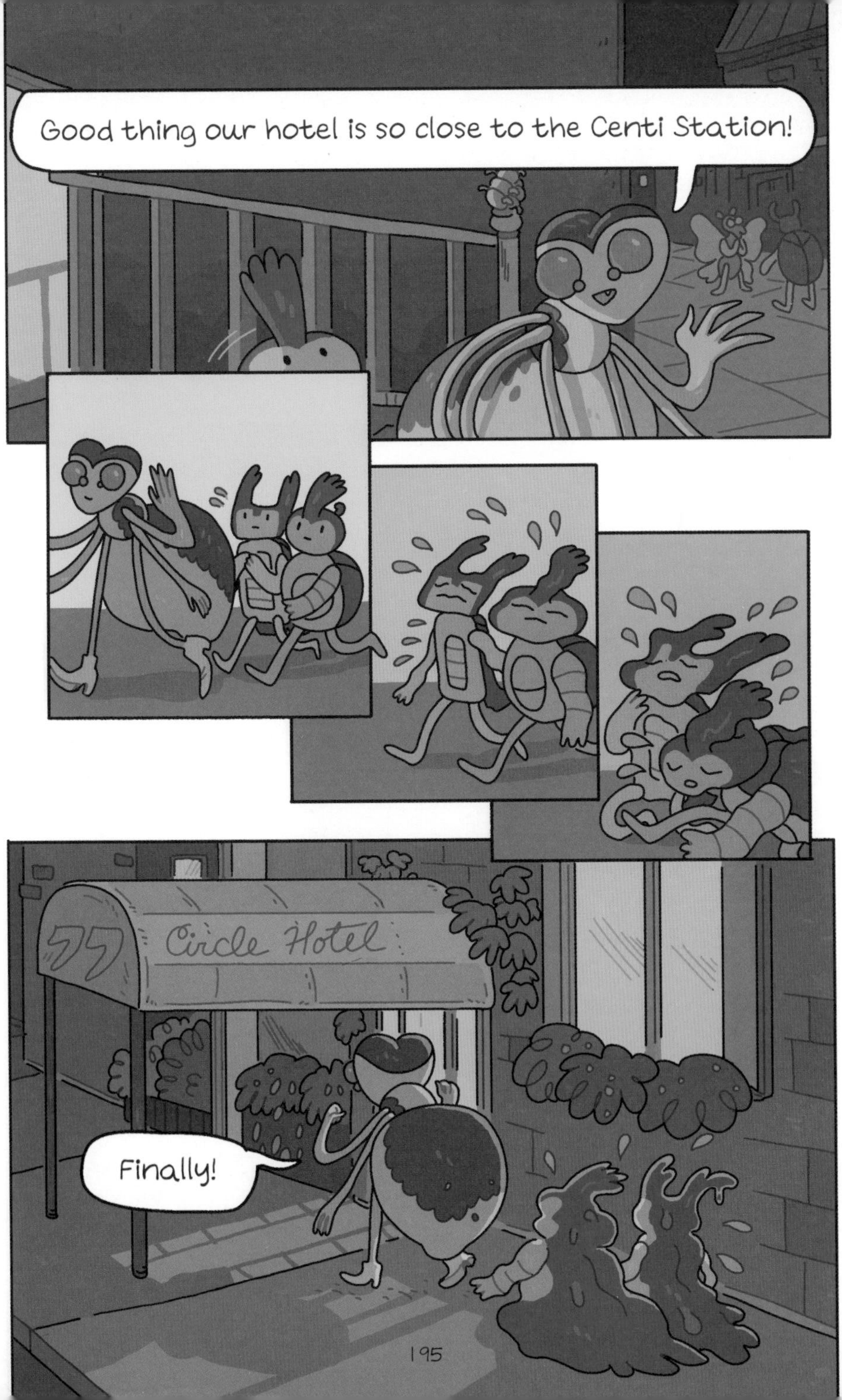
Good thing our hotel is so close to the Centi Station!
Circle Hotel
Finally!

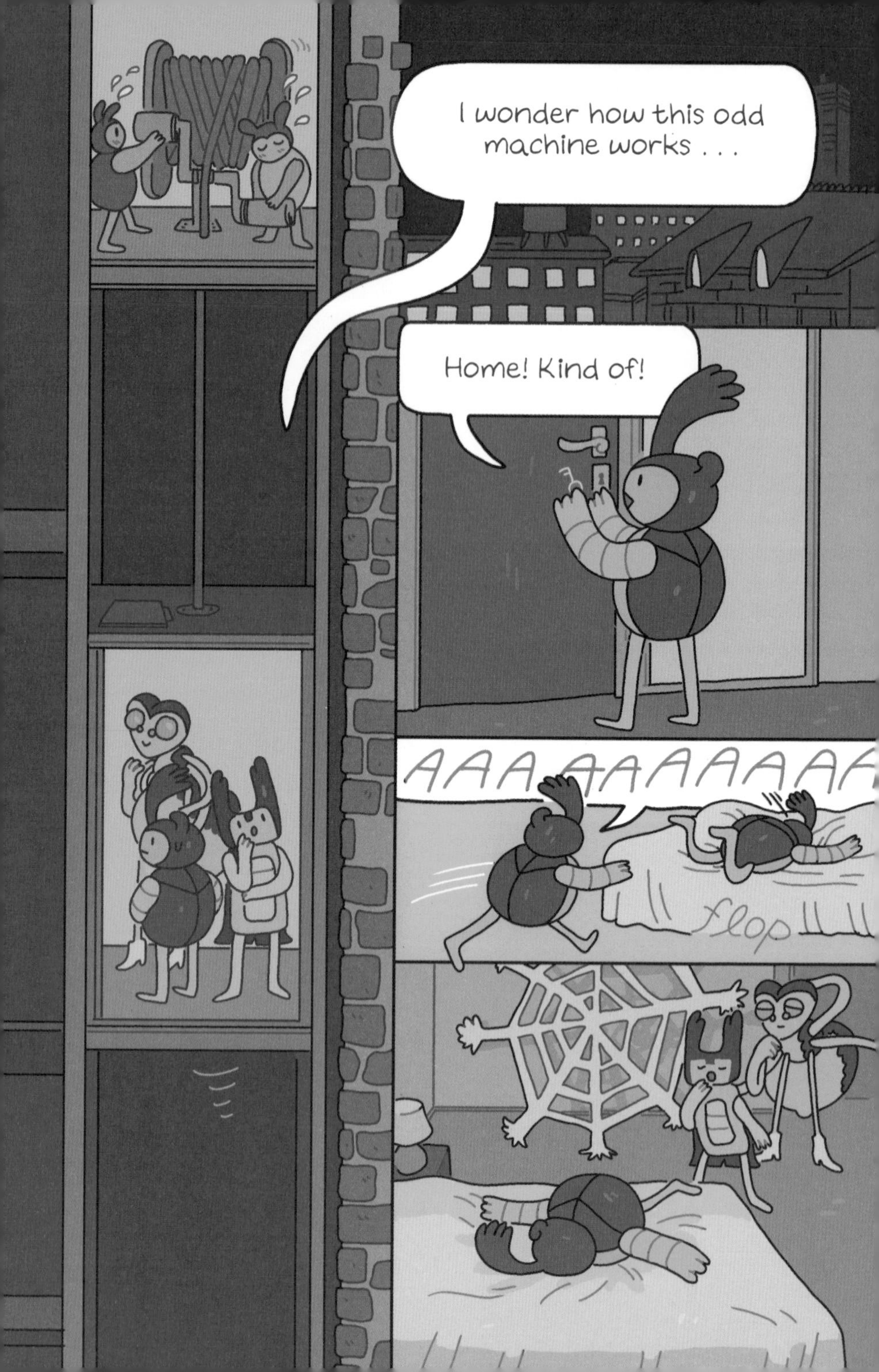
I wonder how this odd machine works . . .
Home! Kind of!
AAAAAAAAAA
flop

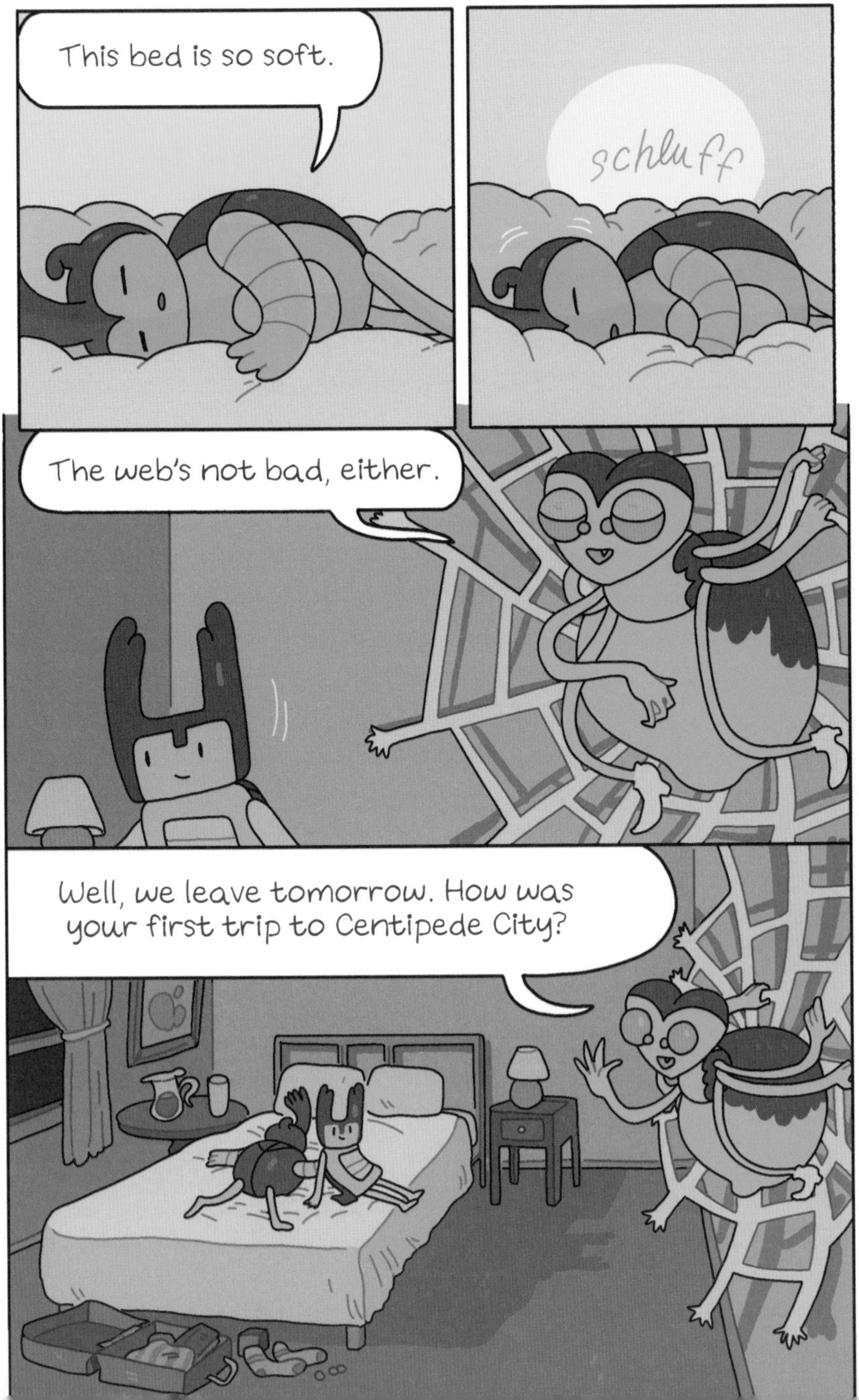
This bed is so soft.
schluff
The web's not bad, either.
Well, we leave tomorrow. How was your first trip to Centipede City?

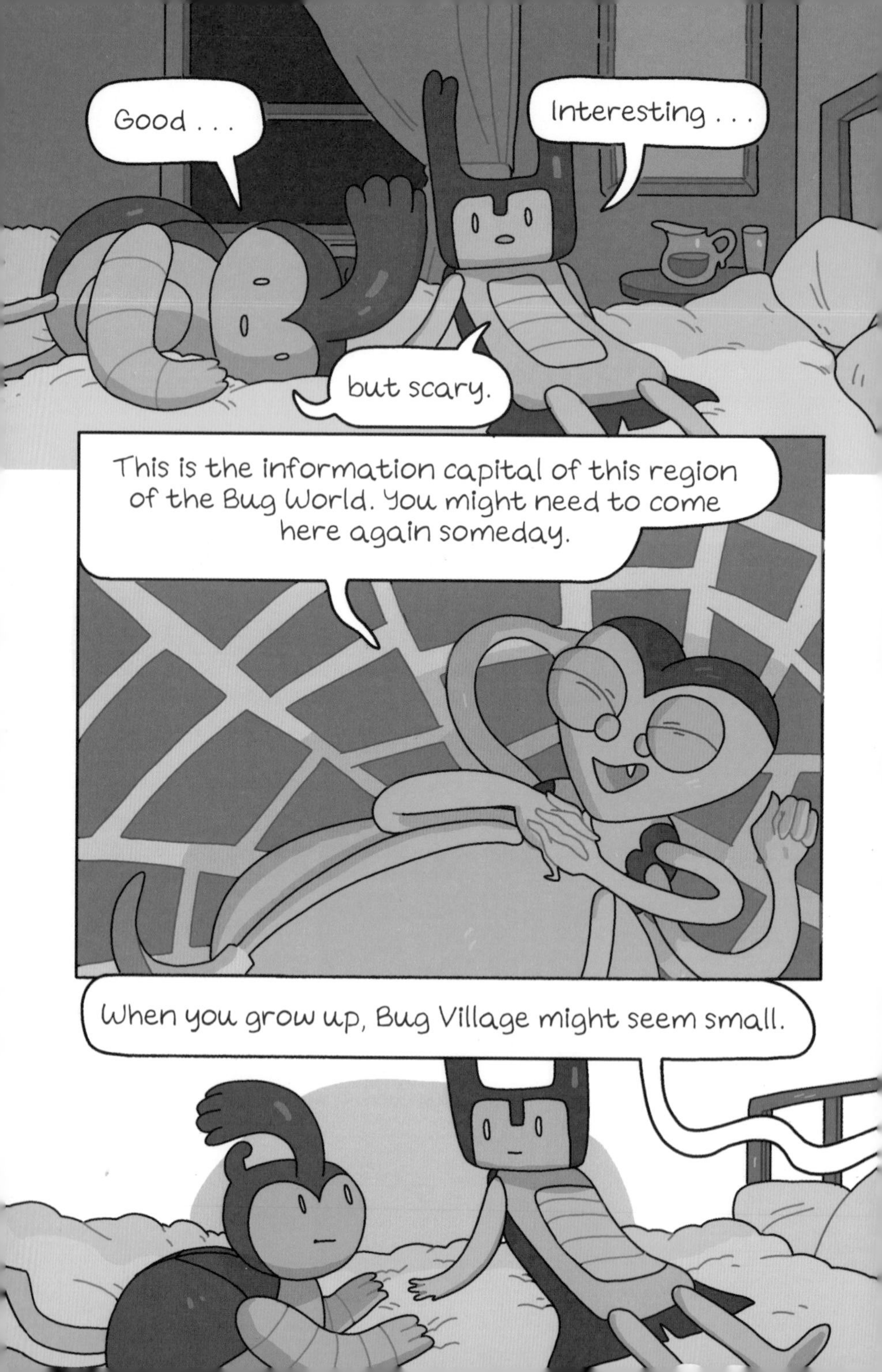
Good . . .
Interesting . . .
but scary.
This is the information capital of this region of the Bug World. You might need to come here again someday.
When you grow up, Bug Village might seem small.

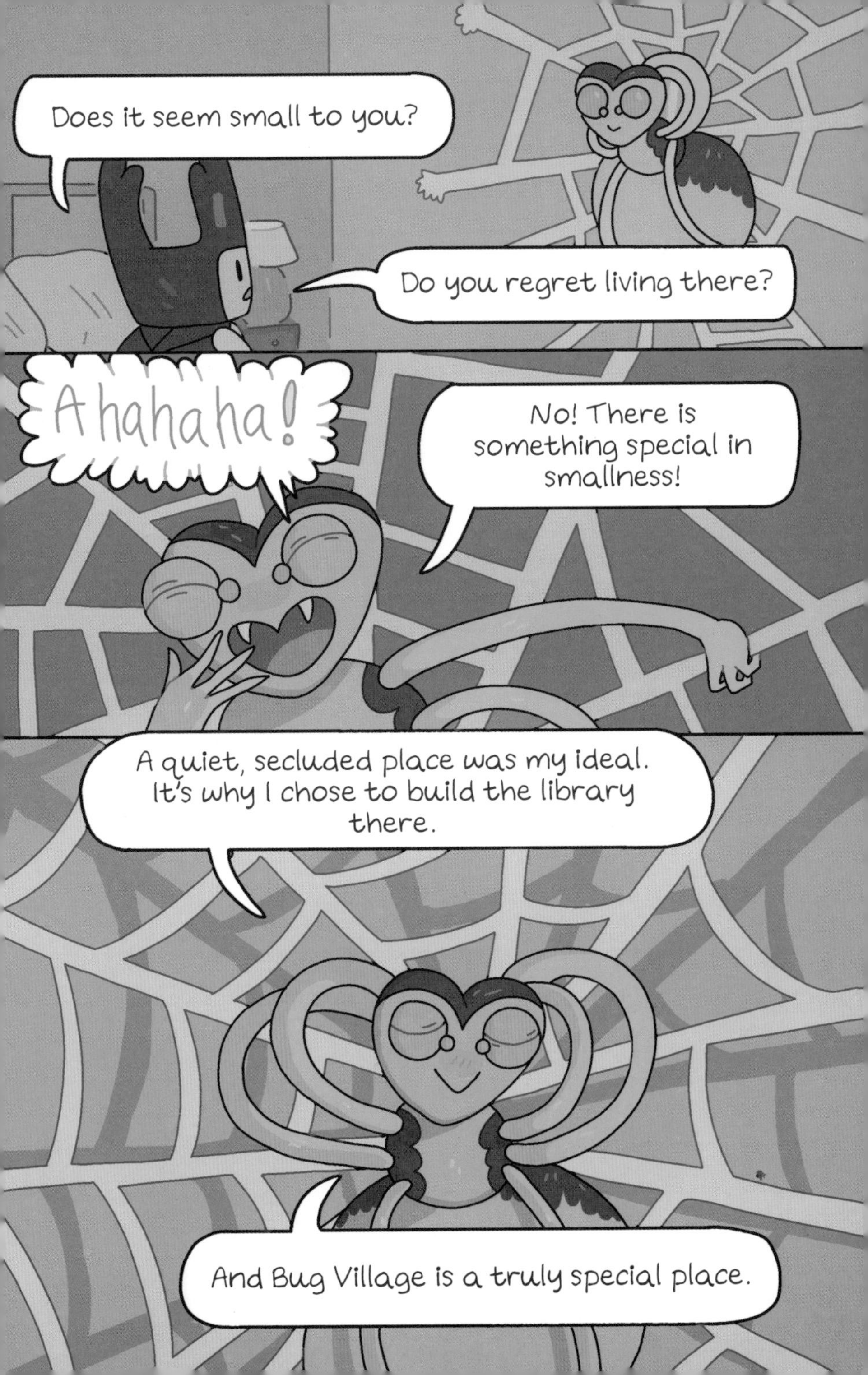
Does it seem small to you?
Do you regret living there?
Ahahaha!
No! There is something special in smallness!
A quiet, secluded place was my ideal. It's why I chose to build the library there.
And Bug Village is a truly special place.

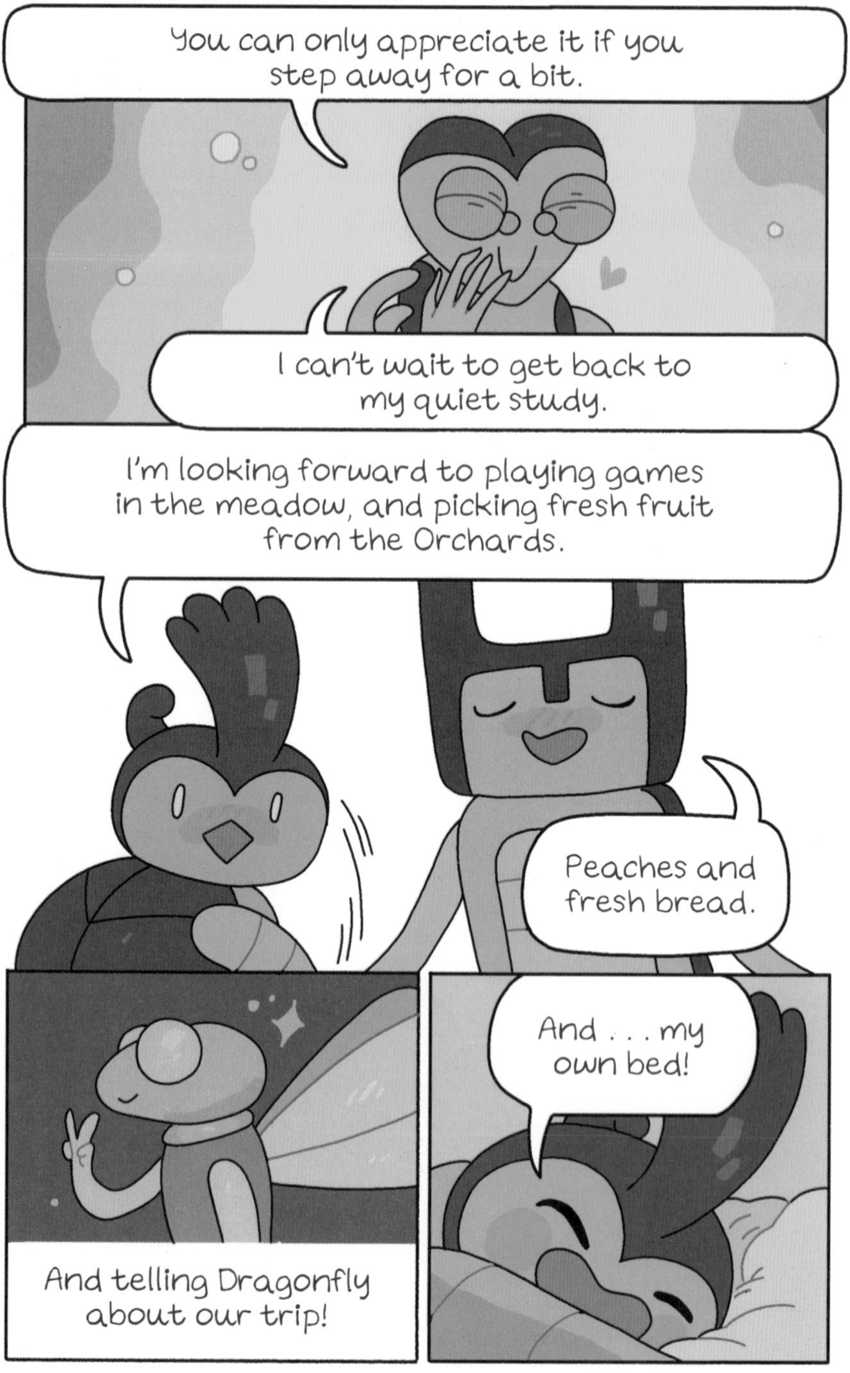
You can only appreciate it if you step away for a bit.
I can't wait to get back to my quiet study.
I'm looking forward to playing games in the meadow, and picking fresh fruit from the Orchards.
Peaches and fresh bread.
And telling Dragonfly about our trip!
And . . . my own bed!

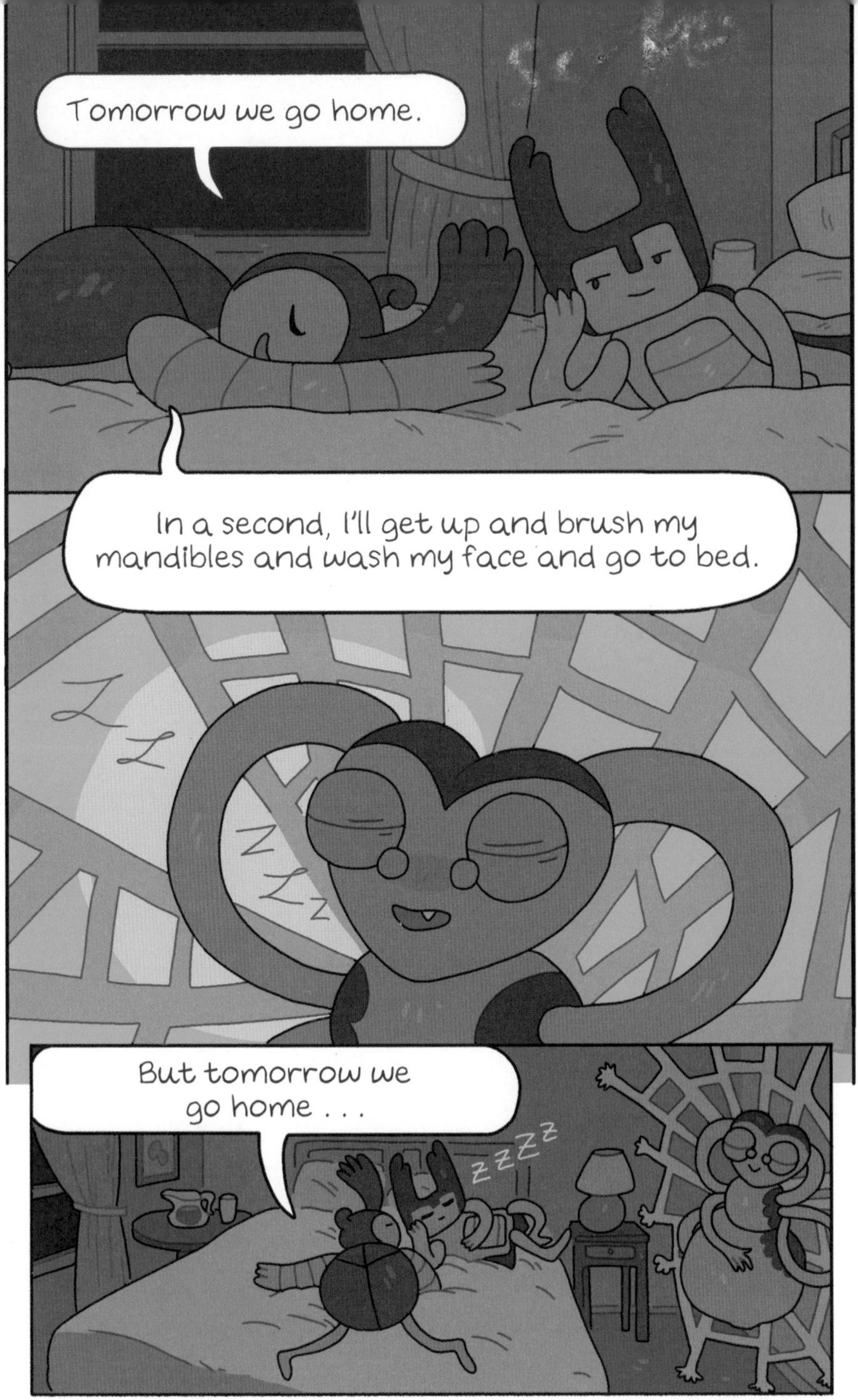
Tomorrow we go home.
In a second, I'll get up and brush my mandibles and wash my face and go to bed.
Z Z
Z Z Z
But tomorrow we go home . . .
Z Z Z Z

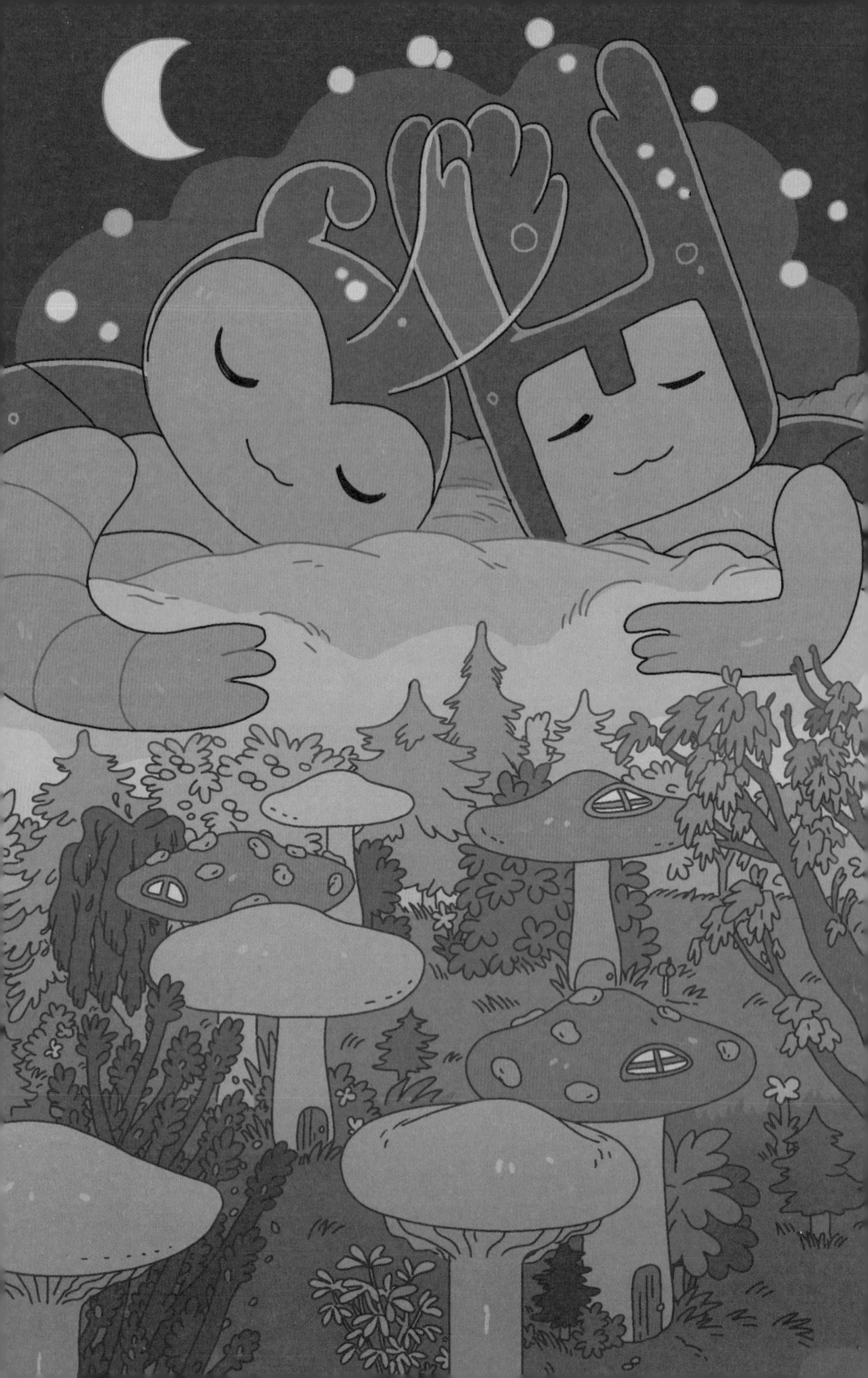

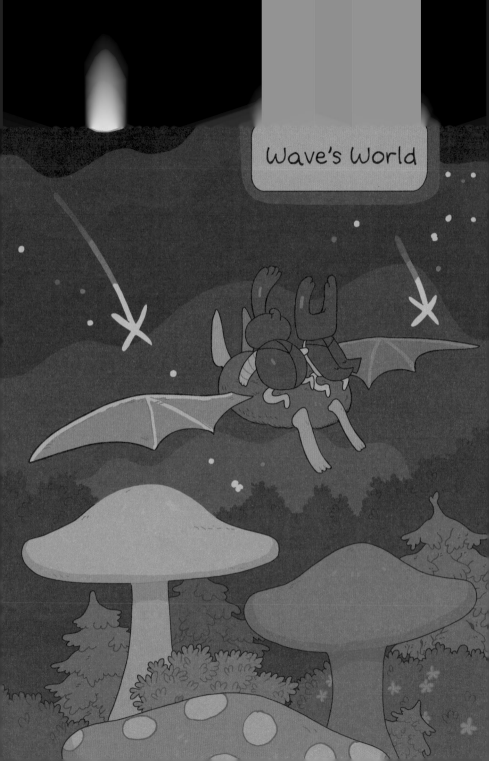

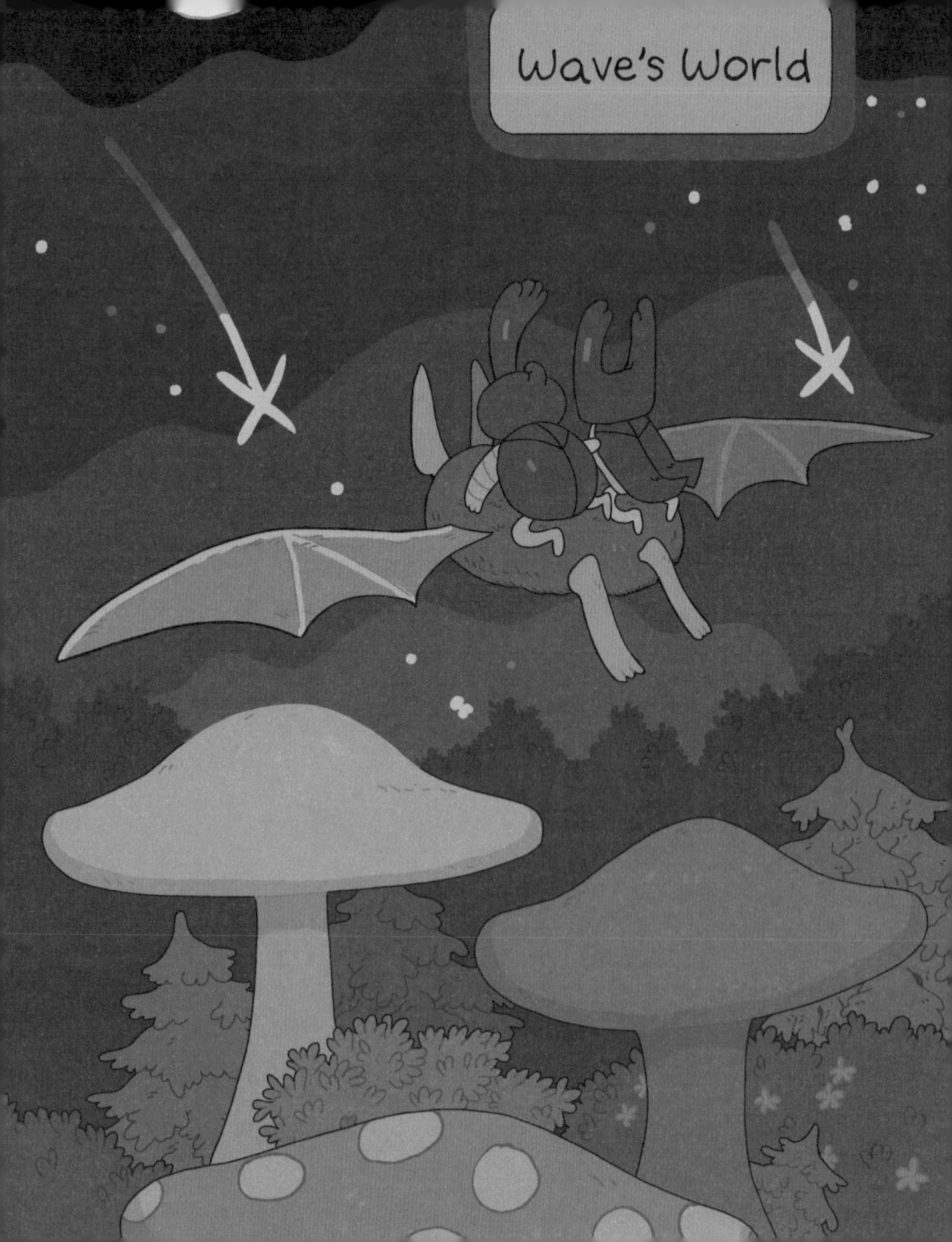
Wave's World

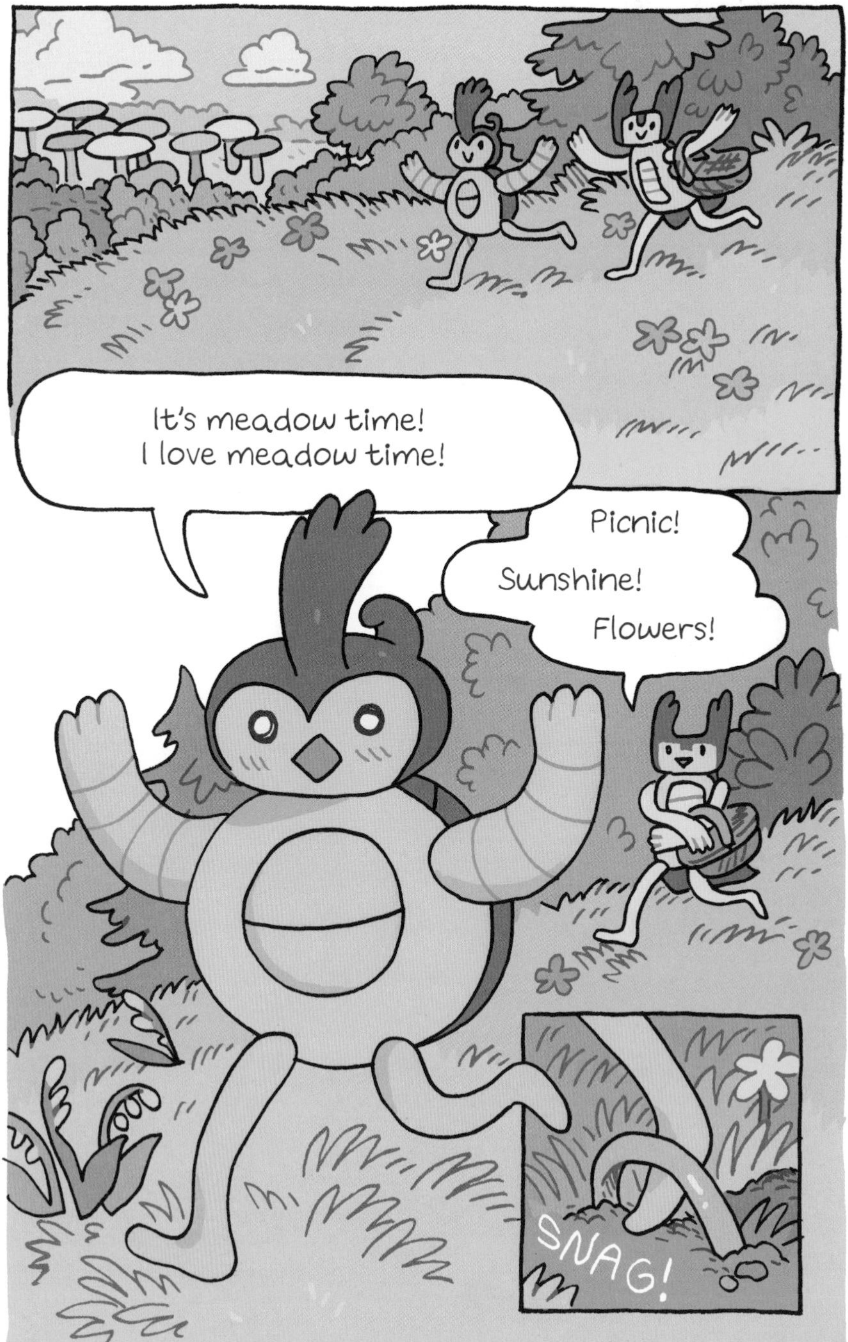
It's meadow time!
I love meadow time!
Picnic!
Sunshine!
Flowers!
SNAG!

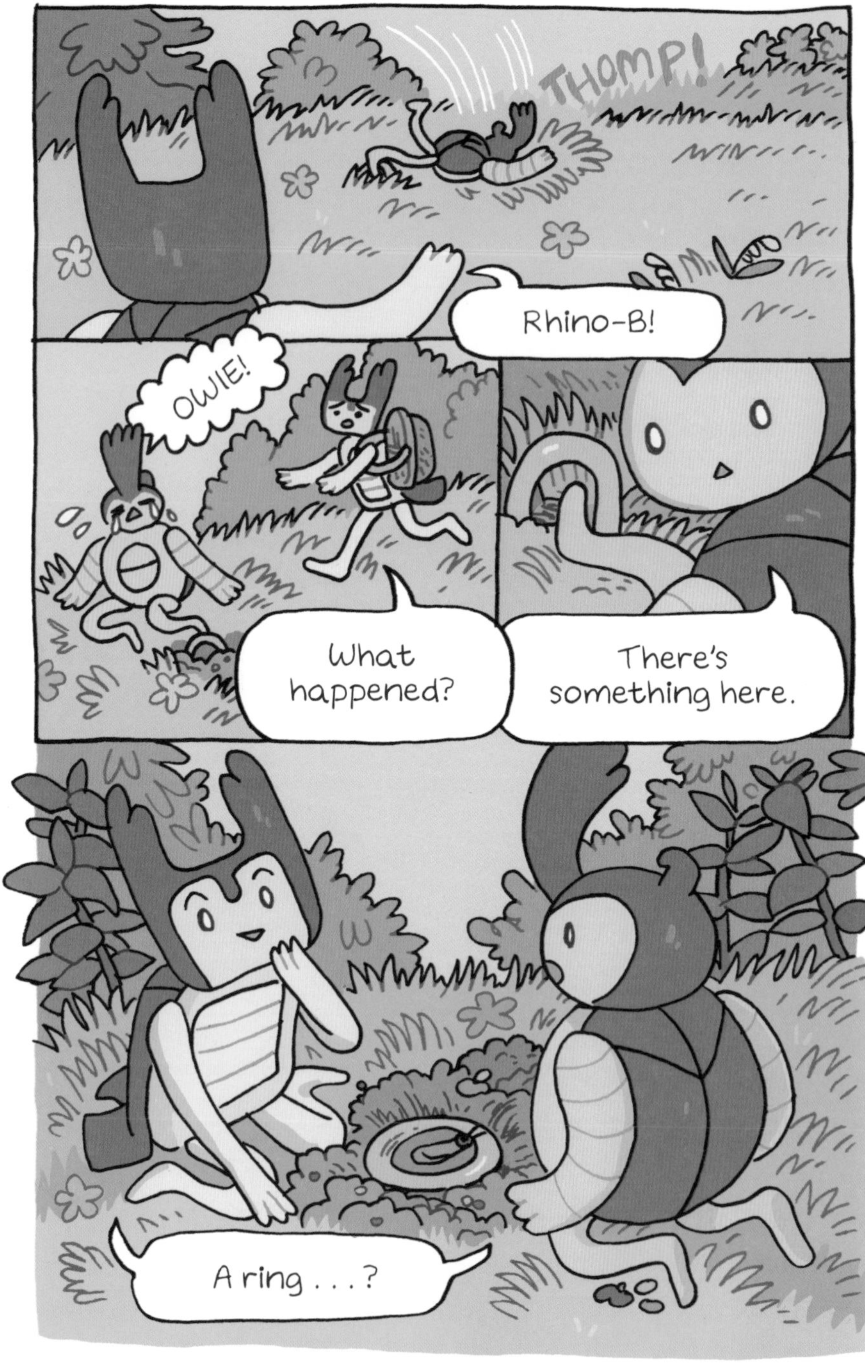
THOMP!
Rhino-B!
OWIE!
What happened?
There's something here.
A ring . . . ?

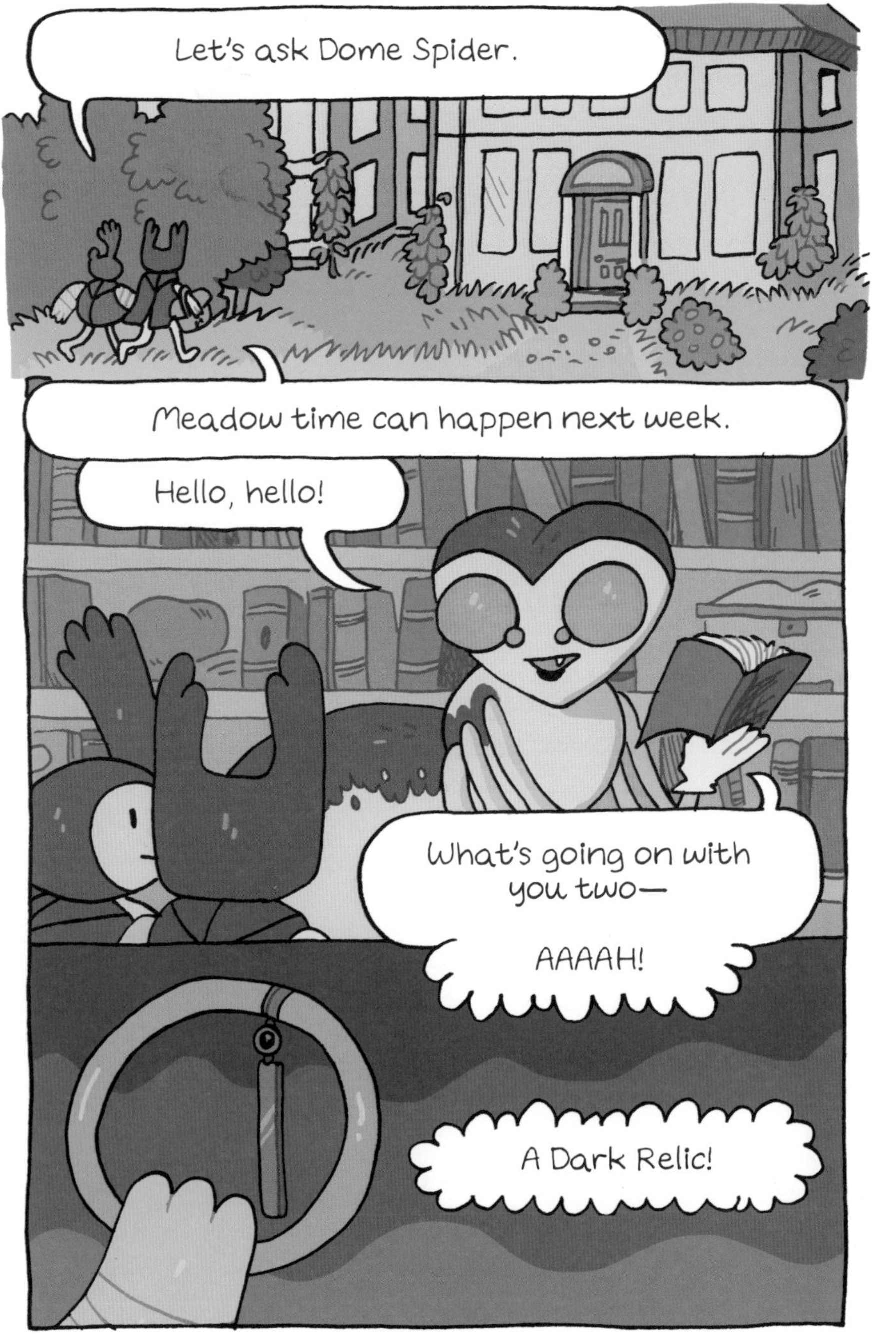
Let's ask Dome Spider.
Meadow time can happen next week.
Hello, hello!
What's going on with you two—
AAAAH!
A Dark Relic!

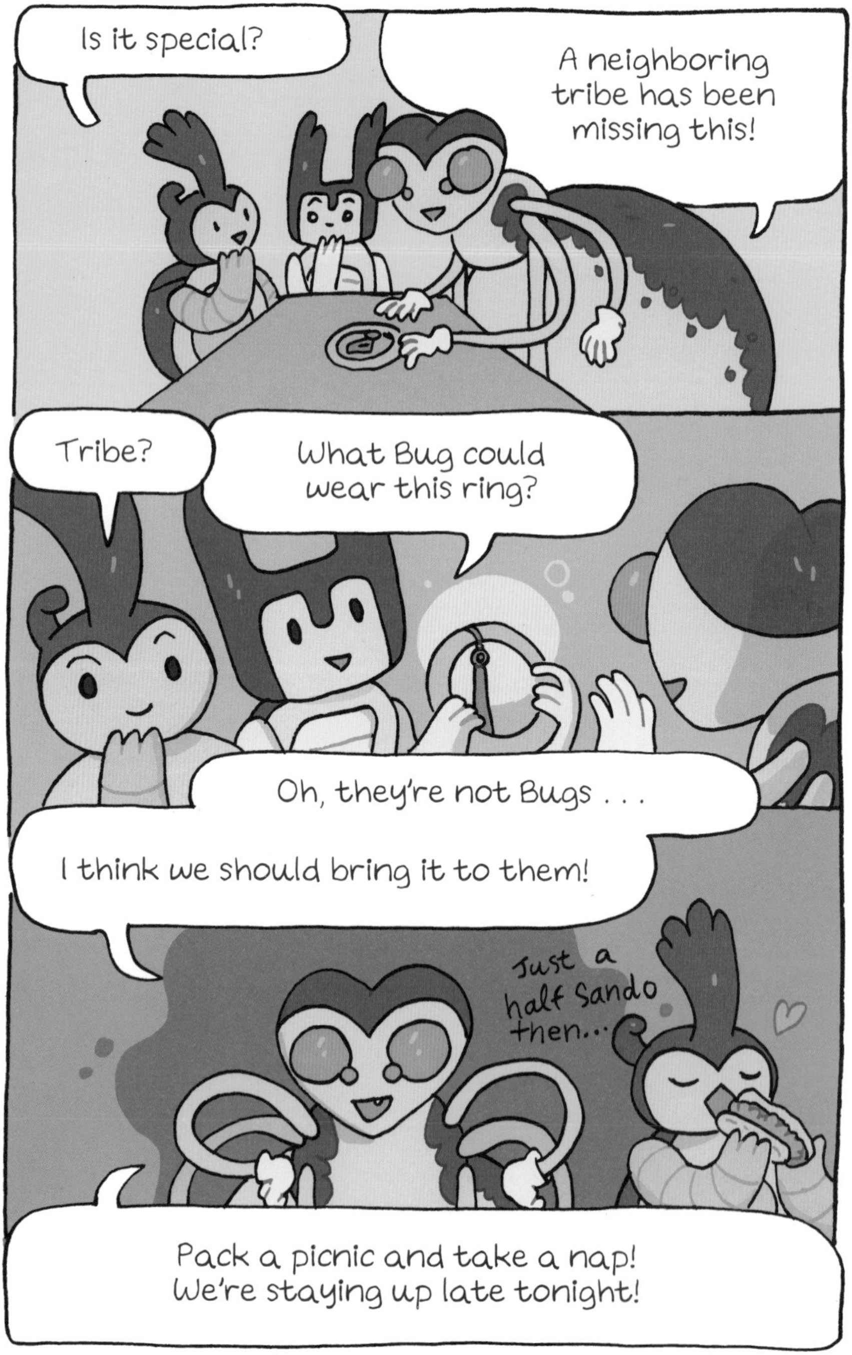
Is it special?
A neighboring tribe has been missing this!
Tribe?
What Bug could wear this ring?
Oh, they're not Bugs . . .
I think we should bring it to them!
Just a half Sando then...
Pack a picnic and take a nap! We're staying up late tonight!

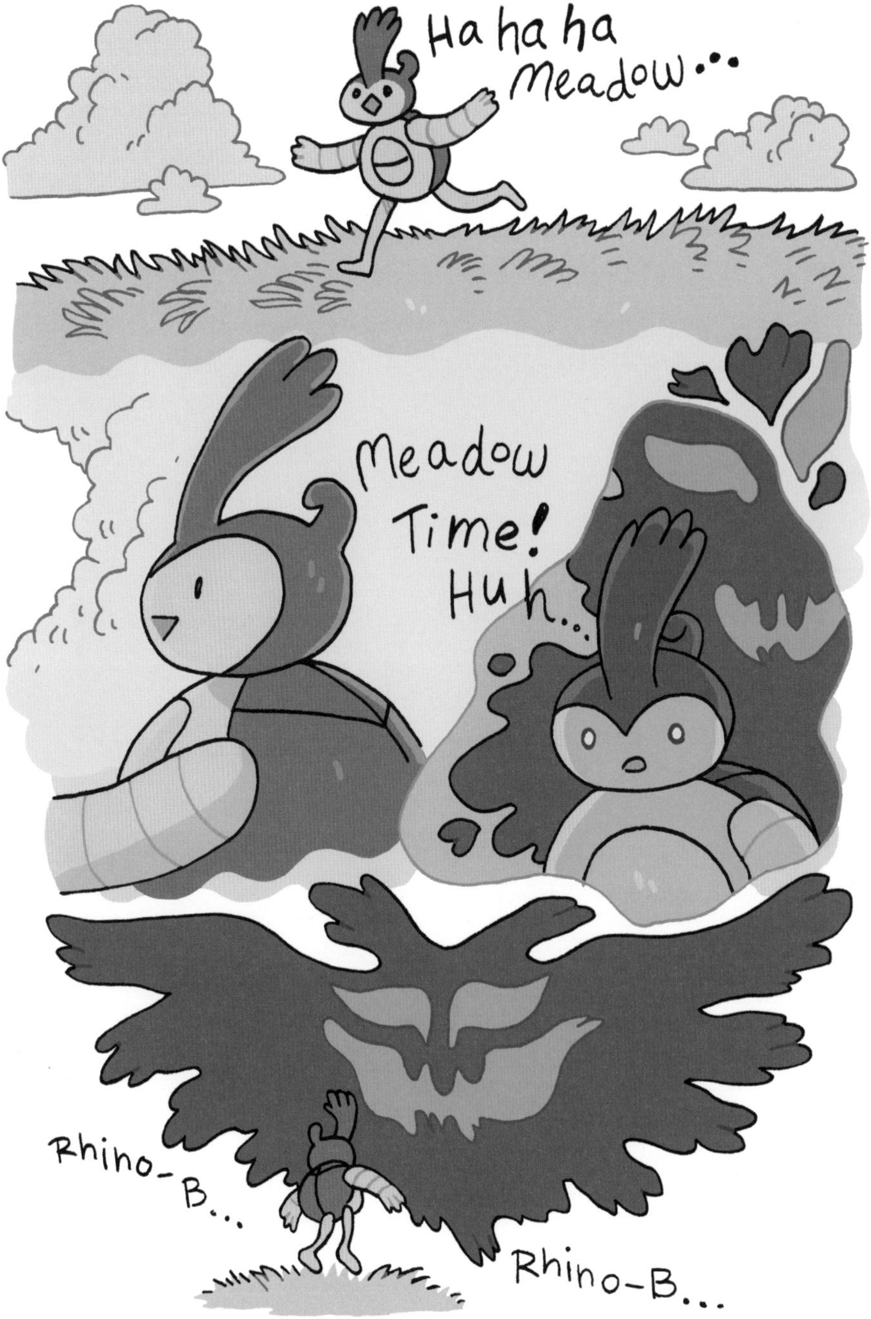
Ha ha ha
Meadow...
Meadow
Time!
Huh...
Rhino-B...
Rhino-B...

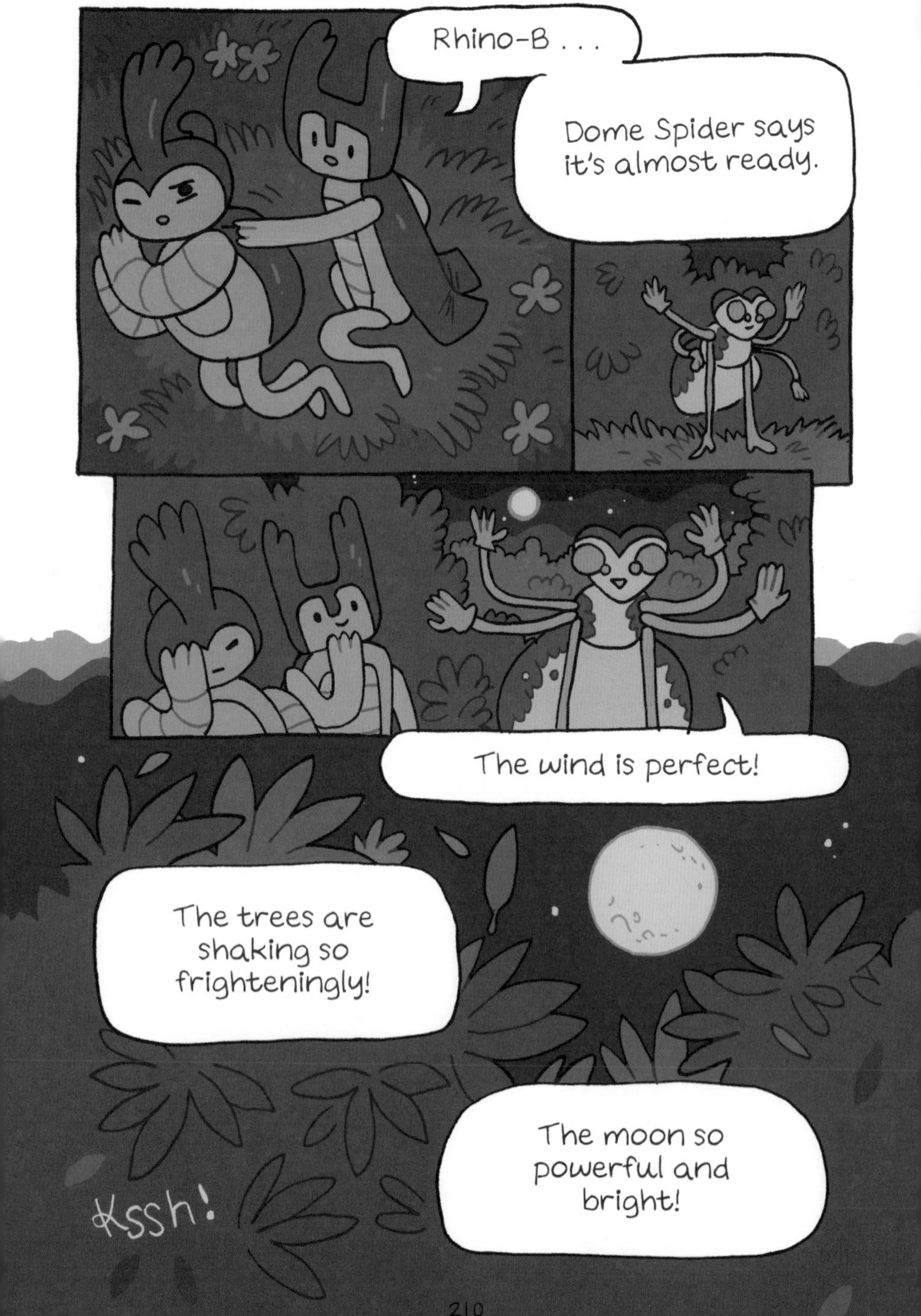
Rhino-B . . .
Dome Spider says it's almost ready.
The wind is perfect!
The trees are shaking so frighteningly!
The moon so powerful and bright!
Kssh!

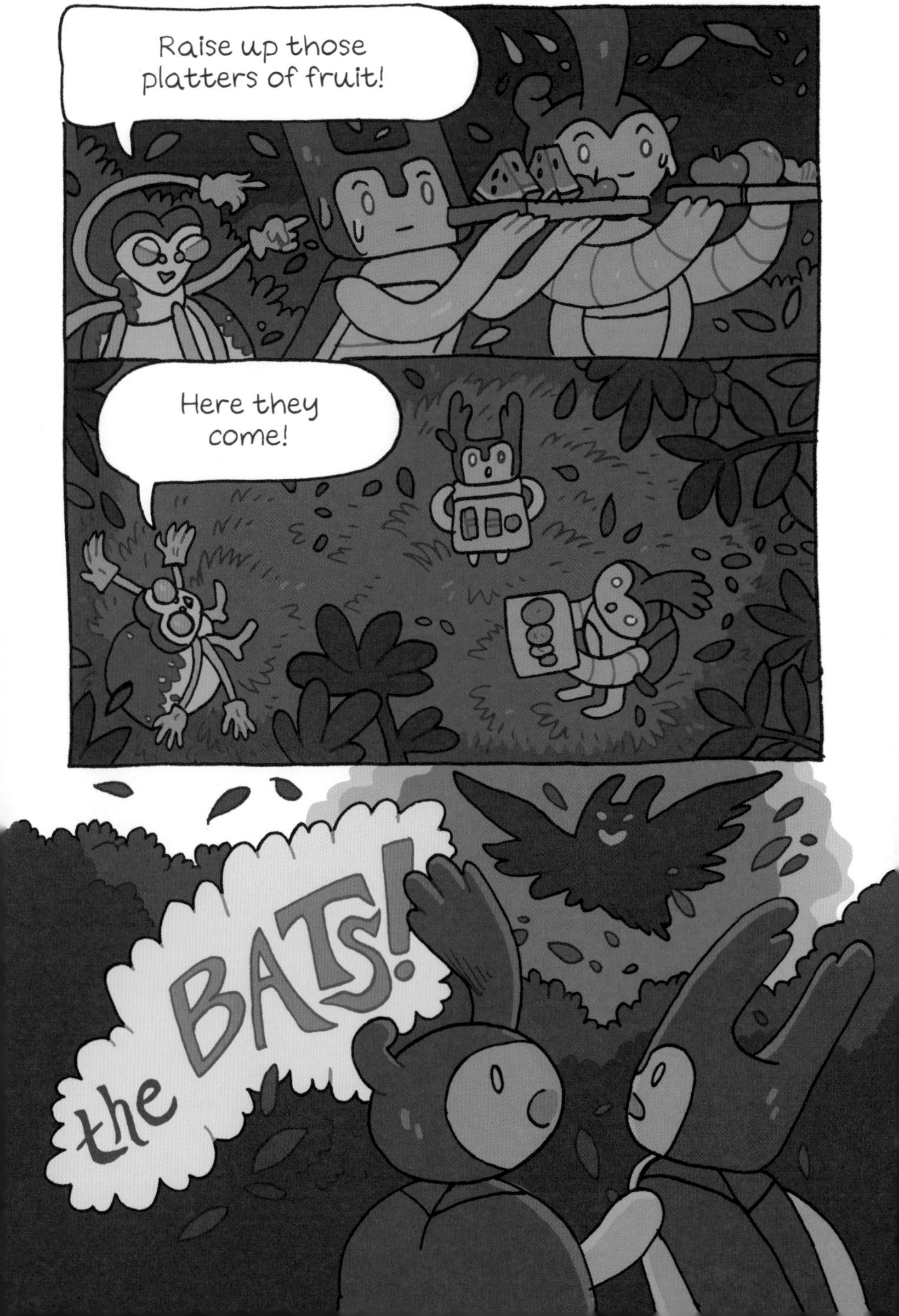
Raise up those platters of fruit!
Here they come!
the BATS!

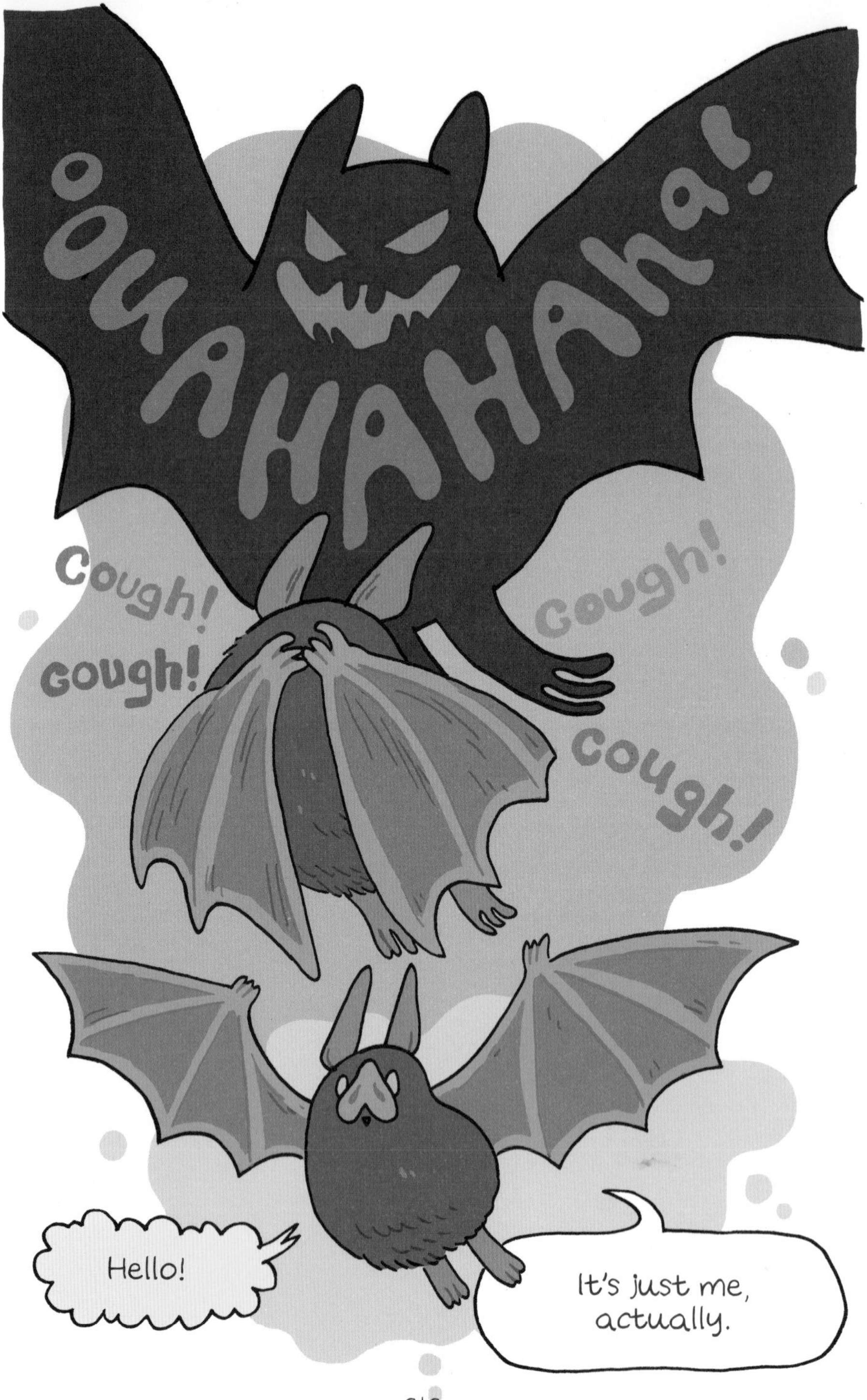

OUAHAHAHAHA!
Cough! cough!
Cough!
cough!
Hello!
It's just me, actually.

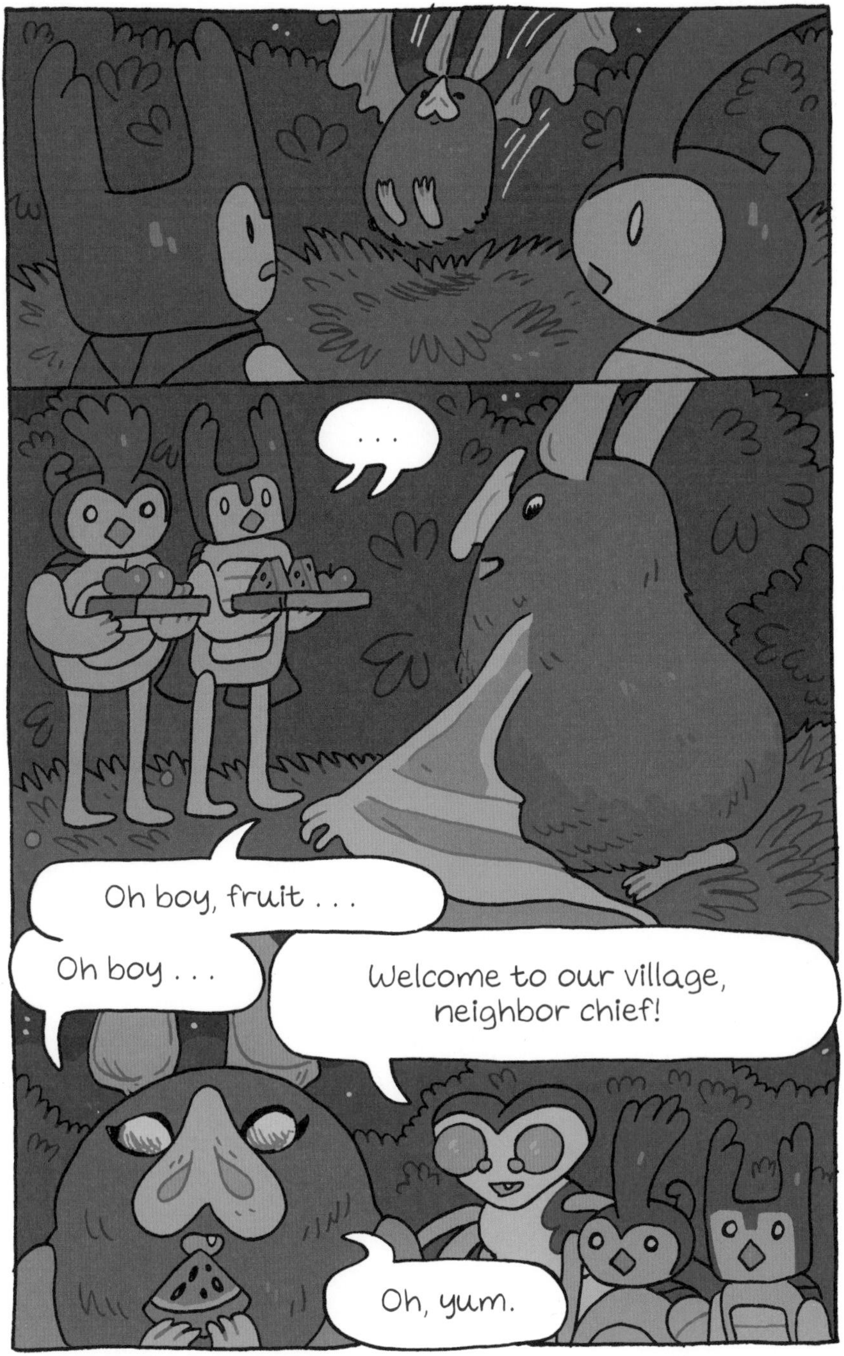
. . .
Oh boy, fruit . . .
Oh boy . . .
Welcome to our village, neighbor chief!
Oh, yum.

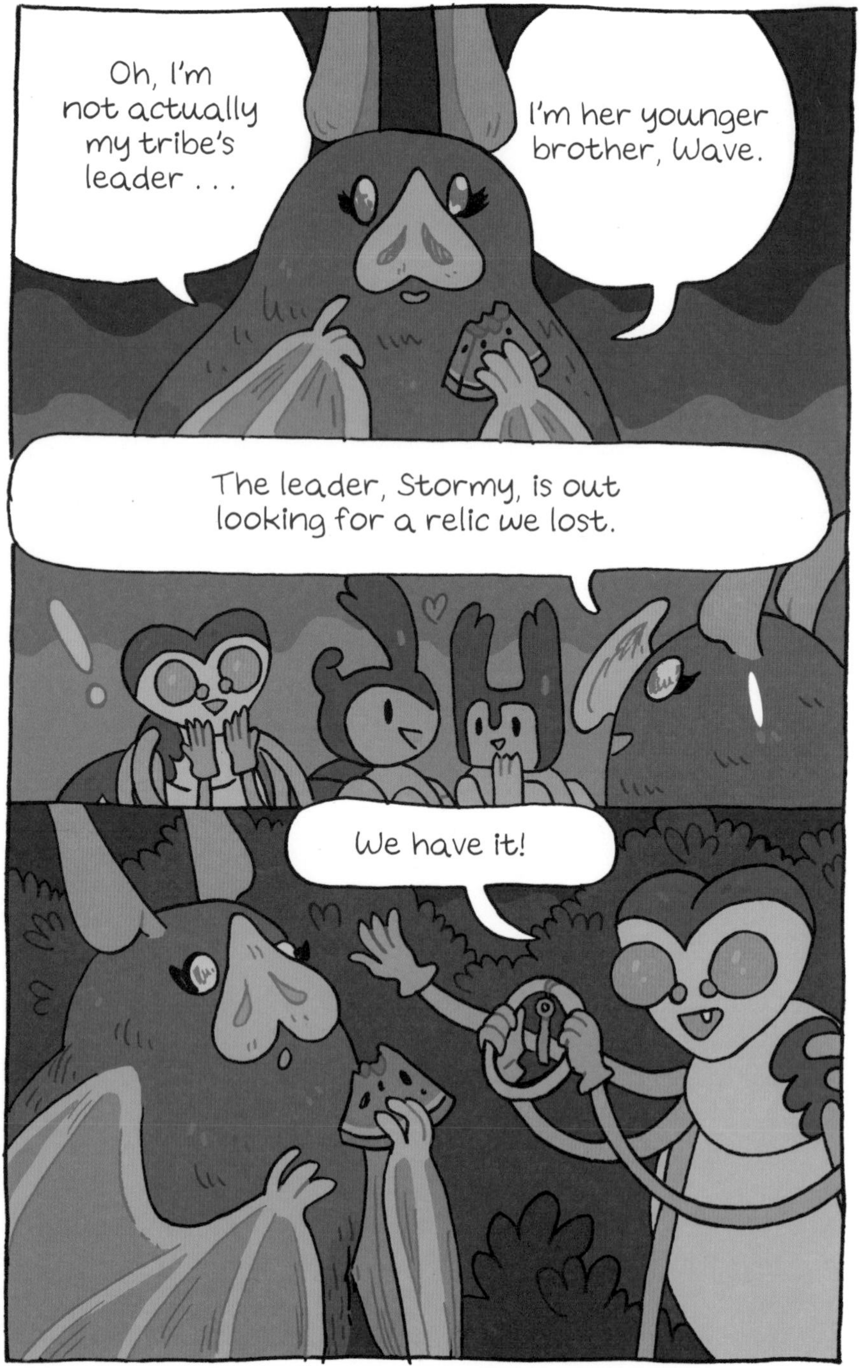
Oh, I'm not actually my tribe's leader . . .
I'm her younger brother, Wave.
The leader, Stormy, is out looking for a relic we lost.
We have it!

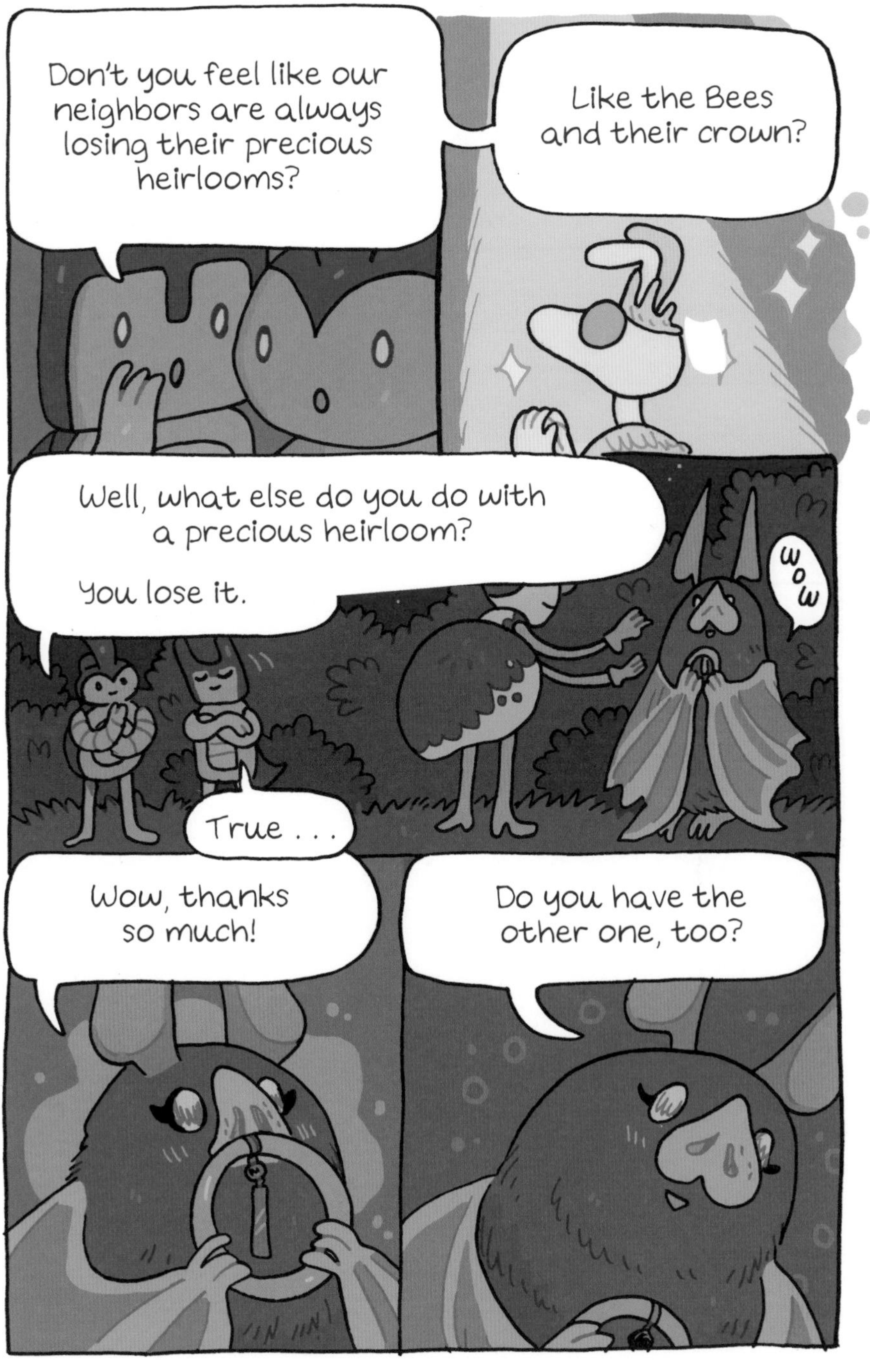
Don't you feel like our neighbors are always losing their precious heirlooms?
Like the Bees and their crown?
Well, what else do you do with a precious heirloom?
You lose it.
WOW
True . . .
Wow, thanks so much!
Do you have the other one, too?

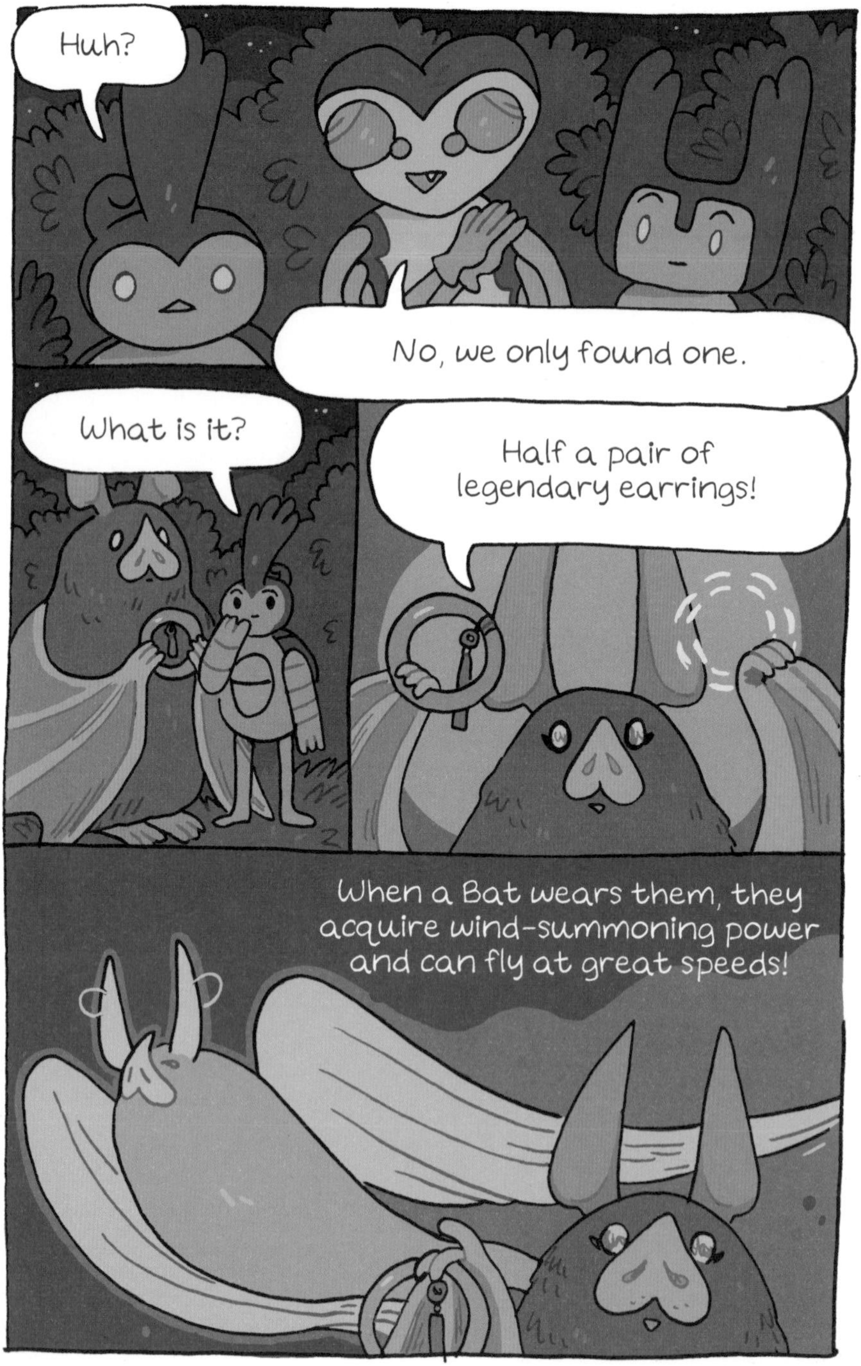
Huh?
No, we only found one.
What is it?
Half a pair of legendary earrings!
When a Bat wears them, they acquire wind-summoning power and can fly at great speeds!

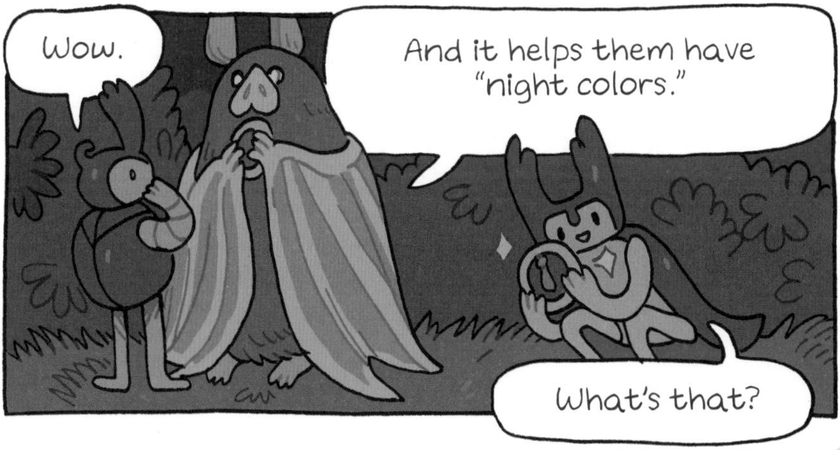
Wow.
And it helps them have "night colors."
What's that?

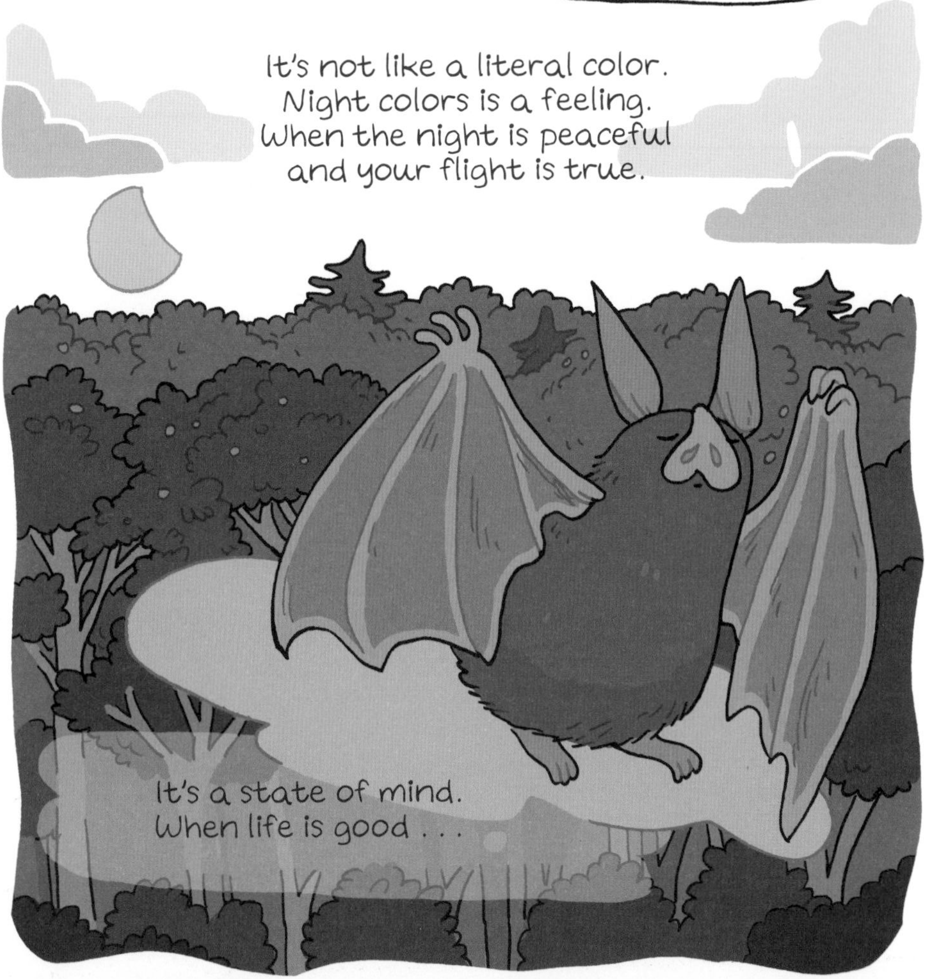
It's not like a literal color. Night colors is a feeling. When the night is peaceful and your flight is true.
It's a state of mind. When life is good . . .

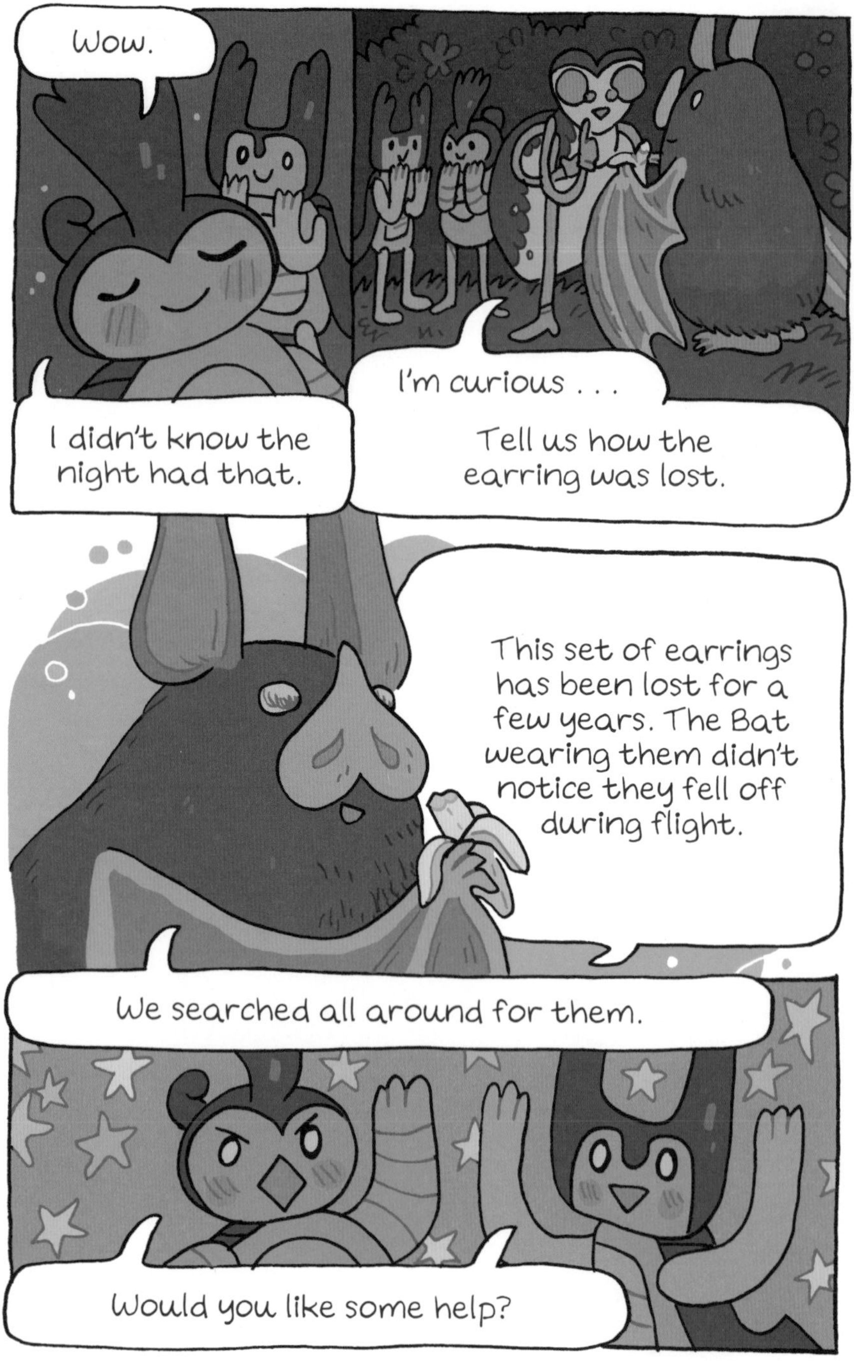
Wow.
I didn't know the night had that.
I'm curious . . .
Tell us how the earring was lost.
This set of earrings has been lost for a few years. The Bat wearing them didn't notice they fell off during flight.
We searched all around for them.
Would you like some help?

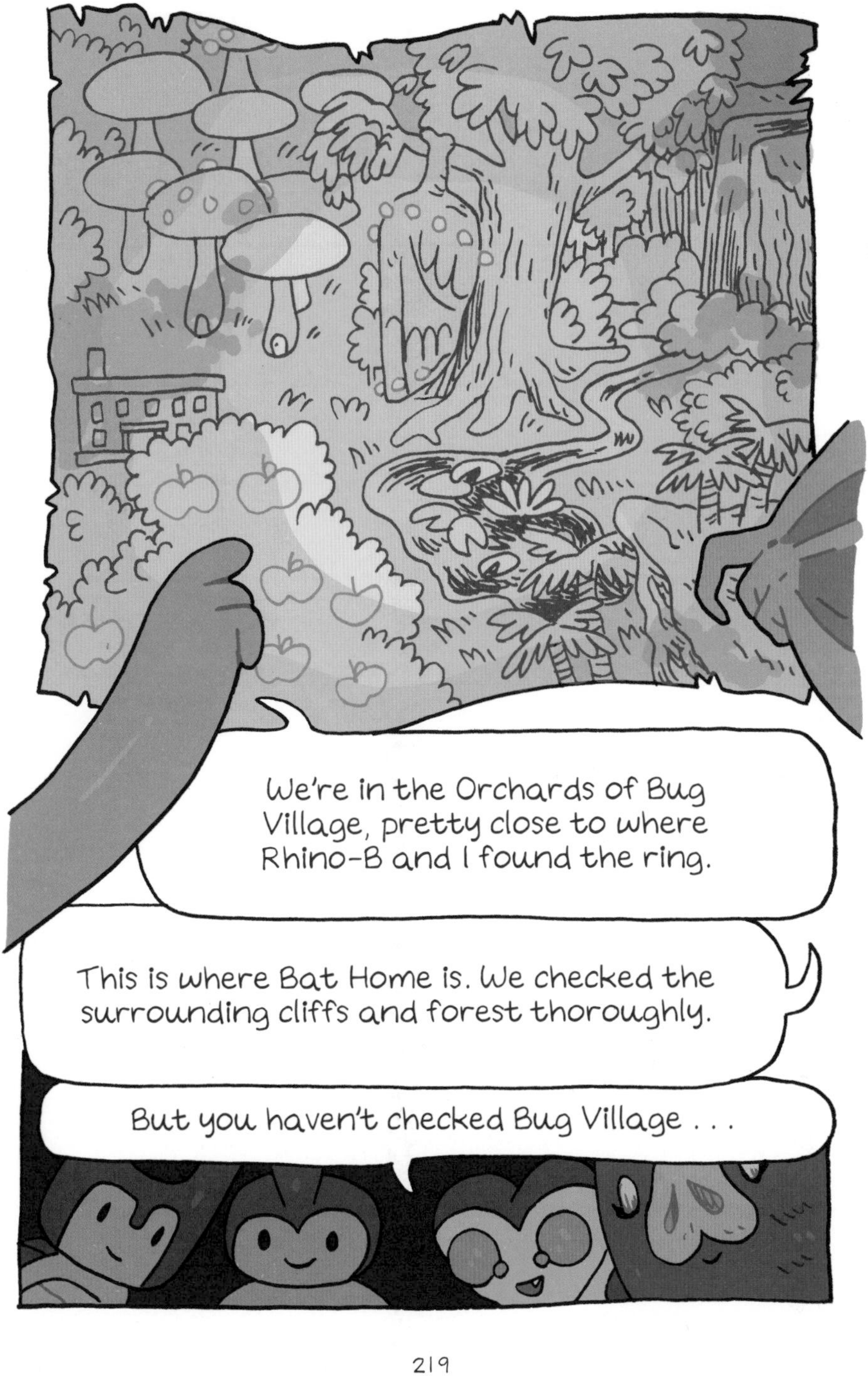
We're in the Orchards of Bug Village, pretty close to where Rhino-B and I found the ring.
This is where Bat Home is. We checked the surrounding cliffs and forest thoroughly.
But you haven't checked Bug Village . . .

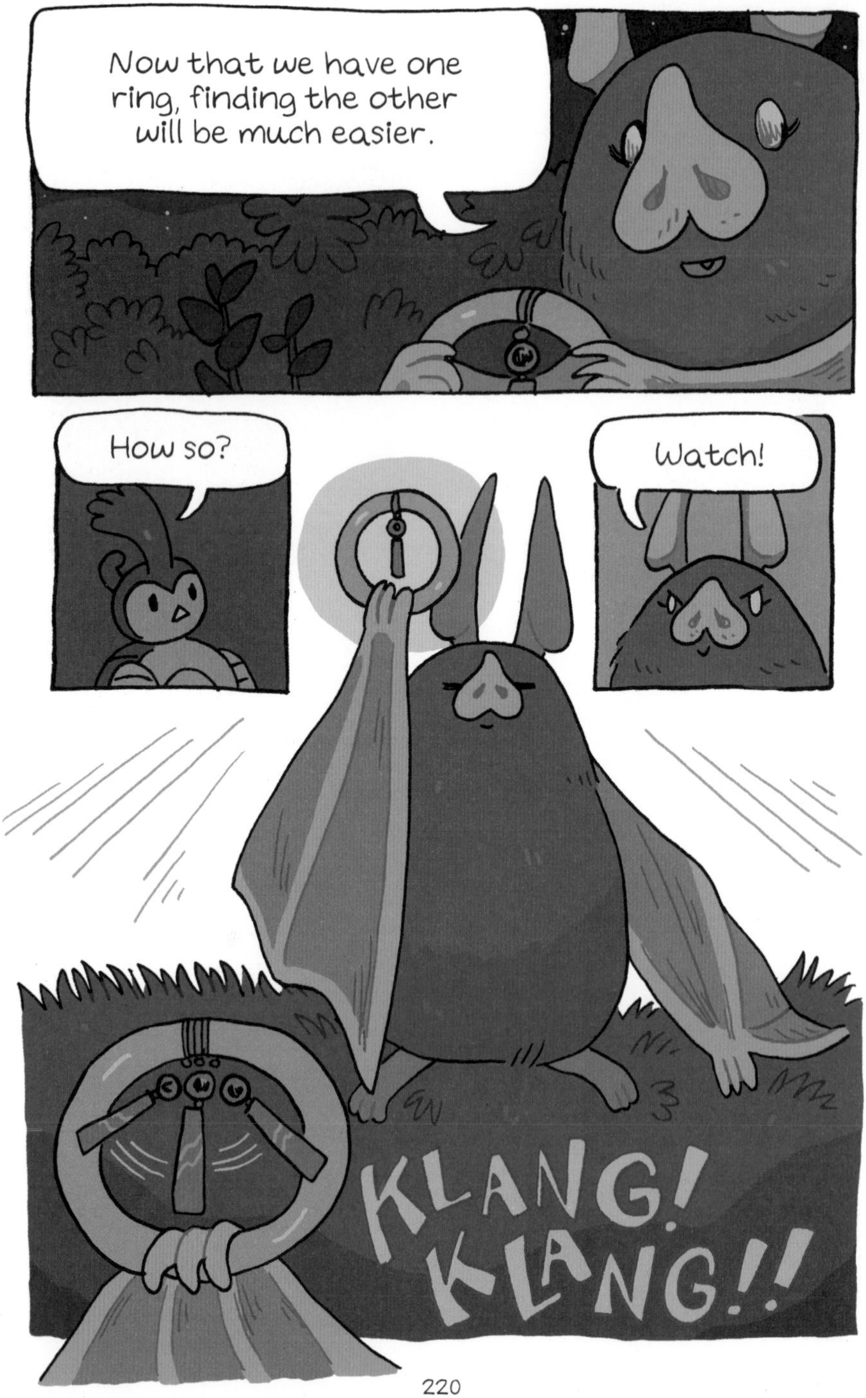
Now that we have one ring, finding the other will be much easier.
How so?
Watch!
KLANG! KLANG!!

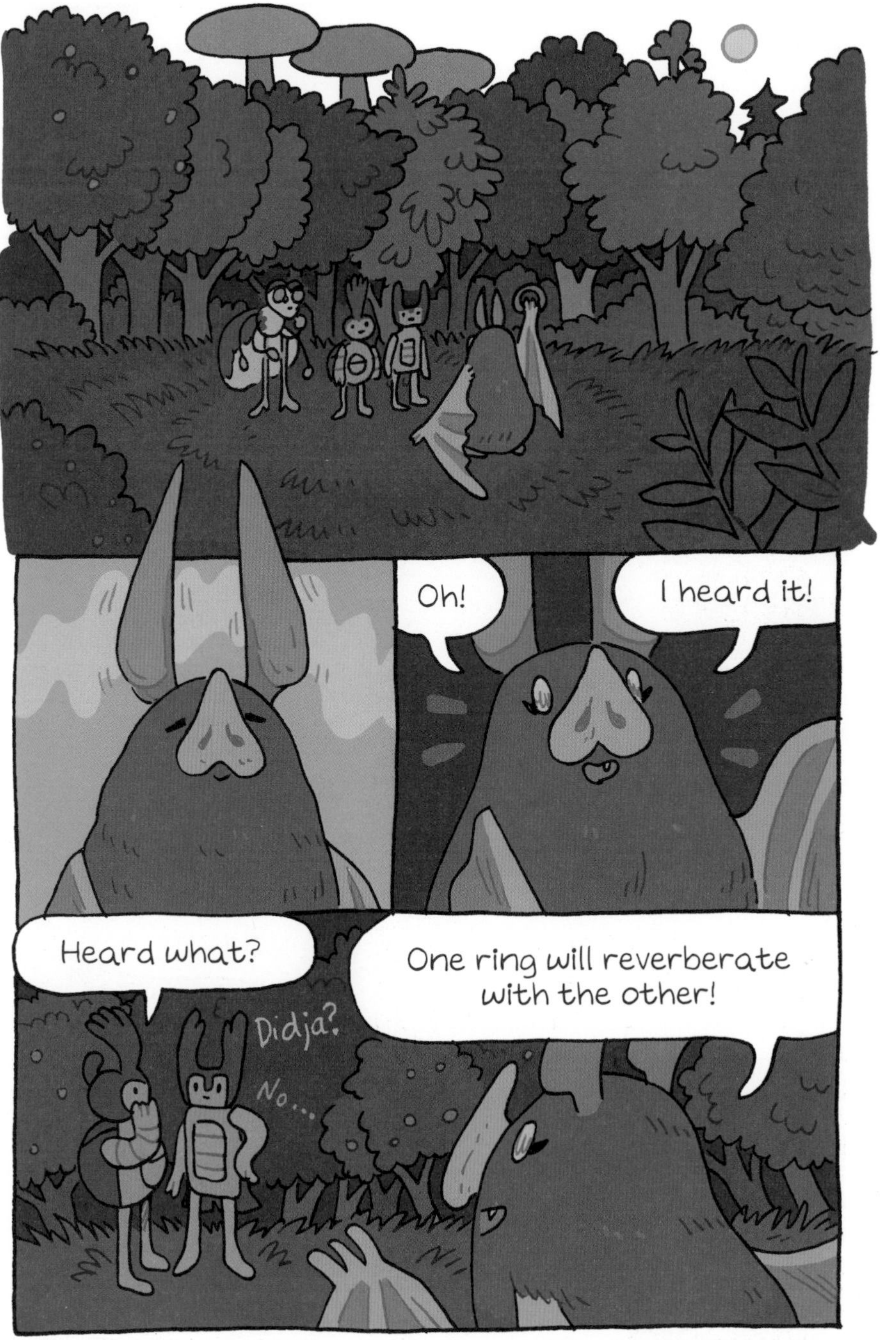
Oh!
I heard it!
Heard what?
Didja?
No...
One ring will reverberate with the other!

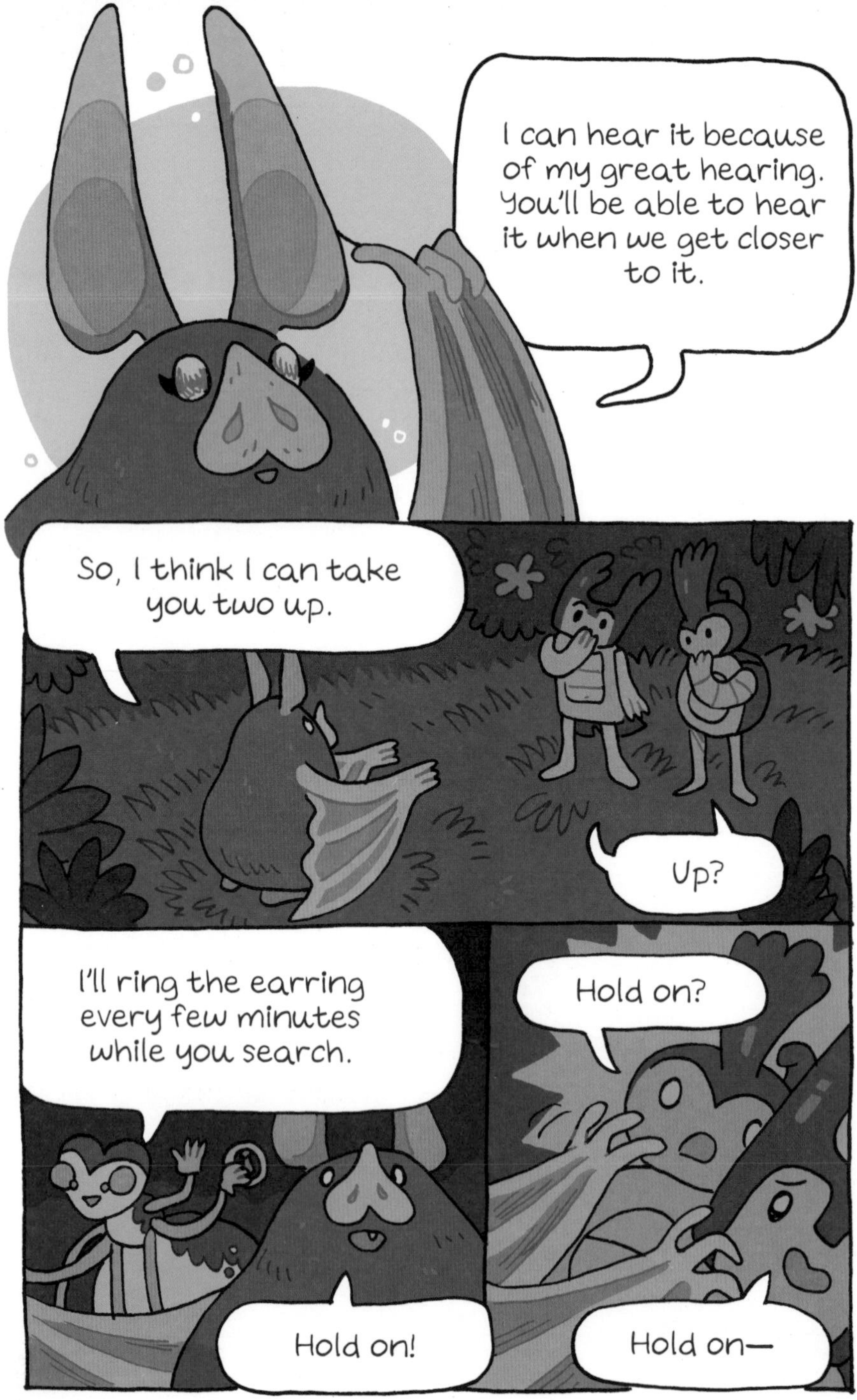
I can hear it because of my great hearing. You'll be able to hear it when we get closer to it.
So, I think I can take you two up.
Up?
I'll ring the earring every few minutes while you search.
Hold on!
Hold on?
Hold on—

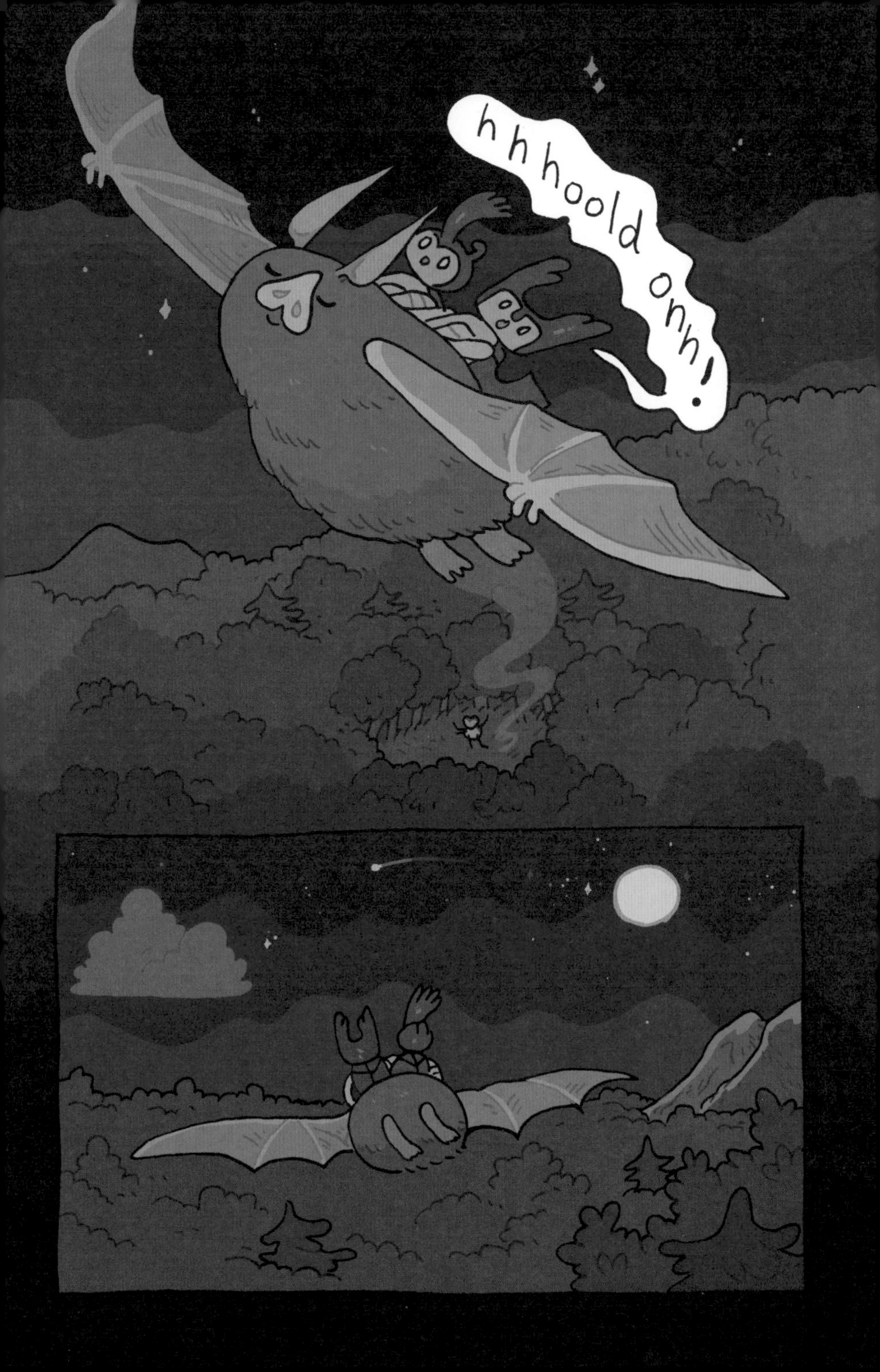
hhhoold onn!

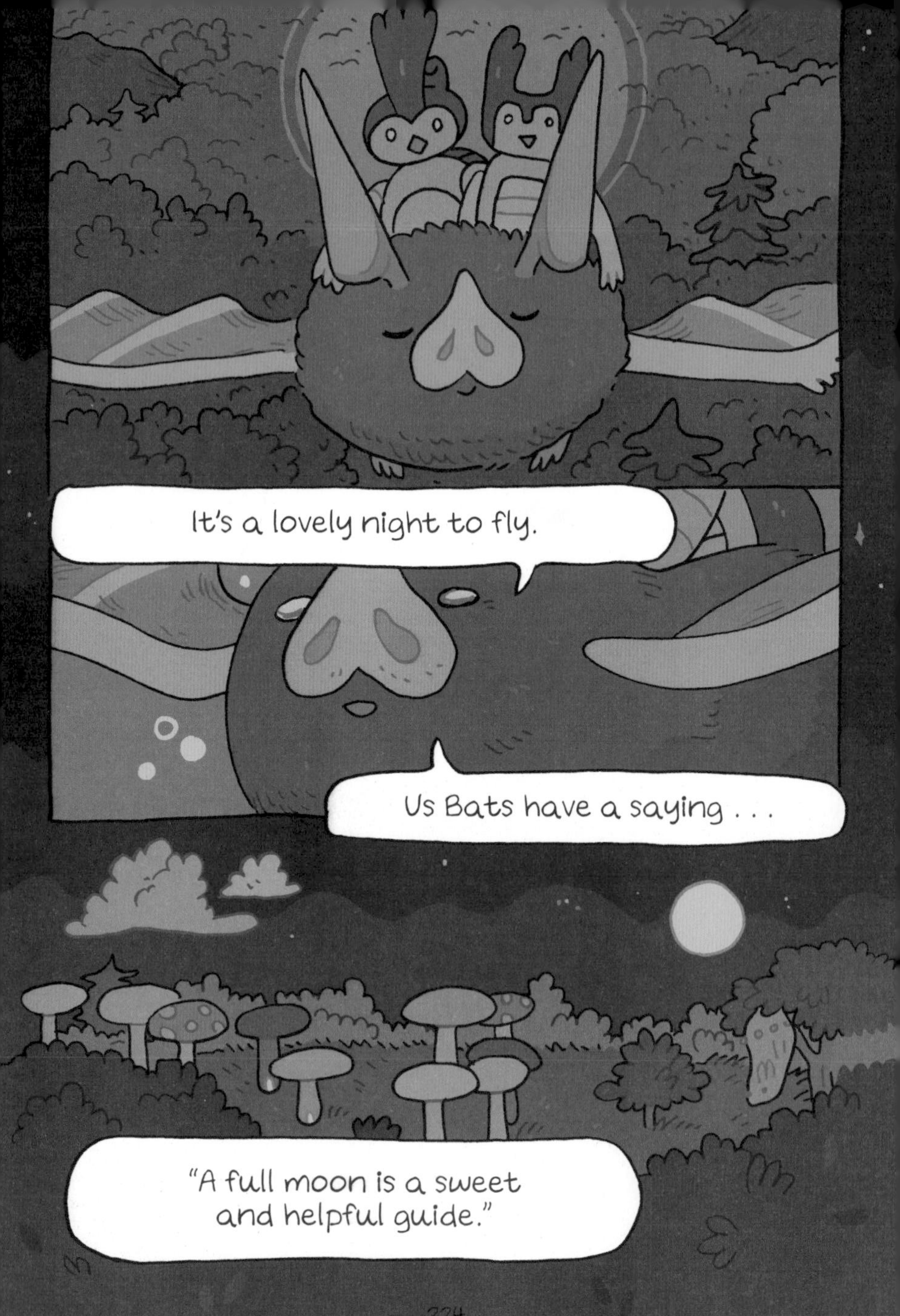

It's a lovely night to fly.
Us Bats have a saying . . .
"A full moon is a sweet and helpful guide."

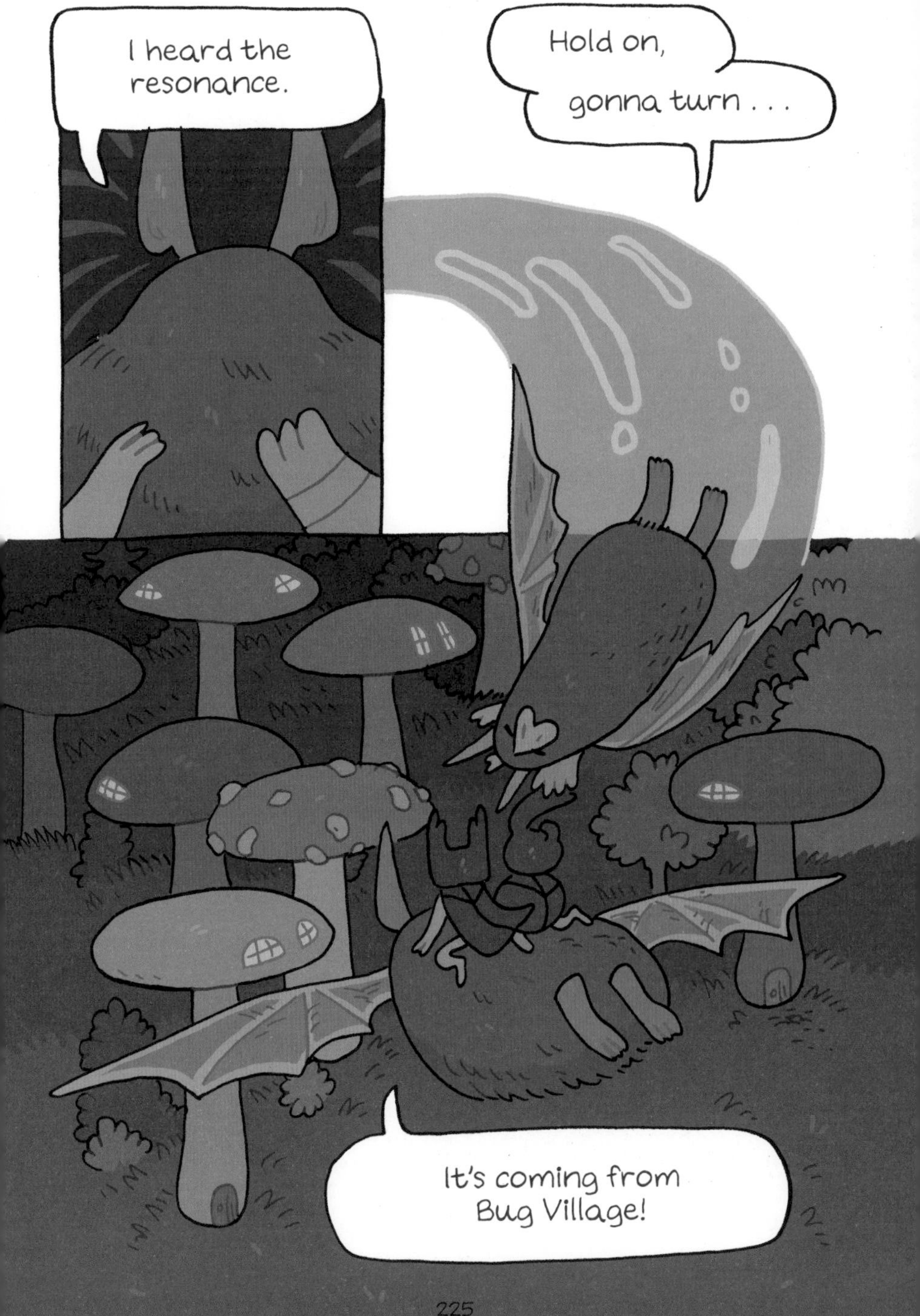
I heard the resonance.
Hold on,
gonna turn . . .
It's coming from Bug Village!

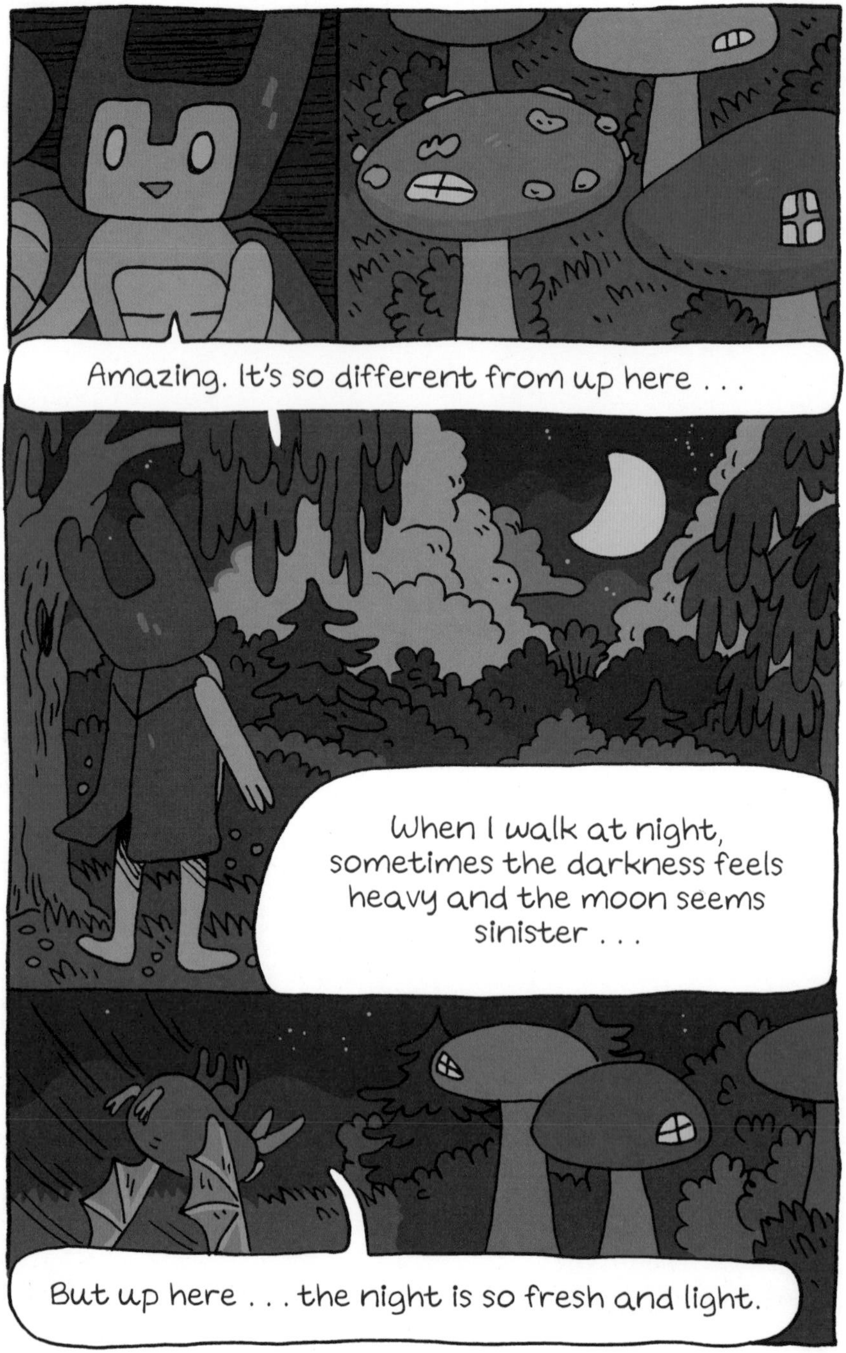
Amazing. It's so different from up here . . .
When I walk at night, sometimes the darkness feels heavy and the moon seems sinister . . .
But up here . . . the night is so fresh and light.

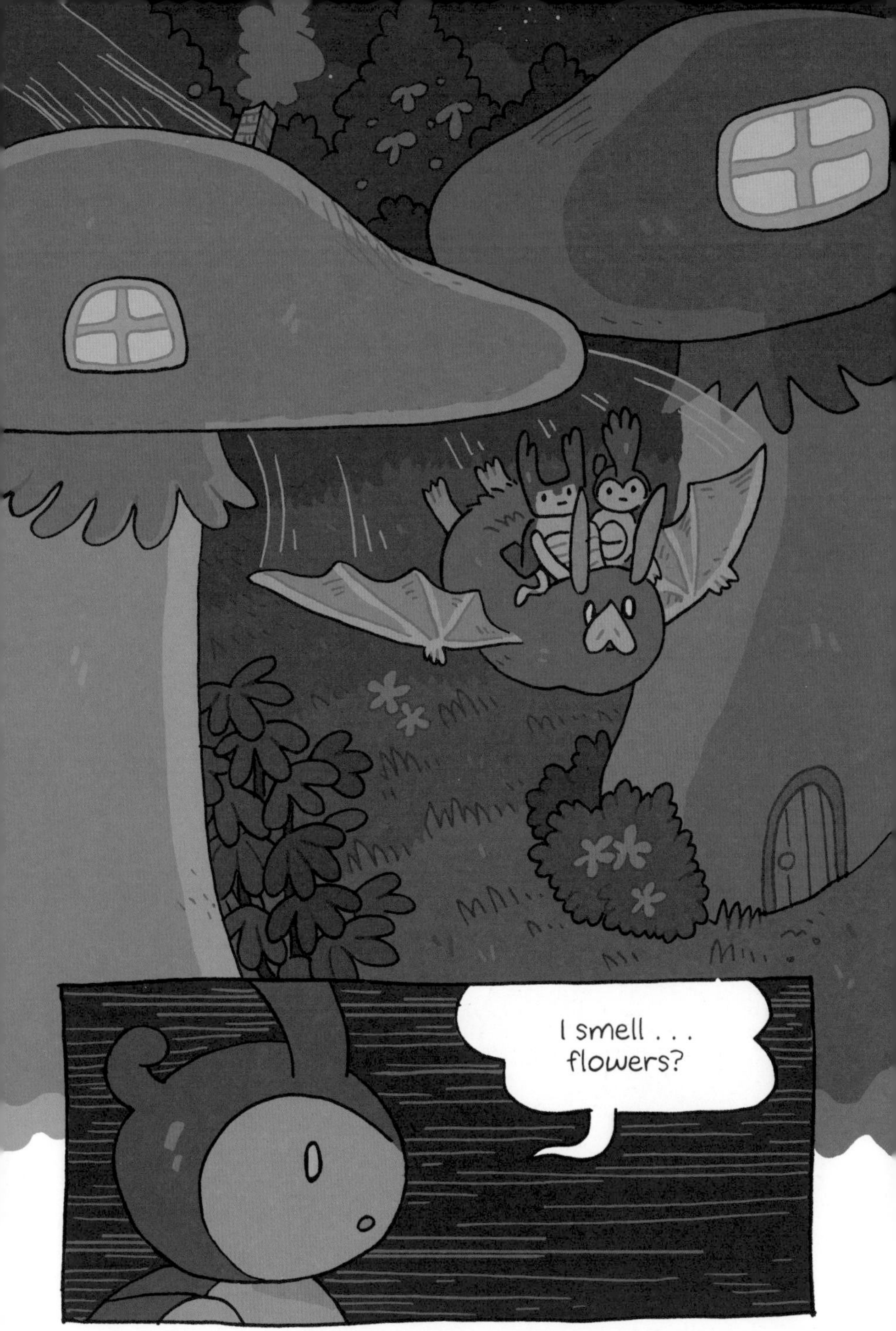
I smell . . . flowers?

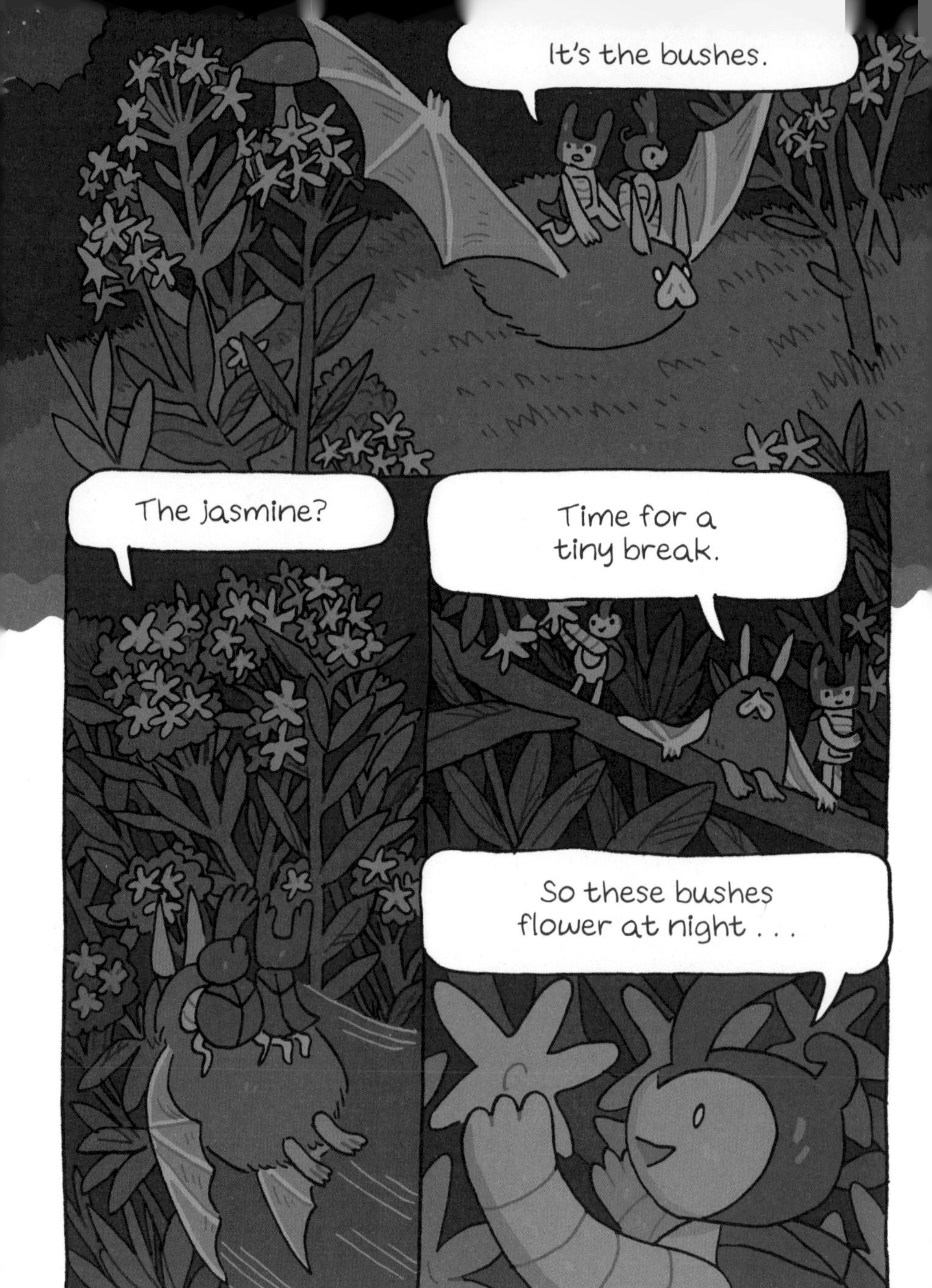
It's the bushes.
The jasmine?
Time for a tiny break.
So these bushes flower at night . . .

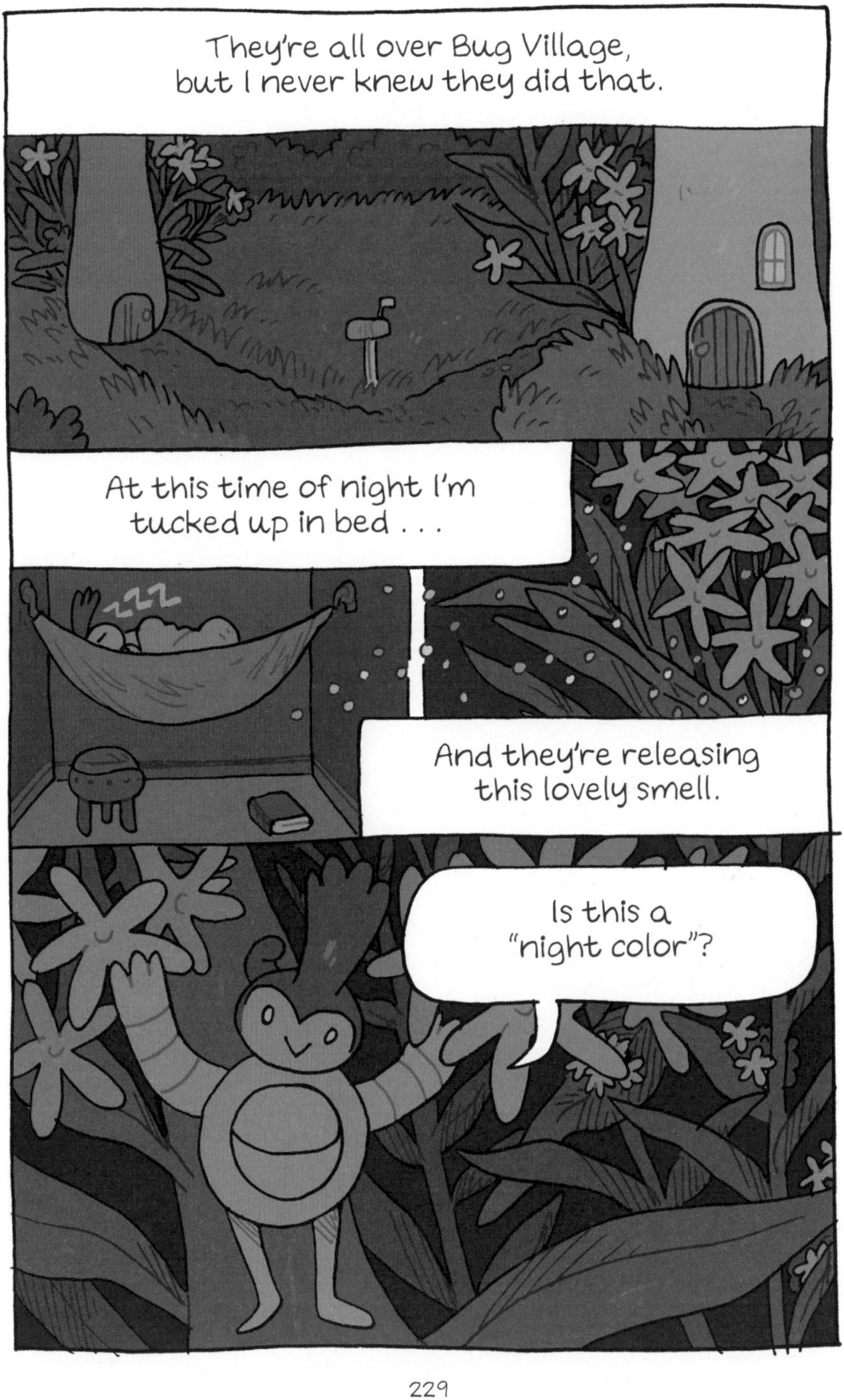
They're all over Bug Village, but I never knew they did that.
At this time of night I'm tucked up in bed . . .
ZZZ
And they're releasing this lovely smell.
Is this a "night color"?

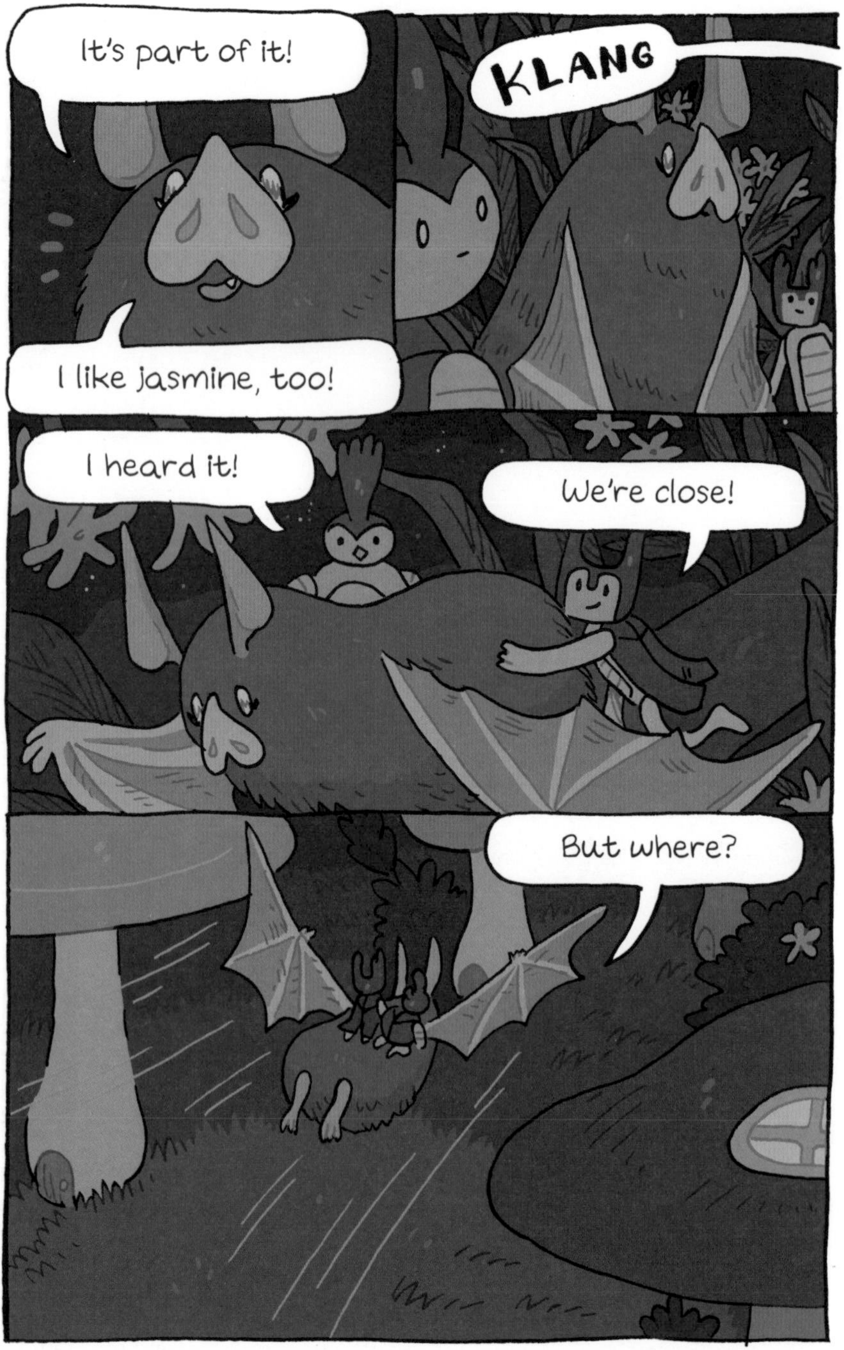
It's part of it!
KLANG
I like jasmine, too!
I heard it!
We're close!
But where?

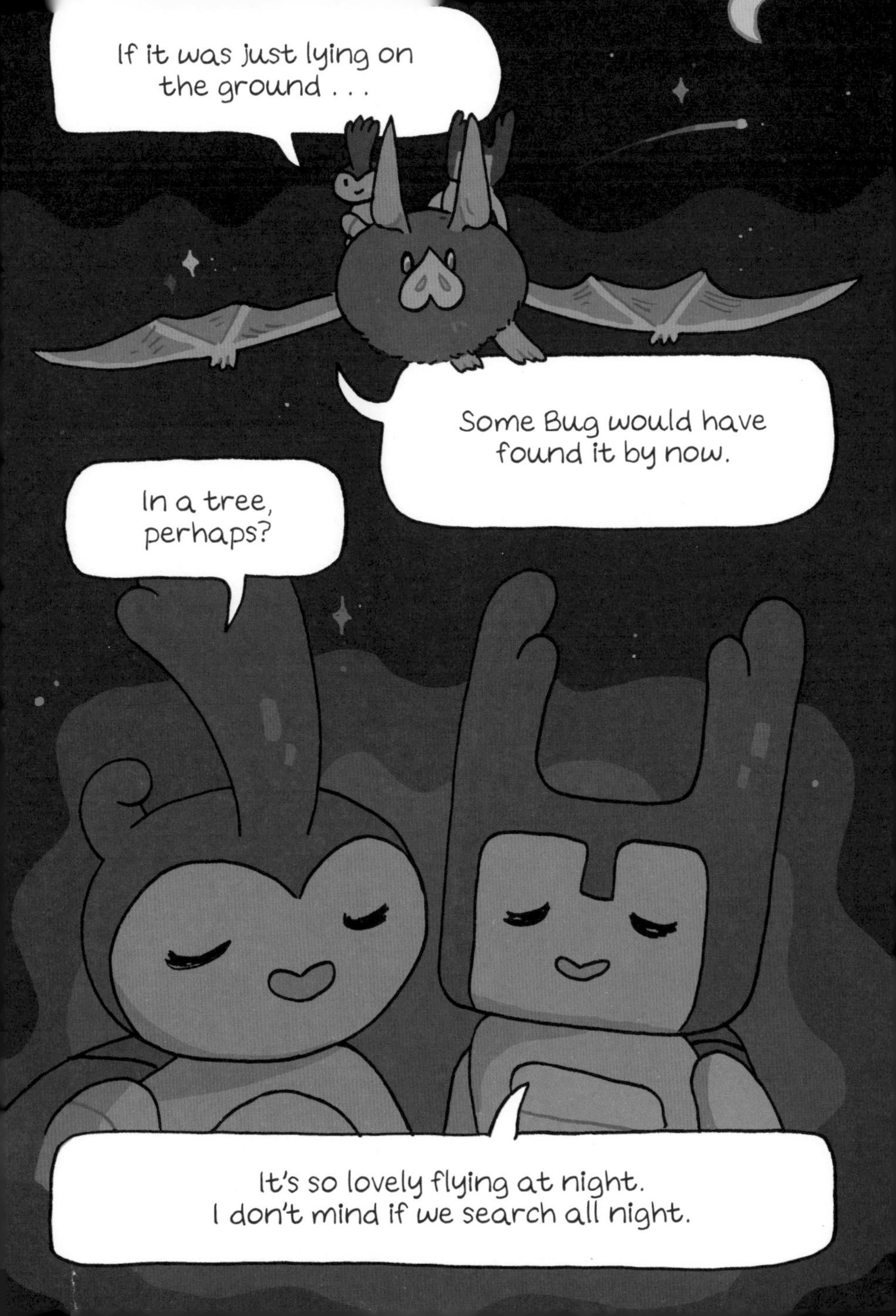
If it was just lying on the ground . . .
Some Bug would have found it by now.
In a tree, perhaps?
It's so lovely flying at night. I don't mind if we search all night.

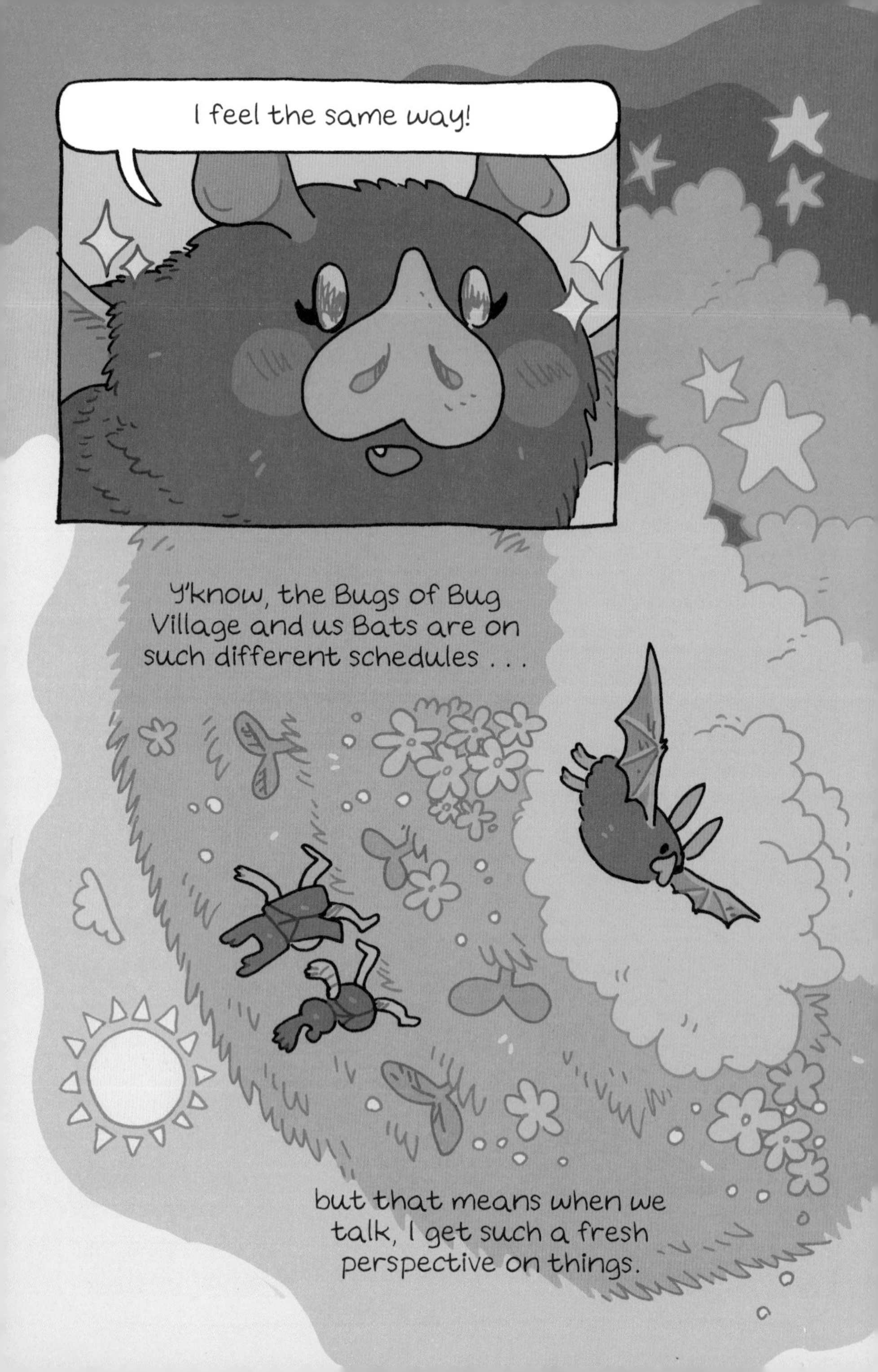
I feel the same way!
Y'know, the Bugs of Bug Village and us Bats are on such different schedules . . .
but that means when we talk, I get such a fresh perspective on things.

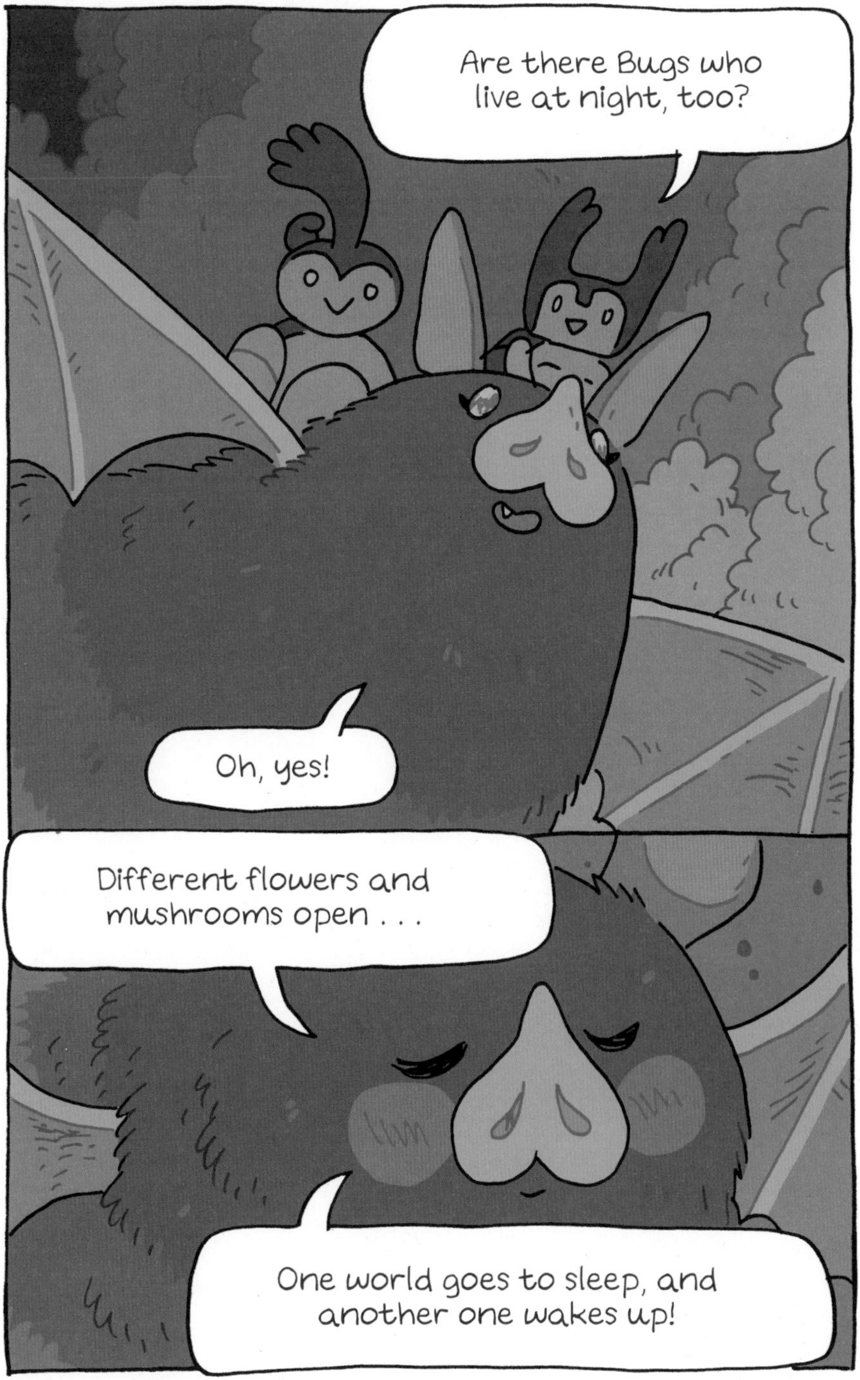
Are there Bugs who live at night, too?
Oh, yes!
Different flowers and mushrooms open . . .
One world goes to sleep, and another one wakes up!

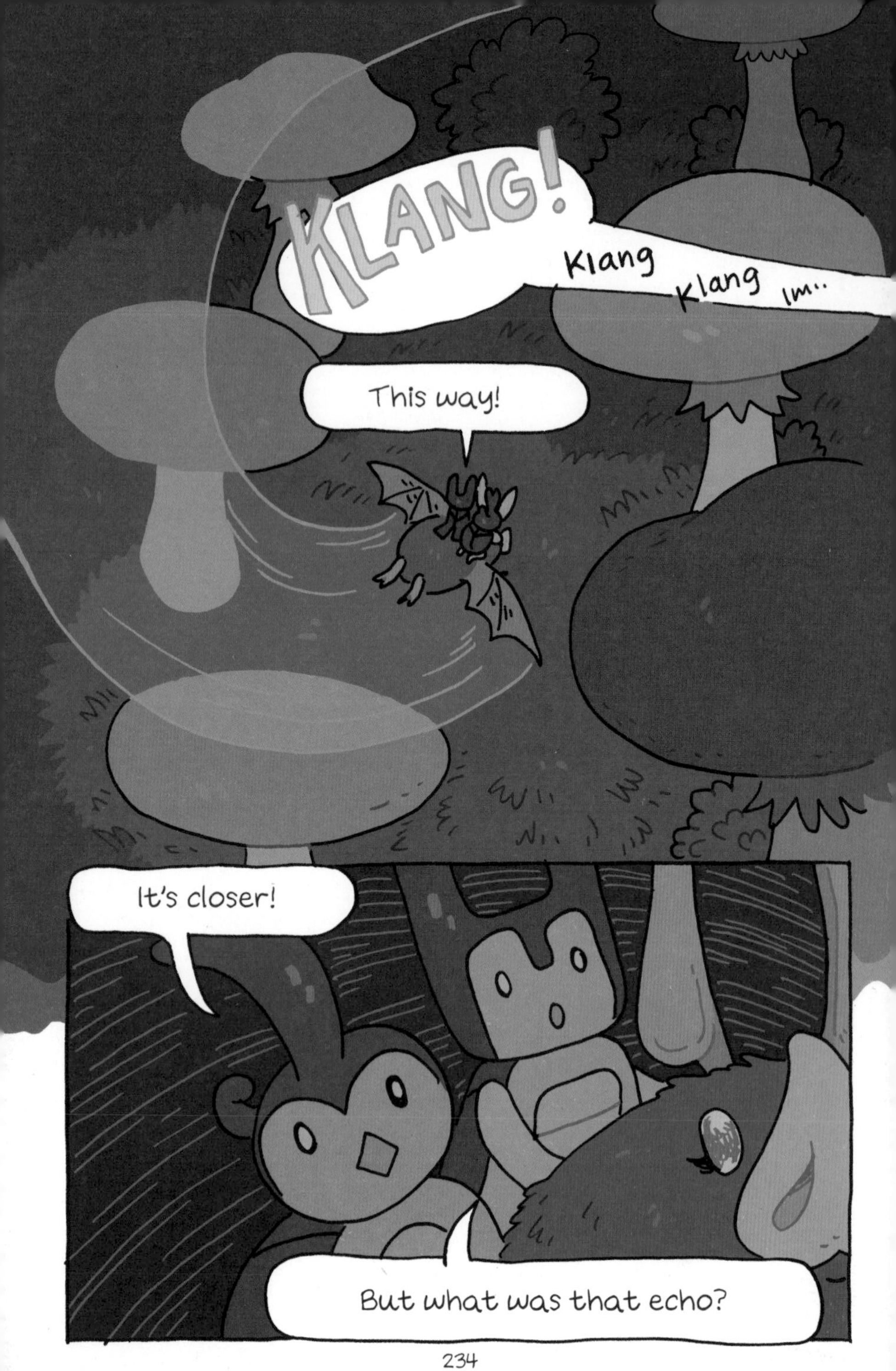
KLANG!
Klang
Klang
lm..
This way!
It's closer!
But what was that echo?

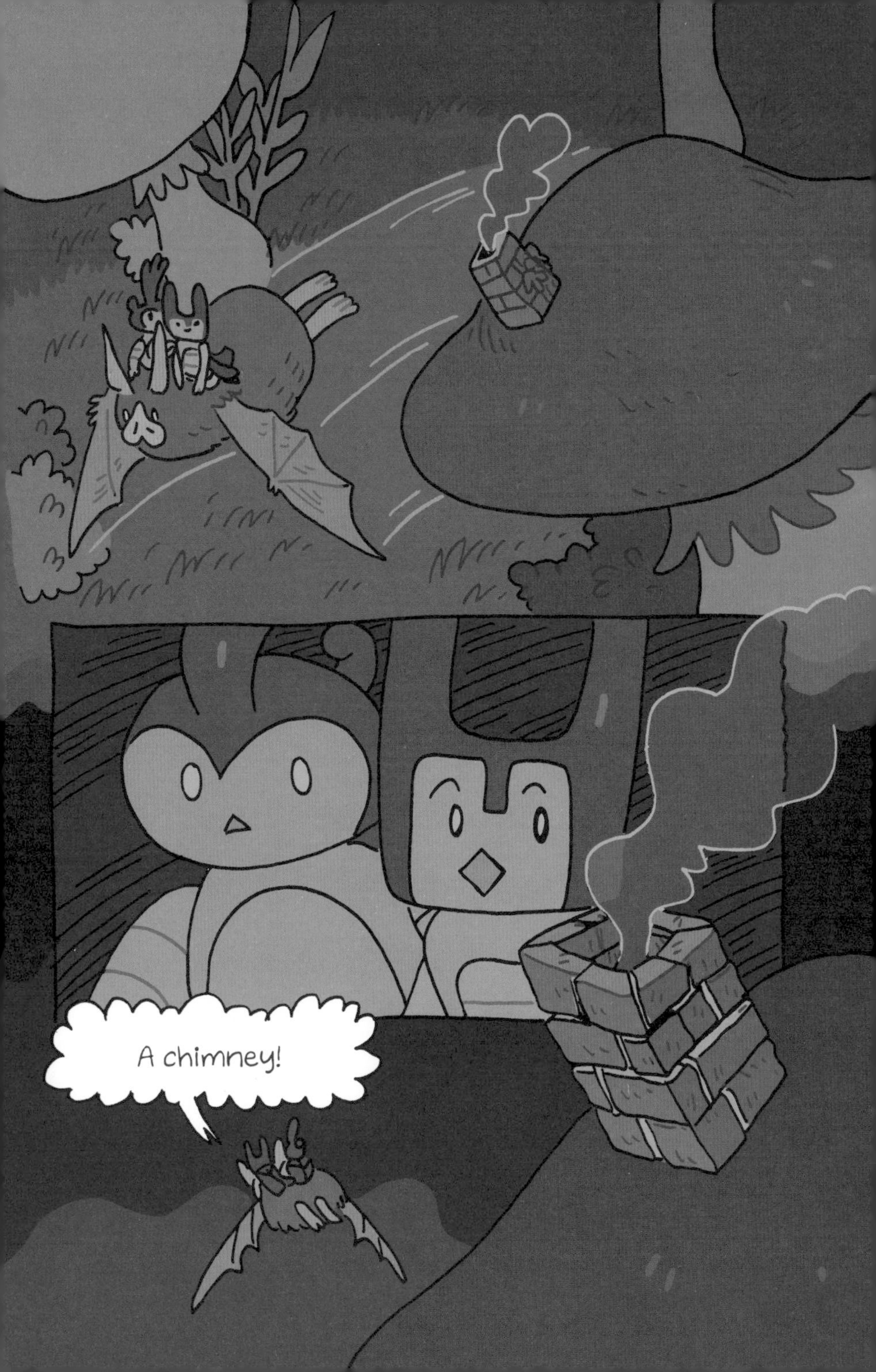
A chimney!

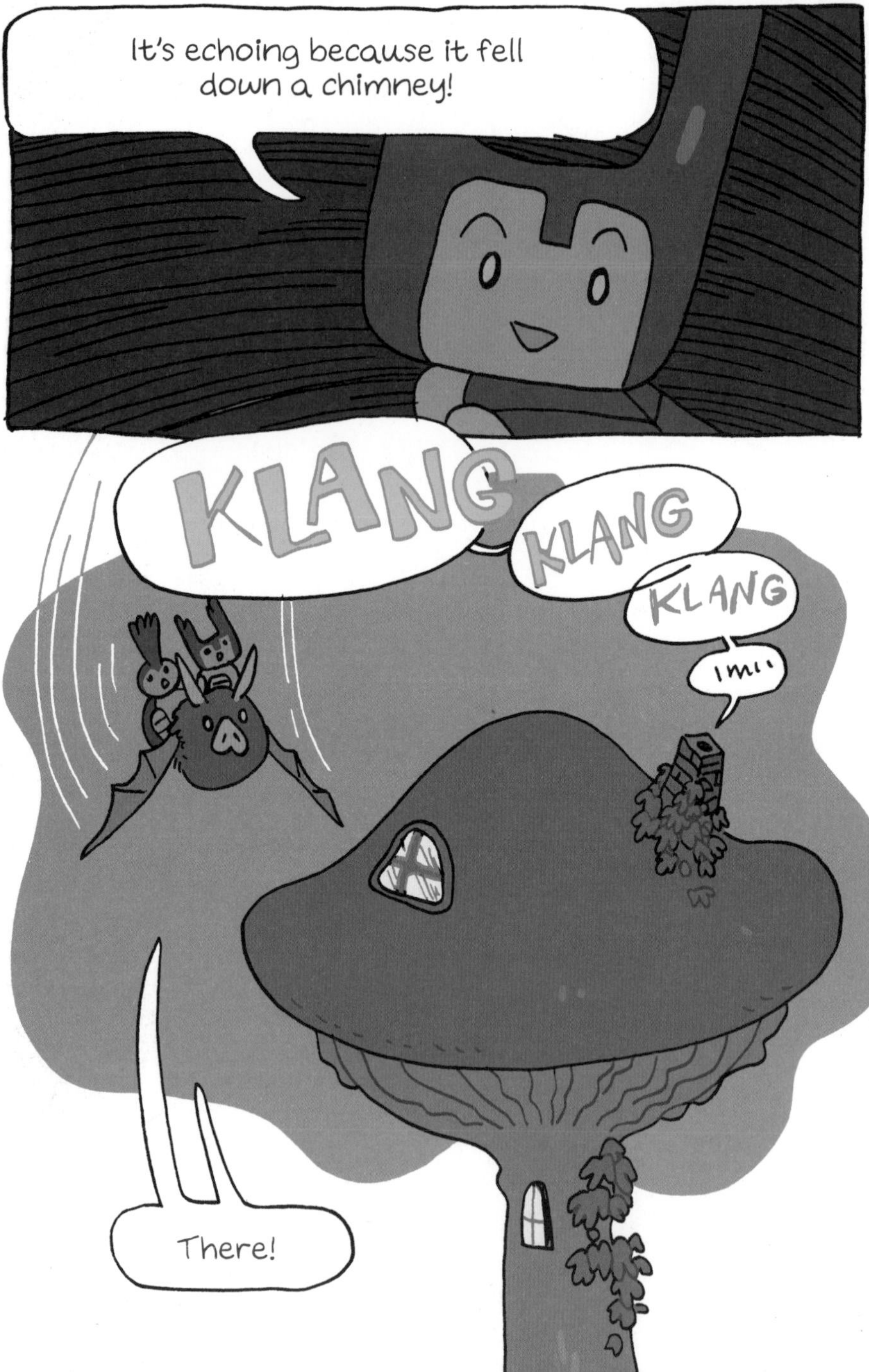
It's echoing because it fell down a chimney!
KLANG
KLANG
KLANG
Imm
There!

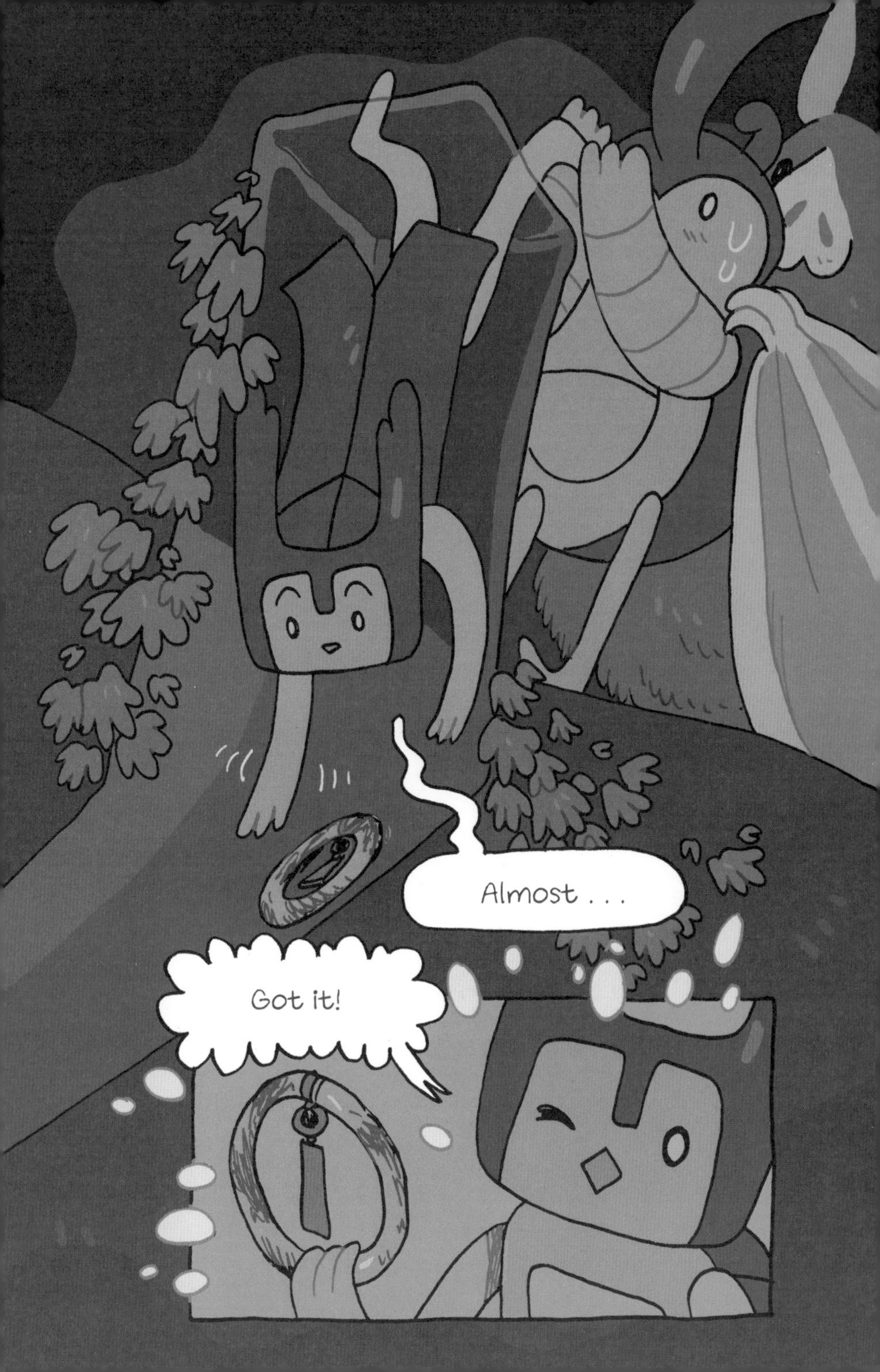
Almost . . .
Got it!

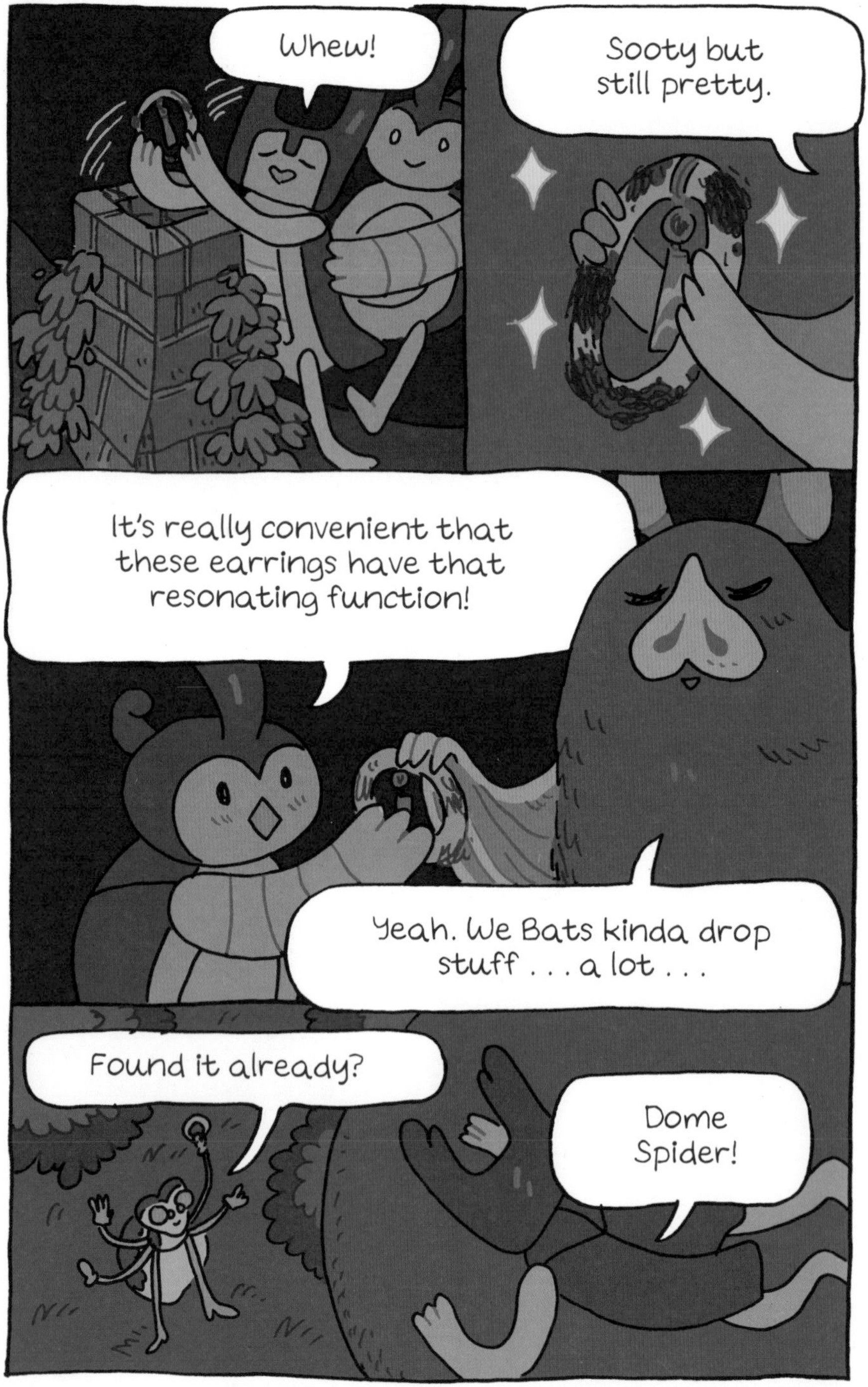
Whew!
Sooty but still pretty.
It's really convenient that these earrings have that resonating function!
Yeah. We Bats kinda drop stuff . . . a lot . . .
Found it already?
Dome Spider!

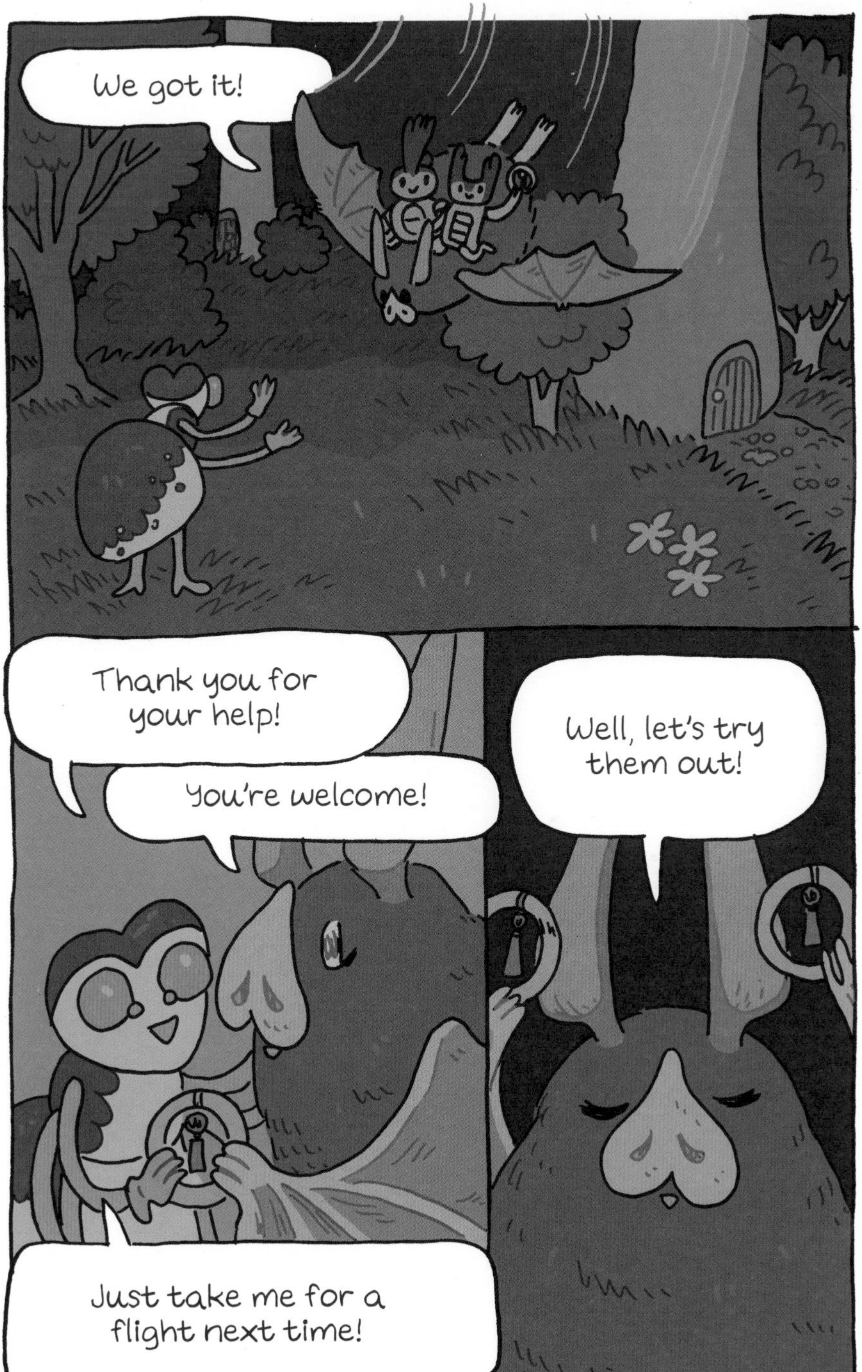
We got it!
Thank you for your help!
You're welcome!
Just take me for a flight next time!
Well, let's try them out!

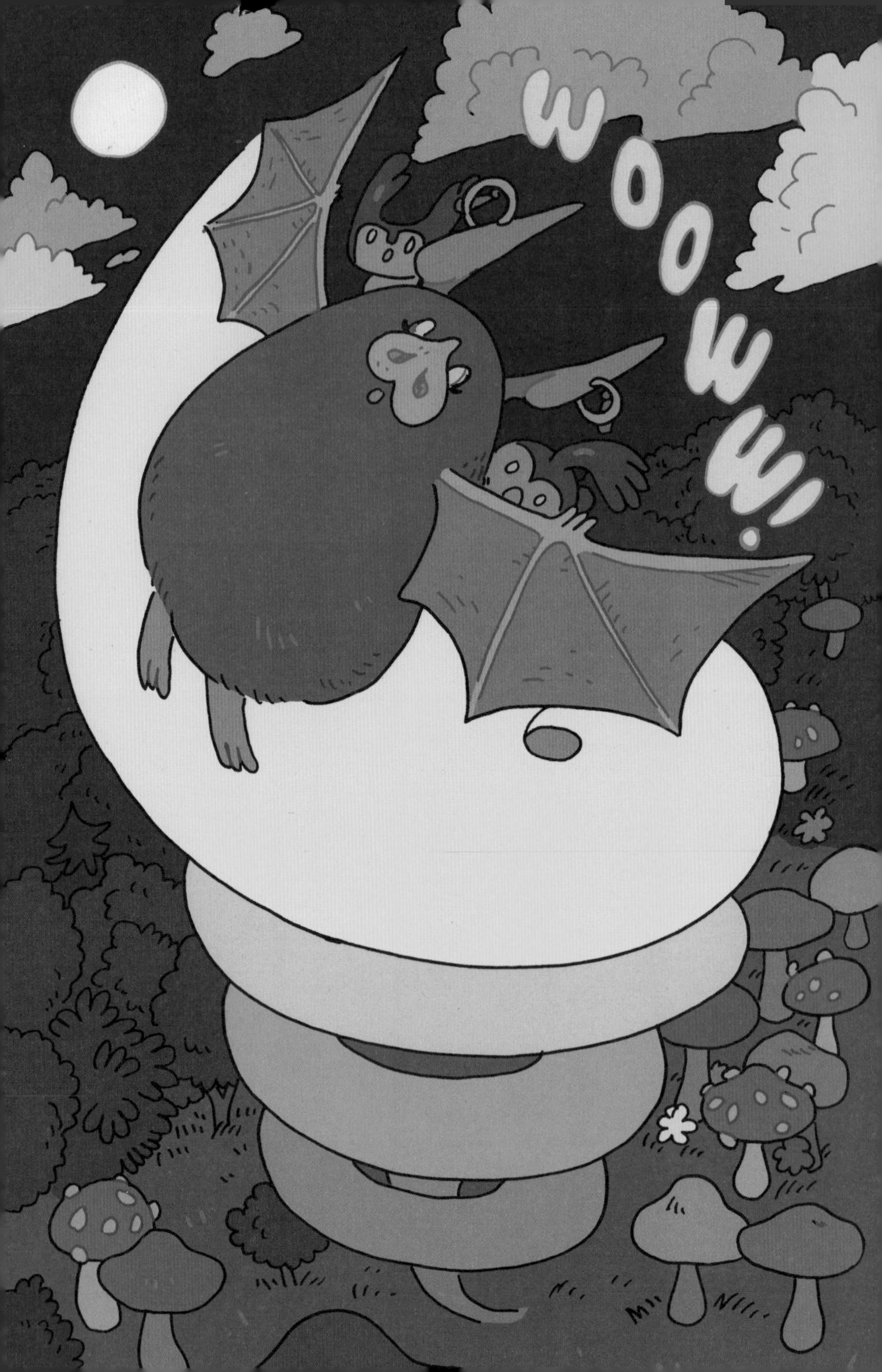
WOOOWW!

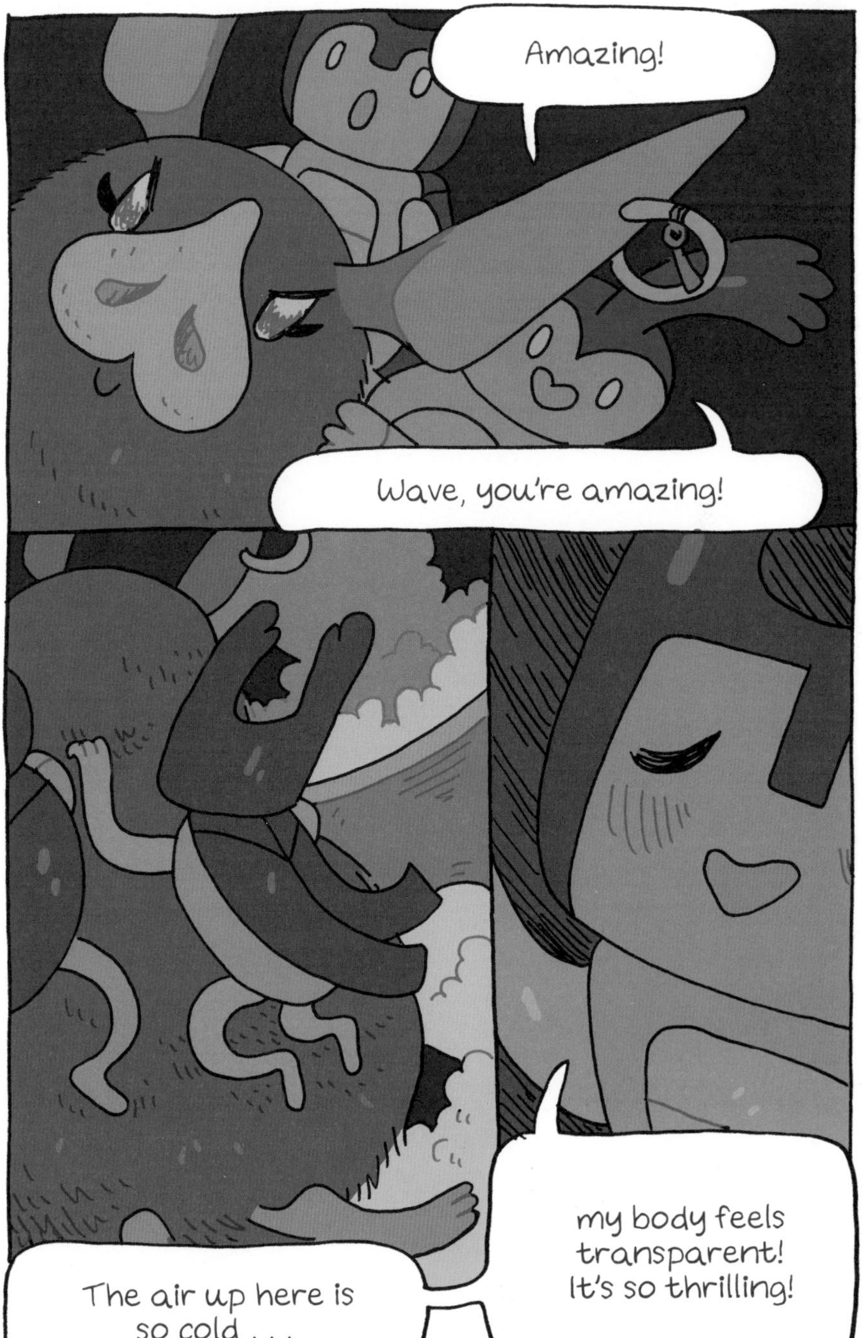
Amazing!
Wave, you're amazing!
The air up here is so cold . . .
my body feels transparent! It's so thrilling!

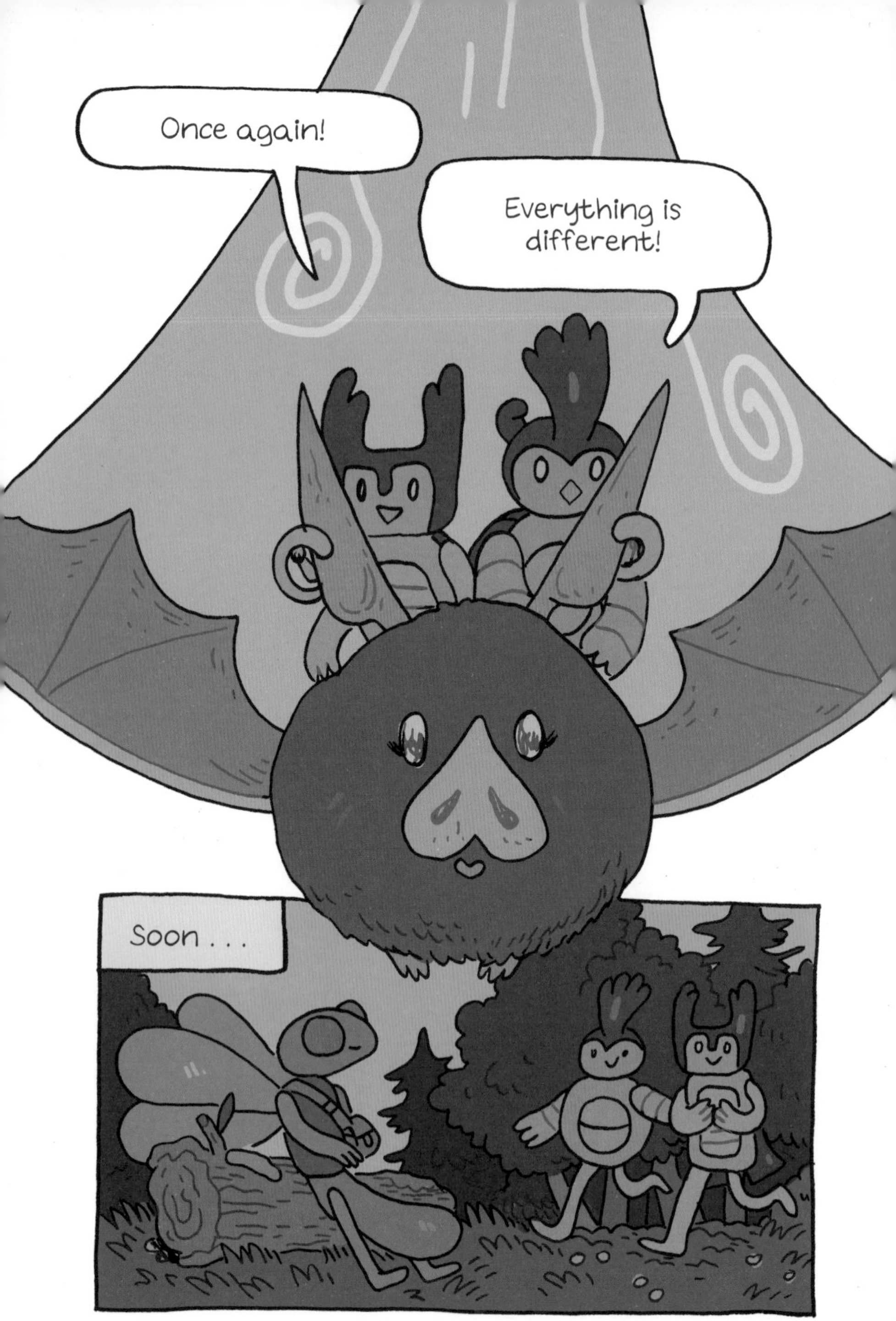
Once again!
Everything is different!
Soon . . .

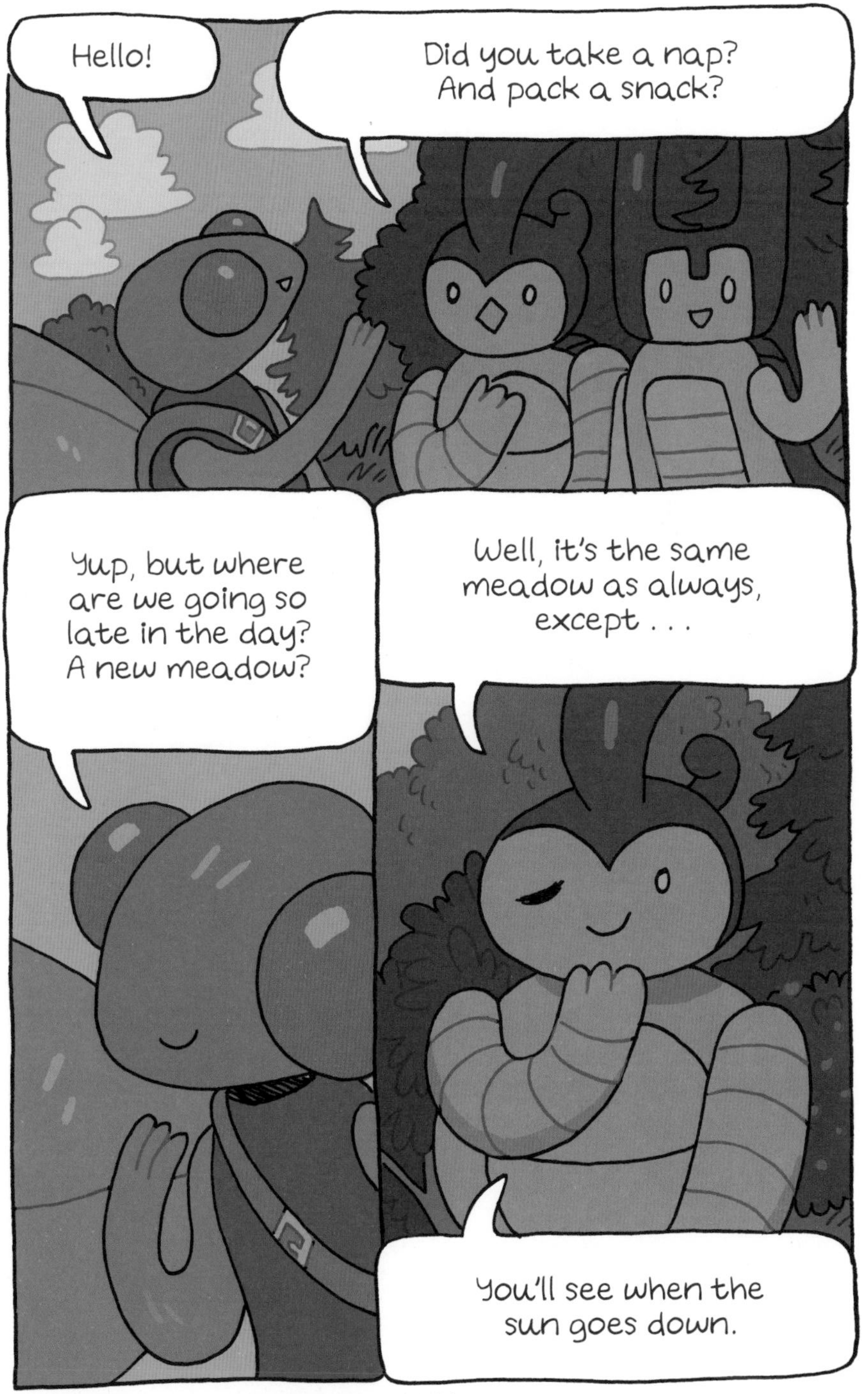
Hello!
Did you take a nap? And pack a snack?
Yup, but where are we going so late in the day? A new meadow?
Well, it's the same meadow as always, except . . .
You'll see when the sun goes down.

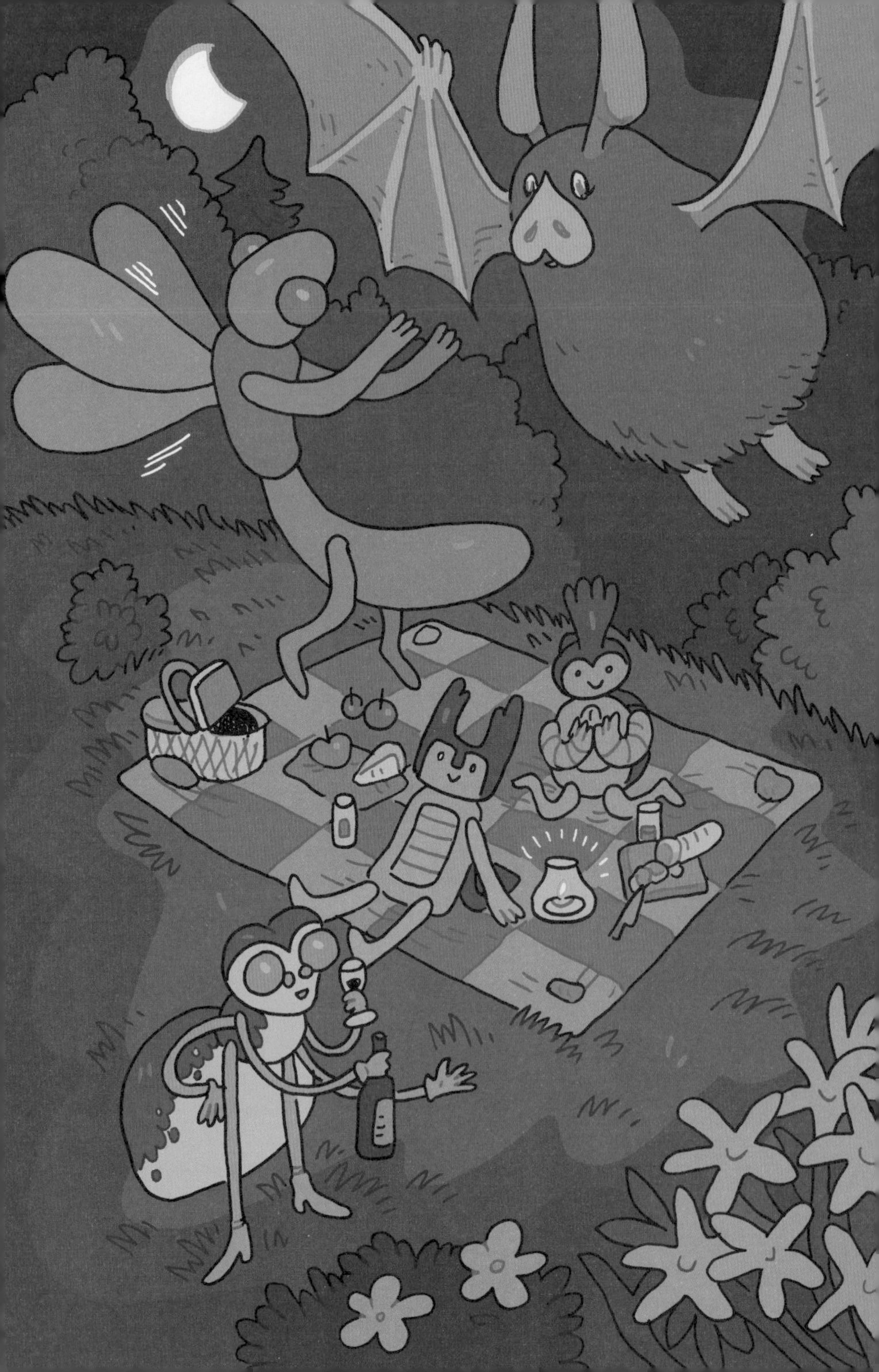

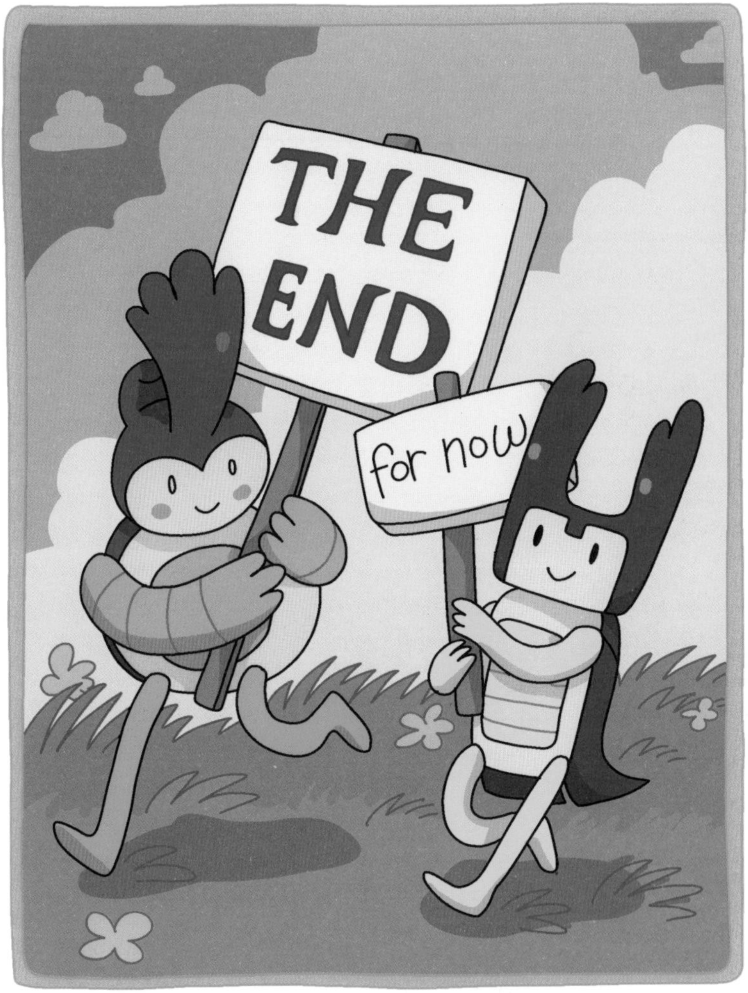
THE END
for now

Laura Knetzger

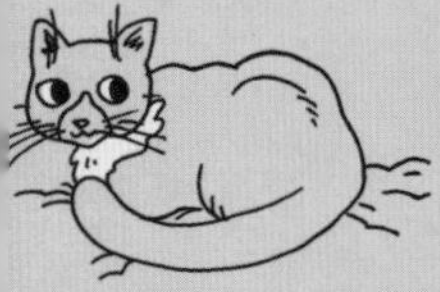

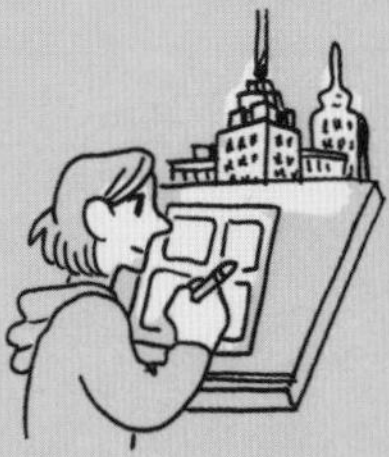

grew up in Washington State, near Seattle. She wanted to be a cartoonist since she was eleven years old. She went to art college in New York City, and now she lives in Seattle.

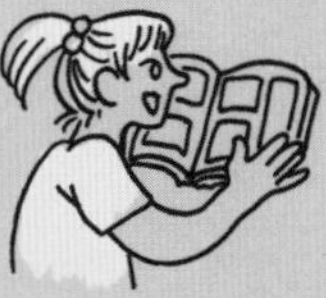

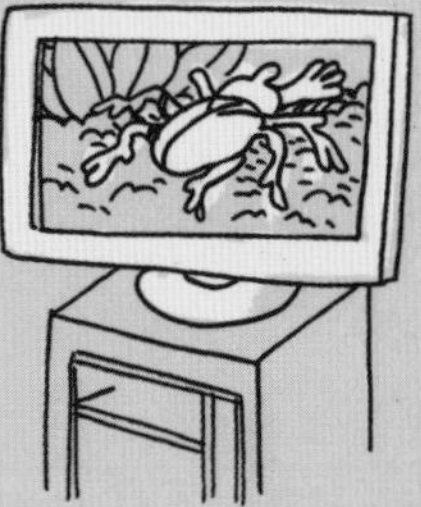

She has a pet cat named Chilly. Chilly is a gray tuxedo cat. Cats are definitely Laura's favorite animal.

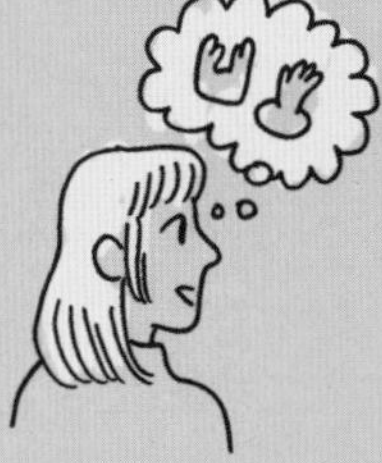

Laura got the idea to make Bug Boys as she was watching a documentary about bug collecting called Beetle Queen Conquers Tokyo. She drew two cute cartoon bugs as she was watching the movie, then tried to make up stories about them.

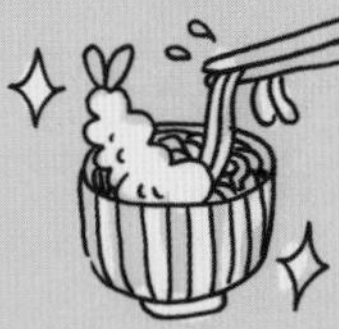

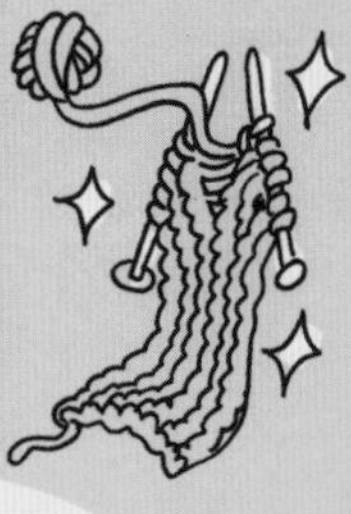

Her hobbies are reading, playing video games, and knitting. Laura's favorite food is udon noodles with tempura on top.

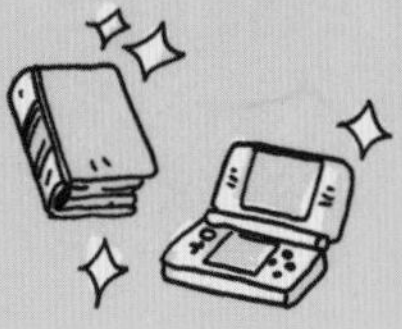

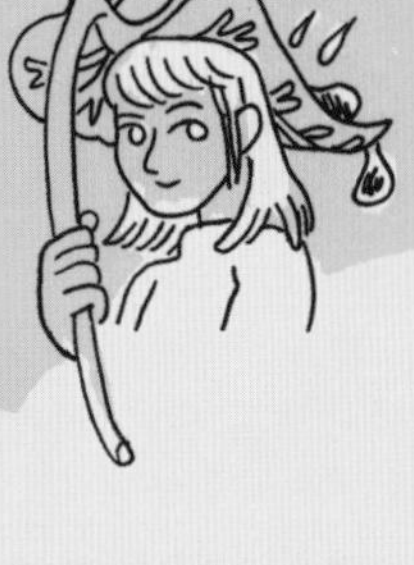

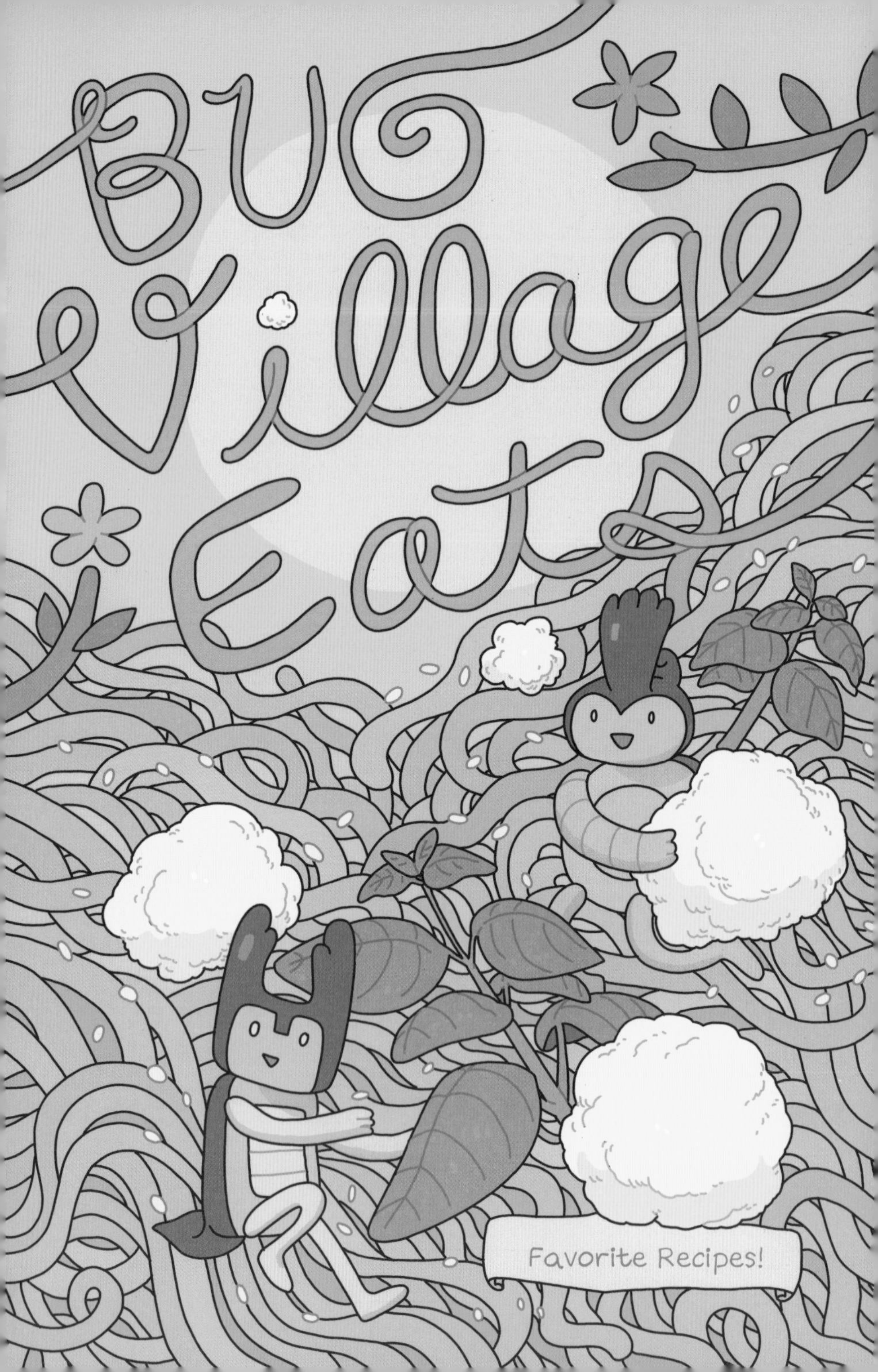
Bug Village Eats
Favorite Recipes!

The Perfect S'more

Gather your ingredients: a marshmallow, a piece of chocolate, sprinkles, and a graham cracker snapped in half.

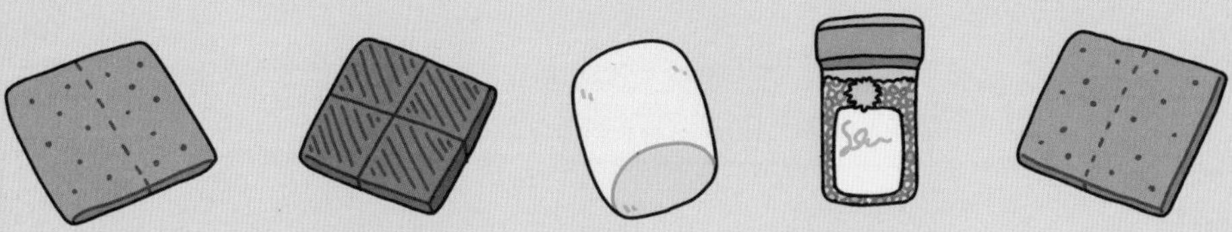

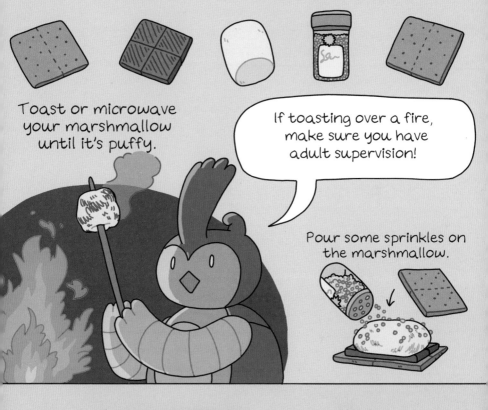

Toast or microwave your marshmallow until it's puffy.

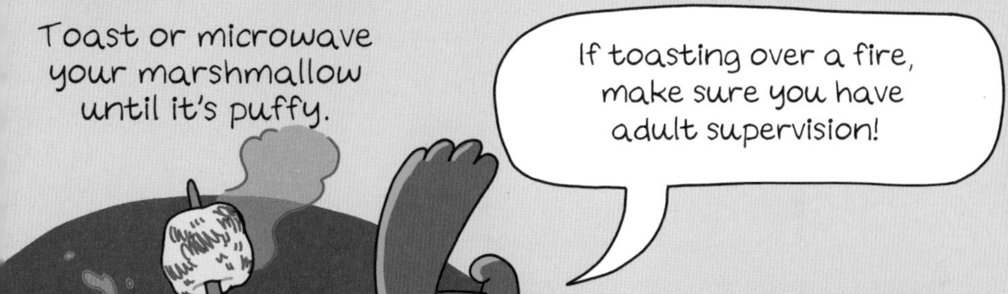
If toasting over a fire, make sure you have adult supervision!

Pour some sprinkles on the marshmallow.

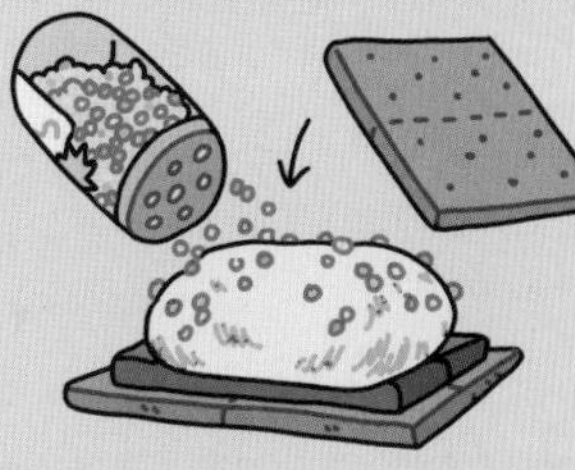

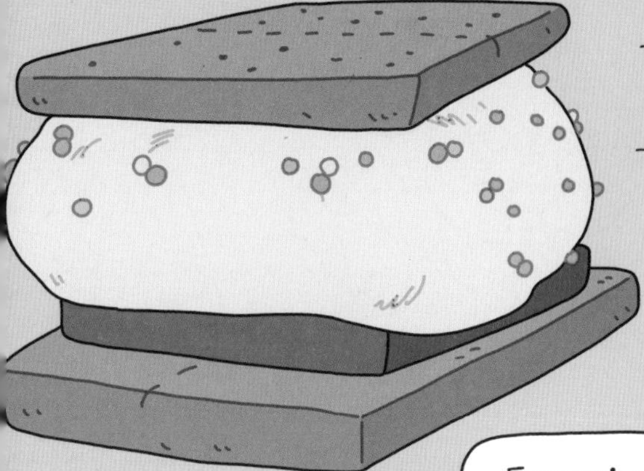

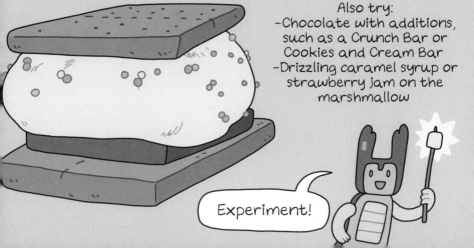

Also try:
- Chocolate with additions, such as a Crunch Bar or Cookies and Cream Bar
- Drizzling caramel syrup or strawberry jam on the marshmallow

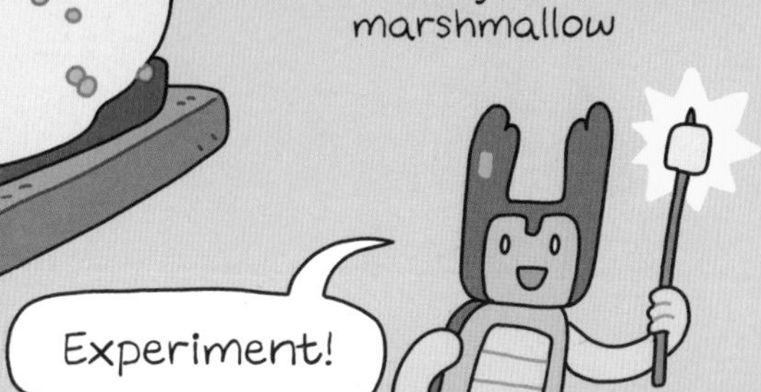
Experiment!

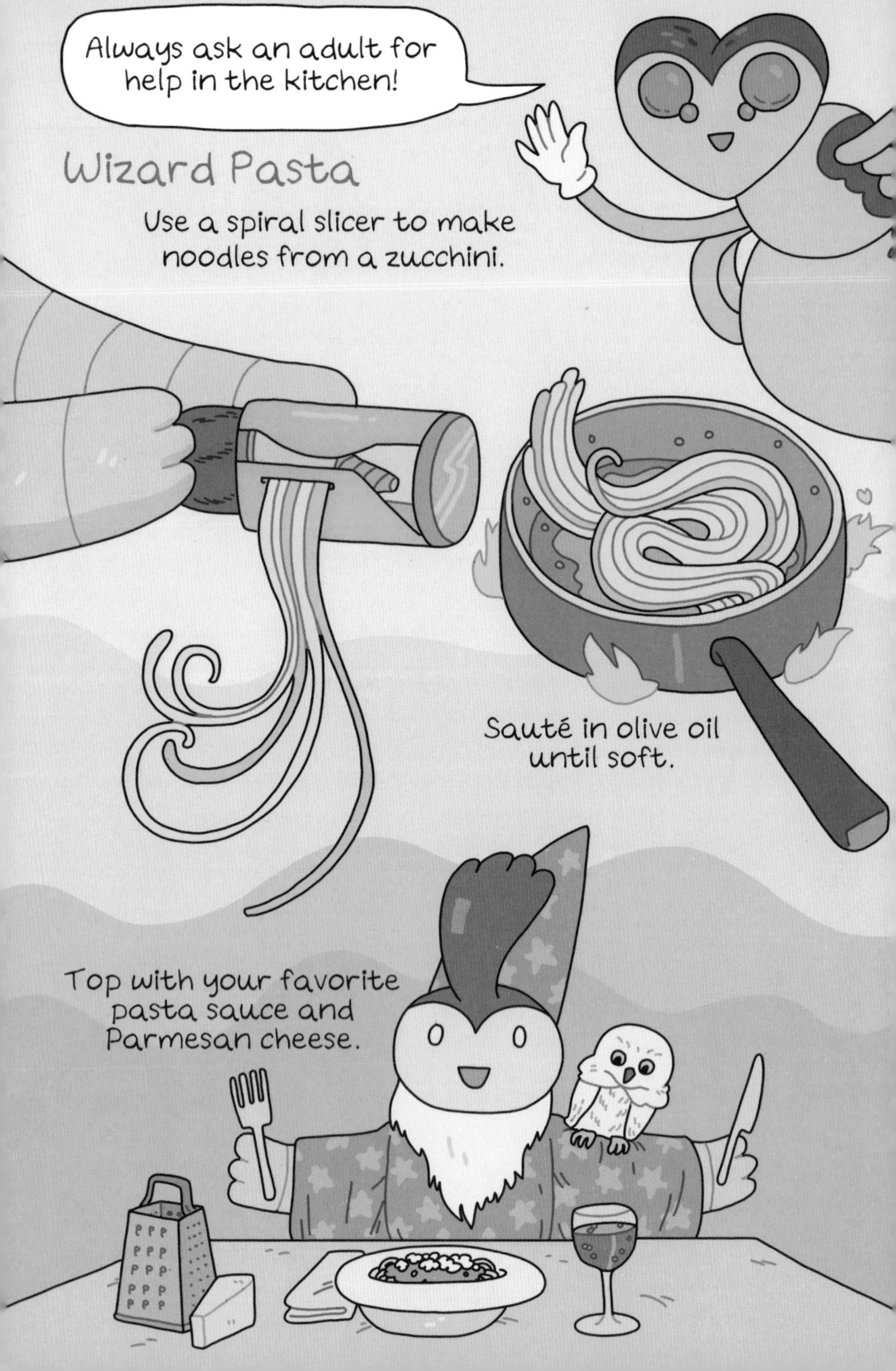
Always ask an adult for help in the kitchen!
Wizard Pasta
Use a spiral slicer to make noodles from a zucchini.
Sauté in olive oil until soft.
Top with your favorite pasta sauce and Parmesan cheese.

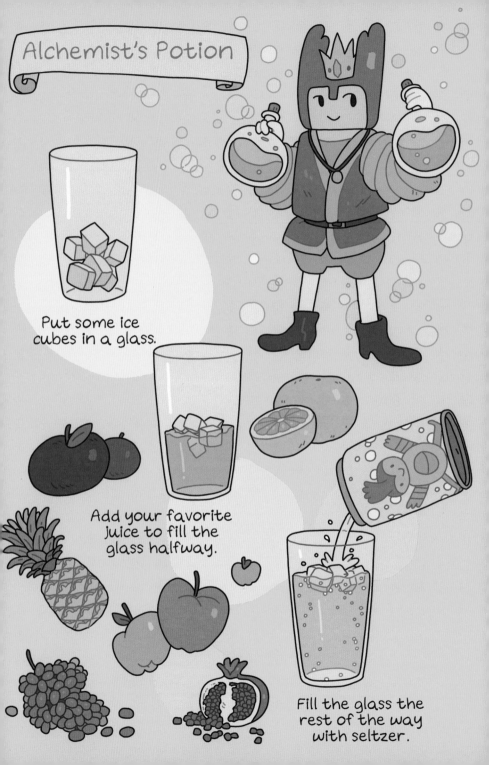

Alchemist's Potion

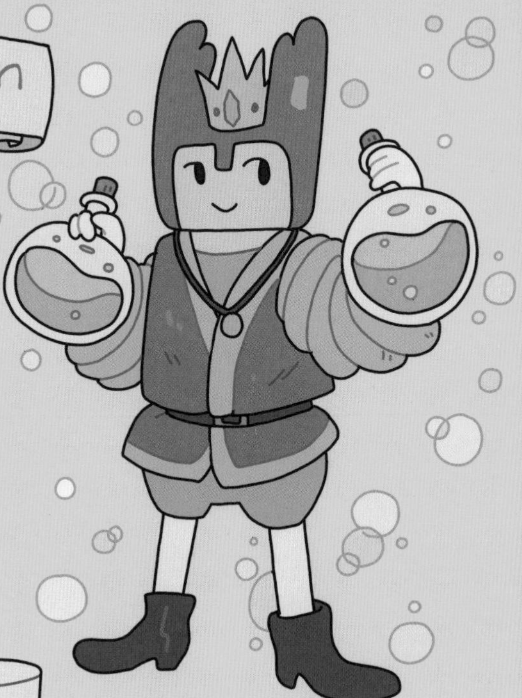

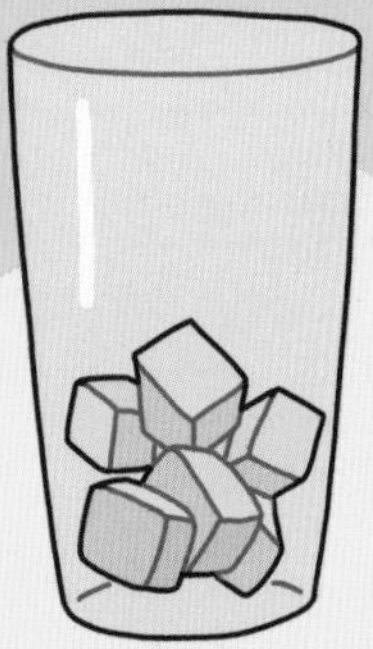

Put some ice cubes in a glass.

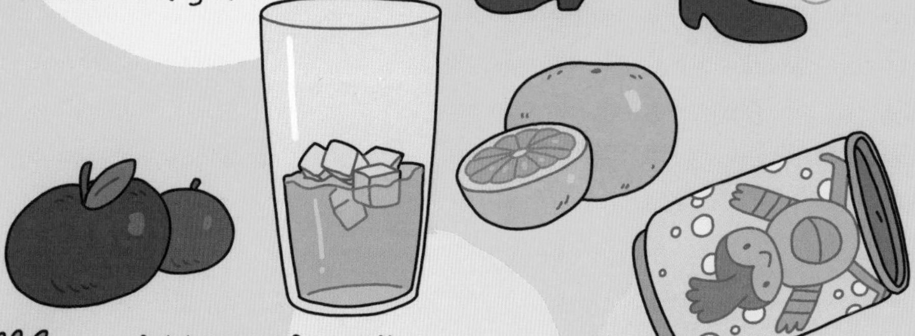

Add your favorite juice to fill the glass halfway.

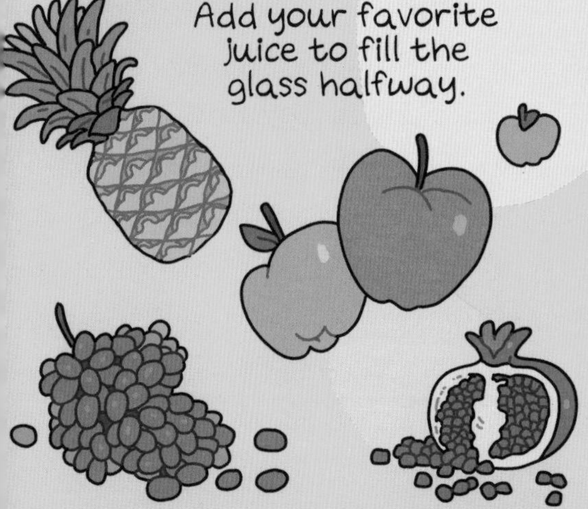

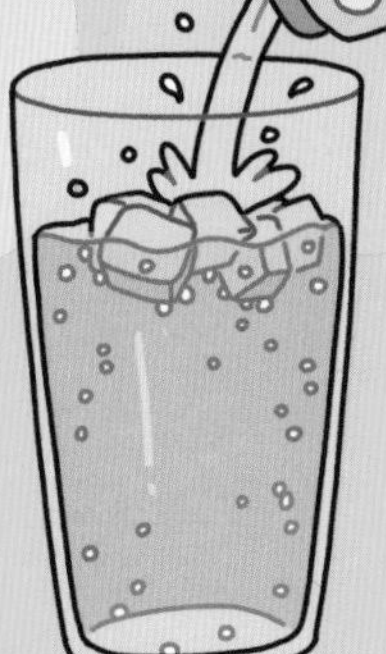

Fill the glass the rest of the way with seltzer.

Bee Queen's Favorite Lunch

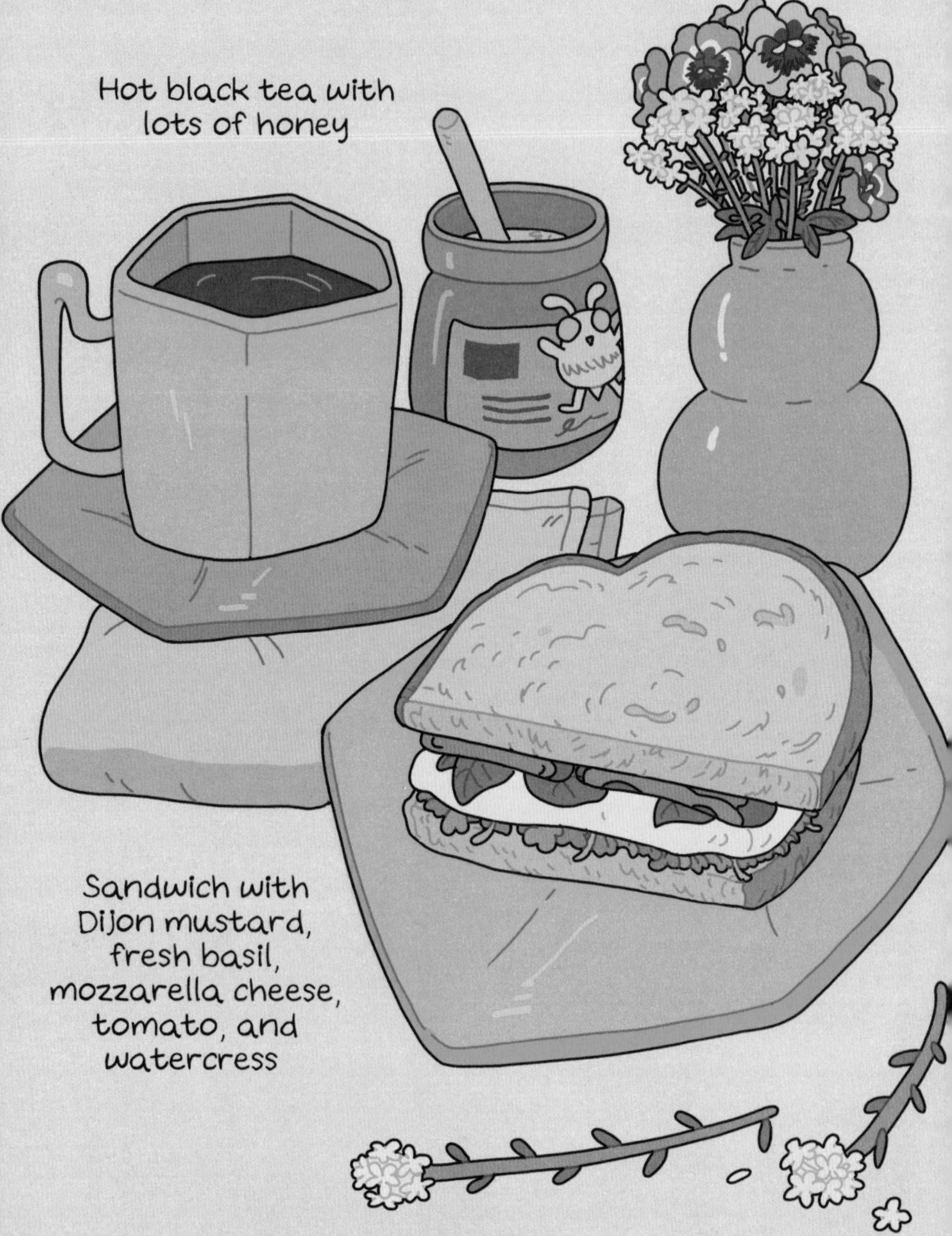
Hot black tea with lots of honey
Sandwich with Dijon mustard, fresh basil, mozzarella cheese, tomato, and watercress

Fruit Bat Salad

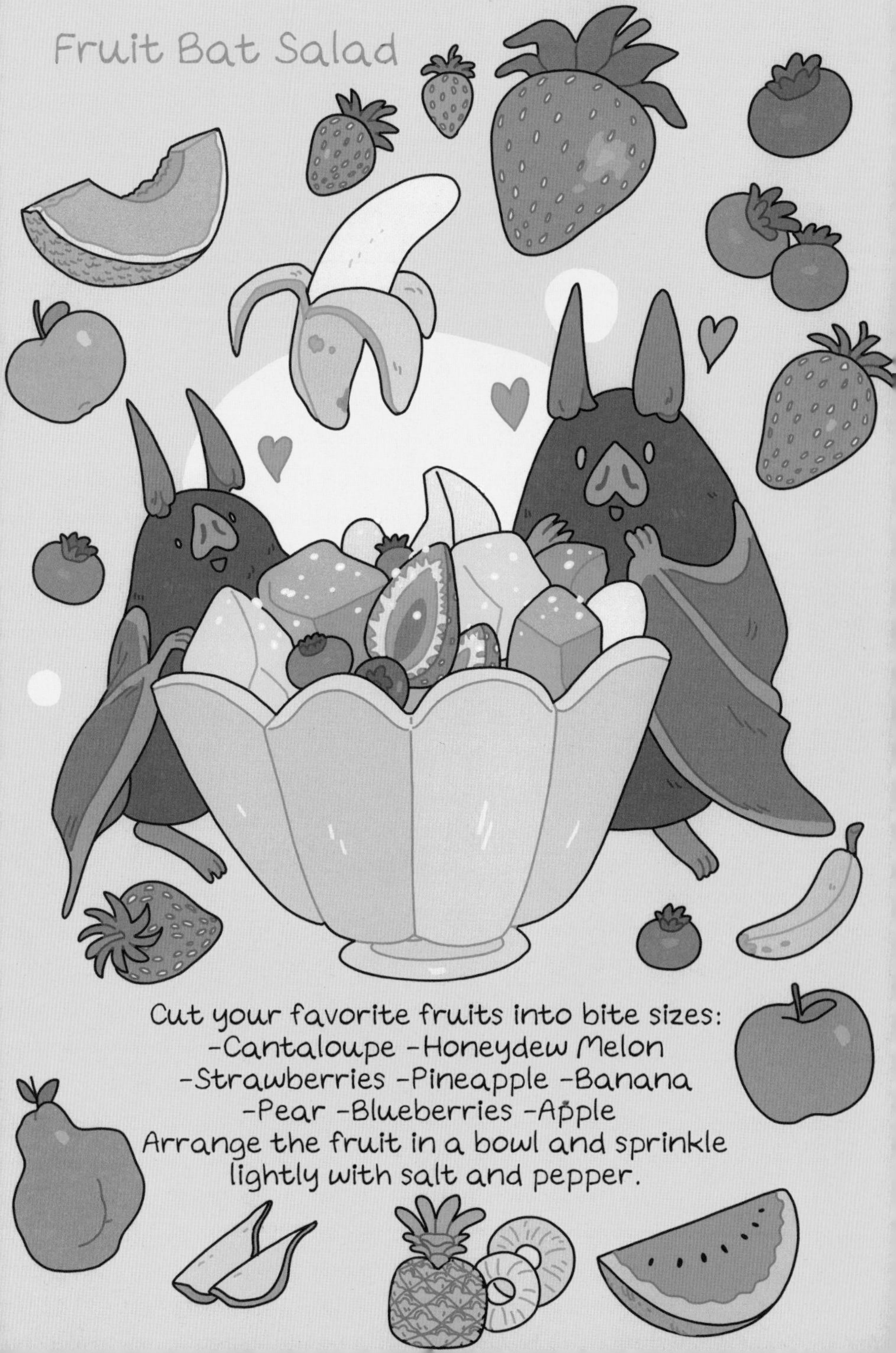

Cut your favorite fruits into bite sizes:
-Cantaloupe -Honeydew Melon
-Strawberries -Pineapple -Banana
-Pear -Blueberries -Apple
Arrange the fruit in a bowl and sprinkle lightly with salt and pepper.

Bonus Comic Part 2

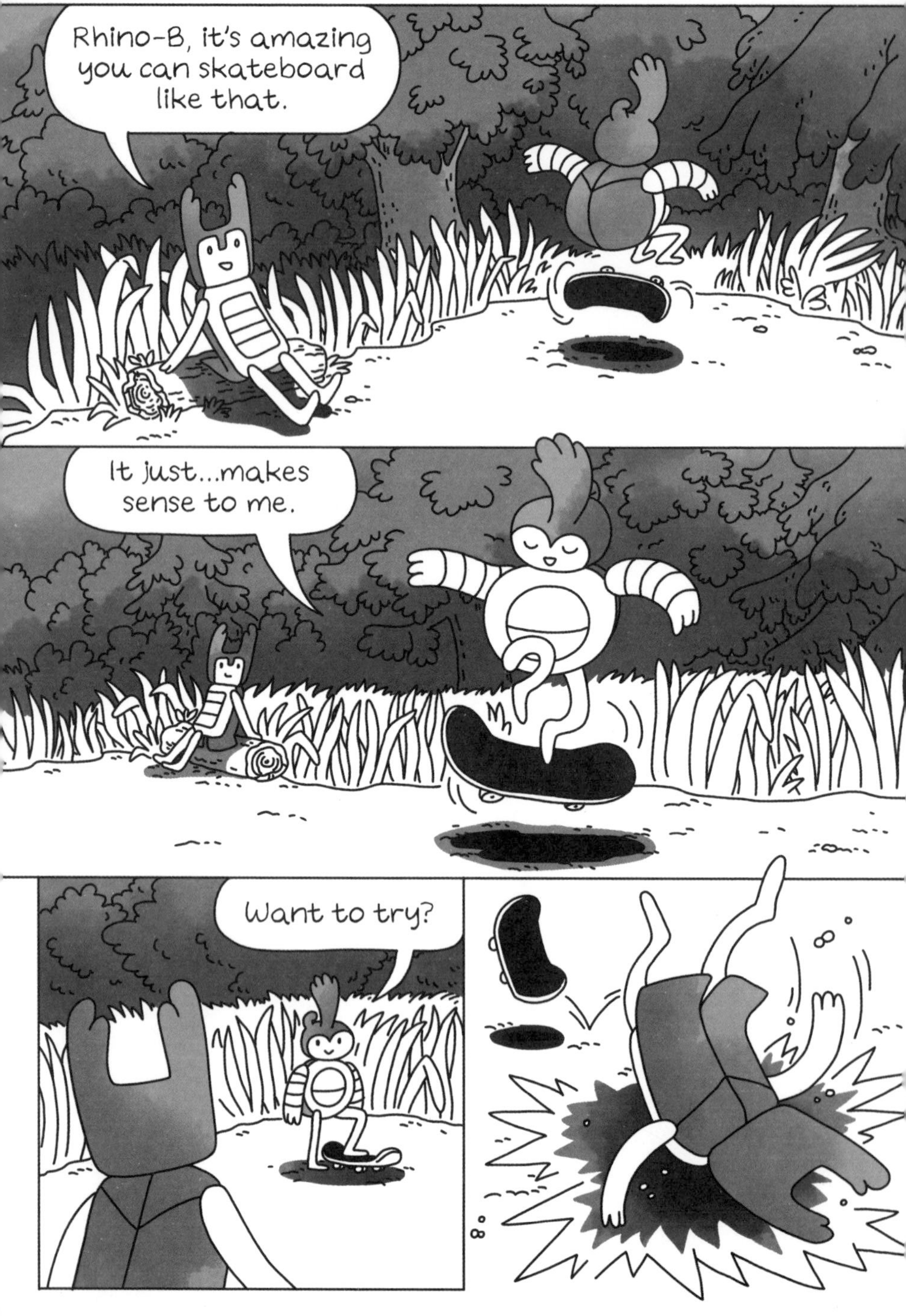
Rhino-B, it's amazing you can skateboard like that.
It just...makes sense to me.
Want to try?

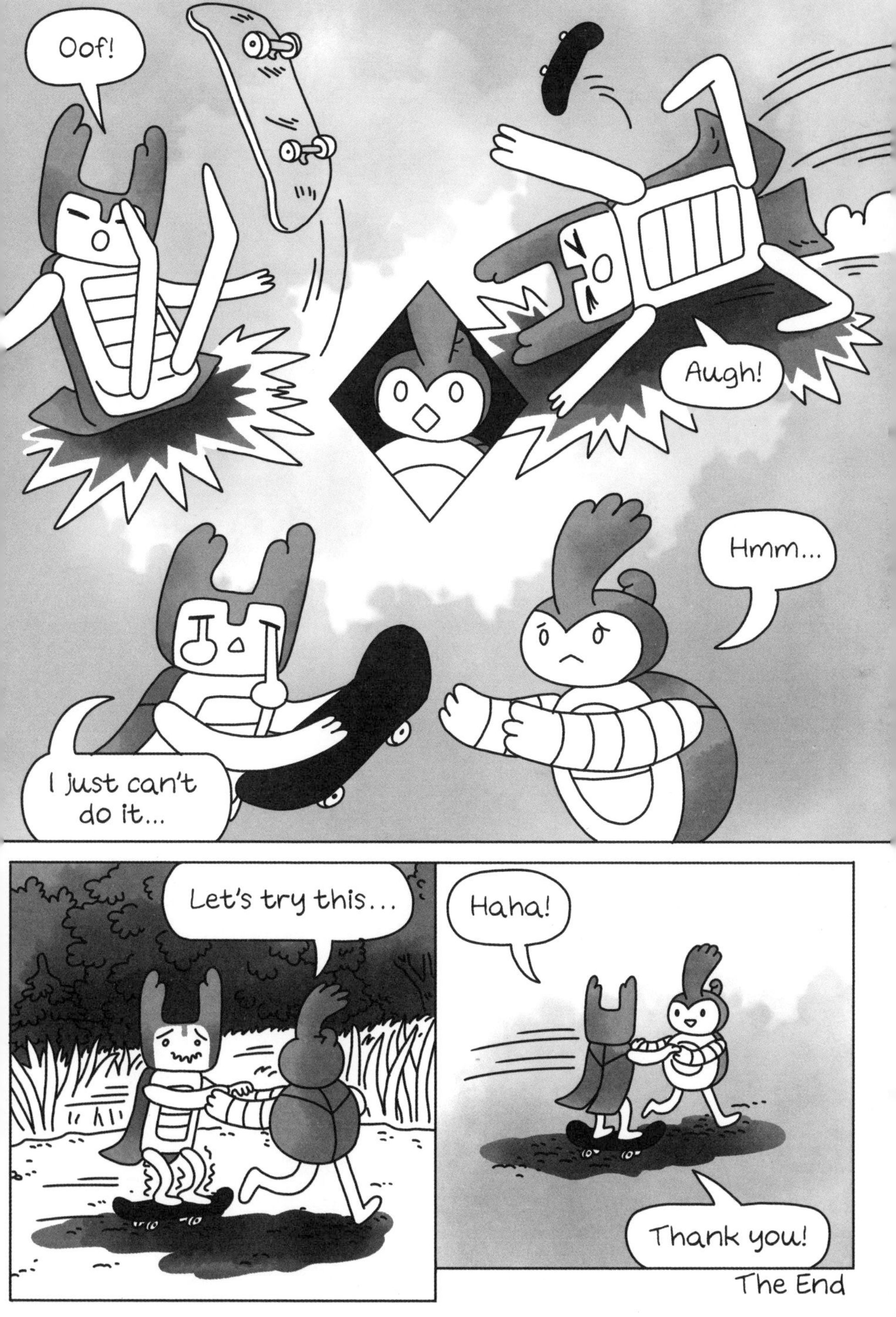
Oof!
Augh!
Hmm...
I just can't do it...
Let's try this...
Haha!
Thank you!
The End

Bug Gallery!

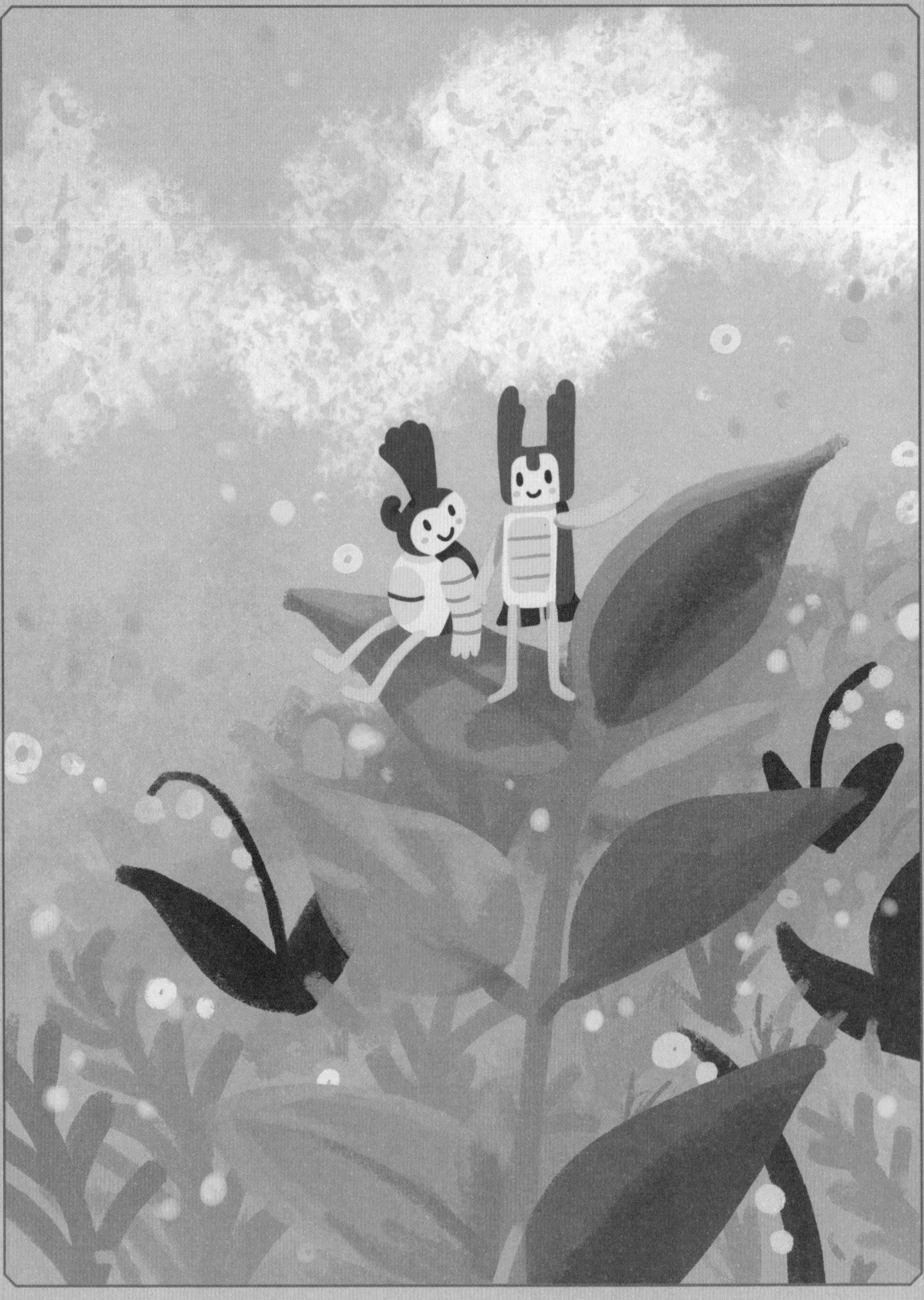

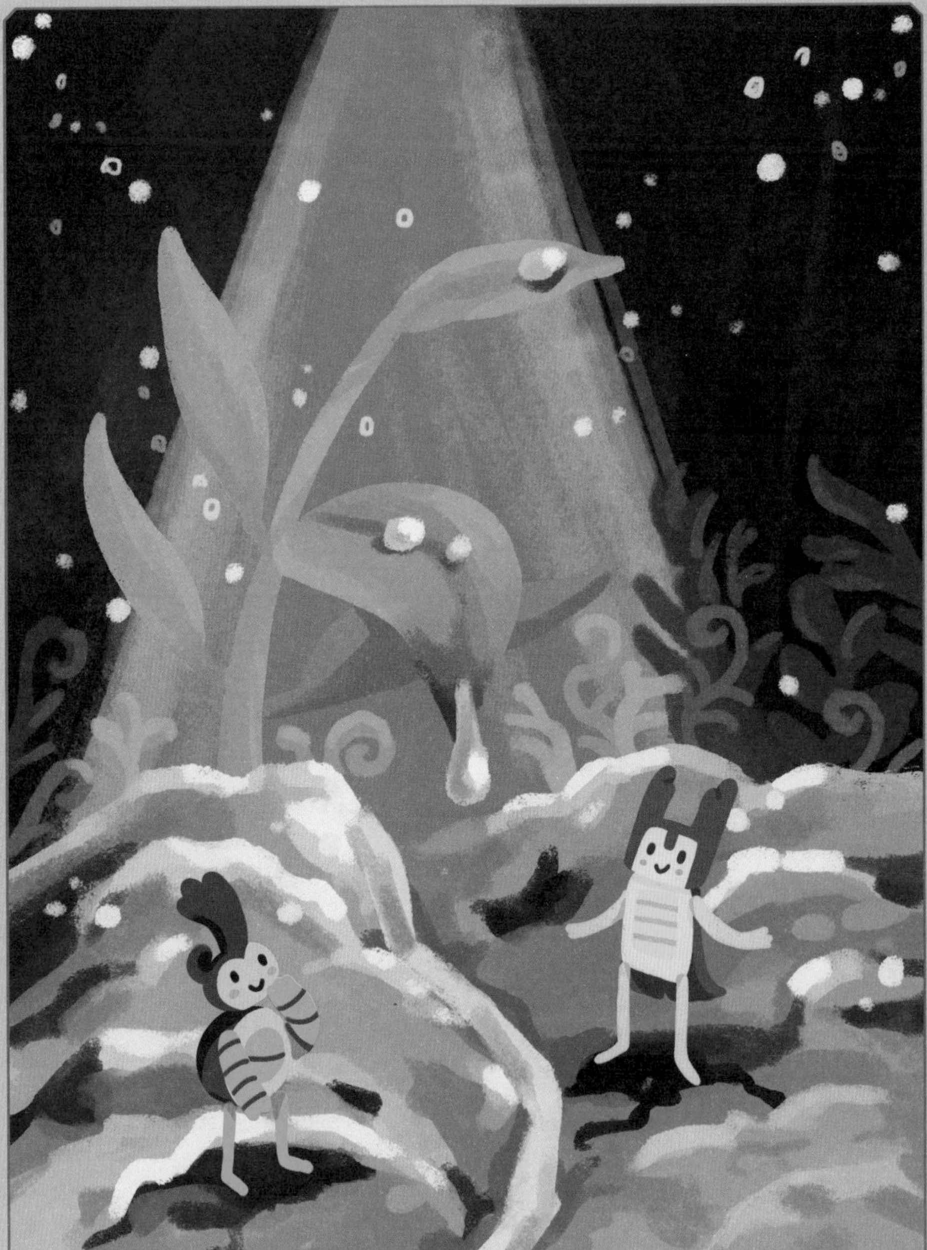

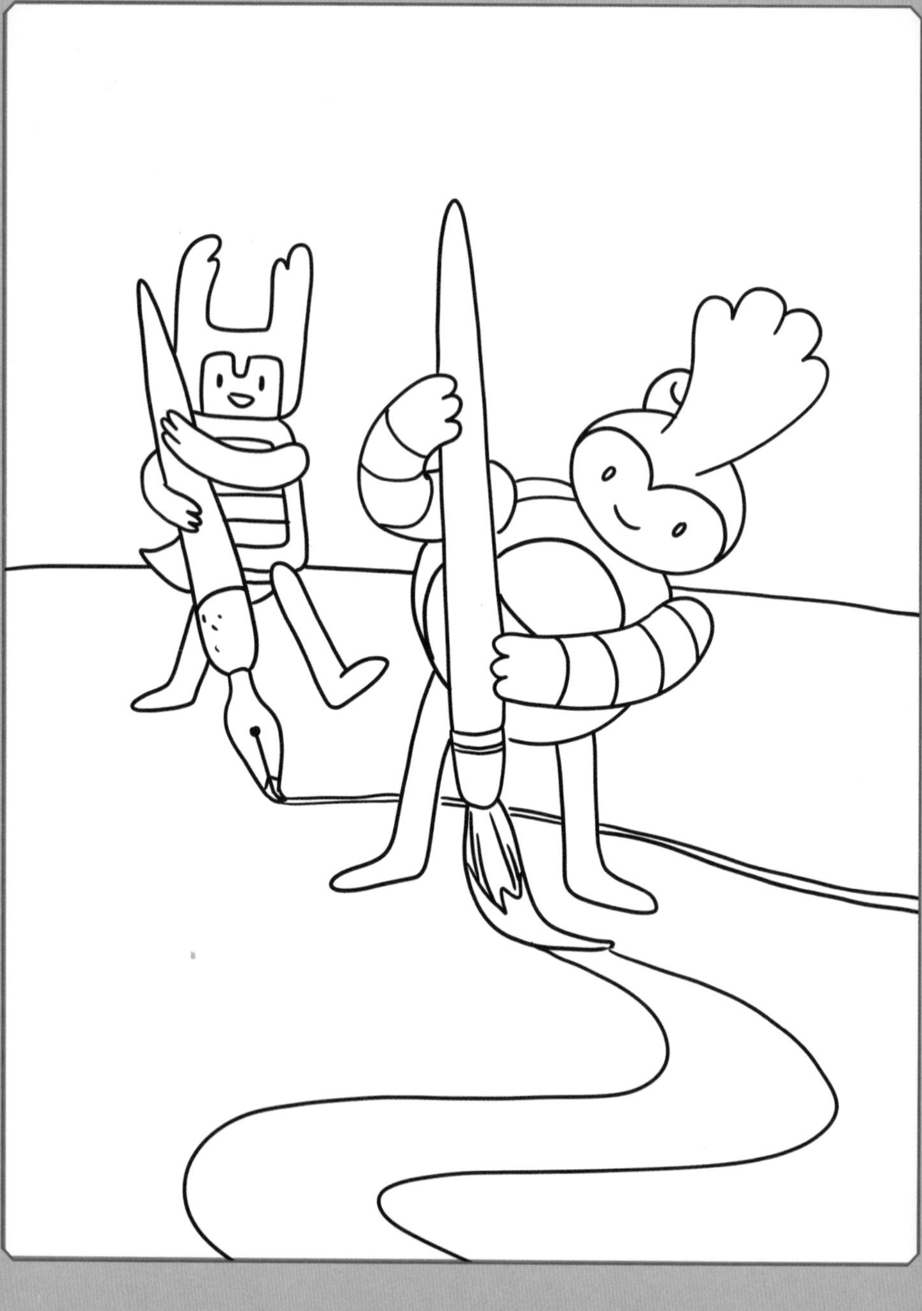

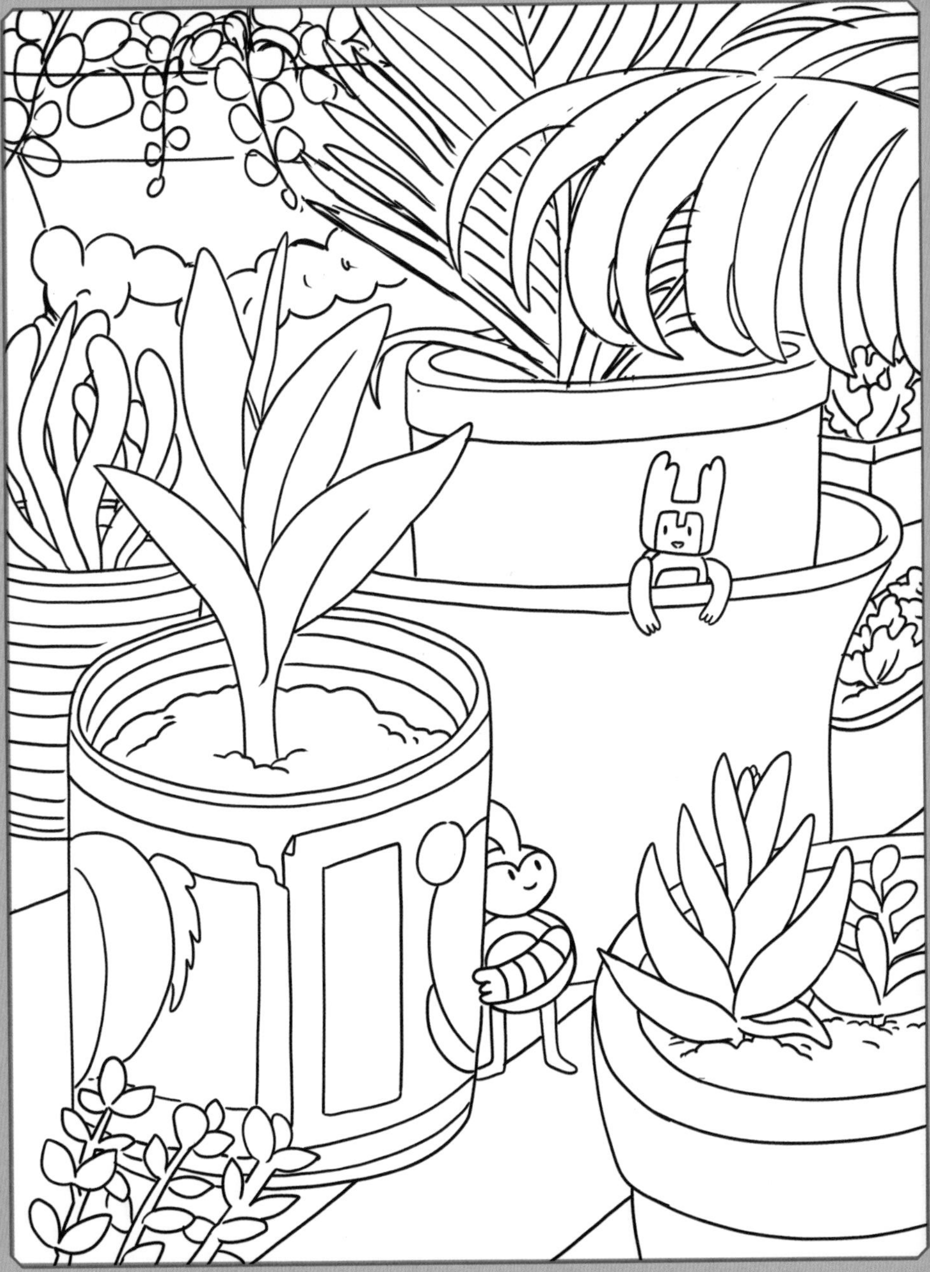

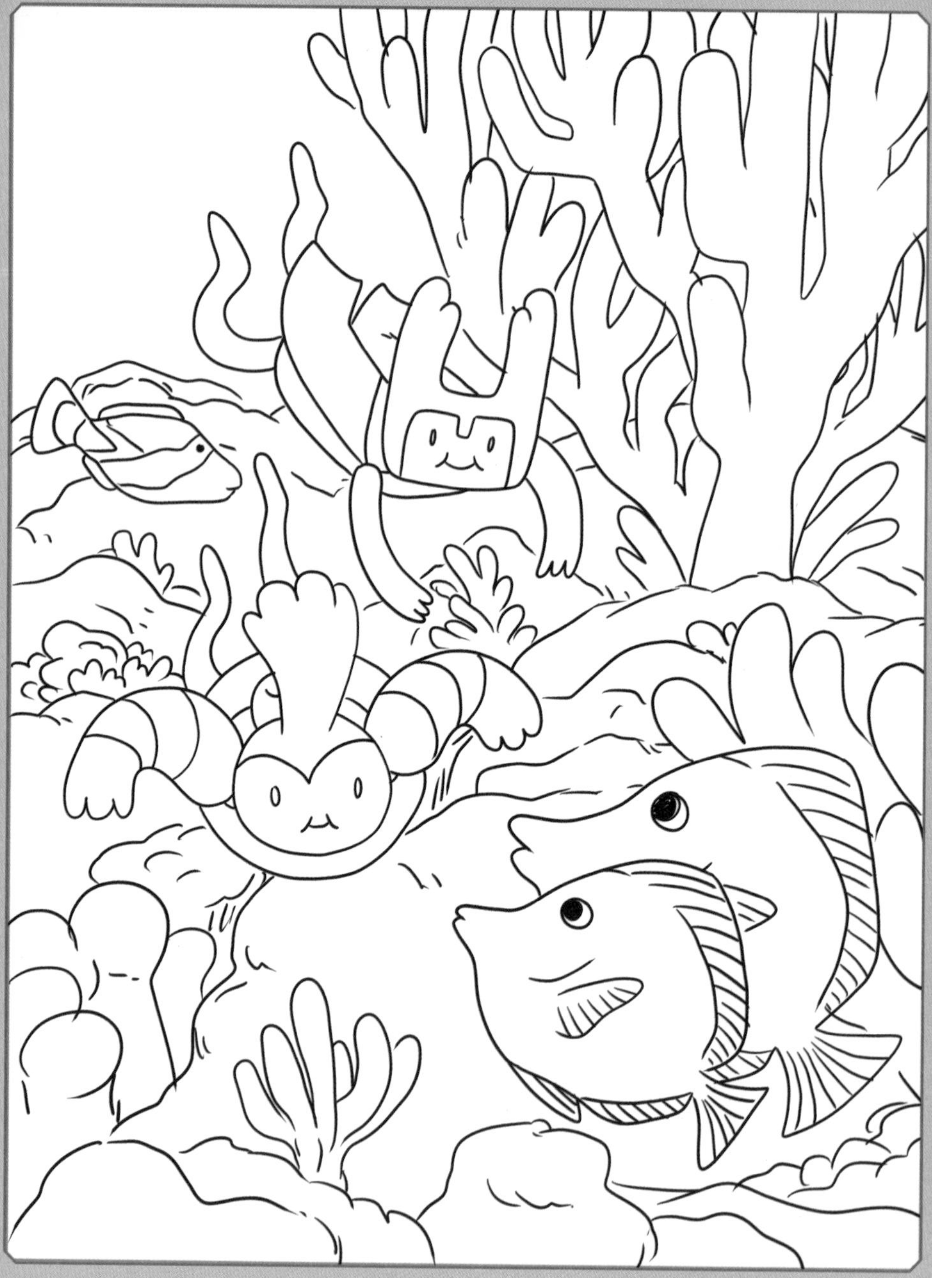

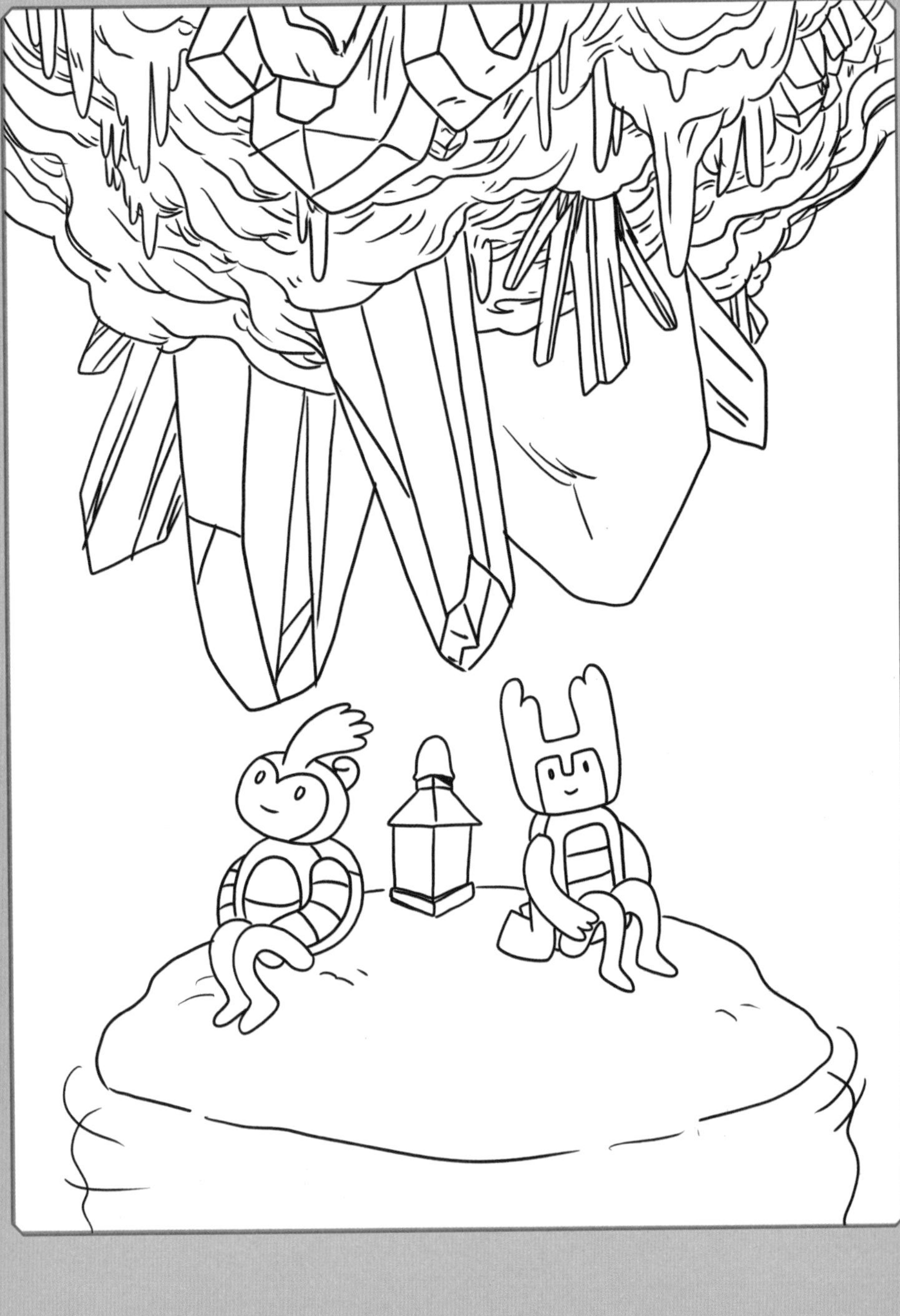

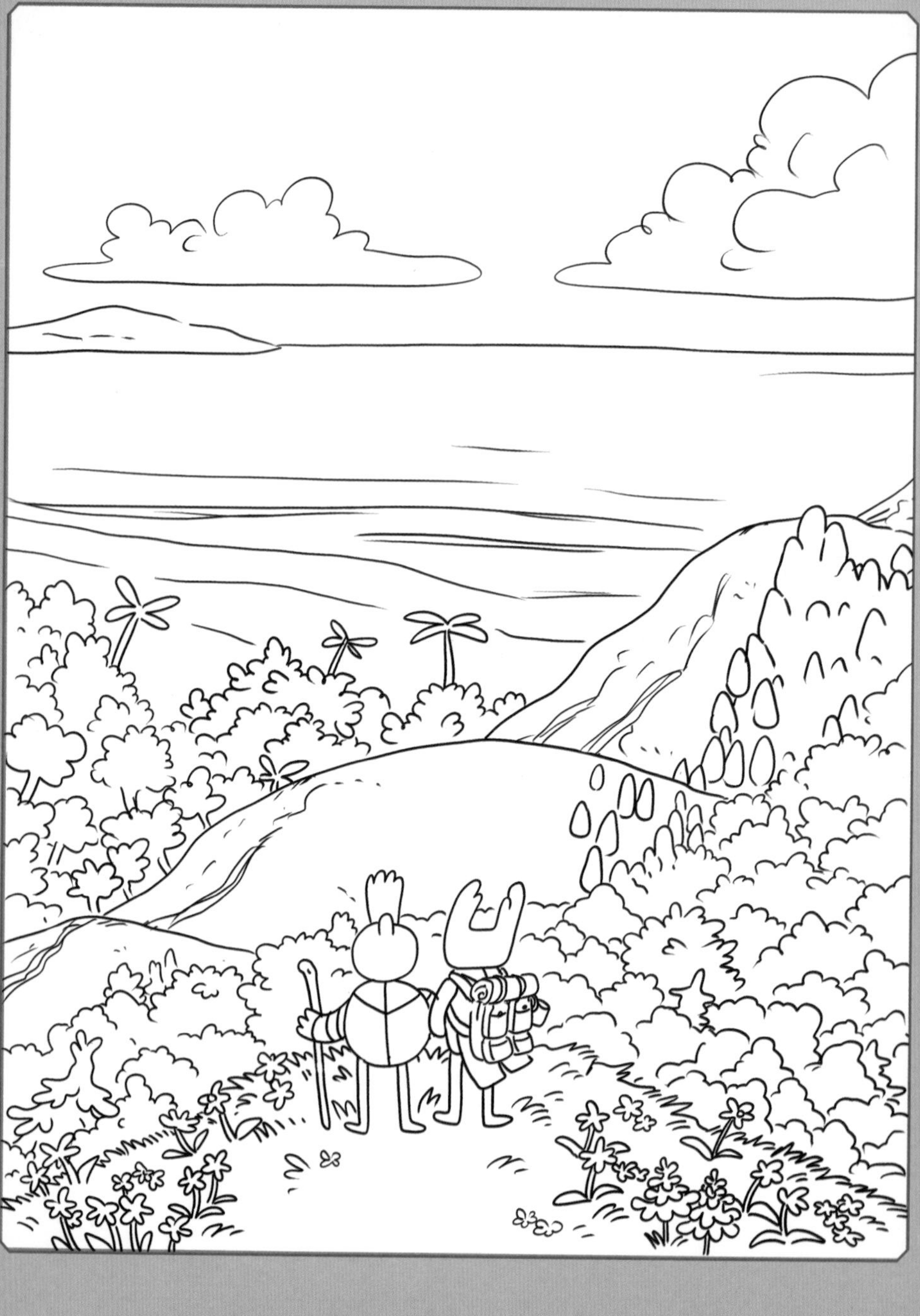

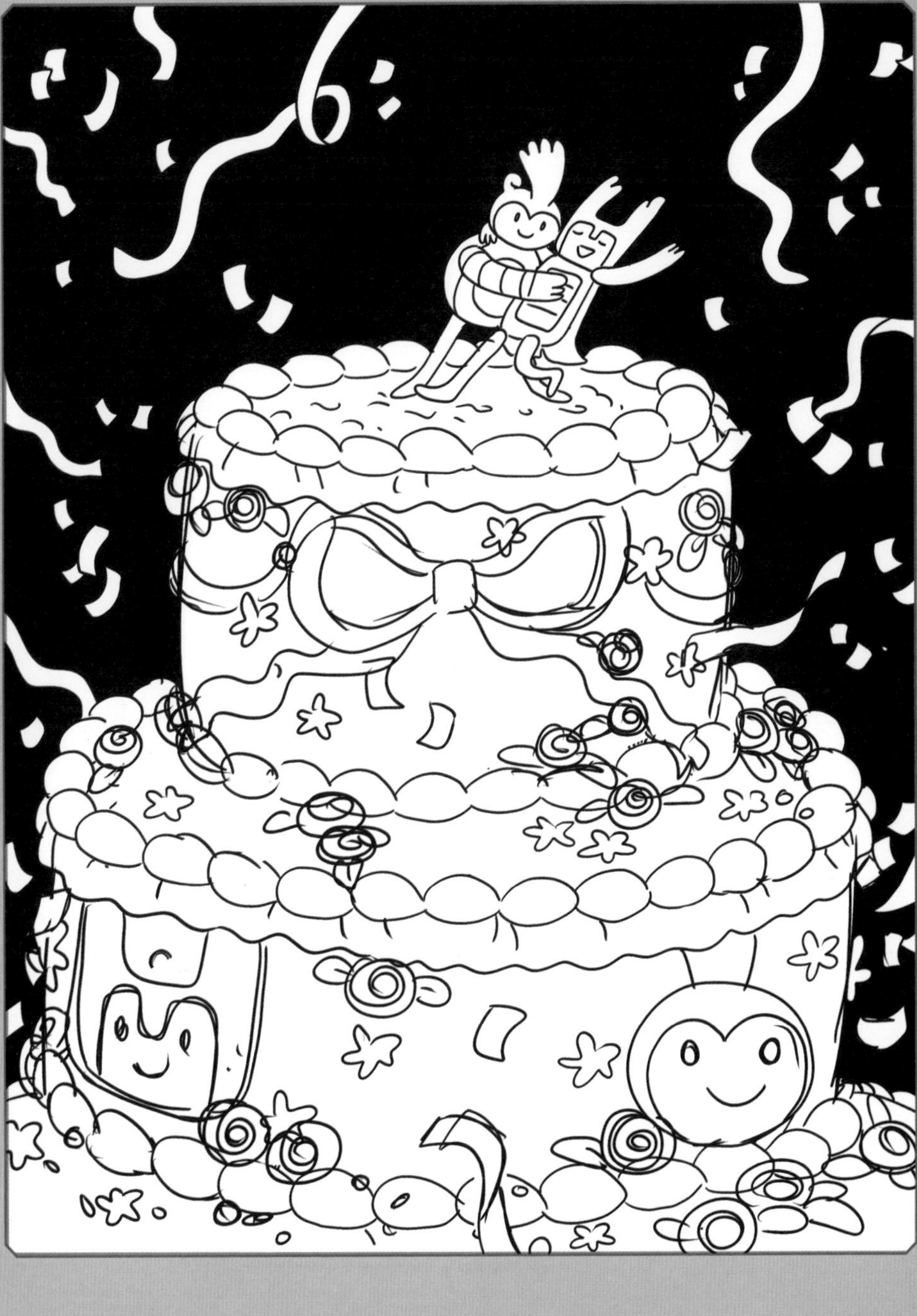

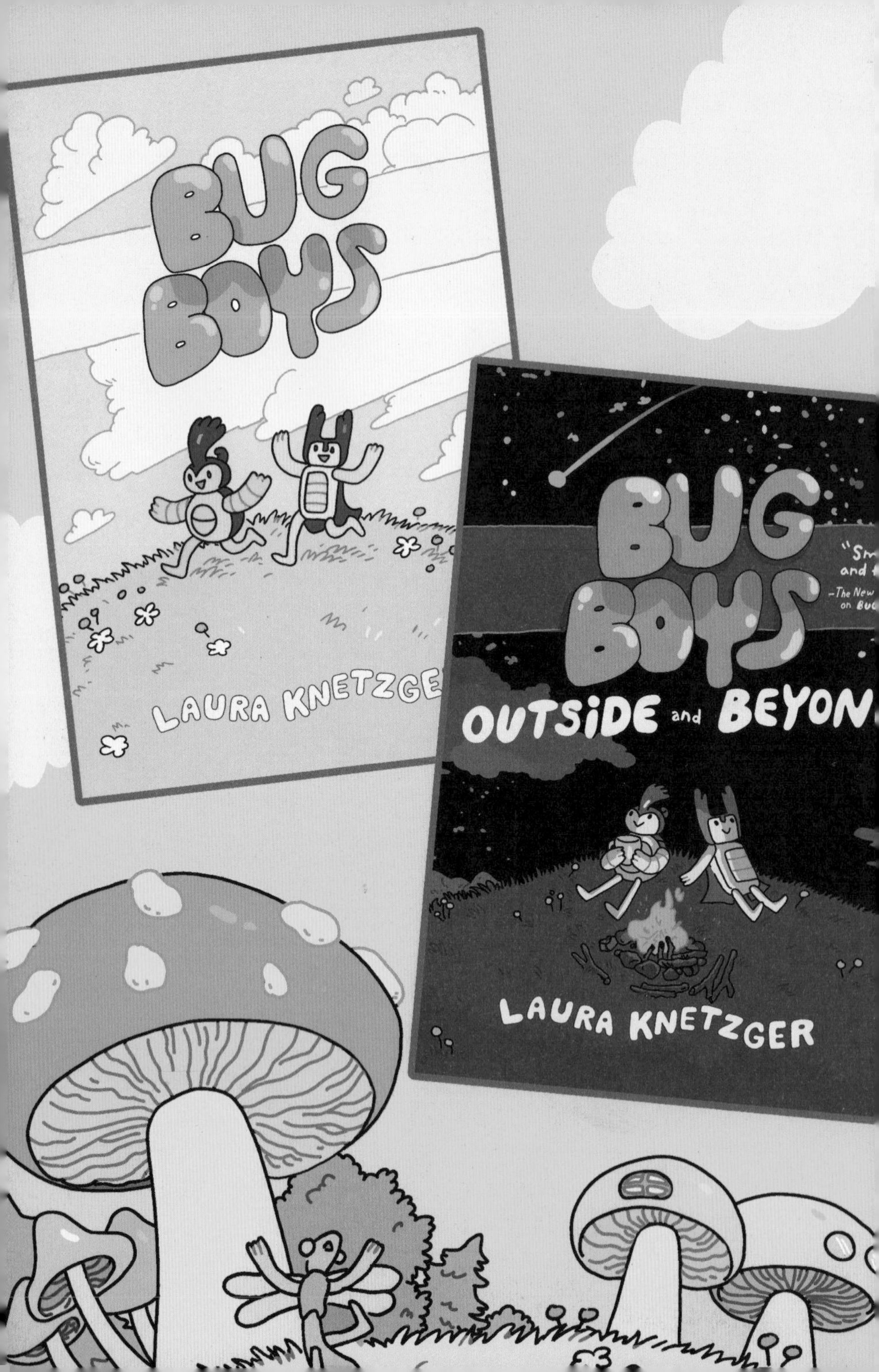
BUG
BOYS
LAURA
BUG
BOYS
OUTSIDE and
LAURA KNETZGER